His
Blazing
Witch

Silver City Series Book 3

Jenny Fox

Contents

Acknowledgments

This time I want to thank my Dreame Team, who first took a chance on the Silver City Series.

I also want to thank all my friends and family, who have been supporting me, each in their own way, in my journey.

Thanks to the foxies who have kindly helped me proofread this third story.

And finally, thanks to you, dear reader, for picking Mara's story.

Thank you.

Introduction

A scream in the middle of the night.

A sharp pain, ravaging my body. A torture I can't handle any longer. I cry out, scream, beg for mercy. I beg her to leave me alone. But she doesn't stop. The poison is spreading like darkness inside me. The darkness takes over me. Let me out. Let me escape this hell…

"Is she awake yet?"

"She struggled earlier, but we think she is hallucinating…"

"How is her dosage?"

"We keep administering larger doses, but it doesn't have much effect…"

Someone sighs.

"This is a tough one… poor girl. Even if she wakes up…"

"Doctor, what should we do? It's already a miracle she is alive, with what happened. It's hard to imagine her waking up at this point…"

"Well, we can try a bit more. I do feel bad for her, but this is not my decision to make."

"Understood, Doctor."

I hear several steps and a few whispered comments.

I open my eyes.

Above me, a bland ceiling. I sit up, completely disoriented. No, I have no idea where I am. What is this… machines surrounded me in an empty room. Is this a hospital? It smells like medicine and cleaning products… I don't like any of it. Moreover, some beeping is annoying me. I want to move, find a way to make it stop, but I'm bound by something.

What are those? Handcuffs? Why would my wrists be chained to the bed?! And my ankles too? I struggle, trying to get out of them.

"Ouch!"

My wrist… When I take a closer look, both my wrists are bandaged tightly. I'm injured? I bend over and grab some of it between my teeth, pulling it away so I can see what they are hiding. …What are those, cuts? They are so deep… Who did this to me?

"Oh my goodness!"

A woman dressed in a white blouse just walked in without warning. She is staring at me with big, frightened eyes.

1

"She... She's awake. She... Doctor! Doctor!"

And just like that, she runs away, screaming like a mad woman. What the... I can't waste time on her. I go back to my cuffs, trying to figure out how to get out of them. My wrists are thin, yet they are bound so tight, I can't even move in them. I struggle again, and one of my cuts reopens, a thin red line staining the bandages.

Let's just burn them.

Good idea! ...But how am I supposed to do that? It's not like I have a lighter or something here. So annoying. I want to try using force again, but before I can do anything, I hear running steps outside. In a few seconds, a handful of people appear at the door. It was high time!

A man and three women are all staring at me, their faces torn between surprise and something akin to fear. What is wrong with them? I growl.

"Untie me."

My own imperious voice surprises me, but it seems right in this situation. Who are they to keep me chained like this? The man walks over, a bit hesitant. Is he a doctor? He is short and bald with small glasses and a dull face.

"Miss, are you alright? How... How do you feel?"

"Didn't you hear me? Untie me now!"

He jumps when I yell, but I don't care. He hesitates a bit but shakes his head.

"I'm sorry, we can't do that for now. Can... Can I examine you? It seems you just woke up. Are you in pain anywhere?"

In pain? Now that he mentions it, aside from my wrist, my legs are... I wouldn't call it painful, but they certainly don't feel good. I would look at them if it wasn't for these stupid cuffs!

"What happened to me? And who are you?"

He looks even more surprised now. I see the bald doctor exchange a glance with the women, hesitant. When he turns back to me, he is fidgety.

"Miss Garnett, you don't... remember what happened to you?"

Miss Garnett? Who is that? And what am I supposed to remember?

I... I don't remember anything. I try to think long and hard, about anything I could piece together, but it's a complete black hole. I have no idea. Who I am, what I am doing here, or what happened.

"Miss Garnett, you look very disturbed. Do you want us to–"

"Don't call me that!"

"But it's your name. Miss Clarissa Garnett."

He's wrong. I know it. I shake my head.

"No. My name is Mara."

"Ma- Mara? You must be confused. I can assure you, your name is–"

"MY NAME IS MARA!"

I yell at the top of my lungs and they all scream in fear. Not because of my voice, but because of this flame that just erupted in my hands. How fascinating…

"Oh my God! Someone call for help!"

"Fire! She… She… She just lit a fire!"

While they are all panicking, I'm absorbed by the little fire dancing on my hands. It's so warm… It dances on my finger in shades of orange and red, and suddenly catches the cuffs that were restraining me. The smell of burning leather fills the room and I watch as the fire slowly consumes my restraints. Naturally, the bed sheets are caught on fire too. While they are eaten progressively by the flames, I can finally see my legs.

What is this… Red. They are a dark, disgusting, and pitiful red. The burn scars run from my feet and up half of my left thigh, while on my right, it went as far as my waist. My flesh was devoured deep enough to leave traces of blood in some places. There is something repulsive about it, yet I can't stop staring. Those two remnants are my actual legs… Are they even of any use in this state? Surprisingly, I can move them just fine. They still hurt a bit, though.

One of the women suddenly returns to the room with something silverish, and she runs to me. I don't react, but she unfolds a cover and puts it over the fire to smother it. Within seconds, the flames die out. They are all acting crazy and yelling about smoke or water, but no one has answered me. So I look for the man and ask again.

"What happened to me?"

"You… Did you just do this? The fire?" he mumbles.

"Not that, my legs!"

Why does he have to be so slow to answer?! Who cares about the fire?! He wipes some sweat from his shiny forehead and looks at the nurses again, completely helpless. Finally, a woman behind him answers.

"You were severely burnt, Miss Gar-… Mara. The firefighters came too late, they found you already unconscious and in… this state."

She is not hinting at my legs, but my overall body. What… Now that my hand is free, I pull up the odd clothing I'm wearing, some sort of blouse.

I was wrong… The burns are not only on my legs. New red flesh flaps appear once you look under my breasts. A large area on my left side up to my breast, and my shoulder and arm is also in the same wretched state. How did that happen… I look at my hands, but the fire doesn't burn me… and neither did the one from earlier. I stare at my fingers, but nothing else happens.

3

"Miss… Mara?"

The nurse took a step closer. She is the one that looks the least afraid of me.

"We need to examine you… Can we? Then you can ask us questions, alright?"

"Why did you handcuff me?"

She hesitates, but after a few seconds, answers with a very serious face.

"It was for your safety. We were afraid you would try to harm yourself."

"Injure myself? Why in the world would I do something like that?"

"But you did, miss. Those scars, and the cuts on your wrists… You did all that to yourself."

#

Chapter 1

Silver City.

A metropolis with over one hundred thousand inhabitants. Despite being rather modern, its unique geographic location makes it rather isolated from any other big cities, as it's bordered by a forest to the east, and the sea on the west. Its most unique feature, however, is probably one-third of its population being werewolves. That's right. Over thirty thousand werewolves, a hundred thousand humans, and... me.

I frown, staring out the window once again. Silver City's dawn is pretty and quiet. The sky shines with the first sunlight, shades of pink and purple in the clouds. I open the window, feeling some nice fresh air. It's really early, we're at the end of May. I wonder what all those people are doing, in the streets and skyscrapers. I'm fascinated by the tallest buildings. I wonder what it's like to see the world from up there. Do you feel like you belong when you watch the streets from so high?

I'm on the second floor, and I can't understand what it could be like down there, or up there.

"Knock knock, I'm looking for the little witch in room five?"

I turn around with a smile.

Kelsi is waiting, pretending to knock on my door with a little frown on. She's wearing her ugly, mint green sweatshirt, the one with a big cartoon cat on it, some jeans, and her usual multi-colored backpack.

"Hi. They let you in so early?" I ask, a bit surprised.

"Yep. Apparently, your sister gave them instructions that I could come in and out as I please. I'm pretty much a full-time VIP plus one now."

"Oh..."

Kelsi drops her bag and comes to hug me gently, being careful about my bandages. She glares at the big bracelet around my wrist, grabbing it with a frown. It flashes with a little green light every ten seconds and is quite heavy too.

"Still there?"

"Still there," I sigh.

5

"Hm..."

She takes a step back, tucking her long, black hair behind her ears, and makes a falsely severe expression behind her thick glasses.

"Alright, Miss Garnett, morning check-up."

"Oh, seriously, Kelsi? Again?" I protest.

"What's my name?"

I sigh and nod, deciding to comply. I take a deep breath.

"Kim Eun-Kyung," I recite, "You've been my roommate for over one year, and as far as I know, you're probably my only friend. You go by your english name Kelsi Kim because you hate hearing people mispronounce your real name. You're two months older than me, a photography student, and a geek... and you like ugly cat sweaters."

"Good girl," she says with a big smile. "How are you feeling?"

"Still like a total stranger to myself," I sigh, sitting on my bed.

"Your temperature?"

I show her the black screen of my watch with a grimace.

"They deactivated the screen since they found out I used it for testing..."

"Oh, crap. No more experiments, then."

"No..."

She nods and suddenly grabs her bag with a spark of excitement in her eyes. It's an old and very used one, but apparently, she loves it enough to have covered the many holes with some funny patches. Kelsi takes out an envelope, barely hiding her enthusiasm.

"You found some new pictures?" I ask.

"Yep! Well, you already know we didn't take many together, but I found some new ones from a party you apparently went to, two months before we moved in together. I had to chat with some weird guy who was a borderline creep, but anyway, I got these and printed them out for you. Look!"

I take the pictures, a bit hesitant. This is already the sixth batch of pictures Kelsi has found for me, but just like the previous five times, I don't recognize anything in them. I spread them out on my bed, and it even takes me a minute to find myself in them. It looks like some party in a big nightclub, with more people I don't recognize. In the pictures, I am wearing a white sequin top with some black leather pants, and I am dancing in heels in the middle of a wild crowd. My hair seems longer too, and straightened. Kelsi only selected the pictures I appear in, but I never seem to be the main focus. I'm always in the middle of a random group or in the background...

"Still nothing?" she asks, biting her thumb.

6

I shake my head. I only recognize myself, and that's because I've spent hours in front of a mirror since I woke up, trying to remember who I am. No one else in these pictures reminds me of anything. It's so infuriating. I can't put a name to any of the faces, or on the place... even what I'm wearing in those pictures doesn't remind me of anything.

"Did the guy say anything about me?" I ask.

"Not really." She sighs, shaking her head. "He had no idea who you were when I found you on his profile picture. He's never heard of Clarissa Garnett, or a girl called Mara. He said he took a lot of pictures because it was his first university party, but he didn't even seem to know half of the people there."

"Okay... Well, thank you anyway for trying, Kelsi."

"I'm sorry it didn't work again, boo."

"It can't be helped. It would be weird if my memory came back all at once."

I really don't want to make Kelsi feel bad about it. She's the only person who comes to visit me almost every day since she's been allowed to, and literally brightens up my whole day. She's been trying hard to help me fill in the gigantic hole that is my past, bringing stuff that supposedly belongs to me, or the pictures she could find. She pouts, playing with her sweater's laces, still staring at the pictures.

"I don't recognize anyone from the university either, but I can ask my friends. Maybe someone knows someone from your department who knows more about you."

"Thanks."

"Well, at least you're sexy! I always noticed you had good taste in clothes. Aren't you tired of the hospital gown?"

I nod. I hate it, but with all the bandages covering my burns, it's the only thing I can put on easily without grimacing all the time. Kelsi did bring me a bag of clothes, but trying to put on a pair of jeans was so painful I cried. She puts the pictures back in the envelope and places it on my bedside table.

"I'd definitely suck as a detective, I could only find thirty pictures of you in six weeks, and I took half of them. I officially suck."

"Don't say that, you're the best. It's not your fault I was a loner."

"I still can't believe you don't have any freaking social media. You're an alien, or born in the wrong century!"

"You still haven't found my laptop?"

"No..." She pouts. "The last time I saw you with it was one morning before I went to uni, you were in the kitchen, typing something. I don't think I saw you with it after that, and then there was the accident..."

7

It's so infuriating. It's already annoying enough that I have amnesia, but now, I can't even retrieve the biggest clues about my own life. I know the smartphone I had got burnt in the fire, along with my belongings, even my clothes. The police officer that came said they only found the remains of a leather bag and a matching purse, but more could have burnt, and they weren't going to spend time analyzing ashes...

"Did your sister come by at all this week?" asks Kelsi.

"No... Too busy, they said."

"Damn, your family is weird. She is too busy to visit you, but she pays for a private room in this fancy hospital."

"I feel like the room is more of a security measure than special treatment. She probably doesn't have time to take care of her crazy younger sister..."

Kelsi frowns, and grabs my chin to lift it and have me look at her.

"Listen to me, boo. You're not crazy. You're a gorgeous piece of woman, and a bad-ass witch, okay?"

Her very serious expression immediately lifts my spirits. I nod.

"With a crazy friend who says so," I chuckle.

She smiles back at me.

"Exactly. Do you want to show your crazy friend your magic trick?"

I hesitate a bit, checking the door. If I'm caught playing with fire again, they'd have an excuse to send me back to an isolated room, with the handcuffs and all that crap. They even put two fire extinguishers inside my room, which is rather funny, I think.

Kelsi is waiting, looking a bit excited. Gosh, if it wasn't for her, I'd go insane locked up in here... I take a deep breath and lift my hand. One by one, I light a little flame on top of each finger. It's like I'm growing nails, and the flame is strangely redder than a normal fire, almost pinkish. My friend bites her lower lip.

"Damn, if only one of us smoked, that would be so cool. It really doesn't hurt?"

"Not at all. It almost feels a bit cold, actually."

"Well, your watch isn't beeping like crazy like last time, so–"

"Mara!"

Kelsi and I jump, and I immediately make my fire disappear. At the entrance of my room, the young nurse is staring at us, her hands on her hips.

"Are you crazy, you know you can't do that in here!"

"Sorry, Bonnie," I mutter.

Thankfully, it's only Bonnie. She's probably the only nurse on this floor who won't freak out about me only doing this much. She sighs and comes in with a large tray, my breakfast.

"You're lucky it's just me... Everyone is scared that you'd do it again. Everything okay here?" she asks, putting it down on the little table.

"Still itchy from the bandages..."

She walks up to the bed and checks my legs mostly, where the large burns are hidden under those damn bandages and layers of cream. I think Bonnie is the only nurse I like. She's just a bit older than us, petite, and very gentle. Her red hair is in a high ponytail today, and she's rather cute with her freckles.

While Bonnie is not looking, busy checking my temperature, Kelsi grabs the coffee from my tray and sips it down. She makes a little victory sign behind the nurse's back.

"Kelsi, put that down, it's not for you," suddenly says Bonnie, still not looking.

I scoff, amused. Kelsi's jaw drops.

"How do you know I took it?!"

"If you open the lid, it smells. I'm a werewolf, I can tell."

I always forget Bonnie is a werewolf. She looks like any normal human being, except maybe for that strange glow in her green eyes sometimes. Also, she never needs to turn on the lights at night, and her sense of smell is very good... good enough to tell when Kelsi tries to get free food from the hospital.

"Damn, I wish I was a werewolf," sighs Kelsi. "It must be so nice to get to shape-shift into a wolf anytime and go around naked."

"That's a bit weird to think about," I say, amused.

"First of all, we are not naked since we have our fur, and second, it's a real pain to take off your clothes and put them back on, if you don't rip them to begin with," replies Bonnie.

"Bonnie, any news of when I can go out?" I ask, a bit more seriously.

She hesitates a bit before answering, crossing her arms.

"Well, medically speaking, you're doing very well. Your skin is recovering from your burn marks very fast, which shouldn't even be possible with third and fourth-degree burns for a normal human or a werewolf."

"That's our little witch doing wonders..." whispers Kelsi with a smile.

Bonnie nods.

"We don't know much about witches, so we can only observe, but yes, you're doing fine on that part. The problem is your amnesia. We have done every CT scan, MRI, and check-up we could, and there's nothing that could explain it. You apparently didn't hurt your head in the accident, so the underlying cause is still totally unknown. We think it's psychological. To be honest, even if your doctor says yes, your psychiatrist will probably refuse, saying you're still mentally unstable..."

"Oh yes, she's obviously some dangerous psychopath," mutters Kelsi, rolling her eyes.

I frown. I'm so fed up with that guy.

"I am stable, Bonnie," I protest. "I've been locked up here for weeks, and I only get to take a walk outside once in a while. I haven't lost control in a while either. Seriously, I have had enough, and my memory is not going to come back by having me locked up here either. Can't my older sister ignore that guy and get me out of here anyway?" I ask.

"I don't think so, Mara," says Bonnie, looking a bit sorry. "I think Ms. Garnett listens to all of your doctors."

"When is my next session with him, then?" I ask, unhappy.

"This afternoon..."

I nod. This time, he is going to have to agree to let me out of here because I'm so fed up. I need some real fresh air, not a walk around the hospital park once every two days like some dog! Bonnie doesn't say anything else, giving me worried glances, but Kelsi has a smirk on.

"Someone's fired up..."

Bonnie shakes her head.

"Mara, if you lose control again, you're going to be sent back to the isolation cell. You know that, right?"

"I know, but seriously, Bonnie, I'm done. That guy is signing my release form or whatever today."

I hear a courteous knock on my door and take a deep breath. A quick glance at the bracelet; still beeping green. Alright.

"Hello, Miss Garnett," he says with his usual polite smile, walking in.

"Hi."

I stay on my bed, legs crossed, and I have a hard time not glaring at that guy. My psychiatrist is in his early forties, despite having lots of gray hair already, a wrinkled shirt, and a crooked nose. His name is Dimitri Epstein. Doctor Epstein... He takes the seat next to my bed, taking out his notepad as always. He does his best to look amiable, but I'm sure that is just part of his job. Not looking at the patient like she's a crazy witch... While he clicks his ballpoint pen, his eyes fall on the new envelope on my bedside table.

"I see your friend found some new pictures? Any luck?"

"No," I reply coldly.

I'm on my guard. I can't get mad because I don't want him to refuse my release again.

"That's too bad... As I mentioned before, I am a bit concerned about this apparent lack of a social life before your accident, Miss Garnett. As you know, your family is worried about what led to this unfortunate incident. Have you taken some time to think about that?"

I frown. Right. The main reason, or excuse, for my family to keep me locked in here is that I was the one who burned that building down in an attempt to kill myself. Thankfully, there were no other victims, but also no witnesses...

"I do have a friend," I note.

"Right, Miss Kim," he nods. "However, Miss Kim herself said you two were not very close before that incident, didn't she? Despite her many attempts to befriend you, she said, and I quote, 'You were not very talkative and our relationship was simply that of flatmates, nothing else.' I'm glad you're on better terms now, but this is not really helping us understand your behavior before the incident."

"Those pictures show I went to a party," I reply, handing him the envelope.

Doctor Epstein opens it and takes his time to check each of the pictures with a little frown.

"Interesting... Do you know when these pictures were taken, Clarissa?" he asks, taking some notes on his notepad.

"...Before I met Kelsi," I admit, "...and I told you to call me Mara!"

Damn it, I hate it when he calls me that on purpose! Epstein jumps, but quickly regains his composure and puts the envelope back, shaking his head.

"That is not your name. Your name is Clarissa Mary Garnett, which is stated on all your official documents, and confirmed by your family. We have already been over this, you saw all those documents yourself, Clarissa. There is no girl called Mara. This Mara is only a persona, a self-defense mechanism you have created yourself. It's nothing to be afraid about, Clarissa; everyone has a different way to cope with a traumatic event."

"I can create fire with my hands. Are you going to tell me my traumatized brain has invented this too?" I growl back.

He stays quiet for a long minute.

"Alright. I understand you do not want to... dissociate yourself from Mara. However, if you are Mara, then what about Clarissa? After all, you are Clarissa. You have seen all the proof of that. Your official documents, statements from your family, your friend, pictures... However, there is nothing about... Mara. No one knows her. So, who do you think Mara is?"

11

I don't have an answer for that. I just woke up, knowing my name, as if it was engraved deep in my head, like the only light I was able to hang on to. Everything else is gone. None of those documents or pictures they showed me reminded me of anything. I have an older sister that does look strikingly like me, but I couldn't recognize or remember her. Same with Kelsi, and she's the person I have been living with for months. Moreover, they all seemed to know me as Clarissa, not Mara.

Who the hell is Mara, then? Who am I...? I massage my temples, annoyed. So many questions and absolutely no answers. The only thing I'm sure of is that I won't be able to find anything out by being trapped here!

"Do you understand?" gently asks Dr. Epstein. "The nurse who is taking care of you mentioned you want to leave the hospital, but Clarissa, I don't think you are ready."

"I need to leave! You won't be able to achieve anything by keeping me trapped here!" I yell, frustrated. "I can read as many stupid cards as you have, do as many tests, I don't care, it's meaningless! My memories are gone, and I have been in here for weeks, with no progress at all!"

"I don't think that's true," he says. "First, your physical recovery was spectacular. I discussed it with your doctor earlier. He has never seen someone transferred out of the burn unit so quickly with the injuries you had."

I already know that. They call it a miracle, but it doesn't feel like that. My body knows what to do, and is healing itself better than any of their ointments or treatments. All of my deeper burns have now changed to lighter ones. Not only do I not feel any more pain, but the process isn't leaving any scars at all. My skin looks as new and smooth as a baby's. They even tried to take some samples to study, but once they removed the skin from my body, it went back to being as burnt as charcoal, which was even weirder.

I'm not burnt by my own fire and my skin heals fast. So why would I have trapped myself inside of a fire?

"If I'm so fine, why not let me out?" I say. "I can even keep this stupid bracelet on if it makes you feel better!"

I can't take it off by myself, and it tracks and records my body temperature at all times. According to Bonnie, this thing was custom-made for me. My personal thermometer tracker or something. It sure is better than the handcuffs, but it's not like it's invisible either. I feel like I'm a ticking time bomb or a prisoner.

Dr. Epstein makes a serious expression, takes a few more notes, and raises his head again to look at me.

"It's not that I don't want to allow you to leave, Clarissa. However, you have to understand that this isn't only about your security, but that of others as well. Since your admittance to the hospital, you've burned two beds and injured several members of the staff as well. This isn't a trivial matter."

"That was weeks ago," I protested. "I haven't hurt anyone or burnt anything in weeks, I can control myself now. Bonnie can tell you, I won't injure someone again!"

He sighs, shaking his head.

"Clarissa, I think you appreciate Miss Bonnie very much. Just like your friend Kelsi, you wouldn't hurt people who don't upset you. However, things are different for people who don't agree to your demands. We both know you have been showing some anger management issues, and this is not helping me trust your self-control."

"When, then?" I retort. "You can't keep me here forever just because you don't trust me! If you never let me experience the outside world, how would you know if I can control myself or not?"

He clicks his ballpoint pen, one, two, three, four times. It's annoying, but I'm more annoyed at the fact that he's not answering me. I want to tell him to hurry up, but I need to keep my emotions in check. I'm already on edge, my hands feel hot. I know I can call my flames out at any second. It's as if my fire is reacting to my anger. I could blast this annoying guy, watch him burn down to ashes, walk out that door, and–

"Clarissa?"

I flinch.

"S-sorry," I mumble.

"You looked lost in your thoughts just now. Do you want to share what you were thinking about with me?"

Oh, that's not the kind of thing I can tell him. That my instincts are telling me to do whatever the hell I want, including getting rid of my psychiatrist by burning him like a piece of toast and breaking out.

"Nothing," I lie.

He frowns a bit, pushing his pen against his lips.

"I've noticed you seem to have those short episodes of absences regularly when you're with me. Does that happen often?"

"I'm not sure..."

It's the truth this time. I'm not even sure what those are supposed to be. It's almost as if I'm... someone else, for a few seconds. Like another voice taking over in my head. Where the heck does that come from? Every time, it's like someone else is in my head, whispering... I close my eyes and take a deep breath.

"Clarissa, talk to me. How do you feel right now?"

"Frustrated. I have a hundred questions and no one is willing to give me the answers I want."

"How about we list your questions down, then?"

I glare at him. Really? After weeks of being locked in here, he thinks everything can be solved with some stupid chit-chat?

"I want to see my sister."

"I know, but she is—"

"Busy, I get it."

It's always the same damn answer. I have only seen my older sister three times since I woke up, and according to everyone here, it's a damn miracle. Kelsi didn't even know I had an older sister, I apparently never mentioned her. I never brought up my family at all, and I didn't bother to keep any pictures of them in my room either. What kind of family is this?

No good family relationships, no friends... No one even knows what the heck I was doing at the university!

He lets out a long sigh and takes out his phone.

"Alright, I guess we won't get anywhere until I actually ask..."

"Put it on speaker."

He looks at me, surprised. I want to listen to what my older sister says, why she won't come to see me. I'm tired of always hearing it from someone else. He nods and calls her. To my surprise, she answers after only two rings.

"Dr. Epstein? Something wrong with Clarissa?"

"N-no, Ms. Garnett, but... I'm with your younger sister, and she insists that she really wants to leave the hospital. I am in one of my sessions with her, and Clarissa insisted that I call you personally."

"I already said no."

He and I exchange a glance. How can she answer so fast? She could at least consider it, or even ask how I'm doing! Why is she so bent on that fucking no? Dr. Epstein sighs and looks a bit distressed with me glaring at him.

"I think it might be better if you... gave a reason to Miss Clarissa. She is a bit sensitive about her confinement, and—"

"I don't have any reason to give. She's my younger sister, I'm her legal guardian. I make the decisions, Clarissa doesn't need to know why. Is that all? I'm busy."

"I understand, Ms.—"

14

I grab the phone from his hand, furious. I don't give a damn about her being busy! This is my life we are talking about, she is not the one locked up within these four walls!

"Tell me why you won't let me out!" I shout.

"C-Clarissa?" her voice is more high-pitched, she almost sounds like she's about to choke. "Why are you listening to this...?"

"Because I want to know why you are not letting me out!"

I hear her sigh.

"You don't need to know. It's also for your security. As long as you stay in that hospital, you won't get into any trouble, and this way, you can be—"

"What security?! You don't tell me anything! Amy, I can freaking make fire with my hands! What is there that I should be afraid of, what trouble?"

"Clarissa, enough! The police already made us pay for all the damages from that damn building, and I have three lawyers making sure no one sues you! Our people already think I have a crazy, pyromaniac, younger sister, and the damn werewolves are all over me trying to get to you! This city is already complicated enough to deal with!"

"...The werewolves? Why would the werewolves want something from me...?"

"Clarissa, stop asking questions. You're staying where you are and that's final. We will discuss it more when I come back to Silver City."

"When is that?"

She sighs at the other end of the phone. Damn, I really feel like a freaking fly trying to squeeze into her agenda. I wait for her answer, a bit too long, in my opinion.

"Give the phone back to Dr. Epstein."

"I'm listening," he says.

"I said to take the phone back. If I need to ask again, you're fired."

Oh, crap... I didn't mean to risk his job. Can my older sister even do that? Does she own the hospital or what? I let the poor man take his phone back, but I already know this is a lost battle. He apologizes non-stop for over a minute before hanging up with a sour face.

"She was a bit... upset," he says.

"Sorry about that."

He shakes his head, puts his phone back, and retrieves his things before getting up.

"Do not apologize, Miss Clarissa. To be honest, I understand your position too. It's not easy to be locked up when you have done nothing wrong... by your own family, no less. Unfortunately, there isn't much I can do to help

15

you. On paper, you are here as a psychiatric patient, and this is hard to overcome when it comes to leaving without your family's approval."

"...Do you think my sister is lying?" I ask.

He seems to hesitate for a few seconds, playing with the pen between his fingers. After a while, he shrugs.

"From the few exchanges I've had with her, all I can say is that your elder sister is probably more stubborn than you are, and very down to earth. However, I do think the fact that she's the only one in your family who does call you and visit you says... a lot about her character."

His words confuse me even more. Does he mean to say Amy cares about me? Does she? What kind of older sister does that? I'm trapped here, she barely visits me... I don't get it.

"I'll get going now, Miss Clarissa, I think we are done for the day. Please try to be a little bit more patient, hm? I sincerely hope it will all be solved soon."

I nod and watch him leave. As soon as he's gone, I let out a long sigh of frustration and lie down on my bed, with a grimace because I rubbed some of my bandages unintentionally. What the heck is wrong with my family... None of this makes sense. What was that about the werewolves too? No one ever mentioned them aside from Bonnie until now. I push the button, but another nurse comes, much to my annoyance. Bonnie's shift is probably over... Crap. I wanted to ask her to see if she knows anything. The old lady leaves my dinner there and almost runs out of the room. They all avoid me when I'm unhappy like this.

I stare outside. Another day lost, trapped here. Is Kelsi at her part-time job? I bite my thumb, nervous and pissed. What am I supposed to do? If things go on like this, Amy will never let me out, or I'm going to go completely crazy before that happens. I should just walk out... I feel the shadow, crawling in the back of my mind. I should walk out that door, follow my instincts, and leave. Burn anything and anyone who tries to stop me. I should just end this...

Suddenly, I hear some sounds coming from outside. What the heck? I run to the window, unsure. I don't see anything, but I can hear someone yelling, a woman screaming. It seems like it's coming from below the hospital, in the park.

Something's wrong. Why is no one coming to help her? The few silhouettes I can see don't seem bothered at all, what's wrong with those people?! I take off running out of my room. I hear someone yelling, trying to have me come back, but I ignore them. I dodge whoever tries to hold me back. I'm almost flying. It's strange, I can hear that woman's screams even from inside the corridor. I run down the stairs, trying to find the way out. A couple of senile grannies stare at me in confusion, I have to squeeze in between them to get out. Two furious nurses are behind me, running after me, but I don't care, that woman needs help!

I finally see the way out to the park. I've been there a few times, so why the heck does it seem so far?! I push through the door to find myself in the park. The... empty park. I look around, completely at a loss.

There is no woman, and no screams anymore. It can't be... I just heard them. It was so clear! Why don't I see anyone? There's only an ambulance at the other end, with a red-haired guy smoking his cigarette, who starts walking up to me with a worried look. Crap, what the heck... What the... What is wrong with me...?

I stay stunned in the middle of the park, completely perplexed. I keep looking around, confused. I don't understand what just happened. All the screams are gone, and even that strange shadow that was haunting me has vanished. It's like I just woke up from some dream... a dream in which I've been very much awake the whole time. What the hell is wrong with me?

The two nurses that were running after me suddenly arrive and grab my arms.

"Where the heck are you running to?! Go back to your room!" they yell in my ears.

I try to defend myself, get out of their grip, but they are stronger than me. Those damn women! They are holding on so tightly, it freaking hurts! I keep struggling. Won't those old hags let go?! I'm just going to burn those damn–

"Hey, hey, easy, easy. Let go, ladies, please. I got it. It's alright, I got it."

The guy I spotted earlier just arrived in front of us, and gently, he takes the nurses' hands off of me. My hands aren't on fire, yet. There is some smoke coming from my fingers, though, and he sees it too. He clearly glances at my hands.

"Don't give me that, little witch," he says. "No fire tricks and I promise these ladies will leave us alone."

I nod, still a bit shaken up. For some reason, I have a hard time containing my fire. I can't stop shaking because I'm so angry. The smoke disappears slowly, and as soon as the nurses retreat away from me, it gets easier for me to control myself. The red-headed guy smiles.

"There we go. No need to get fired up."

"We have to get her back to her room," insists one of the nurses, as if I wasn't there.

"It's okay, I'll watch her," says the redhead. "She can't go much farther anyway, right? She can stay with me for a few minutes, get some fresh air, and I'll make sure she goes back. It's fine..."

I can't believe it... They are actually listening to him and going back inside, despite their dubious glares. I'm confused, who is this guy? I'm rubbing my painful arm in total disbelief. One of their nails really made me bleed... I turn to the guy, unsure who I'm dealing with. He looks like a normal guy, but he clearly knows about my power, and there's something oddly familiar about him too. I'm probably staring too much, because he shakes his head and chuckles.

"No need to give me that look. You don't remember me, do you?"

"You do look familiar," I admit.

"I bet. I'm Benjamin Lewis, Bonnie is my twin sister."

"Oh!"

I can't believe I didn't realize earlier! This guy is the male version of Bonnie, with red hair, big blue eyes, and even her little nose... I feel a bit relieved. Somehow, this guy being Bonnie's twin tells me I can trust him. That doesn't really explain why he defended me against the harpies from earlier, but he does have the attitude of a laid-back guy. He's wearing jeans and a simple shirt too, that actually shows a little bit of a tattoo he's got on his torso. Is that a white circle? Benjamin takes out another cigarette with a little smile. Meanwhile, I'm just in this stupid hospital gown... I wish I had real, proper clothes on, for once. It looks like I'm wearing oversized pajamas like a child.

I suddenly remembered his earlier comment.

"Wait, you said... I should remember you?" I say.

"Yeah, the fire. I was one of the guys who took you out of there. Not that we helped a lot, but–"

"You mean when I was in... that fire?"

He nods.

"Yep. The whole barbecue... To be honest, when we heard there was still someone alive inside, I didn't believe it. We fought the fire like crazy to find you and get you out of there. You're lucky, little witch, because anyone else would be dead."

I feel a bit embarrassed. I never met anyone who was actually on the site of the accident itself. I've only heard a few things from the doctors, my sister, and whatever the nurses would whisper in the corridors. This guy could have died because of me... Is he a firefighter, then? He's tall, and with his broad shoulders and thin musculature, he probably could be one. However, right now, he just has a simple ambulance staff jacket.

18

"Thank you," I mumble.

"Don't thank me, as I said, I really didn't get to do much... You were half-conscious, we dragged you out and sent you here as soon as possible. ...So, want to tell me why you just made those two poor ladies run? You looked a bit lost earlier."

I sigh and look around again. I'm feeling like an idiot now. I ran after something that wasn't there, as evidence shows. If they knew that I'm starting to hear voices, I'd never leave this place. What can I say so he won't think I'm completely nuts?

"I just... needed some fresh air," I lie.

"That must have been quite the emergency," he chuckles.

"Well, I don't get much at all."

Benjamin's eyes get a bit more serious all of a sudden, and he nods.

"I know. Everyone is wary of you... The new witch. I heard your family is keeping you locked here."

"I feel like everyone knows this kind of stuff but me. They are all walking on eggshells, keeping me behind closed doors, and no one is telling me a thing..."

"Yeah... Well, you can't blame them. Silver City has a dark history with witches...."

What dark history? I thought I was the only witch in the city, that's what everyone's been telling me for days!

"There were other witches before me?" I ask.

He looks surprised, raising an eyebrow.

"No one told you a thing?"

"Well, I don't talk to that many people, the staff freak out just by being in the same room... but I'm sure Bonnie never mentioned another witch," I state.

"Ah... It's... Bonnie doesn't really like talking about those things."

"Why?"

Benjamin sighs, looking a bit unsure and annoyed this time. His eyes wander elsewhere while he answers as if he couldn't bring himself to look me in the eye.

"A witch killed our older brother. She's still... not over it."

Oh, shit... Why? What happened? Bonnie never mentioned anything like that! I didn't think there was another witch here before me, let alone one who would commit murder! Their older brother was definitely a werewolf as well, right? Do witches and werewolves usually fight like this? I bite my lower lip.

"Can I ask... what happened?"

"He wasn't the only one who died. Over a couple of years ago, there was a war here in Silver City. A freaking big one that involved werewolves, humans, vampires, and... witches."

"Even vampires? No one told me there were vampires..."

I can't believe it. It was already complicated for me to accept that this city is split between two species, werewolves and humans, with me belonging to neither, but now, even vampires? What kind of crazy world am I waking up into? I feel like a single drop of water lost in an ocean. My lost memories are not getting me anywhere, I'm learning everything, but there is this sort of common knowledge that was left behind, telling me what is normal and what is not. I know what humans, werewolves, and vampires are, everyone does. I'm aware that at least two of those shouldn't even be able to get along.

"Well, they didn't belong to Silver City. They just tried to overpower us. Humans and werewolves united together against the vampires."

"What about the witches, then? Were they on... the vampire's side, then?"

Damn it, do I belong to the bad side? I'm already friends with a werewolf and a human, why do I have to be a witch if our kinds are enemies? Is that why everyone fears me? If witches killed people in that war, why do they even bother keeping me alive at all?

Benjamin seems to slightly regret bringing up this topic. He scratches his chin, which has some hair growing back on it, looking a bit unsure.

"Yes and no... There were only two witches. One on our side, one on the other. They both died in that war, that's why you're the only living witch we know of in Silver City at the moment."

"Oh..."

Well, that doesn't make things much better... I didn't imagine witches would fight against each other. I had actually somewhat decided that, even if those witches were on the vampire's side, I would stay on the human and werewolf one, but I guess that solves the problem... It doesn't help me with who I am or why I'm locked up here, though.

"So that's how you guys all knew I was a witch?" I ask.

"Yes and no. See, we have never seen a Fire Witch, but we know they exist. You were able to survive in a fire that would have killed a human or a werewolf ten times over. And those marks..."

He points at my bandages, the ones that the earlier struggle kind of unraveled. It revealed my remaining markings, a bit red and darker than before. I wrap it back quickly, as I don't like to have them exposed.

"What about them."

"We suspect it's a witch's markings. When witches use their powers too much, those marks appear on their bodies as a sign that they are overdoing it."

"What? Really?"

He nods.

So my scars are some sort of spell? This is insane... I look down. I still remember the charcoal look of my legs weeks ago, the first time I saw them. No sane doctor thought I could heal from that, those were the highest-degree burns possible. The flesh was supposedly dead, yet it started healing and regrowing by itself. Is that how they came to the conclusion that I was a witch? This healing ability of mine is certainly not normal... even I can tell this much.

Benjamin is still smoking his cigarette, looking pretty calm. I'm not calm! I can't believe no one told me my markings were a symbol of witchcraft! I thought my ability to make fire was all they had as proof to say I'm a witch, I didn't even suspect they had more clues than that... or that there had even been other witches before me.

"So, those two witches... They had them too?"

"We never witnessed them getting as bad as yours, but yes. It can affect your internal organs too, so be careful with fire, little witch."

"You said they weren't Fire Witches," I say, ignoring his warning. "What were they?"

"One was a Water Witch, the other one was an Earth Witch. Very different from you, Mara, but the same markings and the same ability to play with their element. We all witnessed it. The two witches we knew about were already frighteningly powerful with just water and earth, so now that we have a young chick like you playing with fire, we are all kind of on our toes, waiting to see what is going to happen next."

So that's why... I mean, it doesn't explain everything, but at least I know why they are all so afraid. I'm not the first one, there were precedents. Those other witches were here before me and left quite an impression on the people of Silver City. This would explain a lot. I'm not just confined in my room, I'm under tight observation. The thermometer, the fact that I can't go out, my doctors, my psychiatrist, everyone watching my every move and trying to understand what happened. It's not just because I'm a freak, it's because of fear. Fear of what I can do... I glance down at my hands. I know this is dangerous, I get it. Even I have trouble controlling myself sometimes.

However, wouldn't it have just been easier to tell me all of this? I'm not an idiot! Why do I have to bump into Bonnie's twin to finally get some answers I've been asking for all this time?!

"Why did no one tell me this earlier?!" I exclaim, furious.

21

I'm getting so mad about all this. At the very least, Bonnie should have told me! She sees me every day, why couldn't she give me that little bit of information right away? She knows how much I'm struggling with my lost memories! I bite my thumb, angry. This is ridiculous! This is about me, yet no one is giving me the slightest clue!

Benjamin sighs, pulling on his cigarette before answering me.

"This isn't just to annoy you, little witch. It's not just Bonnie and our family, almost every human or werewolf living here in Silver City lost a friend or a family member in that war. It was a horrible fight, okay? Some people are still dealing with its consequences, like how my sister is still unable to talk about it. The ones who started it and caused the most damage were the witches. We just don't know how to deal with all of this, with you. It's not that simple."

I am stunned. The witches actually caused that horrible war he's talking about...? The most damage too? He can't mean they were the ones who killed the most people, right? It can't be... I try to process it, but I just don't understand.

"You said there were only two of them..." I mutter.

"Exactly. There were only two witches, but they were the root of everything we went through. I won't get into the details, and I don't want to push it all on the witches, but these are the facts everyone here in Silver City remembers: witches are powerful and scary. They are not human or werewolf, and we don't know that much about them. To be honest with you, we actually thought that your kind had died in that war and that we were done with witches. But you're here now. We have a new witch in town, playing with fire, and she already burned down a building before we even knew she was around. A Fire Witch in Silver City, after the earth and water ones. You're saying you feel trapped here and all, but how do you think people will react once you go out and your existence is made public?"

I... I don't know how to answer that.

I can't even begin to imagine. It's... terrifying. This whole city isn't just split between humans and werewolves. All these people are traumatized by a war that witches caused. Only two of them. If there were as many deaths as Benjamin said, and the witches were responsible for all of it... I'm probably a monster to them. They thought they were done with witches, probably ready to move on, but here I am.

On top of that, I revealed myself in the worst way possible with that big fire. I know it made the evening news for a whole building to go up in flames with one survivor...

"Don't worry," says Benjamin. "It doesn't mean all of Silver City really thinks witches are bad. At least, probably not the werewolves. There was one of them on our side, remember? It's just that we are... wary of witches. Especially the humans, who don't have much affinity with witches. The fight was mostly us against the vampires, but the humans had to participate anyway. Things are... tense, outside. You're not confined here only for people's safety, but also for your own. Until we figure things out."

He means until they can figure out what to do with me... How dangerous I really am. I take a deep breath. So far, I've barely been able to control myself when I get angry. Moreover, there is this voice in the back of my mind that comes up at unexpected times... No, I shouldn't think about it. As far as I know, it might just be my imagination, my own mind playing tricks.

I need to think of something else. I can feel some stares on my back. I probably don't have much time left to ask questions before I'm dragged back to my room. To think Benjamin, whom I just met, is the first one to explain so many things to me... I think about his words again.

"When you say until we can figure out what's going on... Who is this 'we', exactly?" I ask.

Benjamin chuckles and raises his hand with the cigarette toward the building behind me.

"You know this facility is called the White Hospital, right? This hospital belongs to the northern clan of werewolves in Silver City, the White Moon. That's why Bonnie and I work here, you're on werewolf territory, little witch. Your older sister made an agreement with the White Luna, for your protection."

"The White Luna? Isn't Luna the other name for the... Queen of Werewolves?" I ask, remembering what Bonnie and Kelsi taught me only a few weeks ago about the hierarchy among werewolves. "You're telling me my older sister made a pact with someone that important for my sake?"

Benjamin starts laughing, shaking his head.

"Of course she's important, but she's not almighty! Moreover, the Earth Witch, who was the good witch, was a friend of the Luna. So, of course, she's going to keep a close eye on you. She's a good friend of our family, actually."

"What's her name?"

"Selena. Selena Whitewood."

23

Chapter 2

"So... Selena Whitewood?" repeated Kelsi.

I nod. She is lying on her stomach on my bed and frowning next to me, her chin in her hand. After my phone call with her this morning, Kelsi had promised to come visit me right after her classes, and of course, she did. Her bag is hanging at the end of my bed, and her laptop is open in front of us.

"Have you heard of her?" I ask.

"Well, I've heard about the Lunas of Silver City, everyone here knows about the werewolves and their hierarchy, but... he didn't say anything else?"

"No... I wanted to ask more, but the nurses came back and pulled me back inside. I'm pretty sure he was given an earful too, he was called into the director's office right after that."

"Did you try asking Bonnie?"

"I haven't seen her since..."

It's almost strange, actually. It has been two days since I last saw the red-haired nurse, and she has never been absent for this long without telling me before. Did her twin telling me so many things put her in a bad position? I can't help but feel a bit bad about it. Somehow, I feel like this is my fault. What if she really got in trouble? Or does she not want to talk to me anymore because of what I know now?

"So?" I ask Kelsi again. "What do you know about that woman, Selena Whitewood?"

She sighs and sits up, shaking her head with her usual cute little pout behind her glasses.

"Not much, to be honest. I don't have any werewolf friends, so all I know is just general knowledge. You remember how werewolves obey an Alpha and his female partner, the Luna, right? Well, usually, territory is divided among several packs, each led by an Alpha couple. Since Silver City is so big, the werewolves here are split between several packs, but one of the biggest ones is the White Moon Clan, led by that woman, Selena Whitewood. She is basically the boss for all the werewolves living in the northern parts of Silver City."

His Blazing Witch

"So she's still someone super important, right?" I ask.

"To the werewolves, yes. I don't know what she does for a living, though, she isn't really famous or anything. Most werewolf Alphas are often CEOs or celebrities of some sort, usually wealthy too, but that woman seems kind of low-key in comparison."

Kelsi turns to her computer and types that woman's name into the search bar. It only takes a couple of seconds, but when the results show up, we both exchange a look and frown. Only four results? Kelsi starts clicking, biting her hair.

"This one is a birth note for a baby girl born last year, Aurora Reagan Whitewood-Black... Probably that woman's daughter? So if her father's name is Black... Don't tell me, Black like the Black Corporation Group?"

"What is the Black Corporation Group?" I ask, confused.

Kelsi turns to me with wide-open eyes as if I was crazy.

"You don't know who the... Oh, girl, your wiped-out memory is really driving me peanuts! Boo, the Black Corporation Group owns about half of Silver City!"

I grimace and grab my notebook where I've been writing down all kinds of information. I hate missing important pieces of information like that. I have pages and pages of this notebook covered with writing already, mostly from things Kelsi mentioned as "I must absolutely know", and despite my best attempts to remember everything, it's just a lot... though, I'm pretty sure the Black Corporation Group was never mentioned to me before. Kelsi hands me a pen she just took out from her bag and goes on.

"They are a multinational company, their business literally exploded in the last few years. They own several business ventures: shops, malls, restaurants... They are mostly based in Silver City, of course, and famous for being run by the Black Brothers, all werewolves. They are basically the strongest and wealthiest group in Silver City. Probably your sister's nightmare too, in terms of business. They're probably rivals to any other big companies around."

"Wow... So that woman, Selena Whitewood, is married to one of them?"

Kelsi returns to the computer, adjusting her thick glasses with a frown and scrolling down.

"I guess? It doesn't say the parents' names here, just the baby's. Let's see the other links I got... Oh, she's a graduate of our university, in the Business Management Department... Well, she apparently dropped out over four years ago, so maybe not. Next link... Oh, this is just some stupid promo... Crap, that woman doesn't even have a social media account!"

"Maybe she uses an alias?" I suggest.

Kelsi sighs, staring at her computer screen with a frown and putting her hands in her sweater's pocket. She is wearing a pastel blue one with pink kittens today, just as ugly and cringey as the others. She even has little cat ears on the hood.

"To be honest, as a geek, I think it's more like someone made sure to delete her."

"What do you mean? Delete her?"

"You know, like when someone wants to stay private and everything? She probably had someone delete her info on the Internet to be left alone. You don't become this invisible just like that, even with very good privacy settings. However, if she's that influential, she probably paid someone to delete all of her info, or knew someone who could do it."

"This is crazy!" I exclaim. "We are supposedly on that woman's territory! Why can't I find the slightest bit of information about her?"

"Well, at least we know that she probably lives here. Werewolves are territorial, it wouldn't make sense if she lived on the other side of Silver City."

I nod. Kelsi is most likely right. Even if online research didn't give us many results, we are already in the right area.

"Do you think I could find her?" I ask.

"Why don't you just wait a bit and ask Bonnie?" Kelsi insists.

I sigh. I wish I could! I have a feeling that Bonnie will not give me the answers I want, though. If she has avoided telling me anything until now and stopped showing up as soon as I got more information from her twin...

"I need to find that woman," I declare.

Kelsi coughs, looking at me like I'm crazy.

"Are you kidding? After all the things that guy told you?"

"He did say Selena Whitewood thinks witches are not bad."

"He also said most people in Silver City do! Boo, I think you're getting a little bit too impatient here. Why don't you just wait until Bonnie comes back? Maybe she's just on a short leave, or she's caught a cold? Moreover, even if you find that woman, what do you want to ask her anyway?"

"She knew the previous Earth Witch, Kelsi. Benjamin said Selena Whitewood was a friend of hers, and that's why she let my sister hide me here in her hospital. I want to know what she knew about witches, and who that Earth Witch was. No one else seems to know the first thing about witches. At least not the humans around me."

Kelsi nods a bit, glancing at the computer.

"I did try to research a bit about witches, but... nothing really matches you. Well, in ancient times, they did burn the women thought to be witches at the stake, so, not much resistance to fire from them, I guess... I mean, if they were witches at all. I think the actual witches probably did a good job of staying hidden. Even in Silver City, I found no record of witches, none. Not even about those two you mentioned."

"See? I need to find someone who knows, someone who was close to the other witches."

Kelsi is still pouting, but at least, she doesn't protest anymore. She sighs and starts typing again on her computer.

"Alright, maybe I'll find something about her husband, then... If she's with one of the Black Brothers, at least their information should be available, they are pretty well-known."

A website shows up quickly about the Black Corporation Group that Kelsi mentioned. They really are as big as she said. Most of their pages are about promoting their company, though, there really isn't much information about the Black family themselves. Finally, Kelsi finds an excerpt from a web page introducing their staff.

"Oh, here! Damian Black, CEO. He's the eldest brother... I've seen him in magazines. Doesn't seem like he's very talkative, though, he's quite cold and hates interviews."

"You think that's her husband?"

"I don't think so," Kelsi shakes her head. "I'm pretty sure I heard somewhere that this guy is the Alpha of the Blood Moon Clan, a different one. The other biggest clan of werewolves of Silver City, actually. If she's from the White Moon, he's probably not her husband... Oh, here's another one. Nathaniel Black, Vice Chairman and Director of the Black Leisure Group. That might be him... Damn it, there isn't even a photo!"

Kelsi and I spend a while on the website, trying to look for more information about the Black Brothers, but everything is focused on their company, not them. Just like Selena Whitewood, we cannot find their social media profiles either. Finally, Kelsi manages to find pictures of the Black Corporation Christmas party from last year.

"Oh, here! This is the eldest brother... That woman next to him is definitely his wife. Oh, they look so cute together... Oh, she can't be Selena."

"What? Why?" I ask, confused.

Indeed, from their posture, you can see that woman is his wife. Damian Black is a tall man, with dark hair and clear eyes, looking very stern in his black suit. However, he has a protective arm around the young woman next to him.

27

She is really pretty, wearing a dark purple dress and her hair, also black, in a braided bun. However, you can't miss the scar on her left eye... it looks like an old blade injury. That woman looks happy in the picture, though, and she's holding the hand of a young boy that looks like them.

"Look at her dress in the next picture... That one, see? It's not that obvious because of her dress and she's rather petite, but she was pregnant, at least a few months along. The other page we saw about the birth of the little girl said that she was born in late July the summer before. Either they had another baby on the way soon after or she isn't the same woman."

"Oh..."

"This one must be the Blood Moon Clan's Luna then? Damn, the werewolves' hierarchy is super confusing. I mean, if his brother is married or whatever to the White Moon's Luna, he should be the Alpha, right? Can't they just have one big clan? So complicated..."

I'm probably even more lost than Kelsi. I understand the werewolf hierarchy, it's rather simple, but I just want to find that woman, Selena Whitewood. I don't care much about her title or whatever it is. I'm just curious about the woman who can tell me more about witches...

Kelsi and I keep looking at all the pictures of that party, but either the other brother did not attend or we can't find him, I don't know. We end up closing Kelsi's computer, both feeling a bit defeated.

"Sorry, boo... It's okay, we'll probably be able to find more information once we ask around, though. I'm sure there are other werewolves like Bonnie and Benjamin around who can tell us. Especially if she's as accessible as that guy said, maybe you'll get your answers faster than you think?"

"I sure hope so... though I won't get any by staying here, that's for sure." I sigh.

Kelsi nods, leaving my bed to stretch. She opens the window to let the breeze in, taking her hood off with a smile.

"I like being alone so I'm probably not able to experience this like you, but I sure wouldn't mind being able to stay in my bedroom and watch my favorite TV shows all day instead of preparing for these stupid exams!"

"It's not staying here that drives me nuts, it's staying here with no answers."

"Well, it sure is weird. No one knows about your powers, your fire thing came out of nowhere ever since that accident... I'm very suspicious about your sister, though, you know. I swear she never, ever called you before that accident. You never mentioned your family, so I'd bet all of my game consoles that you were never close to her!"

"This much I can tell," I snicker. "I don't even feel close to her. If she didn't look like me, I'd think she's a total stranger..."

"It's been bugging me," adds Kelsi. "She got you this fancy room, negotiated with the werewolves for your sake... Your sis is definitely suspicious. I mean, maybe not bad, like this is not a movie and she's some villain, but... I feel like there's more to it. You think she could know more than she says about your witchy powers?"

I shake my head.

"I feel like she doesn't want to hear anything about it! She almost yelled at the doctors when she heard them calling me a witch in the corridor last time. She doesn't look very... witchcraft-inclined either. More like the modern businesswoman who doesn't have a minute to lose on voodoo and magic spells."

"So, what are you going to do next, boo? I'm pretty sure they won't let that Benjamin near you again, you know. I wasn't sure about telling you, but the nurses were talking about it. I wouldn't be surprised if they add another lock to your door."

"Well, I want to try asking Bonnie or my sister about that woman, Selena, and what they know about witches. They cannot pretend they don't know anything anymore."

Kelsi nods.

"What if they say they don't know again? Or if they don't show up?"

I take a deep breath, scratching my head. I can't wait anymore. I need answers, and it's clear now that they are not going to come to me just by waiting, locked within these four walls. Even with Kelsi hacking the hospital's wifi and sneaking her computer in, we only got this much. They are all working hard at keeping me in the dark, and I'm tired of it.

"Three days," I say. "If I don't learn anything new from my sister or Bonnie within the next three days, I'm breaking out of here."

"B-breaking out?" Kelsi repeated in a whisper. "Boo, that's a little bit extreme..."

I shrug.

"If the answers don't come to me, I'm going to them!"

Chapter 3

I take a deep breath, and open my hands again slowly. I count to three. One, two... A flame appears in the middle of my hand, making me smile. I check my weird watch, but it's still beeping green. My body temperature is probably still on the normal spectrum... I try to focus on the flame dancing in my hand. It doesn't look like a normal fire. It's dark red, almost an odd shade of pink, burnt pink. I put my hands closer together, and slide it from one palm to the other. My heart is thumping in my chest.

I'm getting the hang of this. There is no smoke this time, just a warm, cozy, little fire bouncing between my hands. I can't help but chuckle a little bit. It feels different from the fire I provoke when I'm angry. This one isn't dangerous... I try to bring it closer to my arm, the one without the bracelet. As expected, I don't get burned from that. Even my body hair is just fine. To me, this flame is barely warm. I look around me and grab a dead leaf that's close to my knee. I'm sitting down in some meditation pose, and my back is starting to ache a bit, but I don't care. I take another deep breath and bring the dead leaf to the flame. As expected, it starts to burn right away, until the little ashes fall in between my legs. So the fire doesn't burn me, but it's still hot to everything else. I should have asked Benjamin what colors the flames were from the fire they found me in, but I haven't seen him since.

I sigh and decide to practice a bit more. I try to have it change position, flipping my hand over. Now, it's on the back of my hand, but it's harder to control. I frown and focus on pushing it to the tips of my fingers... As soon as I try to split it, most of the fire dies down, but I manage to have some go all the way up to my index finger and thumb. I pout. Yeah, maybe the roof wasn't the best idea to practice handling fire. There is too much wind here. I put my thumb and index finger together, and the fire goes into the little circle they made.

Why am I fine while doing this? No pain, no headache. My burns are healing just fine too, and more importantly, no voices... I just don't get the voices. What the heck was that? It was my first time actually having this kind of hallucination. Before that, there was always something like a shadow inside my mind. Now, it's outside too. I let out a long sigh. I'm never leaving this place

30

if they find out I'm experiencing that crap more and more. I wish there was another witch around to teach me what the hell is wrong with me...

"Mara! Finally, I found you!"

I jump and extinguish my fire right away. I get up and turn around to find Bonnie, her arms crossed at the doorway of the rooftop's exit.

"Bonnie!" I exclaim.

I haven't seen her in days, I'm excited just to see her red hair flying around her freckled frowning face. She looks annoyed, shaking her head.

"You have a freaking tracking watch on you and you still make me run all around the hospital to find you!"

"Sorry... I needed some fresh air, and they won't let me into the park again, so—"

"You could open the window in your room, you know!"

It's my turn to frown. So much for fresh air, those damn windows barely open enough for me to let my arm out! I walked up to her, trying to hide the fact that I was practicing my fire handling.

"It's been a while," I say while walking back inside with her.

"Sorry. My older brother suddenly asked me to come and help them at the children's hospital, they were swamped, all the kids gave each other the flu..."

"Oh..."

I hesitate, biting my thumb. Should I tell her about Benjamin? After a while, I remembered Kelsi's words. If I want honesty, I'd better make the first step myself...

"I met... Benjamin."

She nods but doesn't stop walking. We are now going down the empty emergency staircase to get back to my floor, and it's awkwardly quiet in here. For some reason, I don't like enclosed spaces like these. There could be room for ten people on each floor, but if it lacks windows and air circulation, I don't like it.

"I know, he told me. As usual, he couldn't keep quiet..."

"...Why didn't you tell me? About... the other witches, and your older brother?"

Bonnie stops, putting her hands in her white blouse's pockets, and turns to me. I see her searching for the right words, licking her lower lip.

"I thought you might feel... too pressured. Everything that happened here happened... before you, Mara. Those witches are dead now, and you're not them. I thought you might feel bad if you knew what had happened. It's not that I have anything against you because of... the loss of my brother. Everyone knows this is a weird situation. We never expected another witch to show up,

31

we don't know what to expect from you either... I also have to watch what I say, I'm under orders."

"Selena Whitewood's orders?"

"Yeah." She nods. "Selena is doing her best right now, but... it's complicated."

I can't help but roll my eyes. I feel like I've been given the same damn excuse over and over again yet no one really explains anything except for "it's complicated!"

"Bonnie, what the heck is going on? I get no one is happy to see a witch in Silver City after what happened, okay? I really get it. However, I also get that there's a lot no one is telling me. I am basically hidden here. Even my own family..."

"Mara, I promise we will tell you things when we can," she says, as she starts walking again, "but your family is also a bit on edge with us, okay? And now that you mention it, your older sister is here. That's why I came to get you."

I stay stunned for a couple of seconds before running after her, almost in shock.

"Amy? Amy is here?"

"Yes, she is waiting for you. She just showed up out of the blue at reception when I was starting my shift, I ran to get you... Why did you have to hide on the freaking roof?!"

I apologize, but we are both almost running downstairs. Well, more like walking as fast as it's allowed in a hospital. My heart is going crazy again, making big jumps in my chest. I haven't seen Amy in at least two weeks, and she finally shows up out of the blue. I'm stressed. Our last conversation was not the best... Is that why she's here? She's mad? We have a seven-year age difference, but I feel like she's miles above me, an authoritarian figure of excellence...

I'm insanely nervous. I didn't have time to check how I look in a mirror or at least tie my hair up or something. I probably look like a damn mess. When we arrive at the entrance, I keep frantically looking around. Bonnie asks the receptionist, and apparently, my sister was already taken to my room. Oh, crap. I don't wait for Bonnie and hurry back upstairs.

I arrive so fast that I almost wreck my face on the floor. I somehow manage to just fall on my knees in front of her, though I don't feel any less stupid for that. I hear her sigh in front of me.

"What are you doing..."

She walks up to me, and one second after her pointy shoes appear under my eyes, she grabs my arm and helps me up. Amy is much taller than me. I think regardless of her being a woman, she's really tall. She has a nice long and toned build. I get back on my feet, a bit embarrassed to face her. Compared to my horrible hospital gown, she's wearing a perfect burgundy ensemble that looks like it just came out of the latest collection of an haute couture store.

Even her hair, unlike mine, is gorgeously shaped in a tight updo, her perfectly tamed curls falling on her shoulders. I probably just look like a big frizzy mess...

"S-sorry," I say.

I probably seemed much more confident over the phone. Amy is gauging me from head to toe with an unhappy expression.

"Why is your gown so dirty?"

Crap, I forgot I sat on the roof. I try to wipe a bit of the dust away, but it's way too late. Amy puts her hands on her hips.

"Clarissa, you can't just walk around like that. I flew all the way here to see you, why do you look like this?"

"You took a flight just to come see me?" I ask, flustered.

"Who else do you think I'm here to see?"

I swallow my saliva, a bit embarrassed. Damn, I didn't expect her to show up after our conversation. Moreover, her makeup and hair are perfect after the flight, while I'm here all day and I can't even manage to keep myself neat and tidy... I feel like a freaking toddler caught doing something bad! I nod and go grab some water to have an excuse to walk away from her.

She crosses her arms, though, her black eyes not leaving me for a second.

"So?" she says.

I nod. You wanted her here, so now, time to get your thoughts in order and ask, Mara...

"I... I want to get out of here. Of the hospital."

"I already said no. You don't need to. If you need anything, you can tell me, I'll have it delivered here. Proper clothes, for starters."

"It's not about some damn clothes!" I exclaim. "Amy, I need my life back. No one is willing to talk to me at all, to help me understand what happened or what's going on. Why won't you let me go outside? No one tells me a thing!"

"There is nothing you need to know about Silver City," she replies. "You've only lived here for a year, Clarissa. I already allowed your roommate to come here when you asked. What else do you need to know?"

"What about before, then?" I ask. "My life before Silver City. Where did I live, and with whom? Why did I come here at all if this isn't where my life was? Why is it that no one in my family cares but you?!"

Amy makes a sour face and massages her temples with her perfectly manicured nails.

"Because I already told you, our family isn't the type to care about each other, Clarissa. Father doesn't give a damn about what you do with your life, as long as you don't bother him. Even now, I don't know where he is or what he's doing. If I want to know, I read the financial newspaper. Otherwise, I'll just guess he is in one of his places with whichever new mistress he's got, alright? Honestly, I don't care either, and same for our brother, I don't care."

"...What about my mother?"

She looks perplexed for a second and looks away from me.

"I... I don't know who your mother is, Clarissa," she says. "Father never said. He just brought you home one day when you were seven or eight years old, saying your mother was dead and you were his daughter, and that was it. I spent half my life seeing him and my mother rip each other's throats apart over their divorce. I never really stopped to research which mistress of my father your mother was."

I take a second to digest it all. That... kind of hurts, even if I don't remember that unknown mother. Since Amy's skin tone is significantly darker than mine, I always figured we may only have one parent in common, but I never imagined even that was pretty much irrelevant.

I drink a bit of water despite my throat feeling tight, thinking about what else I need to ask. I'm really upset about what she just said, but... I can get upset later. I need to get as much information as I can while she's here.

"So... I just grew up with you?" I ask.

"In the same house, yes. Father always sent you to one private school after the other, and I got my own place as soon as I started working so... We didn't have a happy lunch together every day, basically."

"Then why are you the only one here? How...?"

Amy sighs, and leans against my bed, shaking her head.

"I don't know. When you came back from your latest school, father didn't really care anymore about what you did with your life, I guess. I'm not sure what you did for a few months, I think you just stayed home. Then, all of a sudden, you called me and asked for my help to study in Silver City. You had never reached out or asked for anything from me, ever. Maybe you couldn't reach our father... I don't know. Anyway, I agreed to help you, and that's how you ended up here one year ago. I found you a place to stay, told you to let me

34

know if you needed anything, and since then, we have exchanged a few emails, and that was it."

A real loving relationship between sisters, I guess... As far as I can tell, from a father who doesn't give a damn about one of his daughters being in a hospital, our family is really messed up.

"You don't know why I picked Silver City?"

"I think you just mentioned you liked their university program... I had no idea it was a city with half of its population being werewolves, you never mentioned it. I never asked either."

This is really not that helpful. If only Amy and I had a better relationship before... I'm slowly starting to realize how much it actually means for her to be here. If we were never close, I'm probably nothing but a troublesome half-sister to her. However, she agreed to be my legal guardian, so...

"I still want to be able to go out. I know you're negotiating with that Luna, Selena Whitewood, but..."

"Oh, for fuck's sake, who told you that?" she exclaimed. "Can't they just shut up?!"

"Why didn't you tell me?!"

"Because I don't need to tell you, Clarissa! You're supposed to stay here and rest for a while, why are you so adamant about getting out?"

"I'm an amnesiac!" I yell. "I don't remember a thing about myself! I don't remember you, our family, my mother, my friends! It has nothing to do with whether we were close or not, I'm a completely blank slate! All I had when I woke up was you and Kelsi, and this freaky fire thing! How am I supposed to find the answers if you keep me locked up here?!"

"My God, why did I ever agree to let you stay here. You're so stubborn! All I'm doing is trying to protect you, Clarissa! You have no idea how many people are furious about a witch being here! I don't know if you should stay here or leave, I don't know why everyone is trying to get to you while you're desperate to make things complicated for me by getting out of here!"

"What do the werewolves want with me, then? Why don't you just share with me what's going on?"

"Because you know something about werewolves and witches, perhaps?" she retorts, annoyed.

"Well, I get why they don't like witches, for starters, the previous ones killed their people! That much I can understand! But if I could just–"

"Clarissa, it's not just the previous witches."

"W-what?" I stutter, confused. "What do you mean?"

35

Amy shakes her head and walks up to the door to close it. Then, she turns to me with a big sigh.

"I lied, alright? I lied and asked everyone to shut up about it. I... It wasn't just you in that fire, Clarissa. Three people died."

...What?

For a few seconds, I'm completely stunned, staring at my sister. What did she just say? I shake my head, unable to understand. Amy is staring at me with a dark expression, making me even more scared that it is the truth. It can't be.

"No, they said I was the only victim," I protest. "They said it was a miracle that I had survived, and there was no one else in there..."

"Either they lied or they really didn't know, Clarissa. Only a handful of people were informed about it, but the firefighters actually found remains of other human bodies in there. Three of them."

Holy crap... This changes just about everything! I thought things were fine because I was the only victim in that incident. Aside from me, there was only one building burned to the ground. I mean, I could understand why everyone made a fuss about a whole damn building being destroyed, but at the end of the day, it was nothing but material damages. No one ever told me anything about actual victims!

"Do we know... who...?" I mumble.

Amy shakes her head.

"No. The remains they found were unidentifiable. The only sure thing is that they weren't werewolves, as one of the two Lunas would have felt it. The police are still investigating who those people were, though."

I stumble back, trying to take it all in. It's hard. I let it sink in, and my older sister gives me a worried look. I'm unable to say anything. After a few seconds, Amy steps toward me. She doesn't touch me, though; she stays a couple of feet away with her hand falling down in an awkward way.

"I didn't want to let you know so you wouldn't... Clarissa, this isn't..."

"You're saying that I might be a fucking murderer, and no one told me?"

Her eyes open wide in disbelief.

"Clarissa, no! Nothing, and I mean nothing, indicates that you were the one who started that fire! There are a lot of things that were... odd in this incident, alright? The reason I chose not to tell you was that you had to focus on getting better."

"What odd things?" I ask.

Why is it that as soon as I start digging a little, I feel like everyone's been working hard to hide a full mountain of lies from me! Amy sighs.

"The investigation is still ongoing, Clarissa. Until then, there is nothing you need to concern yourself with. I'm handling it."

"Amy, stop saying that! This is all about me! I need to know what's going on! I know absolutely nothing right now, and everyone is treating me like a freak! I can't go on like this, I'm going to go crazy! If I have to prove that I am innocent, let me search for answers!"

"What are you saying?" she says, shaking her head.

"I want to leave this damn hospital. I swear, if you're not letting me out, I will go crazy! You just told me I might be a freaking murderer, and half of Silver City thinks so too! You can't have me stay locked up here hoping everything is going to solve itself. Amy, I am the only person who was there and knows what happened. I just lost my memory, but if you let me look for clues, if you let me try to find out who I was and what happened, maybe I will be able to prove my innocence!"

"Clarissa, you can't be serious. You're just a teenager! You can't–"

"I'm actually twenty, apparently."

She shuts her mouth as if I had just slapped her. Yeah, I guess that's part of being in a not-so-close family, your own sister doesn't care enough to remember your birthday... Amy closes her eyes and sighs.

"Sorry, I must have missed it in my agenda..."

"I don't care much, honestly. But Amy, please, you have to let me out."

She massages her neck, looking annoyed. She suddenly starts walking in circles in my room, her high heels clicking on the floor, which is a first for me to witness. Amy avoids my eyes and keeps shaking her head slowly, though I can tell she's seriously thinking about my words. Strangely, I feel like that comment about my birthday destabilized her, I don't really know why. I start hoping, and don't dare say anything while she's pondering.

After a while, she stops walking abruptly, turning to me again.

"Clarissa, it's not that I don't want to let you out. But the humans–"

"I'll make myself super invisible and quiet, I promise," I immediately say. "I'll be careful about my fire, and I'll stay with Kelsi, alright? I want to at least be able to take a glimpse of what my life used to be. Amy, imagine for a second one day you wake up and you've forgotten everything about your past life, you can't even recognize the people you love. I can't go on like this! I swear, I'm going nuts in here, I–"

"Fine, fine!" she shouts, raising her hands to stop me. "...However, I have conditions, Clarissa."

I can't believe my ears! Really? She's really letting me out? I feel like jumping all over the place right now! However, her severe expression kind of tells me I'm not out of the woods yet. She starts counting on her fingers, reminding me of a strict school teacher, and I have to contain my excitement.

"First, you have to keep coming to the hospital for regular check-ups, as many times as they ask you to. I will know right away from the staff if you don't show up."

"I promise," I say with a nod.

"Second, if you get into even the tiniest bit of trouble with the werewolves or the humans, or I hear about a fire anywhere downtown–"

"You'll drag my ass back here. Got it."

She clicks her tongue, annoyed either at my language or me cutting her off, but making me understand I should shut up for a minute. I close my mouth.

It's hard, though. My heart is beating like crazy. I can finally get out of here! That simple thought is driving me crazy. Not only do I want to go out, but I want to see a million things! The idea that I'll be able to leave the hospital soon is making me want to run out the door right now and do something crazy, dance or shout, I don't know. I'm so excited, I have a hard time not smiling from ear to ear like an idiot. It's kind of insane with what I just learned not five minutes ago, but I've been dying to finally be able to leave this place!

"Clarissa, I'm serious. I can't be here to watch you. If anything happens, consequences will be a real pain to handle. We have an agreement with the werewolves for now, but be aware that we have no allies here, okay? So don't get involved with the humans, and don't do anything reckless."

"I promise," I say, my throat feeling a bit too dry.

She lets out a long sigh and takes out her phone, typing something hurriedly.

"I will let Selena Whitewood know you are about to leave the hospital, she might not be happy with it, though... I need to get you a smartphone too..."

"Can I meet her?"

Amy turns to me, surprised.

"Why do you want to meet her?"

"I heard she... knows about witches."

"No. I mean... Not yet. To be honest, I'm already very reluctant about you leaving the hospital, Clarissa, so I'd like it if you just stayed in your apartment with your friend for now, okay? You can take some time to decide if you want to go back to university, or–"

"Amy, I can't. How am I supposed to study with no memory of what I studied?"

"Oh, right... Well, anyway, you can do whatever you want, but please don't go anywhere without telling me."

"Yeah. So, I can really go?"

Amy waits for a minute before answering me, her eyes on her phone. I keep glancing at the little wardrobe and bathroom, wondering how fast I can get ready. I know I have some shorts Kelsi brought me, and a top I should be able to put on without ruining my bandages too...

"She says it's fine as long as you have someone with you."

"Wait, what?"

I lost the conversation for a second, but Amy is putting her phone back in her jacket pocket, and searching inside her bag, leaving me confused.

"She will send someone to stay with you."

"You were on the phone with Selena Whitewood just now?" I exclaim, shocked once again.

"I was emailing her, yes."

"You're kidding! Can I have her email? Or her phone number?"

Amy glares at me and grabs my hand, filling it with a thick bundle of bills.

"Not today, Clarissa. You can go home after the doctors have seen you, but stay there until whoever Selena sends gets there. If you take one step out of the apartment–"

"I'll be sent back here right away, I get it!"

She really treats me like I'm a ten-year-old or something! As she busily searches through her pockets, I look down at the money she just gave me, confused. She pulled it out of her wallet as if it was nothing, but after checking it a little, there's several hundred dollars here! Before I can say a thing, though, Amy's phone rings loudly, and she looks at the number on the screen quickly with a little glare.

"Crap, I need to take this call... You stay here, okay? I will go see the hospital director as soon as my call is over, and when the doctors say you can leave, they will order you a taxi. And tonight, you stay home with Kelsi, are we clear?"

I nod, trying not to show how excited I am, but my brain is playing "I'm going out, I'm going out, I'm going out" on a loop like an anthem.

She sighs, probably not very convinced by my performance, and gets ready to leave. At the doorway, though, she stops and turns to me despite her phone still ringing.

"About your birthday... I'm sorry."

"It's fine, I wouldn't have remembered either, so..."

She seems to hesitate, then, to my surprise, she declines the call, and turns toward me. Amy sighs, a little uneasy, and talks without looking at me, her arms crossed.

"The... The first year after you came to live with us... Your school had all the children in your class prepare a present for Mother's Day. You apparently didn't tell them you... had lost your mom. When you came home on your next holiday, you came to my bedroom to give me your present. You didn't explain anything, you just put it on my desk and ran away. It... I never really asked you anything about it, but... it was actually my birthday when you did that. You were the only one who had gifted me anything that day."

Wow... I didn't expect her to bring up this kind of moment. I'm a bit uneasy for a minute. Why did she bring that up now? Because of my memories? Or as a... thing between sisters?

"Do you still have it?" I ask.

"It was a very ugly pot decorated with paper mache, blue paint, and beans."

I grimace. Oh, yeah, probably not that nice to keep around for too long... It hurts a bit, but at least, she remembered that for me. I chuckle and nod, a bit touched. Her phone starts ringing annoyingly again. It's usually like this. Whenever she came to see me, it kept ringing until she turned it off or picked it up. Damn, she really doesn't have a minute for herself.

"Thank you, Amy," I say.

"...I'll call you later."

She leaves the room while putting her phone to her ear and starts talking in a tongue I don't recognize.

I'm left alone in my room, and after a few seconds, that wave of excitement comes back. I'm leaving the hospital! I struggle hard not to scream or bounce around my room, I don't know what to do with myself! After a while, I realize I'm still holding on to the bills she gave me. I roll them up, a bit uneasy with all this money in my hand, and leave it on my bedside table for now. Then, I run to the bathroom. I take a shower, being careful about my bandages, and get my body and hair clean in record time. Once I'm out of the shower, I try hard to discipline my hair but fail miserably. Damn it, I guess I'll just leave it as it is. I should have asked Amy how she does it; her hair is perfect compared to my wild mane... Oh, whatever. I jump back into my room, grabbing a sleeveless top and some denim shorts. It feels so strange to be wearing some proper clothes after all this time in a hospital gown... I check myself in the mirror. I guess I have a tall yet bony figure, but the hospital food will do that to anyone. I grab the money and put it in my pocket just as a doctor walks in with Bonnie to check on me.

To my surprise, the check-up is rather fast, though they carefully redo all of my bandages, giving me instructions on how to take care of them, with the cream and all, and I still have to come back to the hospital once every two days so they can check on them. I'm amazed at how fast all of it goes. Bonnie seems happy for me, but we can't talk much with her superior there. When the doctor leaves, she stays behind.

"You finally convinced her," she says.

"Yeah, I still can't believe it!"

"Mara, you have to be careful, okay?"

I nod. Bonnie pats my shoulder gently.

"We have called you a taxi, you can leave whenever you're ready. You can leave some of your stuff here, though, it's still your room for now. Also, Selena will send someone to your apartment tomorrow, so please don't be reckless, before or even after that, okay?"

"Yeah. Thanks, Bonnie."

"Don't thank me yet," she sighs. "Honestly, knowing you, you're going to get in trouble soon enough, so..."

I chuckle. Yeah, I haven't exactly been very patient so far. Bonnie suddenly takes my hand, sitting next to me on the bed.

"Mara, witches are not bad people, but it doesn't mean they cannot do a lot of harm. You have to make sure you remember that at all times, okay? Even if you think you're strong, it means nothing if you end up hurting people instead."

"...Do you think I caused that accident?"

She hesitates for a second.

"I don't know... but what I know is that there are always two sides to every story, so I hope you'll find your side of the story soon."

"Thanks, Bonnie."

She chuckles and stands up, pulling my hand.

"Come on, let's get you ready to go. My shift just ended, so I'm coming over to your place tonight!"

I laugh. So she is supposed to be the one watching me for now, and they are not even trying to be subtle about it!

Chapter 4

I open the window, taking in a deep breath of fresh air. It feels amazing... Just to be in a car, open the window, and watch the streets as we pass by. We are not in a crowded area, but it's still pretty lively. I can't help but stare at all the shops, the restaurants, the buildings. I wish we could stop to check everything out. I feel like I just stepped into a new world and I want to discover it all.

Bonnie chuckles next to me. We are in the backseat of the taxi that's driving us back to my apartment, my bag which was packed in a hurry between us. It's a short ride, but I don't miss one second of it. My heart is thumping like crazy, I'm excited beyond words.

To my surprise, the car finally stops in front of a big modern building. Is this the right place? It looks a bit fancy... Bonnie and I leave the taxi and walk in. I look for my name and ring the intercom for Kelsi to open up. I forgot to let her know I was coming back, so she's overexcited. She's not the only one...

For some reason, I'm nervous in the elevator. I keep fidgeting and twiddling my hair with my fingers until it stops at the seventh floor. Bonnie chuckles when I hesitate, and gently pushes me out.

"Come on, Mara, you were so excited to come home!"

I nod and finally get to the door.

Kelsi opens up right away and literally jumps on me.

"My gosh, Mara! I didn't know you were coming back, you should have told me! I would have gotten you a cake or something! Oh, no, wait, we gotta order pizza!"

I laugh and hug her back, amused. Kelsi's even more excited than I am! When she finally lets go of me, I can see she is wearing horrible, cringey, pink overalls with a gray turtleneck, and her black hair is held in two cute macaron buns behind her ears. With her big glasses, she has the complete cute geek look. Kelsi takes my backpack off my shoulder while I explain my short discussion with my older sister, and how I managed to convince her to let me out.

42

"This is awesome, I'm so excited! I love this place, but it's a bit lonely all by myself..."

I can totally see what she means. I actually have a hard time believing this is our apartment...

I follow Kelsi inside after taking off my shoes. I had somewhat imagined a cute but cozy or colorful place that fit Kelsi's quirky personality, but it's nothing like that. This apartment is big, brand new, and very... bland. I'm standing in a large, open living room, and though there isn't a speck of dust, there also isn't much decoration at all, except for the big photographs in black and white on the walls. The furniture is all white or wood, and I'm standing on a cold marble floor. There are two beige sofas with brown throw pillows, a large TV, and an old rocking chair. We also have one desk on the side, and Kelsi's computer is still open on it, displaying some video game she was probably playing before we arrived. Aside from the packets of snacks on the table and the books on the two shelves, there aren't any touches of color. It's full of natural light from the two large windows. I take a few more steps in, and Kelsi runs to gather the snacks.

"Sorry, I would have put these back in the cupboards if I had known you were coming... The cleaning lady came this morning, though, so everything else is neat."

"We have a cleaning lady?"

Kelsi nods.

"Yup. She's rather nice, she comes once a week."

"Wow... I can't believe this is our place... It looks... expensive. We are renting this?" I ask, still a bit intimidated.

Kelsi scoffs.

"Renting? I'm renting, you're the owner!"

"Wait, what?"

I turn to her, but Kelsi chuckles and gestures at the whole apartment with her open arms.

"Yup, this is all yours. I think your sister bought it when you said you wanted to come study here. You had an extra bedroom, so you looked for someone to rent it a couple of months after our classes started, that's how I came here..."

I don't know what to say. I knew my family was rich, but I didn't think Amy had bought an apartment for me out of the blue... I'll need a while to get used to all of this. More importantly, I supposedly lived here for several months, but nothing feels familiar at all.

Kelsi takes me to the kitchen, showing me the poor plant she was trying to take care of, the grocery list on the fridge, and our arrangement in the cupboards, but none of it rings a bell. I like the kitchen a bit better than the living room, though. I can see we tried to make it a bit warmer, with the random assortments of spices on the side, a waffle maker, and the colored towels.

"Do you want to see your bedroom...?" Kelsi asks gently.

I nod and she leads the way to the next room, but the door is closed and she lets me go in first. I take a deep breath and slowly open it. It's a square room, with only one large window and a wooden floor. I'm almost shaking. This is my bedroom. I have been imagining it so many times, it feels strange to finally be standing in it now. This is Clarissa's bedroom, the one I lived in.

On my right, there's a desk pushed against the wall, with a couple of books on it. Right after the desk, there is one big bookshelf, filled with books, some even piled on top of others, almost overflowing. On my left, there's a standing mirror, a bedside table, and a large bed. I walk up to it, feeling like I'm in some strange dream. The furniture is made of the same dark oak wood, but my room's colors are more vivid than I thought. There's a large, multicolored carpet on the floor, the bedsheets are all dark pink, and there are a few throw pillows , all in shades of white and brown. To my surprise, there's nothing but an alarm clock on the bedside table, but a giant dreamcatcher is hung above the bed. I like it. It's full of black feathers and beads, a bit too many...

"You made it," says Kelsi.

"I made this?" I repeat, a bit surprised.

Kelsi nods and walks to the large wardrobe on the side, kneeling down to open the first drawer on the bottom for me to see. I didn't expect this... It's full of little crafting accessories. Feathers, beads, but also paint, chalk, and paper. There are also little ropes and several different materials, even little stones of all colors. It's very organized, though. Everything is in little containers or boxes, all carefully tagged. It looks like an art student's dream.

I raise my head, a bit lost. If I had so much crafting stuff, how come only the dreamcatcher here seems handmade? The other walls are bare, I don't even have pictures hung up like in the living room. I stand up and open the wardrobe. It's a bit of a mess inside, but there are only clothes, as expected. Most are black or dark gray, but there are some surprising items, like a red sequin top, a sexy black dress, and a cute white skirt. I find a couple of boxes with brand-new jewelry inside, left untouched, but that's it.

"Anything you remember?" asks Bonnie, standing at the doorway.

"No... Nothing."

I'm disappointed. I don't know why, I thought something might come back if I stood in my bedroom, the place I should have felt most familiar with, but nothing, absolutely nothing comes back to me. I keep staring at my clothes for a while. At least I like them, my tastes probably didn't change much...

"I wonder when you got these and why," says Kelsi, grabbing the jewelry boxes. "I've never seen you with jewelry either."

"Maybe you still have the receipts?" Bonnie asks, coming to her side to check with her.

While they are checking the jewelry boxes, I go back to my desk and bookshelf. I have so many books, and a lot of them look used. The covers are torn in some parts, and the pages are yellow for some of them. I check the two books on my desk. One is a book about meditation, the other one is a history book. That's an odd choice, no?

"Mara? The receipts say you bought one of those one week before Christmas and the other in mid-April. Does that mean anything to you?"

"No... Nothing does here, to be honest. Do you think I could be an art student? Or history...?"

Kelsi frowns.

"I've never seen you craft anything but the dreamcatcher, to be honest."

"Most of the paint looks unused," adds Bonnie, looking at the contents of the first drawer.

Damn it, this is all so frustrating! I frown and turn to the books on the shelves, trying to find a clue. Some of them are fantasy books, a couple of old history books, there are a few about psychology, theology, and some I have no idea what the subject is. It's going to take me a while to go through all of these...

"Come on, Mara, no need to agonize over this," says Kelsi, grabbing my shoulder. "You know what, boo? Tonight is your first night back, so we should celebrate properly! Let's order some pizza, get some beer, and hold a proper pajama party!"

To keep me from tormenting myself any more over the questions my bedroom raised instead of solving them, Bonnie and Kelsi kick me out of my own bedroom and take me to the living room, both girls agreeing we need a girl's night. We order from the local pizzeria and decide on a movie to watch. Kelsi goes crazy since I obviously don't remember any of the movies she calls classics, and we spend the rest of the day and evening watching the silliest girly movies I can endure. I know they are doing this to distract me, and it actually works.

Though I am a bit disappointed, at least I am out of the hospital. I get to change into my own pajamas, a dark blue ensemble, while Kelsi puts on a ridiculous pink onesie, and Bonnie borrows an oversized T-shirt. We spend a lot of time laughing at the movies, eating pizza until our stomachs are full, and Kelsi and I drink some nice beer while Bonnie only has tea.

I don't remember falling asleep, but a sudden movement on my bed wakes me up. I frown and struggle to see anything in the dark. After some hesitation, I light a little flame in my hand, careful to control it. It's pitch black in my bedroom, and I'm not familiar enough with my surroundings yet to remember where the furniture is...

I spot a shadow moving right under my desk, and frown. What the heck is that thing? It's small and dark, and I see it rush under my bed when I try to direct my flame its way. What's going on?! I get up, careful about my footing, and rush to turn the lights on. Nothing seems to have moved in my room, but I clearly saw something before. I get down on my knees, and to my surprise, two yellow eyes find me.

"Meow..."

A cat?

It comes out from under my bed, not looking scared at all. It's really a cat. A black one with lots of little golden patches, and those two big golden eyes. It's cute... It walks up to me, not looking afraid, and rubs its back against my leg so I pet it.

"Where did you come from, you...?"

Does the kitty have a name? Kelsi could have told me we had a cat! I wonder how it came into my room, the door is still closed? Did it sneak in before I went to bed? Anyway, it's rather docile, purring while letting me pet it.

After a while, though, the kitty suddenly turns its head toward my bookshelf and walks up to it. To my surprise, it suddenly starts scratching one of the books.

"Hey! That's not your scratchboard!" I protest, taking the cat away from the poor book.

Crap... I take the book out to check its poor state after the ruthless scratching. It looks like an old one too, with a pretty leather cover. It doesn't have a title on it, though? I open it and, to my surprise, there's a picture between the cover and the first page. What is this...?

In the picture is a little girl and a woman hugging her from behind. It looks like it was taken in some garden, probably in a hot season too, as both are wearing dresses. I frown. That girl... It's me, isn't it? I look no older than five or six in that picture. The woman holding me is in her twenties. She looks very thin, with long hair, but the picture is in shades of brown and white. I can only say she's a Caucasian woman... I look at the back of the picture, but there's nothing.

"Meow."

Kitty is purring again and rubbing its head against my ankle. It's funny how it led me right to that precise book. I check the contents of the book. It's all about plants, with drawings of each flower or leaves, their uses, and properties. I keep checking the pages, and to my surprise, there are lots of little notes, handwritten next to some of the book's text. Good for headaches... Use roots for rheumatism... Boil petals for meditation... I grab one of the pens on the desk and a sheet of paper to copy some of it, but it's definitely not my handwriting. Who wrote all these? I get to the end of the book after over an hour of reading. The cat is curled up next to my legs, but I'm more absorbed in all the little notes. Whoever wrote all these was fascinated and very knowledgeable about plants.

I yawn. It's already dawn... A bit late to go back to bed. Too bad, I guess. I keep the book with me and head to the kitchen. Kelsi told me to take anything I needed, but I have no idea of my cooking skills, so I take it easy and simply make myself some coffee while continuing my reading, going back to the first pages once again, hoping I missed something.

"Morning..."

"Hi, Bonnie. Coffee?"

She nods, still obviously half asleep, and sits on one of the kitchen stools. Her red hair is tangled all over, hiding half of her face. Bonnie suddenly notices the cat roaming around me in the kitchen and jumps in surprise.

"Oh, gosh... I didn't see it. Hello, kitty. It's cute... I didn't know you have a cat?"

"Yeah, me neither," I confess.

However, the kitty is well-behaved around us. It's not even grabbing food or anything, just staying around me, its big yellow eyes curious about everything, and rubbing its fur against our legs. Half an hour later, Kelsi gets up, her hair in two braids over her shoulders, and half of her onesie is down to her waist, only wearing a little camisole on top.

"Morning, boo. Morning, Bonnie..." she yawns.

"Morning, Kelsi. By the way, what's the name of the cat?"

She frowns and stops where she is.

"What cat?"

"This cat?" I ask, pointing at my feet.

Kelsi frowns and leans over the counter to look. Her eyes open wide upon discovering the cat, completely awake now.

"What the…?! Where did that cat come from?!" she exclaims.

"What, it's not ours?"

"Of course not, I'm allergic! I would know if we had a cat!"

Bonnie and I exchange a shocked look. Where the hell did that cat come from, then? It couldn't have jumped all the way up to the seventh floor! Meanwhile, the kitty innocently rubs itself against my leg, purring. Kelsi is about to add something when the doorbell rings.

I walk over to open it, still confused about the cat situation. Moreover, I'm a bit surprised to have a visitor so soon.

At the doorway, I'm surprised to find Benjamin, Bonnie's twin, standing there with a big smile.

"Morning, lady! Do you want the good news or the bad news first?" he asks.

"Hi... Uh, the bad news?"

"So, the bad news is that your babysitter has arrived and is going to stick to you like old gum under your shoe. The good news is that it's me!"

His wide smile is not helping me understand at all. He is standing there as if it was completely natural, his hands in his jean's pockets. Benjamin Lewis was sent by the werewolves? Did they pick Bonnie's chatty twin to guard me? I stay speechless at the door, but he gently pushes my shoulder and squeezes past me to enter, still with a confident smile.

"Nice place!"

"You're my... whoever is supposed to guard me?" I ask, following him inside.

From the frown Bonnie immediately puts on when she sees him, she had no idea either. Kelsi too goes from one twin to the other with a very confused expression.

"Okay, please tell me this guy is real. Because after the cat..."

I nod, but Benjamin immediately steps forward before I can say a thing.

"Hi, I'm Ben!"

He extends his hand to her very confidently, and Kelsi has no choice but to awkwardly take it. She keeps sending me totally confused glances over his shoulder as he shakes her hand frantically, and her other hand holding her cup of coffee almost spills on her onesie until Ben stops.

"Okay, is someone going to explain to me what's going on?!" she finally bursts, almost glaring at Ben. "I just woke up, I haven't had my coffee yet, and now I have a cat and a guy in my kitchen! What's going on?"

Bonnie and I laugh. All three of us girls are completely surprised by Benjamin's sudden arrival. As if the cat appearing out of nowhere wasn't enough! Bonnie sighs and crouches down to caress the cat, who seems to like it.

"You could have told me, Ben," she says.

"Sorry, sis, last minute thing. Apparently, they hesitated on whom to send until the last minute."

"Selena decided on you?" she asked with a doubtful look.

Ben rolls his eyes.

"Yes, she did! Don't give me that look, I can do a good job!"

"Hm..."

His sister doesn't look convinced, and neither am I. We watch Benjamin help himself to a cup of coffee. That guy literally spilled a lot of things he shouldn't have the first time I saw him, and now he is supposed to be the one to watch me? While Bonnie quickly explains the whole situation to Kelsi, I cross my arms.

"So?" I ask. "How long are you going to... watch me?"

"No idea."

"And... what else did Selena say?"

"Well, you can basically go anywhere you want," he says, "as long as you don't get in contact with humans and I am with you, that is. Oh, and no playing with fire, of course."

I can't help but roll my eyes and turn to Bonnie.

"No contact with humans, is that a joke? How am I supposed to avoid humans?!"

She sighs.

"Well, we do have a few werewolf-only places, but–"

"We have a lot of werewolf-only places!" retorts Ben with a big smile, suddenly sitting on our kitchen counter despite Kelsi's glare. "Moreover, it's not like you can't walk on the same streets, just avoid getting into any direct contact! After all, no one knows what the Fire Witch looks like."

I raise an eyebrow.

"The Fire Witch? I thought my existence was a secret?"

Ben grimaces.

"It still is, but, you know, between what the werewolves do know, and the rumors... Anyway, most people know there is a Fire Witch in town, they just don't know who it is."

I sigh. Bonnie gets up while carrying the cat, looking a bit unsure too.

"I think you should lay low for a little while, Mara. You just came back..."

I nod. At least for a couple of days, maybe.

"I want to keep searching my room for clues anyway," I declare, "and, speaking of which..."

I take out the picture and show it to Bonnie.

"Do you know who that woman is?"

She takes it with a frown and spends a long minute staring at it, Ben looking over her shoulder as well. After a minute, she shakes her head.

"I've never seen her before... Is that little girl you? Do you think that woman could be your mother?"

I'm not sure. I'm mixed and judging by Amy's skin tone, my mom could be white-skinned like this woman... I try to look for any resemblance between the two of us, but this picture's quality is rather poor... Kelsi takes the picture to stare at it as well, but she doesn't seem to know either.

"I can scan it and look for any similar pictures on the Internet," she suggests.

"Where did you find that picture? It looks old," says Bonnie.

"It was in this book the kitty guided me to. When I looked inside, it was full of notes and there was that picture."

I put the book on the kitchen counter and open it, showing them all the little handwritten notes. Kelsi looks at it while sipping her coffee, but the twins are the ones frowning the most. Ben takes out his phone and takes pictures of the handwritten notes.

"What do you think?" I ask.

"It's... I mean, I am not an expert, but you know, the Earth Witch? She was... the one who knew these kinds of things about plants. And all those notes, there's a lot here that you don't learn in medical school. I think this book might... have belonged to an Earth Witch."

Her brother nods behind her.

"I sent pictures to Danny to get his opinion, but I think Bonnie is right."

"Danny?"

"Our older brother, Daniel," she explains. "He was a bit closer to the Earth Witch, so he might know."

"The one who is Selena Whitewood's friend?"

"That one. ...Did you find anything else?"

"She found a cat," says Kelsi. "A totally unknown cat who squeezed into our apartment. Am I the only one concerned about that?"

"We can go around and ask if it belongs to one of your neighbors?" suggests Bonnie. "Maybe it just walked into the apartment while we weren't looking..."

His Blazing Witch

I don't really believe that explanation, but it's the only plausible one we have for now...

The cat seems rather comfortable, though. It keeps purring in Bonnie's arms while we finish our breakfast and keep looking through the herbology book some more. Once we are done, we leave Bonnie to go ask the neighbors about the cat, while Kelsi and I go back to my bedroom to look for more clues. Ben is left in the kitchen to do the dishes.

"I never really understood why you had this drawer," says Kelsi. "I swear I never saw you use any of this. You've never done a painting, crafted a bracelet, or anything. It doesn't make sense unless you abandoned a hobby without ever starting it."

I don't get it either. That dreamcatcher seems very elaborate for someone who's only done one!

Kelsi and I agree to go through all of my books, hoping to find more of the unknown handwriting in the pages, or maybe another clue about my past. We take out every single book that is on the shelves, put them all on my bed, and start looking for any clues. It's incredibly long and boring to swipe one page after another. I don't know what to look for, and even find the bits we are reading completely uninteresting. It's all theology books, history, some of science or physics. Why did I even have these?

After over an hour, Kelsi sighs.

"Boo, I'm sorry about this, but you had really, really shitty tastes in books," she says, putting another one back on the pile next to her on the bed. "History of the nineteenth century? Theory of atoms? Even the nerdiest person I know wouldn't read these!"

"None of those books look used," I add. "It's as if I had just bought them."

"Even if you bought them just for decoration, there's a lot," sighed Kelsi. "I feel like I'm going to get a headache if I keep looking. There were no notes in all of the ones I looked through, anyway. Just words and words. Even my glasses hurt at this point. I am so used to working on a screen, it feels like the first time in ages I've touched and opened so many books!"

If only we could find my laptop... This is another mystery we have yet to solve. I put down the volume I was skimming through. I'm sitting on the carpet, in the middle of the bedroom. I look around once more, but like this, there is no obvious place for a computer that we haven't already gone through. It's not in any of the drawers or on the desk... I know Kelsi already searched throughout the whole room, but I somewhat hoped I could find it, maybe have some sort of intuition once I got here. Seems like I was wrong...

"You guys have any luck?"

Bonnie just came back, and the black and golden cat jumps out of her arms to come and rub its head against my knee, purring loudly again.

"Nothing so far, Mara's books are boring as a university class," Kelsi sighs. "How about you? No one knows the kitty?"

"No one," sighs Bonnie, sitting on the bed. "They have never seen this cat, including the nice vet on the first floor. The only thing I learned is that the kitty is male, which is apparently extremely rare for a tortoiseshell, and only a few months old."

I chuckle and scratch the kitty's head. So it's a boy? Maybe we should give him a name... I turn to Kelsi, but she's already making a sour face and shaking her head.

"Uh-uh, no. No, Mara, we are so not keeping the cat," she insists.

"The cat probably spent the night in my room, you've been here for over an hour and you haven't sneezed at all..."

"Maybe, but I also didn't rub my face against his fur!"

"He found my first clue faster than you."

Kelsi looks offended.

"That's low, very low. I spent hours in your bedroom looking through everything, I just didn't happen to open the right book! I don't even remember seeing that book; it's like the cat, it came out of nowhere!"

"...Could he be a familiar?"

We both turn to Bonnie, who has her eyes on the cat. He meows loudly.

"A familiar?" I repeat, confused.

"Yeah... It's just a theory, but the other witch had a butterfly that followed her everywhere. I just read a bit about it in one of my fantasy books too... but it's a witch thing. That cat appeared in your bedroom on the day you came back and found a clue about your past right away. I'm just saying, it's a possibility..."

We stay quiet for a moment. I stare at the cat. Is it a magic cat? He looks normal. Bonnie's theory does seem a bit... far-fetched.

"Unless the cat suddenly spits fireballs, I am not believing he's anything but a stray," declares Kelsi.

"Alright, aside from the cat, is there anyone who knows anything interesting about witches that I can talk to?" I sigh. "Can I meet your older brother?"

Bonnie hesitates, and for a few seconds, she stays silent, her eyes blank. Kelsi and I exchange a look, a bit lost. My question was rather simple, so what is she...?

"He's going out tomorrow night," she suddenly declares.

"Wait, what? How do you know?"

Bonnie smiles, a bit amused.

"Mind-linking, remember? I can mind-link anyone from my family or my pack just like that."

Oh, I'm never going to get used to that werewolf thing...

"Anyway, my older brother said he is going out dancing tomorrow night," she says, "in one of the clubs. It's owned by our pack, so you should have no problem going there, as long as you keep your fire in check..."

"Really? We are going dancing in a werewolf nightclub!" exclaims Kelsi.

"It's like any other nightclub," laughs Bonnie, "but yes, if Ben goes, I guess we can go too."

"Then I guess we can—"

I stop and turn toward the door. Oh, crap, did I just hear something break? Did Benjamin break one of the cups?

"Mara?"

I turn to the girls again, but they both stare at me, looking confused.

"Are you okay?" asks Bonnie, coming next to me with a worried expression. "You just stopped talking. Is there something wrong?"

"No, you didn't hear that? I think Benjamin just broke something."

"Oh, crap, Ben..."

All three of us get up and go back to the kitchen, the kitty walking ahead. Once we get to the kitchen, however, Benjamin isn't there. He's actually standing by the TV looking at his phone, and the dishes are done. He raises his head as the three of us enter.

"What is it, ladies? Everything okay?" he asks.

"Nothing," I sigh. "I probably dreamed that or heard wrong."

"Mara, are you okay?" asks Bonnie. "If you think you heard something—
"

"I'm fine," I immediately retort.

Crap, did I hallucinate that? It wasn't even a voice this time, just the sound of something breaking! I heard it perfectly clear too. I don't want Bonnie to think I'm not well, they are just going to send me back to the hospital if they have any suspicions. I need to change the subject.

"Anyway, can we go out tomorrow? To a nightclub?"

Benjamin frowns, but his sister quickly explains the situation.

"Oh, right, it's his night out!"

"His night out?"

"Yeah, Daniel usually goes out once in a while, to relieve the pressure of work. He's probably going to go with his husband too; they haven't gone out much since they had a daughter."

"Oh, so he's..." starts Kelsi.

We exchange a glance and understand there's nothing much to add. The twins chuckle.

"Yeah, he's married to another male werewolf, and they adopted a daughter a few months ago," explains Bonnie. "They met at a nightclub, actually, so it's not surprising that they go sometimes."

Suddenly, behind us, I hear the clear sound of a dish breaking. I freeze. Again? Am I going crazy, hearing things? I hesitate to even turn around to look. Did I dream that one too? It's the exact same sound as before! However, all three of them turn toward the kitchen.

"Crap, Ben! You should have put them back properly!"

"Sorry..."

Bonnie walks past me to go see what happened, and I finally dare to look. One of the cups he washed earlier most likely fell from the kitchen counter where it had been left somehow, as it is now smashed into dozens of little pieces on the floor. I keep staring at it while the twins clean it up, completely confused. My heartbeat is going crazy.

It can't be... That was the exact same sound I heard a minute ago. I'm absolutely sure. I heard that cup breaking before it actually happened. Is that even possible?

"Mara?"

Kelsi put her hand on my shoulder gently, looking a bit worried. I must look crazy, but I can't process what just happened. Either I'm going crazy for real, or...

"Are you okay?"

I nod, trying to calm down.

"Bonnie?" I call, turning to the nurse.

She hasn't seen my panicked expression and doesn't even raise her eyes, focused on picking up the pieces.

"Mhm?"

"The witch you knew, did she ever... hear things? Like... before they actually happened?"

Chapter 5

"I'm really not sure how I feel about this, Kelsi."

"Why? It's your clothes, and it suits you!"

"If you say so..."

I can't stop frowning at my reflection. I know these clothes came right out of my wardrobe, but there's still an odd feeling about showing off my body like this. First, wearing the clothes I saw myself wearing in a picture, from a scene I can't remember is very weird. Moreover, I've only ever worn a hospital gown for most of the time I remember, and since I came here, I've just worn normal clothes, like large pants and simple T-shirts.

This is a bit... sexy and fancy. The white sequin top doesn't hide much skin except for my breasts, and the leather pants are rather tight. With my burns, I wouldn't even have been able to wear such a thing a couple of weeks ago, but now, my scars are fine underneath. They don't itch as much, except at night. I've decided I don't care about my scars. They are there, and they are healing just fine. They are red to dark brown, covering a lot of surface on my visible skin, but really, I don't care.

"You look sexy as hell, boo. One crazy sexy witch right there."

I turn to Kelsi with a frown. She is still in her gray bunny sweater, playing with her braids and staying reasonably far enough from my cat, nowhere near ready for an outing.

"Why aren't you getting all dressed up too? We are leaving soon."

Kelsi frowns and readjusts her thick glasses.

"I don't like dressing up. I'll just put on a T-shirt and stay in my shorts."

I've never seen Kelsi out of her geeky or cute clothes, actually. It's as if she is hiding under her super cringey and oversized clothes. She often has her hood on too, and her glasses cover half of her face. I can tell she is pretty without that, though. She is rather tall and thin too, despite her habit of snacking all day. However, she flat out refused to dress up for this; though, she helped me put my makeup on and happily chose my clothes and a few bracelets for

55

me to wear. She doesn't seem like someone who hates dressing up unless it's just herself?

I turn around to check myself once more, and I suddenly hear a *thump*, and sigh.

"Kelsi, stop freaking doing that, please!" I say, exasperated.

She bites her lip and turns around to grab whatever she made fall.

"I'm just testing..."

"Stop with the testing."

She's been doing that all day and it's getting super annoying... Ever since I brought up hearing that cup crash before it happened, Kelsi has been dropping random things and pretending to let stuff fall, waiting for my reaction. We are already down two glasses and one bowl, and it's driving me crazy and making me jump all day because of it.

"I promise if it happens again, I'll tell you. But please, stop breaking stuff to see if I have some foresight or whatever."

"Sorry..."

Next to her, the cat suddenly jumps down onto the carpet and stretches, scratching it mercilessly. Kelsi stares at him with a confused expression.

"That cat is still the weirdest part..." she mutters.

"At least you don't have an allergy, it's confirmed by now."

"Well, maybe because I make sure to stay away. Or it's a hypoallergenic one, I don't know. More importantly, he hasn't eaten a thing or gone to the loo since he's been here! All he does is follow you like your shadow, meow, and sleep! It's like he doesn't have any needs!"

I'm a bit confused about the cat too. How he got here is still a big mystery. The truth is, Bonnie's theory about the cat is growing on me. Could he really be a witch's pet? What does he do, then? Other than ruining my carpet and finding pictures in herbology books... I've been getting more questions than answers, and the cat isn't even one of the biggest questions right now.

The kitty strolls over to rub himself against my leg.

"...I think I'm going to call him Spark," I decide.

"Whatever you want," says Kelsi with a shrug. "I guess he's your cat, anyway... I wish he'd find new clues, though. Aside from sleeping on the carpet, that cat does nothing with his day!"

I chuckle and crouch down to pet him. Well, that much is true, witch cat or not, Spark is a cat. I guess I can't blame him for living his cat life instead of helping out. Especially since we are both locked here anyway... I wonder if my room could have any more clues we missed.

His Blazing Witch

Kelsi and I searched again today, but we found nothing, and I couldn't really focus. I was mostly waiting for tonight. I really hope we will finally get answers at the club. I don't even care much anymore about going out, I just need someone who will finally tell me who I am, and what happened to me. Someone who knows something about witches. I sigh.

"You okay, boo?"

"It's just... I had high hopes about finding more in my room, you know. All we got was..."

"...A book and a cat. Every witch's starter kit!"

Well, that book got the wrong witch. No matter how much I tried to study it, all those plants and notes wouldn't make sense. I guess I'm really not an Earth Witch... I chuckle. If it wasn't for Kelsi being with me, I'd probably be much more upset about my situation.

She helps me adjust my hair a little and leaves the room to go change into the T-shirt she talked about earlier. To my surprise, it's not one of her T-shirts with a movie picture on it. This one is indeed a bit more appropriate for a club, a velvet turtleneck one. It still looks like she is trying to hide herself, though.

"Ready, ladies?" asks Ben from behind the door.

Bonnie couldn't be here tonight as she had an unexpected night shift, but of course Ben is coming with us. Kelsi and I finally leave my bedroom, Spark following us. Ben whistles when he sees our outfits and me with makeup.

"Sexy ladies! Damn, this is my first time going to a club with two chicks and neither is my girlfriend. Sad."

"At least we're not your sisters!" chuckles Kelsi, grabbing her shoes.

"Any news from your brother?" I ask, putting on a pair of dangerously high heels as well.

"He'll join us there as agreed," nods Ben. "Danny might come a bit later than planned, he's busy with work. It's okay, though, we can wait for them inside the nightclub."

I nod and we go on our way. I can't bring Spark, but the kitty seems to know already. He purrs a bit when I caress his head before leaving, and simply sits in the hallway, staring as we close the door.

Once again, I love the car ride. I'm even more ecstatic that we are finally going to another location! I have been waiting for this all day. I've barely been able to contain my excitement since I woke up. I feel my heartbeat accelerate gradually as Ben drives us toward the nightclub, and I can't help but send worried glances at my tracking bracelet. It's still beeping green, not matching my internal excitement.

His Blazing Witch

I hear the music of the nightclub as soon as we get to the parking lot. It's muffled, but the beat is strangely resonating through me. I turn to Kelsi, but it doesn't seem like she hears it... at least not yet.

"There won't be any problems because I'm human, right?" she asks as we leave the car.

Ben laughs.

"If a witch can come, a human shouldn't be a problem! The club is open to everyone, but mostly owned and frequented by werewolves."

Just like he said, to my surprise, we have no problem getting in. The bouncer barely glances our way and gives us an approving nod. We follow Ben inside.

The music is very loud in there, and I am a bit surprised as we enter.

The place is absolutely crowded with people. Women in short outfits that don't make my top look out of place and many men are bare-chested too, everyone dancing to the wild music. The DJ is on an elevated platform, and the strobe lights are sending flashes in all directions. I'm a bit overwhelmed by all the music, the movements, the violent lights. Kelsi grabs my hand, looking a bit lost too, and we keep following Benjamin further into the club.

We have to squeeze and fight our way through the crowd, and I make sure to stay behind Ben. I didn't expect this. Having so many bodies dancing and bouncing around me, so many faces, so much movement. I don't feel too well, but I try to focus on following the redhead through this battlefield. Finally, we get to the bar, and I let out a big sigh of relief.

"You okay?" screams Kelsi above the crowd.

I nod, but honestly, I'm not at my best. Those flashing lights are annoying. I feel like I see less and less every time they hit my eyes, even though I'm trying to avoid them. I try to take deep breaths and control myself. I'm hot. I don't know why, but I feel horribly hot. Well, it is probably hot in here, but still. My skin is reacting to this, and I feel my own goosebumps sending shivers down my spine.

Someone pushes a drink between my fingers, but I can't focus on the red mixture. I need to go there. There's something going on, across the crowd, something I need to see. I turn around, fighting the flashes and squinting my eyes to try and find it. What is it? I feel just like when I heard those screams. This sense of urgency, that something's going on that I need to latch onto. There's... something.

I detach myself from the bar despite the voices calling me, and I submerge myself into the sea of people. Everyone is dancing around me, ignoring me. Don't they hear it? This... sound. I don't know what to call it. It's like a voice or an echo. Something calling me, telling me where to go. I push someone and struggle to get past another group. I'm squeezed between so many bodies, it's infuriating. Just let me through!

Finally, my eyes catch a silhouette. I stop for a second, but now that I've seen it, I need to go there. I need to see him. I look from afar, trying to print his features in my mind. Black hair and a leather jacket. I can only see his back, though, and everything in my head screams for him to look at me. Look at me, look this way! I'm right here...

What the hell is wrong with me? I'm pulled by a force I don't understand, fighting my way through the crowd. My eyes try not to let go of his silhouette, despite the strobe lights that blind me time and time again. I'm almost there! I want to catch him, grab his arm, I'm just a few feet away...

"Hey!"

I stop, someone just stepped in my way. I glare at the guy, with his drink spilled on his outfit. I ignore him to step aside and go on my way, but he suddenly grabs my arm with his large hand. It hurts!

"You could apologize!" he yells.

"Let me go!"

I glance behind him. No, no, where did he go? The guy is gone, and I'm trapped here with this big idiot! That guy looks like a bear with the face of a rat, and the smell of an empty bottle. That jerk made me lose him! I'm furious and glare at him, struggling to free my arm.

"You should learn to say sorry, little girl!"

"I said let me go!"

I feel my fire get agitated inside. I can't lose control now, not with so many people around, but if this guy doesn't let go...! He still has his hand on my arm, holding it tightly, and he even steps forward.

"Dance with me!"

"Fuck you!"

He makes a shocked face to see me suddenly so angry, but I don't give a damn. I brutally push him and he lets go of me. Finally! Now, where is that guy from earlier...

"You little bitch!"

It's the bear guy again, grabbing my wrist this time. I turn around to glare at him. Isn't this drunkard going to let me go?! I can't cause a scene here, but my anger is dangerously rising. I try to look around for Ben, but maybe he hasn't managed to find me in the crowd. I try to pull my wrist away from that guy using all my strength.

"I said fucking let go!" I shout.

"Hey, what are you doing?!" yells another guy, trying to make the bear guy free me. "Let the girl go!"

Another guy gets involved too, and they all start yelling at each other and... growling. That's right, I forgot this was a werewolf lair. The two guys who just got involved are growling, but the bear guy is definitely human, as he starts insulting them, calling them mutts and dogs. As they argue and growl, they even seem to forget about me. I get impatient. Either Ben or whoever I was chasing, I need to find one of them.

"Let me go!" I yell again, trying to push him away.

"Little bitch!"

Unlike my expectations, he suddenly pushes me, and I fall backward. I don't know if people avoided me or stepped out of the way, but I violently hit the floor. I feel the pain resonate through my head, and suddenly, a flow of voices invades my mind.

It's as if, while I'm getting stoned by the pain, something was unleashed inside. I feel it. This darkness from before, bursting out like a violent hurricane. It's... strangely thrilling. Like a wave of fire flowing through my veins, giving me the chills. I feel... powerful.

Kill him.

I get back up, fire in my hands. I even want to laugh, it's thrilling to see the surprise in that guy's eyes and the fear around us. Everyone who noticed steps back. The lights keep flashing, and I feel the darkness grow around me. I take a step forward. It's so amusing to see that fear in his eyes as my fire dances in my hands.

"A... a witch!"

I snicker. That's right. Did they notice just now?

Kill that human.

Should I? I have a smile on my lips, my fire dancing around my fingers, and ready to do whatever I want... I take another step, my hands raised in front of me, showing the beautiful flames coming out of me. The guy stumbles backward. He hurt me. Why shouldn't I hurt him back? This man deserves it, doesn't he? Men are such vicious creatures. I should–

"Enough."

Someone suddenly grabs one of my wrists, and I fly above a shoulder before violently falling on my back on the floor. I don't understand what just happened, and a sharp pain explodes in my wrist before I do. I hear my own voice screaming, and my body is dragged on the floor.

Something icy brutally pours down on me. I come back to my senses, a bit shook.

His Blazing Witch

"Everyone get the fuck out. Now."

I hear running steps around me, all getting away. I'm cold and drenched. Is that a... an ice bucket? I shiver and look up.

A blonde woman is standing above me, out of breath and looking furious. But what hits me the most is that strange golden, warm halo around her. Like... an aura. She pushes her hair back, shaking her head.

"You damn witch... I knew you were trouble."

"You're... Selena?" I mutter.

Chapter 6

I am drenched on the wooden floor, but at least, I'm now very much... awake. I take a few seconds to come back to my senses, the icy water is quite efficient for that. The club emptied in a matter of seconds around us, the last people squeezing themselves through the doors to get out. Someone stopped the music and those horrible flashing lights too, and now a normal white light is on.

It allows me to see the woman standing above me, looking absolutely furious. She's tall and beautiful, with perfect body proportions, making me feel like a worm under her. The one thing I'm mesmerized about is her... aura. It's a strange feeling, something invisible yet very palpable to me. It gives off a warm yet oppressive feeling... Is this the famous Alpha aura that Bonnie told me about?

"Ben, go close all the doors," she says, ignoring my question.

I hear someone's steps, but I'm still on the floor and a bit confused. I struggle to sit up, shivering a bit. Damn, that water was cold... and I'm soaked. More importantly, I suddenly realize my wrist is painful as hell. I gasp and look down, to find it's at a weird angle. Is it broken? That woman's moves were so smooth, I barely realized what was going on before she violently threw me over her shoulder.

"You–" I start, but she yells at me first.

"What the hell were you thinking?! Didn't we tell you to not use your fire? The first time we let you out, and you try to fucking kill someone? You damn witch, I shouldn't have listened to your sister!"

"Babe..." calls a gentle male voice behind her.

"Shut up, Danny. I'm not done with this witch. She is going back to where she–"

"I didn't do it on purpose!" I yell. "That guy hurt me, and I just... reacted. I wasn't myself."

She rolls her eyes, putting her hands on her hips. I realize she effortlessly kicked my butt while wearing some sexy slim jeans and high heels. The werewolf Alphas really are on another level of strength...

"You weren't yourself? You don't control yourself, you mean! Someone bumps into you, and you light your damn fire right away? You could have burnt the whole building down, killing people! Do you think we need a second time?"

I go white. No, not a second time. I suddenly realize what happened, and remember Amy's words. My fire has already killed people before. I mean, we are not sure if it was actually my fault, but... I can't ignore it. Selena is right. What were those voices? For a few seconds, I really wasn't myself anymore. As if something dark had taken control inside, and was pushing me down that line. It was really dangerous. If Selena hadn't stopped me...

"I... I'm sorry," I mutter.

"Sorry? Sorry, you could have killed people, or sorry you can't control yourself? I decided to trust you because Bonnie said I could, but now, I feel like you belong back in that damn hospital!"

"No!"

I struggle to get back on my feet, holding my injured wrist, but I need to face her properly. I need to tell her she's wrong, that I can be outside. I'm not going back inside that hospital again.

I try to look for words, and while staring at her, I notice the guy behind her, a blonde guy that looks a lot like Ben. Is that their older brother, Daniel? He's scrawny, wearing a white shirt, and looking a bit worried while staring at me. Does he think I'm a freak too?

"It won't happen again," I say. "I came here because I wanted to meet you, to get some answers. I don't want to hurt anyone, I just... I just don't know anything about myself! I have no past, no clue of who I am. How can I control myself if I don't know the first thing about being a witch? No one has told me a thing, and I heard you knew about the previous witches..."

Selena is still glaring at me, but at least, she seems to be considering my words, hesitating. Next to her, the blond guy sighs, putting his hands in his pants pockets and swaying back and forth.

"You know a thing or two about looking for your past, babe..." he whispers.

"Daniel, shut up," she retorts, annoyed.

What are they talking about? Is he saying that to help me? If he's Ben and Bonnie's older brother, he might give me a chance too, right? Though, that means he also lost his older brother to another witch... Selena growls, surprising me. Damn, this is scary... Her eyes are even glowing.

63

"I'm so done with witches," she hisses. "As if we didn't have enough trouble with the humans already!"

What about humans? And what happened with the witches, didn't she like them? I was told she was friends with one of them! But Selena turns to Ben, ignoring me once again.

"And you! Weren't you supposed to watch her?!"

"She kind of ran into the crowd... It was hard to follow, the club was crowded..."

"I'm really starting to question your Beta gene, Ben. Next time I'm having you watch the pups!"

He makes a sour face. Whatever she is referring to, Ben is probably not fond of it. I don't really care to know about their werewolf thing though. I have a hundred questions, and finally, the right person to ask.

"What did you mean, about the witches? I am the only one, right?" I say.

"Thank the Moon Goddess you are! You're already enough of a handful as it is!"

"Will you stop yelling at me?!" I explode. "I'm a handful for myself too!"

She raises an eyebrow, surprised to hear me shout back, but not impressed. I can tell she isn't scared of me one bit, unlike everyone else I've met so far. Either it's because of her knowledge of witches, or her self-confidence, I can't tell. However, I need her to listen to me for just a minute, whether she likes it or not!

"I've had people concealing information from me for weeks! About my family, my accident, my power, the witches, everything about me! I don't care about your werewolf thing or the humans, you guys locked me up in a hospital room for weeks and no one gave a damn about me! I'm tired of all the secrets, I already had to fight my sister to let me know what happened and let me out, you can't simply throw me back there without at least talking to me!"

I'm so furious, I'm panting after that rant. I needed to get it out, once and for all, and for her to hear it. Selena Whitewood might be the Luna or the Alpha to all these werewolves, but to me, she's just a woman hiding things from me. I desperately need answers this time.

She crosses her arms, shaking her head.

"Fine! You want to ask questions, ask. However, I don't trust you. I don't trust a witch who can't control herself."

"I can't control myself when I'm angry!" I retort.

"Why would I answer a witch who can't control herself, then? If I give you an answer you don't like, will you burn me?"

His Blazing Witch

I open my mouth to answer, but there isn't much to explain. I close my mouth, looking for something else to say. The truth is, I'm not sure when those voices will come back. They were too strong. I forgot who I was for a few minutes and yielded to them. I wasn't myself anymore, as if something stronger had taken control.

"I... Something triggered me," I say. "There was this guy..."

I try to remember what happened. Those voices came up the minute I saw that guy's back. Why him? Why that man in particular? Is he linked to my past? It was as if something had been unlocked in my mind, and all my senses were guiding me to him. Yet, I didn't even get to see his face, he disappeared...

I keep frowning, trying to remember until I realize they are still staring at me. Selena is making an annoyed expression, while her friend next to her frowns. He steps forward.

"Babe, maybe you should let her talk," he says. "It's true you haven't been able to meet her once since we found her..."

"You can blame her older sister for that," she sighs.

"Amy said you were close to the previous witch!"

She turns to me again. I blurted that out without thinking, but that was my last resort.

"I wasn't exactly close to Sylviana," she says, "but yes, I knew her well. She was a powerful witch and the only reason you are still here right now. Otherwise, I would have kicked your butt out of Silver City."

Sylviana. So that was the name that everyone avoided saying until now. It doesn't ring a bell at all, as expected... I thought that if I heard it, I may have some sort of revelation, but nothing.

"She... She was on the werewolves' side, in that war, right?"

Selena looks annoyed by my questions, as if answering was painful for her.

"She was, and she died protecting us. She left Silver City witch-less, and honestly, I was fine with that until you appeared."

"Well, I'm here now," I retorted. "If you accepted Sylviana, why can't you accept me?"

"Because you are not Sylviana."

She steps forward, and I feel the pressure of her aura on me. I can't help but retreat a bit. What was I thinking? That because a Luna sounded like a gentle werewolf mom, she would be nice to me or something? Well, I was wrong. Selena isn't even giving me much space to explain myself at all. I gulp as she keeps glaring, and that pressure grows stronger.

"You are not in control of anything. Sylviana defended people. She healed, protected, but you are nothing like that, Clarissa Garnett. You're dangerous, reckless, and, apparently, not even in control of yourself. You don't remind me of Sylviana, you remind me of Nephera."

Behind her, Daniel and Ben suddenly exchange a shocked glance, as if she had just insulted me, or said something horrible. I don't get it. Who is Nephera?

"Babe, that's a bit..."

However, Selena ignores them.

"Nephera was self-centered, untamed, and dangerous. She killed one of my best friends and many, many people here."

"You're talking about... the Dark Witch?" I gasp.

Her eyes get a little bit darker, but the golden shimmer in them is still just as menacing.

"That's right. Just like you, she only cared about herself and what she wanted. She had no training and used her power left and right until she did something she couldn't repair. She became a Dark Witch and attacked us, trying to destroy Silver City. What makes me believe you won't become like that? Can you protect anyone in this state?"

I am utterly shocked. She compared me to the Dark Witch, the one they all loathe. Is that all I am in their eyes? A dangerous witch, another threat?

"You don't know me," I say. "You know nothing about me, you don't even try to. It's true I don't know anything about Silver City, and I can't control my power... well. However, how am I supposed to learn if no one helps me? None of you have tried to help me! All you did was lock me up as if I was going to disappear if you ignored me!"

"I authorized you to leave your hospital room and stay on my territory," growls Selena. "What else was I supposed to do? The humans are just waiting for a reason to jump at our throats already, do you think I have time to supervise a young witch?!"

"Then what am I supposed to do? There is no witch left to train me, is there? I don't want to hurt anyone, but these powers are growing inside of me, and I have no idea how I'll be able to keep them in check the next time an idiot bumps into me or grabs me! Do werewolves learn to shape-shift in the blink of an eye? Do you learn to fight in one day? Well, lucky you, because I'm not like that! I have no memories to rely on, and no one either! You're afraid I'm going to hurt somebody? I am even more terrified than you are!"

I'm tearing up because of the anger and from yelling so much. I'm tired too, my wrist hurts like hell, and I am done with all this crap! I thought I could finally get some answers, someone who could tell me about witches, who I am, where I should go next, but all this woman did was yell and get mad at me! No one is willing to help me, they just try to keep me contained, and this isn't going well so far! I almost killed a guy just now, and I'm afraid of what I'll do next that I might regret if no one stops me!

I don't want to go back to that damn hospital, but I'm starting to realize those voices in my head are going to be a real issue unless I find someone who can tell me how to tame them. There is no witch left in Silver City but me, and those who do know something about witches like Selena won't trust me. The truth is, after what just happened, I don't trust myself either, but I can't give up now!

"Mara..."

I feel Kelsi gently pat my back. I feel a tear running down my cheek, but I wipe it away, still more angry than I am upset. To my surprise, Selena frowns.

"That name, Mara... Where does it come from?"

I raise an eyebrow.

"Bonnie didn't tell you?"

"As far as I know, your name is Clarissa. Mara isn't a nickname for Clarissa, is it? Why is your friend calling you that?"

Kelsi and I exchange a glance, a bit surprised. Why is she getting riled up about that name all of a sudden?

"I don't know," I confess. "When I woke up, I thought that was my name. Mara, not Clarissa. I don't like being called Clarissa, I'm sure Mara is my right name. It's been like that since I woke up... Why?"

She seems hesitant for a few seconds and finally shakes her head.

"I don't know... It felt familiar, as if I had heard it somewhere before. ...Nevermind."

Nevermind? She is the first one to react to that name, no one until now seemed to know anything about "Mara"! However, before I can ask more, Selena suddenly takes off her high heels. What is she doing...? Barefooted, she hands her shoes to her friend Daniel, and from the glances they exchange, I know they are mind-linking.

She faces me and stretches her arms.

"Fine. You said your fire gets out of control when you are angry, right?"

"Yes..."

"Then you can get mad at me. Try to kill me, use your fire."

What is that woman saying? Is she crazy?! Selena snickers.

"Come on, little witch. You want to learn to control it, don't you? You can train yourself on me. We are in a closed building, and I have a bit of time. Try to control your fire to beat me."

"I'm going to kill you!" I protest.

Selena chuckles, getting into a fighting position.

"You can try. ...Don't underestimate a Luna."

I've never fought before. At least, not that I remember. All I've done so far was get mad and light fires I could barely control, so how am I supposed to fight a Luna? Selena seems sure of herself, but behind her, Daniel is giving her looks. I look down at my injured wrist. I can't tell if it's broken or not, but it's still damn painful.

"Wait... You broke my damn wrist and now you want us to fight?"

She rolls her eyes.

"Don't be such a baby. Firstly, you'd be crying in pain if it was broken. Secondly, you're a witch. You should be able to at least heal yourself."

Heal myself? I look down at my painful wrist, but nothing has changed. How can she be so sure? Did the previous witches heal themselves? If so, how? My scars are still there, though they are indeed disappearing slowly. I have an idea, but... it seems a bit crazy. Oh, well.

I light my fire, the one I can control. I can't help but glance toward Selena to see if she will stop me, but she doesn't and is watching me do this without even looking surprised. I guess she is not against experimenting a little... I bring the fire close to my wrist. As usual, the red, pinkish flames are hot, but it's bearable. Nothing like a real fire I could burn myself with. I bring it against my wrist, applying it to my injury as much as I can, though it feels a bit odd. Holy crap... I feel that warmth spread throughout my wrist and the pain lessens. This is awesome, I'm really healing myself! I chuckle, excited. I wait until the pain is completely gone, and make my fire disappear. I try to move my arm around.

"Boo, that's awesome!" squeals Kelsi.

I nod, feeling a bit proud. This is completely unexpected, but it's nice to also discover I'm not just good at destroying things! I can actually heal myself too. Selena smiles, finally giving me something other than a glare.

"That's one witch power you can use. However, don't try it on others until we are sure you won't burn them."

She's right, I don't want to risk burning anyone. Still, that is pretty awesome.

"Alright, you ready, little witch?"

I don't like the nickname, but Selena is already back in her fighting stance, and I'm guessing I don't have time to protest. I feel her aura grow bigger. Crap, is she going to fight me for real? I try to find a fighting position, but let's face it, I have no idea what to do and I am just mimicking her.

How can I fight a Luna? I'm just going to get a beating!

"Try to go easy on her, babe," says Daniel. "She isn't a werewolf..."

Selena snickers and I think she is about to answer him but suddenly, her fist comes right for my stomach. I take the hit, hard. It hurts... I fall back, out of breath. What the heck, she didn't even give me a go signal or anything!

"Get up."

I can't help glaring at her, but I still get up. As if I'm going to let her beat me without doing anything! I light that fire in my hands. She must expect that much, right? However, I'm still a bit afraid I will hurt her. I see Ben pulling Kelsi back and away from me and Selena. He's probably just making sure she won't get hurt by accident. Like, get a burn or a bite...

The next second, Selena moves again, but this time, I'm ready. I try to predict her move, but she shifts her position at the last minute, so fast I can't react, and I get a furious kick. I groan, but I manage to absorb most of the shock by curving my arm and turning. This time, I saw it coming, but I couldn't move fast enough. How the hell is she so fast? Her moves are a mix of martial arts and boxing, it's fluid yet unpredictable! How can I fight that when I'm a complete novice?

"Hold your ground," warns Ben.

I raise my arm, just in time to protect my shoulder from a new kick. I'm sent flying across the dance floor, but this one isn't as painful. I jump back on my feet before she resumes her attack. Selena isn't done with me, but she left me enough time to get up and ready before she runs toward me, a devilish smile on her lips. I squint my eyes, trying to predict her next move. I block one of her punches just in time, but she sends the other one flying right into my jaw. I feel the pain resonate throughout my skull, and I spit some blood.

"Come on, Mara!" Kelsi shouts to encourage me.

I nod and light my fire in both hands. She wants a fight? She's going to get one! Selena smirks, not impressed by my fire. I don't care, this woman asked for it! I get closer, and this time, she's the one to retreat. I need to win this, or else I'm going back to the hospital! I can't send the flames away, but I can hurt her if she approaches me again!

...Or so I thought. I miscalculated that my fire was contained to my hands, while Selena could hit my whole body. Indeed, she quickly approaches me, and

I raise my hands, ready to block a hit with my flames, but she suddenly disappears. What the–

Her leg suddenly swipes me off my feet, and I fall on my butt, my flames disappearing right away as I lose focus.

"Interesting... It looks like you need to concentrate some more, little witch."

"Stop calling me that!" I protest, jumping back on my feet and lighting them again.

This time, my butt hurts and I'm really annoyed! I decide to take the initiative and step forward, pushing my hands and flames forward like some fireball. Selena jumps back to avoid me, but I'm still aiming for her. I follow her, trying to focus on my fire at the same time.

"Come on, little witch, I don't have all day," she chuckles.

Is she doing this on purpose to annoy me? I frown and take a deep breath. Then, I expand my arms, close my eyes, and grow my fire all of a sudden. I can feel this energy burning inside, begging to be used. I expand my flames wider and out of my hands, until they almost reach my shoulders. My arms are on fire, and I see Ben, Kelsi, and Daniel step farther away, leaving a large circle around me. Selena whistles.

"Now we are getting serious. Come on, come get me!"

If she wants to play, I can play! I run forward, ready to use my fist. I'm locked in on her position, aiming at her no matter what. She dodges my first move, but the second one catches a strand of her hair before she retreats. I almost got her!

Kill that Luna!

I jump back, surprised by the voice. No, no, leave me alone! I ignore it and try to focus on Selena. She squints her eyes. She knows something happened, but she won't ask. I'm somewhat glad she doesn't, but this fight isn't over. I need to get ready as her next attack doesn't wait. I barely see her fist coming and try to block it with my arm.

"Too slow."

Just as she says that, she suddenly spins and changes her position, hitting my back instead of my arm. I'm pushed forward, in a stupid stumble, and I end up on all fours, my fire gone again. Oh, for fuck's sake...

I groan and get back up, igniting it again. How the heck is she so fast?!

Kill that woman! I'll help you...

No, I won't, and I don't need you! Now, I clearly hear this other voice in my head, bugging me and crawling like a shadow around my mind. I try to focus on Selena, on her aura and the fight. That aura thing is rather weird. It's not something I clearly see, more like an impression. As if I had an extra layer in front of my eyes that is superimposed with the Luna's image. Maybe I can use that...?

I inhale and get ready for the next attack. As expected, she felt no need to give me room to breathe, and runs at me again. Instead of getting all riled up for the voices to react, I wait, trying to stay calm and focus on that aura of hers.

I feel a gush of wind past my left cheek. I move by mere reflex to avoid the hit, but actually, Selena's fist only arrives one second later. I dodged it! However, I don't have time to celebrate as she throws her elbow in my face right after. Damn it... I feel my nose take the hit, hard, and my own blood is dripping down into my mouth. Oh, gross.

"Holy shit, Mara, you okay?" asks Kelsi from where she stands.

"Yeah..."

"You dodged my move," says Selena, squinting her eyes with interest.

"It doesn't look like it," mutters Ben, looking sorry for me.

"No, my punch. You moved right before I tried to punch you, at the right timing too."

I nod, trying to stop my nosebleed. Seeing that Selena has stopped her attack, Kelsi runs to me, handing me a handkerchief to help with that. It takes a few seconds to slow down the bleeding. It's a bit painful but my self-esteem took the hardest hit.

"Yeah... I think I felt it coming."

"Oh, foreseeing," comments Daniel. "That's interesting..."

"Yeah, let's do that again," says Selena. "Maybe it will come to you again. Moreover, you controlled yourself just fine before, didn't you?"

"But she's bleeding..."

Kelsi's weak protest is ignored by the werewolves, but I also confirm I'm fine. Strangely, that fight sort of woke me up. I feel... alive. Like something in me opened up again.

"Thank you, Kelsi, but I want to continue. I'm good."

"Are you sure...?"

I nod. I'm really fine, and I want to continue this fight. I glance at Selena, waiting for me on the side with her arms crossed. I don't really care if I get a beating, I'm not looking to win. I need to learn to control myself, or else next time, I might do something I'll regret to someone I care about.

Once I feel better and my nose is clear, I give Kelsi her handkerchief back and get into a fighting position.

"Let's continue. Please."

Selena smiles, and we resume our fight.

71

Just as I had predicted, it's more of a beating than a fight. I get back up every time I'm sent flying, and my whole body aches, but at least, I'm starting to control the voices. They are like a storm in my head, but I realize once I'm not that angry and accept the fight, it's not nearly as hard to ignore them. I can do this...

The foreseeing doesn't happen more than twice again. I'm not even sure what it is. The second time, I feel the pain in my ribs before it occurs, but I miss the timing to dodge because I didn't realize what it was. The third one is more efficient, I manage to dive down before Selena sends a flying kick my way. When I'm sent to the ground one more time, I struggle to get back up. I hear her chuckle. Damn it... I didn't even get to hit her once!

"Alright, little witch, let's stop here for today," she says.

"No... One more..." I insist, despite the pain spread all over my body.

"No, you're done and you need to rest for today. Also, I don't have all night to train you. My girls are waiting for their mom and my husband will make a fuss if I'm late."

Oh, so she's really a mom like the information said... Kelsi comes to help me sit. I nod. Indeed, I am dead tired... I could use a long break. I can already feel all the bruises I'm going to get by tomorrow. She really didn't feel sorry for me. Selena smiles and goes to the bar to grab herself a drink. Meanwhile, her friend Daniel sighs and walks up to me. He crouches down to my level. Seeing him up close, I do recognize some of his features.

"She likes you," he says.

I can't help but raise an eyebrow.

"Oh, really? Was the beating a big clue, or...?"

Daniel laughs.

"Don't worry, Selena has no problem beating people she likes a little. You don't have any broken bones, she went easy on you. She used to beat me at training, and I can tell she was nice to you. Be grateful you're a newbie and not a werewolf."

Well, awesome. I survived because she doesn't kill people she cares about. Kelsi and I exchange a glance. The werewolves' dynamics are really different. Actually, that guy Daniel looks rather skinny, I could tell he'd be no match for her. He stands back up and stretches a bit.

"I guess this is how our night out ends, babe," he sighs, taking the glass she hands him.

Selena glares at her drink before gulping it down in one shot.

"I guess so," she sighs. "Damn it, I don't want to go back to all the paperwork and stuff..."

His Blazing Witch

"The paperwork can wait..." suddenly answers an unknown voice.

We all turn toward the door. Who dared to come in? Didn't she order everyone out?

A tall guy just walked in. I've seen him before... Isn't that her husband, what was his name again? Nicolas Black? Selena sighs and frowns, putting her hands on her hips.

"What are you doing here?" she asks.

"I heard there was trouble..."

His voice is ice cold, and he walks past me, but his aura is... terrifying. I shiver. Who the heck is that? I thought Selena's aura was impressive, but this guy's aura is... different. It's not as big, just cold as ice. I feel like he could kill someone without batting an eye. Just standing there, that guy is impressive. He walks up to her, putting an arm around her waist.

I realize it's his only arm. Whatever happened to the other, it's gone. His shirt's sleeve is empty. I try not to look at it, but it's a bit baffling. Though his arm is around his wife, he's still looking down at me. This guy is super scary. I swallow my saliva. I understand what Daniel said when he meant Selena went easy on me. With an aura like this, I would run away, and I'm sure she could have the same murderous aura as him. She pouts.

"What are you doing here? What about the girls?"

"I left them with Isaac. I was wondering what was going on..."

"As if you didn't hear it from the pack," she sighs. "Enough, Nate. We are going home."

"And the witch...?" he asks as if I wasn't here.

She rolls her eyes and slaps his shoulder.

"It's Clarissa, and she is my clan's problem. Mind your own business, Mr. Black."

Oh, so they really are from different packs... Another werewolf thing. He finally breaks down in a little smile and kisses her softly.

"Understood, Madam Whitewood. But let's go home."

His glare is on me again, and I get what he means. He wants her away from me... I don't say a thing, and Selena doesn't seem to mind his attitude either. She puts on her jacket and turns to me.

"You'll train with Ben as we did."

"I might... hurt him."

"He's a big boy and can handle himself. Moreover, if you could control yourself against me, you'll be able to control yourself against him. Just be sure not to burn anything, and work on your self-control. I already ruined one of my nights out, I'm not doing this again."

"I still have questions!" I protest, getting up with Kelsi's help.

"Same deal as before, little witch. As long as you can control yourself, you can go around and ask all you want. I'm busy, though, so we'll chat next time."

I'm a bit disappointed, but she already spent a long time training me. I feel like it's been one or two hours, at least, but I'm not sure. Selena and her husband leave, and honestly, I'm feeling a bit better once that guy leaves. I let out a long sigh. Daniel follows after them too, giving me a wink before exiting the room.

"Alright," sighs Ben. "Who needs a drink? Because I do!"

"Are you sure you're okay?"

I nod, but I can't help but grimace when she puts the ice pack on my forehead. Damn... I didn't realize I would have so many bruises. My wrist is perfectly fine, but every other part of my body has been aching like crazy since I woke up. Kelsi gathered all the towels she could find to make little homemade ice packs... It helps with the bruises, but my sore muscles are probably the worst... It took me forever just to freaking stand up.

Next to us, Ben is loudly eating his bowl of cereal, and Kelsi glares at him. He was the last one up, and not as concerned as she'd like him to be about my current state. Plus, thanks to our drinking last night, she is a bit hungover and not enjoying that... I guess she decided to blame the extra shots of free vodka on him. He chuckles.

"I swear she went easy on you, Mara. Selena is probably one of the strongest wolves in Silver City."

I roll my eyes. Those damn werewolves and their crazy standards. If they could just stop saying that she went easy on me so I can keep whatever self-esteem I have left and suffer in peace...

"I thought she was the strongest?" I retort.

"Well, the top ones have never fought, so..." Ben shrugs with a mouthful, "it's hard to rank. Basically, the King is probably at the top, but I'd say she's a close second."

"I thought there were two Lunas?" says Kelsi. "What about the King's wife? Isn't she stronger?"

"Oh, she's not much of a fighter... I mean, she's crazy strong, but just not as much into fighting. She's a healer, so she's got the other side of the job."

"A healer?"

Ben nods.

"The two Lunas are a bit special... They are cousins and have some super-powerful werewolf blood in their veins. We call them Royals, when a werewolf's blood is almost completely pure of any human blood, though it's extremely rare nowadays. Selena and the Black Luna are like that, and their children too. It gives them something like more strength, better werewolf abilities, and some extra powers."

"Extra powers?"

"Yeah, from all the extra werewolf juice, it makes them a bit special. Well, Selena can mind-link with humans, and the Black Luna has healing powers."

Kelsi frowns, trying to remember everything we learned so far. We exchange another glance. Healing ability and being able to mind-link with people other than werewolves? That does sound a bit special, in the paranormal range; not that I can compare with my own abilities we are learning day by day, but...

"So the... White Luna is the fighter, and the Black Luna is the healer, but the latter is married to the King?" I say, trying to remember all of my notes.

"Yep."

"...And the White Luna is actually the King's sister-in-law...?"

Ben puts his empty bowl down in the sink, still nodding.

"Yeah. The Lunas are cousins, their husbands are brothers. The four of them lead two of the most powerful clans of Silver City, pretty much all of the werewolf territories. Easy to remember, right? Selena's husband you saw last night, he's crazy strong too... He scares a lot of people, actually. But he's the King's brother, so I guess that should be a given?"

I sigh. I'm starting to comprehend the werewolves' dynamics, but this is really not helping me understand their relationship with the previous witches. One they loved, the Good Witch Sylviana, and one they hated, the Dark Witch Nephera. That is all I got so far. I feel like I am gathering more questions than answers...

I suddenly remember a question that has been bothering me since last night, about Selena's husband. I wouldn't have dared to ask them directly, especially since that Alpha was so scary, but... I glance at Ben. He's now cleaning the dishes while whistling a bit, his back turned to us.

"Ben, about... her husband's arm..."

He suddenly freezes and hesitates. Crap, did I ask something I shouldn't have? Kelsi bites her thumb too, glancing at Ben. I'm thinking maybe he doesn't want to answer that, but just then, he shuts off the water tap and turns to me with a sour expression.

"I'll tell you, but... never talk about it in front of Selena, okay? It really upsets the Luna whenever someone brings it up."

I nod and Ben sighs.

"...He lost it during the war with the witches. It was... cut off."

Kelsi makes a horrified expression, a bit shocked. Damn, I knew there was a war, but this is the first time I actually saw a... real consequence of it. It was hard to think about it as someone else's death, but the image of that missing arm really marked me last night.

"Doesn't the Luna have healing powers...?" asked Kelsi.

"No. We didn't find his arm until after the fight was over, so... there was nothing that could be done. That was the kind of injury the Luna couldn't do anything about, and Selena is really mad about that, so never ask again, okay?"

Kelsi and I both nod. I can understand that would make her upset if her own husband was a victim... I guess even a werewolves' power has its limits. Moreover, to think a guy as scary as that suffered such a huge injury... How big of a fight was it really? I shudder. I'm slowly starting to understand the harm that Dark Witch caused here. I saw it in the eyes of that guy. I could tell he was ready to kill me if there was a need. They don't know me, most of them really do see me as nothing but a threat...

I sigh and take the ice pack off my shoulder, trying to stretch a little bit. Kelsi makes a sorry expression and puts the damp towels away.

"Alright, boo, what do you want to do today? No training, I suppose?"

Ben raises his head with a little smile. Oh, hell no. I feel like raising an arm is already a freaking nightmare as it is...

"No," I confirm with a sigh.

We hear a meow, and Spark comes to rub himself against my legs again. Kelsi frowns and steps back a little with a wary expression, but I really doubt Spark will trigger her allergy. Whatever is going on with this cat, he's not affecting her. I pick him up, and he starts purring immediately. Behind Kelsi, Ben tilts his head with a curious expression, staring at the cat.

"Is it me or... does the cat look somewhat different?" he says.

"You think so too?" asks Kelsi, her eyes also on Spark.

Different? I checked the cat, but he looks fine to me. I mean, he's literally stretching his paws and curling up in my arms, looking as happy and comfortable as a cat can be. However, Ben and Kelsi keep staring at him with those strange expressions on their faces. I end up pouting too.

"What is it?"

"His fur pattern. There wasn't that much black before."

Seriously, they think he can change his fur now? I glance down to check, but he's tortoiseshell, he's basically black and gold in random patches all over! His face is mostly gold, while the rest of his body has a bit of black all over. I honestly can't see a difference from the previous days, but Kelsi and Ben keep scrutinizing him as if they are trying to check every hair of that poor cat. I roll my eyes.

"Enough, you two!"

"Okay, wait, let's just make sure!" says Kelsi, running to her bedroom.

What the hell is she doing? She comes back half a minute later with her smartphone and, before I can say a thing, takes a picture of Spark. She checks it and nods, satisfied.

"Kelsi...?"

"Listen either Ben and I are crazy, or your cat's fur color changes, okay? This way, if it changes again, we will have something to compare it with, okay?"

"If you say so..."

"Good idea, nerdy girl!" chuckles Ben.

Kelsi winks at him and puts her phone in her pocket. Those two look like they became buddies without me even realizing somehow...? I chuckle. Oh, well, it's nice to finally have people to talk to whenever I need it! Kelsi turns back to me, crossing her arms.

"So, what is the plan for today? I am not going through all your books again, just saying."

"Don't worry, no more books. At least not here," I say.

"Oh, the university?"

I nod. She guessed right.

Other than my apartment, the other place I was dying to go to was the university. We know I moved here after I asked my older sister to let me study in Silver City... Question is, why did I pick this university? Maybe it was just an excuse, but I need to check if the answers I'm looking for are there.

"You guys want to go to the university?" asks Ben, a bit surprised.

"Yeah. When I was looking for clues about Mara, I found out she was registered in the Sociology Department, but absolutely no one knows about a Clarissa Garnett."

"What? How is that possible?"

"Apparently, I was registered in that department," I explained, "yet when Kelsi asked, no one knew about me."

"Yeah. The secretary found her name, but I tried asking students from that department, no one ever heard of her, or remembered a chick like Mara. Even the professors I asked had zero ideas."

"Now, that's weird," says Ben.

"Well, we can add that to the list," I sigh, "however, I still want to go and check for myself. Maybe I'll remember something once I get there, or someone will recognize me..."

"You did say you were going to the university whenever you left home in the morning," adds Kelsi.

"Let's go check, then..."

Thankfully, the university is on the White Moon Clan's territory, so Ben agrees to take us there immediately. It's a quicker ride than to the club, actually. Kelsi says we usually took the bus, but with Ben's car, we almost spend more time looking for a parking spot than actually driving.

Once again, I'm amazed to discover a new location. All the buildings are very recent, some more than others, but they are sparkling white, except for the greenhouses of the biology department, as Kelsi explains. There is also a weird building that looks like a gigantic cube, covered in graffiti, the art students' lair. More importantly, the place is crowded with students. Young people like us, walking to their next classes or hanging out on the grass.

I feel a bit strange. I used to be part of this world... probably. Maybe I have friends here whose faces I don't even remember. For a few seconds, I feel a bit overwhelmed, almost to the point I want to cry. This should be the university I begged my sister to go to, but... I can't recognize anything, once again. I hate this amnesia thing. I could walk by my best friend and not even recognize them! I don't know what my days were like, which building I walked to in the morning, nothing!

"You okay, Mara?"

Kelsi is glancing at me with a worried expression. I didn't realize I had stopped walking and became teary-eyed... I nod a bit awkwardly, wiping those feelings away quickly.

"Yeah... Let's go."

We drop by the welcome desk of the university first, but they don't give us any more information after seeing me than what Kelsi was already given: the classes I'm registered in. We check them quickly and decide to drop by the next one. It's a class about the expansion of malls in the twentieth century... I find it boring, Kelsi too, and Ben falls asleep in his chair. We wait for it to end, and while the professor keeps talking, I can't help but glance around to see if I recognize any faces. I also hope someone will suddenly walk up to me, greet me like a friend or something, at least give me a hint...

Yet, the full hour passes, and absolutely nothing happens. A couple of girls glance at my remaining bandages and scars, but it's clear they have no idea who I am. After the class ends, Kelsi and I run to the teacher, leaving Ben to snore in his chair.

"Excuse me?" I call to him.

It's an old man, with barely any hair left, who sighs.

"I'm sorry, young lady, I am not accepting any more questions today, you can email me–"

"No, I don't have a question about the class, I wanted to ask if you have... seen me in your class before."

He seems a bit surprised by my question, and glances me over, then gives me a little smile.

"Sadly, no, young lady. I usually remember my prettiest students, and I am quite sure I haven't had the pleasure of seeing you in my classroom before. Have a nice day, and as I said, feel free to email me!"

He gives us a wink and exits, leaving Kelsi and I speechless.

"...What an old pervert!" exclaims Kelsi, outraged. "That guy was basically flirting with you! That asshole shouldn't be teaching anywhere!"

"At least we know he didn't know me," I sigh.

Kelsi keeps ranting about the pervert professor, and we walk back to wake up Ben, telling him about what happened. He yawns.

"Well, I'm glad this wasn't one of your classes; that was boring as hell... Seriously, a class on shopping? What for?"

"Everything can be studied here, Ben, it's a university," says Kelsi. "Now get your butt up, we need to go before the next class starts."

Just like she said, a new batch of students arrives for the next class. Ben gets up, and we have to squeeze through the new crowd to head to the doors. Just as we're about to leave the classroom, me walking ahead and the two of them behind me, I slightly bump into a middle-aged lady.

"Oh, sorry..." I mumble.

I try to make way for her to go in, but she suddenly looks at me with a surprised expression.

"Miss Jones, it's been a while! You're not attending the class?"

I stop, completely shocked. Wait, what? This woman knows me? Kelsi and I exchange a shocked glance. Who the hell is Miss Jones? She seems sure it's me... Whoever Miss Jones is, this woman is smiling very naturally and not averting my eyes. What is going on, why is she calling me that, and who is she? The schedule they gave me didn't include a class after the previous one! I glance at the woman, trying to think of something to say. She doesn't seem to be a student, she looks more like she's the teacher of the next class, with her burgundy jacket and her suitcase... This is so sudden!

"Uh... I..."

She looks down on my body, and her eyes stop on my bandages.

"Oh, dear God! Did something happen to you? I thought it was strange you had missed the last classes, did you have an accident?"

"Excuse me, but... I... You...." I mumble.

All the questions pop into in my head at the same time. What do I ask first? Should I tell her about my amnesia? Or who is Miss Jones...?

"Excuse me, madam, what do you teach?" suddenly asks Kelsi with a smile, putting a hand on my shoulder.

The Indian lady turns to her with a large smile.

"I'm Professor Vutha, I teach parapsychology, dear. My class is full; though, if you want to attend, you'll have to come as a free auditor like Miss Jones."

"P-parapsychology?" repeats Ben. "There's something like that?"

"Of course! My class focuses mostly on all the paranormal phenomenons observed in the world, relationships between the paranormal species, as we inaccurately call them, and the humans, as well as the phenomenons observed by humans yet not explained, and the general beliefs around the Moon Goddess!"

"Could you... tell me what I was... attending your class for?" I ask, my throat feeling a bit dry.

"Miss Jones, don't you remember?" she chuckles. "You were the one with hundreds of questions about witches, for your research!"

...Holy shit.

Chapter 7

"Seriously, boo, you have to calm down," whispers Kelsi.

"I can't calm down after what we just learned!"

I'm trying hard to stop nervously bouncing my leg under the desk, but I can't. It's just too much information at once. The professor had to start her class, so we ran to find spots to sit in before she kicked us out, but I haven't been able to calm down since.

"I was researching about witches, Kelsi. Why the hell was Clarissa Garnett researching witches?! And who the hell is Miss Jones, anyway?"

"I don't know, boo, but we will ask her soon. The class is almost over so please stop doing that, you're stressing me out too!"

I take a deep breath and stop, but internally, I'm going nuts. I thought I had nothing to do with this witch thing. Before my waking up, there was no sign of me having anything to do with witches! How did I come to attend this class, and why did I give a fake name to the professor?

Her class today is about some old tale about a fairy and some knights, but I can't focus enough to listen. A few seats away, Ben is back to napping, as interested in this class as he was in the previous one. We were too late to find three seats in a row, so he had to go to a different spot, though we are not that far away. I glance around. There are even more people than before, almost all the seats are taken... It must be a popular course. A lot of students are frantically taking notes, but I see a few of them sending glances my way... Why are they... glaring? It can't be just because I'm not taking notes, Ben is literally almost snoring on the other side and no one cares. I see some eyes going back and forth between their phones and me. What is going on? Kelsi seems to have noticed too and looks worried.

"Any friends you recognize, by any chance...?" she whispers.

"No, and I don't think we were friends..."

"It sure doesn't look like it..."

Kelsi looks even more worried now. From the glares I keep getting, it certainly doesn't look anything near friendly. I hear some people whisper, though I can't decipher anything. What is their problem?! A girl shows her phone to her friend while looking at me, and behind me, a guy points his finger at me too. What the heck is going on...

"I know those people look like they know you, but to be honest, I feel more like we should get out of here quickly if we can, rather than stay around to ask questions..." confesses Kelsi, sending worried glances sideways.

I look at Ben, but he is still dozing off in the second row and doesn't seem to have noticed a thing. What a laid-back bodyguard... I wish we had a notepad or something at least to pretend we are taking notes, we are sticking out like a sore thumb in the middle of all the other students. I feel like this isn't the problem, though. The ones sending me glances are clearly pointing fingers at me for something else.

Finally, the class ends, and with Kelsi stuck behind me, we almost run to catch Professor Vutha, ignoring the stares following us.

"Oh, Miss Jones! Did you enjoy the class today?" she asks, completely unaware of the tension in the room.

"Ah, yes," I lie, a bit awkward. "Um, Professor, about earlier..."

"Yes?" she asks, gathering her papers.

"You mentioned I was researching about witches?"

She stops, looking at me, a bit surprised. She glances at my bandages once again.

"Are you sure you are alright, Miss Jones? You seem... different."

I exchange a glance with Kelsi. What should I say? I'm not supposed to announce I'm a witch to outsiders! I decide to go with a half-truth, or else I feel like she won't tell me anything...

"It's true I had an accident, Professor, so I'm a bit confused."

"Oh, gosh, I hope everything is alright now? I mean, I don't want to sound impolite, but you do seem different, and with the scars..."

"No, I'm okay. However, I'm a bit... amnesiac, so I was hoping you could help me remember... why I came to your class. According to the university registrar, I'm not registered for your class."

"Oh, of course! Well, no, but I think you did attend my class as soon as the year started, I clearly remember you said you had missed the registration deadline. You didn't seem to mind coming as a free auditor so I didn't think twice about it. It happens a lot, but you certainly were the one free auditor who came the most, you never missed a single class, before your accident, of course."

Kelsi and I exchange glances. It definitely looks like I wanted to hide that I was coming here... that Clarissa Garnett was coming here.

"You said I was studying witches?"

"Oh, you were quite passionate about the subject! Actually, you borrowed some of my personal books when you couldn't find what you wanted in the university library. I think you may still have one, by the way, I would appreciate it if you return it soon!"

"Was it a herbology book?" asks Kelsi.

"Herbology? No, it was on demonology."

Demonology? What the heck?! Kelsi looks shocked too but hides it quickly. So the herbology book doesn't belong to Professor Vutha... What was I studying demonology for?! Moreover, I haven't seen any book like that at the apartment, so where the heck is it? I decide to shift the subject before she asks about her book again, a bit embarrassed.

"Do you know why I was so interested in witches, Professor?"

She pauses a second, looking like she is thinking deeply.

"...I am not too sure, you said it was a personal interest. You had a lot of questions, though. About the three elements, necromancy, the witch hunts, the Moon Goddess, the magic circles..."

"Necromancy?" repeats Kelsi.

"The practice of conjuring spirits! It is very interesting, witches have a different view of the underworld from humans. You were very interested in that, actually. The reincarnation circle too, though I think you had read a few too many fantasy books!"

This is getting more and more intriguing, but not necessarily in a good way... I'm getting nervous now. What was Clarissa Garnett doing with all those questions? And conjuring spirits? Reincarnation? Kelsi looks a bit white too since the professor mentioned necromancy, in particular. Professor Vutha grabs her suitcase and sighs.

"I am very sorry, Miss Jones, but I have another class scheduled on the other side of campus, and honestly, I don't think I can tell you more than that. You only asked questions about the basics of witchcraft, and usually left with the answers or my book recommendations, that is all I can say."

"Thanks..."

Kelsi and I watch her leave, both a bit confused. Kelsi crosses her arms, fidgeting with the ends of her long braids.

"The more we ask, the creepier it gets. Why were you researching witches?"

"I know... I mean, I know it's getting creepy. Still, it actually feels nice we finally found a lead. That woman was the first to actually know me before I... you know."

Kelsi nods with a little smile.

"Other than me, you mean! Plus, she knew about Miss Jones," she rectifies. "It sounds like a made-up name? Though maybe we will get more answers if we look for Mara Jones than Clarissa Garnett."

"Maybe... It looks like I hid the fact that I was researching about witches from everyone, including you."

Kelsi bites her lip, but she eventually puts her hands in her sweater's large pocket and agrees.

"Probably from your sister too. I mean, you lied and apparently never went to the classes you had registered for, and came to this one instead. It's a rather specific course, even for Silver City. There aren't many universities with paranormal-related classes, I'd bet..."

"Maybe I even came to Silver City specifically for this class. Why witches, though? Like why was I researching this before... the incident? It just sounds too..."

A worrying thought is growing in my head, and scaring me more and more. This may not have been as much of an accident as I thought, whatever it was... whatever Clarissa did.

"I know," sighs Kelsi. "You know, we should ask the welcome desk again, for a Clarissa or Mara Jones this time and make a stop at the library. I had asked for Clarissa Garnett, but you may have borrowed books as Miss Jones?"

I nod, and we decide to get Ben, waking him up to get out of here. During the time we spent with the professor, everyone else had cleared the classroom, which I am not going to complain about. I haven't forgotten all those glares from earlier, and I'm not sure I want to find out what the hell is going on.

Kelsi and I explain what he missed to Ben, leaving the werewolf frowning more and more.

"That's..." he says, massaging his neck, at a loss for words.

"Yep, we know," sighs Kelsi, "so now, we were thinking of going to the library to ask about books Mara–I mean, Clarissa may have borrowed under a fake name. But seriously, do all werewolves sleep as much as you?"

"Hey, we burn a lot of energy! I'm not a sit-and-study kind of guy, okay?"

"So far I've seen you store energy, not the other way around," she chuckles.

We finally leave the classroom, the two of them still bickering. They are kind of cute together, but my thoughts are still a bit too dark to join the conversation. I can't help but feel even more nervous than before and repeat the teacher's words over and over in my head...

His Blazing Witch

As we leave the building, I realize the area is somehow more crowded than before... strangely crowded. Little groups of students have gathered around the buildings, and a lot of them are glancing our way. No one seems to be going to class or just hanging out. I feel stared at like a beast in a zoo. I don't like this. Kelsi keeps glancing around too and walks closer to me, unsure. Ben is frowning, his stance like he is on guard, and I'm pretty sure he is somehow scanning the area fully from the quick movements of his eyes. He's positioned himself to stand closer to us too. We are moving next to the building's wall, and Ben is walking between us and all the students gathered around.

I don't like this, but Kelsi and I keep walking in silence, toward the library as we agreed. No one follows us, but I can feel their glances. My senses are tingling, and more importantly, I can feel my fire inside, stirred up too. My fingertips are tingling a bit. I take long breaths, keeping it under control. No voices yet, but I'm just intrigued about what is going on at the moment. We soon arrive at the library building, and we carefully walk along the wall to get to the entrance, but I feel... cornered. It's a horrible feeling, to have a whole crowd with negative feelings aimed at you. I hear Ben growling slightly, warning them.

"We don't want a damn witch on campus!" a man's voice suddenly yells.

We freeze, shocked. How the hell do they know who I am? Kelsi stares at me, her eyes open wide in horror. She is scared about what that mob wants; I do not like that there are so many of them assembled around us already, I really don't. I grab her wrist and pull my friend slightly behind me. If they have an issue with me, they don't have to get Kelsi involved. However, Ben is standing between the crowd and us, and he's not refraining his growling anymore.

They are a bit wary of the menacing werewolf, but just one isn't enough to scare them away. I didn't catch who said that, but there's obviously a general agreement on the matter.

"If you have a problem with me, say it now!" I yell, annoyed at their attitude.

"Mara, don't provoke them!" growls Ben.

"Well, they already know, don't they? They might as well say whatever they have to say and leave me the fuck alone..."

"Just fuck off!" yells a girl.

"Get out of here!" says another voice.

"Mara..." whispers Kelsi, pulling my arm with a worried look.

I am not afraid of them. Moreover, none of them are approaching. They are staying at a distance, even if they are getting more and more people and slowly cornering us. Those damn cowards... They are just trying to surround us? Ben is still growling, and from the way he bends forward with his back slightly arched, I can tell he is ready to shape-shift anytime too.

Somehow, we still make it to the library, and despite the crowd gathered, Kelsi pulls me inside and no one follows. Are they just going to wait outside?

Kelsi lets out a sigh of relief, but she won't let go of my hand. She goes to one of the secretaries, and quickly explains the situation, making up some lost library card excuse and asking if anyone took any books out under the names Mara or Clarissa Jones. The young lady, probably a former student or something, doesn't really seem to care about her explanation. She nods and starts typing on her computer.

"Yes... Clarissa Jones. Oh, wow. Lady, you owe this library nine books! You're at least four months past the return date! Is this a joke?"

Kelsi grimaces.

"S-sorry about that... We will make sure to return them all. Can you give us a list so we can make sure we retrieve them all?"

"You got an email?"

"Sure..."

Kelsi pulls out her phone to give the lady her email address, but as soon as she looks at her screen, she frowns and bites her lip.

"Holy crap, Mara... Look."

She shows me a notification from her social media. I can't believe it. It's a freaking picture of us in front of the library. This was definitely just taken! The caption has several hashtags, including *#burnthewitch* and *#kickthebitchout*. Holy crap... We exchange a glance, and while Kelsi talks to the librarian, I turn to Ben.

"Okay, I may have underestimated that shit a bit. Do you have any reinforcements nearby?"

He nods with a dark expression.

"We have other werewolves on the campus, I already called them for help... Still, let's get you out of here quickly. Kelsi, you got the list?"

She nods, putting her hood back on her head. It's not helping her be more discreet, though, with those furry cat ears on it... I chuckle. Kelsi's quirks appearing in this kind of tense situation are the unexpected comedic relief I didn't foresee. She glances at the door, making a sour face.

"Alright, let's just hurry back to the car?"

Ben nods and walks out of the library first.

This time, the large crowd starts yelling as soon as they see me.

"Fuck off, witch!"

"Die!"

"Nobody wants you here!"

I glare at them and put my arm around Kelsi's shoulders, she is definitely more scared than I am. We walk fast, trying to get back to the parking lot, Ben growling all along. I'm pretty sure he would have shape-shifted into his wolf form already if he didn't have to drive us home.

Suddenly, I feel a bump against my head and see an empty soda can fall at my feet. The yells get louder, and I try to ignore them. I feel the circle of people around us closing in and surrounding us alarmingly fast. We are only a few meters away from the car...

"Let's hurry..." whimpers Kelsi.

I'm following her, but I keep glancing at those people. What the hell is their problem, and how the hell did they find out about me? Another object is thrown at us, and Ben is getting really mad. So am I. That one almost hit Kelsi!

I see a beer bottle flying, and it hits Ben. I clearly saw the perpetrator this time. That asshole!

"Mara, no!"

Too late. I am not letting them get injured for my sake! I take a few steps away from Kelsi, and light my fire in my hand, as a clear warning. I just need them to leave us the fuck alone until we get in the car. All the students suddenly get scared, and a lot of them run away, but the bravest of them are actually angered even more by my power.

"You fucking witch!"

They try to come forward to grab my arm, and Ben growls furiously. I extend my fire and Kelsi whimpers, reluctant to leave me, though she's probably dying to run to the car.

Suddenly, a big, black shadow jumps in between the students and me. The large black wolf growls furiously.

I keep staring, at a loss. Who is that wolf, and why does he feel so... strangely familiar? My heart is beating like crazy in my chest. He keeps growling furiously, and the students are terrified this time. Even the bravest ones retreat, far enough to be away from the black beast.

I don't care much about those idiots anymore. I can't keep my eyes off the beautiful wolf in front of me. I feel a couple of raindrops fall on me, reminding me to put my fire away. I look down at my hands and focus for a second, closing them and extinguishing the red flames. Kelsi seems to calm down a bit, but she grabs and pulls my hand.

"Mara, let's go..."

"Go to the car," I tell her, my eyes not leaving the wolf.

"No, no, Mara, you're coming too," says Ben, though he's obviously glancing at his peer.

Why does Ben look so nervous about that wolf? He just helped us, didn't he? Does that mean he is not from the White Moon pack?

I keep looking and realize what's been bothering me so long: he has this sort of aura thing, too, very similar to that of Selena's husband's. Another Alpha werewolf? His is dark as a shadow, as intimidating as darkness can be... Although, my whole body feels strangely warmer, and I shiver a bit. What the hell is that sensation? I felt it at the club, too... It was the same thing. Is it the same guy...? I glance at Kelsi, feeling a bit unsure. Why are all of my senses tingling like this? I just... I don't get it. I know this is dangerous and I should get out of here, yet...

Whoever this wolf is, I need to know. I glance at Ben, but he is still glaring at the people who did not leave the area, and are just observing us from afar. The black wolf did a pretty good job of scaring them, though. We are no longer in danger, I think. Then... why is my heart beating like crazy? I feel the rain starting to pour on us, and Kelsi pulls me toward the parking lot again. More wolves arrive to stand between them and us. The werewolves are assembling like a wall, and the students understand it's no use anymore. Some of them run back to the buildings to shelter themselves from the rain. No one wants to stick around now that about a dozen werewolves are here to be our bodyguards. I hear Ben's voice telling me again it's time to go too.

I can only focus on one wolf, though.

The black wolf turns around, and I finally see his eyes. One is of a mysterious silvery-blue color, and the other is... white. Like a white veil is covering it. There's some strangely shaped scar on it too, making me think there's something wrong with his eye. He glances at me, his aura scaring me a little, and he suddenly walks away. My eyes follow him without thinking, and my heart goes crazy in my chest. Why is he going already when the other wolves are still here? Where is he headed? I know I should be going, but my whole body is begging me to follow him.

"Mara!"

Kelsi's call wakes me up from this strange slumber, but I can't shake off that feeling.

"Go to the car... Go home," I tell her. "I'll catch up with you later, I promise."

"What? Mara!"

I'm not listening anymore. Rule or not, I shake her hand off me, and now I'm running after the black wolf. He's fast, and I struggle to not lose him. He's headed off campus. He's not a student then? I take one street after another, trying to keep up. Why isn't he stopping? He clearly saw I was following him!

The thunder breaks the sky above us, but I don't care. I don't care about a storm or the downpour falling on me, I just focus my whole being into following this black wolf as if my life depended on it. My clothes are quickly drenched and become annoying, sticking to my skin. It gets darker, but I don't lose sight of the black streak in front of me. I see him glance back several times, and he accelerates. That jerk is trying to lose me!

I don't give up, and keep going. I hear him growling a bit, warning me to stop following him, but I don't care. I need to know who he is. The image of that guy's back in the leather jacket haunts me. I don't know how I am so sure that's him, but I am. I'm so sure, almost as if it's printed into my core.

Finally, we end up at the limit of the city, where the forest begins. I remember, Kelsi said all of Silver City is surrounded by either the sea or a vast forest. A perfect environment for werewolves to reside in, and strangers to stay out. So why would that guy come to the border? We are past the buildings, right at the end of the streets; beyond that, it's nothing but trees as far as my eyes can see. The thunder suddenly makes an awful ruckus above, but even that doesn't distract me. I still have my eyes on the black wolf, who finally stopped running. He's at the edge of the border, almost in the forest. I feel another strange sensation, like something... cold is in front of me. As if I was facing a wall of ice.

I frown and raise my hand. It seems stupid because there's obviously nothing in front of me, but my instinct is telling me otherwise. I extend my arm farther and suddenly, something burns my fingertips.

"Ouch!"

I retract my hand and check my fingers, but there's nothing. The pain is still clearly lingering, though, like a bite or an electric shock... I raise my eyes to look at the black wolf. He is only a couple of meters away from me, still watching me. How did he get out when I can't? That strange field or whatever this is, I'm not risking my fingers again. I can still feel it. Damn it!

"Who are you?" I yell, hoping he'll hear me despite the storm.

He keeps staring at me, not moving. I thought he might run away into the forest or something, but he seems just fine with me being unable to get closer. How petty.

"I saw you at the club," I continue. "I want to talk to you!"

He growls a bit, looking annoyed. What the heck is wrong with him? Does he know me or what? I'm feeling stupid already, yelling at a wolf under this downpour!

"Are you going to talk or not, you idiot?!" I yell, annoyed.

Several long seconds pass. If it wasn't for the rain, it wouldn't have felt so horribly drawn-out and awkward! However, the black wolf is still there, eyeing me, and I just can't leave.

Finally, he moves. It seems like he's standing on his legs, and his body transforms into a human in a few seconds. This is my first time seeing a werewolf shape-shift, and there's something mesmerizing about it. The black fur disappears, showing off a tall, well-built body. His skin is already wet from the rain, but still, he's more muscular and taller than I imagined. I swallow my saliva. Shit, he's... handsome. His fur only remained on his head, showing off his short-cut, silky, black hair, and he runs his hand through it to chase a bit of water from dropping into his eyes. Even his eyes are... mesmerizing. They are exactly the same as his wolf's, one of a cold silvery-blue, the other... blind white. Plus, there are the remnants of a scar that makes a strange pattern around it, like a leopard's markings, or imperfect circles. As if something had been splattered on it...

Despite that, he's really... handsome. Perfectly clean-shaven, and somehow, he looks young but with the charisma of an older man. He has fine features, a square face, and a cute little chin that makes his lips look like he's about to pout. And his muscles... I have a hard time not getting too absorbed in those fine lines. I don't know how long it's been since I've seen a naked man, but he is definitely very well-built, with thin muscles and everything. He reminds me of that young Adonis statue in the hospital's park... Oh, shit, not just the statue, he happens to be naked too.

I make sure to look up, focusing on his face and not on... whatever's below. Thankfully, it's rather dark and he's half standing in the forest's shadows. I try to control my heartbeat, but I didn't expect his human form to be... like this. Or how I'd react to it. I just don't know what's going on, I feel like my whole body is on fire, without any flames. I need to control myself, I need answers first. I see him sigh, making a sour face. He's still glaring at me as if the growling in his wolf form hadn't been enough.

"Who are you?" I ask again.

"Stay away from me," he growls.

I shiver. His voice is deeper than I thought, and surprisingly warm, despite the warning. It's not that intimidating, though. As if I could come any closer! Whatever is keeping me where I am, he knows it's there. That guy stopped right when I arrived at this strange barrier or whatever this is. He knew it'd stop me, so why is he warning me again?

"Do you know me?" I ask.

"No."

"Then why did you come to help me at the university? Ben didn't call you, did he?"

I'm starting to understand a bit of a pattern between the werewolves, enough to know that if this guy isn't from the White Moon Clan, he wasn't called over by Ben to help us. He was the first one to come, though, and right when things took a bad turn.

"You were at the club too. If you don't belong to the White Moon, who the hell are you, and why did you help me?"

He keeps glaring, without answering. What is his problem? He's breathing rather heavily and takes another step away from me. If I didn't know any better, I would even think he's almost... scared of me. However, those aren't the eyes of someone who is scared. I have no idea who this guy is, and yet, he's glaring at me like he wants to kill me. For someone who pretends he doesn't know me, that's a bit too much!

"...I didn't want to help you," he whispers.

"Are you actually going to give me answers or are we playing charades? I've had more than my share, lately," I frown.

He looks away, clearly annoyed. At least, he's still here. I just don't get it.

"Do you know me or not?" I insist.

"I don't know you!" he yells back. "I just know you're the witch, and I don't want anything to do with you!"

Oh, we are finally making some progress here. I cross my arms, completely drenched. Damn it, I wish I had brought a bit more clothing, I'm only wearing this long T-shirt, and I'm soaked all the way to my socks. Surprisingly, I see his eyes go down on my wet figure too and I frown. Seriously, is he fucking gawking now? Our eyes meet, and he immediately looks away, blushing a bit. Wait, Mr. Death Glare is blushing now?!

"Are you sure you don't know me?"

"I don't!" he protests.

"Then why did you run away?"

I can tell my questions annoy him to the core. His eyes are finally going back to me, and his glare is not as intense. What is the deal with him, why is he acting like that, and why am I feeling like this? I'm so tensed up, my heartbeat is going crazy and it has nothing to do with the horrible weather above us.

"I wasn't running away..." he growls.

"We both know you were running away from me," I retort. "You came and you ran all the way here where I can't follow you."

91

I want to try approaching again, but I know this barrier is still there, I can feel it. I look up, but aside from the rain, there's really nothing visible. So annoying.

"Why can't I come closer?"

"There's a protective barrier."

"It doesn't work on you."

"I'm a werewolf. You're a witch. It only stops witches..."

Damn it, that's why he's fine and I'm freaking trapped here. Why the hell is there a barrier outside of Silver City anyway? Did they do this to keep me here? Why? I light up my flames, in both hands, and he reacts immediately, growling.

"Stop it!"

I ignore him. I'm not going to let this stupid barrier keep me trapped like this!

I bring my flames to the barrier, and suddenly, a wave of darkness hits me. I lose all sight for a second, but a horrible, strident ringing pierces my ears. I fall on all fours, completely stunned. What the heck is this horror?! I'm feeling so sick, my stomach is turned all over, and I can't breathe. With whatever strength I have left, I crawl away from that barrier. I can feel the mud underneath, and I just keep struggling to get away, as far as I can. Crap, I feel like throwing up... I've never felt so sick before.

Finally, the ringing stops, and I can breathe again. What the hell was that...? My sight comes back slowly, though it feels like a dark fog more than my actual vision. I'm still nauseous like I was just thrown out of a rollercoaster... Shit...

"...You okay?"

It's my turn to glare at him. He came closer to the barrier, and he has the fucking balls to look worried for me. Do I look okay? I'm lying in the freaking mud, drenched and feeling like someone just hit me with a hammer!

"...I told you," he says.

"Yeah, I got the message..." I mumble.

I take several deep breaths to calm myself down, and after a lot of effort, somehow manage to get back on my feet. He's still there and watching me, and it annoys me. Why did I even follow this idiot? He still looks somewhat sorry, which bothers me even more.

"I fucking get it," I grumble.

"What?"

"You don't like me, you have no name, and obviously, you aren't going to give me any answers. I'm fucking tired of getting dragged left and right by people who want to protect me or kill me, so it'd be nice if you could fucking decide between being an asshole and being sorry for me!"

He looks like I just slapped him. Well, at least, that is satisfying. I feel like crap, and I am in no mood to indulge Mr. Death Glare any longer. As I said, I'm fucking done. I just ran across the city to get hit by an invisible wall and meet a jerk who isn't willing to say anything unless I crawl in the mud. I don't even know why I was so desperate to follow this guy. None of this makes sense, and I feel even crazier than before. And damn bitter too.

I hear him sigh.

"...Liam."

"What?"

"My name. It's Liam Black."

I frown. ...Liam Black, like one of the Black Brothers? Did Kelsi say there were three of them? I stay speechless for a second. I'm tired, and not sure I just understood that right. That guy looks just a bit older than me, not old enough to be some businessman like his older brothers, whatever their names were. So there's a third brother, and that's him? Isn't he part of the other clan, then, not Selena's? Why was he watching me?

He glances sideways, and I can tell he wants to leave. I'm surprised he's even still here when he obviously would rather be anywhere else. I'm shivering, cold, and pretty much fed up with this guy. He's standing there, avoiding looking at me, yet still there. I frown and keep my arms tight around me. I'm so damn cold, dirty, and exhausted. I sniffle.

"Why do you hate me so much?" I ask.

It's the one thing I just don't get. The other werewolves don't like me, but they don't hate me, at best. This guy is clearly strongly opinionated already, and he said he doesn't even know me! He looks a bit stunned by my question and finally looks back at me. At least, his valid eye does? Damn, he's really attractive. Our eyes lock for a few seconds, and once again, my heartbeat goes erratic. Despite the horrible state I'm in, a wave of heat rises from within. I don't understand what the hell it is with this guy that makes me so crazy like this.

Moreover, he seems to be... as conflicted as I am. I see him gasp as if looking at me was giving him the same insane feeling. What the heck is this?

"I don't..." he says.

However, he doesn't finish his sentence, leaving the two of us hanging stupidly. He doesn't what? Hate me? If so, can't he just freaking say it? I'm already feeling like enough of an idiot as it is! Running after some random werewolf guy who doesn't know what he wants?

"Why did you help me?" I ask again.

My tone is more accusatory this time, but he'd better not throw a fucking half-answer at me again. I see him frown a bit, despite the rain dripping down his forehead, and he shakes his head.

"I sensed something was happening, so I came, that's it."

How did he feel a stupid mob going nuts over a witch? I'm done. I agitate my hands, but I can't even bother to light up a flame when I'm drenched like this, it makes no sense. I turn around, annoyed. He's not letting me follow him or giving me answers either. I'm done here.

"Where are you going?!" he yells.

"Why do you care, you were the one running away!"

"You–"

"Anyway, just come and find me when you feel like talking instead of acting like a jerk!"

Just like that, I walk away. I'm so fed up with that guy, these crappy days, and all the half-answers or truth-bomb questions everyone has been dropping on me all day!

I resist glancing back to see if he follows me, and look around for a place to shelter myself from the rain. It's a downpour here, and I'm drenched to the bone. I have no idea where I am either. How am I going to get back to my place? Am I even still in White Moon territory? I keep going, walking around the streets for a clue. With this terrible weather, the streets are empty. There isn't even anyone to ask.

Those tall buildings offer no place to hide either. I feel like a cat, wandering aimlessly and letting myself get completely soaked. Crap, it will be a miracle if I don't get sick. My nose is running already, and I'm cold with the start of a headache. I look around once more, raindrops dripping down my eyelashes.

"Come here."

Before I can turn around, I feel my arm being grabbed, and I'm pulled in another direction. He lets go, but now it's the black wolf that suddenly appears in front of me, guiding me. What, so he changed his mind now?

I follow him, as he does seem to know where to go, but I hope this isn't some crappy trap!

Finally, we reach what looks like an old building. Is this a chapel? It's too small to be a church. There is only one door, but a big lock is on it. However, the black wolf ignores it and squeezes in between the fence to walk inside the chapel's little garden. I frown, but still follow him, climbing over the little fence. Where is he taking me?

His Blazing Witch

He disappears on the side, and I realize that there's an open window. Does he want to squeeze in there? The black wolf easily goes in. I can't see anything past that opening, but if he can get in... I contort myself and finally manage to get in. It's a little jump down, and I land on my bent knees, but at least, we are in a proper shelter from the rain.

I get back up and look around. It looks abandoned... This place obviously hasn't seen any prayers in at least a couple dozen years. There's dust piling up, all the other openings are locked, and aside from spiders, no one alive is around. It's a small place too... Only four benches, a little place for prayers, and a fountain against one of the walls. The window by which we came in sends a ray of light inside, but considering the dark clouds and the storm outside, it's still very dark. So dark, I've lost sight of the black wolf. Where did he go? I frown, looking around.

I actually spot some abandoned candles gathering dust on a shelf. I go get them, and after several attempts, I manage to light them with my fire. I look through the shelves, but there are no more candles, other than those two. That will have to do... I put them in a spot where they can light up the place without the risk of being blown out, and turn around. If only there was a fireplace, it would be even better... At least we are safe from the rain. I can hear it banging against the windows, but the one we came from might be the only one that's protected, there's only wind coming in that way.

"...Take this."

I turn around just in time to receive it. A leather jacket... I recognize it as the one he was wearing at the nightclub. So it really was his back I saw.

This must be a hideout of his because Liam appears back in his human form and is dressed in actual clothes this time. He's wearing some jeans and a simple sleeveless top, but somehow, I manage to find him even more attractive than before... His hair is still wet too, and his muscles are showing under this kind of top. I put the jacket on my shoulders. At least it's a bit warmer... I shiver. It's a bit... awkward. Liam Black sits on the floor, farther away from me, next to the little altar.

I can't help but glance at him. Damn, he's very... handsome, especially in this atmosphere. All the decor strangely suits him. He looks like some fallen angel, with a statue a bit higher above him, and the light of the dark sky shining on the stone around him. I'm mesmerized. Why do I feel this strange... connection to a guy that wants nothing to do with me? I tighten his jacket around my shoulders. It smells like rain, old leather, and... him. Something musky that I like. I feel like a bit of a pervert... I blush a bit and try to look elsewhere. I am still cold, but at least, this is better.

95

We can hear the rain coming down on the roof, and the storm still raging outside. The thunder seems to be right above us, making me worry if this roof is going to hold. The wood is creaking above, but Liam doesn't seem to worry one bit.

I decide to sit on one of the benches, leaving my shoes on the floor and putting my feet on the bench. I curl up a bit, leaning my side against the back of the bench. We stay like this for a long while, and I even feel a bit... sleepy. Hell yeah, I'm tired. Yet, my senses prevent me from actually falling asleep. I just can't relax with this guy here. The rain doesn't seem like it's going to stop anytime soon. I should have kept my phone, but I left it in Kelsi's bag... I'm an idiot. I envy the werewolves and their mind-linking ability.

"Your pack knows we are here?" I ask.

"No."

I frown. Doesn't he keep them informed? Or is it because he belongs to a different pack? I thought all werewolf packs more or less got along...

"You're... the youngest Black brother, then?" I ask.

Without looking at me, he nods. Actually, it looks like he's avoiding looking my way. I feel like he'd climb up the wall if he could... What the heck is with him? It's obvious he doesn't hate me that much if he guided me here, and he doesn't seem scared like all those idiots either. So what's his deal?

"Isn't your pack going to worry?"

"No. They are used to it."

Used to what? Him hiding in creepy forgotten chapels like this? I sigh and shiver under his leather jacket.

"...I met your older brother. The blonde one."

"I know."

So they do talk between brothers... Is it just him acting out, then? I get up and start walking toward him. He notices and immediately tenses up. I knew it, this guy is super wary of me. He glares my way when I come up to him, but he won't move, and he doesn't try to growl either. Even that strange aura of his seems... tamed. I tilt my head.

"Is it because I am a witch?" I ask.

"What?"

"Your reaction to me. Is it because I am a witch, or is there something else?"

He scoffs.

"I am not scared of witches. I am the witch hunter of this city."

"A witch hunter?"

"I keep this city free of witches."

I chuckle. Isn't he doing a poor job of it since I'm here? He rolls his eyes, annoyed at my little mockery. He shakes his head and once again, looks away to answer.

"I mean... The ones outside."

"There are more witches outside?"

"Yeah. Since our... the previous one, Silver City is witchless, and they want to take it over. Several have tried to cross that barrier before."

"...Why?"

He sighs, as if I was asking annoying questions. However, this is of deep interest to me. Aside from the professor from before, this Liam guy is the only one who seems to know what he's talking about while mentioning witches...

"Witches attach themselves to cities with power. Silver City is one of those, and..."

"Since there are no more witches, they want it?"

"Basically."

I nod. No wonder they have that barrier thing, then... With the previous war that involved witches, they are probably done with them. Hence, my being here makes no one happy. Especially that witch hunter guy. I chuckle, realizing how strange my position is. It also explains, even more, why they are all so wary of me: I am the one witch that is already inside. Who put up that barrier anyway? Did they prevent witches from coming in without thinking one could possibly need to get out? How complicated.

"...So you prevent other witches from coming in... How many have tried? Since the war?"

"Just three," he says. "They never got too close, though. They know the barrier is there."

"So, what about me then?"

He growls a bit. Yeah, I'm annoying you with all my questions, aren't I? Somehow, it still makes me chuckle a little bit. I take another step closer, and Liam retreats a little, still frowning. He's not happy with me moving toward him, and there is nowhere he can run away to. Interesting... It makes me want to torment him a little.

"...We still don't know how you were able to get in," he growls.

"You're not pushing me outside."

"We're considering it..." he growls.

"The Luna doesn't seem to think so, though."

"Selena isn't my Luna."

"She's still your sister-in-law, and a Luna, isn't she?"

"I don't obey her, my brothers, or Nora. I do whatever I want."

Is he a loner, then? His brothers and their wives are the most powerful duos of werewolves around, so what does that make him? He said the other Luna's name is Nora. It doesn't ring a bell either, but at least, I know she's the one married to the King, Selena's sister-in-law and cousin. I'm starting to put this whole werewolf thingy together from a better angle, but this guy, Liam, he's not fitting in.

He does act like a loner. He didn't tell them where we are, and maybe they don't know he's with me either. How curious... I sigh. He hates me, but he helps me take shelter from the rain. He's a witch hunter that doesn't hunt me. This guy is just too complicated, isn't he?

A lightning bolt suddenly sparks up the whole room. I jump, a bit surprised, and my headache reappears all of a sudden. I retreat, trying to ignore it. Damn it...

"What is wrong with you?" he asks.

I ignore him, massaging my temples. I can feel it. The darkness, coming back... I need to breathe. Being trapped here with this guy is somehow not helping at all. I feel a bit stuffed, and the voices start to crawl back into my head. They are like echoes of whispers I can't control. They blur my ideas, my senses, my vision, everything.

"Hey."

I ignore him. I feel this shiver crawling up my spine, making me hotter and hotter. What the hell do they want, why now? Why? I'm not cold at all anymore, I'm fighting that fire within. I can feel Liam's eyes on me, and somehow, I feel like it's not helping at all.

Kill him.

What the heck... I don't want to kill anybody! What the heck is that creepy voice... I keep taking deep breaths and try to think a bit more. I try to remember Selena's lesson, but somehow, I don't feel as strong as before. What is this? I feel like this voice is getting crazier than before!

"I... I need to go..." I whisper.

"What?"

Once again, I ignore that guy. I really have to go. I feel sick. As if I was struggling to stay conscious, while that voice is getting crazy strong in my head. I hear her. It's screaming continuously, and all those whispers inside... No, no, Mara, don't let her win.

"I have to leave!" I whimper.

"Hey, hey, calm down."

I feel him, grabbing my wrists. I'm not sure where I am. Probably still inside the chapel. However, my legs are getting weak, and my head is hurting as if it was about to split in two. I want to scream too. I want to scream more. It's so painful...

"Mara. Mara, look at me."

I fight the dizziness and look up. I see him. His ice-blue eye and the white one. He's close, too close. I don't want him so close. My breath shortens, and my head spins again. I know I'm still standing because Liam's holding my wrists in front of me, but my body is falling apart. I hear my own breathing, erratic, and distressed. I can't...

"Mara."

His voice is like a siren calling to me. I fall to my knees, but Liam goes down with me. I have no strength to fight this horrible voice anymore... I hear that screaming, echoing in my head, taking up all that space, and blurring everything else. I can't take it anymore, she's in such distress...

I look up again, fighting my heavy eyelids. I can't let her in now. I need to stay awake... I focus on Liam. Liam Black, the werewolf. He's right here, holding my wrists and waiting for me to calm down. What is that thing thumping in my chest? All I can focus on is him. His face. His fine features, and the way he looks at me. He's worried and cautious. I can tell he's having his own fight too. Something sparks between us. He suddenly avoids my gaze, looking elsewhere, but I need him. I need him to hold me back. If he's not here, I'll...

"Hey, hey! Mara!"

Chapter 8

I hear myself taking deep breaths. I feel like I missed something, there's a blank. Did I lose consciousness for a minute, or a few seconds? With my eyes closed, I try to shut everything else out. I don't want those voices, I don't want those murderous feelings. Leave me alone! ...Why? Why should I feel so angry at everyone else?

It's still there, lurking. I feel the desire to burn something so violently, it's like a monster waking up inside. All my senses are tingling. I struggle to keep it under control, but it's beneath my skin, it's rushing through my veins, giving me shivers and keeping me breathless. Why the headache, why the pain? Where the hell are those screams coming from? I feel like I'm stuck with them echoing from all sides, driving me crazy. It's like an alarm I don't know how to turn off.

"Mara, Mara. Look at me."

I realize I'm crying a bit when I reopen my eyes, and my blurry vision confuses me. Yet, I quickly find the two eyes right in front of me. He's holding my hands, and dangerously close to me. Why is this idiot still here? I can barely control myself right now!

"Don't..." I mutter painfully. "I'll... kill you..."

"I'm not such a pup that you'd kill me so easily."

"I'm a witch," I groan.

Damn it, I have very little self-control right now, and he actually has no sense of danger, does he? Alpha or not, he'll feel it if I burn his pretty ass! I groan again, the headache getting somewhat worse. I need to breathe, ignore it, and control it. I can't endure this crap for too long.

"Mara, what is it doing to you? Tell me."

Why does he care now? He was barely willing to talk earlier!

"It's those... voices..."

"Voices? What do they tell you?"

"I don't know!" I lie. "It just screams..."

I struggle to get out of his grip, but he's stronger than he looks. His hands firmly hold mine and when I want to retreat, he won't let go. What the heck, he

100

was the one who didn't want to stay too close, did that change now? I shake my head, avoiding his eyes, but the voices just become stronger. What the heck is that thing, and why is it reacting now? It only happened when I was upset before, but now, these voices are going nuts over nothing!

"Mara."

"Please, just... shut up, give me a minute," I whimper.

"Breathe deep. Focus on my voice to calm down."

"What the... hell are you... saying..."

"You're not the first witch I've met, so just listen to me. You ought to control this voice and tell her to shut up. You're the one in control, she cannot force you to do anything you don't want to. You understand?"

I nod, but it's easier said than done! I take deep breaths, and instead of my hearing, I focus on his touch. Liam's skin is warm on my hand and wrist. He's got large but thin hands, holding me strongly. I feel that strange spark again, though I can't quite understand that feeling. I don't want to kill this man. I... I think I need him.

"Keep talking," I beg him.

"What does the voice tell you?"

"To kill you. To kill werewolves."

"...Oh, wow."

I glare at him. Is it really the moment to act surprised? Did he think I was having a hard time keeping myself off snacks or what? He sighs and stares at me, even more determined than before. I try to focus on his eyes... mostly the icy-blue one.

"You don't have to listen to the voice, Mara. You're your own witch. Just tell her to shut the fuck up, and control it."

It's like yelling through a hurricane, and it sounds like a piece of very dumb advice from him. Yet, I decide to give it a try. I ignore her mentally, but her voice grows stronger. Then, I confront her, screaming internally for her to leave me alone.

Strangely, it seems to work. I still hear the screams, but they are a bit quieter, and most importantly, that scary voice telling me to kill Liam is gone. I let out a long sigh of relief. I can't believe it actually worked... I give myself a few seconds to get my senses back and calm down; I hadn't realized I was in such a panicked state. I'm still shivering a bit, and some drops of sweat are running down my spine.

When I find the strength to look at Liam Black again, our eyes meet, but it's like an electric shock to him. He lets go of my wrist and retreats immediately, looking stunned. What the hell? He almost falls on his arse while trying to get away from me, and stumbles back until we are a few steps apart. I frown, unsure of what funny game he's playing at. What the heck is it now?

"What the hell is wrong with you?" I ask.

"N-nothing. Just... Please stop looking at me like that."

"Like what? You're the one who came to give me some witch tips."

He growls a bit, annoyed. I didn't realize growling is fully part of the werewolf language until now. I thought it was rather rare to do and only when they are super pissed, but it looks like they can do it anytime to express frustration too. How convenient. Don't wanna talk? You can just growl your unhappiness. It doesn't help me understand, though.

"It's just you're not... very decent looking."

Decent looking? What the heck is he talking about...?

I look down and realize my soaked shirt has been sticking to my body. What, is this what is flustering him now? I chuckle. I thought I was blushing too much, but just seeing a girl's body can make him so perplexed? Now that's a bit of a surprise. I take a deep breath, trying to calm myself a bit more and lean against one of the benches, but I don't try to hide or anything. I can't help but find that a bit... amusing? Liam rolls his eyes and looks elsewhere. I can't help but think he does have something going on with me that I can't grasp yet.

"...How did you know?" I ask.

"About what?"

"How to calm them down. The voices."

He sighs and steps away some more. I'm not too happy about the distance he's putting between us, but thinking about what happened just seconds ago, I can't really blame him either. I was literally tempted to kill him.

"I just... guessed."

"I'm not your first witch, you said. You knew the other ones, right?"

This time, he makes a really sour expression. Does his witch hunter title have anything to do with the previous ones? He avoids my eyes again, looking at one of the murals. After a long silence, he slowly nods, making the piercings in his ears shine a little. Damn, I think I like those piercings.

"Witches have... this thing called the ancestors' blood. It allows them to be guided by their ancestors, especially when they are younger."

I scoff, baffled. Ancestors? The murderous voices in my head would be those of my potential witch ancestors? So far, we haven't found anything to link me to any other witch, other than the fact that I am in Silver City! I shake my head, doubtful.

"I don't think I–"

"All witches have it," he retorts. "It's sort of a... genetic ritual. They hear echoes of the voices of their ancestors, especially when they are troubled, or anxious, whenever they get unstable."

Or dangerously unhappy. Then what triggered it here? I wasn't really in a kind of negative state while chatting with Liam earlier, so why would those... ancestors' voices come up? I don't even believe that is really what it is. Why would my ancestors or whoever the heck those voices belong to push me to become a murderer? It just makes no sense to me!

"There has to be some sort of mistake," I mutter.

"I don't see anything else that could match what you're experiencing."

"What the hell do you know? Are you a witch hunter or a witch expert?"

"A bit of both," he snickers. "I studied the subject..."

I don't like his arrogant tone. I don't like how he seems to know everything yet isn't being clear. He stays away from me, but he's not afraid. He knows an awful lot about witches, yet won't come close to me. I don't want to play charades all the damn time!

"Fine, then does the witch expert have any other tips for me?" I sigh.

"What else do those voices tell you?"

"What? Nothing! All they have told me is to kill or burn people! That, and those horrible screams that give me headaches all the damn time..."

"Screams?"

"Yes, as if... as if a woman was being tortured or something. Just screams of pure fear and pain. It's like having a direct channel to a torture room, it's just horrifying. I have no idea who it is, or why I hear her. Do you really think it's my... ancestors?"

"It could be. Witches have a history of being persecuted, so..."

I nod. Yeah, I know that much at least. All the records of witches throughout history that Kelsi found ended up with women being burned, hung, or drowned. Nothing too funny about it. However, that was ages ago! Why would I have to endure the painful memories of one of my ancestors who died so long ago? It doesn't make much sense...

"Who was your mother?" he asks.

I raise an eyebrow. He doesn't know about my amnesia?

"I have no idea..." I confess.

"What?"

I explain to him quickly how they found me with no memories, and even my older half-sister has no clue about my mother. He seems more and more surprised as I go, but he's still careful to not look at me while I talk. After a while, he nods.

"Well... if you're a witch, it is definitely from your mother's side... Witch powers are inherited from mother to daughter. Actually, a witch can only give birth to a girl witch, and in some rare cases, she'll have a son, a normal human one."

"Now that's something interesting... except that I know nothing about my own mother," I sigh. "Do you think she was a Fire Witch too?"

"No. It's a cycle. A witch gives birth to a daughter born with a different sign from hers. Your mother can't have been a Fire Witch."

"Oh..."

A cycle? Damn, there wasn't anything about a cycle from what the professor told me or in that herbology book I got.

"You do sound like a witch expert, after all..."

"Yeah, well, the lesson stops here for today," he suddenly declares, standing up.

"What? Why!"

"I have to go."

"Where?"

He rolls his eyes.

"Why do I have to tell you, I'm not your babysitter!"

"You can be my witch-sitter for all I care. I still have questions!" I insist.

"Well, keep them for another time."

Before I can add anything else, he ignores me to shape-shift into a wolf, meaning this conversation is really over for me. What a jerk! Completely helpless, I have to watch the black wolf ignore me and jump out of the little window we came through, leaving his clothes behind. I swear, I can't handle this guy. I don't get him! I frown and keep watching that window for a long time, hesitant about going out. I'm not catching up to him now, he's probably already long gone.

What the heck was that...? As soon as he was gone, all of the screams were gone too. I don't get it. Why would that guy be some sort of trigger? I try to remember what Kelsi told me about the Black Brothers, but it doesn't make sense... I hesitate and get up to go and check his clothes. I know it's probably not very fair, but he left them behind, so... Okay, I don't need to check his underwear, though I do notice the name of the brand. I check his jeans pocket and found an ID card. He's really Liam Black, born September 2000... Oh, so he's a few years older than I am. I keep checking. He also has the papers for a motorbike, a driver's license, and a phone. I try to unlock the smartphone, but there's a PIN. Crap.

104

I can't find anything else, but out of spite, I decide to keep everything with me, except for his smartphone. He can come find me if he wants his papers back, I'm done running after him! I feel a bit naughty while putting everything in my pockets, but naughty strangely feels good.

I get up and try to wipe away more of the mud I got on myself. I'm still dirty as hell... I really need to get back and take a good shower. I look up at the window. It's going to be a nightmare to climb out of this. I let out a long sigh, and instead, tour the little chapel a bit. I'll wait until the downpour stops, I am not going back out in this storm. It may be fine for a werewolf, but I'm not risking it. I wouldn't even know where to go anyway.

I look around, but this place is rather... empty. The doors are all condemned, and the bookshelves are bare. Even the little fountain has no water running. It's a miracle I even found some candles... I decide to curl up on one of the benches. If only there was some wood I could burn to warm myself up. Well, at least, Liam left me his jacket. I'm going nuts over his smell... I feel like a pervert, but his smell is so nice and soothing. I start daydreaming, and somehow, warm arms replace the leather sleeves surrounding me. What the hell am I thinking about...

I wake up a while later, with no idea how long I've been asleep. The rain stopped! The difference in sound is baffling. I almost run to the window's opening, and though it looks dark outside, at least I know the storm seems to have passed. I can't help but smile in relief. Good.

As I climb back up, it wakes up all my muscle pains from the fight with Selena, but I don't care much. I need to go back now, I've been gone for a while. I can only imagine the ruckus it's going to be, either from my sister's side or Selena's... I walk through the streets of Silver City, trying to find my way back. One more thing about myself I just discovered: I am the absolute worst at directions. I have a vague idea, but every time I think I'm in the right area, the buildings change just to confuse me. What the hell?

"Oh my God, Mara!"

I turn around just in time to see Kelsi jump at my neck. I hug her back, a bit confused.

"I'm sorry, I just took shelter from the rain, I–"

"Where the hell have you been?! Everyone is furious, they are all looking for you."

"Seriously?" I frown. "No need to be this mad, I was just gone a bit, it's..."

Before I can continue, I realize there's something wrong in Kelsi's eyes. She shakes her head, looking panicked.

"Mara, a big fire started at the university, the humans think you did it!"

...What?

I remain speechless for a long minute. I can barely believe what she just said. A fire... at the university, now?

"I didn't do it!" I immediately blurt out, shocked.

Kelsi grabs my hand, trying to act calm when she most likely isn't.

"Boo, let's get you home first, okay? We can talk once you're dry, you look like you've rolled around in the mud..."

I can't refute that. I see her eyes glance at the new leather jacket covering my shoulders, but she doesn't say anything and pulls me inside the building. Damn it, I was actually this close?

Once we are upstairs, Kelsi gets me in the shower while she grabs some clean and warm clothes for me to get into. I swear I don't remember the last time a hot shower felt this good. I let it pour on me for a few minutes. What a crazy day it's been? First, that professor at the university who knew me, or at least the former me that was asking around about witches under a fake name. Then, the mob that got mad at me out of nowhere, and finally, Liam Black.

I shiver just remembering his cold eyes. What in the world was that feeling I got from that guy? Every time I am near him, I lose control. It's not just my senses, it's as if my whole body was going crazy. I look down at my hand. He held my hand, and it felt... strangely good. I can remember very precisely his gentle but firm grip. How close he was, and even the details of his face. He got dangerously close to mine. Why was he acting like that? One minute, he was running away from me as if he hated me, but then, he got all... caring.

"Mara?" Kelsi knocks at the door. "You should come and see!"

I frown and get out of the shower. I don't even need to grab the towel, my body dries within seconds. I can feel my fire running inside and adjust my internal temperature... I grab the comfy denim overalls and top Kelsi left me, and get out of the bathroom. She's in the salon, watching the TV with her arms crossed. Ben is actually there too, and it looks like he just arrived from outside, his hair still wet.

We don't even talk, I just watch the TV as the local news channel is running. The images speak for themselves. It really is the university; a whole damn building of it caught on fire as if hell itself had unleashed...

"...Of unknown circumstances," says the anchor. "An inferno broke out an hour ago on the campus of Silver City University, engulfing one of the buildings within seconds. The fire took over very quickly according to the witnesses on site, pushing the local authorities to believe this may have been intentional. The chief of the local police just gave a more recent statement, mentioning there are no known victims yet. All parties involved will do their best to resolve this incident..."

Kelsi grabs the remote to mute it, making a sour expression, and turns to me.

"Mara if–"

"It wasn't me!" I retort immediately.

"These are some really strange circumstances," says Ben.

"Stop fucking glaring at me! I didn't do anything, you saw me leave the campus!"

"You've been gone for hours, Mara," says Kelsi. "I don't believe you did it, I swear, but you're going to be in trouble. Where were you? The werewolves were looking all over Silver City for you!"

"Selena is on her way," adds Ben.

I glare at him. So he already told her I was back here. Damn it, if they send me back to the hospital over this, I am really going to lose my shit! I turn to Kelsi, the only one who seems to really believe me.

"Does my sister know?"

She seems surprised by my question and glances at the TV, helpless.

"Well, I don't want to be pessimistic, but... Mara, it's been all over the news for a while now, pretty much the whole city knows..."

Damn it, not only Selena but Amy is going to give me hell. I didn't even do anything! Why the hell did that fire have to break out now? I haven't even been free for three damn days and then this kind of thing happens! I don't know what to do, and honestly, I'm considering running away as one of the options. I start pacing in the room, unable to calm down. This is just impossible, why did this happen? Why, just why? I did not start this fucking fire, so why does it feel like everything is already pointing toward me?

"Mara, calm down..." whispers Kelsi.

"I can't calm down! Someone is trying to freaking frame me, Kelsi, I can't see any other explanation!"

"That's a bit much for framing someone, don't you think?" grimaces Ben, glancing at the TV.

I glare at him, but just then, we hear a knock at the door. Damn it... As I am not moving and neither does Kelsi, Ben sighs and gets up. He goes to open the door while I mentally prepare myself.

As I feared, Selena walks in, looking pretty unhappy and followed by two wolves. I don't recognize either of them, but I guess it's not important that I do. They look like they are her bodyguards or something, but they stay behind her. The White Luna looks angry enough by herself and that's all I'm concerned about. How the hell did she get here so fast anyway? She's in a sports outfit, her blonde hair braided down on her shoulder, a few wet strands sticking out. Was she training or running somewhere close by? She walks up to me, but I step back.

"I did not do it," I declare right away, determined.

"You want me to believe you?" says Selena. "Mara, you went to the university, got caught in some mob of stupid angry students, and disappeared, leaving Ben behind! I said to fucking stay somewhere we could watch you, and not get involved with the humans! Instead, you almost start a fight, and minutes after that, a fire appears in the middle of the university! Mara, what the hell am I supposed to think?!"

I can't help but glare at Ben. I know he's definitely the one who already told her everything. The redhead makes himself as little as possible on the couch, looking a bit awkward. Yeah, I'll make him pay for that later.

"I did not do it, Selena," I insist.

"Then where the hell have you been? What part of 'under surveillance' escaped you for two fucking hours?!"

"I wasn't alone! Okay, maybe I shouldn't have left, but I wasn't alone, I followed Liam Black to the border, we got caught in that shitty storm, and–"

"Liam?"

Her anger suddenly evaporates, I'm thrown a bit off guard. However, Selena's expression has completely changed. She doesn't look angry anymore, but more shocked. Why does it sound so crazy? She puts her hands on her hips.

"Liam Black? You were with Liam?"

"Yes, that guy."

Why does she look so doubtful? Isn't Liam Black supposed to be her brother-in-law? I exchange a glance with Kelsi, but she looks as clueless as I am. Selena sighs, shaking her head. For a few seconds, her eyes look lost, her expression blank, and I get it's their mind-linking thing again. I wait, a bit anxious. She should be able to confirm it quickly if they are family, no? However, after a while, she growls.

"Damn Liam, he's gone again..."

"Gone?"

"Liam knows how to ignore the mind-link. His brothers can't reach him if he doesn't want them to, and he tends to do that often."

You've got to be kidding me? So the only guy who can prove I did not start this fire is off the radar? I pull my hair, so frustrated that I want to scream. Damn that guy! He's been playing push and pull for two hours, and now that I need him, he vanishes even out of his own family's mind-link thing?

"You've got to be kidding me..." I mutter. "I am not going back to the hospital, Selena. I didn't start that damn fire!"

"How... about you convince me after you calm down?"

I'm confused and realize no one is looking me in the eye anymore, but further down. I look down, and my hands... my hands lit on fire without me realizing. Oh, damn it. I shake it off, quite literally, making sure they extinguish completely, leaving a little smoke.

"Alright, what the hell were you doing with Liam then?"

I'm a bit baffled by that question, but Selena sighs.

"Mara, I already know Liam is not fond of you, so you might as well spill it now. Did you fight? What did he say?"

Fight? I saw more of that guy's tail than his fangs! Why would he fight me? Oh, right, the witch hunter thingy... Well, he's bad at it. Is that why Selena was so doubtful? I don't know how to answer, honestly.

"I don't know, we just... talked."

Selena raises an eyebrow.

"Talked?"

What do I even say? I don't want to tell Selena about the voices, and why would she even believe me anyway? After some hesitation, I walk to the bathroom and bring back the black leather jacket to show her. She's a werewolf, she should at least recognize the scent. Upon seeing the jacket, she does seem to relax a bit.

"So it's true... At least I know you were with him for some time..."

"Ask him," I insist. "I did not start that fire, I was caught in the rain and that damn mud, away from the university at that time."

"If Mara didn't do it," says Kelsi, "then who did...?"

"...I want to know too. There are no victims, but the humans are furious. The word is spreading about what happened at the university too. They all think Mara did it, and unfortunately, we have no actual proof you didn't."

Once again, I want to scream about how unfair this whole thing is. At least, Selena seems to believe I'm innocent, but that barely makes me feel relieved. I let myself fall onto one of the seats, exhausted. This is one to put on the list of crappy days.

"I don't have any other proof, but I swear I didn't do it, Selena."

I see her hesitate, but eventually, she growls and shakes her head.

"You stay here until I can find more clues or anything that proves your innocence. I'll go see Nora, I hope she can help me get to Liam..."

Why Nora? Shouldn't she ask his brothers instead? Is that Nora closer to Liam...? I feel a bit upset, but before I can dwell on it, Selena growls.

"I'm warning you for the last time, Mara. I don't want more conflicts with humans, so all three of you better stay here until I say anything else!"

Her last words are clearly directed at Ben with a mean growl. He nods, looking a bit guilty. Well, I did lose him on purpose, but he snitched to Selena, so I'm not feeling that sorry for him.

"Miss Selena..."

We all turn to Kelsi, a bit surprised. She seems a bit shy, pulling the bottom of her sweatshirt.

"A lot of people shared Mara's picture and... ours, on social media. I'm afraid we are going to be targeted again if we go out now, everyone knows our faces."

I had forgotten about that. People were sharing about our presence at the university on social media as soon as we got out of that class. No, maybe it even started earlier, while we were sitting inside. Those girls were doing something on their phones, it bothered me but I didn't think that far. Kelsi looks really worried, though, and she probably wouldn't have mentioned it to Selena if she wasn't.

The Luna nods.

"I know. I'll talk to our people, see if we can do something about it. Needless to say, your sister is furious about this too, Mara. I would expect to hear from her soon if I were you."

Crap...

After that, Selena and her wolves leave the apartment, and I'm left here, exhausted and disappointed. I didn't realize I was still holding Liam's jacket. I don't really want to let go of it either, so I actually wrap it back around my shoulders a bit shamelessly. I don't get how his smell is doing such a good job of calming me down, but it does.

Next to me, still standing, Kelsi turns to Ben.

"Ben, can you go out?"

"Are you kidding me?"

"I was just thinking Mara and I could use some beers, and there's literally a shop downstairs, but if you can't..."

I have to say, Kelsi is a remarkable actress. I can tell when she's acting because I've been with her for weeks, but her pitiful look is totally working on Ben. I see him hesitate and blush a bit. Well, she is hard to say no to when she pouts her lip a little like that, her head a bit low under her pink hoodie.

"Oh... Okay, fine, if it's just... beers..." he mumbles, grabbing his jacket.

"Thanks!"

We watch him leave, and I frown, turning to her.

"What is it? Kelsi, we can't leave now, if I'm caught outside again..."

However, before I can even finish my sentence, she shakes her head and pulls her phone out, taking the seat next to mine to show me.

"Don't worry, we are not going out. I just wanted to show you this without Ben listening. He's cute, but he's a real snitch and I think he basically tells them everything we say..."

"He's cute?" I repeat, amused.

Kelsi blushes and slaps my shoulder with an annoyed expression.

"Mara, seriously! I'm trying to be serious right now and you're making fun of me?"

"Come on, you're the one who said it. Okay, okay, never mind. So, what did you want to show me? Is it about the fire?"

"No, remember the list the library girl sent me? I received it when I got back here, and while you were in the shower, I went through it."

I had forgotten about that list! I look at her screen; she has several tabs open on a public library website.

"The first two I searched were about witches, so you were definitely looking into that... The third one is a bit more concerning."

I need to squint my eyes to read the red letters on the black cover of the book, but I realize it's in a different language. I turn to Kelsi.

"What is that supposed to be?"

"It's an old book, forbidden for sale and printing in a lot of countries. There are a whole bunch of scary restrictions on it I did not even know existed until now. I looked it up, the university library apparently had an old foreign version of it. I translated the title. It reads, '*The Forbidden Art of Necromancy, Blood Witchcraft, and Chthonic Circles*'.

I shiver. A book about fucking necromancy? Why the hell was I researching this...? I turn to Kelsi, and she's making a pretty sour face too.

"You're telling me this was only the third book, and it's about messing with the dead?"

"Yeah. I'll bet we are not going to like the rest of what is on this list..." sighs Kelsi.

Chapter 9

"...You're doing this on purpose, aren't you?"

I snicker. Ben is on his ass and blowing on his arm with a sullen look. I think I'm getting the hang of this, and liking it. Kelsi sighs on the side.

"I don't know if Mara's fighting abilities are amazing or if they gave us the worst bodyguard ever..."

"Hey, she has freaking fire! I can't just ignore that like Selena!" protests Ben. "This is cheating, you should learn to control your fire, not roast my eyebrows!"

I can't help but chuckle. Truth is, I'm getting better at fighting, but the more heated I get, the higher chances are I'll ignite my fire without thinking. After Ben taught me all the basics, I caught on quite quickly. I appear to have very good reflexes, and my foreseeing thing is happening more and more often. The only thing is that it's only short-term, so I have a few seconds to understand what I just heard or felt before it actually happens. I often dodge on the wrong side or do some really weird moves thinking I'll avoid a kick that never came.

We use the parking lot as our fighting ground, though it usually means other werewolves come to watch us. They are not threatening in any way, though. They only watch from afar and leave as soon as Ben and I go back inside.

To my surprise, my sister didn't freak out as much about the fire at the university as she did about my pictures being leaked online. She raised an armada of lawyers to get that issue settled quickly, and all traces of me disappeared off the Internet as fast as they showed up. Amy didn't even bother to come see me, though... again.

"Mara, come and read this."

I frown. After we finished going through the full list of books, though we did grimace at some titles, Kelsi suggested we gather those we could to study them. We only found three books so far, and although the first one gave me a headache on dark concepts of magic, hell depths, lists of numbers, demons, and biblical stuff and such, Kelsi found it fascinating. I think it appealed to her inner geek so much that she has been taking notes for a while now and refused to part with it once we got downstairs to fight.

I grab a towel to soak up my sweat and look over her shoulder. She shows me an image with an illustration of a large circle.

"What is that thing supposed to be? A magic circle?"

"An invocation circle. It's fascinating. According to this book, each family of witches receives their own ancestral powers, transferred through blood. It's what enables magic, like some second, secret DNA. These circles are used to contact the dead, but they are never the same twice. This one belonged to a family of witches who lived two centuries ago; it was found in their attic after the last of them died."

"It's awesome, Kelsi, but even if this crazy thingy is true, I wouldn't know what to draw."

"It does confirm that it's likely your mom was a witch, don't you think?"

I frown. We talked about this before. That herbology book we found, with the picture inside. Kelsi and I raised the idea that it might have been my mother's book, but... we have nothing to confirm that theory.

"The problem is, in all the books I found, the cycle goes the other way," sighs Kelsi. "Water, fire, earth. If your mother was an Earth Witch, you should have been..."

"...A Water Witch," I sigh. "I don't think I ever was. One of the books was about fire demons, Kelsi. Why would I bother with fire demons if I was already a Fire Witch? I..."

Come to me.

I freeze. What the heck? That's... a new one.

"Mara?"

"Yeah, sorry... You..."

Come to me, child.

What the heck is that now? I've never heard that voice before! It's a different feeling from before. It's not making me feel... angry or agitated. It's just as if I was hearing it through headphones or something. I wait a bit, but I don't hear it anymore.

"Hello... Earth to Mara, do you copy?"

I shake my head and turn to Kelsi who, unlike Ben who's making fun of me, looks concerned.

"Are you alright?"

"Sorry, I think I just felt... dizzy for a second."

"You guys have been fighting for a while," she says. "Let's go back inside for now."

113

"We should order pizza!" says Ben, ecstatic.

"My goodness, do you werewolves ever stop eating? And you should take a shower first, you seriously reek of sweat, Ben, that's absolutely gross."

"Rude! It's my manly scent!"

"It's sweat, you idiot, it just stinks. Is it worse because you're a werewolf? Don't get close to me, I hate it!"

Of course, that's all it takes for Ben to have fun chasing her. While they playfully bicker, I retreat to one corner of the elevator, a bit lost in my thoughts. I can't shake off that strange feeling. Why the hell is another voice calling out to me now? Am I just going to keep getting more of these from now on? I haven't even told them about that other voice that wants me to kill people, now I got a new one?

We finally get back to the apartment. It's only been a week, but I'm getting used to this place a bit better now. Living with Kelsi and Ben 24/7 helps a lot too, even if I have been forbidden to leave without a proper reason. Kelsi doesn't have classes as the school year is almost over, so we dedicate most of our time to solving the mystery that is me...

"Oh, crap, Spark!"

Kelsi screeches as my cat approaches us, carrying something in his mouth. I frown and crouch down, and he spits it at my feet. A dead bird?

"Where the heck did he get that? We left all the freaking windows closed and we don't even have a balcony!"

I'm clueless as well, but this is his third prey this week. We have no idea how he does this, but Spark has been bringing dead birds or rats inside the apartment as if he walked out every day. I don't get it. I sigh and grab the cat, who starts purring immediately.

"You're the only thing weirder than me here," I whisper to him.

He lets out a cute meow while Ben gets rid of the poor dead bird. Next to me, Kelsi suddenly jumps.

"Wait, wait, don't move!"

She takes out her phone, and without warning, takes a picture of me and Spark. I blink, but she's already jumping back to my side.

"Look! I'm not crazy, am I?"

I check the pictures she's showing me. I had forgotten that thing about Spark's black and gold fur, actually. However, as Kelsi shows me the picture, I can't help but frown. That's... really strange. His fur has definitely changed. There are more gold and way fewer black spots than in the picture she had taken before.

"What the..."

"Called it!"

Now, that's super weird. The thing about him catching birds out of nowhere was already disturbing, but... Even Ben comes to check, making a frown before opening his eyes wide.

"Wow... That's..."

"See? He is definitely a magic cat!" exclaims Kelsi, ecstatic. "That explains why I'm not allergic to him!"

I look down at Spark. It's true his fur definitely changed colors, but other than that, isn't he a rather... normal cat? All he does is sleep, purr, and bring us dead animals. I caress him, and he just looks like any house cat, purring in my arms.

"Are you sure you're a magic cat?" I say. "You don't have any other tricks to show us while you're at it? Hm, Spark?"

For a second, he looks at me, but then, he jumps out of my arms. All three of us look at each other, a bit intrigued, and follow him as he walks into my bedroom. Wait, is he really going to do something? Or show us a clue? Spark arrives on my bedroom's carpet and suddenly stretches his front paws, scratching the rug. Then, he lies down and looks at us, the three idiots.

"...That was..." says Ben.

"Damn it," pouts Kelsi. "I really thought he was going to breathe fire or something. He's a boring magic cat!"

I'm alright with my boring magic cat, though... I go to sit next to him and caress his fur. It's strange, I feel a lot calmer whenever I pet Spark. He doesn't seem to mind either, closing his eyes and purring.

"Oh, I'm done with this cat," sighs Kelsi. "I'm going to go back to reading my book. Ben, just order pizza, but you better get some beer too!"

"Roger that!"

"...And take a shower!"

They leave the room, and I'm left with Spark.

"They are so cute, don't you think?" I chuckle.

Seeing Ben and Kelsi flirt playfully somehow reminds me of Liam Black. The truth is, I've been strangely thinking about that guy a lot... I can't help but wonder if I should seek him out again. I haven't heard from Selena since she called to say Liam confirmed I was with him at the time of the fire. She didn't tell me when I could go out or see her again, though. It annoys me. I have been diligently training, staying indoors like a good girl, and letting Ben and Kelsi stick to me like glue, but still...

Next to me, Spark gets up and starts scratching that poor carpet again.

"Hey, easy Spark, you're going to rip it..."

I frown. The cat is pulling on one corner of the carpet, and for a second, I thought I saw something... I change positions and go over to where Spark is, meowing again. I lift up the corner of the carpet. Holy shit!

"Mara?"

I suddenly drop it, and one second later, Ben's head comes in.

"Lager or ale?"

"I'll have what you're having," I mumble.

"Lager it is, then!" he says while getting back on the phone.

I feel a drop of cold sweat run down my temple. I listen for a second, making sure he's gone for good, and raise the carpet again. What the heck...

A large circle is drawn on my floor using something dark and brownish, I don't want to know what. However, that thing under my carpet is clearly one of those circles Kelsi showed me before. Why the hell is that here?! What the heck is going on... Spark rubs his head against my knee with a new meow, and I grab my cat, stand up and put that carpet back down. I can't believe we missed this, but most of this carpet is under the feet of my bed; we didn't think about moving it while searching my room for clues... Should I tell Kelsi? I hesitate, biting my thumb. This is bad. An actual magic circle thingy is right in my bedroom, it's a whole other thing than just some creepy books!

"Mara, come pick your pizza!"

I go back into the kitchen, and Ben is showing me the flyer.

"Just order the usual for me, I'll... I'll go take a shower," I say.

"...With the cat?"

I ignore him and go to my bathroom, keeping Spark with me. I feel like I'm going crazy... I take a deep breath and open the shower tap, making sure the water runs loudly before turning to the cat. He's sitting there and looking at me with his big golden eyes.

"Spark, if you have other stuff to show me, I'd really appreciate you showing it to me now," I whisper.

He's still looking at me, and I do feel crazy for a second. I sigh.

"You're really not helping me, are you?"

He's agitating his tail lazily, and I sigh again.

"Mara, who are you talking to?" asks Kelsi from the other side of the door. "You okay?"

"I'm talking to Spark," I bluntly answer, exhausted. "I'm taking my shower now!"

I turn back to the cat.

"Fine, I guess you're not talking, but next time, you could show me stuff like that earlier!" I whisper.

His Blazing Witch

He yawns, and I guess that's all I'll get. I sigh and finally get in the shower to actually get cleaned. I'm going insane, talking to a cat, magic or not. That and hearing the voices too. How much crazier can things get now? Suddenly, I hear a ruckus as I'm still under the water. I try to see through the steamed glass, but I need to open the shower door. What the heck is going on now?

I open the door, and to my surprise, I find Spark there with his back arched, furiously hissing at something. I realize something white is curled up in the opposite corner of the bathroom. I approach, feeling anxious. What is that thing…? Holy crap, that's a freaking snake! That reptile is already showing its little fangs, threatening my cat and hissing. Damn it! Without thinking, I ignite my fire and send some its way. Spark suddenly decides to jump on the snake at the same moment. Shit, I'm about to roast my cat!

I wait, in shock and scared, but suddenly, I see him. Spark is perfectly fine, and comes out of the smoke, waddling his butt and holding the snake in its fangs… What the hell now…? I let out a long sigh, retreating until my back is against the bathroom door, and let myself sink to the ground. I can't believe it. What the hell just happened, where did that snake come from? Spark sits up and starts biting the snake like it's some treat. I frown and grab the snake before he gets himself sick. Holding it at arm's length, I burn it between my hands. I don't know what that shit was, but from now on, I hate snakes, that's for sure! I keep burning it until it's reduced to ashes and I can throw it in the tub.

After that, I let out a long sigh, exhausted.

What the heck now…? Magic circles, fireproof cats, and now a snake? What the hell is going on…

"Mara?"

"I'll be out in a minute!" I retort, a bit annoyed.

"Sorry, it's just… Selena just called. The Black Luna wants to meet you!"

"Add that to the list…" I whisper to myself.

Spark turns to me and meows again, coming to rub his head against my leg. Yeah, I officially love this magic, fireproof cat.

I take a few seconds to catch my breath. Just when I thought I wasn't making any progress, so many things happened all at once. It's always like this, lately. Just when I start to think I'm out of clues, something crazy happens to remind me I'm not out of the woods yet. I caress Spark, trying to calm myself down. My magic cat just killed something that probably was magic as well, didn't he? I stare at the black spot in the corner of the bathroom. What the heck was that thing? If Spark attacked it, I'm pretty inclined to think it was something we needed to get rid of, but still, what the hell?

"We are so in trouble…" I whisper.

I put the cat down, and grab the little sponge from the drawer to try and clean the blackness left by the burn on the wall. I don't know why, but after this and the magic circle, I've decided I'd better not tell Kelsi or Ben. At least, not for now... I'm done with everyone doubting me and watching my every move. I need to do things by myself for now. Werewolves or humans, they are not me. They don't get this, and they consider me crazy at best, dangerous at worst.

Once the stain is pretty much gone, I grab the towel to wrap myself in it. My scars are becoming more scarce... I still have some long, dark patches, but it's far from the charcoal and blood from weeks ago. I look like a tiger now, or a leopard, the black patches stand out on my brown skin. They are not painful either, even if I rub the towel on them. I'm even more annoyed at my new bruises from Ben's training. At least now I'm actually good enough so I can get back at him for that...

At my feet, Spark meows and rubs himself against my leg. I glance around, but aside from the slight burnt smell, there is no trace of what happened here. I take a deep breath and leave the bathroom. Kelsi jumps as I come out, almost dropping her phone.

"You okay?" I ask.

"Yeah, yeah... Um, the pizzas are here."

"Cool. I'll get dressed and be right back, you can start eating."

"We'll start drinking too!" yells Ben from the kitchen, where he's behind the counter, busy opening some bottles.

I give them a little smile and go inside my bedroom. I close the door behind me as soon as Spark is inside too. I stare at the carpet for a few seconds, hesitating. Maybe I just dreamed the last hour... or maybe I'm really going crazy with voices, magic circles, and nasty snakes. I get closer and lift the carpet with my foot. Damn it, it's still here. Alright, not dreaming then.

I bite my thumb. What next? I don't know the first thing about these damn circles! I put on some silk ensemble and walk back to the main room while trying to think of my next plan.

Kelsi and Ben are already on the couch, fighting over which movie to watch tonight. This has become pretty much the routine for our little trio, but for some reason, tonight, I'm not really into it.

I sit on the big armchair and grab my bottle of beer. Kelsi frowns.

"You okay, Mara?"

"Yes, yes... What was it about the Black Luna, by the way?"

"She wants to meet you," says Ben. "Don't worry, she's super cool. I mean, she's not nearly as intimidating as Selena."

Great, then maybe I'll have a meeting with a member of that family where I don't end up on my ass or in the mud...

"When?"

"Tomorrow late afternoon, at her house."

"Why is she interested in me all of a sudden?"

They exchange a look, both a bit surprised by my cold tone. Crap, that one didn't come out well. Still, I'm getting suspicious of everyone now. No one cared about me for weeks, and all of a sudden, I have to meet both of the werewolf Lunas in the same week?

Ben, who was about to eat his slice of pizza, is left hanging with his mouth half-open and hesitates, a bit at a loss.

"Uh... I think she was curious to meet you, now that they've pretty much determined you're... not dangerous..."

"So they have determined I'm not dangerous?" I repeat, a bit confused. "I thought everyone was doubting me after the fire at the university?"

"More like they think you don't have bad intentions?" says Ben, shrugging. "I don't know. The Black Luna isn't really the kind to doubt people either, she isn't like Selena or the Black Brothers, to be honest. On the contrary, she's seen as the pacifist."

"Didn't you mention she was the strongest, though?"

"In terms of werewolf blood and power, yeah, but still, she's not much of a fighter."

Oh, right, she's the healer... I keep getting confused. I don't really understand how she's got some magic healing power. Maybe she's a bit like me in that aspect? I doubt it's similar, though; she heals others, while I only heal myself super fast. I nod and grab myself a slice. My tone was a bit too harsh earlier, and now there's a heavy atmosphere. I need to act normal, not clue them in on the fact that I just killed a magic snake in the bathroom!

Spark hops on my lap, interested in my pizza, so I quickly eat it, while Kelsi grabs the remote to select the movie. Ben is sending me glances, still at a loss.

"She's a bit of a legend to all the packs, you know."

"How so?" I ask, genuinely interested. "Because of her noble blood thing?"

"It's Royal Blood. And yes, there's that, the fact that she's... super filled with Moon Goddess power."

The Moon Goddess... The deity all werewolves believe in. According to Bonnie, she's not only the werewolves' goddess, but all witches are also under the Moon Goddess' protection too, whatever that means. All creatures of the night, as opposed to humans. I find it pretty ironic that all three species, if I include the vampires, believe in the same goddess, but can't see eye to eye with each other.

"Nora was abandoned as a baby, she grew up in the slums and then in a pack that had no idea of her real status and used her as a slave, you know. She found her mate, our Alpha King, years later. She had no idea she was a Royal, but she fought in the war, the one against the vampires, and she was so, so good. A few years back, the clans were super divided, and the King wasn't super popular, but once Nora took her place as his Luna, all the clans got along!"

"You're saying it as if things had gone smoothly," says Kelsi. "Wasn't there a big fight between all the clans at first?"

Ben frowns and shakes his head.

"No, one fucking clan wanted to overthrow the Blood Moon Clan and they tried to make a mess out of the alliance the King and Nora offered."

"What happened to them?" I ask.

Ben hesitates, but eventually, he grabs his beer and shrugs.

"They were killed."

He gulps down his beer.

What the hell...? Did they kill one whole pack that didn't agree with them? I shudder. Is that how things are done in the werewolf world? If you don't agree with them, you're killed? And he said that Luna was possibly the nicest one...? Or is it because they like her so much, their judgment is clouded? It sounds like she came out of nowhere, became the King's lover, and suddenly everyone loved her. I don't really get it. I thought they liked her because she was a mother figure to their pack, but now, I wonder if werewolves don't value strength and their Royal Blood more. I'm a bit confused...

Selena had that strange blood too. The Royals...

I keep thinking about it while we watch some dark fantasy show about a mutant guy who fights monsters. I don't really grasp the story, but I think Ben just enjoys the action scenes, and Kelsi is into the magic stuff that happens to the lead female character. I'm half asleep in my seat, and petting my cat doesn't help me fight the drowsiness. Spark is already sleeping like a regular, content cat.

"Oh, shit, Ben!"

I open my eyes, a bit surprised as I was almost asleep. I missed the action, but Kelsi's pajamas are covered in beer, and Ben's sorry expression pretty much sums it up.

"Seriously, can't you just enjoy it quietly!" she yells while walking to the bathroom.

"Sorry... Wait, I'll grab a towel!"

While Ben runs to the kitchen, I sigh and wonder if I should get up to help. Still, Spark is happily sleeping and I don't feel like waking him up, he's had some action today.

In any case, I think they are pretty fine with yelling at each other and arguing from both sides of the apartment while I pretend I'm still dozing off. They really fight like cats and dogs... I wait until they are done. I've given up on understanding the show, dead people are back in the next scene and I'm completely lost with their crazy timeline. I sigh and caress Spark again, who immediately purrs loudly.

"Mara, can you pause it, I'm coming! Damn it, Ben, that's my favorite one!"

"Sorry... Do you want a T-shirt?"

"No, I–hey, stay out of my bedroom! Pervert!"

"Ow! Don't throw your stupid plushies at me, you crazy woman!"

"You're the stupid one! Go and fetch, you better bring them back!"

"I am not a freaking dog!"

I chuckle and lean over to grab the remote. Crap, they had to put it just far enough away that I have to contort myself to grab it! Just as I'm leaning over, I feel Kelsi's phone vibrate with a notification. I frown, and after a hesitation, I look over. It vibrates a second time, keeping the screen on for a couple more seconds. Three texts from... Amy Garnett?

I glance back, but they are still arguing. I grab Kelsi's phone to try and read it. Crap, it's still locked. I slide down to at least see the latest text, even if it's just a bit of it...

"I talked to Selena. Just let me know what time she goes. I want Clarissa to..."

...What the hell? I put it back down. Why the hell is Kelsi texting my sister? I don't even get to talk to her! Plus, Kelsi? Why Kelsi? Is she working for my sister? I thought she was my friend, but... what if she isn't, what if she's just working for Amy and keeping an eye on me?

I hear them coming back, and drop the phone on the table, standing up to grab my bottle of beer and drink it down. Ben and Kelsi return and both stand there. They watch me empty my beer in one go with wide-open eyes. When I'm done and I put it back on the table, Ben chuckles nervously.

"Wha-... You were thirsty. You want a second one...?"

121

"I'm good," I say, getting up. "I think I'm going to go to bed, actually. Kelsi..."

"Yes?"

I stare at her, a bit lost. Crap, I feel like I'm not seeing the same person as I was before. It's still the same Kelsi, but now, I wonder if she's really my friend, or if she is just another spy sent to watch me.

Is any of this even real? Is this really my flat? Has anything I've been told until now been the truth in any way?

"Mara? Are you okay?"

"...Can I have the book?" I ask, pointing at that book she left on the table.

"S-sure..."

I grab it, and after whispering something like a good night, I go to my bedroom and close the door behind me.

I need to breathe. If I don't take a break, I'm going to cry, or scream, or something. It hurts. It fucking hurts. I thought Kelsi was the one I could believe. The one who had no interest in this, no side to take. I'm such an idiot, after all. I can't believe any of them, can I? Was she even my friend, all this time? Or just my sister's spy? I feel the fire burning in my fingertips, begging to come out, and I need to calm down. I can't burn this damn book.

I get down on my knees and open it. I try to push my bed and pull the carpet over as much as I can to see that circle. Spark sits on the side, watching me make all this ruckus with curiosity. I hope this leads me somewhere!

Chapter 10

I keep checking page after page frantically, making sure I didn't miss one, but it doesn't match. None of the circles are like the one painted on my bedroom floor. At best, there's a couple of similarities, but that's it. I don't even have one that looks close to it that I could use as a reference. Damn it. I'm not a bookworm like Kelsi, I don't understand half of this stuff... I'm a failure of a witch! I glance at Spark, who's crouched down, his paws under his body like he's some big bundle of fur with just the head sticking out. I frown.

"Are you going to help or not?"

He squints his eyes very slowly, almost as if he's about to fall asleep. I guess that's a no...

I really need to sort this shit out. What did Kelsi say earlier about these circles? Something about families of witches... Could it be, this one is unique to me, then? I scratch the mess that is my hair, trying to remember more. She said this power was transmitted through blood, that those magic circles were made to invoke the dead. I am not sure I am up for a medium session right now.

I sigh and push the book aside. I know I am not going to read this thing now, but that circle intrigues me. I roll my carpet back some more until I even have to push my bed against the wall. I guess it's useful to have a large bedroom, you can hide magic circles under the carpet... Once everything is out, I stand above the circle, at a loss for what to do. It is about my wingspan in diameter. What is the point of this thing? It doesn't look much like the invocation circle in the book. Does it really help to call the dead? Who am I supposed to call?

Next to me, Spark meows and stretches, but when I think he's about to do something interesting, he just sits. I pout.

"Don't get my hopes up like that if you aren't going to be useful, dude," I whisper. "It's mean."

After hesitating, I decide to step inside the circle and sit down. It fits me just fine, but now, I feel stupid. I really have no idea what to do.

"Alright... Spirit, are you there?"

Of course, nothing freaking happens. I wait a couple more seconds, but it's very quiet, except for Ben's snoring coming from the living room. I sigh and massage my temple.

"Damn, I shouldn't have drank that damn beer so fast. I'm going crazy... Hey!"

Before I could do anything, Spark suddenly jumped to scratch the back of my hand. I push him by reflex, but the cat has gone back to sitting right outside of the circle, and even licking his damn paw! He really hurt me, that stupid cat... The back of my hand has three deep scratches, all bleeding. I see a couple of drops fall on the floor as if the scene was slowed down and suddenly, something happens.

The circle. It started moving. I watch it spinning around me as if I had just unlocked a wheel. I don't dare move a finger, mesmerized by this thing. The marks are moving on my bedroom floor as if the ink has a life of its own. It keeps spinning at the same speed, and I realize it's waiting for something.

"Sh-... Show me the truth," I mumble, with no idea what I'm saying.

Around me, everything suddenly becomes gray. I freeze, completely taken by surprise. What the hell...? It's like I'm seeing everything through a filter, like in shades of gray, but not just that, as if there was some sort of disturbance. I turn to Spark, and instead of a cat, a large, red shape is there. I almost jump back, shocked by its size. Yet, it still has a cat form, just... much bigger. Like a tiger made of fire, but it's sitting just like Spark was seconds ago. What is this thing doing to me...? I get up and look down. My body... Something is different. My skin tone! What the actual hell, I'm whiter now? No, it's... changing. I feel like throwing up, but it's as if my body is morphing and can't decide on which appearance to take. What the heck? I stand up and turn to the mirror on the wall.

Oh... Wow. I look different. My hair is much longer and falling on my shoulders, all over the place. My face... keeps changing, and I can tell one part is my face, but why is it trying to change like that? What is going on? Even my eyes look like they are trying to change color, they are turning more gray, or perhaps blue... More importantly, when I look down, there's something big radiating from my chest. It looks like a core, radiating in red. The same red as the creature in Spark's spot. What is that thing...?

Suddenly, I realize the reflection isn't just a reflection. She is moving when I'm not. Oh shit, this is getting into the real creepy stuff. I see her lips extend into a smile. It's not scary, it really looks like a gentle... smile. I don't dare move. I'm too shocked to move or react. Then, I see her raise her hand, and with a face that looks like mine, she puts an index finger on her lips.

I fall back on my rear, still in the circle but out of the mirror's view. What the fuck was that?!

"Meow..."

I fucking jump. God, I had forgotten about Spark being replaced by a giant fire feline or whatever that thing is! Did it just seriously meow like my cat? Take deep breaths, Mara, deep breaths... Oh, hell, this really turned creepy real quick. Plus, everything around me is still in that gray filter, how do I stop this?!

I look down. The circle is still there, except that it is now white for some reason. Is it because it's activated or something? Crap, I thought I was a crappy witch, but now, I may have jumped to level nine or ten without knowing how the hell to handle this thing! How do I stop it? I try to step away from it. I get both feet out of the circle, but nothing changes. Oh, crap, crap... I can't stay like this! Maybe if I'm far enough...?

I walk to all four corners of my bedroom, but it doesn't change a thing. Don't tell me, this is going to work everywhere? I go to my bedroom door and open it, very slowly. I grimace as soon as I hear Ben's snoring, but when I glance down at the couch, I see a big wolf sleeping on it. Did he go to sleep in his wolf form? Don't tell me that's a circle thing too? From the snoring, that definitely comes from human-Ben, not wolfy-Ben... What the hell did you do, Mara? I see the giant Spark following me, and his tiger size apparently doesn't care about my door frame. Guess it's just my vision, the real Spark has no issue going through that door... It's horrible to see everything in gray but the living beings in that room, I feel like I'm trapped inside some broken old TV screen...

Suddenly, I realize. If this shows me Ben's werewolf form, what about Kelsi...? I hesitate. That's probably not a very cool thing to do, but since I have a unique opportunity to check... What the hell am I checking for anyway? Kelsi is a human, what else is there to find out with this thing? I'm about to bite my thumb when I remember my hands can't decide on what to look like. Yeah, no, that's kind of gross to chew a finger that's not really mine.

I take a deep breath and walk to Kelsi's door. I hesitate again. Well, she is the one with secrets, to begin with... I open the door very slowly. She sleeps with night lights on? Three rows of fairy lights are lit up above her bed, but Kelsi is soundly sleeping and... looking exactly like normal. I'm a bit disappointed, and feeling even more guilty now. I sigh and close her door. My mistake, then... Apparently, this thing gives humans their normal appearance and shows me a werewolves form, but I'm the one with a creepy appearance.

I get back into my room quickly, closing the door behind me. Spark is already ahead. I can't get used to this giant-shaped thing, but from the way it starts scratching the carpet on the side, it's definitely my cat.

"Alright, I've had enough of this," I say. "How the hell do you turn it off?!"

Spark is just staring at me. I walk to the circle, doing my best to avoid looking in the mirror. I am not ready to see that girl again, not yet. I glare at that stupid circle, clueless as to how to go back to normal. There has to be a way!

"Stop!" I say, sitting back inside it.

Nothing happens. I frown and for a dozen minutes, I keep saying all the words I can think of to make it stop, including a couple of swear words and foreign ones. I really feel like the kid who made a mistake and has no idea how to repair it. After I'm out of ideas, I sigh.

"I swear you're getting a treat if you help me shut this thing off, Spark."

I see my cat come over, and under my shocked eyes, he starts licking the pattern. What the heck? He keeps licking, and I suddenly get what he's doing. Don't tell me it was that easy! I grab the end of my sleeve and start rubbing too. As soon as we erase a portion of the circle, everything is suddenly back to normal. Wow...

I look around, a bit shocked. It's really back to normal. At my feet, the circle is still there, with a chunk wiped off. Damn, I hope I'll remember whatever was there in case I need it again.

"Meow."

I turn to Spark, who's sitting there and waiting.

"Seriously, Spark? You let me say all that stupid stuff for ten minutes and waited until I promised a treat to help me?"

"Meow..."

I let out a long sigh and lay down on the floor.

So, I've found a new way to use my witch powers... A magic circle. I didn't know it could do that, aside from invoking demons... I'll be careful not to mention that next time. I don't want to have a goblin thingy all over the room. Damn, Kelsi would be proud.

I feel a pinch in my heart, thinking about Kelsi. I really thought she was my friend... Is she? The image of her sleeping in her bed comes back to me. She sleeps with fairy lights on... What kind of villain sleeps with fairy lights on? Maybe I'm just trying to convince myself she isn't really bad. My sister isn't a bad person. She's just... Oh, whatever.

"Meow."

"Oh, I get it, Spark, stop it..."

I get up and grab a Sharpie to try and draw in the circle as it was. Spark even tries to grab the pen a couple of times, though I don't know if he's telling me I'm wrong, trying to play, or just getting impatient about his treat. When I think I'm done, I roll the carpet back down and move my bed into its usual spot. Damn, that's a lot of exercise just for one magic circle; I guess that's how it wasn't found until now, though... I hear something just as I'm moving my bed, like a little creak or something. What the hell?

I look down under my bed, and suddenly, I spot something brown between the slats. Crap, more secrets? I need to crawl under the bed to go get it. It's a kraft envelope... What the hell now? I wriggle back out and agitate it in front of Spark's whiskers.

"And that one, you couldn't have helped with that one? Or were you hoping to extort me for a tuna can with this? Hm?"

The cat gets impatient as I keep teasing him with the envelope, and pushes it with his paw, sniffing it a bit too. Well, maybe he only helps with witch stuff. I open the envelope. What did I hide now...? To my surprise, a big bundle of money falls out and a little key. What the heck? Every time I think I find an answer, two new questions pop up just like this. Where the hell did this money come from? What is this key for? It looks too small to be a door key, more like it's for a locker or something?

"Meow..."

"Oh, fine, fine, Spark, I'm getting you your treat! Anyway, I'm thirsty after you let me say all that stuff without helping..."

I leave the money on my desk; from the thickness of it, I can already tell it's a lot more than a twenty-year-old should have. I keep the key with me, though, putting it in my pocket while heading to the kitchen.

Ben is still there, though I see him in his human form this time. I chuckle for some reason. Human or wolf, he's the same... sleeping with his mouth wide open and his horrible snoring. I walk to the kitchen and find an olive left from the pizza, giving it to Spark to play with while I pour myself some water and find a real treat for him. Didn't we have a bag somewhere?

"...Mara? What are you doing?"

I turn my head toward Kelsi, who just stepped out of her bedroom, rubbing her eye.

"I don't know," I retort. "If I tell you, are you going to text my sister about it?"

She stares at me, completely stunned like a deer in headlights. Even I am surprised by how calm and composed my tone was, despite the hint of irony. Kelsi opens and closes her mouth a couple of times, at a loss.

"I... I don't know what you're talking about..." she mumbles.

She's such a poor liar. It's written all over her face and in the way she nervously pulls down on her T-shirt too. I sigh and close the cupboard, putting the bag of treats on the kitchen counter a bit too loudly. Ben's snoring skips a bit, but he doesn't wake up. Meanwhile, Kelsi is still standing there and looking guilty as hell.

"H-how... How do you know...?"

"I saw your notifications," I admit.

Spark jumps on the kitchen counter, too curious to wait, and I give him a couple of treats while waiting for Kelsi to say something. She walks up to me, looking absolutely devastated, which I didn't really expect.

"Mara, I really didn't mean... You weren't supposed to see–"

"To see what, Kelsi? That you're spying on me for Amy? That the one person who I thought was my friend is not? Are you even my flatmate to begin with? And I thought Ben was the snitch!"

"It's not what you think!" she protests. "I really am your friend, Mara, I... I didn't lie to you."

"Then what? You're best buddies with my sister too? Forgive me, but Amy doesn't look like the kind of person you could chat about your favorite video game with."

She sighs and crosses her arms as if to protect herself.

"It's not like that... Okay, m-maybe I lied a couple of times, but... most of it was real, Mara."

"As in?"

"I'm really your friend."

I take a deep breath in.

I don't know how to react to this. I'm angry and upset. Yet I want her words to be true, for some reason. It's hard. Now that I've seen the text, I can't trust Kelsi like I used to. I can't look at her, so I look down at Spark, who's attacking the bag of treats. I push him off to grab it and put it back into the cupboard despite the loud meows of protest. I just don't want to look at Kelsi right now...

Damn it, I didn't think I'd be this upset, but she's been my only friend for weeks. She came to see me almost every day, we spent so much time together, watching her silly videos and chatting about stuff of the world I had to learn again... I take a deep breath to keep myself from crying. Shit, I had no idea I was actually a sensitive crybaby.

"Mara... Let me explain..." she sobs.

I turn around. She took me turning my back on her as a sign of rejection. Now, she's crying silently, and it's ugly. She's got a runny nose, big tears, twitching lips, and red eyes, the whole package. Damn it... She's really upset, then. I don't know why I expected more of a fight. It turns out, Kelsi is also quite the crybaby. I sigh and cross my arms.

"Fine, then, I'm listening."

She nods and takes off her glasses for a second to clumsily wipe her nose, looking for her words. It actually takes a full minute before her breathing calms down enough for her to start speaking.

"I don't know where to start..." she mutters.

"Start with the part you didn't lie about," I suggest a bit rudely.

"I didn't lie about anything, Mara! I mean... n-not really. It's true we weren't close before the incident. You... barely talked to me, and to be honest, I also worked too much to worry about that."

"You worked too much?"

She slowly nodded.

"Yeah... I don't want to get into the details, but... unlike you, I came to Silver City completely broke. Their university was offering this super alluring program where they paid for your expenses if you got the right kind of grades, so I moved here penniless and I found a job right away. I spent my first year of university working like crazy... I had a part-time job in a fast-food restaurant, and I gave private tutoring lessons to some rich brats whenever I could squeeze them into my schedule. I lived in a flat where I had four roommates, and three of them had no idea what personal hygiene or private space is."

I grimaced. I don't know why until now, I had thought Kelsi came from some rich family, like me. Not as rich, but... aside from her geek stuff, I definitely saw her wear some super expensive brands sometimes. I would have never thought she had struggled like this before.

She sniffs, rubbing a bit of her snot on her sleeve, and continues, looking down.

"I could barely make ends meet in the first months. I was tired of studying, working, and all of it. I ate at the university cafeteria because it was cheaper, skipped breakfast, and ate some cup noodles for dinner when I couldn't get food from my job. I had a really shitty year. During the summer, I took even more hours at the fast-food restaurant in the hopes to have enough to pay rent, but with so many students coming here, the prices boomed... That's when we met."

"When you started renting here?"

She nods.

"Yeah... I was standing in front of one of those panels at the university where you can put offers, lost stuff, and so on. You were about to put up that note saying you needed a roommate. I asked you how much it was, and you asked me how much I could afford. I told you a very low sum on purpose, I thought I could find a way to negotiate like that if I started super low, or you'd just turn me down... I was shocked when you agreed right away to what I said. I thought you'd laugh at me."

Wow, I didn't expect that... She had simply told me we met through an online thing. I don't think I ever asked her how much she was really paying to stay here either.

"We started living together... I finally took it easy on my job, until I only worked on the weekends. It was a really... nice change of pace, to not have to worry all the time about money. I focused on my studies, and I managed just fine. Although, as I said, we never got close. You barely talked, I'd just run into you from time to time."

So that part was true, at least. She could have embellished it a little, now that I think about it. Saying we're buddies or something. I still don't really get what role my sister has to play in this, though. Kelsi sighs and I hear her dry throat. I sigh as well and take her almond milk out of the fridge to make us some late-night chocolate milk.

When she realizes what I'm doing, she looks a little bit relieved and comes to sit on the stool across from the island. I am impressed that Ben is still snoring like a pig while we're chatting a few steps away from him like this. We are speaking rather softly, but still...

"One day, I ran into your sister while you were at the university. I have to say, I literally freaked out. I am not super confrontational, and your sister is... a bit..."

"...Scary?"

Kelsi grimaces. Yeah, Amy tends to do that to some people. She is so imposing, everyone else feels like ants next to her. I can easily imagine Kelsi, in one of her silly, fluffy sweatshirts, coming out of her room and meeting Amy. A close encounter of the third kind. They are almost like two species that were never supposed to live in the same environment...

"So, what happened?" I ask, grabbing my cup.

She sighs and pulls hers closer, frowning a bit at the pink mug.

"She asked me what I was doing here, so I spilled the beans... I couldn't tell if she was upset about it or not, she didn't get very... talkative. She said I wasn't really supposed to be here, so I understood she wanted to kick me out or something. That's when she gave me her card."

I frown, confused.

"Her card?"

"Yeah, her business card." Kelsi nods. "Your sister said to call her if anything ever happened to you... Back then, I was a bit surprised, so I just took it without saying anything."

"...That's it?" I ask with a frown. "That's how you started to... spy on me?"

She almost drops her cup, shaking her head.

"No, no! That's not how it went. I put her card into my agenda, and I decided not to think too much of it... She had told me not to tell you too, so I didn't think twice about it. That was at the end of February, months ago! To be honest, I forgot about that stupid card until you disappeared."

"What do you mean?"

She grabs her mug to sip a bit, clearing her throat, and lets out a long sigh.

"One evening, everyone on campus started talking about some big fire that had happened, with some people inside. All of social media was going crazy about it. There was news about a girl who had survived and had been rushed to the hospital. At first, I didn't think twice about it, but... when I got home that night, I felt super uneasy. You weren't home, and it wasn't like you to stay out at all. I decided to stay up, in case you were just late, like at the library or something."

She keeps turning her mug nervously between her hands as if she was feeling the stress from back then all over again. I can just imagine it. A nervous Kelsi, pacing around in the living room and hesitating.

"The university library closed around 10:00 p.m. that day," she continues, "so I waited until then, but I had this feeling, you know? When you still didn't show up by around 11:00 p.m., I grabbed your sister's card and I rushed to the E.R. to ask about the girl they had brought in. They hadn't been able to identify you yet, so they let me in when I explained that my roommate was missing, with your description."

"You saw me... like that?" I mutter, shocked.

Kelsi shivers and nods.

"Yeah... I recognized you... Gosh, you had tubes everywhere, it was so... scary... They only showed me your face, though, don't worry, I didn't see... you know, all the ugly parts. I mean, no, I don't mean ugly!"

"I was burnt to the fourth degree, Kelsi, you can call it ugly," I shrug, shaking my head. "I've seen it too, it wasn't pretty. Then, you're the one who called my sister?"

"Yeah, and the hospital did too. She was out of town, so I texted her about your state throughout the night and into the next morning about how you were doing."

"You stayed the whole night at the hospital?"

"Yup, with a lot of coffee... I met Bonnie this way, actually. She let me use the nurses' resting room to get coffee and some food."

Oh. Now that I think about it, I had assumed those two met at the hospital, but not really... that way.

I'm a bit surprised. So far, Kelsi doesn't really look like any kind of spy I had imagined. I don't really know where we are going from there, though, we have already caught up to the point where I was hurried to the hospital, after the incident... Kelsi drinks a bit of chocolate milk and wipes her chocolate milk mustache with her sleeve before continuing.

"I felt pretty bad, you know. I kept wondering what would have happened if I had been worried sooner, if I should have tried to befriend you more. A part of me kept thinking that maybe, I don't know, if we had actually become friends..."

"That sounds a lot like survivor's guilt, Kelsi," I stop her. "You said it yourself, I wasn't the friendliest roommate either."

She pouts a bit, staring at her pink cup.

"I know, but... you still let me live with you, and with all the money issues I had the previous year, I couldn't help but feel like crap about all of this. You basically picked me up out of the dirt, and I was fine not making any efforts. It's just... You know, after you spent the night between life and death in that hospital room, I had a lot of time to think."

I chuckle.

"A bit too much, maybe."

She pouts, with the beginning of a smile.

"Don't mock me... It was a really shitty night."

"Alright, you big crybaby. So what happened next and how the hell did you start keeping my sister updated?"

She lets out another long sigh, pushing her glasses up on her nose.

"As I said, your sister didn't arrive until the next day, but she was pretty panicked... That's the only time I've seen her panicked, actually. She was really worried for you, it seems. I explained everything I knew to her, and she harassed the medical staff for a while after that."

I can imagine that easily. I did see some of the nurses were nervous whenever my sister was around, let alone those who basically cleared the ward whenever she came. Same for the doctors, actually. It takes a werewolf Alpha

132

or Luna to not be afraid of Amy Garnett and her army of lawyers, from what I have seen. It explains why Kelsi isn't too intimidated by her, though, if she saw Amy be more... human.

"That's... kind of how it started."

I raise my head, a bit confused.

"What? What do you mean?"

"The texts, with your sister! She asked me to keep her informed of your state because she couldn't stay any longer after a couple of days... At that time, I really didn't think much of it. I thought it was just informing a parent, no big deal. The thing is, I kept doing it for weeks until you woke up. That's when it really started. One day, she asked me why I wasn't sending her more updates if you were alright, so I told her that I thought you were fine, but she should come more often because I wasn't too... comfortable on keeping that up."

"Then?"

Kelsi hesitates, biting her lower lip and avoiding my gaze.

"Kelsi, what did my sister do?"

"...She said she'd pay me if I kept... updating her..."

I slam my mug on the table.

"Kelsi, seriously?!"

"Don't get mad! I swear, I wanted to refuse, but... she really insisted, and I didn't think there was anything wrong with updating her, it just kind of went a bit overboard..."

"You shouldn't have taken any freaking money!" I yell back.

She grimaces, looking down and really sorry. I'm mad at her, but before I say anything else, I see Ben sit up, half-asleep, staring at us with a sour face.

"Hey, girls... If you want to fight, can you do it in your bedroom? I'm trying to sleep here..."

We both glare at Ben, and he shrinks on the couch, grabbing his blanket a bit awkwardly.

"O-okay, I guess I'll just... go back to... sleep... quietly..." he mumbles.

However, something catches my attention behind him. Why is it so bright outside? I exchange a glance with Kelsi, and we both rush to the bay window to see what the heck is going on. Ben sees us walk past him, and frowns, following us too.

"It smells like..." he whispers.

"...A f-fire?" mutters Kelsi.

We both freeze in front of the window, completely out of words. It's... a fucking nightmare.

A fire. A gigantic fire is happening right under our eyes, in the building directly next to ours. The flames are devouring at least two levels already, and the black smoke covers the upper levels. Kelsi gasps.

"Oh, God..."

"Shit," says Ben. "The firefighters, we gotta call the—Mara, fuck, no!"

It's too late; I'm already running outside.

"For Moon Goddess' sake, Mara, you can't!" Ben yells behind me.

I'm already smashing that stupid button to call the elevator, impatient. Why can't this damn thing come any faster? I run to the stairs, the two of them following me.

"Mara, you're going to get in trouble!"

"You two were with me before that fire started, you know it wasn't me!" I yell back.

All three of us are running down the stairs as fast as we can, I'm focusing on not breaking an ankle. Why the hell is the apartment so high?! I hear the two of them trying to catch up to me. Ben is fine but I can hear Kelsi losing speed and running out of breath quickly; she is not good with exercise.

"You're supposed to stay the fuck away from these kinds of things!"

"It's a fire, Ben, a building on fire with people inside! I'm a Fire Witch, when am I supposed to do anything if not now?"

"You're not supposed to do anything!"

"That is not what I decided!" I retort back.

If I could, I'd glare at him but for now, I'm just glaring at those endless damn stairs. I don't care what the werewolves or anyone else says. I am not sitting back and doing nothing when people are in danger right under my nose!

We finally run out of the emergency exit, and immediately, we are faced with a gigantic blaze. I hear Kelsi gasp behind me, and I'm just as shocked. How did the flames even get that tall? The building next to ours is about ten or twelve floors high, and the flames have already engulfed up to the fourth floor. Some windows have shattered and are letting out thick plumes of black smoke. It smells horrible, and there is a ruckus outside. The inhabitants of the building who managed to evacuate are gathering in the parking lot. A lot of them are in their pajamas, looking up at the fire and in a state of total panic. I hear people crying and screaming, some pointing their fingers up.

Ben and I exchange a glance. He knows we can't possibly go back, not after we just witnessed this. He shakes his head and growls.

"Damn it... Come on," he says.

We run to the crowd, and though I'm unsure what to do, Ben is the first to spot someone in the crowd.

"Jayce!"

A man, with an arm around a younger girl, turns his head and seems to recognize Ben. He meets us halfway, shaking his head.

"...What happened?" asks Ben.

"No idea! I woke up barely half an hour ago. People were fucking screaming, I grabbed Yuri and we ran downstairs to see this... Selena is on her way, though, and the firefighters were called too!"

"Do you know if there are people inside?"

Jayce shakes his head, at a loss, looking around him with a desperate expression.

"I don't know, dude, I... It was complete chaos, everyone ran down..."

He sighs and looks around. The girl, his sister or girlfriend, I don't know, her face is covered in tears but she looks around too.

"I don't see the family from the sixth floor," she cries. "The old man from the fifth floor either..."

She starts crying louder, completely panicked, and she isn't the only one. I glance at the building. The fire is progressing quickly, and we can see people screaming on the upper floors. Damn, I hope everyone tried to get upstairs as fast as they could to win some time, but even so, with all the damn smoke...

"Ben, I'm going in," I declare.

"Mara, you..."

He doesn't finish his sentence, and I know he's conflicted. This is their neighborhood, their territory. The firefighters aren't here yet, there is no one else to help.

"Mara, you can't!" Kelsi protests. "You've never handled this much fire, you haven't created yourself! You might get burned again this time!"

"Well, time to figure this out," I sigh.

I am not waiting for anyone's permission. I push Ben out of my way and run inside. I hear them call after me, but I have made my decision already. It might not be too late for those people. If I have just one chance to save someone from this with this ability of mine, it would be a nice change for once. To not be the one who injures others, but someone who can save them. No one stops me when I enter the building, but I hear some shocked screams behind me.

The main entrance was left completely open, and with the fire being four floors up, I have no issue climbing up the stairs. At least for the first two floors. I can feel the heat, but it's nothing unbearable, probably even for a regular human.

It gets hotter on the next floor. I can endure the heat, but the smoke quickly starts stinging my eyes and making me cry. I didn't think the smoke would be a bigger issue than the fire, but it's burning my throat more efficiently than the first flames I see. I'm getting to where the fire started and has already quieted down to get to the floor above. I only need to kick a door for it to fall down. God, everything has been turned into charcoal... I look around, but if there is anyone around here, there is no way they survived...

"Meow..."

I look down, almost thinking I dreamed it, but Spark is seriously at my feet! Where the hell did he come from?!

My cat looks completely fine in this mess, though he is sticking to my ankles like glue, and looking up at me as if he was waiting to see where I'm going next. Damn, if I needed more proof that this cat is just as fine with fire as I am, here it is... No other living thing apart from us would be fine in this nightmare. I keep walking, looking around. I never thought a fire would be this loud, I hear the creaking all around us. I fucking hope that the structure doesn't crumble or something...

I keep progressing inside, not sure what I am looking for. I can't hear anything precise, and all the screams coming from the outside or upstairs are confusing me.

"Spark," I cough, "if you wanna play search for the humans, it's now, buddy..."

He meows back, but once again, I have no idea how much my magic cat understands... I walk into what must have been a living room before it was turned into a freaking oven. I'm starting to sweat pretty badly, but I'm still fine despite the flames engulfing the walls around me. I guess it means I should be okay if I go on, but this goddamn smoke!

I go to each room I can find, but thank God, all the beds seem empty. I would only be looking for bodies around here anyway... I run out and go to the apartment across from this one. It's even worse here. Is this where the fire started? There are pieces of plastic melted all over the living room. Did the freaking TV explode?

I freeze in front of the bedroom. Oh, no... This poor guy is done for... It must be the old man the girl was talking about. He is lying in his bed. I hope he didn't wake up to suffer... I sigh and turn around, there's nothing I can do here. I run to the floor above, and this time, I hear very distinct cries. The fire just got here, but it's all over their front door. I cover my eyes and kick down the damn door. It takes several kicks, waking up my muscle pain, but it finally breaks down.

I run to the living room, but although the smoke is filling the room, it's empty. The bedrooms then? I finally find what I assume to be the master bedroom.

"Help! Please..."

I finally spot them, crouched down on the other side of the bed. It's a young Hispanic couple, holding each other with wet towels on their heads, looking at me with shock. Yeah, I'm probably not what they expected. I run to them and realize they are holding a baby, the source of the loud crying I heard earlier.

"Are you alright?" I yell over the noise.

They both look terrible, covered in water and sweat, their eyes red and hair stuck to their faces. The woman grabs my wrist, her tears running down her soot-covered face.

"Our daughter! My Eréndira!" she cries out, coughing too. "She went to play next door! To our neighbors'..."

She has to stop and cough loudly, something black coming out of her mouth. Oh, crap. I need to get them out of here. The fire is only in their living room for now, but I need to get them upstairs and there is no other way.

"Stay behind me!" I yell. "I'll get you out!"

They don't react, but they probably think I'm crazy too. I turn around and run back to the door. I need to do something about these flames, or they won't be able to get through here and upstairs. I take a deep breath and extend my arms, and try to extinguish that fire like I'd do mine.

It doesn't work. The flames get agitated, which means it got worse. Shit... I can't put it out? Because I didn't cause it? Shit, shit, shit... I hear the couple screaming behind me. It's not helping! I need to find another solution. I get to the flames, and after a hesitation, put my hand in them. It really doesn't burn, I ought to be able to do something with them!

As I leave my hand in the fire, I realize the flames wrap themselves around my fingers, crawling up my hands. Maybe I can't put it out, but I can... absorb it. That's right, I don't usually extinguish my fire, it's more like I recall it inside. Come on, Mara, time to tame an actual fire...

"Oh, *Dios mío*..."

I focus, and as if I was pulling on two large ropes, I bring the fire to me. I feel it wrap around my arms, and I have to control it. It tries to get higher on my body, but I need to contain it inside. I try to control my breathing, despite the smoke, to focus on this. Finally, I feel it. The heat increases, but the fire gets redder and melts against my skin. I'm not sure if it's really... safe, though. I grimace. It gets hotter. Much, much hotter than before. Is it because I can't absorb too much? My sleeves are long gone and burned, but more worrying, I see my actual burn marks extending, turning back to a darker color. Crap, I guess this means I can't hope for unlimited fire absorption...

"Get ready!" I yell to the couple.

From the corner of my eye, I see the woman get up first, her husband following her, and they slowly come behind me. I start walking, my arms still extended, and I keep channeling the fire to me. It's hard. I feel my skin starting to burn, really bad. I have to endure, we are almost at the doorway... We cross the living room and finally, as soon as we get to the door, they run to the stairs.

I can finally let go, and bring my arms down. Crap, that really hurts... Just as I'm taking a second to breathe, I notice the woman running back down to me. She has to stop a few stairs away, the fire is starting again behind me, and the smoke is horrible.

"My daughter!" she screams. "My Eréndira..."

I nod and go to the next apartment. The door breaks without any effort from me, and Spark jumps inside. Thankfully, the flames aren't there yet, looks like they took over the other apartment first. I run inside, hoping to find that girl still alive...

I follow Spark without thinking. The cat runs ahead, looking like he knows where to go, at least. He guides me to a bedroom and sure enough, I hear some crying. Two little girls are curled up in one corner of the room, holding each other's hands. Oh, poor things, they look terrified. Both run to me as soon as they see me. They hug me and start talking so fast, I take a full minute to realize it sounds like Spanish or something.

"*Mi Abuela*!" cries one of them. "I don't know where my grandma is!"

Wait, she's talking in a full foreign language and I understand? Did I know Spanish before? I don't know how but I get it all and even surprising myself, I nod immediately.

"I'll look for her, girls, but we have to get you two out of here first. Follow me really close, okay?"

Both nod and stay stuck to me. Spark meows and guides us out. If I had known, I would have given him a whole can of tuna! We make it to the living room, but something falls from above and the girls scream, panicking.

"It's okay, it's okay!" I yell.

There's no use, they are pulling my hands and panicking. I crouch down to carry them. They must be six or seven, I don't know, but it's hard for me to carry them both, especially when my arms are so burnt already. I bite my lower lip and ignore the pain to run to the staircase. The mother is still there, and her eyes brighten up when she sees us three coming out. She runs to grab her daughter out of my hands violently, but I'm not complaining about carrying less weight. The other girl gets down too, but she won't let go of my hand.

"My grandma..." she cries.

I nod.

"I'll go get her, but please get upstairs!"

The mother and I exchange a glance, and she understands right away. She nods and pulls the two girls upstairs with the strength of a lioness. At least those two are safe, but where the hell is the grandma?

I run back inside, ignoring the pain in my arms and this horrible headache. The smoke is definitely getting thicker, and the flames are growing. I need to find the old lady... I run to one of the bedrooms, but it's empty.

"Spark! Spark!"

Damn it, I lost the damn cat!

I'm really starting to not feel good. I need air, but I keep coughing from these disgusting ashes. I feel the heat in my arms getting worse too. I can't take in any more fire, I can barely feel my arms. I finally stumble to the kitchen. Oh, no... The grandma is unconscious on the floor. Is she still alive? I try to walk over to her, but the truth is, I'm not too good either. I see black dots obscuring my vision.

"Hey... Grandma..."

My throat is raspy as hell. I try to grab the grandma's arm, but she isn't moving at all. Oh, no, no... How do I check someone's pulse? Crap, I've seen Bonnie do it a hundred times... I keep pressing on her wrist. There! I can't believe it, the grandma's still alive. I let out a sigh of relief and at the same time, I want to cry. How the hell do I get her out of here? I can barely walk... Shit.

I look around for a solution, but there's nothing...

"Mara!"

The window next to me suddenly bursts open. I see two human silhouettes coming in, but just then, I can't help but close my eyes. Damn it... I feel that I'm being carried, and suddenly, a wave of fresh air enters my lungs. Someone puts me down on the asphalt, but I am too tired to do anything.

"Mara! Mara, can you hear me?"

"Can you do something?"

"I don't know, I've never healed a witch before... Boyan, bring the ambulance here! Come on, Mara, you have to hang on..."

Chapter 11

My arms hurt. It's my first sensation as I slowly wake up, and find the way back to my senses. It's not unbearable, though. More like a slow ache, as if someone was applying constant pressure on an open wound. It stings a bit. I grimace and open my eyes. I'm expecting the white ceiling of the hospital, the one I've seen for months and months, but instead, it's a wooden one. My head is a bit heavy and slow to remember what happened. I try to put the pieces back together.

Everything comes back to me all at once, and it's not pleasant. The fire cat. The fight at the university, and my fight with Kelsi at home. The circle under the rug, the magic one. The face smiling in the mirror. The confrontation with Kelsi, in the kitchen, and the fire... Now, that explains why my throat feels like sandpaper. It's dry as hell.

"...Mara?"

I turn to Kelsi's voice. She is sitting close, looking worried. Why does this feel so familiar...?

"Water," I gasp.

"Oh, sure. Here."

I drink down the full glass in seconds and immediately need a refill. Kelsi keeps topping up my glass and helps me get hydrated as much as I need until my stomach feels so full I can't drink anymore. I let out a long sigh of relief, feeling a little bit better. Still, my throat feels pretty dry when I finally speak up.

"W-where are we?"

"At the Black Mansion," she whispers.

"The... Liam's house?"

"Uh, no, his older brother's."

I'm confused. I vaguely remember episodes of the fire in that building. Faces flash before my eyes, and I try to sort out the mess, a bit lost for a second. Then, I suddenly remember something else.

"The grandma?"

"What? Oh, you mean the old lady from the fire? She is still in the hospital, but she is doing fine, from what we heard of her. They say only an old man died. I don't know anything else, though..."

I nod. That's still good enough for me. All this crap wasn't in vain... I didn't go back into that apartment for nothing. I feel a lot better after hearing that. I hope the grandma lives a few more years, her granddaughter is cute. I look at my arms, and they don't look too bad... They are wrapped up in bandages, and someone changed me into a simple white tube top. I get up, and with Kelsi's help, put on the baggy denim pants they also prepared.

"So... This place is..."

"The Black Luna's home," explains Kelsi. "They decided to bring you–I mean us, here after the fire. The Luna tried to heal you, but it didn't work on your burn marks."

"Really?"

I'm surprised. From what they had all said, I kind of imagined her power was absolutely limitless or something like that. Kelsi shakes her head while I glance in the mirror to see what I look like. My hair is a whole mess of frizz, as usual, but I don't look too bad for someone who almost got killed last night... I frown.

"Wait, what time is it?"

"Oh, just about midday. You only slept through the night, actually."

That's good then, I had a little fright for a second. I don't feel like losing weeks or days of my life to a coma again. Kelsi guides me out of the bedroom. I realize we really are in some big family house. It has a very nice and warm feeling, with a nice smell of warm bread and coffee in the air. We walk past a large living room with a fireplace and a big sofa. Based on the rug with some random stains on it and the little toys scattered around the room, there has to be at least one child living here. I remember the pictures we found, with the little boy stuck to his mother. For the house of the most powerful werewolves in Silver City, it feels strangely cozy and welcoming.

We arrive in a large kitchen, empty as well. However, that delicious smell is stronger here, and I see a row of freshly baked croissants that cruelly remind me that I haven't eaten in hours... I must be the only one because Kelsi walks right by them without even sending them a glance. Damn...

We finally leave the kitchen through the back door and enter a very spacious garden. Wow... It's a really nice one. The green grass has been roughed up a little, but there are patches of wildflowers scattered everywhere, and a little vegetable garden on the side too. It looks like we left the city to be in a little bubble in the countryside. I can't tell where this place is in Silver

City, but it's... peaceful. Just as I'm following Kelsi, we are surprised by a little wolf that runs right by us.

"The puppies are so cute!" she exclaims.

Indeed, they look adorable. I follow the black wolf, who is running wild in the garden and being chased by two other wolves, brown and exactly the same size. As I glance around, I spot another pup, a white one this time. The little puppy gets up and comes toward us, walking gently. Kelsi looks excited and wants to approach it, but before she does, a large beast jumps in front of us. Kelsi yelps and I can't help but retreat too.

For a second, I wonder if that thing really is really supposed to be a wolf. It's large and brown, more like a bear! The large wolf growls as a warning, standing between us and the pups. I realize the warning is for me, as it has its green eyes on me.

"It's okay, Bobo."

I see Selena walking to us. She's in jeans and wearing a simple off-the-shoulder top, but she is still dazzling. She smiles at us, glancing at the large brown wolf.

"Sorry, Boyan is just cautious because of the kids. Stella, come here."

The white pup runs to her, and I realize she's actually Selena's daughter? Wow... The werewolf world is amazing. Selena smiles and grabs her daughter to carry her. I hear Kelsi squeal next to me, and I can't blame her. Stella is as white as snow, with two adorable, big blue eyes; she looks like a little plushie. Selena smiles.

"This is my daughter, Estelle," she says. "Come, we are having brunch. Nora wanted to meet you, too."

I feel a bit nervous, following her into the garden. Bobo the big wolf seems to have completely accepted us now, he actually goes back to play with all the younger wolves.

As we arrive in the middle of the garden, I suddenly feel really nervous. Those are the most powerful werewolves in town, the Black family... Liam's family. Strangely, I had imagined them in some scary underground location or an impressive building, but instead, they seem to all be gathered for a family brunch in the garden! There are several adults present, and for a minute, I'm a bit intimidated and also trying to figure out who is who. It's hard to recognize people from a picture where they were all dressed up...

However, a beautiful, young woman immediately stands from the table and walks up to us with a bright smile. She is wearing a short cotton dress with floral patterns and a pretty headscarf. She looks even younger than I thought...

With her long scar on her left eye, it's impossible not to recognize her. She's the Black Luna.

"Hi, Mara, nice to meet you," she says with a gentle smile. "I'm Nora!"

I want to open my mouth to say something, but before I can, I see their expressions sink.

"M-Mara, are you okay?" Kelsi asks, looking confused too.

What's going on? I realize I'm crying.

What the hell? I feel big tears running down my cheeks, and before I know it, I'm sobbing uncontrollably, as if I was completely overwhelmed by sadness. What is going on?! I can't control myself, it's just unstoppable. I wipe my tears, completely lost. I'm making a complete fool of myself, crying for no reason, and I have no idea why!

Selena hands me a tissue, but I can tell she has no idea how to react. She glances toward her cousin, frowning.

"You don't normally have that much effect on people..."

Nora seems really sorry, but I have no idea why I am reacting like this either. I just keep sobbing uncontrollably despite my attempts to control myself. What the hell is this? I glance at her again, but I'm overwhelmed with this pain. I thought it might come from her aura, as I see that white, bright halo around her, but that's not it.

Damn, this needs to stop. I close my eyes and take deep breaths, trying to control my emotions until I can stop sobbing like a baby. Just as I finally calm down, I hear someone else sobbing. I re-open my eyes, and Nora is glancing down at the little boy holding her skirt, who looks like a mini male version of her. The boy looks like he's about to cry too. She chuckles and crouches down to hug him.

"Will, it's okay, honey, it's okay. Do you want to go play with James and the others for a bit?"

The little boy shakes his head, and tries to hide behind her skirt, stuck to his mom. She gives me a little apologetic smile.

"Sorry about that, Will is a bit sensitive, and he is too young to shape-shift, so..."

"He can't turn into a wolf yet?" Kelsi asks, looking interested.

"The youngest shape-shifting we have seen so far was around three or four years old," explains Selena, pointing at the wild pack of pups running around in the garden, "and those were very precocious."

"Anyway, are you alright, Mara?" Nora asks.

I nod, feeling totally embarrassed to have cried for no reason in front of her. I don't know what came over me, but it was damn weird and unwelcomed, especially with so many strangers around... They probably think I'm the weirdest witch ever. I take a deep breath to repress my tears and turn to Nora.

"Sorry about that... So you are... Selena's cousin, right?"

"Yes, and her sister-in-law too."

I nod. I'm starting to understand more about their family tree now. Actually, the two men behind them with scary auras help... They really stand out from the group. I recognize Selena's husband instantly, with his ice-blue eyes. Nathaniel Black. He is sitting at the table, but instead of the deadly glare from last time, he is actually focused on the baby girl on his lap. She's blonde, just like her parents, with big blue eyes... I remember the little announcement on that website. This must be little Aurora... She looks like any happy little girl, smiling at her dad like he's the sun itself.

It's actually rather easy for me to tell which children are the Black children, even among the pups: they all have the same pure white halo as Nora. It's such a strange feeling. It's not something I can actually see, yet it is so clear, it feels like I could even touch it... I only feel Estelle and another young black wolf with this, though; the other pups look... like regular wolves.

"I'm... Mara," I sigh, "but you already know that."

"Yes," Nora chuckles, "I do know who you are. Actually, do you want to sit with us? I'm sorry we brought you here without asking, but I wanted to get to know you, and from what I heard, you're not fond of hospitals."

"That's the understatement of the year," I sigh.

I hesitate to give her a definitive yes about sitting down with them, though, because aside from Nathaniel Black, there is another dark aura, and I really, really don't feel like getting closer to that monster. He is standing a few steps behind his wife, but it's like he's her shadow. This man really feels like a dangerous beast. Although, the fact that he is holding a little baby so tenderly offers a very strange contrast.

Nora seems to notice my glance, and unaware of my fear, she smiles.

"Oh, this is my husband. Damian Black."

I nod, but Kelsi and I exchange a quick glance. There is no doubt: that man is the Alpha King of Silver City. His aura is the very definition of imposing; I didn't feel like I was affected, and yet, if I get any closer, I feel like I'm going to be crushed by the darkness. Strangely, the only solution is to stay close to Nora and Selena. I don't really get how that whole aura thing works for werewolves, but for me, it's as if theirs are nullifying their husbands.

I only feel like it is safe for me to come close when Nora walks up to her husband, a smile gracing her face. I quickly glance toward Kelsi, but she looks unaffected. If anything, she is slightly blushing, probably just a bit intimidated. So this is definitely a witch and werewolf thing...

Nora smiles at her baby in her husband's arms. Oh, right, she was still pregnant just months ago.

"Damian, you should put her to sleep. She looks tired."

"She can sleep here," he replies with a surprisingly soft and warm voice.

"In her crib," insists Nora.

The Alpha frowns, and for a second, I catch a glimpse of how scary that man could be if made angry. Yet, he sighs, and plants a light kiss on his wife's forehead before heading inside the house.

"Sorry about that," says Nora, taking a seat at the table. "He is literally obsessed with our daughter..."

"You guys need to stop making babies," suddenly says a voice behind me.

Liam walks past me and grabs some food from the table. His older brother, the blonde one that is sitting there, gives him a glare, but he ignores it, and walks farther away. Nora shakes her head.

"Ignore him, Mara, he's been pouting all day because I forced him to be here. Come on, take a seat! Do you want anything to eat?"

She starts listing everything they have and filling my plate, but I'm a bit concerned about the other people around the table that no one introduced to me. There is a woman with long brown hair, extremely pretty but looking a bit stiff and quiet. There is also a Black woman, focused on eating a full plate of meat, and right next to her, a man with a shaved head that has to be her sibling. He is talking to another woman, probably his wife, but I struggle to keep up with everyone. It's a big table, and no one really seems to be bothered by me or Kelsi taking a seat here. Even Nathaniel Black isn't bothered, and he is talking to a red-haired guy next to him.

As if it wasn't enough, there are a lot of wolves scattered in the garden. At a glance, about a dozen, but they are moving a lot, some playing with the children like Boyan, or going in and out as they please. I recognize Ben among them since I saw his wolf form before, and he is playing with the younger wolves too. I suppose their house is some sort of headquarters too... Selena catches me looking around and smiles.

"Relax, Mara."

It's hard to relax in front of so many strangers! I'm feeling a bit nervous, but Nora doesn't seem to have noticed, and finally puts a full plate down in front of me. She lets her son climb onto her knees and play with her long black curls. I had noticed in the pictures, but she is a really beautiful woman... although she is the exact opposite of Selena. If it wasn't for her aura, I wouldn't have guessed she is the Luna. I can imagine she is not the fighter of the duo. While Selena is tall, with a very fit body and an outspoken attitude, her cousin is more petite, with a gentle and caring expression. Truthfully, I wouldn't be able to tell that they are cousins. Selena has tanned skin, blonde hair, with amber or light brown eyes, I can't tell, while Nora is completely white with blue eyes and black hair. I can only see a very slight resemblance when they are together, mostly in their facial features, like their nose or the shape of their eyes...

"How do you feel?" asks Nora.

"I'm... fine."

"I tried to heal you, but just as I feared, my... ability doesn't work on witches. I think it's because your burns are related to your magic."

"It's okay," I say. "Thank you for trying to save me..."

"Oh, you should thank Liam more! He jumped into that building to save you!"

I am stunned. He did what? I turn to him, but he's obviously ignoring us, eating his food and standing away from the table, his back against the tree. Now that I think about it, I don't remember how I got out of that building... I keep staring at him, but he is definitely pretending he doesn't hear our conversation.

"I'm sorry, I don't... remember what happened."

"Well, you didn't listen, for one," says Selena with a frown. "However, you did save lives, so I'm not going to scold you for this one."

"Thanks... How did you get there so quickly?"

"Werewolves tend to relay the information very fast," she explains with a wink. "Although, no one was as fast as Liam to get there..."

She says that while staring at him with insistence, but once again, the younger Black brother ignores us. So he was there first? Again... just like at the university. I can't believe that guy just happens to be hanging around every neighborhood where I am in trouble. That's a bit too much of a coincidence. ...Is he watching me too?

I keep glancing his way, but no matter what, Liam Black won't look at me. He is eating away from the table, his back against a tree, watching the children play around. His figure is starting to feel familiar to me, but not those feelings when I see him. It's rather strange.

Moreover, why is he always hanging around me? It makes no sense, he is supposedly trying to stay away but when I need help, he is always there. I don't understand this guy, and those are more questions to add to my long, long list.

"You should eat," gently says Nora.

146

Her voice reminds me I have been sitting in front of my plate for a while without moving. I nod and start eating. It's strange but I don't really feel out of place. Nora Black is very welcoming, and none of her guests are staring at me or anything, it's as if they were expecting me to be here, and didn't mind it... That's a nice change.

"To be honest," says Nora, "I was a bit eager to meet the new witch."

"The new witch?" I repeat, a bit intrigued by her choice of words.

"Yes... You know about... Sylviana, right?"

Yeah, I do. Somehow, I feel like that name is starting to become a shadow, following each of my movements and looking for a mistake. I glance toward Liam Black again.

"She was the previous witch watching over Silver City," says Nora.

I nod, although I already sort of knew that. I just don't get how they went from a witch that seemed to be loved around here to me, whom they only fear or hate so far... Once again, I feel like that witch left a big hole in her place that I'm supposed to perfectly fit in. However, all they have is a crazy Fire Witch that can barely make a move without going crazy.

To my surprise, Nora notices my expression and smiles.

"Don't worry, Mara. We are not expecting anything from you."

I frown and glance toward Selena.

"Are you sure...?"

"As long as you don't burn anyone," retorts the blonde, "and you learn to control your fire frenzy. I am not pulling off a firefighter move again, I won't always have a bucket of ice nearby..."

"So far I've barely lost control a few times," I respond.

"Have you seen the color of your arms, girl? You almost burnt yourself to death last night, and believe it or not, we don't want another dead witch in town."

I'm about to reply, but Liam suddenly growls. We all turn our heads toward him, and he is glaring at Selena. Just then, he suddenly shape-shifts into his black wolf like before and runs out of the garden. Nora shakes her head.

"That was not very subtle, Selena. You know Liam is still sensitive about that..."

"It's been two years, Nora. He can't keep acting like a child. I know he hurts more than anyone, but we need him to act like an Alpha around here. You can't keep treating Liam like a rogue teen, he should start taking care of his responsibilities."

"Isn't he fighting off witches past the border?"

They all turn to me, looking surprised.

147

"Liam does that? How do you know?" Nora asks, perplexed.

"The question is, why the fuck does he go beyond the barrier?" growls Nathaniel Black.

Oh, crap, did I say something I shouldn't have? I go quiet, but my eyes drift toward the direction he left in just now. That guy... He tells me stuff he didn't tell his family, yet he won't talk to me when I need him to. What's his deal?

"What was his relation? To the witches?" I ask. "He called himself the witch hunter, but..."

Nora grimaces.

"That is not really something for me to tell you, Mara. You should ask Liam directly... when he is ready."

I sigh. I do have a feeling, from the way they all react. I want to go back to my place and eat in peace, as I'm rather hungry now, but after a few minutes, while everyone else is having their own conversations, I realize Selena's eyes are riveted on me, and Nora is looking at her. Are they having another one of their silent discussions?

"What is it?" I ask, a bit annoyed.

"That name, Mara. I really can't remember where I've seen it, it's annoying..." growls Selena.

"That's been bothering you for a while," notes her husband.

"I know, I'm usually good at remembering stuff but I'm struggling with this. Mara, Mara... Damn it, I know it's going to take forever!"

I ignore her and turn to Nora.

"I understand I should ask Liam directly about his relationship or whatever, but... can you tell me more? About Sylviana? I don't have a witch to give me guidance here, and... I feel like she should have been the one to, if we hadn't missed each other."

She seems to hesitate but then, she turns to Selena.

"I'll be right back."

The White Luna nods, and Nora gets up, letting her son down. The little Will is about to follow us, stuck to his mom's skirt, but then, he sees his dad coming from the house and runs to him. Nora exchanges a look from afar with her husband too. He frowns slightly but doesn't stop us. She probably told him what this was about... Sometimes, I'm a bit jealous of their mind-linking thing. It's like being in a room with strangers who speak another language and you don't understand a thing despite them being right next to you.

"Come on."

Nora guides me away from her family garden, and I realize their house is located in the outskirts of Silver City. Near the forest... and that barrier from before, most likely. When we arrive close to the barrier, I stop.

"I'm sorry, I won't be able to go further..."

"I know. Liam told me. Come, it's close by."

She changes direction, and I realize we are headed toward some... impressive tree. I slow down my pace, completely surprised. That tree is not just a regular tree. I see something sparkling around it, like little lights, but it's not something from this realm. I get the same sensation from when I was using the circle, like I was seeing through some strange, colored glass. I see this extraordinary halo around it, moving like a cold wind and extending around. I couldn't see the barrier before but now, I realize this tree is the source. It's extending like some veil along an invisible line between us and the forest. I gasp, impressed. Is this... magic too?

Nora doesn't seem to see that strange veil like I do. She walks up to the tree and gently puts her hand against it. I'm... surprised. The tree seems to react to her aura, as if it was channeling it.

"That's..."

"This is the barrier Sylviana left to protect us," Nora explains. "When she... died, she used her magic to be reincarnated into this tree, to protect us."

I'm speechless. The previous witch is... within this tree? I do feel as if it is living... I mean, not like a tree, but as if it had a different presence, something more imposing. I glance at the barrier, surprised. So this is what witches can do too. Create barriers like this. I think about that magic circle, could I be able to produce something like this someday too? I bite my thumb, a bit unsure, and continue to observe it.

"It's... breaking."

Nora turns to me, surprised.

"What?"

"The barrier," I whisper, a bit unsure. "It's weaker in some parts, like the tree can't... maintain it. I think it's already been damaged."

Nora gasps and looks at the tree, confused. I know it may sound crazy, coming from the novice witch, but I'm pretty sure about what I'm saying this time. It's like I can perfectly see that bubble, now that I have seen its source. I see the halo that emanates from Sylviana's tree and spreads wide to shelter Silver City, but it's not even. Some parts look like they're thinner, or the tree can't get to them. I look for one of those weak spots and walk up to it. I take a deep breath and bring my hand to it. Yeah, it's not as painful as last time. If I persist a bit, I could perhaps push through it, with a lot of effort...

"You can see such things?" asks Nora, looking impressed.

I shrug.

"Apparently... This is new for me too. I'm only guessing at all this witchy stuff most of the time. This barrier sent me on my butt just days ago, but now that I have seen... her tree, I think I understand it better. It's like everything else, I'm learning without the right tools for that. However, it is rather obvious to me that this... your barrier isn't in good shape."

Nora frowns, and tries to look at this invisible wall with a worried expression.

"To be honest, I had that feeling too. That's why Liam has been guarding the border... To be honest, I don't think Sylviana's tree was meant to protect us forever. She always said that Silver City needed a witch."

She turns to me, looking very serious.

"I think this is exactly why you are here, Mara. I think Sylviana knew... someone like you was going to come and take over. As Silver City's new witch. She always said she couldn't see the future past her own death, but I don't think she would have... acted the way she did if she wasn't sure someone would be able to come and take her place."

I take this a bit hard. It changes... a lot of things. I always felt like the outsider in Silver City, the strange and unwelcome witch no one wanted. Because there was someone before me, who fit the role of Silver City's witch, and I am not a good replacement. However, this woman, Nora, she makes it sound like it's the other way around... I shake my head.

"You might be overestimating me," I mutter. "Selena wasn't wrong, earlier. To be honest, I'm barely getting the hang of it, it's a miracle I haven't... burned something else yet."

That's an understatement, actually. Not only can I barely control my fire, but I haven't forgotten those voices. For some reason, they have been strangely quiet for a while, but I know they are still there, lurking. I am in no hurry to hear them mess with my mind again, but I wish I knew what the heck is going on and what I am dealing with.

"I don't think your witch... that Sylviana expected me at all." I sigh. "If she did, why wouldn't she have told you? At least, I would have liked to have some sort of guidance. How to become a good witch in ten lessons or something. I have nothing, I... I don't even know who I am. I don't think anyone smart would entrust a city and its people to a girl who can't even solve her own issues."

Nora suddenly bursts out laughing, making me jump. What the hell did I say that was so funny? She takes a few seconds to calm down, and I'm a bit nervous. Did I say something stupid or what?

"Sorry," she says. "It's just that... your sentence... I think I relate to it so much, it's a bit funny."

I try to remember what I just said, and suddenly, her own story comes back to mind. Right... They did say she came from the slums and raised to her position almost overnight. No wonder she felt this was relatable. I shake my head.

"It's not the same thing. You knew you were a werewolf, and what a werewolf was! I am starting from nothing."

"I didn't shape-shift until I was seventeen, you know. Compared to my son, I'm a very late bloomer. I only found out the truth about my family and my lineage around that time too."

I sigh, biting my thumb nervously again. Damn, I need to stop doing that. I take a deep breath.

"I get it, but I don't–"

"You're going to find answers, Mara. Maybe you are just trying too hard to be someone else. Sometimes it's more about the journey than the destination."

"I'm not... I don't have a starting point. This isn't a journey, it's a sandpit. If I knew what to do, anything at all, I'd gladly do it. But for now, my only direction is being used as a barbecue or signing up as a firefighter. There is nothing much about being a witch that I have been able to find so far, I'm trying to find the smallest clues, but..."

I sigh and look at the tree.

"If... if she really meant for me to come here, to take over Silver City and help you, why didn't she give me any clues? I'm just... lost. All of the time. My own family is a pathetic mess and close to non-existent, except for my elusive but overbearing sister. I just found out that my only friend is basically a spy, and Bonnie and Ben work for you werewolves. I am absolutely nobody so far."

Nora makes a sorry expression, finally nodding to my words. I bet she heard about all of this already, from Selena most likely. Her eyes go back to the tree.

"...What about Liam?"

I blush a bit.

"What about him?"

"You feel a connection, don't you?" she asks gently. "I saw it... in the way you looked at him. You and Liam might have more in common than you think."

"An obsession for witches?" I scoff.

Nora chuckles.

"Well, that's a start!"

If only he wasn't trying to run away from me all of the time. He hasn't been very cooperative so far. Yet, I keep repeating to myself that he did come to help me... twice. First, at the university, he appeared out of the blue to help me. Secondly, in that fire. What kind of guy runs into a fire to save someone they have been trying to avoid? A lot of this doesn't make much sense to me...

"I really think you should try talking to Liam. He might be the one you need to help you. He does know a lot about witches, so if you can convince him..."

So far, I have been thinking about how to actually capture this guy and trap him to make him talk. He is annoyingly nice but enigmatic, and as I am slowly finding out, patience is not my forte.

"Maybe I need to be a bit more... convincing." I sigh.

"Oh, feel free to chase him all you want. He hasn't been helping much with the packs lately, his brothers will be happy to see him busy instead of just roaming around..."

"How come he isn't... you know, an Alpha like them?"

"He is an Alpha, he just... doesn't feel like leading a pack. Liam has been in Damian and Nathaniel's shadow most of his life, I think he just... might be struggling to find his own way. He likes to have some alone time, and it's been worse since... the war."

I nod, understanding a bit. He does seem like a loner. Somehow, even though it's his family, he didn't seem to fit in during their family time earlier. I remember a detail I'd been meaning to ask about.

"His eye..."

"He lost it in the war too. It was an injury caused by magic, so unfortunately, I wasn't much help... like your burn marks, I suppose."

I glance down at my charcoal-tainted arms. I guess it would be too easy if the Luna's healing power could heal everything. I don't really mind, though. These markings are a part of me... somehow. Plus, I am learning to live with them as proof that I am a witch. If anything, I'm learning to be proud of them.

"Alright," I say. "Do you know where to find Mr. Runaway?"

"You should check the docks. He is often at–"

We both turn our heads at the same time. Something just creaked on the other side of the barrier, and there's this strange feeling too. Instinct doesn't lie. Nora and I exchange a glance, but she is mostly glaring at whatever is on the other side in the forest. I can feel it. Someone is staring at us, from the shadows.

His Blazing Witch

My skin is crawling, and I feel my fire crackling at my fingertips. We wait a little longer, but they don't reveal themselves. Nora is growling, warning them not to approach. Definitely not a wolf, then.

It lasts a while, but then, that sensation vanishes all at once.

"What was that...?"

"You mean who was that," mutters Nora. "Come on, let's not stay here... I don't like this."

Chapter 12

Why does it have to be her? Moon Goddess, why did you do this to me? I did not ask for this. I was fine with being alone, I was fine with taking care of my family. That's all I ever asked for. For Damian and Nate to be happy. So why now? I can't help but glance up at the moon, a bit annoyed. I wonder if she's really there. Mom used to say the Moon Goddess isn't the moon, she just uses her light to shine on us... I'm still a child, thinking about Mom's words.

"Liam, where are you?"

I ignore my older brother. Nate is worse than a helicopter... I know they are all worried about me, but they don't have to be. I am fine. Perhaps it's because of my eye, they just can't forget anytime they see me. About what I've lost. What would they think if they knew... that I knew?

I wasn't sure, but I always had that hunch. It always felt a bit off whenever I was with her. As if she wasn't letting me in. We were a couple, but... there was always something that never felt quite right, as if she was keeping that distance between us. I would act blind, tell myself she was just into her witch stuff, that she wasn't like us. Or maybe, it was the age difference. She'd joke about that sometimes. Yet, I pretended not to notice. I thought it would go away after some time, or maybe once everything was over, once Syl was done with her life mission... and it was. It did end.

I look around and decide to aim for the docks. I like that place, and I'm a bit hungry. I can drop by and grab a bite... once I've changed. Silver City has changed a lot, the streets always have one or two wolves hanging around. The humans are used to it, but I still get glares. They blame us for keeping that witch... Mara.

I want to kick myself for thinking about her again. My stupid instincts are driving me crazy. I wish I had never seen her, never crossed her eyes, or got a hint of her smell. I don't want this, I don't want

154

to be that guy, slave to his wolf. I've seen Damian and Nate go crazy over it, I always thought I'd be fine without a mate. Moon Goddess, you're really a bitch sometimes.

I jump above a few of the docks' containers to find the one I need. There, I open the blue one to find the bag with my clothes and get changed. It's damn hot and humid around here, I'm sweaty. I brush my hair with my fingers a bit, and they get just as wet. I need a haircut soon... I should ask Nora, Tonia almost fucking chopped my ear off last time.

I grab my bag and get out of here, jumping back down to walk on the docks. There is a light drizzle starting, plus that salty breeze. I like being close to the sea, it helps me calm down. I walk down the docks, only crossing paths with a couple of people. The clouds are dark, it smells like a storm is coming. No one wants to stay around with this kind of weather.

"Liam, where are you?"

I sigh. Nora.

"Come on, don't ignore me."

"You probably already know where I am, you can sense my aura, can't you?"

"...True. Sorry, I just didn't know how to reach out to you without... you know, being too awkward."

I shake my head, even if she can't see it. That's Nora for you. Always trying to care about others' feelings... unlike her cousin.

"If you're worried about what Selena said, I'm good."

"She gets a bit cranky sometimes..."

"Nora, I'm fine, really. Selena's a kitten compared to Nate, and I know she's just trying to push me a bit."

I'm not that close to Nate's wife, but I get how she works. Selena is just that kind of person who will take on the bad girl attitude if she needs to, just to make me react. I know she's actually the one who was the closest to Sylviana after me, she just hates to show her pain even more than I do. She probably thinks I need to get angry once and for all or something like that, and she's trying to provoke me on purpose. However, that's how she reacts, but that's not me. I am not one of her pups to be trained, to react to that... I don't deal with the pain with my fists like she does.

"Do you want to come back? You can stay for dinner."

"I'm good, Nora, I just... want to be alone for tonight."

155

"...Alright. I understand."

Really? I know she probably wants to say something else to try and convince me, but she doesn't. Usually, Nora would try to coerce me by mentioning my nephews or whatever she is making for dinner, but strangely, she gives up easily tonight. I feel our mind-link disconnect as she really leaves me alone.

I take a deep breath, and lift my chin up, letting it rain on my face a bit. It feels so refreshing after these hot days. I don't remember Silver City ever being that hot when I was a kid...

"Hey!"

I frown and turn around.

What the fuck is this girl doing here? She is standing a few steps away from me, staring at me and a bit out of breath. Did she run all the way here? How did she...? Oh damn, Nora has to be the one who told her.

I can't help but sigh. I have a strong feeling of déjà vu. The two of us, staring at each other under the rain. And once again, I have this horrible feeling in my gut. My wolf wakes up, like a wild beast in my stomach. I never knew it would feel like this. It's as if my whole body is suddenly woken up by an electric shock. I get the chills, my hair standing up almost. Like last time, I can't help but worry that she is going to feel it too.

Mara's eyes are even darker, like the skies above us. Why the hell do I feel so shaken up just from looking at a woman I barely know? Because she is a woman, not a girl. It's an odd feeling, to find her whole being so attractive, like an irresistible pull. I want to run to her, but I don't. It's not even about her body. If I'm being honest, she's pretty average. She has full lips, a lean body without many curves, and long limbs. Because of her bandages and scars, she's only wearing a tube top, but it's not her exposed skin that drives me crazy.

It's something else, something more intricate in an insidious way. Like the little frown between her eyebrows, her movements, or the way she stares at me. Her eyes are like those of some feline, always so dark, defiant, and full of questions. I feel like she's about to jump away every time someone says something.

She steps closer, and I want to run away. Don't come near me, leave me alone. She has no idea the torture I am going through every time she opens those damn lips.

"You werewolves have no idea how annoying it is to walk across the city, do you?" she says.

If she was a werewolf, she'd probably be growling right now. I glance down, and she is wearing some ugly gladiator sandals. Oh, she probably had to borrow them, she was bare-footed when we brought her out of the fire, for some reason... I sigh and stare at her.

"Nobody asked you to follow me," I retort.

Her frown disappears as soon as I open my mouth, which is somewhat not helping. I can't help but notice her hair is losing some of its volume as we are really starting to get wet, the rain increasing.

"I have more questions."

Well, I don't want to answer them. I am not a witch coach, and especially not for this one I don't want to be around the most. I glance to the side. We are almost at Nina's. I sigh and turn around to get there.

"Hey!" she calls after me, annoyed that I'm ignoring her.

I know I don't need to say a thing. That girl is stubborn and will definitely follow me. Meanwhile, I feel like I am digging my own grave, bringing her with me. Every word I pronounce, it's like I'm letting her in a little more, and I don't feel too good about that, really.

We get inside Nina's restaurant. I missed this place. It's still vintage, with the red neons and the overused leather of the chairs that smell like fritters all the time. It has barely changed since I was a kid. Nora and I come here from time to time, but since Lily's birth, it's been months since we came to have one of our little "dates"... Nina jumps, recognizing me from the bar, and comes to greet me with a big hug as usual.

"Oh, Liam boy, how come you're here with this weather?! And it's not Nora today! Do you have a new date, boy?"

I turn around to Mara, and for some reason, I expected her to be blushing, like Nora the first time she was mistaken for my girlfriend. Instead, Mara is smiling a bit shyly, and I just felt that. Oh, Moon Goddess, I'm in real trouble here...

"Hi, I'm Mara," she says with a dangerously warm smile.

"Nice to meet you, sweetie! Oh, kitten, you're soaked! Give me a second, I'll bring you guys some towels. What's with this weather, really?! Just pick a table, you two, I'll be right back!"

Nina leaves, and I immediately show Mara to a table where we can both sit before she gets a say in this. The truth is, the restaurant is pretty much empty, but the spot I picked is one with a table large enough that we won't be elbow to elbow. I am a total coward for that one, but I slide myself onto the chair, keeping myself far from the table and far from her.

It doesn't help much. She's still way too close, with her eyes fixated on me, even a bit too much. I can see the details of her face, the little brown marks on her skin. At some point, I can't ignore it any longer.

"Can you stop staring like that?" I sigh, almost begging.

"I'm waiting for the minute you're going to try and run away," she replies back.

Oh, so she's pissed about last time. I sigh and look away. Sure, it wasn't nice, but I already stayed with her longer than I intended to. I just... I couldn't walk away after noticing she was in trouble. Seeing her under the rain was the first pull. I just... I felt this urge to do something. She was like a soaked kitten, and my instincts were making me feel like shit for witnessing that. I didn't think we'd end up spending that long in my hideout, or the kind of torture I'd experience there. Like a dog trapped in a cage with a bone... I shiver just remembering that. I think my own self-control surprised me that day, but also those new feelings I got there. I just can't.

"Here, my lovelies," says Nina, handing us two towels. "How about some hot cocoas, hm? Are you hungry? It's not too late for lunch!"

"We are fine, Nina..." I declare, but I shut my mouth since Mara is glaring at me.

"Can I have a cheeseburger?" asks Mara. "Since Mr. Runaway right here made me walk all the way here, I'm starving now."

Did she eat at all at Nora's? I don't dare say a thing; the more she glares at me, the more I feel my wolf getting ready to poke his nose out. Stay down, boy.

Nina leaves with a chuckle, sending me a glance as if to say good luck with the feisty one. Yeah, I'd need luck and to run very fast and very far... Mara starts trying to dry her hair, and I put my towel on my face too. Why do I have to go through this...? I'm feeling crazy enough already. I don't want to be in the same room as her, but my entire body is saying otherwise. My heart goes crazy as if I'm about to have a panic attack. Why, why another witch? Why a witch, of all people? It wouldn't even have felt half as bad if Mara was a wolf or at least a human!

"Why is it always such shitty weather when I see you...?" she sighs, taking the towel off.

Oh, damn it. Her hair is more tamed because it's wet, and this drop going down her neck is driving me crazy too. She's fucking pretty like

158

that. I need to take a deep breath and look away. Once again, there are crazy fireworks in my stomach and Mara is staring at me, making it even worse. It's like my senses are getting corrupted by this.

Thank Moon Goddess, Nina comes back with our drinks, because I need something to tame my thirst. I'm going freaking nuts here. Why is she so persistent about me? She can't feel the bond, she's a witch. I wish she could also experience half of the trouble I'm in... or wait, maybe not. That'd be worse...

"So, are you going to answer my questions today?" she asks, playing with the metallic straw, making it click against the glass.

"I'll answer whatever I can."

"About Sylviana's tree, for example?"

Oh, freakin' fuck. Of all the questions... I want to growl and run the hell away from this place, from her.

"No."

"You're the laziest witch hunter I've ever met," she sighs.

She takes a sip of her hot cocoa, and the whipped cream gives her a cute mustache. Oh, damn, not cute, Liam, stop thinking shit like that. I don't want to, but I can't help but notice she is still frowning a bit, even while staring at her drink.

"What's wrong?"

"I have a headache..."

"...The voices?"

"No, not this time. Just a damn headache..."

She massages her temples and closes her eyes, giving me a little break. How come she's feeling unwell now? She wasn't well last time we saw each other either. I stare outside. Is it the rain, perhaps? Water should be her weakness after all...

"It may be the rain," I explain. "Witches are weak to their opposite element."

"Sylviana was weak to... fire?"

I nod. Syl hated anything related to fire, including candles or cigarettes... The smell of smoke gave her nausea, though she tried not to show it. I guess Mara is just as weak to rain, especially downpours like these...

"What about the other witches?" she asks.

I don't really want to talk about that... I didn't want anyone else to know, actually. Especially not Nora. I thought I could fight them off by myself with what I know. Direct them toward where the barrier is stronger, make them feel like they are not welcome, keep them at bay.

"The barrier is weakening, don't tell me this won't be an issue," she suddenly declares.

I turn to her, surprised. She looks a bit proud.

"Yeah, I can feel it," she adds before I say a thing. "Nora took me to see Sylviana's tree and the barrier. It's getting weaker. I think whatever she was trying to do, she knew there would be another witch to take over someday. Sylviana knew it wouldn't last."

...I don't want to listen to that.

I had a hunch Nora was thinking the same thing too, that Sylviana had planned all of this. She was always two steps ahead of everyone, planning for the future. I kind of never understood why she felt like she had to protect everyone, almost as if she was guilty of something. She was guilty of nothing, but only... She tried to protect us from her sister, from one crazy Water Witch that went wrong.

Yet, to think she knew enough about someone like Mara coming?

"No, she couldn't see the future past her death," I protest.

"Regardless of what she could foresee, she ought to have known there would be a time needed for a tree like that," she says. "It means she also knew it wouldn't last, and there would be another witch no matter what. Maybe she wanted to pick which one."

I glance at her, unsure. What is she implying? I had always wondered about that tree. Somehow, I thought she'd be there forever, that she would continue to protect us even in her death... until Mara came. Then, my doubts appeared, tormenting me with two black eyes, and my heart was thrown into her fire.

Sylviana did talk about how each city had its witch, but... she never mentioned her own replacement. I'm doubting everything now, and I have more questions than I can bear. She knew she would leave me. She knew we would never be together forever, but could she have predicted this? Predicted that Mara would appear?

"This barrier has been here since the end of that war, right?" says Mara. "Yet, I am here. And I came to Silver City less than a year ago. One way or another, Sylviana's barrier let me through. Don't you think there's a reason for that?"

I remain silent. I don't like this theory. It's even crueler coming from her of all people, and she has no idea. Mara takes my silence for doubt, and she bites her thumb.

"It's not even my theory, to be honest. I talked to your sister-in-law, Nora. She is the one who thinks... this might have been Sylviana's plan. She may have foreseen me coming. I didn't really believe it at first, you know. However, while I was coming here, I couldn't stop thinking about what Nora said, and... so many things don't add up. Do you know what I found out? I came to Silver City to ask questions about witches. My mother could be a witch, from what I know. And... I am a witch. I am the only witch in Silver City, and all the others are kept out. What else could it be?"

I shake my head. I don't want to hear this...

Nina arrives with Mara's cheeseburger, and I watch her start to eat, regretting I didn't order something too. My werewolf stomach is unhappy only being able to watch. Why the hell did I choose to be so stubborn anyway?

"So, are you going to help me or not?" asks Mara.

I frown.

"What are you talking about?"

"I want to know more about Sylviana," she says, "and about the other witches you fought too. I have no witch to teach me anything, just a grumpy witch hunter, so you'll have to make do for now."

Oh, Moon Goddess, this has to be my personal hell.

Chapter 13

Dang, even if I don't remember the last time I had an actual cheeseburger, this one has to be the best. Maybe it's because I am damn near starving after coming all the way here. This is just so good, and warm too. I feel myself getting a bit better, after being exhausted and drenched...

Facing me, Liam stares at the burger, but I can't tell if he's hungry too or just avoiding my eyes. That guy is really not willing to talk or help me out. I feel like I need to push him to say every single word. Moreover, how dare he be so... sexy? I don't think that guy has any idea what he looks like right now. His sleeveless shirt shows off his muscular arms, and his wet hair is a bit too much for me to handle calmly. He keeps brushing it with his fingers, and every time he does, he looks like one of those pop stars Kelsi likes to fawn over on the TV. He has that kind of effect, and it's damn dangerous when I am trying to have a serious conversation with him. To stop looking, I focus on my meal. Thankfully, it's rather easy. I eat with my fingers, a bit shamelessly, but as Ben says, there is no bad way to eat a good sandwich...

"...What do you want me to do, exactly?" he asks. "I am not a witch teacher, I am a witch hunter."

I roll my eyes. This guy needs to win an award for most negative person around.

"You knew Sylviana, for starters," I say. "All you werewolves did, from what I understand. Plus, as I said, I think she knew about me, or she was suspecting it. Is there any way she left something for the next witch who came to town?"

He sighs and shakes his head.

"I don't want to talk about Sylviana," he says.

"Well, I don't care, because I need to know and I'm going to stick to you like glue until you spit it out. I'm not asking you about personal stuff, Liam Black, I want to know the witch stuff. How did she use her powers? Did she have some books, some wand, a magic spell, or something?"

He looks at me like I am a child and rolls his eyes.

"No, Mara, it's not like in books..."

"What about a magic circle?"

162

Ah, there we go. His expression changes immediately. I kept it to ask at the end on purpose and it worked. Even if he denies it now, it's too late. He definitely knows something about magic circles.

"Spill it," I say, licking my finger.

Liam makes a strange expression, gulping down while looking at my fingers covered in ketchup, and has to look elsewhere to answer.

"Yes, I know she had one. How do you know about magic circles?"

"I have one too."

"What?"

"Hey, I'm the one asking questions," I retort. "You didn't want to answer so let me ask before you get yours. What else did Sylviana use? We found an old herbology book at my place. Ring a bell?"

"Yeah, she had a ton of those... She was an Earth Witch, so everything was related to that. She had dozens of plants, a few herbology books, and... just stuff like that. But no magic wand or whatever that you could use. You're a Fire Witch, I doubt any of her stuff should get in your hands!"

"You don't know that," I shrug.

I bite into my burger, thinking. Could that previous witch really not have prepared anything if she knew I was coming? The more I chat with Liam, the less I'm convinced by Nora's theory, it's a bit disappointing. I was really hoping that there would finally be some clues for me to catch on, but it looks like Sylviana may not have been as prepared as I thought after all. Or maybe she just couldn't know it would be a Fire Witch after her? I'm getting more and more lost now. And this damn headache... I try to eat a bit more. If I knew it was going to be so painful to walk under a downpour, I wouldn't have followed this idiot here.

"...I don't think Sylviana had anything ready for you," he says. "Her house is condemned anyway."

"Condemned?"

"No one has been able to get in since she... Anyway, it's just condemned. Not just physically, like no one can get in, and we really tried. There's a barrier on her house too... I tried several times, but it didn't work."

He shakes his head, and I get this heavy feeling again. For someone who supposedly hates witches, Liam has a rather painful expression whenever we mention Sylviana. I feel this little pinch in my heart, and I'm torn between wanting to know more, and thinking I'd rather not know. I'll pick the latter for now.

"What about the others?" I ask, trying to shift the subject.

"As I told you, there have been three so far... I mean, three attempts. Only one of those witches came close enough that I saw her, but she didn't try again. I think they can feel Sylviana's barrier and the Royal Aura inside."

"You're talking about Nora and Selena?"

"More about Nora. She is powerful enough to help strengthen the barrier, but she is more of a... battery. Sylviana's tree channels a part of Nora's aura, but it should be able to withstand on its own. The barrier was perfectly fine until a few months ago."

I'm slowly starting to understand all of this... I grab a napkin to wipe my mouth and think a bit, my stomach full. So that barrier should have been just fine but as it appears now, without a witch, the barrier is bound to disappear in a while, and the appearance of those foreign witches is not helping at all.

"Do you think they could be the ones affecting the barrier? If those witches have been trying to attack for a while..."

"Or a witch getting in could have done that too," he retorts, staring at me with an accusatory look.

I can't help but roll my eyes. Why is everyone always thinking I'm going to blow up the whole city just by breathing around here, it's getting annoying now. I slam my hand on the table.

"Listen, grumpy hunter. So far, the barrier has been fine with me inside it. I didn't even know it existed until a while ago, so chill. I didn't do anything to it. Although I am a newbie witch, I felt that barrier and it didn't seem more bothered by me than that."

"I did see it send you on your... you know," he says.

"Alright, maybe I played with it a little. But if that barrier was that strong, I'd have probably lost a few fingers then. I felt its power and it wasn't very witch-proof to me. So even if you're not fond of me, I'm probably still a better option to help you strengthen it than the other witches lurking out there. Hm?"

He makes a bit of an annoyed expression, but we both know I'm right. I am the witch that's already in the house. We both know I also happen to have plenty of firepower in stock, but I need to learn how to use and control it. Liam stares at me for a long while, looking unsure, but it's just making me more determined.

It's not just about getting my answers. I also have this... pull toward him that I need to sort out. I still feel it, like an invisible thread that binds me to this guy without asking my opinion. Of course, he is handsome and all, but there is more to it. It is a really strange feeling, like my whole body reacting to his presence, permanently. I can't shake it off, it's just there. I don't know what it is. Like some force, a natural attraction toward him. I have no idea why, why him of all people, but I do think there is something I need to unfold about that bond I feel between me and him... something I have to decipher. I know he probably feels it too. I see it in the way he looks at me, but he also looks like he's ready to run away every single time.

I feel like if I say something about it, he will deny it or run. I didn't realize until now, how scared I actually was about... putting it on the table and facing his reaction. I'm not ready, not yet. Whatever this is between us, I need time. We both do.

"So you've never actually... seen or fought those witches," I say, clearing my throat a little.

"I had them run off. Witches are still just women."

"Now you're being rude," I retort, lighting up my middle finger as a warning.

"I didn't mean it like that," he says, rolling his eyes. "It's just that aside from their powers, physically, they are close to human women, weaker than werewolves. They hate direct confrontation unless they are very strong and sure to have the upper hand."

"So what, you're saying we are dealing with... novice witches, like me?"

"Maybe. Or maybe their element isn't too suited for a direct fight. They ran away pretty quickly when I found them."

It does make sense. I can probably barbecue a whole building, but I doubt any witch can provoke a massive flood or an earthquake. Moreover, I've seen werewolves fight, and they are quick. I wouldn't want to have to fight Selena head-on if I was really her enemy, for example. And seeing how Liam's aura is about as dark as his brothers', the other witches probably didn't feel like it was worth risking a bite... at least not while the barrier is up.

"I get it," I say. "So, we can't get out and chase those witches, but we still need to sort out the barrier issue. I want to see Sylviana's house."

He suddenly glares at me.

"I said the house is condemned."

"From what you said, it's condemned with magic, right? Lucky you, there's a new witch in town, and she's curious about that house. So, I want to go there and see it. Maybe Sylviana made sure her house was locked for a reason."

He seems hesitant, but I ignore him and get up.

"Come on, you said you wanted to get in there," I add. "Maybe it's your chance!"

Truth is, I'm probably an idiot for saying that. I don't want to know why he wanted to get into that house, but for now, I have other things in mind. I do want to get into the previous witch's house. I hope she'll forgive me from wherever she is, but I believe this house might be my biggest clue and give me more.

After a few more minutes, Liam looks out the window. The weather is still shitty, and I had forgotten that bit. I guess I'll manage... He looks at me, but I try to look like I don't care about the damn rain or the headache I'm going to inflict upon myself. Eventually, he sighs and nods, getting up.

"Fine, let's go there. Nina! Can you put all that on my tab? I'll pay next time!"

"Of course, sweetie!" says the nice waitress lady, coming back to our table. "Are you sure you'll be okay with all that rain? Oh, don't stay out too long... See you soon and be careful! You too, Mara, come back anytime, love. I like girls with a big appetite!"

I smile at her. Indeed, I emptied that plate in a flash and Nina looks happy about that.

"I will!"

His Blazing Witch

I follow Liam outside, but as soon as we get past the door, a wave of regret hits me. Oh, God, the rain... He chuckles, taking out a cigarette as we stand right against the wall, sheltered by the roof of the restaurant a bit.

"Having second thoughts?" he asks.

Damn, this guy only smiles when it's a smirk to mock me. I shake my head, I can be damn stubborn too. I cross my arms around me. This is the worst summer weather I could have imagined. At least my body temperature keeps me from actually being cold, but still, I don't want to get wet. Liam chuckles and takes his time to smoke his cigarette. I didn't even realize he smelled a bit like tobacco until now. He notices my eyes on his cigarette.

"Sorry, I can't smoke around the kids, so I usually wait until after the family lunches..."

"Sounds like you're a decent uncle."

"I try to be. It's my family..."

"Lucky you," I scoff. "The only member of my family who cares enough to talk to me pays my best friend to spy on me."

He coughs a bit, surprised by my words. I feel a bit bitter about the Kelsi-gate, but I'll sort that out later. For now, I think I still need to cool off on the matter, and staying away from my friend, where she can text my sister about my every move, helps...

"Okay," he says, crushing his cigarette into the outdoor ashtray, "wait for me here."

He's about to walk away, but I grab his top without thinking. He suddenly stops, looking at my hand with surprise. Oh... I just grabbed him without thinking, but now, I actually get to see his abs. Nice one, Mara. He growls a bit and pulls down his top, forcing me to keep my hand off.

"You're not leaving me, are you?" I ask.

He looks a bit more surprised by my question than I expected and blinks a couple of times before answering. He already stepped out, letting a bit of the rain get into his hair again. He shakes his head.

"No, but you're going to get sick if we go like this! I'll be right back, wait for me here."

I'm not sure I trust him to come back, but I don't say anything and watch him leave. Is he going to get us a taxi or something? I keep looking around, hoping to see his figure come back soon. He wouldn't really ditch me, would he?

He's going to abandon you...

Oh no, fuck no, not now. I take deep breaths, but the headache is really not helping this time. I feel that voice, the other voice, slithering in like a fucking snake into my mind. I try to ignore her, but it's insidious, like a voice whispering right into my ear.

He hates you... They all hate you... The werewolves... They are going to use you... like they used her...

What the hell does that damn voice want now? Is she talking about Sylviana? What does that mean, they used her? I take deep breaths, trying to ignore the voice. I know she's just there to torment me, and I don't know what the hell she wants but I won't give in. I don't want to give in to the hatred, those voices full of spite in my mind. The werewolves are good to me. I know they don't hate me. Fuck off!

"Hey! Mara!"

I look up, and Liam Black is there, looking at me with a worried expression. I realize he's even got a hand on my shoulder. Did he call me several times already? I feel a bit... off. The rain is really making me so much weaker. I take another deep breath to try and calm myself down and nod. I don't know what those voices want, but it's really not the moment. Of course, they had to freaking come out when Liam was gone and I'm feeling so nauseous...

Just as I try to get back to my senses, I realize what I am looking at, and my jaw drops.

"You have a bike?" I ask, impressed.

Liam chuckles.

"You're only seeing it now? It's noisy, though!"

Well, whatever sound it's making, I couldn't hear it until now. Gosh, I already love that bike. It's a big red bike, a Japanese brand, and it's roaring like a tiger. I feel like I'm seeing the best toy of my life, and I really want to play with it. I bite my thumb, unable to take my eyes off this beauty. Would he let me drive it if I ask...?

Liam chuckles.

"Wow, I didn't think my bike would have that much of an effect on you."

"Please tell me we're going somewhere with this gorgeous thing," I say.

"Yeah, here."

I grab his biker's jacket. Oh, that good smell of leather... I love it. Liam nods and helps me get behind him. Okay, next time I need to ask if I can try driving it... Crap, this helmet is going to be a nightmare to put on with my hair. I stick my head in, but Liam doesn't wear a helmet or even a jacket. Did he not have a spare? I'd like to think he hasn't had someone behind him in a while, but...

"It's not that far," he says a bit loud over the sound of his bike, "but I figured it might be better for you if we get to Jones' territory fast!"

I space out for a second.

"Wait, what? Whose territory?"

"Jones, the Jones family. It's another family of werewolves, Sylviana's house was... I mean-- is on their territory. Why?"

Jones. I did not expect to hear that name again. Could it be a mere coincidence? Did I use the name Jones back then simply because it's rather common? Though, that's a big coincidence to think about. The previous witch's house is on the territory of a household name I used as an alias? How much did I really know before I lost my memories? I know I couldn't have met Sylviana, she was dead before I came here, but still... I picked the name Jones when I went to that library. Was that a clue? If so, a clue for... whom?

"Mara?" he calls me.

167

"Sorry, it's nothing. Let's go."

Liam gives me a suspicious glance, but I flip the helmet visor down, hiding my eyes. He gives up and starts driving. Damn, I'm on a bike with Liam, of all people, but I'm going to ask myself hundreds of questions instead of enjoying this now...

The ride on his bike makes me feel a lot better... in a lot of ways. First, I think my headache lessens a bit. Maybe it's because I'm protected from the rain with the helmet and jacket, but it definitely isn't as bad as it was a while ago. Or maybe the ride soothes me in a way. It's pleasant, to say the least. Despite the rain, the roar of the engine makes a reassuring noise, and the driver is actually pretty good. I had heard it's not recommended to use a bike in rainy weather, but Liam doesn't seem to care one bit.

Even without his helmet, he rides his bike as if they were just one being. What disturbs me the most is that I love both. The good leather smell and the heat are getting to my head. Moreover, I have to hold on to him for the ride, and it is the first time we have enjoyed such proximity since we met. I feel the heat of his back, despite the clothes between us and the rain. I know I could just hold on to the back handle of the bike, but damn, this is one rare opportunity where he can't brush me off... I hold on to him and, a bit shamelessly, rest my head against his back to look at the city passing next to us.

We have left the docks to get back to the heart of Silver City. I can't help but feel a bit strange, seeing all those tall buildings from down here. I used to watch them from my hospital room's window, think about how tall they are, and wonder how it would feel to walk next to them. Now that I'm here, it's a bit of an eerie feeling. Dozens of windows lined up, some with lights on because of the dark clouds above us. The neon signs mix into funky colors, making some pretty images with the bike's speed. I don't think I'll ever get tired of this. I hate the rain, but I have to admit, it suits the atmosphere of this city.

Finally, Liam stops in front of a different neighborhood. Here, all the buildings are either gray or covered in graffiti. It looks like a giant skate park or one of those backdrops in gangster movies. We left the skyscrapers behind us too. Here, the tallest buildings are ten floors at most. There are strangely a lot of people in the streets. Standing in front of the shops, sipping bottles of beer in front of pubs, and smoking cigarettes, no one seems to care about the downpour. It lessened, actually, but it's still heavy rain.

Liam stops in an empty parking lot, and I have to get off first and unwillingly take off the helmet. Damn it, my hair is an absolute mess... I try to tame it a bit while Liam puts a lock on his wheel, and actually, I'm hiding my blushing a bit too. We were so close during the ride, it's a bit awkward now. Liam too, I feel like he's taking a bit too much time just to park his bike. When he finally gets up, his eyes look elsewhere.

"Alright, let's go..."

His Blazing Witch

I follow him, keeping his biker jacket on me. I really like the feeling of that heavy leather on my shoulders, the mixed smell of leather and Liam. ...Is that creepy?

He guides me toward a street full of houses, all in a row but of various colors. It's probably a lovely street under good weather, but now it's just averagely gloomy. Just as we get into the street, I can already tell which house we are going to. It really stands out, with all the green. It has a rather impressive fence, with ivy or bushes covering it all. To my surprise, we get in without any issues. The gate is open, and I was expecting something magical to happen, but we just step into a large garden. The grass is growing freely, with wildflowers everywhere. On the side, rows of vegetable crops have been taken care of and seem to be growing fine. Same for the little greenhouse, nothing inside indicates that its owner has passed.

"The neighbors have been taking care of the garden," explains Liam as he notices my gaze. "Most of what Sylviana was growing is still doing fine thanks to them, so they can use the vegetables and herbs..."

"Is that alright?"

He nods.

"She liked to grow everything she consumed herself. A lot of people on this street have started doing the same, actually. This street is one of the greenest in Silver City..."

Now that he mentions it, all the houses we walked by had little gardens that looked well taken care of. I guess she did leave her mark around here... Maybe everything is growing faster and better because an Earth Witch was living in the area too.

I keep looking around in Sylviana's garden, but we are already at her house. It's a rather normal house, actually. I don't know what I was expecting. Once again, it's covered in so much ivy, I have to guess the original exterior color was white. There is something a bit more interesting, though; the whole house is covered with this thick layer of ivy, including the windows and door. We stand in front of it, under the rain, a bit at a loss on what to do.

"I suppose you tried tearing it off?" I ask, turning to Liam.

He nods and steps forward. He grabs some of the ivy on the door to pull it, but indeed, as soon as he even touches it, more ivy suddenly grows at an accelerated speed, covering the door with a new layer of leaves. And he hasn't even plucked one leaf off yet. I bite my thumb. She really didn't want anyone to come into her house after her... at least, not the werewolves, not even Liam. But what if I try?

Just like Liam, I step forward and try to tear a branch off. I pull one, but as expected, at least ten more grow to replace it before I can do anything. Damn, I'm not going to accept that we came here for nothing. Liam shakes his head, glaring at that ivy.

"I've tried countless times," he says. "I've tried cutting it, burning it, even digging out the roots, but nothing works. It regrows no matter what and won't let me in, or anyone else..."

169

His Blazing Witch

Well, despite being nothing but vegetation, her protection does look pretty pervasive. Although, I haven't tried yet. This rain isn't helping, but at least, it's not as heavy as earlier. I take my arm out of Liam's jacket and start a fire between my fingers. Liam frowns.

"Hey, what are you doing? I said I tried burning it!"

"You haven't tried magic fire," I retort. "It's worth a try."

He seems hesitant but steps back despite the frowning. Well, I guess we will know soon enough. Either it doesn't care and regrows, or...

I approach with my fire, and to my surprise, the leaves get consumed right away, despite being drenched by the rain. Actually, it propagates very quickly, all the nearby branches catching fire at once. I just had to burn one! We watch the fire spread, but it doesn't just act like any normal branch burning. It's very... orderly, the leaves disappearing one by one. The ashes even disappear into thin air as soon as they get burned, meaning there's definitely some sort of magic seal I just broke. We wait a few seconds, watching all of the ivy on the door and windows disappear. It looks like even if she unlocked the door for me, Sylviana never intended to let her house run out of Ivy. The branches that aren't on the door or windows are just fine.

We exchange a glance, and I put my hand on the door knob, a bit nervous. I have no idea what I'm going to find inside. It could even be some sort of trap. This is an actual witch's house, the last one before me.

I walk in first. The house is smaller than it looked on the outside, probably because there are a lot of things everywhere, even hanging on the walls. Plants, of course, are absolutely everywhere. I was more or less expecting so, but still... They really are everywhere our eyes can stumble upon: on shelves, hanging pots, in front of the windows, and on every piece of furniture, table and stools included. It's as if she had tried filling every available spot with something green. I walk in carefully. The entrance is actually a walk-in to the open kitchen and a large living room after just a couple of stairs.

"How long has it been since...?"

"Around 2 years," he says.

Liam looks around, as confused as I am. It doesn't look like this house has been abandoned for 2 years... more like 2 weeks, at most. Every plant here looks perfectly fine and hydrated, there's only a thin layer of dust, and nothing is out of place. Even the kitchen looks like we could use it right now, except that there is no fridge, only storage for dry food. Now that I look around, I only see about a quarter of the appliances one would find in a normal house. No TV, just an old radio. The light must only come from the windows because I don't see a lamp of any sort either. It looks like she lived in the fifties or sixties... I bet her electricity bills were in the single digits.

"It feels... weird," sighs Liam.

From his expression, I know he's not just talking about the overall feeling of the house, more like his personal feelings. Again, I feel this little pinch in my heart. I walk further inside, starting to rummage through her belongings for more clues. I actually need to keep myself busy instead of seeing this abandoned puppy expression of his.

"So... are we going to talk about it?"

"About what?"

"About your relationship with that witch. Not the bullshit from earlier."

He sighs, still looking around without stepping inside as if he didn't feel allowed to.

"There isn't much to say..."

"I'm not blind," I retort. "If you don't want to talk about it, say it. Or tell me the actual truth, but please, don't serve me a lie or some half-assed answer. I've had that all week long already."

"Fine," he sighs. "We were together."

Damn, I fucking knew it. And even if I knew it, it still hurts. I grab a big bundle of books to look at, anything to avoid looking at him. Although, I feel my anger rise a bit. I glare at the pages, one after another. I know I have no right to be angry or even remotely jealous, but I can't help it. I ignore him and keep looking through the stuff here.

I hear Liam coming closer, but I don't know if I can endure looking at him right now.

"...Are you... upset?"

Is he being insensitive on purpose? Or is he just that dense? I wish he didn't ask, because I hate having to lie. I don't want to lie.

"I don't know," I retort. "Does it matter?"

He has nothing to answer to that, and it suits me just fine. Guess I am the one serving half-assed answers now. I shake my head and ignore that part of the conversation. To think I'm going through his ex's stuff... What a unique and weird situation.

For one, if I had any doubts, it is clear Sylviana was an Earth Witch. There are countless books on pretty much anything related to plants, soil, ground, everything. Just like the one I found in my bedroom. Moreover, all the books look used until the cover is starting to fall apart. I doubt any of these will be of any help to me, though, I'm no Earth Witch...

"Anything that looks changed?" I ask, realizing he probably already knows this place very well.

Liam shakes his head, looking around.

"No... It was never very orderly, to be honest. This is just the usual, from what I remember, I didn't come for the books or the decoration either, so..."

Now I feel like barbecuing this insensitive idiot. Seriously. I'm starting to get hot, so I take off his jacket and almost throw it at his face. He makes a sour expression, maybe realizing his mistake. I ignore him and go to check another corner of the room, mostly to be away from him.

I'm a bit frustrated too. I know there is something here, there has to be. Then, how come this house looks so... normal? I wasn't waiting for magic fireworks, but still. I keep searching for clues, and he starts helping out, no matter how reluctantly.

"By the way," he says, "why did you react to the name Jones, earlier?"

I was so excited to finally discover the house, I almost forgot about that. I put down the book and scratch my head.

"I apparently used it as an alias," I say. "At the university, I gave the name Jones instead of Garnett, and I was hiding which classes I went to. Classes about witches."

"From the time before the... incident?"

"Yep, from the whole part I don't remember, it looks like I used a fake name instead of... Clarissa Garnett."

"How many aliases do you have, and why?"

If only I knew! Even the name Clarissa Garnett doesn't ring a bell, and instead, I have been Mara all along. Now that new name, Jones? Is it supposed to mean Mara Jones? It doesn't make sense... It feels more like a hazard. Did I pick any name just to hide from the university? Jones is rather common, but of all places, Sylviana's house is on the territory of a werewolf family named Jones.

"Was Sylviana related to the local werewolves?"

"Not that I know of. They knew she was living here, but they weren't sure she was a witch, they never cared enough to find proof either. She was living a very quiet life until the war.

"So the... Jones' couldn't have had any kind of tie with her?"

"Only knowing where her house was, but..."

Crap, that might be it! What if I had picked that name on purpose? Aside from that idiot Ben, most werewolves would have been able to tell me there was a werewolf territory led by the Jones family! From there, they would have guided me to the witch's house, it comes back in a circle! I can't believe I lost so much time because that idiot couldn't even react to an alias! Was he even listening back at the library? I am so going to kick his useless ass.

"Mara?" Liam calls, noticing I am lost in my thoughts for a while.

"I think I really was meant to come here," I explain, looking around once more. "I picked the name of the territory Sylviana lived in, it can't be a coincidence. I... the previous me, the me from before the incident knew something and left clues behind."

It sounds crazier as I say it. Because it would mean I knew I was going to lose my memory and left clues on purpose. It can't be, right? I mean... so far, it did seem like I was hiding some things from the people around me. The circle under my rug. The classes I was truly attending. That fake name too.

I stand up, leaving the books there, resolute. It has to be something bigger. I look around the house. It will lead to nowhere, just looking through all these damn books one at a time. What did I miss? I keep looking around, but it's really covered in plants. Actually... literally covered. One of the walls is covered in ivy, just like outside, from floor to ceiling.

"What are you doing?" asks Liam. "That ivy was already there years ago!"

"It doesn't mean it wasn't meant to be undone later," I retort.

His Blazing Witch

Who cares if I burn that ivy down anyway? If it doesn't like being burnt, it will probably regrow just like the one outside. I light my fire on the tip of my fingers, hoping I'm not about to burn down the house with us in it.

Just like before, my fire spreads through the leaves quickly. Very quickly, actually, I worry a bit as I see all of the leaves catching fire so fast. It's not like outside, where they were wet and disappearing as ashes as soon as they got burnt. A strong smell starts coming off, but my fire isn't disappearing.

"...Mara..."

"I know!" I retort, a bit annoyed to have him watch my failure.

What the heck is going on? There is definitely something going on here, because that fire stays within the ivy wall, thankfully, but still, all this smoke is not good, and my fire isn't disappearing at all, the leaves keep burning. What the hell is wrong now? I spread out my hands, and take deep breaths, trying to call back my fire. It doesn't calm down at all, and my fire doesn't respond to me. What the hell?! I made this fire, why can't I control it now? I keep trying to bring it back, but it's like it's glued to that ivy and resisting me.

I stop trying to pull it back in and look at it. The fire stays on the leaves. It doesn't burn, but it doesn't go away either. The effect was just the same as before, so why aren't they disappearing now?! If I don't do something, we aren't going to burn, but the damn smoke will be just as efficient in killing us... I try to recall what I did outside. What is different?

"The rain!" I yell.

I'm such an idiot! This isn't just about me burning some damn leaves! Fire, earth, water, this is just like some weird witchy riddle! I look around for water, but Liam got it before me. He grabs an empty pot lying in a corner and opens a window to fill it with rainwater. After a few seconds, he comes back and splashes it on the burning ivy on the wall.

Finally, we see it. The leaves disappear in a new wave of ashes, thankfully taking the smoke with them as well. We can finally breathe some fresh air, even more so with Liam opening all the windows. I'm getting nervous all of a sudden, wondering what I will uncover this time. Liam grabs more water, as only the wet and burnt leaves have burned away. Meanwhile, I'm trying to decipher the image that is left behind. It's a drawing on the wall. Not just a childish drawing, something done with water paint. A very large tree? There is stuff written, some have even faded and disappeared over time. It takes me a little while to get it. It's a family tree.

I remain in front of that wall, baffled. Liam is still filling the pot with rainwater to put out the fire on the remaining leaves, but I'm mesmerized by what we uncovered. A very, very large and complicated tree. I didn't expect something like this, but now that I'm seeing it, I have this strange feeling in my heart. Like I just found something epic, something really, really important. Why was it hidden underneath that ivy wall? Why was Sylviana trying to hide this...?

Once he's done splattering the water, Liam stands next to me to stare at the tree, still looking shaken. He seems just as lost as I am. We are both scrutinizing that tree. The branches go in all directions on the wall, and it takes me a while to understand how to read it properly. The leaves are going toward the floor, while for some reason, the older branches, closer to the roots, are almost on the ceiling. It's like a waterfall of leaves, but not just leaves. The little figures painted on that wall are symbols, three different ones: a leaf, a flame, and a water droplet. They definitely represent each sign the witch was born under. It's really... pretty. It's a simple painting on a wall, with nothing complicated about it, but the repetition of those three elements, over and over again, going in all different directions on the wall has something beautiful about it, like a mosaic.

Moreover, there are names on there. Lots of names, one per symbol. It's written so small because there is a lot, so many that it covers a full wall. Hundreds, at least... I gasp.

"Are we supposed to look for someone specific?" I wonder. "It's going to take ages..."

Shall I search for the name Mara? Or Clarissa? I glance sideways, and Liam's ice-blue eye is already going around, most likely looking for Sylviana's. I take a deep breath. Oh, well, I should start looking now...

The most ancient witches are probably the ones whose names are closer to the roots. I even recognize a few famous names, some I have seen in the book about witches that Kelsi brought. Medea, Circe. I thought those were only tales... What part is true? Curious, I try to look up the oldest names of all, the ones that are on the ceiling. Strangely, they are almost faded. As if they had been written there for ages, and been erased by time. Didn't Sylviana supposedly write them all at once? Or could it be, this house is much older than we thought? I find the oldest names and take a few minutes to decipher the old handwriting. ...Lilith... Hecate, Cybele, and... Luna? For real? Or is that some coincidence? Could the oldest witch have been a Luna? A werewolf as well?

"Mara."

I turn my head, and Liam is frowning in front of one end of the tree. I walk up to him and look at what he is showing me. Oh, of course.

Sylviana.

Her name looks freshly painted, adorned with an ivy leaf. I feel a strange heart-warming feeling, seeing that name there. Why is that? I never knew her, but I still feel... happy that she is here. As if I was seeing a friend I know, a picture of somebody I recognize. Now that I think of it, I have no idea what that woman looked like. Could there be a picture or something somewhere?

"Wait a second..."

"What?"

Liam is frowning and looking around, confused. I look at Sylviana's branch. The name above hers is Danica. A Fire Witch, according to that little flame symbol behind her name. Her name follows a long list of what are probably her ancestors, just like any end of the tree. The branch stops with Sylviana's name, though...

"Liam, what's wrong?" I ask, annoyed to see him squinting all around.

174

"Nephera. Her name isn't... with Sylviana's."

I suddenly realize. Weren't those two supposedly sisters? Yet, the branch doesn't split in two ways. According to this tree, Sylviana was Danica's only daughter, nothing comes after her, or between those two... no one.

"Maybe Nephera was born after?"

"No, no," says Liam. "Sylviana was years younger, Nephera was... the older sister, that's what they said... They were half-sisters, but still."

Half-sisters? With the same mother? But if she was the oldest, Nephera should have appeared above Sylviana's name! I don't get it either. Or could it be because she turned bad, they removed her name? I look around. Actually, some names are indeed erased. A few branches further, a witch's name was burnt by something and is unreadable. Somewhere else, some mold has taken over to erase a witch's name too. They are either replaced with a new witch after, probably a second child, or the branch ends there. Liam notices too.

"Maybe because she was a Dark Witch? Are those all the Dark Witches that are erased?"

"Dark Witches?" I repeat.

"Yeah... Sylviana told us about them. Witches that used their magic... in a bad way, to do bad deeds, were deemed as Dark Witches."

This is getting very fairytale-like... The good and bad witches, Light and Dark Magic... I don't think those were bad witches, though. It doesn't make sense. All those names end their branch. Why would no bad witch have children, ever? I keep staring at the tree, thinking there's something I've missed.

Suddenly, I recall Kelsi's words.

"The cycle!" I exclaim.

"What?"

"The witches' cycle. My friend Kelsi found out about it. The three elements are essential to witches."

"Yeah, I know. What about it?"

"Nephera was a Water Witch, right? There's no way she was Danica's daughter, according to that sacred cycle thing, her firstborn had to be an Earth Witch! Look, the tree has the exact same pattern all over. Each branch. Fire, earth, water, fire, earth, water, it's all the same. There's no way a Water Witch was a Fire Witch's daughter."

Liam stares at me, dumbfounded. He probably didn't even think of doing the math until now. Looks like his ex wasn't anywhere near done with having secrets.

However, it doesn't explain to us where the hell Nephera the bad witch came from. Why would they claim to be half-sisters? From the same father, then? However, there are no male names here. The witches only kept track of each other's daughters. So much for the patriarchy, I guess.

"Here."

I found her, just a branch higher. Because of the way the tree is composed, her branch happens to end farther away, but Nephera is there, and... she is not alone. I frown. Right after her, there's a burn mark over the name. She had a daughter...?

"Oh... She mentioned a stillborn child," whispers Liam, as I put my finger on the burn mark.

"Really?"

He nods slowly and sits down next to me, looking bitter.

"She... Nephera didn't really have the happiest life. She said it a bit... before the fight, while talking to Sylviana. She was chased out of Silver City by my father, the previous Alpha King, and he basically sent vampires... to attack her. She was pregnant at the time, and the baby... died."

"...Vampires killed her child?"

Liam looks really uneasy, staring at that burnt spot with a sour expression.

"It was my father's fault, mostly. He... didn't want Nephera to have his child."

I'm lost for a second.

"Wait, his child? What the heck? You're telling me that the Water Witch, the one that attacked Silver City, was pregnant with... your father's child, and he had her attacked by vampires?"

"Yeah, my father was that kind of asshole," he growls.

"Fucking messed up seems like an understatement. So that burn mark is basically your... stillborn half-sister?"

He nods.

"And your ex's niece...? Seriously, how fucked up is this, exactly?"

And they are telling me Nephera was the bad witch in the story? After losing her baby to a fucked up ex, who happens to be Liam's dad? I turn to Liam.

"You guys just told me it was two sisters having a spat, you never mentioned that kind of fucked up history."

I don't know why I feel so upset about this? Is it because this is another half-truth the werewolves served me? Or because those women were witches? According to this tree, we are all related, all cousins, all sisters. Mothers and daughters. Why do I feel so upset about Nephera and Sylviana's story? I didn't suspect they were so closely related to the werewolves, especially to the Black family. They made Sylviana sound like a friend and Nephera like an enemy. Why?

"Mara, we barely met Nephera before the war," he says.

"You mean before you killed her? Why? Why do you even call her a bad witch at all? Because she wanted to get to Silver City? She had grounds for her revenge, didn't she?"

Liam rolls his eyes, starting to look angry too.

"You know nothing, Mara. Sylviana was Silver City's witch, and her sister just wanted that spot. She was ready to kill for it, and not just a few people. You know she killed some loved ones we had."

Yeah, that I know. Selena mentioned she lost one of her best friends, Ben and Bonnie's older brother. I saw her husband's missing arm too, and Liam's eye is blind, right in front of me. I sit down next to him.

"I want the full story, Liam Black. Stop giving me pieces here and there. I want Nephera and Sylviana's story, as it was, not just the part that accommodates the werewolves!"

"Fine, fine," he growls.

I see him glance at Sylviana's name on the wall.

"Nora and Selena are Royal werewolves, you know that, right?"

I nod.

"They weren't born here, in Silver City. Their family lived far away, to the north, in an unknown location. Their grandmother was a sacred werewolf, with powers akin to the Moon Goddess herself."

"Alright, this is all very interesting but with all due respect to those two, I want the witches' story!"

He rolls his eyes again.

"Moon Goddess, Mara, can you shut up for a second and let me speak? How the hell are you so damn stubborn? Let me talk and listen!"

I don't like his tone, but I decide to shut up. I can always light up his fine ass later if I don't get what I want... He sighs, shaking his head with annoyance.

"It's not just about their family. Their grandmother had a witch, a friend of hers that was in that city with them."

He points his finger toward Sylviana's mother.

"...Danica?"

"That's right. Danica, the Fire Witch. She was the witch on the Royals' territory, the Blue Clan. And that's where she raised both of her daughters, Nephera and Sylviana. Until today, I had no idea Nephera wasn't her daughter, but that's the story we were told."

"...What happened then? You said it didn't all happen in Silver City?"

"Right. Because of the Blue Clan's Royal Family's powers, they were targeted, especially Selena and Nora's parents. They were twins, and their grandmother, Diane, wanted to protect them at all costs. So, many years before Selena or Nora were even born, Danica sent Nephera, her first daughter, with Diane's younger sister, a werewolf lady named Cynthia, and a portion of the Blue Clan to settle elsewhere."

"...Why?"

"Danica believed they could find a place with more witch power, some sort of magic source or something, that would help them protect the children. Nephera was sent here with Cynthia before Sylviana was even born. Their little pack settled in Silver City. However, she didn't really do her witch duty. She fell in love with my father, helped him become the next Alpha King, and..."

"And he threw her away when he didn't need her anymore?" I guess.

Liam makes a sour face and nods.

"Trust me, I know this part has to be true. My father was the worst kind of scum."

It sounds like Liam and his brother's childhood wasn't all happy pup play... It would also explain why they are so inclined to protect their family, though, or why they fell for strong women like Nora and Selena. I remember seeing the two couples, and how close they looked... Liam was the only one sticking out.

"Nephera never fulfilled her duty to find that magic source, and things here were... messy for a while. My father wasn't the best kind of King Silver City needed. Cynthia's pack had to fend for themselves among many others. They became the Sapphire Moon Clan, but meanwhile, Nephera completely detached herself from them. I think she said she tried to get away from our father and left Silver City while pregnant..."

"That's when she was... chased by vampires?"

I don't know much about vampires, but I do have a feeling they are probably not the nice kind. So, she was driven out of Silver City... and attacked while pregnant. No matter what, I feel extremely sorry for her. I can almost feel the pain, that anguish she must have gone through. Falling for the wrong man, losing her family, having to fend for herself... Maybe it's because I am also a witch, and isolated at that, but I can really feel Nephera's pain as my own. Somehow, I understand why the werewolves can't feel sorry for her, as she abandoned the Blue Clan her mother served, but I do...

"If she left Silver City and Sylviana was still with... Diane and her kids, how did things lead to a war in Silver City?" I ask, confused.

"The thing is, Nephera was supposed to be the guide to bring the rest of the pack to Silver City. All of this happened about thirty or forty years ago. Silver City or their birthplace wasn't developed like it is now, no phones or computers to communicate, and without knowing where the other was..."

"They lost contact?" I realize.

"There might have been some magic involved too, as Danica was probably protecting the place, but basically, yes. So, while a portion of their pack was settling in Silver City, Diane never got to come here with her children. That's how Nora and Selena were both born in that place, wherever it was. However, through Nephera, the vampires learned about it."

Holy crap. So that's when things went wrong... Liam looks up at Sylviana's name.

"What Diane had feared happened. The vampires attacked, and Nora and Selena's parents were killed. Queen Diane and Danica, also. However, Sylviana managed to save Nora and leave, while Selena was saved by another werewolf... Both of them were brought here to Silver City and raised in different packs. It wasn't until they met my brothers that we found out they were Royals, and... the awakening of their powers brought Nephera back too."

"What? You mean she tried to come back to Silver City?"

Liam sighs.

"She wasn't coming back with good feelings, Mara. Our father had chased her out and killed her baby. The Blue Moon Clan, now called the Sapphire Moon, hadn't helped her. She was dead jealous of Sylviana, who had been raised by their mother, and most of all, she blamed Nora and Selena's family for what happened to her."

Now everything is becoming much clearer...

"So that's it," I whisper. "The war... It was caused by all of this?"

"By Nephera," Liam says. "She wanted revenge. She wanted to kill all of us, for what she had suffered. She was... tortured by vampires for years, Mara. Vampire venom is extremely painful for witches. A werewolf can save themselves from it under certain conditions but for a witch... Even if she could heal herself, she must have gone through hell. It... wrecked her. She was just so full of spite, I think blaming us for everything was her way to cope, but it also made her crazy."

"I would have gone crazy too if I had gone through all that shit." I sigh. "I get that the werewolves and Sylviana were lucky, but I feel sorry for Nephera. Your father was the bastard in the story. If he hadn't chased her out, and killed her child... What kind of bastard even does that to a woman carrying their child?!"

Liam rolls his eyes.

"I don't want to talk about that... jerk, Mara. But yes, deep down, my father probably caused it."

I feel pretty sour about that. Their half-sister was killed in such a horrible way, and Nephera... In the end, she was just a pawn, wasn't she? How young was she when Danica sent her here? No wonder she envied Sylviana, to be sent away from her mother to some unknown location, with no one like her? I can feel that.

I glance at the tree again, while Liam resumes his explanation.

"Basically, the war occurred because Nephera wanted revenge. She... somehow turned the vampires to work for her, but she was coming back to kill us, as the sons of the man who had betrayed her, and Selena, Nora, and Sylviana for what she had gone through, Mara."

"I get it," I retort, still absorbed by that tree.

"...You don't look very... concerned."

I turn to him, a bit annoyed.

"Being sent somewhere without any family or friends to explain to you how to be a good witch? Well, I can relate to that. For the record, werewolves didn't exactly welcome me with open arms, nor did the humans. So if you're waiting for me to take sides, for now, I won't, okay? Nora and Selena were nice to me, I get it. But look at this tree. Sylviana liked her sister, didn't she? No matter what, I don't think she saw Nephera as a villain."

"She was a bad witch!" he retorts. "Do you know how many people she killed?!"

"You said it yourself, she had gone nuts from being tortured! Moreover, are you going to tell me your father had no victims? I heard the story, Liam!"

He looks at me, shocked.

"Why the hell are you defending her so much? Just because she was a witch too? This is ridiculous!" he yells, standing up.

179

"And why are you hating her so much?" I retort. "Look at this tree, look at what Sylviana was trying to show us! She knew Nephera wasn't her sister! Yet, she said otherwise, to the point even you thought so too! Why, if she did not consider her family herself?!"

Liam glances at the tree, upset.

"You're just looking for someone to blame for what happened to you," I say. "To Sylviana."

"You're talking as if you were there," he says. "You know nothing."

"I know I am a witch, and those sisters were too. Maybe their family mattered more to them than what happened."

We stare at each other like this for a long while, both angry and stubborn. I didn't expect that kind of reaction from him, but I didn't even know I'd react like this either. Why am I so affected by the sisters' story? Until now, every time it had been mentioned, I thought this wasn't of any concern to me, something that happened two years ago, when I hadn't even set foot in Silver City, wasn't related to me in any way.

So what has changed now? Why? Why am I reacting like this, to the point where I'm even fighting Liam about it? I was supposed to look for my name, so why do I care anyway? I need to stop doing this... I take a deep breath and step back, away from him. He seems to calm down too, shaking his head. A long silence comes between us, and now, it's awkward. I'm a bit ashamed of my reaction too, it was overboard...

"She... cried."

What is he talking about? I cross my arms but glance at him, unsure. His clear eye is still fixated on that portion of the wall, where the two witches have their names close to each other. Liam takes a deep breath.

"When... the battle was over. Sylviana cried for Nephera. I had forgotten that... until now."

That's a... strange detail to think about. Somehow, it makes me a bit relieved to hear that. I follow his gaze to the two little symbols. An ivy leaf and a water droplet, not that far from each other. I guess there really was that sister bond after all. Maybe that's why Sylviana hid that the two of them weren't actual sisters until the end... Whether she learned of it late or knew from the start, she chose to keep this lie alive until now.

"...Let's look for you," he sighs.

I nod, still a bit too embarrassed to say anything else. I guess that means this matter is closed. ...What about me, then? I keep looking around for a long while, checking one name after another. It's almost a headache to read so many female names at once. I start from the extremities and work my way up, again and again, checking each end of the tree, but there is no Mara and no Clarissa written anywhere here. Stubbornly, I keep checking, thinking I may have missed it. What the heck is going on? Sylviana's name almost popped out to my eyes, but I can't find mine? Liam keeps frowning too. We both scrutinize the hundreds of names on that tree until our eyes hurt, and I shake my head.

"There's something wrong with that tree," I sigh. "I am a witch. I should be here, so why...?"

Liam nods, but he has no answer either. Something here just doesn't make sense... There are hundreds of names on this tree, but the two of us checked all of them at least twice. Even if we are tired, I don't believe we would have missed it! What is that supposed to mean...? I glance back toward Sylviana and Nephera's names. They look a bit lonely, each at one end. I get closer, looking at the burn mark beneath Nephera. That poor child... She would have been a Fire Witch, just like me. I look on the other side of Nephera's name.

"According to this tree, her real mother's name was... Sadia. Ring any bells?" I ask Liam.

"No." He shakes his head. "I really didn't know anything aside from what Sylviana shared with me. She never even told me her mother's name until Nephera appeared and gave us the whole story."

Well, for once it sort of feels good to know I am not the only one being kept in the dark. ...Why hide this, though? Was she really trying to save Nephera from herself? What would have changed if Nephera didn't know about her real origins?

"I wonder what happened to Sadia, for Nephera to be in Danica's custody so young," I whisper.

I trace up their branches, and indeed, they are related, by an older witch, three or four generations before... one of the few to have her line split in two. So that witch had two daughters instead of one. I had noticed already, but it seems like most witches only had one daughter, not two or more. It seems rather unusual for them to have another girl... Did they have boys too, just not recorded on this tree? The witch Sylviana and Nephera have in common, something like their great-grandmother, was an Earth Witch named Beatrice. She had two daughters, the first one being a Water Witch, Sylviana's ancestor, and the next, a Fire Witch and Nephera's grandmother... I keep studying that tree. The cycle logic is still there, and aside from those two being cousins instead of sisters, nothing seems amiss. I feel a bit of pain as their branches stop there... and my name isn't anywhere to be found. What am I missing here? Where am I even supposed to be? What about my mother?

"Hey... Who was the witch of Silver City? Before Sylviana, I mean?" I ask.

Liam frowns, glancing at the tree.

"I... I don't know. I mean, I don't even think there was one?"

Really? I stare at that tree, but from the looks of it, it doesn't seem so. Even in this house, I have that gut feeling about it. I look around, and no matter what, it's way too old. Sylviana couldn't possibly have built it, it would look newer. Why would she have picked a house in the middle of a werewolf territory too? Moreover, the Witches' Ancestral Tree has been there for a very long time. Why would it be here, if it wasn't a witch who painted it in the first place?

"Wait..." whispers Liam, "Sylviana and Nephera did mention something like their ancestors being here, long ago... That's why they were sent here in the first place, their family has a history in Silver City."

So that's it. Probably Beatrice or one of her ancestors painted this. Somehow, her daughters must have left... It looks like witches aren't the best at sharing. If it's one witch per city as I heard, then... Beatrice's daughters probably parted ways as well? Did Danica figure her daughters couldn't co-exist without trouble either?

Even so, it doesn't tell us where I fit into that tree, though... I keep looking stubbornly at each of the tree's ends, looking for Mara or Clarissa, but after a while, I have to admit. I have seen hundreds of names, but there is none that matches. My neck and eyes even hurt from looking all around so much, and I'm a bit disappointed. Why does it feel like I'm missing something? Liam shrugs and goes to sit on one of the kitchen stools, probably having reached the same conclusion as me.

"So? You're not there. What now?"

"I wonder why," I sigh. "I'm younger than Sylviana... I should be there."

"She may not have known of your existence and simply didn't add you."

I frown, not happy with that explanation. It makes sense in a way, but not for a witch. If so, how would she have been able to complete all the other ends of the tree? Some of the branches are longer, meaning those witches at the end might be younger. Most probably live far, far away from here too. I have a hunch that what I am staring at is nothing ordinary, either. This tree probably doesn't wait for a witch to simply put in each name one by one, all by hand, to fill itself...

"Wait..."

I remember the herbology book Spark found in my room with the picture. According to the cycle, my mother had to be a Water Witch. What if the cycle went wrong somewhere? Could my name have been put under one of those disrupted spots, where the names were erased, like Nephera's daughter? It wouldn't make sense, though... That child was stillborn.

I bite my thumb, a bit annoyed. This is so frustrating! I count. From those who could possibly be in my generation, around twenty names are burnt or hidden somehow, with mothers being Earth or Water Witches. However, none of those ring a bell. How sad is it if I can't even recognize my own mother's name... I shake my head.

"This is..."

I take a few steps back and let myself fall on the couch, a bit disheartened.

It's still pouring outside, but somehow, my headache isn't as bad here. Is it because I'm in a witch's house? Is there some sort of protection going on against the elements? I close my eyes. The voices are leaving me alone here too, but I'm bummed enough to feel upset anyway.

"Mara, are you okay?"

I sigh and shake my head.

"No," I admit. "I... I'm dying to know who the hell I am, and every time I get the tiniest clue, it raises more questions than answers. Like this stupid tree, I get to learn about any witch I want but me. No one is helping me, I feel like I'm just sent left and right and no one who has any answers actually cares enough to give them."

I hear him move and get closer to me, making me a bit anxious. He's been avoiding me all along, is he fine with coming close now? I was fine as long as we were focused on that stupid tree, but hearing Liam come over here makes me all nervous again. I didn't even stop to think it was the two of us alone in this house... his ex's house.

"...How did you meet her?"

"Are you sure you want to know?"

I take a deep breath. Do I want to know? Somehow, I feel like my jealousy is still outweighed by my curiosity. I am probably some weird kind of masochist, to ask him about his ex. However, it feels like an itch that needs to be scratched, a band-aid that needs to be taken off for me to properly see how bad the injury is underneath.

"Yeah... As long as you spare me the saucy details, if there are any."

I hear him chuckle.

"Okay. I... I kind of met her at a low point in my life. My brothers protected me my whole life, and when they finally killed our father to have Damian become the King of Silver City, then–"

"So that story was true? About your... older brother killing your dad?"

"Yeah. As I told you earlier, he wasn't... Anyway, Damian really had no choice but to, it would have been him or us in any case. I was too young, though, so I was mostly kept out of it. I wanted to help, but I felt like the useless, weak younger brother. That's when I began wandering a lot in the streets of Silver City. I wanted to prove my strength to them, so I'd get into fights pretty often to show off."

"Let me guess, you got your ass kicked?"

"Only a couple of times. The... Purple Clan here has the best warriors, so they were my favorites to pick fights with. Although, they took me for a kid just playing, so they never really saw me as a threat or anything like our pack provoking them. A couple of times, though, I did go overboard and got my ass kicked for real. I was too proud to tell my brothers, so I would go off the grid until it healed."

"That's the dumbest idea I've ever heard..."

"I was a teenager. Moreover, wolves heal fast, as long as it's not too bad. Anyway, that time I did end up pretty badly injured, an older lady found me and took me to Sylviana to be healed."

"So they knew they had a witch here?"

"More or less. They thought she was some sort of... natural healer, something like that. She liked to take care of the kids in that neighborhood, so... Anyway, that's how I met her in the first place. From then, I'd come here sometimes, tell her about my brothers, all that anger I had in me that wouldn't go away. We were friends for a long time, but I was the one who..."

"You're saying you fell first?"

"Yeah... She was older and more mature, so I guess she saw me as a brat for a while."

I chuckle. From how I've seen him interact with his family, Liam is probably still in that younger brother spot he was. Although, he's definitely a man to me. I blush a bit, thinking about the bike ride that we shared earlier. Stop thinking about it, Mara, not the moment!

"So that's how..." I say.

"Yeah."

It's not the big *Romeo and Juliet* kind of romance story that I had imagined... although I can tell why he misses her so much. I wonder how things would have been different if... Sylviana had never been with him, or if I had arrived in Silver City earlier. I still don't really get what is going on between me and Liam.

Sometimes he will get close, like now, and sometimes, he pulls away. It's like there is no way either he or I can avoid this, but neither of us can easily accept it either. I wish I knew what's going on. Everything that happens, I fear a trick of my own mind, like the voices, something that isn't right. I don't know if our relationship is right, but I... like what I feel. It makes me want more.

"Your... role as a witch hunter. Did you start because of her too?"

"Yeah. I wanted to fill in that void, no matter how. I don't trust any witch, and I have seen what they are capable of. I don't want anyone to hurt my family again."

So even though he plays the loner, he is still watching out for them...

I'm a bit envious of that. My whole world is confined to an estranged sister, a lazy werewolf bodyguard, and a friend who isn't telling me the truth. The rest of this city is torn between seeing me as dangerous or crazy... I don't know how much more of that crap I can handle out there. At least here, I feel strangely calm. There's definitely something about this house that keeps me calm.

"So? What are you going to do next?" he asks.

I finally open my eyes, only to find him dangerously close. While I'm still lying on that sofa, Liam is next to me, sitting on the floor with his arms crossed. I frown a bit and look away, unable to endure that stare of his.

"I don't know. This was more or less my best lead until now... I still hope to find more, actually."

That's right, I'm not done searching here. Even if that tree was probably the biggest clue so far, I may have missed something else. I get back up on my feet and look around. The plants are definitely not my domain, but it can't be all there is around here. Even though my name isn't on that damn tree, I bet Sylviana left me some other clue, if she had any idea about my existence. Even if this wasn't about me, she ought to have known there would be another witch coming sooner or later. From what I learned until now, it seems like some sort of rule, but... why Silver City, anyway? If I wasn't related to the sisters in the first place, why would my past self have become obsessed with witches here?

I'll ignore the books, they are not telling me anything I need to know, from what I've seen. There has to be another clue somewhere. Liam watches me rummage around with a frown.

"So you're really not done."

"Liam Black, are you going to stay on your ass or help?"

He puts on a grumpy face, but I ignore him. This is something I must do for myself anyway. I take a deep breath and keep looking around. If only I had that magic circle thing to show me where to look, or even Spark. Now, I'm searching blindly with no idea what I am even supposed to look for...

Would Sylviana have used a magic circle as well? I don't see anything that could have been of use for that... I don't dare go upstairs; based on the layout of this house, it would be the bedroom. Although I'm doing my best to be open-minded, I am not ready to see the place where she and Liam had... whatever was going on.

"Have you ever seen her do actual magic?"

"Yes, but it depends on what you are looking for."

"Something like a magic circle?"

Liam frowns, looking a bit unsure, but he eventually shakes his head.

"No... Wait. She didn't have a circle, but she did use something like a map. Would that help?"

"A map?"

He gets up and goes upstairs; I don't follow him, though, and wait until he comes back, carrying something that looks like an oversized... painting? I am a bit confused until he lays it down on the floor. Wow... It's beautiful. This painting is entirely acrylic, with gentle colors. It takes me a few seconds to observe it and realize that it's... an actual representation of Silver City?

Chapter 14

I take my time to observe the map. It isn't as simple as an actual map, but if I look at all the details carefully enough, this is obviously some representation of Silver City. I recognize the forests, an apple-green area, and the sea, some indigo blue. Silver City is split into different colors and shapes too, like a wide circle. They are probably representing the different neighborhoods or werewolf territories? It would seem so; what I think could be the White Moon territory is a bright orange… Moreover, there are some figures and shapes that make it easier to figure it out.

The hospital, first, is represented by little squares, and I see the park I would occasionally be allowed to go to. It's like Sylviana picked some landmarks of the city and represented them as if she was seeing them through a magnifying glass. One big black rectangle must be a company headquarters, maybe the Black Corporation? I keep looking. Why did she pick those spots in particular? There are over twenty, including one little greenhouse that must be here, her house. So how do I figure out which ones are important?

I am tempted to try and burn that painting, to see if something stays behind like with the leaves, but there isn't any ivy on there, so it might be risky to assume this will be the same kind of system... My pyromaniac tendencies might cause trouble again. What, then?

"How did she use this?" I ask Liam, who has been observing me for a while.

We laid the map down on the floor for me to see it all, but while I'm on my knees and almost on all fours to try and decipher this, he is just standing on the side, arms crossed and looking at a loss.

"I don't know!" he says. "That thing was always hung in her room, I don't know if this is actually useful, or how... I know she did use it, though, she would add some important places as time went on."

"Like what?"

"Like the Sapphire Moon House from the former Blue Moon Clan, our company building, Selena's hideout in the forest, East Point Ground where Nora's powers appeared for the first time, that kind of stuff. The hospital, and the... the location of the war too."

Oh, I can see it. A big red zone in the northwest area… So that's where it happened? According to the scale of the city, it was a very wide area. No

wonder they all consider it a big war. Of course, she chose red to represent it...
It's kind of sad and depressing to think about. Probably not too useful either...
I spot something else too.

"This white mark, it has to be her magic tree."

Liam nods, although a bit sour.

"Yeah, that's right at the border and on the right spot too."

He comes to sit next to me on the floor, and once again, I feel that little
spark between us. Is it really just me? Whenever he's near, I feel like something
is waking up inside... His smell, mostly, drives me nuts. I never thought I was
particularly sensitive to smells, but it's like a conditioned response whenever
he's near. I keep staring, losing my mind for a second. I don't know how
ridiculous I am, staring at him and being struck like this, but I feel like if I don't
learn his facial features by heart, I'll be losing something. His straight jawline,
that eye between a gray and a blue sky, his thin lips...

"M-Mara?"

Crap, I really did end up staring! I'm so dumb... I feel like an idiot, and he
probably thinks I'm some weirdo too. With his strange attitude toward me, I
still can't tell how he feels about me, and this is not even the right place to think
about it! I shake my head and look at the map again, blushing and feeling dumb
as hell. The only thing that makes me feel a bit better is that I am pretty sure
Liam was blushing too...

"Alright," I say, clearing my throat a little, "help me out, I don't know this
city that much yet. There's a lot of stuff I don't recognize, you're the specialist
here. Anything else you can point out?"

We are both happy to change the topic to something else. For a while,
Liam helps me figure out what is what, and we try to understand why she
pinpointed those buildings in particular. As it turns out, a lot of them are
actually important buildings in the city overall, like the two hospitals, the
cemetery, a few parks, and buildings. Some are related to Nora or Selena and
the packs they were raised in too, or the Blacks Brothers' past like the cemetery
their mother lies in, or the docks his older brother apparently used to work at,
the same one we ate at for lunch...

"So you recognize everything," I sigh.

"Yep. I grew up here, Mara, what were you expecting?"

"Well, not something like a big cross pointing at some treasure, but still.
I don't know... If there was one you did not recognize it would have been the
next spot for me to look at."

"I see..."

He stares at the map again for a while. We are now both at a loss and
honestly, I don't even know what to say next. It's getting a bit uncomfortable,
and I'm upset to be left without a clue again. Suddenly, Liam points out two
locations with his fingers, making me confused.

"What?"

"Well, I do recognize everything, but these two are the ones I actually
don't really understand."

I frown, staring at the two locations.

"What do you mean?"

"All the other locations she put make sense for Sylviana to have pointed out. Like, she's been here before, it's related to her past with Nora, Selena, or me... but these two, I was actually surprised she painted them when we figured them out. This one is the North Cemetery. I don't recall her ever going there at all. That location is originally for Selena's clan, the northern werewolves. A lot of deceased people from the war are all there, that's why I know about it. Although, I don't know why she would have been there before, and if they are victims of the war, they were buried after Sylviana..."

He can't seem to say it, but I get it. So she never saw those people being buried there, which makes no sense as to why this place would be relevant to her.

"No one she knows is buried there...?"

"No... Only werewolves she was never close to, like Selena's adoptive parents. I think the only wolf she did know from the north was Selena's godmother, but she isn't buried there either..."

I check out the other spot.

"What about the docks? No link either?"

"Yeah," he says, shaking his head. "I mean, I can't figure that one out. It's more a thing of my past and my older brother's... I never took her there, to be honest, she wasn't a... cheeseburger kind of person."

"Vegetarian?"

"Vegan."

I bet. Liam keeps frowning.

"I thought it might be because I told her about my brother working there, but it makes less sense to her... less than any of the other spots."

So we do have two new leads... After a while, though, I'm somehow more intrigued by that cemetery situation. Why is there always something related to death lingering around...? That professor from the university mentioned something like necromancy, was Sylviana into that too?

I glimpse at the Witches' Ancestral tree again, at the burn mark after Nephera's name. Did her child even have a name for it to be erased? What about the others whose names disappeared from the tree? I suddenly realize something else. It looks like only the stillborn children are erased, as all witches whose name is a few branches above must have died by now too. If it was just the dead ones, most of those names would be gone, but only a few are erased.

"Oh, crap..."

I see Liam stand up, frowning, and looking toward the window. I stand up too, confused.

"What?"

"One of our wolves spotted something outside the barrier. I have to go."

"Wait, I'm coming with you," I say, walking to grab his jacket.

However, to my surprise, Liam comes and gently takes his jacket back from my hands, shaking his head. Our eyes meet and for a while, I feel that spark again, between us and down to my stomach... I see him gasp, and for a second there, I'm even more troubled. I didn't realize he had come that close to grab his jacket, and that space between us is full of something I can't describe.

"No," he suddenly says.

"Wait, what? Why not?"

He carefully steps back as one would back away from a dangerous tiger. He glances outside.

"It's still raining, Mara, at best, you're only going to get a new headache and come out for nothing. Even if there is something outside, it is not for you to deal with."

"How would you know?" I protest. "I'm a Fire Witch, I have plenty of firepower to defend myself!"

"Defend yourself against what? You know nothing about other witches, and if it's one of them, they have years of experience compared to a newbie like you! No, you stay here and wait."

I really don't like that, and I keep frowning as he leaves his jacket on the couch. Seriously? If he was going to leave it anyway, he could have left it to me! He even takes his shirt off, and I lose my attention for a while. His eyes follow my line of sight down to his abs, and he sighs.

"I'm going to shape-shift, Mara."

"Yeah?"

"So, would you mind, you know, not watching me undress?"

I blush and turn around, but despite the nice view from just then, I'm still not happy with his answer. I cross my arms, shaking my head while I hear him take off his pants.

"I still think I could very well come with you," I protest. "You're about to leave me alone. Is Selena fine with that?"

"Well, they are probably more fine with you being alone than me, to be honest, and Selena isn't my mom, my Alpha, or my caretaker. She can't spank me because I've been a bad boy."

Great, so I'm the only one she likes to give a good beating. Although, I bet Liam would shut up in front of his older brothers. I fight the urge to turn around while he keeps undressing.

"Still, I don't see the harm in coming with you. I can do well despite the headache..."

I suddenly feel a cold wind blowing in, and despite my blushing, turn around to check what's going on.

Damn it, that jerk is gone already! The entrance door is wide open, hence the damn wind, rain, and cold getting inside. I'm left with his pile of clothes on the floor, including his... oh, crap. At least he took a second to fold it a bit and push it to the side. I shake my head, annoyed. Damn it, he really ran away while I wasn't looking. Again. Shall I chase after that idiot? He's still pretty damn fast, and I have no idea where that stupid wolf boy went... He only said the border, that's rather vague. I should avoid being where I'm not supposed to be for a while too.

189

I sigh. Fine, but now, I'm left alone here and I don't know what to do. I've already studied the map so much, I feel like I could repaint it myself, although I am pretty sure I wouldn't have Sylviana's talent... I grab Liam's jacket to wrap myself in and fall on the big couch again. This time, I am facing that gigantic tree, my feet on the couch, and my arms around my knees, observing it one more time. What were you trying to tell me...? I keep staring at it for a long time as if something was going to happen. Nothing changes. I'm alone in a big, silent house, left to stare at this painting like a clueless idiot. No, I gotta do something. Nothing will happen this way, right?

Come on, Mara, don't stay on your ass. I get up and go to look around the kitchen, searching the cabinets for I don't know what. I find some cutlery, dishes, and that the water is still running, but my progress is zero. I sigh and walk over to get down on my knees and face the map again. It can't be a simple map. I am sure I missed something and it annoys me. So what now?

I light the fire in my hand, but nothing happens yet. If only I had my cat! I bet Spark would have found the trick long ago. I am surprised I couldn't find a magic circle. Unless...

The city is sort of shaped like a circle. It isn't regular, but it is still sort of a closed shape. Moreover, it isn't just a painting, it is on a thicker kind of fabric, something I can step on without damaging it. I ought to try. I put my cup down and run to the kitchen to grab a knife and return to that map. I take my shoes off and, with a deep breath, knife in hand, I step inside Silver City to sit. Nothing happens, but at least, I know what is the next step to try.

I use the knife to stab my finger, deep enough for some blood to appear. I hope I'm not doing something crazy, but I bleed on the map.

Damn, the colors are really changing, I knew it! It takes a few seconds, but instead of simply staining that map, the red drops run to different locations. What the heck is that supposed to mean...? One stops right on the cemetery, and a second one on the docks, I was almost expecting it. So Liam's hunch was right. What's next...? I follow three more drops, but one stays right here, on the spot of Sylviana's house. Is it because I'm there? The drops keep rolling around that spot, pretty useless.

"...Show me where Liam Black is," I say.

Immediately, they change directions, making me smile, satisfied. Damn, this thing is just amazing. The drops run straight toward the north, and they suddenly slow down but are still heading toward the north. So Liam is probably running there, and that is his position. Now I know where the idiot went. However, one of the drops goes ahead to stand on a different spot. What is that supposed to be? It's moving too. The other witch, outside? I glance at the tree. According to that thing, I have some blood in common with all the other witches anyway.

So now I know where he is headed. I hesitate a bit, but my decision is made quickly. I look around and find a bag to fold the map inside, along with that knife. I take several pictures of the Witches' Ancestral Tree with my phone, and like a good girl, I even quickly text Kelsi about where I'm going.

His Blazing Witch

Better than having half the local population of werewolves looking for me... I don't wait for a reply, though, and put my shoes back on to go outside.

It's still raining, but I have Liam's jacket on and his helmet in hand. I suddenly come face to face with his bike.

...It can't be that complicated to drive, right?

I am not sure what's come over me. Liam left his bike here, his keys, and I can't forget that sensation from earlier. It was thrilling. That sensation of absolute freedom, the wind fighting us, and the power of the engine running anyway, stronger and faster. I just want to try again, and I have a once-in-a-lifetime opportunity, waiting right outside that door.

I am playing with the keys in my hands, but now that I'm facing the beast, I can't help but weigh how wrong this could go... I have seen him start that bike, I can tell how it basically works. It's still theft, though, right? I take a deep breath and start by putting the helmet on. It feels a bit heavier, but I feel more legitimate once I have it covering my head. I keep Liam's jacket on, and I try to act normal. Not that I'm afraid anyone's going to call me out for riding this thing.

There is no one out in this kind of weather. The storm is getting worse above my head. I see lightning strike a bit further away, and although it looked okay from Sylviana's house, the downpour really isn't showing any sign of stopping soon.

The headache is back.

I wish I could pretend it isn't and I'm fine, but it's still there, pounding and painful. As if to remind me this is dangerous and I don't know what I am doing... I take a deep breath and get on the bike, mimicking Liam's gestures to the best of my abilities. Up until I turn the engine on and get the bike roaring, I am actually doing pretty good. I could get used to this sound... I take another deep breath and put both hands on the handles, determined. You can do this, Mara.

It takes me a couple of tries where the bike almost runs away without me, but after a few uneasy attempts, I get the hang of it. A little pressure and I get the engine purring like a kitten and ready to take me wherever I want. Could I possibly have a knack for this? That would be awesome... however, I don't have time for fun. I need to get to this bike's owner. Liam is always so adamant about leaving and staying away from me, but I am fed up with it this time.

I shyly start the bike and get farther away from Sylviana's house. I am thankful for the clues she left me, but somehow, I know my heart isn't there. I have Liam's current position stuck in my mind, and I know I gotta go there. I have no idea what is waiting for me, but I just know I need to get to wherever he is. He left so fast, and I still have a lot of questions. The ones at the top of my list are actually about our relationship, so...

I finally dare accelerate a little once I recognize some of the buildings of the White Moon Clan. Selena's territory, basically. I keep heading north. A few crazy people still outside glance at me with curious eyes, but I ignore them. I just want to find one werewolf, I don't care much for the others who are starting to follow me.

Driving a bike is even more amazing than I had thought. It follows my every move, ready to take any direction or turn at my demand, and feeling my weight merging with the motorbike is simply amazing. I enjoy this ride, careful of my surroundings. I can't afford to kill anyone, I think. Moreover, although I have a rough idea thanks to the map, I need to find that location by myself... It's easier than I thought, but not in a good way.

I can't describe that feeling, it's like something is constantly pulling me toward Liam. I'm not even aware of it sometimes, but it's like a knife, planted deep inside my heart. An aching pain, whenever he ignores me or leaves. Does it make any sense for me to fall for a stranger? Who supposedly hates me, nevertheless. I don't get it. I don't understand why I'm always craving his presence, looking for him subconsciously, and even worse, always able to tell where he is. Moreover, I can't help but think he feels the same. Why else would he always be around whenever something happens to me? He is strangely caring toward me for someone who so often tries to avoid me.

I follow my instincts and that pull until I get back into the familiar part of the territory. One bonus to riding a bike is that, with a helmet and a leather jacket on, no one can recognize me. People glance at the shiny engine, but they don't care much about who's driving it. Moreover, in this rain, the few pedestrians I see are just running to find shelter from the rain or get to their destination quickly.

I really like gloomy, rainy Silver City. For someone so sensitive to rain, I'm strangely fine with the downpour. My headache is still there, but it's not a pulsating pain like before, just a slow one. I can manage just fine, and I have other priorities too. I keep going, past the northern territory, until I find the border. Thankfully, I feel it right before I hit it. I suddenly hit the brakes, and the bike stops right there.

I almost forgot about that damn thing. If only there was a way for me to get past it! I know Liam is out there, and it's horribly frustrating that I can't get to him. What do I do now?

I keep telling myself I need to sort things out. I'm aware of how hot-headed I am, but this time, I need to find the solution without burning myself. I take off the helmet and leave it with the bike. Keeping his jacket to hide the keys in, I get closer to the barrier. I can feel it, as if some electric tension was stopping me. It's somehow... weak. Weaker than next to the tree. Is it because it's farther from the source? Or someone weakened this area? I decide to walk alongside it, looking for some sort of weak spot. I remember feeling it was weaker in some parts when Nora showed it to me, and if the overall wall is even weaker here...

Bingo.

I find one spot where I can barely feel anything. It's tiny, but there's definitely some hole here... Is this what that witch was looking for to try and sneak in? I check it with my arm first, and it goes through. It's like pushing into something buttery, there's a slight resistance, but nothing I can't take.

I slowly squeeze myself in, fighting a bit. I don't want to enlarge the loophole, but it requires some strength for me to push my way out. I almost get on all fours since I have to crouch so low.

Once I'm finally out, I get up, a bit tired. It must have looked ridiculous from the outside, seeing me crouch and squeeze myself through some invisible wall. Even now, everything probably looks normal to most people. Seriously, I wish she had added some sort of door to this. With a "no visitors allowed" kind of sign, even...

I don't have time to lose. I'm not supposed to be out, and I still haven't found Liam. I run into the forest. I have no idea where I'm going, but somehow, I have no issue finding my way in. It's like some strange instinct, telling me which area to avoid, which path to take. Like a mute, quiet voice inside guiding me. It's nice, but I have no idea how to deal with all these new feelings; I'll add them to the list...

I suddenly slow down. I hear something on the side, and growling too. I feel more movements, like branches shaking suddenly, and bushes and the ground being hit violently. I hold my breath and get closer, trying to stay as silent as possible. I can recognize Liam's wolf growling, but nothing about whoever he is fighting!

"Oh, who do we have here...? The baby witch..."

I stiffen and glare at wherever the voice came from.

To my surprise, a woman suddenly steps out, looking completely unafraid and staring right at me. Her clothes are dirty, probably from the fight with Liam, but she has that cunning smile on... Overall, she's really pretty. Her long, brown hair is braided over her shoulder, and she's wearing a long, sleeveless tunic with a unique patterned design. She has a mix of Caucasian and Hispanic features and skin color, but her heavy makeup blurs my guesses.

She smiles wide with her brown-colored lips.

"Who are you?" I ask, defiant.

"One of your sisters, of course! Little witch, did no one teach you anything? You look so lost..."

What the heck is she saying now? I don't like her manners or how she acts. She looks out of it, with her arms moving around and her strange mannerism.

Suddenly, Liam jumps out of the bushes, still in his wolf form. He briefly growls at me but comes right away to stand between me and that woman. While he only growled softly at me, most likely annoyed by my presence, he is furiously threatening that witch. I frown at his muddy paws and the injury on his shoulder. He looks furious and not in good shape. The witch loses her smile a bit, seeing us together.

"Oh dear, did that wolf already get to your head? Don't let them corrupt you! Werewolves are known to use witches to their hearts' content..."

"What are you talking about?" I ask, a bit baffled.

"Long ago, us witches used werewolves as allies to protect us. Despite our magic, we are still women, physically weak. So, we'd use werewolves to help us stay away from the greed of men. Yet, the werewolves are now allying with humans and getting greedy as well! I had no idea this city was taken, but... you work for the werewolves, don't you?"

I frown. Is this city taken? Does she think I am Silver City's... official witch? I am not sure what I am supposed to say.

"I don't work for the werewolves," I retort. "I've only worked for myself so far."

"Oh... So how did you make this one so attached to you? He looks like he's protecting you like they protect their fated mates! Witches can't be a werewolf's fated mate, so... did you compel him to do this? You don't look like a Dark Witch, though... No, you're too green for that, aren't you, dear?"

What the heck is that woman talking about now? Fated mates? What's that? I've heard werewolves talk about mates and all, but the way she says it, I feel like I missed a chapter. About that Dark Witch thing too. The way she says those words do not match the little bits of information Liam gave me. I glance down at the black werewolf.

What did he hide from me? There are some things I just don't understand, and this woman doesn't look like she's about to cause me any harm either. I am a bit... lost. She notices and smiles a bit more.

"You've never been properly trained, have you? I can see it, you have that spark in your eyes, that little flame all young witches have that says you have no idea what you are doing... Shall I teach you, darling?"

Liam growls even more at her, not fond of that proposal. I'm a bit confused, all of a sudden. She is definitely weird, but I can't feel any ill intent from that woman toward me. I have to tell myself she was still fighting Liam until minutes ago because I can't tell from her words and actions.

She tilts her head.

"Little lady, you look a bit lost. Is that really your home city?"

"Yes, and how about you leave it alone!"

I don't have as much spite as I tried to make it sound. I am a bit confused, and she doesn't even seem upset at my answer. She crosses her arms, gauging me with an amused look.

"You're a feisty one. A Fire Witch, aren't you? You are all always so hot-headed. However, you'll get burned if you don't learn how to really play with fire, darling. All witches need training, and you don't seem like a trained one."

I frown and light my fire in my hands to show her. I'm getting annoyed with all her nagging and belittling me. I may not have been trained by a witch, but she'll be the burnt one if she keeps insulting me. I raise my arms, the fire dancing in my hands with some deep red flames. She raises an eyebrow.

"Impressive..." she whispers. "Still, mastering your element is only the beginning, young lady."

She does something with her fingers, agitating them like someone would play air piano, and suddenly, big roots emerge from the ground. She has them mimic her finger movements, and I have to admit, I am impressed. She can really master those at a level I am far from... I'm still at the stage of not trying to injure anyone. I must have let my emotions show because she chuckles.

"You're cute," she says. "I was glad to have finally found a city, but it turns out it's not witch-less, just wrongly taken care of. Shall I teach you, then? Who is your mother?"

"...I don't know," I admit.

She suddenly loses her smile, and the roots fall down to the ground.

"...You don't know?" she repeats. "Interesting... Although, that explains why you're roaming around like a child and playing with fire. Well, I am Ravena, daughter of Cathleya. Do you at least have a name?"

"...Mara."

Maybe I shouldn't have given her that, but I had a glimpse of hope that this woman might know something, and react to it. She simply nods.

"Well, Mara, I am an Earth Witch, but a wiser and older one than you are. I won't pursue this city any longer... if you properly claim it."

"How do I do that?"

"Learn your powers. Assert your dominance over the wolves, and... keep greedy ladies like me at bay. I don't mind killing a wolf or two, but I am not really desperate to steal from a child. Earth Witches like me are not the confrontational type, but some of our sisters are. Like the two other ones roaming around here..."

I frown. So there are other witches looking to get into Silver City, as Liam said! Damn it... Ravena chuckles, shaking her head.

"So interesting. You're really lost, aren't you? You can't even sense them?"

I feel a bit ashamed, but I can't. I can't figure out who the other two witches are, or where the hell they are. I don't like knowing we have two enemies hidden around here, waiting for the right time to attack. Ravena shrugs.

"Oh, well. I will probably stay around a little while longer then. I don't like fighting, but maybe I won't have to if you guys kill each other first."

Wow, talk about not being confrontational, this one sounds more like some vulture! I glance down at Liam, but he is still growling furiously, probably not giving a damn about whatever that witch says.

"...Why aren't you even trying? You even offered to teach me," I ask.

"Witches are selfish, but we also have strong maternal instincts. We are not as many as we once were, either. It is a bit of our duty to protect the little ones like you... especially when it looks like they are in trouble. This city is crowded with wolves, isn't it? I can tell. We can't have a little witch get killed by werewolves, it would be a loss for us."

"So you're only fine with me dying as long as you guys do the job?" I mutter, a bit annoyed at these weird witch rules.

Ravena hesitates for a second, but she smiles.

"Sort of? Well, it's better than dying by the fangs of werewolves. Personally, I don't like those dogs, considering they betrayed us long ago. You should be thankful you met me before you met the other two. They wouldn't have let you or that dog go back alive. I just happen to be the laziest and weakest of the three. I am not interested enough in a city infested with werewolves to dispute it with a Fire Witch."

I realize she's probably aware that, as untrained as I am, I'm still probably stronger than she is as a Fire Witch. She would be at an obvious disadvantage, fighting both me and Liam. So her giving up is not just about goodwill, but she is also smart enough to not provoke me. Maybe her little talk from earlier was also to test if I would be able and willing to fight back or not...

"Anyway," she continues, "I'll stay around to watch. You can just come back here and call me if you're interested in a lesson. It won't be free, though. And please, spare me the dog next time. This one is feisty, territorial, and annoying."

I glance down at Liam. I can't say she is wrong about any of that... Ravena's words are stuck in my head. Liam and I have some serious talking to do. I watch her go, still full of confidence, and as she glances down at Liam with a sneer, he suddenly starts growling.

"Hey!"

I see him about to jump at her, and I try to hold him back without thinking. He reacts immediately to my hand on his fur, but not in a good way. He bites me.

Chapter 15

The pain is somewhat worse than I would have thought, but not as much as the shock. I keep staring at my bleeding hand, the bite mark pretty deep. I glare at Liam, but the black wolf already looks sorry, whimpering a bit and retreating.

"Seriously?!"

"See? Werewolves can never be trusted."

I glare at Ravena too. Why is she not freaking gone already? Seeing her sneer at this situation infuriates me, and I light up my valid hand with a big flaring fire without warning. Her expression immediately drops, her fear painted all over her face. So this is what it's like to be the advantageous witch.

"Fuck off," I hiss.

She doesn't wait for me to ask a second time. Maybe she knows that bite was destined for her, but she suddenly loses all of that confidence and she runs off into the woods, disappearing in seconds. I agitate my hand to get my fire to stop, and it's rather easy with the downpour around us.

I'm left with a bleeding hand and a sorry wolf, his tail between his legs and his ears down. It doesn't change anything, I'm still fucking mad at him for that. Why the hell did he have to bite me? It's so damn painful too, he didn't even hold himself back! As if I needed any more injuries! I hold my hand, shaking because of the pain. I can't take the sight of Liam right now. I glare once more at him and walk away.

I came here to fucking help him, and this is what I get! Alright, maybe there was some selfish curiosity in the mix, but still! I walk away, furious, drenched, and in pain. Is it supposed to hurt this damn much? I don't even know how to stop the bleeding, and I'm feeling dizzy from seeing this much blood. I never got that with the burns, but apparently, blood just isn't my thing, or maybe because it's mine.

Moreover, it's muddy around here, and I progress with difficulty back to Silver City. I shouldn't have left the house, I shouldn't have crossed through the border, and I shouldn't have followed that idiot. I'm an idiot, Selena had everything right when she called me clueless and reckless. I fucking am.

"Mara! Mara, wait!"

I don't stop.

I'm too mad at that idiot. Plus, he's apparently shape-shifted so he's following me naked. Probably not the best time to look back. I don't want to look at him; right now, I just want to see someone who could do something about me losing blood.

"Mara!"

I feel his hand grabbing my shoulder, and I finally turn around to push him away.

Damn it, he's really naked, and I'm just too angry to even care. I just glare at him, holding my injured hand against me. His eyes are going back and forth between my injury and my face, looking at a loss. Even if I can tell he's really sorry, the pain is just too much to forgive that puppy face he's making.

"S-sorry," he mutters. "I reacted without thinking, I didn't really mean to bite you..."

"Well, so much for being cautious," I retort. "If you didn't want me here, a growl would have been enough!"

"I'm sorry, but you shouldn't have been here in the first place! How the fuck did you get past the barrier?"

His eye is reflecting the storm and thunder above us, and now there's anger mixed with his apology. Seriously, he's going to lecture me too?

"Why is everybody always so keen to tell me what I can and cannot do, but no one gives me an actual answer? I have to threaten people into telling me what I need to know, and now that I finally meet someone like me, you're going to give me hell too?"

"That witch isn't your friend, Mara! She isn't going to become one, she's the enemy!"

"Well, at least she didn't fucking bite me!"

My last sentence hits him hard, he loses his anger again and takes a step back. I frown and turn around, continuing my way back to Silver City. I get to the barrier, so I guess he'll have his answer this way. I find that hole from before and, cautious with my injury, I squeeze myself back in with a groan. That thing is fluctuating and presses down on me a bit for the five or ten seconds it takes for me to get back inside the dome. It doesn't stop me, though, and I stand a few steps away from the barrier, glaring at a shocked Liam.

"How did you...? Hey, what the fuck did you do with my bike?!" he yells, recognizing the gorgeous machine a few steps away.

I forgot I had left it there. I wish I could show him, ride his own bike away, and leave him to eat my dust, but I can't, not with my hand in this state. Instead, I look around to find shelter. I'm surprised the voices aren't back, but maybe Liam's presence is keeping them at bay. Or maybe I'm just in too much pain already for them to add to it.

It's a residential area, but I spot a little convenience store. I walk in, looking for something for my injury, and mostly, to be sheltered from this cold rain.

"Mara!"

I stop and turn around. Don't tell me that idiot walked in naked?

He's naked indeed, but only from his waist up. I frown, completely confused. When and where did he find a pair of jeans to put on? Liam follows my glance down to his pants and sighs.

"Werewolves shape-shift at the border all the time, we have several hideouts with clothes... just in case."

No wonder. I guess that would be the most convenient for a city inhabited by thousands of werewolves. There are probably hundreds of pairs of jeans hidden in random spots in the forest. It's a bit weird to think about, but it does make sense. Anyway, I am a bit more upset that he can now follow me without getting glared at by the lady at the counter. I take a deep breath and walk away anyway, still looking for the pharmacy aisle or something like that.

I finally find it, but they only have band-aids... I keep looking up and down. Damn it. Should I drop by the hospital and ask Bonnie? Crap, she's probably still at Nora's. I bite my thumb, at a loss for what to do.

I can hear Liam walking up to me, but I pretend I don't.

"Mara..."

"What?" I retort, a bit annoyed.

"I'm really sorry... about the bite. Okay?"

I finally look at him.

He's dangerously close, and with that sad puppy look again. His eye is bluer under the convenience store's light, throwing me off guard for a second. I am not sure what to do or say anymore... Is he doing this on purpose? My angry heart is at a loss. I don't wanna stay mad at this face, but the pain is still there. Not the one aching from my hand, the one in my heart. Did that idiot realize the damage he's done?

Being so close, I can see the drops running down his skin, the shades of his wet hair, and hear his breathing. It's a bit... confusing. His smell is driving me crazy too. That, mixed with the leather of his jacket I'm still wearing. We must be one weird duo, standing alone in this convenience store, him half-naked and me with my oversized biker jacket and a white tube top. I swallow my saliva, trying to focus.

"F-... fine," I mutter.

I don't want to look at him, he's confusing me. The sparks are back again, and it's worse, it's a whole firework in my stomach. I feel hot, more than even a Fire Witch should be. I glance back at the shelves, wondering why those aisles have to be so damn narrow all of a sudden...

"I just... reacted out of surprise. We are not entirely in control, sometimes, when we shape-shift into our wolf form."

Is he trying to justify himself? I'm not sure he's making his case better. I slowly nod, still unable to look at him, and holding my hand with no idea what to do with the injury. I feel a bit helpless. I feel like I'm going to melt if I look at him, but I don't want my anger to go away so simply. It hurts and he should regret it some more, I think. I just don't feel like letting that idiot off the hook so easily.

"Come," he whispers.

That whisper sends shivers down my spine, and before I can react, he gently takes my hand.

Oh, crap, he's making those eyes again. There are some fleeting seconds between us, we stare at each other like two idiots waiting for the other to react. Maybe I should whack him or something, but I can't, and I don't. He gently pulls on my non-injured hand and takes me to another aisle of the convenience store. He grabs something from the shelves, but even when we get to the cashier, I can't take my eyes off him. Damn it, he's a bit more handsome than I can handle. The rain and sweat combo is damn dangerous.

We leave the store, still hand in hand, and we find ourselves against the wall, the downpour a step away. I glare at the gray skies. Is there only that kind of weather in this city? I feel like Silver City is mocking me, getting so damn dark every time I am in a bad mood or confused. Right now, it doesn't quite match my emotions, though. Liam's large hand is still on mine, and the heat and size difference is perturbing. His fingers are cold, yet they still manage to send shivers down my spine. I'm probably blushing too, but I can't take my eyes off our joined hands, like an idiot.

"Okay... Wait for me. I'll go get the bike."

"Okay."

With a feeling of déjà vu, I watch him run away under the rain to get his bike. I let out a long sigh as soon as he's gone. You should get your feelings in check, Mara, before you really regret it. Yeah, as if I could hold them back. I can't stop my feelings any more than I can stop the rain from falling. I look up at the skies, a bit at a loss.

The worst thing is that little, tiny bit of hope that Liam is actually feeling the same. It's confusing, the way he looks at me sometimes. As if he's scared, but still cares more. I can't quite name it. I get this itch that I'm eager to follow, yet I feel like it's on the crazy and dangerous side. I'm barely pulling the few pieces of my life I have back together, yet Liam is like a headlight right in my field of vision, distracting me from everything else when he's there. Moreover, I'm even questioning my attraction to that guy. It was so sudden yet so intense, how is that even possible?

I hear the sound of the bike's familiar engine.

Liam is riding his bike, half-naked in the rain, and I'm on the verge of collapse from that vision. That is not something any male-attracted being can ever forget. ...Damn, is it even legal to be that sexy? I have to force myself to look elsewhere before this gets any more embarrassing.

Strangely, I've never felt more self-conscious than I am now. I'm waiting for him on the side, not looking like anything decent or attractive. I don't even want to imagine the mess my hair must be in with all that rain, plus my clothes are drenched, muddy, and bloody. I kind of wish I had put on something a bit more attractive or learned the first thing about makeup.

He stops the engine, but somehow, my feet can't seem to get me there.

I don't know what holds me back, but all of a sudden, I'm scared. Scared that this is just temporary, that he's just being nice before he throws me away to go back to playing the little werewolf soldier, the righteous vigilante.

"Mara, come on!"

I mentally kick myself in the ass and walk up to him, swallowing whatever was holding me back. Without a word, I sit behind him, but I try not to touch that naked torso, holding the back handle of the bike with one hand. Yet, he doesn't start it and turns to me.

"Mara, hold on to me."

"No."

The answer escaped my lips before I could give it enough thought. Liam stares at me, a bit surprised. With what's going on above our heads, it feels a bit more awkward than it should. He opens his mouth, then closes it, distraught. His eyes fall on my injured hand, and finally, he frowns.

"Mara, hold on to me, otherwise, you'll hurt yourself or fall off."

"I'm good."

He growls, a bit annoyed. I still avoid looking at him, my hands resolutely nowhere near him. I am such an idiot. As if avoiding him now was going to change anything!

Moreover, I should know better than to play with that idiot. All of a sudden, he makes the engine roar and drives off without warning. The start is so sudden I indeed almost fall off, and by reflex, I grab his waist. Damn it. I take a deep breath and swallow my pride, finally holding on properly. I should avoid touching him, but the only way to not touch my injured hand is if I hold on to my wrist, and that leaves very little space between me and Liam's back. I blush a bit more, the heat getting to my head quickly. Damn it, he got the last word this time.

He rides off, and I do my best to focus on something other than his skin, his smell, the movement of his back in front of me. Neither of us has a helmet on this time, but it's a short ride, and Liam is good. He takes the highway, speeding a bit between the cars, and we are soon back to Silver City's high buildings. I'm glad I kept that map with me, it looks like we are not going back to Sylviana's house. The rainy afternoon has the roads crowded, but we slide in between the cars, Liam making the engine roar from time to time so the cars let us through.

I wonder if we are going back to Nora's, but it doesn't look that way. Liam takes us deeper into the busy streets, between fancier buildings. I have flashes of seeing those buildings before, from my hospital bedroom window.

Liam suddenly rides down to an underground parking lot, and I get off his bike almost as soon as he's parked. I feel a bit guilty when I see the leather of his bike, stained by my blood. He sees it too, but doesn't say a word, and gestures for us to walk to the elevator. I hesitate a bit but follow him inside.

He pushes a button to one of the highest floors, and an awkward silence surrounds us. It feels even more cramped than in the convenience store. I realize he still got that plastic bag from his little shopping earlier. Now I'm curious about what he bought. Not bandages, that's for sure.

The elevator stops, and unlike I thought, we arrive directly at the entrance of a very large apartment. Liam walks ahead, but I freeze.

"This is..."

Liam stops and turns around to stare at me, confused at the entrance. He shrugs.

"Yeah, it's my place. Uh..."

He seems to suddenly realize he's bringing a girl into his place, from his expression. Sometimes he's really clueless like this, and it kind of hurts. He doesn't even see me as a woman? Just as my stomach gets knotted from that unhappy thought, I suddenly notice his ears are a bit red. Oh, so he's... blushing? At least, he looks too embarrassed now to look at me. I tilt my head.

"Why not the hospital?"

"I thought you hated hospitals."

"Oh... thanks."

He's not wrong. I'm in no hurry to go back there again. Does that mean he can treat my injury here? I see him walk off to another room, so I carefully step into the living area, a bit curious.

This is somewhat larger than I thought, and a lot cleaner too. I don't know why, I imagined him living in a garage or a little studio, something smaller. He doesn't look the fancy type... but then again, his family is rather rich. Moreover, as I look around, it doesn't really look like anyone lives here. There are family pictures on the walls, of his brothers, their wives and his nephews and nieces, but aside from that, nothing shows Liam actually lives here. The whole place is sparkling clean, and... somewhat cold. Even with his jacket on, I can tell it's cold in here. I look around until I find the lights to turn them on. It's so dark outside, I have to guess we are now in the late afternoon or something. It's hard to tell, the sky is super gray and dark. Strangely, it looks like all of Silver City has turned into its name's color from here. I get closer to the large bay window, curious. There's a balcony, but it's flooded.

"Mara."

I turn around. Liam is back with an impressively big first aid kit. I raise an eyebrow.

"Wow. You dated a nurse too? Or robbed a hospital?"

He rolls his eyes with a smirk, visibly relieved to hear me joke. He puts the box on the table and invites me to come sit next to him on the sofa. I take a deep breath.

"Are you sure inviting a witch over is a good idea?"

That's probably the dumbest question I've ever asked, but I do have an underlying question. Is he fine having *me* over, of all people? Liam sighs.

"You don't like the hospital, and as you noticed, I have robbed a hospital. It may sound extremely surprising but werewolves are used to treating werewolves bites. And..."

This time, he looks at me, his eyes darken, more serious than before.

202

His Blazing Witch

"Yes, I am fine with having you here," he whispers gently.

Chapter 16

A wave of relief comes over me after hearing those words. I don't know if I was waiting for some confirmation, but now that I have it, it feels so much better to be sitting next to him.

We are still staring at each other, but this time, there's no awkwardness, no embarrassment. Only a bit of shyness, and the mutual feeling that we are alright being here together. Liam gives me a weak smile and grabs the box to pull it closer, breaking our eye contact first.

I don't take my eyes off him.

He didn't lie when he said werewolves know how to treat bites... I watch him as he carefully takes care of my injury. He cleans the dried blood with a wipe, disinfects it, checks how deep it is, and carefully applies some sort of balm over the little holes. I can tell he's done this a few times before. I frown as he applies some gel; that stuff stings. Liam notices my grimace and makes an apologetic expression.

"Sorry, I know this one isn't too nice, but it's efficient."

"You're speaking from experience?"

"Yeah... You're not the first victim of a temperamental werewolf."

I can tell he knows exactly what he's talking about.

Liam is still half-naked, and under the lights, I see the thin lines of some old scars. It wasn't too visible under the rain and dark clouds, but now, I can clearly distinguish the whiter lines on his body. There's a lot, it's even covering a very simple black moon tattoo he's got on his chest. The black moon tattoo looks old and its original shape is damaged from all the scars covering it... I can't take my eyes off of it. A lot of them look like animal bites, but... some seem worse and with a different shape, like he was stabbed with a sword or something. The most impressive one is on his flank, and there's another one a bit below his other arm.

"...Did you get those during the war?" I ask.

He slowly nods.

Once again, that war is like a dark shadow over all the inhabitants of Silver City. His blind eye too... Even if its movements are almost normal, the white layer over the blue-gray color cannot be missed. The scar over it as well. I realize I can stare at Liam for so long because he doesn't know I am. From the way we are sitting, I'm in his blind spot. It's a bit shameful, so I get self-conscious and look down at my hand on the table.

He gently blows on the gel covering my injury for it to dry. The movement of his lips throws me for a loop again. I need to stop staring at them, it's dangerous. I'm getting hot and I don't know if this is something I can contain.

"Alright..." he says.

He grabs some bandages, and gently takes my hand, wrapping it slowly and carefully. The movement of his fingers around my hand is driving me nuts. He's just touching my hand, but every time he does, it sends more of those amazing sparks into my soul, and this warmth spreads fast. I want to smile, jump, scream, do something to let the excitement out. I'll go crazy, at this rate. Yet, I love this. A new kind of fire is about to burn every time our skin touches, and it's strangely addicting.

I let him finish, my throat terribly dry. I even try to focus on the little bit of pain left because I need something to cool down my imagination. I'm always on edge, wondering if I'm crazy, or if I can hope, even just a little. It's very strange. I am not sure of anyone since I woke up, yet Liam is there, eclipsing everyone else, and I'm irresistibly pulled toward him.

"Does it still hurt?"

When he suddenly looks up at me, I almost jump, like an idiot. I nod, even though it's a lie. That damn bite still hurts despite the medication and all the bandages. He smiles a bit, looking a little relieved.

"Good. I'm really... sorry, Mara. But I told you, werewolves can be really dangerous. When we are mad and about to attack, aside from our peers, we're a bit... on edge with everyone."

"I get it, but... I didn't really think before holding you back, either. I just didn't want you to attack her."

He frowns.

"Mara, Ravena isn't going to help you," he says, standing up to walk to the kitchen.

I stand up and follow him, unable to remain seated and wait. It's a big kitchen, but the only thing Liam seems to use is the microwave... and the kettle, which he's now filling with tap water. I'm about to cross my arms when I remember my injury. I sigh.

"I'm a big girl, I'm not going to trust her out of the blue just because she's a witch..."

"It's not just about that. She may use you to get into Silver City. By the way, how did you...?"

"The border? It's full of holes, and getting weaker too. I just found one I could slip through."

Liam looks more shocked than I thought he would. Doesn't he already know this? He makes a sour expression and glares at the boiling kettle for a few seconds. After a while, though, he seems to calm down by himself.

"I see."

That's all he says, and the silence invades the room again. A bit at a loss, I watch him take the shopping bag and take out some big plastic cups. Instant ramen? I chuckle, but I'm hungry, I'd eat anything. Moreover, there isn't just one, but five cups, and he took the biggest ones too. I watch him pour water in all of them before putting the lids back on. ...Is he seriously going to eat all that?

He sees my confused expression and chuckles.

"Sorry, werewolf appetite. I got one for you, though. I mean, two even, if you're hungry..."

He looks a bit unsure and nervous now, but it's my turn to chuckle.

"Witch stomachs are pretty normal, I'd say. I'm good with one, as long as you leave me the spiciest noodles."

"Deal."

We both chuckle after that, and I sit up on the kitchen counter, waiting for our noodles to be ready. It doesn't smell really tasty yet, but as we're waiting like idiots in front of the cups, I realize I am a bit hungry. I glance toward Liam again. He looks tired, but judging from the glances he keeps sending at the time on the stove, he's hungrier.

A few more seconds pass, but once again, I'm a bit too impatient. I have so many questions, as usual, and... I don't like the awkward atmosphere when we are not talking.

"Liam... What was Ravena talking about earlier?" I ask. "I know about mates, but... she said something about witches can't be... fated mates. What does that mean?"

Liam suddenly stares at me, looking a bit more shocked than necessary. Did I say something wrong? The way he's staring at me, he looks really... shaken up, so much so that I almost regret my question, and worry about something gone wrong instead. After a while, he averts his eyes, as if he couldn't look at me. I'm... even more confused now. I see him run his fingers through his hair, looking a bit unsure.

"It's... It kind of bothers me too."

"How so?"

Still avoiding my eyes, he glances outside. The dark skies are turning darker as the night starts to fall. I hadn't realized how late it is now, but we had a busy day indeed, with the search at Sylviana's house and those rides through Silver City. Liam sighs a bit, with an expression I can't decipher. I wish I could get into his head like those voices in mine and see what's going on. What he thinks, where his mind is at. After some more long seconds, he goes to one of the drawers to grab some chopsticks and comes back to put them between us on the counter. He leans against the kitchen counter and starts playing with one of the bamboo sticks between his fingers. ...Isn't he going to put on a T-shirt at all?

"It's a... werewolf thing," he sighs.

"I'm all ears," I reply, not letting him off the hook.

Liam finally glances at me, but I'm not dumb. He either says too much or not enough, and we're getting to the bottom of it. He makes a bit of a sour expression before opening his mouth again.

"In... the werewolf culture, we all abide by the belief that the Moon Goddess oversees everything going on in our lives. She... decides our ranks, how strong and healthy we are at birth, stuff like that. The most important thing for us is the mates' bond, though."

"It's when two werewolves get together as a couple, right?"

"It doesn't have to be... two werewolves, but yes. We consider that when we have found our lifetime partner, we have to bond with them, to mark them."

"Mark them?"

He nods and taps his nape with his finger.

"Yeah, here. We bite them while we are... mating."

Oh, wow. I take a second to take that information in, hoping I'm not blushing as much as I think I am.

"A bit... savage."

He chuckles.

"A little bit. However, a marking is sacred to werewolves. There is no turning back once it's done, so... better get it right the first time, because it's also the last."

It does sound like a lifetime thing. If they bite each other the same way Liam bit me, on purpose and in such a place, it probably doesn't disappear easily... It must be freaking painful too, better not get it wrong. I can't help but think it's still a bit... gruesome.

"What if the mate isn't a werewolf?"

"We usually mark them too, it's a bit of a territorial thing, but they don't really need to mark us back. A werewolf will be faithful to the mate he or she has marked anyway."

I slowly nod. I do remember seeing those distinct bite markings on some werewolves we've met... Not that I was staring at those areas in particular, but it's a rather visible spot, not really hidden or anything. Especially for men, as I guess female werewolves have theirs covered by their long hair. I didn't think it had such a deep meaning until now, though. I unconsciously touch my own neck, caressing the naked area of my nape. I wonder why they picked such an area to bite their partners. I still think it ought to be rather painful...

"So... what about this fated mate's thing?"

Liam clenches his fingers a bit more, almost breaking the bamboo stick between his fingers. The younger Black brother looks a bit tense, and even more unable to look my way. Once again, my heartbeat accelerates, making me worry about what he has to say about this.

"It's something a bit more... instinctive. Since we are young, we are told that the Moon Goddess has chosen someone for us, our fated person who is supposed to be our perfect mate. Our fated mate."

For a second, I feel the strange need to laugh nervously, but all I can do is grimace. ...Is there really such a thing? I mean, the mating thing is already a bit alien to me, but this is on a different level. Liam sighs.

"It's real," he says, as if he was reading my mind. "We have some sort of... special instinct that allows us to feel who our fated mate is."

"Like a radar?" I ask, confused.

He chuckles nervously and shakes his head.

"No, it's... it's something a bit deeper than that. It's like some... bundle of feelings that come all at once and grips you from the inside. You just know, when you see them, that this person is for you. It's a higher form of attraction, a pull you can't resist. It's... It gives you everything you imagined and worse. Sparks every time you touch that person, crazy feelings about wanting to be with them, yet wanting to run away."

...Now that sounds familiar. A bit too familiar, actually...

"It... sounds like you have felt that..." I mutter with a blank voice.

My head is ringing like crazy, and my heart even more.

Why does everything he's talking about perfectly reflect what I've been feeling for him all this time? I don't get it. I'm not imagining this, am I? It's not just my own expectation? The spark, the push and pull, that desire to see him again... I don't think I would have explained it differently, but hearing it from Liam's mouth is worse. I'm going nuts and in an absolute panic right now from the way he described it. Should I tell him? And would he believe me anyway? I can't even breathe normally, I feel like crying and screaming. I'm not a werewolf, so just... how? And why? Why the hell would I feel that fated bond thing?

I see him slowly nod. I'm glad he's avoiding my eyes right now because I can't contain my emotions and I'm probably not hiding them well either.

"I... I've been feeling that way for a little while now," he admits.

Oh, gosh, Moon Goddess or whatever, this is it. If she is the one deciding this thing, it has to be reciprocated, right? I suddenly stand up and back away, a bit at a loss.

"Mara?" he calls me, surprised.

I shake my head, and cross my arms around me, careful of my injury as if to protect myself. I shake my head as if everything was normal, as if I just needed to take a walk. The window. I need some fresh air. I walk over to see what part I can open, even if it lets some rain in. I need to breathe or I'll just suffocate and break down right here. I hear him come behind me, but I don't turn around. I can't face him yet.

"How... how can you be sure?" I ask, almost gasping for air.

"I... I just know, Mara, it's not really something you can ignore. To be honest, I... I already knew what it's supposed to feel like. Both of my older brothers experienced it already, so they told me about it."

"With their wives?"

"Well, yes and no... Nora was Damian's fated mate. It was a bit different for Selena and Nate."

I nod, but I don't need the details right now. I guess it's not exactly always a highway to getting with your perfect person or something. It just can't be that simple. Yet, here I am, walking in circles, alone in a room with a guy who could be my... fated mate. Gosh, even to me it sounds absolutely crazy. I'm not a werewolf, it doesn't work that way. Even Ravena said it. I can't decide to go back to the table or look at him, so I just take deep breaths in front of the window.

"Mara, are you alright?"

"What if you don't want it?" I ask. "What if... you're paired with some bitch, someone you hate, or someone you can't date? I don't know, someone super old, or... someone you can't love."

"...A fated bond can be rejected."

So that's it. He can just... reject this, refuse it? Ignore those feelings, throw them away like some dirtbag? If so, why... why wouldn't he have done that already? I'm in a state of panic and confusion I can't describe. Fear crawls into my mind like another shadow I don't need. What if Liam rejects me? Or what if he's just been testing me all along, waiting to see if he should throw me away or not?

If he's feeling like I do, why didn't he tell me earlier? He could have said something, but instead, he kept pushing me away, avoiding me. And now, does that mean he only cares because of that stupid bond thing? Is he chained by it, unable to deny this? Maybe he doesn't feel it, I'm the one making a scene for nothing and getting all worked up. I keep thinking of so many scenarios, and the more I do, the more frightened I am. I feel like something is crumbling inside, someone is... whimpering. I try to ignore that sound in my head, like some wounded animal, but it just echoes my heart perfectly.

I don't feel well. I'm a bit dizzy, and I need to do something about it. I take one last deep breath, and I turn to him.

"Is it me? Your fated mate, is it me?"

In other circumstances, that shocked expression of his may have been funny, but I don't feel like laughing at all right now. My heart is about to burst or collaps, I don't know. It's just thumping like crazy. I turn around to face him, to see when he will answer me, but now, I'm regretting it a bit. The answer doesn't come, Liam just stares at me with that dumbfounded expression. I know what that means, though. I nod, shocked despite what I already knew.

"So I was right... I'm your fated mate," I mutter.

"H-how do you..."

"Sorry to break it to you, but you just made it kind of obvious, on top of everything else," I chuckle nervously. "Come on, you appearing at random times when I was in a bad position? Patronizing me, trying to run away from me, yet always being around somehow? What does it sound like to you?"

He closes his eyes and runs his fingers through his hair, a bit at a loss. I can't blame him, I'm not too comfortable having this discussion either. I feel like we're jumping too many steps at once, going from a walk to one crazy sprint. Like we're about to hit a wall. It's all going a bit too fast for me, hence my erratic heartbeat and dizziness. I'm not feeling well, and I'm crazy with the fear he might... reject me. Because that's what it all comes down to. I don't want Liam to reject me, and I'm scared I've just flipped a switch I'm going to regret flipping. Once again, I spoke without thinking twice. I've just thrown my own feelings out into the open... If this is what I'm feeling now for him, what will it feel like when he rejects me?

He massages his eyes for a brief moment, and finally, lets out a long sigh.

"Yeah, that's... right. You're... my fated mate," he says.

Even if I was almost fully sure, I still feel a little bit relieved to hear that. Thank the Moon Goddess I'm not the crazy one... I nod slowly, but that leaves one big question between us. I'm not really sure how to ask, but Liam actually speaks first.

"Mara, I didn't mean to hide it from you, but it's... it was too sudden for me. I didn't know how to deal with it, and..."

"Why didn't you just reject me?"

My question seems to shock him. He raises his eyebrows and crosses his arms.

"Why? Did you expect me to reject you?"

"...Sorta," I mumble.

He stares at me as if he is trying to understand the mess I am inside. It's hard to justify myself and every question I ask, but I really need to. I don't want more secrets, I'd rather have it all out in the open and face the pain. I don't think I've ever doubted myself this much before, but faced with the idea that Liam might reject me, I'm... petrified. It leaves too much uncertainty, and I don't want to be focusing all of my feelings on a guy I barely know just because some unknown entity made us infatuated with each other.

Liam takes a deep breath and clears his throat a bit.

"Alright, I'll admit, I did think of... rejecting you."

Wow, just hearing that hurts a bit too much... I nod. I had expected that much, at least. He would have definitely been lying if he said he didn't consider it. Some amnesiac witch, hot-tempered and dangerous at times? Yeah, I'd probably consider the emergency exit too.

I want to step back, away from him, but he actually steps forward before I do.

"But... I don't want to regret doing that," he resumes. "Mara, I've seen both of my brothers go through the whole thing. I know it's not easy, but... I also know it can be pretty damn good if it works out. Even before I met Sylviana, I always thought I'd make an effort if I met my fated mate. Among werewolves, it's a really, really rare thing to happen. Those who do meet their fated one have the luck a hundred others only dream of having. I'd be an asshole if I didn't even consider that much."

"Still," I say, "it's not like you won the lottery. I'm not exactly the best... girlfriend material."

He chuckles and tilts his head.

"Mara, to begin with, we barely know each other. And you barely know yourself. That's the other reason I decided not to reject you. The Moon Goddess... She does things for a reason. I believe Nora and Damian found each other because they really needed that person. I... Yes, I know it's one surprising match that you're my fated mate. Still, I don't want to be that douchebag who says no before he has any idea who his partner is. Maybe... maybe there's a reason we don't know yet. Sure, you're not exactly who I imagined. The reason I considered rejecting the bond is that you're a witch, we don't know the first thing about you, and honestly, you're a piece of work when you're stubborn."

Yep, that's all of me in one sentence... At least I can't say he's not being honest with me. I wrap my arms around myself once again, waiting for the rest of it. I can't decipher his expression right now. His voice is surprisingly gentle, but this whole time, he's barely looked at me. Although, his feet do draw him closer, one step at a time.

"But... I'm fine with... trying to get to know you."

I raise my eyes. Seriously? I wouldn't have blamed him if he had decided to reject me after this conversation... After we both came clean with what the hell is going on with our feelings.

"I know it's not even that big of a deal because you can't feel the fated bond thing, but..."

I breathe in and bite my thumb, a bit embarrassed.

"Yeah, uh... Liam, about that..."

"What?" he asks, frowning.

"I think I... feel it too," I confess.

He pauses for a second, a bit surprised, before chuckling nervously.

"You can't, Mara, even if you're a witch. It's a werewolf thing. It's not..."

"I'm serious, Liam. The whole... sparks, the pull, the heart beating crazy and wanting you very strongly regardless of whether you're actually there or not. I may not... feel it with the same intensity as you do, but... I swear I've felt that way since we met too."

Liam shakes his head with a rictus.

"No, you can't. If it was the case, you'd have felt me when I was—"

"In the nightclub," I say. "The night I met Selena and her husband. You were there, right?"

He doesn't answer, but he doesn't need to. This time, he knows I'm not kidding. He stands there, frowning and opening and closing his mouth, at a loss. I sigh. Yeah, I guess I should have... said something, maybe earlier.

"Until you described it earlier, I really didn't know what it was," I explain. "I've just been feeling that way since I saw you that night, and ever since, every time you're near, I get that crazy pull toward you. That's why I followed you, at the university, and even this afternoon, to the border. I know it's not... in your rules that a witch feels these things too, but I do, okay? I really do."

Liam remains speechless for a few seconds. I guess he really had no idea. Is there really no record of a witch being a fated mate before? It can't be that surprising. Even if Ravena said so, my bond with Liam shows they were all wrong... or there's something wrong with me. Which would only add another thing to the long list, but...

"It's not possible," he suddenly says. "No witch has ever been able to feel the mate bond, Mara. I didn't know it was possible to happen with... a werewolf and a witch to begin with."

"Why not? It happens to human and werewolf couples, no?"

"It's not the same! Werewolves and witches are natural enemies. It's like... I don't know, the food chain. Werewolves fight vampires, vampires bite humans, humans hunt witches, witches–"

"Kill werewolves?" I snicker. "Sorry to disappoint you, but I think Sylviana already wrecked that previous-century logic of yours. I don't know how it happened, if the Moon Goddess drank too much or what, but this is what things are at the moment. I am your fated mate, and... as far as I can tell, you're... mine. It comes as a pair anyway, so..."

"It isn't that simple, Mara. It changes a few things," he mutters, frowning.

He looks almost upset now, but I don't really get it. We just confirmed I feel the same thing as he does, right? I don't understand his problem, and it annoys me a little. For once, things are becoming a bit clearer, but Liam looks unhappy with it while I'm still nervous about being rejected, like an idiot. Suddenly, I get it.

"It means I can reject you too, then?" I ask.

His eyes go wide, and I know I just hit the mark. I chuckle a bit nervously. Seriously? I cross my arms, a bit amused by his reaction.

"So that's it? Because I can reject you, is this what upsets you?"

He frowns, really unhappy this time. His eyes have taken the color of the storm outside once again. He steps closer, but he doesn't intimidate me, not in a scary way when he's half-naked like this. I stand up to him, raising an eyebrow.

"This isn't a game, Mara. The fated bond pairing is something sacred to werewolves. All of us want it, everyone wants to experience that just once. I've seen both my brothers lose their ground and go crazy because they had lost their fated mates, okay? You can't play with that."

I sigh.

"Liam, you're the one who said you considered rejecting me just seconds ago. Right? Well then, isn't this crueler? You get to decide if we keep this bond or not, but I wouldn't even have been aware of you tossing me away? I'm glad I get this thing too. Sacred or not, I'm glad I get the choice too. Now you can't reject me just like that."

"You don't know what happens to a rejected one, Mara. It feels–"

"I don't want to know how that feels because I don't want to be rejected!" I yell, stepping forward and closer to him. "Liam, I literally have no one. Everyone around me has an interest in being my friend or my family. There is no one I can really trust, but I get this thing with you, and this is the most real feeling I've been able to experience so far. I don't want to lose it. I don't want to lose you, I don't want to lose this thing we have together. I don't care if it's artificial, I don't care who put it there and why. I want it. I want someone to whom I feel attached to, someone who has real feelings for me."

Our faces are so close right now, but I don't care anymore. I have a mix of crazy emotions guiding me, making me tremble and tear up. I'm glad I could form the words and say them out loud. I can see his facial features from this close, betraying his messed up feelings. I see a hint of fear in his eyes, but also something warmer, something that grips my entire being. His lips are half-open, and his breathing erratic.

"I have... real feelings for you," he whispers.

"...Good."

That's all my tiny voice could utter after that. We are both staring at each other from really close, and what should be awkward feels strangely... inviting. I see him glance down at my lips, and then look away. I know he wants to, but won't. Liam swallows, taking one step back with a bit of an embarrassed expression, and those cute red ears.

I'm about to retreat too, but... my heart doesn't take that well. In a split second, a million things go through my head. Is that it? Is this all? What next? Are we going to be awkward like this from now on? Why doesn't he? Why don't I?

"Oh, damn it..."

I take a deep breath and grab his neck, pulling him toward me, and kiss him.

It was so sudden, our lips collided a bit too brutally, but what comes next is much smoother. As if that was all he needed, Liam starts kissing me back, avidly. I put my hand around his neck as if he was already mine, reaching out for his large shoulder. I had never realized how hot his skin is, but I like it. I feel his arms wrap around me, pulling me closer, caressing the skin on my back. I feel my fire inside almost purring from this kiss, as if it was spreading gently throughout my whole body. It doesn't feel like some wildfire I have to tame, but some embers slowly radiating from my chest, gently warming up everything.

Liam's lips are intense to follow, he doesn't stop. I feel pulled toward him, wanting more of his embrace, more of those savage lips on mine. I can't believe I started this kiss when he's the one being so restless. I barely catch any air, kiss after kiss. His hands still on my back, he keeps me trapped there, and for a long while, nothing can be heard but the rain outside and the two of us, making out passionately.

I know it's silly, I know it's risky. We barely know each other, and we are just pulled toward each other like two magnets charged by desire, a desire neither of us can control. But Moon Goddess, I don't care. I just want to enjoy every second of his lips on mine. I want to learn the taste of his kisses, the way he touches me, and how he frowns cutely while we kiss. I can almost hear his growling, his voice getting deeper as he takes pleasure in our lips. There's something animalistic about this, but it just feels so good to go along with our instinct. I don't care if I'm human or witch, woman, wolf, or feline. I just want this, want him. Liam's lips on mine, our bodies against each other. His warmth melting into mine, and his fingers caressing me.

After what seems like forever, our lips naturally slow down. We are not even out of breath, just a bit dizzy. After one last long, slow to part kiss, we both exhale, still in each other's embrace. Liam gently puts his forehead against mine. I chuckle.

"...Interesting."

"...You're welcome," he sighs, making me smile some more.

I wrap my arms around his neck and put my head against his shoulder. I don't want to let go of him, not yet. Liam must feel the same, because I feel his arms hugging me tight, and his lips against my nape.

"...I really like your smell," he mutters. "It's unique."

"...What do I smell like?"

"Some... chimney fire," he says after a few seconds, "or burning wood. ...And like rain, a little bit."

I nod. It does sound nice, but I have no idea... I find myself wondering what a werewolf's environment feels like. It must be a crazy world every time they enter a new room... I'm a bit jealous. I suddenly think of something.

"...No cheeseburger smell?"

"...Yeah, maybe that too."

I chuckle. Of course, he'd like that one. We slowly put some space between each other, but I can't take my eyes off him. I may be simply imagining this because of our kiss just now, but... I feel like his eyes are more on the blue side now, and have a bit of a softer look in them. A little wave of nostalgia hits me for no reason. I extend my arm to caress his cheek, and he smiles, looking down.

"Alright... Should we try the ramen before they get super soggy?"

Damn that werewolf stomach...

I can't stop staring at Liam while he's eating. It's almost scary to think my lips were against that mouth just minutes ago. I know he was hungry, but this feels almost dangerous to watch... I'm chewing my chopsticks, almost not feeling like eating myself. Not that I had any doubt he would eat all of the ramen, but still, he's eating them scary fast while I'm still here trying to take my time. It looks like I won't need to, he'll be done before me.

Somehow, I wasn't really prepared for what comes after a kiss like that. I thought it might be awkward, but now, it's almost as if nothing happened. Liam is back to his usual self, a bit more relaxed maybe. I'm sitting on the kitchen counter next to him, only a couple of feet away, but I can't stop sending glances his way. What are we now? Where are we at? It's a bit too soon to be, like... a couple, right? I sigh. We should have cleared the air earlier. Now I feel like asking a thousand questions while he's completely absorbed by the ramen.

I keep reliving our kiss, and I feel my heart swoon every time. It was really... nice. Not like a professional kiss like in those movies I watched with Kelsi, but simpler, more... realistic. Something that isn't perfect, but still felt crazy good. I wonder how much that fated mates thing blurs our judgment. What would have happened if I wasn't Liam's mate? Maybe he would have kicked me out of Silver City already. Would I still have these feelings for him?

...Why do I have them in the first place? Liam seemed absolutely sure it's impossible for witches. I would have thought he was simply wrong if it wasn't for Ravena saying the same thing. So why? Why me? I sigh and stare outside. It's still one hell of a downpour outside. Silver City is one of those cities that doesn't do things half-assed. It's either gorgeous weather or some crazy ugly downpour outside. I hear the storm breaking again, and I see some lightning far in the distance. His nephews probably didn't get to play very long outside...

"Are you done?"

Surprised by his voice, I turn back, and he's pointing at my half-empty cup of noodles in my hands. Liam is done eating his, but judging from his expression, he didn't ask out of concern for me. I frown.

"No, I'm not done. Let me eat my ramen, you glutton."

"Sorry... I had to watch you eat lunch, so..."

"You could have eaten if you weren't so stubborn."

He chuckles and leans forward, putting his elbow down on the kitchen counter to stare at me from up close. Damn, now he's going to be all I can see when I close my eyes again...

"Fine, fine, finish your ramen. I'm full anyway."

I frown. Why the hell did he ask if he was full already? I watch him throw away all his empty cups while I hurry to finish mine. There's unfairness in this world to see a guy with abs like that eat like he does every day without blinking. What the hell are werewolf stomachs made of?

Liam walks over here, making me all flustered again. He's not going to steal it, is he? I frown a bit and hurry to slurp the last of those noodles, leaving the soup. I'm stuffed already and I don't want to risk throwing up in front of him...

Yet, he's getting close, a bit too close for my poor heart to handle. Shouldn't I have developed a little immunity after that kiss? I mean, I touched those abs, that torso, but it's still so... hot. I gasp a bit as Liam walks up to me with a little smile. He finally puts his hands right next to my knees, one on each side, and faces me with a faint smile.

"So? What else is on your list?"

"M-my list?"

"Of crazy things to do?" he says, tilting his head. "You've gone through the barrier, got into a witch's house... I feel like there's more coming. I am not going to get bored with you, am I?"

"Probably not..." I mutter, my voice slightly raspier than usual.

I take a deep breath, looking around. Damn, this place feels... big and empty, with the two of us facing each other like this, so close.

"So this is your place?" I ask, a pitiful way to change the topic.

"Yeah... My brothers bought it for me, though. I don't really like to use it now, since I didn't actually... pay for it."

"I know what that feels like..."

I'm in such a similar situation, it's easy for me to relate. I still don't really get what my sister meant by buying me my own place either. Is this their way of looking after us, of keeping control over our lives? I wonder... I don't really like it, though. I mean, the place is nice, but it's not like I paid a cent for it. Even this place. Liam doesn't really... fit in here, and I understand why he hasn't been really using it, aside from microwaving food and crashing on rainy nights.

I glance outside. It's not like we will be able to go out anytime soon, either. The downpour doesn't slow down, and the storm seems to be coming our way. I'm surprised my headache has subsided. Probably because I'm inside a building and behind double-pane windows. Perhaps because I'm very distracted from the pain too...

"...I keep wondering how you can possibly feel the bond," suddenly whispers Liam.

I turn back to him, surprised. His eyes take me a bit by surprise. He's close, a bit too close... I need to stop myself from staring at those lips and close my mouth.

"What?"

"You're not a werewolf," he mutters. "I mean, we would know, even complete stranger werewolves can feel each other, we recognize our kind. Yet, you're my mate, and there's... something odd about you."

"Thanks... How odd, exactly?"

He frowns, coming a bit closer, making me even more self-conscious. I almost regret asking now... He sighs, shaking his head.

"I don't know. There's something strangely familiar. Werewolves have an aura, some sort of... halo. It lets us know who is friendly, who is dangerous. Our statuses, like, Alphas have scary auras, and Betas have a much less... menacing one."

"Oh... Like your brothers?"

He looks surprised for a second.

"My brothers?"

"Yeah," I nod. "When I saw them, earlier, they had that... scary dark halo around them. If it wasn't for Nora and Selena being next to them, I don't think I could have approached. It looks like some dark cloud, right?"

Liam stays speechless for a few seconds, making me realize there's something wrong again. I bite my thumb.

"...You're going to tell me I shouldn't be able to see that either?"

He slowly shakes his head.

Oh, crap... I gasp. Another thing not normal to add to the list? I feel the headache coming back. I try to relive that morning, remembering what I saw... what I experienced. I take a deep breath, and Liam suddenly grabs my hand.

"Mara, calm down. Explain to me what you felt, okay? And then we'll try to sort it out."

I nod, and trying to be as precise as possible, I detail everything. How I felt the first time I saw Bonnie, and how his brothers, Nora, and Selena felt different to me. The whole thing, my senses, the halo, all of it. Liam listens to me, without expressing anything. He does frown from time to time, but not in a too-shocked way, which I appreciate. I'm tired of feeling like an alien and realizing I experience more than I should is kind of disturbing enough in itself. Liam gently rubs the back of my hand the whole time, which both calms me down and excites me. Yet, I need to stay focused.

"...Like snow?" he repeats.

"Yeah... I don't know, like something very soothing and quiet. Nora's aura is really special... I don't know about the whole... Royal thing, but I can see what you mean. She's different."

"No, I think you're right, but you even see it... differently from what werewolves experience. It's like you feel the auras, not the wolf behind it. It's curious. I mean, it makes sense you can't feel our wolves, but... our auras?"

"But, I thought Sylviana could feel them too?"

Liam shakes his head.

"No, not that way. She just had a good instinct about it, as most witches should, but you... you experience the auras. It's different from what I've seen until now..."

"Another thing to add to the Mara is a weirdo list, then..." I sigh.

Liam shakes his head, and suddenly pulls himself a bit closer. This time, his waist is truly between my legs, and he puts his hand on my cheek, making me burn at that very place instantly.

"You're not weird, okay? You're just... out of the boxes we know."

"...That's a really nice way to put it, but let's be real, I'm a new kind of freak."

"We will sort it out, alright? Didn't you get some clues already today?"

I nod. I can definitely use some of his optimism. Sylviana's house did give me some new leads... First, I need to dive into that genealogy thing again. I feel like I missed an answer there, and that map thing, as well. I just used it quickly to find Liam, but now that it's with me, I know I can do more. I have a hundred questions to ask those magic circles, and there's going to be a proper answer coming sooner or later. There has to be.

However, I don't say a word about the magic circles to Liam. I won't tell anyone... for now. I feel like I should be careful about everything and everyone. It's a bit sad, but even right now, when we are so close, I can still feel that wall between us. Something that won't allow us to completely give in and trust each other. Liam smiles gently, and I smile back too. I'm glad we got it sorted, but I don't want to be naive. I'm still a witch, a clueless witch with a lot of questions.

"So, uh..."

This time, he's the one to glance outside, and I'm a bit confused for a minute.

"I guess you're sleeping here?"

I chuckle. Is it me or is he the one being nervous this time? Not that I'm gloating, I do feel a bit... shy about the idea of sleeping here as well. I glance around, and his hands go around me, circling my waist without being too intrusive.

"...Do you have a guest room?" I ask, my throat a bit more hoarse than I wanted it.

Liam hesitates, but then, he slowly nods.

"Yes, I do... if you want to use it."

Oh, Moon Goddess mother, I'm in trouble. He's making those eyes again, and I'd rather be outside in the storm than have to face that from... up close. I know he is tempting. He's half-naked and basically offering me to share his bed, which is probably a whole new definition of temptation. I take a deep breath. Do I want to use the guest room? I know I'm the one who... initiated that kiss, but Liam brought the passion without a second thought. I don't know where my heart is at the moment, and I don't even know about my body. Maybe I'm not even a virgin? Gosh, what kind of crap am I thinking about now? Liam chuckles.

"You're cute when you're thinking deeply, but I haven't heard your answer yet."

"Is it alright if we... sleep, like sleep together?"

I put a clear emphasis on the sleeping, indicating which kind of sleeping I'm talking about. He frowns a bit. Is he disappointed or trying to figure out my cryptic question? I bite my thumb, nervous, but he clicks his tongue and grabs my wrist to make me stop.

"You mean... just sleep?" he asks.

"Just sleep... but together," I nod, feeling damn embarrassed already.

He stays silent for a minute, and my heart goes nuts. It's not bad that I don't want to have sex with him right away, no? I mean, we technically just kissed so far, and the previous time, we'd been playing push and pull on an edge so... I don't consider myself a nun, but seriously, even my own body is akin to a stranger to me. Seeing that he's staying silent, I lose patience and slap his shoulder.

"Say something!"

"I'm just considering if I can reasonably tame the wolf or not," he finally says, cracking up.

"Not funny, Liam!"

Yet, that idiot is laughing, and suddenly, he comes to give me a quick peck on the lips. I stupidly smile a bit, despite still being a bit mad at him.

"Alright, it's a pajama party in my bed then. I promise I'll be a good boy. Anyway, you can burn my ass if I don't, right?"

He said that with a smile, I can't help but chuckle and nod too. True, there's always the bad witch option, although I'd like to spare him that. He probably doesn't heal from burns as fast as I do... I get a bit of my confidence back, seeing that he's back to his playful self again, and this time, I'm the one to kiss him back, making this a bit longer and enjoyable. I hear him chuckle against my lips, and his fingers get to my tube top... I push him with a frown.

"Hey!"

"Sorry, Mara, but you really shouldn't play with fire if you can't handle the heat..."

The red gets to my cheeks super fast, and I push him away again, a bit annoyed that he's making fun of me. He's laughing while I jump down from the kitchen counter.

"I'm going to take a shower now if you're done teasing me..."

"Second door on your left, tiger."

"Tiger?"

He shrugs.

"I don't know, that came up first."

Well... I don't hate it. Although I'm still a bit mad, I give him another peck on the lips, just to have the last one, and run off to his bathroom. It's a nice bathroom... and I'm in a hurry to close the door behind me. Moon Goddess, what's going on with me? The mirror takes up half of the wall, and I see my reflection, all flustered and a bit out of breath. Is it still me, acting boldly like this? I touch my cheeks, they feel hotter than ever. I'm going a bit crazy, aren't I? Is it the bond thing making me like this, or just half-naked Liam playing on my twenty-year-old hormones? I need a cold shower...

I leave my clothes on the floor and hop in the shower. I'm dirty as hell, now that I think about it. Sweat, mud, plus the smell of gasoline and cheeseburger... How the hell does he feel like kissing me? I don't go easy on the shampoo and soap, but damn, it feels so good to take a cold shower... I think my temperature is crazier than usual because of that idiot. No matter what, I can't calm down. Easy, Mara. But still, I'm taking a shower at Liam Black's place! Moreover, about to sleep with him as well. How the hell did I even get here...?

I step out of the shower, only to realize I have nothing to change into. A bit embarrassing... I grab the largest towel I can find, noticing it smells like him... not that it bothers me. Quickly putting just my panties back on, I wrap myself in the towel, take a deep breath, and leave the bathroom, trying to not look like I'm panicking about walking around half-naked...

The main room is empty, and our cups are gone from the kitchen counter too. I look around. This place is big, but there aren't that many rooms, actually. I finally find him in the master bedroom, looking in his wardrobe. And he's still half-naked, of course. Is that a werewolf thing? I barely step inside before I have to open my arms to receive some clothes.

"Here."

I look at what he just threw at me, and frown. The top is a simple short-sleeved shirt, but he also gave me a large sweater, and the dark pants look like some huge sweatpants.

"I'm going to be too hot in this," I shake my head.

"Maybe, but if you don't put those on, I'm probably going to be the one who is too hot..." he sighs.

His eyes are on me, and go down to check out my exposed legs, then back up again to my cleavage. Alright, the towel is definitely still too freaking short on both ends. I gulp. Okay, I guess that means I'd better get dressed quickly now before the beast takes over...

I let out a long sigh. It's only been a couple of minutes since I put on the oversized gym clothes or whatever this is, and I'm too hot already. I shake my head.

"This is ridiculous."

"Agreed," he mutters, checking me out from head to toe. "How is it that this looks cute on you?"

I roll my eyes, but I know he's joking a bit. I walk over to push him, a bit annoyed, and he plays back, pushing me so I fall on his bed.

"Good girl," he says, pointing a finger at me. "Stay."

"Seriously?" I raise an eyebrow.

He laughs.

"Don't worry, I'll take a shower, and turn the heat down so you don't get sick or whatever."

"Fine... Can I borrow your phone? I just want to text Kelsi."

"Oh, you can take this one."

He throws the latest smartphone at me. Seriously? He's got such a good phone and he just leaves it in a drawer in an apartment he barely uses? Liam quickly leaves the room, but I don't even have to ask for his password, there isn't one. This thing looks brand new, he really mustn't use it often... I guess their whole mind-linking thing is much simpler to use from one wolf to another, but still. Thankfully, Kelsi's number is super easy to remember... I quickly text her about sleeping elsewhere, that I'm fine, but I don't give any more details. For all I know, my sister could very well be paying for her phone too...

I wonder what Amy would say about me staying at a boy's place, sleeping in his... bed. Now I've just realized I'm already lying in Liam Black's bed. Not that he seems to use it often. I turn to lie on my back, looking around. There isn't much. A super large wardrobe, a mirror, and two bedside tables. Plus this very large bed, all in a dark blue. It's comfortable, but it seems a bit big, even for two. It's like twice the size of my hospital bed.

I hear the shower running, meaning Liam just got in. I'm feeling strangely calm, being in here alone. Perhaps the sound of the rain against the windows soothes me, instead of giving me a headache for once... A bit curious and bored, I quietly check inside the drawer of his bedside table. There's a magazine, but nothing too spicy, just some luxury magazine with only brand items. It feels like this could have been left here as part of the home staging or something. I turn the pages, not really understanding how some people can be that beautiful. Liam could be in these pages... while I'm just here, with my half-wet, messy hair and boring proportions.

His Blazing Witch

I pause on a page for some perfume. I don't care much about the brand or the picture, but the Asian model feels strangely familiar. Yeah, that girl looks a lot like... Kelsi...

I sit up, staring at the page until my eyes hurt. It can't be Kelsi, can it? Seriously, it looks a lot like her, but that girl has a ton of makeup on, bold colors too. I can't tell. I grab the page and take a picture of it, sending it to Kelsi's number, asking if that's her. I know it sounds silly, but I'm starting to know the face of my only supposed friend. This has to be her, but why the hell would she be featured in some high-end magazine? She reads the text but doesn't respond. Seriously, Kelsi? More secrets? I click my tongue, grab the page, and tear it out to take with me. I hope Liam won't mind, but anyway, I don't want him to have a picture of my friend in his drawer, it's a bit... disturbing to think about.

I check more pages, but that's the only interesting thing, so I put it back. Liam sure is taking his time in the shower... I sigh. I grab his phone to play with, but there really isn't even an app I can play with. A bit bored, I decide to look for that restaurant we ate at today. I could leave a good review, I've never done such a thing. Plus, I want to go there again someday. Maybe we could have a proper date there... I put in the name of the restaurant, but they don't even have a website.

As I scroll down, something else catches my attention.

Associated with the name of the street, some news headlines are popping up, from... a few months ago. I frown. The sixteenth hanger disappears in a fire? A miraculous victim taken out, three bodies found...?

A shiver crawls down my spine, as I open the article. I had no idea it had happened there, on the docks. What was I doing there? I check more of the news. It made so many headlines because of how violent and sudden the fire was. It happened on the same street as the restaurant, farther down... yet, in a place where there were no inhabitants. Who were those three bodies...? Why has no one been identified yet? There should have been at least a witness, or a family member calling in if it was a disappearance. Yet, it looks like no one cared about what happened to those people. Who the hell could it have been?

"Hey, what are you reading?"

I glance up from the phone. Liam just came out, with only a towel around his hips, trying to dry his hair with another one. I let out a long sigh.

"Why am I the only one who needs to wear clothes while you get to hang around half-naked?"

He chuckles.

"I'm the big bad wolf around here."

"And I'm going to be the big bad witch if you don't put something on."

"Oh, really?" he mutters, coming closer.

He puts his hands down on the bed, coming very close with those dangerous eyes of his getting a bit darker. Moon Goddess, help me deal with this kind of demon... He smiles and leans closer until we can exchange a quick kiss. Gosh, he smells like fresh mint shampoo, I might get used to this. Our kiss stays reasonably innocent, but I know I'm not trouble-free yet. He retreats and opens his wardrobe, hopefully to put on something I can bear to look at.

"So? What were you doing? Checking on my secret texts?"

"There were secret texts to find?" I ask. "Thank Moon Goddess, your life looks incredibly boring if I believe this phone."

He laughs.

"Yeah, I think Damian gifted it to me last Christmas, but I really haven't used it much."

Out of curiosity, I open up the call history, but indeed, the most recent one was six months ago from his brother. Missed call too. I guess they gave up after a while. He's definitely more wolf than human, technology-wise. I play with the phone.

"I... found some articles. About the fire."

"Which fire?" he asks, glancing over his shoulder.

"Mine. I mean, the one they... found me half-dead in."

"Oh..."

I see him take out some pants, and I only have a second to look away as the towel slides down his legs. Oh gosh, I thought his butt was fine under the jeans, guess it wasn't just the jeans... I clear my throat loudly, but I am pretty sure he's doing this on purpose. I focus on the phone, ignoring that childish demi-god a few steps away.

"Alright, what about those articles, then?"

"I didn't know it had happened on the docks," I say.

"Yeah... Seaver was pretty crazy about it."

"Seaver?"

Liam nods, and turns to me, finally wearing some sweatpants. I guess he really has a thing against T-shirts, because he's half-naked once again. He comes to sit next to me on the bed, and I'm torn between getting away and appreciating the view... I try to tame my hormones and hand him his phone back.

"Yeah, he's the Alpha who watches over the docks..."

"How many Alphas are there? I'm confused, I thought it was just your brothers and Selena."

"No, they've got the biggest packs, the Blood Moon and White Moon Clans, and Nora is kind of temporarily looking out for the Pearl Moon while their... Alpha is still too young. I mean, she could take over the Pearl Moon, but it's complicated. Then, we have Jones who still has her Purple Clan, the fighters. Seaver's family has always been on the docks, so he's still in charge there."

I nod, but I wish I could take notes, I'm never going to remember all that. I sigh.

"...Can I meet him? That Seaver guy?"

Liam frowns.

"I'm not enough already?"

"No, you idiot. I want to ask him about the incident."

"Oh. Well, I thought you might want to ask Jones instead."

"Jones? ...The Purple Moon Alpha?"

"Yeah, she was there also."

I pause, a bit confused.

"Also? So that Seaver guy was there too at the time of the fire, right? Can't I just ask him?"

Liam makes a grouchy face, and it takes me a full minute to get it. I smile.

"...Are you jealous? Is that why you don't want me to speak to that guy?"

"He's just a douche!"

I start laughing uncontrollably. My God, Liam Black is jealous of a guy I haven't even met yet! I can't stop laughing, but he's back to his grumpy face and goes to lie on his stomach, his face in his pillow. I can't help wanting to tease him. I crawl to get next to him, leaning on his back. I pull on the lower strands of hair on his nape.

"Why? Is he handsome? More handsome than you? Is he tall?"

I'm so excited to see Liam Black jealous, I can't stop. Liam turns around suddenly, annoyed and pushing me off his back.

"He's not handsome! He's average and an ass!"

I can't stop laughing. Gosh, now I have to meet this guy! For him to make Liam so pissed and jealous, he has to be his rival or something. I'm so curious now. Moreover, his expression is so grouchy and cute, I can't take it. I keep laughing, trying to fight him off as he pushes me down.

We keep bickering like this, Liam trying to stop me from laughing, me laughing even more to see him so annoyed. We start fighting for real, like two kids playing on this gigantic bed. I try to push his torso, but he's holding on to my wrists and trying to get me off of him. I know he's being gentle because size-wise, he's much larger than me. After a while, though, something slowly changes in our movements. We are pulling more than pushing. We gently caress each other. I put my hand around his neck, and he slides his arm under me, wrapping me in his embrace. His lips venture on my neck, making me tremble. He can't go any further, though, the sweater covers everything else... which doesn't stop his hand. I feel him venture under my heavy clothes, caressing my back. I shiver, wondering if I should say something or not.

My heartbeat may not be able to endure this for much longer, but my stomach is going even crazier. When did I eat a bunch of butterflies for it to go all crazy like this? It's resonating all the way down to my toes, making me curl up a little under him.

Yet suddenly, Liam stops moving. What the hell? I glance down, and he is frowning, his eyes lost and staring at nothing. I'm confused until I realize.

"Seriously?" I whisper.

After a couple more seconds, he sighs and shakes his head.

"Sorry. I didn't exactly tell them I had company tonight so..."

I bet. I think Nora might have caught on to something between the two of us, but for his brothers, it will probably not be so well-received that I'm spending the night here... Liam sighs and rolls on the side, still frowning, apparently not done mind-linking whoever is disturbing us. I sigh, and roll to the side to face him, although now we have put a clear safe distance between our bodies. I put my hand under my head and stare at him. Even when he's frowning, he's super attractive... it gives him that serious bad boy look. I bite my thumb nervously while staring, but he grabs my hand away from me, locking his fingers with mine. I really need to stop that bad habit of mine...

Now that I have to watch him frown and make all kinds of expressions without anything happening, I'm getting a bit sleepy. It was a rough day indeed. I'm hot with all these clothes on, I don't even need to roll under the covers. I feel like I'm going to fall asleep like this, but I fight it, staring at Liam. After a while, he starts to smile, probably noticing my heavy eyelids.

Gently, he keeps caressing the back of my hand.

"Go to sleep, bad witch," he whispers.

"I'm... okay..."

He chuckles and brings my hand to his lips to kiss it gently. I should slap myself for falling asleep with that guy half-naked next to me... It feels like a crime.

"Okay, they are done," he suddenly whispers.

I re-open my eyes. I hadn't noticed they were half-closed already. Liam comes closer, wrapping an arm around me.

"I'm really letting you off easy," he chuckles.

"You're the one getting... calls," I yawn. "Who was it?"

"My older brother... Sadly, his voice is too strong for me to ignore. He wanted to ask what happened at the north border today, some other wolves told him about that other witch."

"Oh... What about me?"

He sighs, and gently kisses my forehead, coming closer.

"...I didn't tell him you're with me. I think your friend Kelsi lied and said you're back at the apartment because they seem to believe that."

Did she? What about Ben, then? Is he lying with her? Those two idiots... I chuckle. Now that I'm not with them, I realize those two have been a big part of my life for the last few days. The two little snitches. I close my eyes again, but Liam suddenly moves. I open an eye to see him get under the covers.

"You don't have a right to be cold when you make me dress like this," I mumble.

"It's an extra precaution. I'd roll myself like a burrito if I could..."

I chuckle, but I know he's half-kidding. An extra sheet between us probably wouldn't be enough to tame the big bad wolf in him if he truly wanted to do anything... I close my eyes once more, and feel Liam coming back closer to wrap an arm around me, the other sliding under my pillow. Gosh, I'm snuggled against his chest, cozy and warm. Heaven must feel something like this, or it's a scam...

I'm in a bubble.

A big, pink bubble. I feel a bit strange. It's warm. I feel like I'm floating in something... something like water. There are lights dancing around. But there are sounds too.

Someone is screaming. I want to cry. The voice of that woman screaming in pain is making me so sad. I want to cry, but I can't. I can't move, I can't talk. I can't do anything. I want to stop this... I want to help her. I'm sorry I'm so weak. I'm sorry. I want to help you, I really want to.

I hear those screams again, and something violent hits me. It burns... It burns so much, I'm suffocating. All of my body burns, it slowly disappears. Somebody help me. Somebody let me out of here. Help me. Help me. I can't breathe, I'm hurt. It's so painful. I'm sorry. I'm sorry...

"Mara! Mara!"

I suddenly open my eyes, Liam holding both of my arms, looking panicked.

"Mara, for fuck's sake, breathe!"

I open my mouth, and suddenly, a big airflow comes in. I take several deep breaths, realizing I was out of air until just then. I keep gasping and trying to calm myself. Liam looks crazy worried, rubbing my arms and not letting go of me for a single second.

"W-what happened?"

"I think you were having... a nightmare. You kept crying, and suddenly, you stopped breathing. I freaked out..."

"S-sorry..."

"What were you dreaming about?"

I look at him, a bit out of it. I need to wipe my eyes, I realize they are wet, so are my cheeks... I take deep breaths again, and take off the sweater. I'm drenched in sweat, but Liam helps me get it over my head.

"Sorry, I shouldn't have made you wear so much clothes to sleep... You probably had a nightmare because you were too hot..."

"No... No, Liam, wait. Did I say anything?"

"What?"

I grab his shoulder, trying to calm myself a bit. I don't want to let that nightmare go. It felt so... familiar...

"Did I say anything?" I ask again.

He pauses and shakes his head.

"You kept saying sorry... and... I think you called out to your mom once."

"...My mom?" I repeat, shocked.

"Yeah. You said, 'Sorry, Mom,' at least once."

Chapter 17

"Here."

"Thanks..."

I grab the glass of water he just brought back from the kitchen, but my hand is still shaking. Liam sits right next to me, looking concerned. I feel... sick. The fever from that nightmare still isn't gone, it's like this pulsating headache. I force myself to drink, just to realize how dry my throat is. I'm extremely hot too. I hand him the glass of water while I take off that stupid T-shirt; it's drenched in sweat, but at this point, neither of us cares. I just need a few deep breaths and some fresh air.

"Come."

As if he could read my mind, Liam gently takes my hand and guides me to the balcony. The rain must have stopped while we were sleeping, but it's humid and cold out here. This feels good... We both step barefoot onto the terrace, and Liam takes me to sit on the little bench, finding his place next to me. I rest my head against the bay window behind us.

The fresh air feels so nice... The clouds are still heavy and dark, but the lights of the city are enough to see. I almost wish it'd rain, to wash away all that angst. Liam is still holding my hand, gently caressing it with his fingers.

"Better?" he asks softly.

"...Yeah."

We stay a little while longer just like this as I calm myself down. I don't know how late it is, but I still feel tired. That nightmare has exhausted me. What was that, anyway? I usually don't remember most of my dreams, or they don't make any sense. Yet, this one was so clear and vivid... I try to hold onto it before it fades away.

"...Are you sure I called out my mom?"

"You said it once or twice. But mostly, you were just apologizing and crying... You were already in complete panic mode when I woke up. I actually shook you for a while before you finally snapped out of it."

I can tell. I feel the sides of my arms aching, where Liam held me to try and shake me awake. I'll have bruises tomorrow, but honestly, I couldn't care less about it.

"Do you want to tell me about it?"

I glance at him. He's even sexier and cuter with his messed-up hair and those dark gray eyes. I can tell he's still tired, yet he wants to listen to this crazy

226

witch's nightmare. I nod slowly and start talking. I don't have much to say, but I try to do my best to describe it to Liam. It's not just about telling him, I hope I'll remember it better if I put words to those visions, and not forget them yet.

He listens to me without saying a word. I can't tell what he's thinking, he doesn't move an inch. Still, I feel better just talking to him, as if I was finally letting go of that pressure, taking the dream away from reality, putting a nightmare back to where it belongs.

When I'm done, I glance down at our hands, still intertwined, and suddenly, I want to feel him a bit more. I don't dare move, though. I just wait to know what he's thinking.

"...You said you have no memories of who your mother is?" he asks.

"I don't... We only found a picture at the apartment. Of a child who is... very likely to be me, and a woman."

"Could it be your mom?"

"I don't know..." I sigh.

It kills me to not even be able to remember my own mother. I shake my head, mad at myself. I hate this black hole in my head, I hate running after the answers.

"Hey..."

Liam notices my expression, and gently comes closer. Pulling on my hand, he makes me sit right against him, my legs over his, and wraps his arm around my shoulders. I am not so hot anymore thanks to the fresh air outside, so his warmth is more than welcome. He gently kisses my lips, a brief kiss.

"Don't worry, we will find answers soon, okay? Let's go check the docks again at dawn, and the cemetery too. I bet we will find some clues there."

I nod, but the truth is, I want to go now. My heart can't contain all of this anymore. I look at the city beneath us, and for once, I'm not amazed at its beauty. I just wonder which part of this world I do fit in. I can't find the right spot for me, that place where I'd say, "Ah, this is where I belong."

I feel like I'm just trying on some shoes that don't fit, one after the other. As if mine had been broken, and I was just gathering the pieces... I let out a long sigh, and curl myself into Liam's arms, trying to repress those dark feelings. I will get my answers. The wait will be over soon. Liam gently rubs my back, my shoulders, letting me calm down until I fall asleep there. I have a vague sensation of him putting me back to bed, but I'm not really sleeping.

His arms around me, I try to find comfort in them. We don't care about the distance anymore. Liam is falling back to sleep next to me, and I want to snuggle in his arms, breathe his smell, and hear his gentle breathing. I take deep breaths too, trying to calm down. Our bond is all I need for now... Right? I will be fine. As long as Liam is with me, I will be fine...

I try to, but I can't seem to fall back asleep. Liam starts gently snoring, and that's all I can focus on for the next hour.

When he finally moves, I decide to get up while he has released his grip around me. I watch him sleep for a while, a little smile on my lips. Moon Goddess, if you're real, I have to thank you just for allowing me this vision.

There's a demi-god half-naked in the same bed I slept in, snoring with his mouth open and expression as innocent as a young boy. I bite my thumb for a bit, and grab Liam's phone, taking a picture silently. This has to be illegal, but I don't mind being a criminal for this... I smile and get up, looking through his wardrobe to borrow some clothes I won't sweat in. I find a gray T-shirt and a pair of jeans. Of course, they are too large for me, but with a belt, I manage to make it work.

As I wash my face with some cold water in his bathroom, I check my appearance, but my dark circles aren't that bad... I do whatever I can to tame my hair with a comb, and finally head to the kitchen, hoping to find some coffee at least.

The oven timer says it's almost 5:00 in the morning. So I probably did sleep a bit before that nightmare... I pour myself what tastes like the worst coffee I've ever had, but it's strong enough to finish waking me up.

What do I do now? I'd rather let Liam sleep after that shitty night, and from the snoring, he's doing fine with that. I walk up to the bag I abandoned in the kitchen yesterday, taking out the map. I should have told him I brought that thing here, maybe. I spread it out on the floor, watching Silver City again. This time, I make sure to orient the map so that north matches our current position. I don't need a knife, my previous cut is still there... I pull on it until it reopens, and a drop of blood falls on the map. I sit cross-legged in front of the map, curious to see what happens.

Once again, the drop spreads toward three points, but this time, one has moved from Sylviana's house to what ought to be here. We have already confirmed we have to check out the cemetery and the docks, probably the point where the accident happened.

I take a deep breath. What do I ask it now?

"...Where is my mother?"

I wait a while, but nothing happens. Either she is somewhere outside of Silver City, or she isn't anywhere... I sigh, a bit disappointed. I have no idea what to ask that stupid map now.

"...Where are the other witches?"

This time, the blood moves and, curious, I watch it go up north. It divides into... two, two dots right next to each other, while a third one goes southeast, behind the territory in green. Shit, so there really are three witches. One of those two up north has to be Ravena, but then, who is she with? I bite my thumb. Is she planning something? Crap, if only witches could communicate like werewolves...

"Meow."

I jump and turn around.

"Spark!"

My cat is there, walking toward me naturally. How the hell did he get here? He definitely has to be a magic cat, I have no idea how he found me, but no normal cat could have gotten into the building, let alone the apartment, like that. He comes up to me, rubbing his head against my knee and purring.

I scratch his head.

"Are you here to tell me something, perhaps?"

It may sound like one damn crazy idea, but... If Spark really is my familiar, could he have appeared because I was talking about contacting another witch? He sits in front of me, his furry butt on the map, like he doesn't care much about the magic stuff going on there. I caress him.

"Spark, can you do that? Can you go talk to that witch for me?"

He meows, and for a second, I wonder if it would be really crazy to try... Should I give him a note or something? He doesn't have a collar I could slide a paper in. Yet, he's still here, staring at me with those big orange eyes. I hesitate, biting my thumb again.

"Spark, if you could speak, that would be so much easier, you know," I sigh.

Another meow, of course. I can tell he's a smart cat. And a magic cat. Why couldn't he be a courier cat...?

"Hey, do you think you can ask Ravena... No, wait, what should I ask?"

She didn't seem to know who I was either when we met...

"...Mara? Who are you talking to?"

I didn't realize the snoring had stopped. Liam arrives, still looking half asleep. Damn, he's just irresistible with his messy hair and grouchy morning face... I get up to go greet him, and to my surprise, he immediately wraps his arms around my waist, putting his head on my neck.

"Morning..." I gasp, blushing a bit.

"Mornin'..."

I chuckle. Is he still half-asleep? Well, I guess it is early, after all... I caress his hair, his breath on my neck tickling me a bit. He starts kissing my shoulder, making me shiver a little. Damn, a clingy Liam isn't bad... After a while, though, he stops, and I hear him growl a bit.

"...What is that smell...?"

"A smell?"

Do I smell bad? Perhaps I should have taken a shower? He keeps sniffing and stands up straight, frowning.

"Yeah, you smell like a... cat."

"Oh."

I glance back, about to explain, but... Spark is gone? I look around, a bit confused, but I really can't see the cat anywhere, and moreover, the map has disappeared too? What the hell is going on now? Don't tell me Spark took it? Even if I could imagine such a crazy scene, it's too freaking big for a cat to transport!

"Mara?"

Liam stares at me, noticing my confused expression. I chuckle nervously, not sure what to tell him. Is there a reason Spark disappeared? He's never done that around Kelsi!

"Coffee?" I suggest.

Liam nods, and we both head toward his kitchen to make another round of coffee. I hadn't noticed, but the sunrise had just begun outside. The big wolf yawns loudly while we wait for the kettle to be ready. He really only uses that to feed himself... A couple of seconds later, I hear his stomach complain. I raise an eyebrow.

"Seriously?" I chuckle.

"Werewolf stomach..." he grumbles.

Well, the werewolf stomach will have to wait, because I'm pretty sure there's only coffee here. Liam suddenly glances at me with a smile, and I wonder what he's up to. I step back as he steps forward, but my back hits the kitchen counter. He grabs my waist before I can do a thing, and lifts me up to sit on it. I like it... I'm a bit taller than him now, and I easily wrap my hands around his neck, pulling him in for a kiss.

He gently chuckles against my lips, and we exchange a morning kiss, the water slowly boiling somewhere on the side. I swear, those lips can make me forget anything... His taste is so unique and addictive. I can feel the little spikes of his growing beard too, a little scratchy against my hand, but more than this, I love caressing his hair. He still smells a bit like sweat and rain, I hadn't noticed that before... I feel his hand going under my shirt, caressing my back, and I pull in a bit closer, my waist against his abs. He groans a bit, biting my lower lip.

"You're making me crazy," he whispers.

"...Really?"

"Yeah. You're a sexy witch."

I chuckle. A sexy witch, me? I'm dressed in oversized male clothes, probably not too fresh either, and I have nothing to pretty myself up with. I shake my head.

"You're crazy for sure," I chuckle. "...You're the sexy one."

To add to those words, I caress his skin, my fingers going down the lines of his abs. He growls a bit. I love it when he makes that sound. It's animalistic, but it really gives him that... Alpha male thing. Liam grabs my wrist before I get too far, and intertwines his fingers with mine, coming back for another kiss. The kettle hisses behind us, but who cares. We kiss some more, caressing each other, trying to tame that growing desire. I'm so glad I'm wearing these jeans, otherwise, his hands would be wandering around more than just my butt... and I don't hate the thought.

After a while, though, we both pull back, a bit out of breath. He smiles gently, his eyes driving me crazy again. I caress his scar with my finger, trying to imagine what he'd look like without it...

"So, are we going back to the docks?" he whispers.

I nod.

"The cemetery too."

"Weird place for a date," he sighs.

I tilt my head.

"Are we dating...?"

Liam looks at me, a bit surprised.

"You don't want to?"

I stay quiet for a while. It's not that I don't want to, I just feel there's something... wrong with that. How will his family react to this?

"...I'm not sure your brothers would be fond of the idea," I mutter.

I can almost hear my self-confidence crashing to the floor. I can see his older brothers' eyes again, both filled with something dark and scary. They don't like me. No, they don't like the witch I am. They don't trust me at all, why would they trust me with their younger brother?

Liam looks shocked, staring at me with a baffled expression.

"Seriously? You're afraid because of my brothers?"

"...Maybe she should be."

We both freeze and turn our heads.

His older brother is standing at the entrance of the apartment, the blonde one. Nathaniel Black, dressed in a black suit. Of all people, the one I wouldn't want to have to face the most in this position... He's with a little girl, who is holding his hand and she's carrying a cute school bag. She has her mom's hair, but her dad's bright blue eyes. I immediately push Liam and jump down from the kitchen counter.

"Hi, Uncle Liam!" says the little girl. "We brought you croissants!"

"Hi, little star."

She's super cute, but the atmosphere between the adults isn't as warm as her... I feel really bad. I guess this is the feeling of being really unwanted... especially since his brother's blue eyes are glaring at us. He's definitely not happy to see me here. I can almost hear them talking in their strange way of communicating, even if there are no words exchanged that I can really hear. What do I do? I want to walk away from Liam, maybe step back a bit, but he holds on to my hand.

"...Daddy?"

As the two of them are still glaring at each other and it gets more uncomfortable, I exchange a glance with the little girl. She smiles at me, looking very sweet. Damn, she's really cute with her ponytails... even cuter than her cute white wolf pup appearance.

"Hi, Estelle," I greet her.

"Hi..." she answers shyly.

Yet, those two don't stop. I sigh and pull on Liam's arm for him to finally let go.

"Have breakfast with them, Liam, I'll get going."

"What?" he says, turning to me. "No, we said we're going together. You're staying here and you can eat with us."

"No, I'm good, I'm full with the noodles anyway..."

I notice his brother raising an eyebrow. I hope it's because I mentioned the noodles, not because he realized I slept here... I mean, we didn't do anything wrong, but still. If a glare could kill... I step away from Liam, and with my fists clenched, I go to grab my bag and shoes before he says a thing, almost running to the door. As I walk past his brother, he and I exchange a glance, and once again, I get that chill down my spine...

"Mara, wait!"

I run to the elevator, still barefoot, a bit confused, and my heart thumping like crazy.

I am not sure where to go, but I feel a lot better once I'm outside. The atmosphere of the apartment was so stuffy with Liam's brother in it... I don't know why he's so scary to me. Both of his older brothers are like terrifying monsters I can barely look at. Their auras are... oppressive. Would I react to Liam's the same, if we weren't mates? I take a second to breathe in.

The rain from last night has left a fresh smell in the air, and some little puddles in the streets. Some rooftops are still dripping a bit, and people are wearing jackets because of that little breeze in the air. It's still early, though. I left in such a hurry, I barely took a minute to put my shoes on in the elevator. I crouch down to redo the laces and realize my bag is heavier than it should be... I frown and check it.

The map! The map is back inside. What the hell? How did it get back here? I'm sure I had left it on the floor before Spark disappeared along with it...

"Meow..."

I chuckle. Of course. The black and gold cat is right there, coming out from under a car like any regular stray cat would. I smile and grab him to carry him. He stares at me with those big innocent eyes.

"You smart boy, Spark... Did you help me hide it?"

He purrs and rubs his head against my chest. I pet him for a while, taking a little walk with my cat. At least I can count on him... My heart aches a bit when I remember the look in Liam's eyes when I left. I didn't want to leave him, but his situation with his family isn't for me to handle. I have a lot on my plate already, I can't face his brothers for him. From the way Nathaniel Black glared at me, there's definitely more going on. He needs to tell them about our bond too... I guess we should have known this relationship wasn't going to be easy.

I look around, but I don't have anything on me. Can I walk back to the docks from here? It should be closer than the cemetery, but it still took us a long while to get there with Liam's bike... I grabbed his phone, but I don't know Kelsi's number by heart. Should I go back to my apartment? I'm not even sure which way to go. Oh, I can grab a cab and pay at the destination, right? ...If I can find one. I decide to keep walking, Spark in my arms, trying to look around for a solution. I really feel at a loss at times like this.

"Mara!"

I stop and look around, only to find a familiar old Toyota with Ben and Kelsi inside, waving at me.

"Guys!"

I run to them, and they park to come and meet me. Before I can react, Kelsi suddenly hugs me, looking relieved. I hug her back, a bit surprised. We've only been apart for a few hours, I'm glad to see her... although I have questions. Ben nods with a big smile behind her.

"What's up?"

"How the hell did you find me?"

"Selena texted me," explains Ben. "She said you'd probably be in this neighborhood, but she didn't explain much."

Oh... Was she expecting her husband to kick me out or something and told Ben to come and get me? I nod, a bit thankful. Kelsi checks me out from head to toe, a bit confused about my attire.

"You're trying the boyfriend style?" she asks, raising an eyebrow.

"I... have a couple of things to explain. And so do you, by the way. I know you saw that text."

Kelsi pouts but still nods. We both turn to Ben, who's waiting for us, clueless, his hands in his pockets.

"So, where are we going, ladies?"

We find a nearby café to stop at and have breakfast as those two apparently left in a hurry. I take another coffee while, as usual, Ben orders a lot and Kelsi only has a bowl of granola. I fill them in on everything I learned so far. Not only my strange relationship with Liam Black, but also Sylviana's house, the map, and that short meeting with Ravena at the border. They both stay mute but listen to each word, concerned, letting me do all the talking for a while. When our orders arrive, my throat is so dry again, I have to order a smoothie.

"I don't know about that witch, Mara," says Ben. "I mean, no offense, but there are reasons werewolves don't get along with witches, and I don't think this one is going to be on your side..."

"I agree," sighs Kelsi. "The fact that she was lurking at the border isn't reassuring."

I nod.

"I hope she doesn't get any closer, but... I keep thinking I could use someone to help me. I keep second-guessing everything so far, and the progress is super slow."

"Well, you would have progressed faster if this idiot had paid attention to the clues earlier," says Kelsi, glaring at Ben.

He almost spits out his coffee, shocked.

"What, me? What clues?"

"Mara Jones! You're a werewolf, couldn't you have told us there was a Jones family of Alphas when you heard that name?"

"Hey, it's a super common name, and I was only half-listening back at the library! Plus, I'm not involved in any way with that pack, why would I make the connection?!"

Kelsi rolls her eyes, and this time, I agree. Ben can be super slow, for a werewolf. She turns to me, shaking her head and playing with the lace of her pink sweatshirt.

"If any smart werewolf had heard that name, they would have told you to go see that family, Mara. I bet it's another clue you left for yourself. You should meet them and ask if they know anything about you. Plus, isn't that witch Sylviana's house right on their territory? Isn't that too big of a coincidence?"

"Maybe that's what I was meant to find by asking them," I sigh. "The house."

"Anyway, you have to ask," says Kelsi.

I nod, petting Spark who's purring on my lap. I've been thinking the same thing too. It looks like Mara Jones, or Clarissa Garnett, definitely left a few clues behind, voluntarily or not... I didn't tell Ben and Kelsi about the actual magic behind the map or the circles. I made it sound like Sylviana's map was just as it is, with the cemetery and the docks popping out. I didn't say a word about the circle in my room, either. I have a feeling Spark hid the map on purpose, but from whom? Nathaniel, or... Liam? Anyway, maybe I shouldn't trust anyone so fast. They already doubt me and watch my every move...

"So, what now?"

I glance up at Ben, but he already looks a bit excited.

"What?"

"Aren't you going to go there? To the docks? Or shall we go see the Jones' first? I think we should give them a heads-up, but they are rather... open to visits."

I look at both of them, looking ready to go and follow my every move. I am a bit baffled.

"You are still going to accompany me? After what I told you?"

"Why not?" asks Kelsi, looking confused.

"I mean... you don't have to follow me anymore, no? The werewolves know me now, Nora and Selena probably agreed to let me go anywhere, and with Liam Black being my... well, my fated mate, Ben, you probably don't have to watch me anymore, right?"

He slurps his fruit juice slowly, looking at me with a little frown.

"Mara, why do you think we came to get you?"

"...Because Selena asked you to?"

He rolls his eyes and ruffles his hand through his hair.

"Little witch, I may be a poor bodyguard, but I'm a very good friend. Kelsi and I got ready in like ten minutes to come and get you. You barely gave us any news since last night, I was a tad worried. Mara, I may not show it, but I do worry about you. And Kelsi. You know, I don't really have to sleep on the couch of your apartment, they rented an apartment for me in the same building. I also insisted they don't change your designated bodyguard wolf, aka me, for someone else even if I got an earful for losing you a couple of times. Because I really do consider you my friend. It's fun to hang with you chicks, and to play detective looking for answers too."

His answer makes me smile. I always forget because Ben doesn't express himself often, but... at least he's here, and staying around. I appreciate that. I nod slowly. Kelsi too is rubbing the ends of her sweatshirt sleeves together, and blushing a bit.

"Me too, Mara... I know I probably wasn't the friend of the year, but... I really want to help you too."

I glance at her, a bit unsure. I sigh, still having this picture in mind.

"...Are you sure we are done with secrets?" I ask.

She gasps, and looks down again, hesitating a bit. Then, she glances toward Ben, biting her lower lip. He is back to eating his meal like an ogre, although there isn't much left on the plate. I don't think he cares much or listens anymore now that he said what he wanted to say. I sigh.

"So it was really you?"

"...Which one did you see?"

"Can I borrow your phone?"

She nods and hands it to me. I remember the name of the magazine and the ad, so I quickly find the picture. It actually looks like there was a full campaign, the same picture appears repeatedly all over the search results. I hand it back to her, and her expression immediately sinks.

"So... I was right? That model is you, right?"

She frowns and nods, but immediately closes the window and puts her phone back into her pocket. She seems upset... Kelsi shakes her head.

"Yeah... This one was taken a couple of years ago, I had forgotten it. I didn't really mean to hide it from you, I just... wish I'd forgotten about it. Like, all of it. I hated that... I hated being a model."

"Wait, who is a model?" asks Ben, his mouth full.

Kelsi glances at him, and from our expressions, it takes him a full minute to get it. He starts coughing, almost spitting out his food.

"You?" he asks Kelsi, laughing. "You're kidding, right?"

I glare at him. How much of an idiot is he? Even if she covers herself in oversized, ugly clothes and hides behind those glasses, Kelsi is obviously pretty. She is taller than me by half a head and rather thin too, her legs look like chopsticks... His expression falls, he stops laughing.

"What...? Seriously? Hey, can I see that picture?"

However, Kelsi glares at Ben once more before turning to me, the two of us ignoring that idiot.

"I always knew I was really pretty," she says. "My... dear mother would brag about it all the time. She made her friends jealous because she had such a pretty daughter, her daughter had naturally good skin, pretty hair... I was skinny too. I mean, more than now. Hearing my mom say it so much, I got sick of it... I hated being the pretty girl. If I could have chosen, I would rather be normal. I tried to eat more to gain weight and not stand out so much, at some point. I was just tired of it. There are so many labels around pretty people, and it stuck with me until I got fed up with it. I could never make friends, and I never fit in at school."

"...How long ago was that?" I ask.

"I don't know... since I was eleven or twelve until I moved here. I really wish I could leave it all behind me.

Kelsi shook her head, glancing at her empty plate with a bitter expression.

"...Everyone assumes you have some eating disorder because there's no way you're naturally skinny. You should eat more, you are unhealthy. You had surgery. You must spend all your time in your bathroom. You must be so popular. ...It made me sick, hearing all those people think they knew me, but my mother was the worst."

I notice Ben has stopped eating, sending us glances and not daring to say anything. Spark too moves under the table to go from my knees to Kelsi's lap. I don't think I've ever seen him act this cuddly with Kelsi before... She smiles and gently starts petting him, but I can tell Spark didn't just go there on a whim. She is probably even more sour about those memories than she looks...

"When some guy from a model agency scouted me on the streets, my mother went nuts... She had me sign right away after her lawyer had double-checked everything, of course. As soon as the contract was signed, I was taken from photoshoot to photoshoot, during whatever free time I had. I took so many pictures, probably hundreds of thousands like this one. I... I never really felt like saying no. When I did, everyone would remind me how it was such a waste, how I was so pretty and should be grateful someone wanted to make me a model, how lucky I was, how famous I could become... I don't know. It was all glitter and bright lights in front of my eyes, so much so that I felt blind and just followed their instructions."

I... feel sorry for her. For that young Kelsi. I've always known her as introverted, a bit quiet, and she never had any strong opinions other than to support me, but I would have never imagined she went through so many things before meeting me. I had just assumed she had come to Silver City on a whim, not to escape an overbearing mother... She puts her hair back.

"My mother controlled every aspect of my life. What I ate, how much I slept, where I went... I was terrified, sometimes. If I had dark circles, or if I gained a bit of weight, she went crazy. She'd cry that we were going to lose that contract, or that I didn't care anymore about her... She made everything about us or her. I started getting scared of that, so I just went along with her whims for several years. It was the worst part of my life."

She sighs and plays with Spark's ears with a bitter smile.

"I didn't make any friends for years... I was too busy with being a model, my career, and my mom's ambition, school became my only refuge. Yet, I couldn't make friends. I was the pretty girl who was a famous model. It was hard... They had all made up their minds about me. I was pretty and famous, so I was probably some self-centered bitch. I was acting too mighty, I thought I was better than them... To be honest, the only girls who approached me were just interested in getting free makeup or wanted to ask if I could help them become models too. I got so fed up with that, I stopped talking to anyone and just studied like crazy to avoid them. If I had an exam coming up, it was the perfect excuse to stay at the library and avoid my mother."

I think I understand her feelings a bit... feeling it wasn't worth the effort, that no one would acknowledge her anyway. No one cared about her situation or tried to really know her. They all had their assumptions, and Kelsi didn't have the strength to refute them.

"At some point, I went crazy at a shoot. The lights were too bright and close to my skin, I got burnt and collapsed. My mother and I had a huge fight at the hospital. She wanted to sue the agency. I told her I wanted to stop, and she lost it..."

"What happened then? She agreed?" I ask.

Kelsi shakes her head with a bitter expression.

"No... The fight went on for several days, and I begged my father to help me. I said I'd die if I didn't stop. My mother said she'd kill herself rather than see me ruin my career and future... Eventually, my older brother intervened too and talked to my dad. They agreed to send me away for a while. My father said I could do whatever I wanted for a year, as long as I came back knowing what I wanted to do with my life. They didn't leave me anything but the savings my mom hadn't taken. I took a plane to Silver City. They have some great scholarships if you're willing to work hard, so I registered at the university, picked some subjects I wanted, and looked for a place to rent... You know the rest of the story."

So that's how she arrived here before she and I met. That explains a few things... also why she stays home or wears those kinds of clothes and those ridiculously big glasses outside. Also, why she was in such a bad situation with money, despite some of her brand name clothes. Probably had been bought during her modeling period. Strangely, it makes me feel a lot better to finally know more about Kelsi's past, and all the real reasons behind her attitude.

I'm about to say something when we both turn our heads. Ben has his eyes almost full of tears. ...Seriously?

"Moon Goddess, that is so unfair... Don't worry, we are your friends, and we won't judge you!"

"Thanks..." says Kelsi, a bit confused by his attitude.

"...Ben, weren't you the one who was laughing about Kelsi being a model just minutes ago?" I whisper, slapping his knee.

"I didn't know the whole story!" he protests. "...Can I see those pictures now?"

"No!" we both yell at him.

He shrinks in his chair with a grumpy expression. What an idiot... I shake my head and turn to Kelsi.

"Sorry for–"

"No, Mara. You were right for doubting me. To be honest, it felt good to have someone who didn't know about my past, and... had something else to focus on rather than my looks."

"So... all the cute sweatshirts are all... a facade?"

She chuckles.

"No, I really love them! It's comfy, better than wearing tight jeans and crop tops. I love my stupid geeky shirts, I'm not going to stop!"

I smile back. So, after all, I already knew all I needed about Kelsi. Even with her past, she's still that introverted, cute, and geeky Kelsi. We chuckle for a while, a bit relieved. Finally, Ben finishes his plate.

"Alright, ladies. Let's get going to our next adventure. So, where to now?"

Chapter 18

"So you just left?"

I nod. We are both sitting in the back of Ben's car as he's driving us toward the seaside. Kelsi has finally dropped those stupidly huge and thick glasses, but that's all. She is still wearing her large sweatshirt and has her hair in two macaron buns, cute and childish as usual. It's not a big change, but it does feel a lot better to see her face.

"I couldn't stay there with his older brother glaring at me," I sigh. "That guy, Nathaniel... I already had the feeling when I met them before, but he and Nora's husband freak me out."

"Girl, you're not the only one," chuckles Ben. "The Black Brothers are known to be absolute monsters among werewolves. They are almost legendary in Silver City. Not only because they got rid of their father, Judah Black, but also because they are exceptional Alphas. You're lucky to be immune to Liam's aura. For us regular werewolves, all three of them give us chills like that."

He takes a turn down a smaller alley, and we can already smell the familiar sea breeze coming into the car. Ben finds a place to park his old car, and we get ready to leave, but Spark jumps down from my lap to curl up on the seat between us.

"Spark, come on, kitty!"

However, my cat doesn't move from the backseat, staring at us with his enigmatic big golden eyes. Kelsi and I exchange a glance, at a loss.

"Not fond of the sea perhaps?" she suggests.

"If he's like me, he probably doesn't like the area," I say. "Maybe we should leave him here."

"I don't think we should leave him in the car," says Ben, glancing at us in his rear mirror. "As someone who knows what it's like to be on four paws, trust me, no pet likes to be trapped in a car."

"I'm not worried about him," I sigh. "If he knew how to appear in a skyscraper without human help, he can probably get out of this car in a blink too."

"...I don't think I'll ever get used to that magic cat," sighs Kelsi. "Oh well, at least I can pet him and not sneeze and cry for hours..."

Agreeing to leave the windows open since there's nothing to steal in the rundown Toyota, we leave it there and exit the car. Kelsi immediately gets the chills and comes to wrap her arm around mine.

"You're lucky you're not cold," she says with a shiver.

Although my unique body temperature protects me, I can still feel it's rather fresh outside. I have a bit of nausea again from all the humidity, but nothing I can't endure so far. Ben comes to us with his hands in his pockets, still frowning.

"I don't like being here," he sighs. "Seaver is a real asshole..."

I chuckle.

"What?"

"It's funny, Liam said the same thing."

"What's wrong with that guy?" asks Kelsi, curious too.

Ben shrugs.

"You'll see if we run into the Sea Moon Clan... which we probably will."

Kelsi and I exchange a glance, a bit curious, but we still follow Ben. He takes off his jacket, handing it to me, and shape-shifts into his wolf to walk ahead of us. Kelsi grumbles while grabbing the clothes he left behind, putting them all into her backpack.

"I hope that was necessary, Ben. Now we can't talk to you!"

"We can talk, he just can't answer," I say. "It's probably because we are not on his clan's territory. Liam shape-shifts every time he's not on his family's territory too."

Kelsi sends me an amused glance.

"Look at you. Becoming a werewolf expert already, are we?"

I ignore her, and we keep walking along the seashore. Unlike Liam and his bike, Ben had to park a bit farther away than where we wanted to enter. The docks are privatized, for the most part, making me think this is also the Sea Moon Clan's doing. I keep glancing around, but there are no other wolves in sight. Ben is calmly trotting in front of us too.

As we keep walking, Kelsi is a bit excited to see a part of the city she had never been to before, and we chat about the fish market and the little shops around. It's a nice area, except for the fact that it makes me sick by nature. Finally, I spot Nina's diner and stop.

"This is where we ate. The hangar that got burnt must be in the area..."

Before I can look around, Ben is already one step ahead of us, heading farther down the street. He probably smelled it before us, but now that we've been following him for a few more minutes, I do notice it. The smell of cold ashes. My heart starts beating a bit faster, and I get anxious. I have no idea what I'm going to find there. What am I even looking for?

I bite my thumb, but Kelsi grabs my wrist and gives me a little smile to help me calm down. I feel a bit better because she's here with me, and Ben too. The two of them are so... normal, compared to me. It helps me keep my feet on the ground.

We finally spot a large building, and it really stands out compared to the rest. It's pitch black, although most of the roof seems to have collapsed inward. It has been burnt so badly there's nothing but the studs of the walls, even the metal was scraped, layer by layer, by the flames... The local authorities put a little security perimeter around it, some fencing panels, but it is not much of an issue. As we look around, I can tell even the nearest buildings barely escaped the flames. They have large dark spots, where the flames touched.

Kelsi gasps next to me.

"It looks like that building from the other night... No offense, girl, but I've seen enough fire for a lifetime."

I nod. I had seen the picture from that news website, but it's still more impressive to see in person. There's the horrid smell too. It's clogging the air and so thick, I feel like I'm breathing in a full box of soot. Thankfully, the sea breeze is enough to make it breathable, but still. Even Ben has his ears down, sniffing around the area with a cautious stance. I don't feel too good about this place either.

Kelsi looks around, but the closest buildings are apparently deserted at the moment. They are probably used for storage, there are dozens of boxes and empty fish traps piled up around. There aren't even that many boats on the port, and none near where we are. This seems like a rather isolated area. ...Why would I have come here in the first place? There are no habitations nearby, no real public areas either. Aside from fishermen, I don't know who would come here.

"...Shall we try going inside?"

Kelsi is whispering, and I can see why. This whole burnt building has something rather solemn and intimidating about it. I just can't tell why. Maybe it's because we both know three people died inside... I can't really forget that information, somehow. I take a deep breath and walk closer to the entrance, ready to go in. Something scares me about going inside that place. Will my memories come back if I do?

As if he could feel me hesitate, Ben suddenly crouches down and squeezes himself under the fencing panels ahead of us to go in. Seeing the red-brown wolf go inside before us gives me a little bit of courage, and Kelsi's grip tightens around my arm too. We help each other climb over the fencing panels, and we quickly step inside. As expected, it's a bit of a mess in there. With parts of the roof collapsed, we have to be careful to not step on fragile pieces of wood, or make anything collapse even more. It is probably still a dangerous area, as mentioned outside. It's larger than I thought, though. It looks like this was a two-storey building, but I can't see how to get upstairs. It probably wouldn't be a good idea, anyway...

"...So, are we looking for anything specific?" asks Kelsi, still looking a bit worried.

"I have no idea," I sigh. "Let's look for the origin of the fire. They said they couldn't find what started it."

Ben stops and glances at me with his big black eyes, and I can tell exactly what he means even without him speaking. I roll my eyes.

"Ben, from what we know, Clarissa Garnett had no signs of being a Fire Witch before this incident, and there was no Mara either. I want to see if something here can explain what the hell happened."

He growls softly but speeds up inside. Kelsi nods and finally lets go of my arm to start looking around as well.

"It's going to be hard to tell," she sighs. "Everything is charcoal now. I bet even the firemen had to use some specific tools to find any clues about what happened in here..."

I stop.

Well, maybe they are not the only ones with specific tools. My fire had a strange reaction in that other fire already, maybe I can do something here as well? I extend my arms and glance at Kelsi. She knows me well enough by now to back away before I light the fire in my hands.

My flames appear, bright red as usual. I glance around, but of course, nothing really happened just because of that. I have to be careful to not restart another fire in here. I walk ahead, trying to see if I feel something. There is no magic circle here, but there has to be a clue...

Suddenly, I feel it. As if my flame is attracted to one specific point. It's faint, but there's definitely a slight pull, like a magnet on the other side. The problem is, it's directed toward an area filled with collapsed parts of the roof. Kelsi grimaces next to me too.

"I guess the two of us and Ben can squeeze under there, but–"

"No, let me go alone," I retort. "I'm not going to risk you guys being injured if something falls or collapses. Just stay back, I'll try to clear the path a bit."

Kelsi hesitates but eventually nods. I know she wants to help me, but she's human and she can't be as reckless. Ben, however, already has his snout in a little gap between the pieces of wood, sniffing around and testing it with his front paws.

"Ben, I'll take care of this alone," I protest.

He ignores me and starts grabbing a piece between his fangs to tear it away. I sigh. He's probably going to play deaf... The two of us start pulling the chunks of burnt metal or wood out of the way, careful about the overall structure. Kelsi helps behind us too, trying to push away the pieces to the sides so we don't end up having too much around us. We get a couple of scares as all of the other debris grinds and trembles, but I'm ready to jump to the side or throw some fireballs at any moment. Ben is on alert at all times too, even sending glances to Kelsi's side from time to time, making sure to know where she is.

"Ben. Here."

He helps me push out of the way what must have been a barrel before it got burnt, and finally, something interesting appears. A darker area on the floor. It's barely noticeable, but there are tons of ashes here, an abnormal amount. As if something burnt completely before the fire itself and stayed there. Moreover, it makes a human figure...

"Please tell me we're not going to find a dead body under that," mutters Kelsi. "I only like gore in video games..."

"Ben would have smelled it, don't worry. Also, they probably took all the bodies out already."

However, I still feel a strange pull toward those ashes... as if it was calling me. I get closer, Ben helping me clear more of the little debris around. I finally put my hand in the pile of ashes, and it's... strangely warm. I have a strange feeling in my body, as if I was familiar with this. Like I've been here before.

No, I've definitely been here before. I get down on my knees, my heart beating like crazy. It's like I can feel my memories, waiting behind that thin wall to return to me. It's... like a dark cloud, something buried that begs to get out. I want to know. Those ashes... I bring my fire closer to it, and they start moving. Kelsi squeals behind me.

"Oh, God, I don't know if this is creepy or cool, Mara, but it's impressive..."

I nod, but I'm more focused on what is going on. The ashes start moving as if something underneath was controlling them. Anywhere I bring my fire close, they suddenly move to go to that designated spot, as if it was pulling it back into a very special spot. It's not just going away, it's like the ashes are going back to their original place... I light both of my hands and bring them closer to the ashes, making all of it move. The wind starts to pick up around us too, and Ben growls nervously.

My heart is beating like crazy, but I know exactly what to do. My fire is sharing its memory with the ashes, putting the whole picture back in place. I keep my fire vivid and watch the ashes move around until finally, a shape appears. It's so familiar it's crazy.

A new circle.

This one is even more complex than the one I discovered in my room and much bigger too. Ben has to keep clearing the area around it as some of the ashes struggle against some of the wood to go to their designated spot. However, a few seconds later, I can really see the full circle. The design is so complex, it looks like it was done with incredible precision. Did I do this? It feels oddly familiar...

"It looks like the one from the book..." mutters Kelsi. "This one looks much more complicated, but... Wait, let me take a couple of pictures, okay?"

She takes out her phone and makes sure to get the entire circle in several shots. I don't even think of stopping her. Actually, it's probably a good idea as I feel like I will need to remember this. I can't transport it either, the ashes will probably not move anywhere to do this.

However, now, the circle is done, and I have to activate it. I guess this is a bit like déjà vu... I reopen the wound on my finger and let some blood drop on it.

"Mara! What are you doing?!"

His Blazing Witch

"Stay back, both of you," I tell them, very sure of myself.

As soon as a few drops get on the ashes, they immediately turn to a strange silver color, almost as if they were becoming liquid. It's different from the previous circles, and... I have an odd feeling about this circle. Not just in that it's more familiar, but also... more dangerous. I don't know what this one will do. It's probably risky, but...

Once the whole circle has changed color, it looks ready. Ben is growling at it, but I came here exactly for this. I take off my jacket and shoes to hand them to Kelsi, who looks worried as well. I take a deep breath for some reason. I have this feeling that things won't be as quiet this time...

"Stay back, and no matter what happens, you two, don't intervene, okay?"

"Mara, what are you going to do...?"

I bite my thumb, a bit nervous. I'm not even sure myself, I just have a hunch I'm about to get some answers, but not for free. I can't explain. I'm simultaneously excited, nervous, and wary of this thing. The fact that the circle is bigger and more complex is probably a sign in itself. I hesitate, and turn to Ben.

"If something looks... wrong, wipe away part of the circle, okay? It cancels whatever is going on with it."

The wolf nods, standing on guard and ready for me. Alright, let's do this.

I take one step inside, but so far, nothing happens. I get in completely, and sit like I did with the others. I'm sitting alone in the middle, but nothing happens. Should I try a question like last time?

"...Show me the truth."

I wait a few seconds, but nothing happens. Alright, wrong question? It's a bit nerve-wracking. What am I doing wrong here? First, the circle feels a bit too big to be sitting... I sigh and lie down, Kelsi making a grimace. I don't care about how dirty the floor is at the moment, I just need to work this thing out. Stupid circle, aren't you going to answer?

Now both my head and my feet touch the circle, and it feels like it's the perfect size... I take a deep breath.

"Alright, show me what you've got," I mutter, more to myself than the circle.

Then, everything suddenly goes dark.

The sudden darkness takes me completely by surprise. I try blinking several times, but I realize I'm not even sure I am. It's like I'm suddenly dreaming, but very aware of it. I can't even feel my own body, or it's more like I'm some doll. This is the weirdest feeling, like I'm floating.

I try to move, but my body won't react. It's as if I'm not really there. Something warm surrounds me, though. It's not a bad feeling, just... strange. Like nothing I have felt before. What's really going on...?

"...I miss you..."

I shiver.

His Blazing Witch

That voice... It feels like it came from my mouth. My mouth I can't control. I don't get what is happening, but someone else is controlling my body, as if it were theirs.

The scene starts forming around us. It looks like a bedroom... a child's bedroom. It's not warm or cute, though. It looks like the basic furniture was put there, but there is no trace of anything family-related. I wish whoever talked would move, so I could see more, but her eyes are riveted on the floor. She... We are curled up in a bed. I can feel tears running down from our eyes. Why am I in a child's body? We're in the dark, there's only a faint light coming from the window. Is this night time then?

"...Mommy..."

I feel a pain striking my body. No, my heart.

Is she missing her mother? I wish I knew mine... Why am I in this child's body? I don't understand. She moves her head a little bit, and I can see more of the room. Her bed sheets are dark blue and smell fresh. Actually, everything in this room looks new, and almost... staged, like one of those furniture magazines. Decor that only belongs in some glossy paper. That room is too freaking big, as well. Even that huge teddy bear across the room is more lonely than cute.

I hear more crying, and realize it's us again. She's whimpering against her pillow, as if to muffle her crying. Suddenly, someone knocks at the door. She freezes and hides under the covers, making my vision go dark again.

I hear some steps. Someone walks into the room and sighs. We are silent, trying to hide. Is she scared of that person? I wish I could read her emotions too.

The room stays silent for a while, then more footsteps come.

"...Amy, what are you doing here?"

Amy? Is that my older sister, then? The one who spoke to her sounds like an older man. His voice is stern and cold. I'd be scared too if I was a child.

"Father. I thought I heard–"

"Leave her alone and get back to your room."

"...Yes, Father."

The footsteps quickly go, and someone closes the door shut. The whole room goes silent again. After a while, we dare look again, but as expected, the room is empty. She starts crying again, more silently.

Was that really Amy? Then, was that voice our father? I really can't remember him. Who is the child, then? ...Is it Clarissa?

The whole scene changes again.

This time, we are at a dinner table. There's a plate with some potatoes, broccoli, and a steak in front of us, untouched. The tableware is so fancy... yet, we are just looking down at our hands. They seem a bit bigger than before. Is this much later, then? I try to analyze everything I see. As she moves her head just a little bit, I can catch from the corner of her vision that there's someone else at the table.

There's a set for another person to our left. That's the only other one. How long is that table, anyway? I can't see the other side, but it can seat at least eight to ten people... even that person on our left is pretty far away. Who is it? I wish she'd raise her head so I could see! I hear them eating, but aside from that, there isn't even a bug flying. This room is only echoing that other person's eating. It feels so intimidating. She glances at her plate again. What, we don't like it? Not hungry, or a stomachache? I can't tell. I mean, that steak looks yummy...

"...Why won't she eat?"

That male voice again. Is that our father, then? Moon Goddess, I wish she'd just look up once so I can see what he looks like! I can just barely see his dark hands. He has long and thin fingers, with one big gold ring on.

"I think the young lady doesn't like broccoli, sir..."

Who is that lady talking? Moreover, why is she calling him sir, this is the twenty-first century! Is she an employee? The voice came from behind us, I can only tell she sounds a bit older than our father...

"She is too difficult. Her mother should have raised her to eat everything without complaining."

...What an ass.

She didn't complain, she's not even talking! I'm feeling angry just having to listen to this. If that's our father, I understand better why Amy always talked about him like he was some heartless douchebag. Oh, no, I can feel her lip twitching. Is she about to cry? Don't cry, don't cry...

"Tsk. When is school starting?"

"Tomorrow, sir."

"...You'd better not embarrass yourself there."

I hear his chair move, and he leaves the room loudly. Just then, Clarissa bursts into tears. She covers her eyes, and for a while, all I can hear is her erratic sobbing. Moon Goddess, I feel so bad for her... Is no one going to console her? She seems so young, and no one cares! I wish I could do something... Although I'm seeing everything through her body, I don't even know what exactly she is crying about. Is it because of her father's harsh words? Is she scared about being sent to another school? And... why am I seeing all this as if I were a third party?

I'm borrowing her senses, but... it's like there's a glass between her world and me. I'm just a passenger in this body, I don't control anything. I don't feel what she feels, I don't understand any of her actions or reactions. Aren't these supposedly my memories? Or is it because I'm using magic to see this instead of actually recovering my memories? It really feels like I'm seeing the past of a stranger, but I'm in their body...

"You're such a stiff!"

The scene changed again.

I just had enough time to hear some loud banging, and the hit on my back. What the heck is going on? I can hear her breathing badly, as if she was out of breath. Clarissa looks up, and I realize her blurry vision is due to the tears in it. She's crying again. I take those few seconds to try and catch sight of the room she's in. We're in a bedroom, but this one is even more stern, like a dorm... The bed has metal bars too, and that desk has nothing but books for studying. Nothing here seems personal except for that picture on the bedside table. Wait, is that the picture Spark found? We're too far away for me to see the details, but it does look like it.

So she had that picture with her; it does belong to her. I hear her sniffle, and she locks the door behind us. The banging on the door continues.

"You freak! Go home to your dead witch mother!"

She closes her eyes, and the room goes dark again. Her dead witch mother? What the heck is going on? People keep banging against her door, and while she cries more, I feel the anger rise inside. Are those teenagers? Are we in that boarding school?

"I'm okay... I'm not a freak... I'm not a freak..."

It takes me a few seconds to realize she's talking to herself. How long has this been going on? She is shaking so much, even her voice... She slowly lets go of the door handle, and the banging ceases too. I hear people laughing on the other side of the door and going away. This is so messed up.

As Clarissa steps forward, I catch a glimpse of a red uniform. She walks up to that picture, still crying silently. I recognize my own hand, a few years younger, grabbing the little frame. It's actually broken; she put some tape on the lower corner. Clarissa sits on the end of her bed, that picture in her hands.

"I miss you, Mom... I know those weren't dreams... I want to see your magic again..."

Her mom's magic?

So her... our mother really was a witch? And we witnessed it. How old were we when she passed again? Amy mentioned we changed households around seven or eight years old. Was Clarissa still holding on to those memories? If she was bullied at school and in such a cold environment at home, it may have been the only thing that worked... She cries for a very long time while looking at her mother's picture. So long, I wonder if this is it, or if that scene is about to change again. I want to see more, more of our life before *Mara* appeared. Hopefully, I'll see what happened in Silver City too...

Yet, we stay in the bedroom until she gets up, still holding that picture. She walks up to her desk and takes one of those notebooks. The pages are darkened with lines and lines of notes from what must be her classes. There's even some languages I recognize as French, German, and Spanish. Wow, I didn't even know I could read that much. There's algebra too, and the more pages she turns, the more I realize how high-level this must be. Clarissa must be fifteen or sixteen in these memories, but this calculus is something else. Is she in some specialized school? She finally finds what she wanted, and this time, it's not her tiny handwriting anymore, but drawings. All those were done with a ballpoint pen, but it's... beautiful. She even managed to make some gradients.

This scene she drew is the first heart-warming thing I get to see in these memories. It looks like a little apartment, with furniture, and lots of plants... flowers, plants in pots, leaves... It reminds me of Sylviana's house. I even thought that was what I was looking at for a moment, but the layout is different. This apartment looks much smaller than her house, and the windows are smaller too. Moreover, a woman is drawn in the middle of that scene. She's definitely the woman in the picture... Our mother. She is even more beautiful than in that picture. Clarissa's drawing details her facial expression more precisely, and I can definitely recognize some similarities...

She grabs her ballpoint pen and I realize that's all she has to draw with. Four exact same blue stupid ballpoint pens are on the desk, and that's it... Is this a prison or a school? I think she's about to add more to the picture, but her fingers freeze. She stares at the picture for a very long time. Her breathing gets so quiet, I feel she's managed to calm down.

That's when a teardrop falls on the picture, messing it up. Oh, no...

She starts crying again, and her hand frantically tries to wipe down the soaked picture while more sobbing comes to my ears. It's getting harder and harder to witness this. I can feel her loneliness. I wish there was at least one person by her side to tell her she is fine... Didn't she have any friends at all? She suddenly gets up, and goes through her bag, taking out a phone. Finally! Is she going to call a friend? Or Amy?

She opens the list of contacts, and I'm in for another shock. Father? That's it? Her only contact is that frigid father from earlier? Oh, crap... She hesitates a long time before pressing the call button. I get nervous, probably like her, as we wait for the ringtone. It rings for a hell of a long time...

No one picks up. I swear internally, but Clarissa is in for more crying.

The scene finally changes again.

I'm pretty sure we are back home, or wherever our father lived with us; it's that horrible cold and empty background again. We are sitting on the floor of our bedroom, with some news articles lined up before us. Wait, isn't that a picture of... Silver City? I recognize that skyline. It's from a different angle, but it's definitely Silver City. What are we looking at? It looks like she's compiling dozens of news articles and taking notes. I see several headlines with the words "magic" or "witch"... Is that what she is looking for?

"Miss Clarissa, you should... put an end to this... If your father finds out..."

"As if my father cares."

I'm surprised by her cold voice. It actually sounds like mine, but... she speaks with a hoarse voice, as if she was sick. I actually hear her cough a couple of times, and it sounds pretty bad. The nice lady sounds like the one from earlier too.

"...Do you want me to call the doctor? Is your headache worsening again? You barely slept last night..."

"I'm fine... Did you find anything else about this?"

"N-no, miss. Those are all the articles we could print about Silver City. Miss Clarissa, I really think you should stop looking for witches... If you keep doing that, you'll just make yourself sicker..."

"Sicker? Didn't you hear the family doctor? I'm as good as dead, anyway. I might as well die proving I was telling the truth. I don't want to be remembered as crazy... Just once, I want to be able to tell my father, 'I told you so.'"

Wait, what? What does she mean about being as good as dead? I hear her cough again, and a chill goes down my spine. I don't like the sound of that and I don't feel good about this. Clarissa's even headhunting for witches. It does sound like she had some unhealthy obsession, but does that mean she... really wasn't a witch? What the hell, then...?

She grabs another paper, but her hand freezes. I wonder what's wrong, and she starts coughing again. It sounds painful even to me, and I can't feel the pain of it. She coughs, again and again, and something red suddenly stains the newspapers. Oh, crap...

"Miss!"

However, Clarissa suddenly grabs that woman's wrist and shakes her head.

"Don't tell my father."

"Miss, please! You should have been hospitalized a while ago already! Your... I know your father doesn't really show his feelings, but I promise he can take you to a very good hospital if you just tell him..."

"No. I don't care about that man. My father doesn't have feelings. He didn't have any for my mother, and he doesn't have any for me, either. He left her to die, didn't he? Why would he care more about his daughter? As soon as he knew I was sick, he just brought me back here and left again. He just hopes I'll die in silence and not bother him."

"But... still, your health... You can't keep suffering alone like that..."

"I'm fine. I don't... I don't care. The family doctor promised not to say anything, so please, don't do something stupid in my stead either."

"Please, miss... At least tell your sister, Miss Amy. I'm sure she could help you..."

Clarissa remains silent for a minute. Is she going to tell Amy? Well, does that mean Amy knew about Clarissa's... about our sickness? Or didn't she?

After a while, she lets go of the woman's wrist, her gaze going back to her notes and pile of newspaper articles. I hear her chuckle, and she takes out her phone.

"Give me my sister's number."

The woman recites each number, and I'm a bit anxious. Is that how Clarissa left for Silver City...? To my surprise, Amy answers after only two rings.

"Clarissa?"

Even Clarissa stays silent for a few seconds, and I wonder if she's hesitating.

"...Did you know my number?" she asks.

Wait, is that the first time they... I mean, Amy and I are calling each other? No wonder she's surprised. Even I feel a little bit happy that Amy answered so

249

fast and had her younger sister's number... I mean, our number saved. However, that pause is a bit more awkward than it should be. I swear, this family...

"...I had your number saved on my phone, that's all. What is it?"

Clarissa hesitates, and she goes through the pile again, until her eyes stop on something else. There's a brochure of the university, as well, and I'm pretty sure that the woman on the front is Professor Vutha... She takes it.

"...I ...C-could you help me? I want to apply to a university..."

"A university? ...Why don't you ask Father?"

"...I just thought... I could ask you... No, nevermind, sorry, I shouldn't have asked you..."

"No, no, Clarissa, wait!"

Amy's tone surprises me too. Another awkward silence happens between the two sisters and I could almost feel her heartbeat going crazy. That silence on the line is a bit heavy, until we hear Amy sigh.

"Sorry, it's just... I was surprised you called. ...I'll help you. Which university was it?"

"It's in Silver City. The name of the program is..."

Mara!

I jump, feeling a strong pull. What the heck is going on? I hear my name being called again and again. I feel like I'm pulled away from the memory, I hear her talking to Amy, but I can't make out what she's saying, as if I was going away. No, no, not yet, I need more answers! Stop!

Mara! Mara, come back!

Chapter 19

I have to watch the elevator doors close on her, annoyed. Why did she have to go? I turn back, glaring at my brother.

"Seriously, Nate? Did you really have to?"

He raises an eyebrow, trying to play innocent.

"We only came to bring you breakfast, since your culinary skills are still non-existent..."

"Stop that, you know I'm talking about your attitude toward Mara."

"Mara? You're already so close that you'd call her by her first name and let her sleep here?"

I frown and walk up to Estelle, ignoring him. I know what I used to say, but things are different now. My niece smiles and opens up her arms for me to hug her. Damn, how did they make such cute kids? It has to be their moms' genes, although Estelle is much sweeter than her mom. I lift her up and take her to the kitchen. She already knows how to put the little croissants in the oven to warm them up a little and she even takes out a baking tray I had no idea was there.

Meanwhile, Nate walks over too, still with that dark expression on, his eyes as cold as ice.

"I texted you we were dropping by," he says.

Seriously, that's all he's got for an excuse?

"I didn't check my phone."

"You never do. And you complain when we mind-link you too."

"Because you guys wake up at dawn when I'm usually asleep!"

That, and the fact that I don't need a helicopter brother either. He and Damian have barely changed, always trying to control everything, especially me. It used to be fun to escape their surveillance, but now that I'm getting older, it's becoming seriously annoying.

"Did we wake you up?" asks Estelle, looking a bit concerned.

I sigh, Nate putting a little bit of a smile on. He knows I can't resist my nieces, so now he's going to make me feel guilty in front of her? I shake my head and kiss her forehead gently.

"Don't worry, little star, I'm always happy to see ya."

She smiles back, looking relieved, and goes back to staring at the oven and the croissants inside. A nice smell is slowly coming out of it,

251

and it's hard to keep a cold atmosphere this way. I turn to Nate once again, my brother stern as usual in his dark business suit.

"I'm allowed to have whoever I want over. This is my place."

"It may be yours, but don't forget we bought it for you, Liam. Moreover, that witch is dangerous. Why would you want her close? I thought you didn't like her. Weren't you avoiding her just days ago?"

I sigh. Of course, they're using their money to control people, as always. This is going to be a complicated one, but... I can still see Mara's expression when she mentioned my brothers. She's genuinely scared and wary of them. She should be. They are Alphas, and although they now have families and all, they're still the most powerful wolves around. Even I watch my actions around them, or at least those they know of.

However, they are still my brothers, and I want Mara to be my girlfriend. Those relationships are equally important to me. Things are going to have to change, and I need to face the truth head-on. I take a deep breath to talk to Nathaniel seriously.

"I like her, Nate. Seriously."

"...Like her as in...?"

"I really like her, as a woman. I..."

I glance toward Estelle, but she isn't listening, taking out some little plates.

"I want her, Nate. As my mate."

He sighs.

"...Do I need to give you the full lecture about witches? Again?"

"Mara isn't Sylviana," I growl, a bit annoyed as to what he's implying.

Moreover, I hate how he still treats me like I'm a child. We are far beyond the time where I had to hide from our father and he and Damian had to protect me. I'm an adult now, I can make my own choices and live with them. Actually, I'm probably more involved with Silver City's security than he is now. He and Damian only have time for their families and the Black Corporation Group nowadays, but I'm the only one patrolling the border with the regular wolves. What right does he have to tell me whether Mara is dangerous or not?

Nathaniel and I glare at each other for a while. I don't like that he's gauging me like this and testing me. He has to stop freaking doing that.

"The croissants are ready now!"

I help Estelle take them out of the oven to distract myself from my older brother's attitude. I wish he'd let go a little and mind his own business. Why did he come here anyway? I don't believe he's just cautious of my diet. For a little while, I try to ignore him and help Estelle set up the table for breakfast, but really, there's nothing much to do anyway. She can prepare her own little hot chocolate, as I always have her box of chocolate powder somewhere, and Nate makes more coffee.

His Blazing Witch

We finally sit at the kitchen counter, and I remember the good time Mara and I spent there last night.

I miss her already. I'm an idiot for not following her out, or stopping her from going. Why couldn't I tell Nate to fuck off for once? I fucking miss my fated mate. I don't know how Damian endured this for years, it's been a few minutes and I'm resisting the urge to run outside and find her. My inner wolf is upset too. I had such a good sleep next to her, until she had that nightmare... Moreover, I got to see her wearing my clothes. Does she have any idea how sexy she is when she has my shirt on? I don't know how much that bond between us is corrupting my mind, but damn, I'm so done for. I'm addicted already. I need her scent like a junkie. I want to touch her hot skin again. I can't even believe how well-behaved I kept myself when we were so close. My own self-control is getting better with each minute we spend together, but it doesn't help that I still always want more. I want to touch her, to caress her. My animal instincts are getting the best of me. Is there anything I can do to tame my wolf before I do something she won't be able to endure? She's not the dangerous one, I am. I'm the beast that craves its witch.

"So, what have you found?"

I raise my eyes from my cup, my croissant still dipped in my coffee. What does he mean? Nathaniel tilts his head.

"About that witch," he adds.

"Her name is Mara, for f–"

I suddenly remember my niece is here, and although she is busy drinking her hot chocolate, she has werewolf ears too. She may not be listening, but she can still hear. I take a deep breath and glare at Nate.

"...*For fuck's sake*," I growl, using our mind-link to finish my sentence.

"Language, Liam."

"Is that what you came here for? You knew she spent the night with me, so you came to dig around for some information? Is it not enough that Selena is watching her? Hell, half of the city is!"

I hate how they are scrutinizing all of Mara's actions, waiting for her to make a mistake. The worst part is that I did the same thing not too long ago. Watching her from afar, waiting to see how dangerous she is and how we should handle her.

Dangerous? Hell, she's her first victim. You can tell she doesn't know what to do from that pure look in her eyes. I love everything about her eyes, and most of all, how they genuinely express all of her emotions. I can tell when she's sad, when she's upset, and when she's surprised. Mara is a blank canvas and all her thoughts go into her actions. She doesn't have an ounce of evil in her.

Nathaniel is still staring at me, but I can't read him. He's always had that thing about him, he's so good at hiding his emotions. In a way, he's the opposite of his wife...

"...I only came to bring you breakfast," he coldly retorts. "You may not remember it often, but you are still our younger brother."

I calm down a bit. I know he resents me for distancing myself from them. Or more like, I'm not as invasive as I once was. I like being around my nieces and nephews, and even my brothers, Selena, and Nora. But they have their own lives now, and I need to have mine.

I needed some time after Sylviana left us. They respected that, but now it's been over two years and they don't understand. Things have changed. I cannot be like I was before, the goofy and easy-going Liam...

I glance at Estelle. They probably decided to drop by to check on me before he took her to school. I shouldn't have reacted so coldly. I'm just upset he made Mara go. I take a deep breath. Crap, I know Nate better than that. He may be an ass and not trust people, but he's my older brother.

"Fine, I'm sorry..." I sigh, "but please, don't talk about Mara like that again."

I'm serious, and he knows it. He doesn't make fun of me or retort that he doesn't care about that witch. Nate simply gazes at me for a while, looking intrigued. He sips a bit of his coffee, his blue eyes still on me, probably trying to decipher whatever is going on with my sudden change of attitude.

"...So you're really serious about her?" he asks gently.

I nod.

"She's... my fated mate, Nate."

He opens his mouth, shocked. Yeah, that's a big bomb to drop over breakfast, but here we are. He puts his cup down and frowns.

"Are you sure?"

I can't help but roll my eyes.

"Hey, I've seen Damian, and we've talked about this. Trust me, there is no mistake."

"A wolf being paired with a witch is..."

"New and unheard of? I know. Trust me, I'm just as confused as you are. I didn't even want to believe it for a while, but... it's no mistake. The more I tried to stay away from her, the more I felt like I needed her. Moreover, that's not all. It seems like... Mara feels it too."

"...What do you mean?"

I sigh, shaking my head. I can't blame him, I doubted it too...

"The fated bond, Nate. She seems to feel it as well. As if she were a werewolf, she described it to me and everything. That's... why we keep finding each other. She somehow found me again when I left her to go to the border too."

He remains silent for a while, frowning. I think he trusts my word, but not Mara. I wish he'd just lower his guard already, but my brother just seems even more confused.

254

"Daddy, I'm done!"

"We'll get going soon, baby star. Go wash your hands."

"Yes!"

While Estelle runs off to the bathroom, Nate checks his watch and turns to me.

"I'm not... going to doubt you about the fated mate thing. We both know that's something that can't be faked or mistaken, at least I hope. However, that witch–"

"Mara. Please call her by her name. She isn't the first witch we've met."

He makes a sour expression, but reluctantly nods.

"Mara. There are still a lot of things we don't know about her, so be careful, Liam."

"You don't trust me?"

"I trust you, not her. Sylviana hid a lot of things from you too, and we both know the result. She was a good witch, but it still left you in a bad state. It's not about their nature, it's about their intentions. Witches are self-centered, Liam, and nothing tells us Mara will always care about your bond as much as you do... I don't want to patronize you, but I certainly don't want you to go through that kind of shit again."

"I know."

It took me a while to get over her death. Even now, I feel sick whenever I see that tree. I don't know how many times I went through the whole scenario, over and over again, asking myself why. Why didn't she trust me more? Why couldn't I have stopped it? Even now, I wish I had the answers. I resent her for dying. She left me no choice, I had to witness it. It's just not fair.

"...What did she say about your fated bond? Does she... want it?"

"I think so. Actually, it hit me hard when I realized she might be able to reject me... I hadn't thought of that. I just kept running away from her. Maybe because I knew, or I thought, that she'd never really be apart from me. But now that I know that she can, it's..."

"It hurts, right?"

I glance at my older brother. He's the one who went through the pain of being rejected once by his fated mate, a real rejection. He was so devastated after that, it was painful just to watch him. He wouldn't even let us see it because Damian was missing his own mate at the time, but I still cannot forget how dead his eyes looked at the time. His first woman was the most cruel bitch to him. He never really explained what had happened or why. We just had that silent agreement to never mention her again.

Selena made him go through hell too, but they both had their wrongs and eventually sorted it out. They are the mismatched couple that still made it work, unlike a perfect pair like Nora and Damian. I wonder what kind of couple Mara and I would be.

I can just imagine us as a free-spirited pair, like two wolves that only need each other. Moon Goddess, I miss her badly.

"I guess you'll go see her whether I stop you or not," he says, standing up. "However, Liam, remember that I warned you about her. Don't get yourself involved too deeply before we know exactly who she is."

I nod, but it's still a bit sour. Mara cannot trust the werewolves, and they can't trust her either. When will those walls break? Is it because we don't know the truth about her identity?

I accompany my brother and Estelle downstairs. I'm happy to have seen them both for a short while, but inside, my wolf is just going crazy. I wave goodbye and act like a good uncle until the car leaves, but then I immediately run back inside to the parking lot, grabbing my bike.

I don't even have to think. I know where Mara is.

That feeling is absolutely incredible, it's like a force constantly pulling me in the right direction. The closer I get, the more this warm feeling spreads throughout my body. Moon Goddess, I want my mate. I can feel her, and I know she went to the docks. How did she get there so fast on foot? Did she find someone to take her there? My wolf growls, unhappy at the idea of another male with her. No, no, she's ours. She's our mate.

I finally park my bike in a familiar spot near Nina's diner, but Mara is nowhere to be seen. Did she find the building already? I almost run there, my heart thumping loudly. My wolf is excited at the thought of seeing his mate again. It's crazy, we've been apart for what, less than an hour? I try to tame myself, and go past the fencing panels.

I can tell something is wrong.

Mara's friend, in flashy pink, is standing on the side looking panicked. Ben Lewis is there too, in his wolf form. How the hell did they get so deep into the building? I struggle to make my way across to them, realizing they pulled a lot out of the way already.

Finally, I see it. Some strange circle with Mara, unconscious, in the middle of it. She's on the floor, looking as if she were peacefully sleeping. What the hell is going on? Her friend spots me, and just when I'm about to run to Mara, she puts out her arm.

"W-wait, please," she says with a tiny voice.

"What the fuck is going on?" I growl, furious to see my mate in that state.

"She's fine... I think. Mara found this magic circle, and she wanted to try it out, but she passed out, and then this happened. C-can you wait a few more minutes...?"

How the hell do they know she's fine? This circle of red flames around her doesn't look fine to me!

His Blazing Witch

Chapter 20

I try to fight it, to keep my eyes closed and hold on to the memory a little bit longer, but I can feel his hands on my arms, shaking me. It brutally stops, and I open my eyes, unable to fight it anymore.

It's a strange sensation. Like I just woke up from a violent nightmare, but without the harsh part. I'm out of breath, feeling a bit lost, and nauseous.

Liam's eyes immediately meet mine, he looks panicked. I realize he's the one who's been holding me and shaking me like crazy. My neck and shoulders even feel weird. He sighs in relief, falling back to sit on his rear, as he was crouched down in front of me.

"Moon Goddess... You gave me one hell of a fright..."

"Are you alright, Mara?" asks Kelsi, rushing to my side too.

Even Ben looks worried on the side, his ears down.

"I was almost going to get all my answers! Why did you wake me up?!"

They stare at me as if I was crazy, but I'm too shaken up, at the moment. The adrenaline from the dream is still coursing through me, I can feel my heartbeat still thumping erratically.

"I swear, I was living Clarissa's memories, my memories! I was almost to the part when I moved to Silver City and–"

"Mara, Mara, wait," says Kelsi. "We didn't stop you for a long time, I promise, but... boo, look at your... I mean, just look at your body."

What about my body?

Oh... Oh, holy crap.

The burn marks are back. My legs look like they are taken over by growing tentacles, black like coal, once again as if the burns had occurred yesterday. ...Or just now. They are running all around my legs, and as I look up, my arms have some mean ones too. As if my brain had been waiting for me to see, the pain suddenly hits me like a wave, and I scream uncontrollably. How the hell did I not feel that before?! It burns, it burns! It's like someone piercing me with a hot needle, ripping my skin off slowly. It's unbearable, I want to cry and scream. I do. I feel like they all waited to attack at once, making the blow so much worse. It takes me a full minute to calm down and tame it, as they all panic around me. I know this is just the first wave. I can endure this, I can do it...

I hold on desperately to Liam's arm, and listen to his voice.

"Mara, calm down, calm down."

I nod.

I need to control the pain. It's familiar, I've been through this shit before. I can do this. I take deep breaths, trying to focus on his voice. Grabbing his arm and holding on to it firmly helps me. The burn marks stop progressing on my body, and the pain subsides slowly too. It's like trying to find my little flame among the fire raging inside. I need to tame my magic and have it calm down before it kills me for real.

Liam keeps whispering into my ear, caressing my nape and rubbing my shoulder, careful where he touches. It feels so good to have this to help me. I can lean my forehead on his shoulder and focus on this. I don't care that we're sitting in that dirty hangar, I just need a minute, and Liam.

"Do we need to call an ambulance?" asks Kelsi somewhere above my head.

"No... I'm fine," I protest.

"Boo, you don't look fine..."

I know she's worried, but I've been through this before.

Or at least, I think I did. These marks are so much like the ones I had before, after the first fire. The one that happened here. If I had used this circle before, what did I see back then? What happened that almost killed me? Is that why? I didn't have someone to stop me, so I went overboard and... did this to myself without knowing? But the memories I saw were Clarissa's, and it doesn't explain who Mara is...

"Come on."

I feel Liam put an arm under my knees, and lift me before I can say a word. Either I'm thinner than I thought, or he's strong, because it looks like he's completely fine while taking me across the room.

"...Where are we going?" I ask, my voice a bit raspy.

"Let's go to Nina's," he says. "You can sit down and explain what the fuck was going on here..."

He sounds angry, and I don't even dare protest. He really looked panicked earlier. Is it okay if it makes me happy? Liam doesn't say a word as we leave the building. I'm so tired, actually, I'm happy to just be carried around. Why the hell am I so tired already? Is it because of the magic from earlier? Moreover, I'm so comfortable in his arms, I could shamelessly take a nap there if I wasn't fighting this.

Kelsi and Ben are following us, exchanging worried glances. I must really look like crap... I'm fine with it, though. I already got a lot of answers. Or did I? I may have gotten even more questions, actually. But I do know where to start next...

"Oh, fuck..."

What's going on? Liam starts growling, and I turn my head to check what's going on ahead of us.

Wolves. Two dark gray wolves appeared, and between them, a young man is standing there, his hands in his pockets with a smirk on. He has ash blonde hair and a little goatee, and a lot of piercings too. One is a little anchor. The fact that he's half-naked probably means he's a werewolf too...

"Hey, Black. You're coming into our territory and not even coming to say hi?"

"I'm busy, Seaver," growls Liam.

The other guy sounds arrogant, and I already knew who it was before Liam said it. To my surprise, he looks about our age, not older as I had imagined. He smiles, shaking his head.

"You should greet old friends even if you're busy, kid."

"You're only one month older than me, you idiot," growled Liam. "Fuck off."

Ignoring him, Liam starts walking again, still heading toward the diner. I think this is fine, until the two wolves start growling at him, warning us not to come closer. Ben is growling too behind us.

To my surprise, Liam doesn't stop or even slow down. He obviously doesn't care about those two, and still goes to enter the diner behind them. When the wolves start growling even louder, he suddenly turns around and growls at them. He's in his human form, yet his growling is much louder and impressive, and they both immediately back away, their ears and tails down. I guess this is probably how I'd react if I were a werewolf and could be impressed by his Alpha Aura... Behind the wolves, the Seaver guy seems to not like that either.

"Careful, Black. You forget this isn't your territory."

"Call your cousin if you have an issue with that. Technically, it isn't really yours either," growls Liam.

That Seaver guy grimaces, unhappy, but Liam walks inside the diner, Ben and Kelsi quickly squeezing themselves in behind us. Ben is growling at the other wolves the whole time and not turning his back to them, even as he enters the diner.

Nina walks over, immediately catching hold of the situation.

"Liam, boy! Did you fight with Johnny again?"

"Not yet... Sorry, Nina, we just need a bit of quiet to discuss for a while."

"Of course, honey. Grab any table you want, it's early, anyway..."

Indeed, the diner is empty, except for an old man snoring at one end of the bar and Nina. Liam carries me to the other end of the restaurant and helps me sit next to him, careful not to touch my injuries. I can barely put my ass on the end of the leather, thankfully my burns aren't spreading too high. I suddenly realize most of my pants are gone. I don't know why I didn't realize earlier that the denim had burned all the way up to my thighs. Now it looks like I'm wearing shorts, but it's not as eye-catching as the obvious burn marks.

Nina seems to only spot them now that Liam let me down too, and her eyes go wide.

"Oh, dearie, what happened?! Should I call someone?"

"I'm fine, thanks..." I mutter, a bit embarrassed.

"...Actually, can we get some ice?" asks Kelsi, a bit shy.

"Of course, darling, give me a minute!"

Nina is obviously used to werewolves, she doesn't even blink at Ben sitting at Kelsi's feet, or the two still glaring at us from outside. That Johnny guy too is standing there, not coming in but not walking away either. I try to ignore him, but Kelsi looks uncomfortable.

"...Should we be worried?"

"Don't mind him," sighs Liam. "It's just a rivalry thing, he's an Alpha too..."

I do feel a bit of an aura from that guy, but it's not as intimidating as Liam's older brothers. More like some gray cloud compared to a raging storm.

"Your rival?" I ask.

"He thinks so. He's just fixated on me, for some reason. It's old."

So those two have some history together? I wonder why Liam won't tell me more, but honestly, I can't afford to care much. I'm still in a shit load of pain and trying to control it. Kelsi takes the seat in front of me, still with that worried look on.

"What happened there?" she asks.

"Well, it worked, for one..."

"We saw that! Boo, there were red flames all around you, it was really scary... I thought it might be normal since you didn't look in pain or anything, so we waited until, um... your friend arrived."

I glance at Liam. I forgot he didn't really get to introduce himself, although Ben definitely already knows him. I sigh and nod weakly, but it's hard to focus. I want to sleep, scream in pain, and cry. All the emotions from earlier are still haunting me. If it wasn't for those three around me, I'd be falling apart right now... and dead, probably.

"How long did it take?"

"Not long, actually. Maybe less than five minutes?" says Kelsi.

Ben nods next to her.

That's it? I felt like I was having those nightmarish memories for hours! They all seemed so real too. I mean, it was probably real in some ways, but to me, they just felt like dreams, as if they could disappear at any given moment. I keep trying to remember each detail, afraid I'll forget something important.

"...Are you sure you don't want to go to a hospital? You're all sweaty..."

"I'm fine, Kelsi, just... tired."

"You need to learn to control your magic, Mara," says Liam. "You're going to kill yourself at this rate."

I nod.

Actually, it feels a bit unfair because I have no idea what I am doing. I wouldn't have known I was in trouble, and even if I did, I may not have known how to stop it. Nina comes back with a bunch of ice and a towel, and both Liam and Kelsi thank her. She reaches to take it, but Liam is faster.

He grabs the towel to wrap some cubes in, and Kelsi and I exchange a look. Her eyes are full of questions, but I silently move my lips to say I'll give her the details later.

"So? What happened?" Liam asks.

He applies the towel on my legs, and I'd surely blush if it didn't feel like a horrible slap on my legs. I gasp, but after a few more seconds, the cold finally kicks in, and I feel a lot better. Oh, Moon Goddess, that feels good. Liam doesn't seem embarrassed one bit about applying ice on my thighs, but I do. Even Kelsi is blushing across the table, pinching her lips with her eyes wide open on Liam Black and his hands...

Ben growls a bit and puts his head on her knee. I see Kelsi frown, confused.

"Mara?"

I almost forgot his question. I nod and start explaining.

I try to detail what I saw as much as I can, not just for them but also because I need to vocalize everything to be sure I don't forget. They remain quiet the whole time, even Kelsi makes a sad expression from time to time. I detail everything, not just what I saw but my sensations, the feelings of being trapped in someone else's body. Liam frowns the whole time, but I try to ignore it until I'm done.

Nina comes back to give us a bunch of colored drinks just when I finish, and I grab one to quench my thirst. In front of me, Kelsi is still making that upset expression, as if she was about to cry.

"Poor Clarissa... I mean, poor you. What a douchebag her father was! Even to... Amy..."

"You mean is. He's still alive, as far as I know..." I grumble.

"It explains a few things, though," she says. "You probably didn't come for the university program, you were really looking for witches. Probably had to do with your mother..."

"There are some things that still don't match, though," says Liam, rubbing his chin. "You being a Fire Witch, and your name. There was no sign of a Mara in those memories?"

"Nothing. Something definitely happened here. Whatever Clarissa did made me awaken as Mara. As I said, the name Clarissa feels... strange to me. Even the name Mara, I don't know how I know that. We are still missing pieces, and those pieces are between the time Clarissa came here and before the fire in that hangar."

"...Moreover, she was... sick, right?"

I nod. That's the strangest part. I felt a part of Clarissa's pain in that last memory. She wasn't just sick, she was in pain, and in really bad shape.

"From what she said, it sounded like she was... supposed to die," I say. "I mean, she was coughing up blood, and she said something about being as good as dead. It doesn't sound right to me."

"But you're... fine," says Kelsi. "I mean, your doctors wouldn't have lied about that or Bonnie. I overheard your sister talking to them too, I never heard anything about you being... terminally ill."

"Which makes me think either Amy had no idea, or she knew and hid it."

Kelsi gasps. She slowly starts nodding and frowning.

"It would explain why she was super... I mean, really on top of things at the hospital... She didn't even want to let you out, I thought it was because of the fire incident, but if she thought you were supposedly sick and had miraculously healed, she may have been scared you found the truth? Or could get sick again?"

"I have to ask her," I nod. "Moreover, I'm curious about what she'll have to say about those memories. I..."

Ben suddenly starts growling at the door, and we all turn our heads. Seaver and his wolves have stopped glaring at us. In fact, they're busy looking elsewhere, toward the sea. What's going on? I'm about to stand up, but Liam gets on his feet first and holds out his arm to stop me.

"No, Mara, wait here."

He goes ahead with Ben to see what's happening outside. We see the two of them go, but once the door is shut, we can only watch through the windows, and I don't like it. I stand up, and Kelsi does too.

"Mara... You should stay put, you're not in any shape to get up..."

I know, but I have a bad feeling about this. I walk up toward the door, to at least see what the heck is going on. I had only seen Liam this bothered a few times before, and it was always about a witch, even myself. I try to see what's going on, and the first thing I notice is the sea.

It's way too agitated, even more so than earlier. The weather has gotten worse, but it doesn't really explain those tall waves I see. What the fuck? I don't like this at all... Kelsi grabs my hand, scared, but my eyes are outside, trying to see what the werewolves are growling at. There's more of them, actually. A dozen more werewolves have appeared, but they are not growling at each other anymore, they look like they're all on the same side and angry at something else. I keep moving around the windows to see, trying to follow their line of sight, until I finally spot it. A woman, standing alone in the middle of the waves.

What the...? I can barely believe my eyes. I rush outside, trying to look for whatever that woman is standing on, a boat or something, but those waves wouldn't even make this possible. She is moving strangely, as if she was riding the waves, but with the minimum amount of effort. How does she... No, aside from that. This can't be good. I did not expect to meet another witch so soon. Moreover, this one probably isn't just here for a chitchat. Ravena had warned me that her peers wouldn't always be so... passive. I don't like that this rain is seriously getting worse too, and bringing my headache back.

"You two, step back!"

I ignore Liam growling at me and stare at that woman. She spots me too, and her eyes snap toward my markings. She's standing a few meters away, and I see her slowly bringing her fingers to her lips, looking intrigued. Is she staying at a distance because of the barrier? Or because she's at least a little bit wary of all the werewolves assembled here? What is she looking for?

I take a deep breath, and look for my inner flame. I glance around, trying to find the barrier, but it's not quite what I wanted to see. I don't know if I'm too tired, or the barrier is too weak, I have trouble finding it. Maybe I'm too far? Does it even go into the sea?

I can barely focus with all the wolves growling around me, the sound of the furious waves, and the wind around us. This turned from a calm morning to the beginning of a mean storm on the shore...

"Fuck off, witch!" yells Johnny Seaver, his fists closed. "Or we will attack!"

She barely glances his way, as if he was some insignificant insect. The threat doesn't seem to have any effect on her. This woman... her clothes are all black, with a lot of silver jewelry on her. And her eyes too, there's something strange with her eyes, like they are not human... Reptilian eyes? What the heck is this now? She lifts her hand, and a wave suddenly stands over us. Holy crap. This is going to be one hell of a shower if she releases it on the shore.

All the wolves start growling even louder and retreating.

"Kelsi, get back inside!" I yell behind me, but she pulls on my arm.

"Mara, you too! You can't fight in your state!"

Among all the other wolves, Ben suddenly sticks out his head, having heard our voices. The large young wolf runs to us and stands in front like a guard dog. I feel like he's bigger now that he's in an actual defensive stance, growling furiously with his fangs out at the witch. I don't think I've ever seen him this impressive or serious before, but the situation calls for it.

This woman by no means looks like an ally or anything remotely close. I don't like judging by first impressions, but that wave looming over us looks pretty mean. Liam runs to stand in front of the wolves, still in his human form. He's the only one.

"What do you want, witch?!" he yells.

The ruckus of the wind and waves is astounding, but she still heard him. She turns her head toward him, shaking in disagreement. She starts talking, and I have to figure it out from the movement of her lips, or what I can make out of it.

"You damn dogs... Always barking for nothing..."

So, it's a "no" with the werewolves. I exchange a glance with Liam, and she seems to notice it. Her stare is on me now. I'm not sure how brave I am supposed to be at the moment... I don't step forward, as Kelsi is still holding on to me, and she's probably not completely wrong either. I am tired as hell. It's really the worst timing to pick a fight with another witch, I'll admit that much.

For a second, I think she is going to talk, ask me something above the ruckus, but in a fraction of a second, I see her expression change into a haughty smile. I can almost tell what's going to happen.

She suddenly moves her hand, and the wave brutally falls on us. It's not just a little splash; the wave falls on us like a dead weight, and I'm brutally smashed against the diner's window. I hear a *thump* sound right next to me, and I find Kelsi a fraction of a second later. I don't feel her holding my hand anymore. My head, my shoulder, and my right flank hurts. I need to gather my thoughts and get back up. I'm down on my knees, and completely disoriented.

The wave retreated as fast as it came, but I see it standing above us again, ready for another strike.

Holy shit...

It happens again before I can do anything. It's like getting a hundred-pound rug dumped on your whole body, except that it breaks apart a second later. Plus, the water gets into my nose and my mouth, and I start throwing up violently as soon as I get my head out of the water, on all fours. The worst part is, I hear a laugh somewhere farther, from a feminine voice.

That. Damn. Bitch!

"What is it, little one? Tired already? Or did I go too easy on you?"

So I'm the target? I gather my senses, and whatever is left of my stomach. I get back up, wiping my mouth. I glance around, only to see two dozen wolves spread all around, most lying down, half-conscious or looking groggy. She fucking struck all the werewolves...?

I find Liam, and thank Moon Goddess, it looks like he's getting back on his feet too, probably in the best shape out of all of us.

Kelsi! I had almost forgotten her. She's unconscious right next to me, her body lying against the diner. She's got blood on her temple too, she must have hit that wall hard. Damn it... I spot Ben as he gets back on his feet, like the other wolves, and stumbles back to come stand next to me. Poor Ben, it's not like he can perform a miracle against that kind of attack!

"What the fuck do you want?!" I yell with a raspy voice, mad as hell.

She suddenly pulls her wave to come closer, but, very strangely, she seems to hit something. The barrier! So she isn't able to get in after all, she can only attack from afar. How is her magic coming in, though, I thought we were fine! Or did I miss something? The sea... She's just using natural waves and making them bigger before they get in the barrier! I'm no expert, but you don't need magic to make a fucking big wave. Although, the good news is, that's probably all she can do for now. From Liam's injury, the other Water Witch, Nephera, could do much worse than that. I hate to say it, but those big scary waves are probably all she can do... I mean, she can send as many waves as she wants, perhaps rinse the people on the shore a hundred times with those, but there's all of Silver City left... She makes a grimace, annoyed by the barrier, and stops smiling to glare at me.

"I want this city. You don't deserve the power... How is a child like you even able to maintain a barrier like this?"

She thinks I'm the one maintaining the barrier? Moreover, what power is she talking about now? Is this about Sylviana's tree, or the Royal werewolves? I'm lost. Liam slowly retreats to stand in front of me, but I don't think the Witch Hunter will be useful in this case. She can't get in, but we can't do much to physically get to her either. ...Or, actually, the werewolves can't.

I take a deep breath, clearing my thoughts and ignoring everything that hurts right now to focus on my inner flame. I bring it out, showing my flames in my hands. Liam frowns.

"Mara..."

I know. I know I'm probably going to regret exhausting the very last supply of magic and energy I have left, but this bitch isn't going anywhere, and she needs a lesson about washing people out.

"Oh?" she says, smiling. "So you want to play with fire?"

"I can do more than play," I growl, and suddenly launch one of my fireballs at her.

However, I'm not that precise and strong that I would hit her on the first go. My flame almost felt dull and too slow, she doesn't even bother to step aside, and lets her new wave extinguish it first.

"Come on, little one, I know you can do better than that!"

She is provoking me on purpose. I know she sees the black markings on my arms, how weak I am as I try to stand on my own two feet.

"Liam, Ben, tell everyone to get the fuck out of here. She can only send more waves, but she's still behind the barrier."

Liam exchanges a glance with Ben, and the red-brown wolf suddenly howls loudly. All wolves, still down or already up, turn toward him. Some growl, but some are happy to scurry out of the witch's reach. I need to win time so that everyone manages to get out. Kelsi is still passed out, and only half the wolves leave, Liam and Ben not included.

"...Who the heck are you?" I ask the Water Witch.

"Why should I tell you?" she frowns.

"Because this is my city you're threatening!"

"Your city? It doesn't belong to a Cursed One like you!"

Cursed One...?

"What the hell are you talking about?" I mutter, shocked.

"You were born without magic, weren't you?" she hisses, squinting her eyes, full of anger. "Cursed Ones like you aren't even real witches! How the hell did you get your fire power?! No Cursed One can acquire such power by themselves! Whose witch's powers did you steal? You witch thief!"

I'm shocked beyond words.

Not only do I have no idea what she is talking about, but it makes zero sense to me.

Cursed One? No powers? It doesn't sound like me, but it does sound like... Clarissa.

I keep reliving those memories. She was desperate to prove her mother was really a witch. She knew about magic, she knew Silver City had witches. Yet, if Clarissa's mother was a witch, what happened to her? She was clearly born without any powers, from what I saw, so... how did it come to me, to Mara? There were traces of Clarissa using magic, or at least studying it. If she was powerless, what happened? Why was she born without powers despite her mother being a witch, and how did I come to have this fire?

I remember Kelsi's words. According to her, the cycle didn't make sense for Clarissa to have an Earth Witch as a mother, but... what if we had it wrong from the start? What if it didn't make sense for her to have the powers of a Fire Witch?

Once again, I get more questions than answers, and this Water Witch bitch is probably not in the mood to answer them.

"How would you know I'm cursed?!" I yell back.

She shakes her head.

"You know nothing, and you call yourself a witch! Look at those burns! Would a real Fire Witch have those?!"

From the way she glances, she isn't talking about the black markings, but about the older scars, those of the first fire that have still not disappeared. The pinkish ones I still have left, visible on my legs under my burned shorts. ...So those shouldn't be there? I'm confused. I always thought those were due to the fire, and the doctors said I was healing crazy fast, but, judging from her words, it's not enough.

"You really know nothing, do you?" she hisses.

"Liam!"

A gigantic shadow suddenly jumps over us, and three of the most impressive wolves I've ever seen stand like a wall between the witch and us. The largest one is as big as a fucking bear, and I recognize it immediately. It was the one I saw in Nora's garden, watching the children. However, it's not the most impressive... even without seeing his face, I recognize the King, his aura is as dark and scary as his wolf form. His growling even scares me enough that I unconsciously step back. And I'm only seeing him from behind...

The third wolf is cream white with golden eyes, and I'm pretty sure that's Selena. Moreover, her husband and Nora arrive next to us, running.

"Are you alright?" asks Nora, looking worried.

"How the hell did a witch get inside the barrier...?" growls Nathaniel Black.

"She isn't inside," says Liam. "Just waiting right outside and having fun sending tsunamis at our faces..."

As Selena is standing before him, Ben whimpers and retreats a bit, pulling back to go and check on Kelsi. To be honest, I feel bad for not doing the same earlier, but I can't be in both attack and defense mode, or whatever this is.

We turn our eyes to the witch, and Nora is impressive. Her blue eyes are strangely shining at the moment, and I can feel her white aura growing stronger. It's as if she is spreading her strength to all of us, and the dark clouds are about to retreat just because she's standing there. The witch notices it too, and squints her reptilian eyes.

"A Royal..." she mutters, looking very displeased by the arrival of more allies.

It's not just them. So many werewolves arrive out of nowhere on the docks, some going to help out the ones still lying on the ground, some taking defensive positions. I'm not sure this is what we need, but it does make us feel a bit stronger.

"Yes, and this wouldn't be our first time getting rid of a witch," says Nora. "So, I strongly suggest you leave my family and my city alone and go back to wherever the hell you came from."

"Your city?" repeats the witch, frowning. "This city doesn't belong to werewolves or humans!"

"Well, it does now."

"You bastards, killing your own witch and replacing it with a Cursed One?! How dare you!"

Nora frowns and turns to me.

"A Cursed One?"

"I have no idea, either," I mutter, shaking my head.

Nora sighs and glares back at the witch.

"Well, cursed or not, we don't care. Mara is Silver City's witch, and we don't need a replacement at the moment, so you're welcome to leave and never come back."

The witch seems shocked. What? Is this because Nora is a bit too polite despite their current situation? Yet, the witch turns her head to me, looking stunned. She stays silent and stares at me for a long time. It's really weird, until Nora and I exchange another look. The King suddenly steps forward, growling loudly, and it wakes the witch from her slumber.

"...What did you just call that girl?" she asks.

Nora frowns, unsure how to respond. Is it bad if she says my name? Yet, before she can decide, the witch brings her wave closer, looking like she wants to take a better look at me.

"Mara? You said... You're being called Mara?"

I slowly nod, a hint of hope appearing. Does this witch know about Mara? No one has been able to tell me anything about that name so far, not even the slightest clue! Yet, that witch is shocked. She ought to know something.

She suddenly starts laughing hysterically. ...Seriously? Her laugh goes on and on... Crazy as hell, until she has to hold her flank, almost falling off the wave she's standing on. Then, her eyes return to me, and this time, she's clearly glaring. Not just a glare... I can feel her murderous intent.

"Mara! How dare you use that name... How dare you use that power, you Cursed One?! You monster!"

"What the... What do you know about me?" I ask, completely lost at her sudden change of attitude.

"Oh, I know enough! Cursed Ones like you are always preying on others' power! How dare you take the powers of that child?! You should rot in hell! I hope that flame burns you down and kills you!"

I'm the shocked one now. What the hell is she talking about...? They are all staring at me now, but I feel like the child in the middle of a class accused of something she didn't do. I have no idea what's going on and what the hell caused her to suddenly freak out...

"What about Mara? What child? I am Mara!" I protest.

"You're Mara? How dare you use that name?!" she yells. "I should have known! A Fire Witch, in Silver City, a Cursed One? How dare you steal those powers?!"

"What the fuck are you rambling about, I didn't steal anything! I don't even know why my name would be Mara, who am I?!"

"You're not Mara!" yells the witch. "You're not Mara, Mara is dead! She died in her mother's womb, she died because of the damn werewolves you stand next to, she died because of vampires!"

"Holy shit..." suddenly mutters Nathaniel Black.

I turn to him, but I realize he's not the only one making that face. They all know what she is talking about, but I don't. Even Liam looks like he's about to throw up. I turn to Nora.

"What is she talking about?" I ask, desperately.

"That's right, you know... don't you?" hisses the witch. "You caused all of this. Of all people, you dare steal Nephera's daughter's powers!"

What the... Nephera?

It takes me a little while until I take the full measure of what she just said. Nephera's daughter? Mara was the name of... Nephera's unborn baby? Everything Liam and I found comes back to me, like dozens of flashes in my mind. The Witches' Ancestral Tree. That burn mark next to Nephera, that strange feeling I had every time I saw that erased name. No, even before that. Why did I feel such unfairness toward Nephera, to begin with? When they told me her story, I was... angry, and sad for her. To the werewolves, that woman was a defeated enemy, an evil witch that caused more harm than good, and yet, I was the only one who possibly felt pity for her.

...Was it all because of Mara?

"You're saying... Mara was the name of Nephera's daughter?" mutters Nora, as shocked as I am.

"That child was never even born," protests Nathaniel Black next to her. "This makes no sense."

"Oh, we don't need to wait for our physical envelopes!" roared the Water Witch, still furious. "You werewolves think you know anything about witches? There's incredible potential in a witch's womb, from the moment her child is conceived, magic is gathered! Mara's name appeared on the Witches' Ancestral Tree like all of her ancestors before her!"

So I was... right, and wrong at the same time. So much of this finally makes sense. This feeling I have toward Silver City, is it because... Mara was conceived here? It's her birthplace, in a way. However, there are still a lot of questions. What about Clarissa, and what is this Cursed One thing? Because Clarissa was born powerless?

"You're the scum of witches..."

I wish I had more time to wonder and could ask more questions, but that witch definitely has me at the top of her kill list right now. She's glaring right at me, as if the werewolves had suddenly become a secondary matter. I light up another fire in my hands, but I'm almost out of fuel, it's a dim flame. I'm literally exhausted too. The memory trip from earlier drained all of my energy, and although my burns have subsided a bit by now, I'm not in any condition to face a witch, a water one at that.

"I think we got the message," Nora retorts. "It doesn't change our answer. You get away from Silver City and our territory before I get seriously mad."

The Black Luna's sapphire eyes are shining, and despite her petite figure, she's much more imposing than any normal werewolf present. Nora has that white aura that is impossible to ignore. The angrier she gets, it feels like being in the middle of a snowstorm picking up.

Right ahead of her, Selena is growling too, and her golden eyes are burning like a fire. Both Lunas are furious and ready to fight. I know it's not for my sake, but I'm still a bit happy to hear that. Having those two powerful, strong women by my side was what I needed to spark my courage again. I focus a bit more on my inner flame, and bring my hands together, making my fire stronger, as if I was about to hammer it.

"You're all pathetic," hissed the Water Witch. "I'll have Silver City, and I'll never leave it to a Cursed One."

"Unless you stop whining about all that shit and start explaining what you mean, you can fuck off!" I yell, annoyed.

How can she call me a Cursed One and keep insulting me, when I have no idea what she's rambling about?!

"Hmpf! I have nothing to discuss with the likes of you! I'll crush a fake witch like you anytime!"

"Come on, then!" I yell back.

However, before I can raise my hands, an arm blocks me.

"Mara," says Nora, stepping in front of me. "The barrier is doing its work, don't be reckless now. You're tired too, you can't fight in this state. Don't worry, let's just make sure she leaves."

"But–"

"Nora's right," adds Liam. "She can only send waves at us, but she'll get tired faster at that rate. The barrier won't grow weak because of this kind of attack."

I wouldn't be so sure about that.

The werewolves may not spot such details, but for me, the barrier is like some translucent paper, and I'm getting better at determining how strong it really is. It may be thicker and stronger than at the north border, but I wouldn't say this is completely fine either. I am not sure how it works, but my fire ball crossed it to hit beyond that witch. Isn't that proof enough that the barrier isn't doing so well on this side too? I'm not as optimistic as they are, although Nora might just be trying to dissuade me.

Finally, the witch starts moving her arms again, and in front of me, Selena growls louder, in warning.

The witch seems to hesitate. ...Is she scared because of Selena's aura? Can she sense the Royals? Or the Black Brothers' dangerous auras? Damian Black, the King, steps forward too, unafraid of the pending waves.

"You damn dogs!"

This time, we are all prepared for the attack. Everyone moves at the same time. Out of the corner of my eye, I see Selena and Damian crouch down, while the gigantic brown wolf jumps between us and the wave, blocking it with his body. Just then, Liam suddenly gets in front of me too, taking me into his embrace.

I'm shoved in his arms, unable to see anything, but I feel the violence of the new wave. It hits in several shock waves, like a hurricane, and I feel Liam's body move. I grab his shirt to hold on to, making sure he stays close to me, and we wait for it to stop. It only lasts a few seconds, but I'm worried for everyone. I keep thinking about Kelsi, half-conscious behind me. Isn't she going to drown? I should have done something for her instead of withstanding that attack! Yet, it's too late. I have to wait for the next moment we can move.

"Is she gone?"

I didn't recognize the voice, but I know I can finally look up behind Liam's shoulder. The sea is still wild, the waves going in all directions, but there's no sign of the witch. Liam steps back to check all around too, but she is nowhere to be seen. Did she really leave? For a few seconds, we are all alert, cautious of a new attack.

But the harbor is strangely silent now, and the sea is slowly returning to its natural, peaceful state.

I see Nora and Nathaniel run to their respective partners, but both wolves seem fine. Selena is even still growling toward the sea, looking mad. To my surprise, she starts shape-shifting back into her human form, and all the males around turn their heads while her husband hands her his shirt.

"What a bitch!" she growls as soon as she's able to. "What the fuck was that?"

"I didn't do anything," I immediately say out of reflex.

"No, but it turns out you may have more... issues than we thought," sighs Nora, draining the water from her hair.

"...Do you think it's true?" suddenly asks Liam.

Everyone turns to him. I don't like the tone of his voice, or how pale he looks. I turn to him, but he's not looking at me, he's staring at Nora and the others. The Lunas exchange a look, and Nora glances my way briefly before looking back to him.

"I... I mean, there's no way to be sure for now, Liam."

"About what being true?" I ask him, a bit annoyed.

Why is he acting like this now? Despite me staring at him, Liam is still stubbornly staring at his sisters-in-law, not me. I don't like that at all.

"Mara," says Nathaniel Black, "it would mean you're... kind of our half-sister."

"Yeah, I caught on to that part," I retort. "However, did anyone else catch the part where I only have her powers, not her body? Or is it just me?"

"W-well, we are not sure about anything..." mutters Nora.

"Why did you call yourself Mara, then?"

I glare at Liam. Now he's looking at me, and to talk to me like that too? They all take one step away from us, probably a bit embarrassed about the situation, but right now, I don't care. I'm not ready to take this kind of attitude, not from Liam. Why the hell is he mad at me all of a sudden? He was protecting me not five minutes ago, now he's staring at me as if I'm some gross monster!

"I don't know," I retort back. "Like a shit ton of things, I don't know. I don't know why I woke up with that name in mind, or why I have no memories. I don't know why the hell I'm paired with a guy who could be the half-sibling of a deceased witch whose powers I'm using, but as far as I know, I'm still getting answers, and waiting before judging a fucking thing!"

"Mara, maybe the whole let's-find-who-I-am thing is a funny little quest for you, but this is fucking serious! You carry the name and parts of that witch's child! I feel sick about how my father treated that witch, but–"

"Her name was Nephera!" I suddenly yell.

Liam stares at me, shocked at my reaction, but I'm so fucking done now.

"Stop with 'that witch' thing!" I go on. "We have damn names, all of us! Why is it that the only one you can use is Sylviana? All of you! That witch, this witch, the witch! Do I always call you guys werewolves, that wolf, wolfie guy? Or is it because it makes it easier to forget we are actual living beings as well? Yes, her name was Nephera, and yes, she was evil and a mean bitch, but she wasn't just a witch! Stop linking us all together like we're the same kind of freak! Witch is not my identity, it's part of who I am, and as far as I know, I am not Sylviana, I am not Nephera, and I am not her baby!"

A long silence follows my words as they all go quiet. Even Selena lowers her head, they all know I'm not just talking about Liam's attitude at this point. Yet, he's the one I'm most mad at.

"If you could forget for a minute that I'm a witch, you'd see that finding my real identity is not a fucking joke to me. Yes, I'm shocked that I'm somehow bound to your unborn half-sister, and I don't know anything about that! However, one thing I do know for sure is that I'm bound to you! For Moon Goddess knows what reason, I'm bound to you, not anyone else! I don't know about Clarissa Garnett, and I don't know about Mara either, but I do know the feelings I have for Liam Black are real!"

The more I talk, the more his anger seems to dissipate. He still has that darkness in his eyes, but it looks different. We are no longer that playful couple from earlier. I feel like we collided before we could even find out which part of the puzzle we are, and it's now brutally coming back to us.

I take a deep breath, trying to calm down.

"Mara, I'm–"

"No, listen. I don't know what my relationship to... *that* Mara is for now, okay? I don't know why I woke up with that name, and I still don't know what happened to Clarissa either. I'm still looking for answers, and if you're not ready for what I might find, I can just do this alone."

Without letting him answer, I turn around and finally go to Kelsi's side. I'm just too angry to even listen to his answer now. I'm tired, worried for my friend, and fed up with all this shit. I haven't had time to put everything I learned today together, and I feel like everyone is back to sending daggers at me because of what happened, because there was another witch attack and once again, it was my fault, somehow.

Thankfully, Kelsi is just unconscious. Ben covered her during the previous wave, and aside from a mean bump on her head, she looks fine. We help her get back to her senses, slowly, but she just seems a bit lost and groggy.

"...I think it's better we go back for today," sighs Selena. "Seaver can... Where is that idiot, for starters?"

I turn to look, and a young pregnant woman arrived at the docks, leaning over a big gray wolf. Selena walks up to her to explain the situation, but this is werewolf business, and I've had enough of that lately. I help Kelsi get back on her feet, Ben's fidgeting next to us, obviously worried.

"I'm fine... Oh, my head... It hurts... Is it ugly?" she asks with a grimace.

"Kind of? Boo, you're going to need ice."

She chuckles despite the pain.

"You called me boo... Oh, I'd love some ice cream right now..."

"No, Kelsi, I meant some actual ice. Are you sure you don't need a CT scan or something? Shall we stop by the hospital and have Bonnie look at you?"

"No, no, I'm fine..."

I'm not sure of that, but she doesn't seem completely lost either. Nina, who must have been hiding during the attack, comes out of her shop to bring us another pack of ice for Kelsi's forehead. Meanwhile, I can't help but listen to the werewolves, who have apparently decided to ignore the private matters for now and focus on the big ones.

"Seaver's handling this for now," says Selena, coming back, "but I don't think that witch will be coming back anytime soon."

"We can never be too sure," sighs Nora. "I will go check on the tree right away. You should watch out for the north border, if anything happens again, she can use the river there against us..."

"I know. I'll have more wolves on patrol for a little while, just in case."

"...Babe, you still don't remember where you heard or saw Mara's name?" suddenly asks her husband.

I turn to Nathaniel Black, surprised. Of all people, I didn't expect him to care about that, as well... He sends me a quick glance, but then, his eyes go to Liam. So he's actually worried about his younger brother. It is pretty legitimate. Is he trying to figure out my relationship to Nephera's daughter, then? I can't be the only one thinking that would make no sense if we are fated mates! ...Did Liam already tell his brother? Is that why he's the one curious?

Selena growls and crosses her arms, visibly frustrated. I don't know how she can be that sexy and confident while only wearing a man's shirt in the middle of a harbor...

"No fucking idea, and it's annoying as hell. I know I saw it somewhere!"

"...Wasn't it at Sylviana's house?" asks Liam.

"No, I'd know. Damn, this is why I usually stick to numbers, I have a shitty memory... I'll ask Danny, maybe he'll know. He's like an elephant with those kinds of things."

"Alright, then let's just go home."

Although she's still frowning and looking upset, Selena nods. Nora is standing next to her partner too, and still staring at the sea with a complex expression. She looks lost in her thoughts, until she notices me staring, and smiles faintly.

"Do you want to come with us, Mara? Or we can drop you off somewhere...?"

I exchange a glance with Liam, but we are both terribly awkward at the moment. I shake my head.

"No, thanks. You guys should go back, I'll go home with Kelsi and Ben."

"Are you sure? If you need to go to the hospital–"

"I can take you," says Liam, stepping forward.

This time, I'm the one who backs away, shaking my head. I'm not really ready for that.

"Sorry, Liam, I think it's better if you go with your family... for now."

We exchange a long stare. I'm not pushing him away, but it's been a... confusing day for the two of us. I think we need some time apart. Things have been going too fast until now, and now, they're going backwards. Everything is messed up between us. It's not like I don't want to hug that idiot and tell him we're fine, but... I'm not sure we are, for now. I'm not really sure of anything, and I need to be.

"Alright," he says.

He turns his back to me a bit too quickly, and follows his brothers. Nora gives me a faint smile before leaving too. Slowly, all the wolves leave, and it's almost as if nothing had happened. I sigh and turn to Kelsi, who's still making a grimace, the ice pressed against her forehead.

"...We are not going home yet, are we, boo?" she asks.

"I was going to ask if you're okay with that."

Kelsi shrugs.

"I'm getting a bump, but if you're fine, I can hold on a bit longer too. So, what's the plan?"

I turn to Ben and sigh.

"...Do you think you can take me to meet that Alpha, Jones?"

Chapter 21

"Wow... I thought I had passed out for like ten seconds, but now it feels more like ten good minutes..."

I nod and apply some more of the ice on her forehead, making Kelsi grimace again. We are back in Ben's car, driving toward the Purple Moon Clan territory. It left me enough time to update Kelsi on everything she missed while unconscious, but I'm still a bit worried, her forehead has one serious bump growing and it's a bit blue too.

"I really think we should stop by a doctor's or something to have you examined," I say.

"No need, just the ice and I'll be good. It doesn't even hurt anymore."

"It doesn't hurt because you're numb from the ice," I protest.

"Don't worry, I mind-linked my sister," says Ben. "She'll meet us there."

I nod, feeling a bit better that Bonnie will take a look at that ugly thing growing on Kelsi's head. Actually, taking care of her is also a bit of an excuse so I can focus on Kelsi instead of thinking about Liam and the other werewolves.

I don't like the way we parted. I don't like the fact that we parted at all, to be really honest. However, something tells me it was the right decision for now. Everything's happened so fast since last night, and I need to take a step back to reconsider the whole picture. Although everything went... incredibly well between us, and we had an amazing evening together, I know this is like learning to run before we walk. I don't have all the answers to my questions and with what we just learned, it looks like those answers might even end up hurting Liam. Which is definitely the last thing I want.

Very selfishly, though, I feel a bit happy that one thing was revealed, another clue about my identity. Mara was Nephera's unborn child. It explains why no one knew about that name, only the witches could have seen it on the Witches' Ancestral Tree. However, where did Selena see it, then?

Those words from the Water Witch haunt me too. What is a Cursed One? Is it because Clarissa was born without being a witch herself, but I am one somehow? Clarissa was sure her mother was an Earth Witch, and with all the clues we've got so far, I'd be keen to believe it too. So why wouldn't she be one herself...?

"We're here, ladies," Ben suddenly says.

His Blazing Witch

I was curious to go back to the Purple Moon territory. Liam and I came here briefly, but since we only scouted out Sylviana's house, I didn't have a real chance to meet the local werewolves and humans. The first thing that hits me is that just like before, all the houses look the same, aligned in colorful rows. I think we arrived on the other side, where it looks more like family houses, with people in the yards. Someone is grilling a barbecue, is it Sunday morning? The smells in the air are nothing like the fishy ones from the harbor over half an hour ago. Kelsi keeps looking out the window too, just as curious as I am.

"Oh, here's my sis."

Indeed, Bonnie is waiting for us in front of a large building, her arms crossed. For once, she is not in her hospital blouse, and quite nicely dressed. She's wearing denim pants and a white embroidered top, her long red hair held by a hairband. All three of us get out of the car, and I notice she has little heels on too.

"Mara, what's with that outfit?"

I forgot I was wearing Liam's clothes... What didn't burn, to be more precise. It's been a rough morning, now that I think about it. I could really use a shower after this, I probably smell like a not-so-fresh mix of seawater, dog, and... barbecue. Is it okay to meet an Alpha looking like this?

"Hey, sis, can you take a look at Kelsi? She hit her head badly..."

"I heard what happened at the shore," says Bonnie, walking up to Kelsi to check on her. "Are you guys alright?"

"Yeah... Just tired," I sigh.

I check myself out in the car's window, and I do look like a bit of a wreck, to be honest. I'm tired, my burns still hurt a bit, and I have a lingering headache because of all that humidity earlier, most likely. Bonnie suddenly growls.

"You call yourself a bodyguard? How come you're the only one who's fine?"

Ben makes a grimace and looks down, a bit embarrassed. She's not wrong, but I really cannot blame him. It's been a tough start for everyone, and I was probably the most at fault out of the three of us. After a while, Bonnie nods.

"You're just bruised, Kelsi, from the looks of it. Here, take this. And if you still have a headache, or you feel nauseous or dizzy in any way, you tell me, okay?"

"Sure."

"What about you?" she asks me, her eyes going down to my new scars. "How come you have more of... those?"

I glance down at the black marks on my body. I know they are nothing like normal burns, which is why Bonnie can immediately tell I have been playing with fire.

"We put ice on it. I'm fine."

"You're lucky those kinds of burns are fine with ice! What are you going to do if Kelsi or Ben get burned? They don't heal like you from fire!"

All three of us are looking down now, as if we were scolded by our preschool teacher. After a while, though, Bonnie sighs and crosses her arms.

"So? Why are we here now?"

"Come on, sis, I'll update you on the way."

Still not so happy, Bonnie follows us into the Purple Moon Clan territory.

With all the people around, our arrival did attract some glances. Not only because of my appearance, but because Kelsi, Ben, and Bonnie are the ones who stand out, for once. We are clearly in a neighborhood where Caucasian skin isn't the majority. I see all shades of brown skin around us, and strangely, I can't help but glance around wondering if anyone knows me here. Is it a coincidence that Clarissa borrowed a name from a community that looked like her?

A lot of people look our way, but they don't approach or seem hostile at all. In fact, the few wolves on the grass or sidewalks barely glance our way. I would have thought that the twins' presence would agitate some of them, but in terms of territory, the Black Brothers' territory is literally next door. I guess there's nothing too surprising, and the packs are indeed at peace in Silver City.

"So, what now?" asks Bonnie.

"We need to find Lysandra Jones, the Alpha," says Ben. "I don't know the Purple Clan too well, but I guess we can ask–"

"No need," I say.

I can feel her. Just like the other Alphas, Lysandra Jones' aura feels something almost physical to me. It's not as strong as Nora's or Selena's, but I can still feel it. It's a bit stronger than Johnny Seaver's, and it's guiding me toward those buildings with the graffiti. I start walking, the three of them following behind me.

I'm feeling a bit... numb. Maybe I'm just tired from all these events today, but I feel a bit strange, thinking I'm going to meet yet another person who could have the answers. However, she could also have none at all. I mean, I'm only meeting that woman based on the assumption that Clarissa picked the name Mara Jones on purpose... although it's a relatively common name. I could be completely wrong, or I could be on my way to meet someone related to Mara, the original Mara, Nephera's unborn daughter. After all, if it was her real last name, does that mean she was connected to that Alpha, to the Purple Moon Clan? All the questions are rushing in my head, and I'm making too many assumptions.

We arrive at the entrance of the bunker-like building covered in graffiti. It's more like an abandoned building, actually, but the walls inside have been torn down to leave only the main structure, and inside, a giant skatepark has been established. It's not just a skatepark, though. To my surprise, there are about as many humans as there are wolves. I can't tell if they are doing some strange dance, fighting, or pursuing each other, but there's a lot going on. It's echoing like crazy in there, making the whole place crazy noisy compared to the quiet neighborhood just before.

"Oh, shit..."

I feel just like Ben, a bit overwhelmed. This place is crowded with people. Most look young, but there are some older ones too, who seem to be training them. Is this some sort of training area? I keep glancing around, following that aura I felt. It guides me toward a woman, sitting on a pillar, like a panther watching her territory. There are two men standing at the foot of that pillar with angry pit-bull faces, making me think I definitely found the Alpha. Moreover, her eyes are already on me.

She doesn't act or say anything, though, she only has that smirk on, and swings her leg around, waiting for me to come to her. She's wearing only sports clothes, and her long hair is split into two very long braids. She looks much younger than I thought. Her skin color is darker than mine, but she has gold tattoos on her arms and gold rings too. She even has a few piercings. I navigate between all the wolves and humans in the area to approach her, trying hard not to get hit or bumped into. I didn't think it would be this hard just to come and talk to an Alpha!

Finally, I arrive below the little pillar she is seated on. She smiles.

"Hello, little witch. Got lost?"

"I just came to ask you a few questions," I say.

"Let me guess. You're curious about Sylviana, right?"

I hesitate. Sylviana's house is on their territory. It makes sense they were... closer to her. Their pack probably knew of her existence long before others. I take a deep breath, and decide to be more direct.

"...More about Nephera, actually."

She loses her smile, and I see her frown a bit. Crap, maybe that was too direct? She doesn't look like the kind of woman I should mess with. Her aura seems quiet and tame at the moment, but I have a hard time reading her facial expression, and it makes me nervous. She's definitely gauging me, and I can feel her bodyguards, or whoever those two massive guys are supposed to be, glaring at me.

"...Why would you ask me about Nephera?" she finally asks.

"I... wondered if she had ever been associated with the name Jones."

"Jones?"

She stays silent for a moment, and I can tell she's scrutinizing me again. Although she doesn't seem to trust me, at least she's rather honest. After a little while, she comes down to the ground with an elegant little jump, falling silently on her feet like a panther. When she stands back up, I realize how tall and muscular that woman really is. Her aura seems more impressive from up close too.

"Come with me."

She guides me out of that place, and my friends follow after us as soon as we are out of there, all three of them rather quiet. However, Lysandra Jones doesn't seem to care about them. She goes toward one of the houses in the area, a large blue one. It has an old lady sleeping outside on a rocking chair, with some young pups sleeping at her feet like it's nap time. Lysandra walks past them and takes us inside.

It's a family house, but surprisingly empty. I would say it's a bit smaller than Nora's, more closeted too. It has a strange choice of decor, though. Some of the old items hanging in all corners reminds me of that old movie that took place in Louisiana, with the voodoo stuff, scented candles, and the likes... There are old pictures everywhere, it looks like the Jones Family has been around for a while... However, the furniture has been changed into something more colored, more modern that clashes with the rest. A big, black leather sofa is in the middle of the room, and Lysandra points her finger for us to quietly sit on it. Then, she turns around, leaning against a large mantle.

"Alright. What about the name Jones?"

"I don't know if you heard, but... Mara is basically looking to find her memories, and who she is," Bonnie starts explaining. "The White Moon Clan was... helping her until now, but..."

"You mean watching her," Lysandra interrupts her. "I know Selena, she is a good Alpha and a good woman, but she is too stubborn and wary of people to simply take pity on a young unknown witch, not after what happened. I already know all that, do you think Tonia and I don't talk?"

Bonnie stays mute and looks down, a bit embarrassed. I sigh.

"If you already know, then, do you know anything about... Mara Jones?"

She frowns, crossing her arms.

"Mara Jones? Who by Moon Goddess is that supposed to be?"

I gulp down my saliva and, in a few words, tell her about our little quest at the library for answers, how that name came up, and more recently, our new revelation about Mara's affiliation to Nephera.

"...I don't know much about Nephera, but... in my opinion, it feels a bit strange that Judah Black would have been the father of her child."

"Why not? He was enough of an asshole for that," she growls.

"Liam Black and I are... fated mates."

A few seconds of silence follow; Bonnie's jaw drops though no sound comes out. Kelsi and I exchange a nervous glance, when finally, Lysandra Jones chuckles

"Wait... you're the young Black's fated mate? That stubborn little punk got himself a mate, and a witch, to boot!"

"Yes, I mean we are not technically mates yet, but... You seem to... really know Liam?"

"Know Liam? Girl, I trained with his little ass since he was a kid! He would come every single week to our territory, looking for trouble. He just loved to brawl behind his brothers' backs, he would come and train in that very same arena you saw just now."

Arena, she means that deserted building? Is that really their training ground, then? I wouldn't exactly call that an arena... Lysandra laughs, putting her hands on her hips.

"I don't know how many times he and I almost killed each other, but my father didn't care as long as he didn't go over the line. Liam had so much energy to spare... plus, that's how he met Sylviana."

"You knew Sylviana well too?"

Lysandra nods.

"Of course. My pack is one of the oldest packs in Silver City. We are familiar with witches, we knew they were here long before us. Sylviana knew we were probably one of the only packs with nothing against witches at the time she came to this city, before... Black got rid of his father and Nora Bluemoon became the new Luna. She never asked for anything, but she was useful to our community. We let her settle in that house, protecting her identity from other packs as long as we could."

"Th-then... do you think that before Sylviana was around, Nephera could have... I mean, if your pack is familiar with witches, and she could have been acquainted with your... family..."

As she slowly understands what I'm trying to imply, she opens her eyes wide, staring at me. After a while, she scoffs, but frantically shakes her head.

"I'm going to stop you right there, young lady. My mother died when I was a child, but she was my father's fated mate. Bless their souls, there is no way he would have ever gotten involved with another woman. I have no idea if she had an affair with those three's piece-of-shit father, but there is no way it ever happened with my dad."

"Then... why would I–I mean, Clarissa pick the name Jones? Was it just a coincidence?"

"I don't know about Nephera, but I have never heard of her being associated with our pack. If she hid from Judah Black long enough to have a kid with someone else, it wasn't with my father."

My hopes crumble with those words. So Mara was really... Judah Black's child? It... still doesn't feel right. I was so sure her father could have been someone different, another man. Everything would have made sense too since the Purple Moon was familiar with witches, but it feels like something went wrong, both with my conclusions and Nephera.

"...I think you're looking for the wrong witch, hun," she sighs.

Just as I was about to ask what she meant, Lysandra suddenly walks to one of the portraits, a black and white picture, a family portrait. She takes it off the wall and brings it to me. I notice a young couple, posing on a bench, both with little girls on their knees. If they are not twins, the two girls ought to be very close in age. The picture looks very old, a few decades old at least. I am confused.

"...Sorry, but who are they?"

"Lucian and Beatrice Jones, my great-great-great-grandparents."

...Beatrice? A vision of that name flashes in my mind. The Witches' Ancestral Tree. I remember clearly, the name Beatrice was there. Her name was among Sylviana and Nephera's ancestors, the witch who had two daughters! I stare again at the picture. Two daughters... two young witches. Sisters who got separated and each formed their own line of descendants, giving birth to new witches.

"That woman you see right there? The little girl on her knees was the last known witch of Silver City before Nephera and Sylviana. And she was also my great-great-grandma. Her name was Sadia Jones."

280

I hesitate a few seconds, replaying the events in my head, but... something's just not right.

"No, no, it's not possible," I mutter, completely confused.

"Mara?" asks Kelsi, a bit lost.

"Sadia was marked as Nephera's mother, in that tree," I explain. "She was right next to her name. If she was your great-great-grandmother, she can't be Nephera's... mother. It makes no sense, that would skip more than two generations!"

"Could it be another woman with the same name?" suggests Bonnie.

"No, darling, there was only one Sadia Jones," says Lysandra. "However, who told you it was necessarily going from mother to daughter?"

"But..."

"Think again. There were no male names on that tree, right? Sure, it's extremely rare for a witch to birth a son, yes, but it does happen. Like my grandfather, one of Sadia's sons. She had three boys. So, why would that tree not record those men too?"

"...Because they are not witches."

The answer just hits me. I had already noticed there were no male names, but I thought that was because it only recorded the girls, not necessarily only the witches. I wasn't interpreting that tree the right way. I thought all witches gave birth to witches, but I should have known better. No, I should have realized where I was mistaken after seeing Clarissa's memories this morning!

I can feel the wheels spin and turn at a crazy speed in my head. A lot of things are starting to make sense. Or at least, it does fill in a few holes. Not all of them, but it does feel like I just got a few clues I was missing. I was thinking about all this in the wrong way. A too... linear way. I was too focused on the witches themselves, I didn't even consider the rest. I mean they had families, partners. Why did I think they'd only have daughters?

"So... witches don't always give birth to witches?" asks Kelsi.

"They obey the same laws of genetics as we do," says Lysandra. "A werewolf and a human's offspring won't always turn out to be a werewolf, either. Moreover, witches have no male counterparts. It makes sense their blood could weaken. Especially if they pick wolf mates, we have pretty good genes."

"So you're saying, instead of her daughter, Nephera must have been... Sadia's descendant?"

"One of her descendants, yes. I told you, Sadia had three boys, and they all had children as well, from what I know. If what you're saying is true, and she was next to my great-great-great-grandma on that tree, she ought to be."

"...That could explain why Clarissa used the name Jones," says Kelsi. "If she didn't know who Mara's father was, she may have... used a name from her mother's family line."

"Yes, but that would mean you–no, Clarissa had found out about Nephera's link to the Jones'," adds Ben, turning to me. "Doesn't that sound odd to you? It was a pretty big... mystery until now. How would she know?"

I agree. Something here just doesn't feel right. Let alone the Jones' Family tree, I'm getting more and more curious about Clarissa. If she didn't pick that name by chance, how the hell did she find out?

"Did anyone else come around to ask questions? I mean... have you seen me before? " I ask Lysandra.

She shakes her head slowly.

"No, girl, only the night of the fire. I came with my wolves to see if they needed help, but you were in a bad state. I'm not going to say the piece of charcoal I saw was anything like you, girl. I wouldn't have recognized you. And I had never seen you before that."

So she has no memories of me as... Clarissa.

Then, if she never met Lysandra, where did Clarissa get so much information about Nephera and Mara? How did she know about their relationship with the Jones Family? It's strange. Even if she found another Witches' Ancestral Tree, the name Jones shouldn't have been anywhere on that tree, it only kept the first names. How in the world would she have found such information? From what I have heard so far, even Nephera herself ignored who her real mother was!

Lysandra sighs.

"I'm sorry I can't help you more than that, little witch. However, Sylviana was the only witch I knew, and even she had her own secrets. The few things I do know about witches, I learned from my grandpa. We may not have witches anymore in the family, at least not on my side, but we don't forget our ancestors. Moreover, he always said it was important to pass that knowledge onto the family, in case another witch would appear. We swore to protect the good witches here in Silver City, even if they are not Jones'; that included Sylviana, of course. However, Nephera may have been a Jones, but she was an evil witch. We only help good witches. If you intend to stay on the right path, I'll help you whenever I can."

I slowly nod. In other words, she'll be keeping an eye on me too... I should be used to it by now. However, that good witch, bad witch thing bothers me a bit. It actually reminds me of another matter I had in mind.

"Actually, I do have another question to ask you. That witch... the Water Witch we just saw on the harbor, she... called me a Cursed One. Do you have any idea what that means?"

Lysandra raises an eyebrow, looking surprised, but she nods immediately.

"Yes, I know, but even among witches, that is not a very... According to my grandpa, mostly evil witches used that term. It is a bit of a... an extremist way of thinking among witches. Cursed Ones are the name they use for girls born from a witch, but without any powers. It is a rare phenomenon, but it does happen, just like them giving birth to boys."

"Why call them Cursed Ones, though?" asks Kelsi. "It's not their fault they are born like that..."

"Like I said, it's quite extremist, and most witches don't use that term. I am not too sure, but it does sound like the blood of the father has something to do with it. Long ago, witches made sure to have children with witches' sons, to make the magic in their blood stronger. However, this is not the middle ages anymore. Witches marry whoever they want, human or werewolf. It is only a theory, but there are probably less and less witches in the world. Hence, some witches like the one you met probably don't like that. Girls being born without power means less witches. They consider them failures to their bloodline, or something like that."

"It's really cruel..." mutters Bonnie. "They are already born in a weaker position, but they are even rejected by a part of their own community..."

"Excuse me if I missed this, but you keep using the terms good witches and evil witches," says Kelsi. "I thought that was just a thing of fiction, but you make it sound like there's a real difference."

To my surprise, Ben is the one to answer that, turning to us.

"It's about the way they use their magic. Mara, you probably don't... I mean, I don't really know how that works, but from what Sylviana had said, good witches use their body as their source of magic. Like, when you get those burns? They appear because you use your own strength, right?"

I nod, glancing down the black markings on my body.

"To be honest, I didn't know there was any other way..."

"Well, the other way is the way of evil witches, like Nephera. Instead of their own... forces, they use other people to make magic."

"Wait, what? Other people?"

What the heck is he talking about? Ben glances toward Lysandra, but she doesn't react, and when he looks at his twin, Bonnie slowly nods. So she knows about this too. Of course.

"They... I mean, I'm no expert, but they apparently use the life force of other people to do magic..."

I remain quiet for a few seconds. What the heck is that now? Using other people? He means doing... those burns, that pain, and pushing it on someone else? This is...

"That's pretty fucked up..." mutters Kelsi.

It's the first time I've heard her swear, but Moon Goddess, I couldn't agree more with what she just said. This would make me want to freaking vomit. How can you inflict this onto someone else to do magic? I mean, it's already painful enough for me whenever I try to do it, I don't wish this on anybody else! No freaking way!

"Okay, when were you guys going to give me that information?" I ask the twins, a bit annoyed.

"I didn't think you'd need it," says Ben with a grimace.

"Of course I don't, but it doesn't mean I shouldn't have freaking known sooner! Bonnie, you too!"

"Hey, I thought you knew! You guys have been doing a bunch of research, and you talked about evil witches a while ago, I really thought this wasn't breaking news for you!"

"Well, it is," I sigh.

That certainly explains a bit better why everyone is so allergic to Nephera's name. Her being a... bad witch does resonate differently with me now that I know this. So whatever her power did to her, she... did it to other people? She probably didn't get burns like me, but it likely wasn't much better... I shake my head.

"Alright, I get it. So they... use other people to deflect the secondary effects? Like my marks?"

"I don't think it was anything like your burns," says Ben. "It just made people sick, like poisoned. They'd cough up blood or vomit, be super, super sick, and die."

Oh shit, it does remind me of someone... I try to think about it, but... Clarissa should have been a Water Witch, right? What if a Cursed One wasn't just about... the lack of power?

"You mentioned that the Cursed Ones tend to be... weaker? How is that?"

"I don't know. That's all I heard, but apparently, it isn't just the fact that they don't have magic. They often don't live long, either."

I remain silent for a little while, taking all of that information in.

Clarissa was sick, very sick. With her mother being an Earth Witch, she would most likely have been a Water Witch, but no, she was a Cursed One. What if the Cursed Ones weren't just magicless, but unable to handle their amount of magic? If it forcefully... I don't know, attacked them? It was a similar sensation this morning. When Liam woke me up. I didn't realize the amount of pain I was in, my magic was working against me. It's not something that's just a part of me, it sometimes seems to have a will of its own. Maybe Clarissa's powers never came to be because she could never control it. Not only did she not have the necessary training she should have gotten from her mother, but she ended up with a power that was too strong and was consuming her life from the inside.

That's what that witch saw in me, she probably saw the powerless Clarissa, a Cursed One, using the unborn Mara's fire powers. Of course, it wouldn't make sense. Even if she had been a witch, Clarissa wouldn't have been a Fire Witch.

The question is, what happened? That witch implied that I... that Clarissa had stolen Mara's powers. Is that even possible? How did she do that? Mara was never even born! How could Clarissa have found out about an unborn child, whose very existence was concealed, and discovered a way to take her powers when she couldn't even endure her own? Regardless of how she got those fire powers, was Clarissa really able to handle it?

Something just doesn't make sense here. ...Did she get help? Did something happen that I missed? The hatred that Water Witch had was so intense, I felt like she was staring at some murderer, she made me feel like a damn criminal! However, it doesn't add up. If Clarissa stole Mara's fire powers... Why do I feel more like Mara than Clarissa? What really happened in that fire? Damn, I wish I had been able to see more of those memories...

"...Any more questions?" asks Lysandra.

I slowly shake my head. No, I think I'm done. Still with a lot of questions, actually, but those I won't find answers for here. Kelsi and the twins get up with me, and I politely thank Lysandra for all of her help until now.

"No worries. Come back around if you need anything... As I said, the Purple Moon Clan has nothing against witches... good witches, of course."

Just like that, we leave her house, and find the four of us slowly walking around the neighborhood.

The truth is, I'm a bit disappointed and torn inside. I didn't get the answers I really wanted to hear. That Mara wasn't the Black Brothers' sibling, Liam's half-sister. Instead, what I got was more questions about Mara, Clarissa, and Nephera. I keep thinking something happened, but not as bad as what all the evidence points out. How desperate was Clarissa, and why did she get Mara's powers? The Clarissa I saw in that memory was... ready to die, if I may say so. Her quest was only to prove her mother was a real witch. She had no thirst for power, I felt nothing like that. So how did we get to where we are today? With Clarissa Garnett's body and Mara Jones' powers?

We slowly walk back to the car, and from the long faces following me, I know I'm not the only one who's doing some deep thinking. From the frowning, I'll guess Ben is updating his sister on everything she's missed. Kelsi walks up to stand next to me.

"So, Clarissa was a Cursed One, and... Mara Jones was actually Nephera's daughter, but she was never born into this world, and so far, we... I mean, it still seems like Judah Black was her... biological father?"

"We are not sure of that yet."

"I know..."

She doesn't dare add anything else, respectful of my feelings. She probably knows I'm quite disturbed by that. I know I acted tough and like I didn't really care until we had valid proof earlier, but... the idea is still haunting me. It just doesn't feel right that I'd... partly be Liam's half-sister. I mean, regardless of the whole body thing. I'm not Mara Jones. But was Judah Black really her father? Something just doesn't make sense here.

We finally arrive back at the car, and all get in, the twins in front, Kelsi and I in the back. I am still thinking about our conversation with Lysandra and Kelsi's words when Ben starts the engine. He stops at a red light, and suddenly, another thing hits me.

"Moon Goddess, that explains it..."

"What is it, Mara?" asks Ben, glancing in the rear mirror.

"I just thought, when we were talking about biological parents... Sylviana and Nephera thought they were half-sisters, because they had been raised by the same witch, Danica, right? But, it turns out Nephera wasn't Danica's daughter, she was... probably a human's daughter."

"Yes, that's what we determined from the fact that she was... Sadia Jones' descendant. But what about the relationship with Danica?"

"That's exactly the thing. Danica was a witch. Sylviana was a witch. If you were born with a child that's a witch, without being a witch yourself, what would you do?"

The twins exchange a look, but Kelsi is faster to catch on this time.

"Oh... I see where you're going, boo. You think whoever Nephera's parents were, they entrusted her to Danica because she was a witch?"

"Well, that would make sense," says Bonnie. "Perhaps Danica didn't want to tell Nephera she wasn't her biological daughter, but she still sent her here, to Silver City, where her roots were? Maybe she was hoping Nephera would reconnect with her past?"

"It didn't happen, though," sighs Ben, taking a left turn. "Nephera never connected with the Jones', Lysandra had no idea she was a... distant relative."

"But... how could Clarissa have found out, then?"

That's the one thing I am most disturbed about. How, indeed? The only people who could have made the link never crossed paths with Clarissa, or they were dead long before she came to Silver City.

It's strange, that the more I research about Mara, the more things point to Clarissa, and not in a good way. She knew way too many things. How did she even get the name Mara Jones, supposedly unknown to everyone? She couldn't have met Nephera, or Sylviana, so who? Who helped her? I can't believe she only found her answers with a bit of research. Something happened, someone who knew the whole truth helped her out, and it just drives me crazy.

Because I feel like this is the one question I really need to answer to unveil everything.

Chapter 22

I keep tossing and turning in my bed, unable to find sleep. The room is completely dark, though, only a glimmer of light comes in through my curtains. I'm staring at the moonlight, my heart filled with questions. It must be pretty late... I sigh again, I really don't feel sleepy at all. I glance down and curled up next to me, Spark is there. The black and gold magic cat is sleeping innocently, his fur moving with his breathing. Even after I've been petting him for what feels like hours, I can't sleep a wink...

Too many things happened today. I keep reminiscing about my night with Liam, and everything we talked about. I miss the feeling of his arms around me, the gentle look in his eyes. His eyes are always so expressive, even if one is basically dead. I even forget he's half-blind sometimes. I just get lost in them, in the way they change color without warning, how good they are at expressing his feelings. But then, there was that attack at the harbor, and the look in his eyes when we parted... Something hurts inside every time I remember that scene, his back as he walked away. I felt abandoned, although I had agreed to it. I feel a strange echo of my feelings. Sorrow, angst, that feeling of somebody abandoning us. Who is us?

I wish we could have gone to the cemetery today, right after talking to Lysandra Jones. However, Bonnie told us it was closed, and she insisted we all go home for today. To be honest, I would have probably attempted to get in anyway if I hadn't been worried about Kelsi and feeling really, really tired myself. Bonnie checked our injuries at home, and I fell asleep without realizing, completely exhausted as I was. I woke up in the late afternoon, and the four of us had dinner, but the topic of discussion was all about today's discoveries. Although we learned nothing really new just by talking and making countless theories about it, I was happy to see the three of them basically taking my side of things on each matter, and genuinely trying to help me figure it out. Moreover, everyone carefully avoided talking about Liam. The twins probably understand how deeply our bond affects me and the issue with the name Mara that comes with it...

No matter what, I don't believe he and I are related in any way. It just wouldn't make sense... However, everything we found out so far points to Judah Black being Mara's biological father.

Something inside me tells me this is completely wrong. I just know it. I need to find out why, a clue. Nephera was many things, but if I've learned one

287

thing, she was a smart and cunning witch. Would she have had a child with a man she loathed in the end? Would she have kept the baby? I remember that dream I had, at Liam's place... What was that? Was it memories of Mara or Clarissa? I sigh. I need answers.

I get up, waking up a grumpy Spark, who doesn't appreciate it. I check my markings by reflex, but they look fine. As expected, the cold patches Bonnie gave me already calmed down the burning sensation.

That's another thing. The Water Witch implied I wasn't using my magic correctly, I was getting burned more than I should... for a Fire Witch. It does make sense. From what I've experienced so far, I get two types of burns: the real burns from fires that aren't mine, like the one in the building before I woke up and from the fire a few nights ago. Then, there are those black marks. They burn like regular burns, but they are black on my skin, and they look different. Both heal faster than normal, though. Should I be healing even faster? Or is there one kind I shouldn't be suffering from at all?

I crouch down, rolling up the carpet to reveal the circle. Should I use it again? I'm seriously tempted, but I've probably exhausted my magic for now. Maybe tomorrow morning, once my markings have reduced more...

"Meow..."

Spark is rubbing his body against my leg, but his head is turned toward the door. Is someone up? Kelsi and Bonnie are sleeping together next door... Is Ben up, then?

I step out of my room, and indeed, Ben is up. He's sitting on our little balcony, staring at the moon. I silently walk over to him, a bit curious. He has left his phone on the couch, and he's just outside, with a deep expression.

"Hey," I say.

He turns his head to me, visibly surprised. I realize his eyes are red and teary. Was he crying? He clumsily rubs his eyes and sniffles, trying to act normal.

"Hey," he replied. "You're up too?"

"Yeah... I think I napped too much. I can't sleep."

It would be a bit awkward if I left now, so I just grab the other chair and sit on it. Spark immediately jumps on my lap to make himself comfortable and resume his sleep. Ben looks a bit embarrassed and avoids my gaze, staring away. For a little while, we stay silent. I feel sorry I caught him crying. That's not the Ben I know...

"...I can't sleep either," he finally says.

"Well, we had a pretty big day."

"Yeah... but once again, I was worthless."

I'm surprised to hear Ben being so harsh on himself. He's usually so... joyful and encouraging, I never thought I'd hear him say something like that.

"Ben, what are you saying, you... you protected Kelsi during the attack."

"Have you seen her forehead?"

"It's not that bad..."

However, he keeps shaking his head.

"No, it's bad, Mara. Kelsi is human. She isn't a werewolf or a witch. She doesn't heal easily like us. What if she gets a scar? It's going to be all my fault."

"Ben, she followed me," I retorted. "If anything, you're the one who tried to stop us. I'm the one to blame, Kelsi refused to go back inside the diner because I stayed outside. I'm to blame, and she's a bit to blame too."

He sighs loudly, and the way his shoulders fall, I know I haven't been convincing enough. Why is he being like this tonight? He seemed okay this afternoon. Or was it all an act? Is he the type to brood when he's alone?

"...Ben, you're doing a good job, you know."

"Stop lying, Mara. It's nice of you, but I am not that dumb to think I'm anything you can call a good bodyguard."

I stay silent. I'm not good at comforting people, and I really don't know what to tell him. I feel sorry for Ben because I'm probably not the easiest witch to watch in the first place. Maybe Bonnie was a bit too harsh on him this afternoon too without realizing it. He was dragged into this morning's mess, and anyway, Kelsi could have been hurt either way. She's a human sticking to a witch and a pair of werewolves. I've come to love her, as my first and best friend, but she's just about as stubborn and reckless as I am, and it's really not the best combo.

"Bonnie was right... I'm a shitty excuse for a Beta," he sighs.

I feel like if we had any alcohol in the house, he'd be drinking right now, and I don't really like that.

"Bonnie can be harsh with her words sometimes. She scolded me a lot too..."

"No, she's... You know, she's my twin. She knows me better than anyone in this world, and when she says I suck, I truly believe it. The truth is, I... I haven't really been myself for a while. I know Selena gave me this job as a... way to make myself useful, to prove myself, but I haven't been up to the task lately. I've disappointed my Alpha, my sister, and myself. I just... don't really know what I want anymore."

So this isn't just... about me or Kelsi. I look down at Spark, who's shamelessly purring and making himself comfortable there.

"Then... what do you not want?"

He frowns and looks at me, a bit lost.

"What?"

"You said you don't know what you want. What do you not want, then? Let's start there."

Ben sighs, but he eventually nods, and goes back to staring at tonight's full moon.

"For you girls to be hurt. Kelsi, you, my sis... If anything happened to you guys, I don't think I'd be able to forgive myself. I'd feel like... I truly failed him this time."

"...Your older brother?" I guess.

"Yeah... Moon Goddess, I fucking miss him so much... I feel like... I feel like I've lost my way since Levi's death. That I'm worthless."

"I feel like you all really, really loved him."

"He was the best older brother, Mara," he says, looking at me with a little smile. "Levi was kind, strong, fucking brave... The kind of guy everyone wants as their brother. He was like that to our whole pack. He would have been Selena's Beta. To me, he was my older brother, the one I was always looking up to. There's a fucking void in our family since Levi's gone, and in me too. You know, since Levi was so perfect, and Daniel is the total study nerd, a beast of a brain, I was fine being the goofy third brother. Just making the family smile on hard days, spending time with our little brother, making Bonnie, who's the most serious and stiff, loosen up sometimes too. Now, everything is just... so fucked up."

I can imagine that, if their older brother was such a great guy... It does feel like he left a big void behind.

"Until you experience it yourself, you feel like... When someone dies, it just hurts when they pass. Maybe a bit after the funeral, and then a bit of time later. I realized this is bullshit. You can never forget. You just... learn to live with that fucking hole in your life. It's not like someone's going to replace them, or things get better after a set amount of time. It never does. I... How do I keep being the goofy brother, if no one feels like laughing anymore? Bonnie wasn't so harsh before, and she wasn't one to get mad at someone. Even Selena. She's changed. Everyone has changed, and I don't know what I should change into."

I can hear his voice cracking, but Ben doesn't let go and cry. Instead, he looks... angry. I don't know at what; maybe at himself, or at his deceased older brother, or at the Moon Goddess. I keep staring at him, surprised to see him so mature. I had forgotten Ben was an adult too under his usual laidback and cheerful attitude.

I let out a long sigh, a bit at a loss on what to tell him. It's hard to advise someone in a position I've never been myself...

"You know, I like the cheerful you."

He glances at me, surprised.

"You mean the one that lets you get away with pretty much everything you shouldn't?"

I can't help but chuckle.

"Yeah, there's a bit of that too. But, you know... I don't think your family will resent you for staying you. Even if it's hard for them to smile or laugh, at the moment. There was a time I was pretty depressed, at the hospital, you know. The days are very, very long when you stay between four walls, with no family to visit you. Bonnie couldn't be there all the time, and she was my nurse, not exactly there to be my friend. However, the fact that Kelsi visited so often... She didn't have to, but she spent so much time there. I know no one likes to visit hospitals. It's... unfamiliar, buzzing with people between life and death and people who don't have time to care about you. The cold white walls, the smell of disinfected rooms and weird products... Still, Kelsi always came to see me and never complained. She was always smiling, overflowing with joy, excited for new research or something. I think... I think this is exactly what people going through shit need."

I can't help but smile a bit, reminiscing about our days together in that hospital room. I was always so looking forward to when she'd come and visit. Wondering what stupid outfit she'd have on that day, if she had found anything new... Maybe that's also why I was quick to forgive her about those texts. I knew Kelsi couldn't really be bad, just... wrong.

I glance down and pet the ball of fur on my lap. Spark doesn't care about our moonlight discussion, he's just wrapped up in a perfect bundle with only his tail out. Ben is looking down too, but I know he's listening to my words.

"From... someone like me, it may sound odd, but I really think we need all kinds of people in this world. You don't have to worry about how your parents or siblings deal with the loss. That's something you cannot do anything about, and they'll overcome it themselves in some way. But... I think it's sadder if they lose the goofy Ben too. I think Levi would be happy, if you keep trying to make them smile, if you keep being yourself. It's just... okay, Ben. Things are hard enough without your brother, you don't need to add pressure on yourself too. If you do your best, that's all we need."

He slowly nods, but stays silent a very long while. I don't mind, though. I don't think I'm the best listener, and probably not the best person to give advice to people. It was more of my own personal opinion than any real advice too. I just needed to tell Ben what I really thought of him.

I don't really care that he's not a good bodyguard, or if he messes up. I do too. I actually like it better that he's letting me do what I want most of the time, and regrets it later. How much longer would it take for me to find my answers if I had someone constantly on my back, watching me from up close and preventing me from doing what I needed to, keeping me away from where I had to go? In a way, I was lucky. Or maybe, Selena knew exactly what kind of werewolf should be with me. I don't think she overestimated Ben. Or maybe, she underestimated me instead...

"...Thank you, Mara."

Ben has a faint smile on, but at least it's a smile, and he does look a little bit better now. He takes a deep breath.

"I think I needed to hear that... and from someone who wasn't from my family."

"You're welcome," I reply. "I'll send you my bill as a therapist?"

"Very funny..." he chuckles, "but you're right. Maybe I've been... putting too much pressure on myself lately. Selena was never mad at me either, not really. I just think we're all... trying to figure out where we are now, what to do."

"Trust me, I know the feeling," I sigh.

"...Don't worry, girl."

I turn to him, a bit surprised, but Ben gives me a faint smile.

"You have us. Even if... you don't get all the answers you want, or those you want to hear, at least you have us. Kelsi, Bonnie, and I. We are not just here because we feel like we have to, you know. You're one hell of a spunky witch and I love that."

I find myself chuckling at those words. They do feel good to hear, and I nod.

"Thanks, Ben. I like my goofy bodyguard too."

"At your service. But please warn me next time you're trying to die. I'll try to help."

"Will do."

Suddenly, Spark seems to wake up, and jumps down from my lap, stretching on the balcony. Is he done sleeping now? I shake my head and get up too.

"I'm going to get something to drink... Do you want anything?"

"No, thanks."

"Okay."

I step back inside, but to my surprise, Bonnie is standing there. Not only that, her arms are crossed, and she has tears in her eyes... Did she overhear us? I hesitate, but she sniffles, and points at the balcony.

"Do you mind if I... chat with my brother for a minute?"

I shake my head and step aside, letting Bonnie take my seat on the balcony. Well, maybe it's a good thing. Maybe she needed to hear that her twin isn't as alright as he seems. I think Bonnie might be more harsh because that's her way to deal with it too...

"Come on, Spark."

I go to the kitchen to grab myself a cup of water, feeling very thirsty all of a sudden. I really want to go to that cemetery first thing in the morning. I glance at the clock, but it's still too early. Instead, I stay in the kitchen, slowly drinking and thinking a lot. What Ben said about family made me think of my own sister.

I didn't stop to think about it again, but I can't forget about Amy trying to come and see her younger sister who was crying... I sigh, and go to grab the phone. I tried to call her earlier, but she wasn't answering. She hasn't called back since. I check the voicemail, but there's nothing.

I hesitate, and push the call button. It rings one, two, three times. I glance at the clock, a bit nervous; I shouldn't have called at such a time but then again, who knows which side of the world she is on...?

"Amy Garnett speaking. Who is this?"

For a couple of seconds I'm surprised. Shit, the phone! I forgot I took Liam's, Amy doesn't know this number.

"It's Ma-... I mean, Clarissa," I say, a bit embarrassed.

"Oh. ...Is everything okay? What's this number?"

"Yeah, uh... I borrowed a phone from a friend."

"I see."

She doesn't say anything after that and I'm a bit at a loss on what to say. My eyes go to the clock again.

"I'm not... waking you up, am I?"

"No, I was working on something."

"Are you busy?"

"No, it's fine. Clarissa, what is it? Are you sure you're alright?"

"Yeah, but, uh... I need to tell you something."

I take a deep breath. I'm not really sure how to bring the subject up without making Amy freak out. If anything, I don't want to tell her about the magic circles and even all the trouble I got into today. She'd most likely have me on the next plane out of Silver City...

"Amy, I had a dream about... when I was younger. Before the accident."

"What, really? Is your memory coming back then?"

The tone of her voice surprises me. I can tell she sounds happy about it but also... cautious. I know I have to ask, but somehow, it's just not easy. I don't know what Amy knew or not, and I'm afraid I'll reveal something she shouldn't have known. Why am I so cautious with her all of a sudden?

"I can't really say," I explain. "It's just... dreams and I think they are memories from the past. Did my room have... dark blue walls?"

"Yes. Yes, your room at our father's house was like that."

"And... my bed was in the corner opposite to the door."

"Yes."

"I just had a memory of... me crying under the bed covers. You... walked into my bedroom, but a man... I think it was our father, he told you to leave me alone."

"Oh..."

She stays silent for a little while and I hear her close a laptop.

"That's... after Father brought you home. You really cried a lot and I would hear you when I went to the bathroom. Our father is a strict man. He didn't like seeing me out of my bed, for any reason at all."

"Yeah, he didn't seem... very concerned."

"No. I told you, he's not really the... doting type."

She sounds almost sorry, and it makes me smile. If anything, I'm happier to learn that Amy was more concerned about the crying Clarissa than she was sad about our douche of a father.

"It's fine, I'm not really surprised at this point."

"Do you remember anything else?"

"There was a meal with our father, but it wasn't very... happy. You weren't there. Also, I remember when I... asked you to help me apply to the university here."

"Yes, like I told you, it was the first time you reached out to me to ask me for anything."

I nod, although she can't see it. Clarissa probably didn't give her more details about her reasons, it sounded like Amy helped without asking too much. There's still one thing I need to ask though.

"...Amy, did you know I was sick?"

She stays silent for a long while. It can't be that she didn't know. It would explain a lot, about basically everything. Even her reactions at the hospital, how she was being over protective of me. Will she lie? I wait, even checking if she might have hung up at some point but I can hear her breathing, very faintly.

"...I didn't know until your accident."

"How so?"

"You had put me as your emergency contact so they called me when it happened. I flew over and was taken to the Emergency Room and so on. When I did the papers for your admissions though, I saw your health records..."

So Amy really had no idea until then, as I suspected. Clarissa did one hell of a good job in hiding so much from her older sister... She hid that she was sick, probably terminally ill, and she flew to Silver City under false pretenses too. Of course. If Amy had known about her health issues, she probably wouldn't have let her... I mean let us fly here.

"I thought there was a mistake," she continued, "so I called our family doctor, and she confessed everything."

"Amy, what did she say?"

"...You had a strange form of lung cancer and lymphoma. Not only that, but your organs were failing one after the other. As if your body was destroying itself from the inside. You also had some form of blood disease. Our family doctor said you... refused to be treated and refused any medication."

It does sound like Clarissa dismissed all the concerns of the people around her. The few that actually cared about her. Why, though? Did she really not care about dying? Or did she know there would be a way to survive...? I hear Amy walking on the other end of the phone and some coffee machine running.

"I called Father, to ask if he knew," she sighs. "I couldn't believe our family doctor wouldn't have told him at least."

"He knew, didn't he?"

"Yes. I... I fought with him over the phone."

Wait, what? She fought with that stiff father of ours? For my, or Clarissa's sake? I'm shocked. I had felt like Amy was the most implicated but I never thought she'd go that far. She had said so herself she really didn't care much about her father...

"Really?"

"Yes. I couldn't believe he was that unconcerned. I had always assumed... that he somewhat cared a bit more about you. He had kept you home longer than he did with me, before sending me to boarding school, so I don't know why... I should have known better. Anyway, it made me mad so I figured if I was mad at our father I had to at least do better than he did as a parent. I mean, I know we are only half-sisters but you're still much younger than me, and without any decent parental figure."

I have to keep myself from chuckling when she says that. Despite her very strict tone, I guess that's her way of showing she cares. I think I'm trying to understand how it works in our family... I'm completely fine giving up on that asshole of a father though. From the bit I remembered of him, I'm not missing out on much. I nod and take a deep breath.

"Amy?"

"Yes?"

"...Thank you. For being my family."

She goes silent on the other end of the phone, but that's fine. I didn't expect any cheesy response from her. I just wanted her to hear it from me at least.

I hear her clear her throat and I smile. Is she touched?

"A-alright," she says. "...Anything else you remember?"

"Uh, I don't think so. That's pretty much it."

"I see, I don't know what happened in that accident but... Clarissa, your disease..."

"I know. I'm healed, aren't I?"

"Yes. I asked them to check and double-check everything. They said aside from your injuries, everything is... gone. I am not really knowledgeable in the medical field, but they said it's like all of your cells had regenerated. Your lungs are as good as any healthy person your age, your blood is clean, everything is... fine."

"I remember how I felt before the accident, a bit. I know I wasn't feeling well."

"Clarissa, you were terminally ill. Our family doctor said you should have... died within a couple of years. I don't know what happened in that accident but it saved you."

Magic saved me.

I don't know what happened, how Clarissa got ahold of Mara's powers, but... somehow, she found a way to survive. Not only did she heal herself but she... we acquired these powers in the meantime. A Cursed One's body who should have died now is as good as the body of the Fire Witch who should have lived instead. How the hell is that possible?

I lean against the kitchen counter, my head filled with questions. I'm mostly uneasy because I'm afraid to know what Clarissa did, the price she paid for this new life. Why I don't remember myself as Clarissa, and why the name Mara is the one that sticks in my head. Something about all of this scares me. As if some truths I still have to uncover are going to hurt more people...

"Amy... Why didn't you tell me? That I was sick before?"

"Oh. I..."

She sighs.

"I don't know. I didn't have any plans to actually hide it from you at first, but then, before you woke up, I guess I just felt like maybe it was better you didn't remember. I thought... you might be happier if you had a chance to start over. You had... a new life given to you. I honestly don't care to know how it happened. I just felt you deserved it after... everything. You were in a new city, you had a new friend, a new life away from our father and everything you went through as a child. I felt like maybe this was a chance I should give you. I know if it had happened to me, I would have taken it. So, I made the choice for you."

I nod.

I can't say I fully agree with her decision but... Clarissa and Amy weren't close enough to tell each other their secrets. Her dying, younger sister came to Silver City and suddenly, she wasn't ill anymore but an amnesiac. I don't know what I would have done in her stead, but Amy knew Clarissa wasn't happy. No matter how far apart they were, she couldn't ignore the fact that her little sister was unhappy with her previous life.

The bullying episode... I didn't tell Amy. She probably doesn't need to know that but maybe, she would have been comforted in her decision if she knew.

"...Are you upset? That I didn't tell you?"

I hesitate. I probably am a bit. I mean, I wish she had been much more honest about everything, earlier. It's not that I really resent Amy. I do understand she was trying to do what's best for me, but it's just that our relationship was too... awkward to begin with. I guess she and Clarissa never really learned how to behave as proper sisters, so she just acted the way she felt was the best for her estranged sister. It's not wrong, it's just... not really right, either.

"I understand," I simply reply. "However, I'd appreciate it if you... asked me things directly, from now on."

"I will."

"...And not pay my friends to do it."

"...Oh."

Yes, I know about that. I want to roll my eyes, but it probably wouldn't do much. I hear her clicking her tongue.

"Sorry, Clarissa. I just... felt it might be more convenient that way."

How is paying Kelsi to report to her more convenient than asking me directly? Is it because she can't be bothered to call? But if she texts Kelsi she should be able to text me also, right? I sigh. I just don't understand how she thinks sometimes.

"Well, don't do it anymore," I say. "I really don't like it."

"I understand. I won't."

I nod. I guess this is it for tonight's awkward sisterly conversation... I try to think of something more to say, but I don't think I can ask her how her work is going or something like that. I really don't know much about my older sister... How do you work on that?

"Did you find anything new?" she suddenly asks, taking me by surprise.

"Oh, uh... yeah, a bit. I mean, I found a picture of my mother and a book that probably belonged to her. I... I also met someone, who is like... a distant relative. On my mom's side, I mean."

"Really?"

I'm a bit shy, but I decided to detail a bit of my findings to Amy. I feel like she's making an effort by asking and acting genuinely interested, so I just let her know how it is going so far. Of course, I spare her all the details about me hanging out with werewolves, the whole witchery situation, and the fact that I almost died a couple more times this week... I just make it look like the research has been rather easy and simple, like a trip to the library and a bit of luck.

"It sounds like you've been busy," she says.

I almost grimace. Oh, Moon Goddess, she has no idea...

"Hm, yeah. I do hope to find more soon, though..."

"Clarissa, what about university?"

I'm so surprised, I stay mute for a few seconds. What about university now? Who cares about university?

"Uh..."

"You went to Silver City to study also. At least, that's what you had told me. Are you going to your classes?"

I'm almost sweating, and I'm cringing. Who cares about university?! Clarissa was the one who made up that lie so why do I have to answer for that now? I have no idea if I've missed classes! Did Kelsi miss hers to be with me too? What do I tell Amy now?

"I'm... considering changing majors."

Awesome, Clarissa.

"Why?"

"W-well, with my amnesia, I just... I guess my tastes have changed a bit, I don't think I like what I'm doing anymore."

"...What are you going to do, then?"

I have no idea; why do I have to worry about properly going to a university now?! I look around, looking for some kind of answer but I have no idea!

"I... I'm still thinking."

"I see. Well, let me know once you've decided. You should see if you can save your credits for the end of the semester, at least. It might be useful later."

"O-okay..."

I glance toward Kelsi's room hoping she'll help me figure this out in the morning. University, seriously? As if I could afford to add that to the long list of things I need to take care of!

"Alright then. It's... almost 6:00 in the morning here, I have to get ready."

"Oh, okay," I say, relieved she's not pushing this further. "I... Is it okay if I call you back later? I mean this week?"

"Of course. I'll save this number."

"A-alright. Uh... Have a good day, then."

"You too. Stay out of trouble."

Ugh, I can't guarantee anything about that.

We hang up, and I let out a long sigh. Although this conversation was a bit strange, I somehow feel a lot lighter. I feel like we've cleared some air between us. I think... I think I'm starting to understand Amy a bit better. She doesn't have bad intentions, she's just trying to do her best with the little bit of knowledge she had about what a real family is supposed to be like. If Clarissa grew up alone and depressed, maybe Amy became cold and detached as her own result... and is fighting through it with the only real bond she has.

Spark suddenly jumps on the kitchen counter next to me, staring at me with his big golden eyes shining in the dark. I pet him, a bit unsure of what to do next. I don't really feel like going back to bed now... although I should probably try to get some more sleep. The twins are still chatting on the balcony. I rinse my cup and turn around to grab my cat and my phone, but just then, it vibrates. I frown. Did Amy text me?

I open it, but to my surprise, it's from another number.

"I miss you. And I'm sorry. Can we talk tomorrow?"

I hesitate a bit. Liam? My heart skips a beat in my chest. Damn it, I really hope that's him and not one of his other secret girlfriends... I think about what to answer, not to sound too cheesy or too nice. I'm still a bit mad at his reaction earlier...

"Are you learning to use phones now?"

"I had to. My girlfriend isn't a werewolf."

I bite my thumb. So he still considers me his girlfriend... Hmm. Does that mean he got his family's approval? Or he doesn't care? I haven't found anything about the other Mara yet. What does he want to talk about? I'm a bit nervous now. I try to think of an answer while I glance at the clock again. My conversation with Amy comes back to mind for some reason. What would she think of me going out with a werewolf? After a while I sigh and type an answer.

"I miss you too. Can you come get me after my classes tomorrow?"

I take a deep breath, and walk back to the balcony where the twins are silent. They both turn their heads toward me as they hear me arrive.

"Ben, do you think you can take me to the university tomorrow?"

He opens his eyes wide and he exchanges a look with his sister, both baffled.

"Sure, but... why are you going there? You have a new lead? What about the cemetery?"

"I'll go to the cemetery... after my classes end. And Kelsi's too."

"You're going to your classes? Seriously?"

I sigh, a bit embarrassed.

"I talked to my sister, and I figured... although I don't have all the answers yet, I'll have them someday. And then, I'll have to get back to... a normal life as much as possible. So, I want to go to the university, find something I might want to do. It doesn't have to be anything too meaningful. I just want some... normalcy in my life."

"Normalcy. Got it. Yeah, sure."

"Thanks..."

A bit awkward, I walk back to my room with Spark on my heels, and look through the stuff on my desk to find an agenda or something. Damn, I have no idea what my schedule is like... I guess I'll just have to accompany Kelsi to hers tomorrow and ask the secretary.

His Blazing Witch

Chapter 23

"...You want me to help you put on makeup?"

"Hush! Kelsi!" I protest in a whisper.

I am already dead embarrassed, but her over-excited expression and the glares we are getting from all the nearby students is not helping.

She is smiling from ear to ear and barely glances at the professor behind her laptop. This class is dead boring anyway, I don't even know why I wanted to accompany her... I found out my classes ended an hour earlier than what I had told Liam at the last minute. This is what I get for not checking my schedule properly, I guess. Anyway, I didn't want to look too impatient, so I joined Kelsi for her class, but now, I am regretting this a little...

"So you really have a date with Liam Black after?" she asks.

"We are going to check out the cemetery, you can't call it a date..." I grumble.

"Anywhere with Liam Black is a date, boo! Plus, you are the one asking me to help you with your makeup. This is so a date."

I frown and bite my thumb, a bit annoyed, but Kelsi slaps my hand. I really need to lose that habit...

I sigh instead, and go back to fidgeting my pen above my blank notepad. Aside from a few doodles, I haven't actually done anything... I just keep drawing the same symbols over and over again, some of them were in that book Kelsi found. I don't know why those three just stick out to me. There's a simple spiral, a circle with two moons on each side, and one with a moon and three tear shapes.

"Alright, I'll help you," Kelsi whispers, "but you have to tell me everything afterwards!"

"Yes, yes... What about you and Ben, by the way?"

She freezes over her keyboard, and turns to me with that deer in headlights look.

"W-what about Ben and me?"

...Seriously? Is she blind or just pretending not to know? I doodle again.

"Yeah. Aren't you two a thing?"

"What thing?!" she exclaims.

Everyone turns around to glare at us once more, and the professor clicks his tongue.

"Ladies, can we be quiet for a few more minutes?!"

Kelsi mumbles an apology, embarrassed, but I see some glares still aimed at me. The whispers too, I can hear that.

"That witch... She really thinks she can do whatever she wants..."

"Arrogant bitch."

"Why do the werewolves decide if she can stay or not? Fuck them!"

I glare at the asshole who said that, and just as our eyes meet, he makes an obscene gesture my way. I take a deep breath and remain quiet and avert my eyes, but he continues, making his friends laugh.

...Kill him.

Oh Moon Goddess, no, not the voice again. I slam my pen down. It's been a while and I did not miss it! The guy continues, and he is not even hiding himself. I catch the professor's eyes, and I realize he saw it too. As soon as his gaze crosses mine, he composes himself and goes back to his lesson. ...Really? He doesn't react, and goes on with his class. Is he seriously going to pretend he did not see that? What the hell is wrong with these people?!

"Hey! Fuck off!" yells Kelsi, who noticed it too.

"What are you going to do about it, freaks?!" a girl next to him says with a sneer.

...We should kill that bitch too.

I take deep breaths. No, we are not killing anyone, at least not today, not here. Putting the murderous intent aside, I do not like this at all. They are not just provoking me, but Kelsi has to go through this crap too? This is her classroom, I shouldn't have come. I knew what it was going to be like since I returned to class, but I didn't think my friend would have to go through this shit as well. What shocks me even more than those jerks targeting me is that no one else is saying anything. They clearly know, but those who do not participate all stay silent, some even smirking.

...Humans are rotten... They should all just burn...

Agreed.

As the guy starts making some dance with his middle fingers, I put mine up too, but with a flame dancing on my fingertip.

His smile disappears instantly.

"Y-you bitch! She is going to kill me!"

"I am sure going to fire your ass if you don't leave me the fuck alone!" I retort, not bothering to whisper anymore.

"Mara... Let it go," whispers Kelsi.

"Why should I? This guy has been provoking me on purpose, no one stopped him, neither did the professor. Why should I stop? He's the one who played with fire!"

"Miss, you are disturbing my class! Please leave!" suddenly yells the professor.

To my surprise, Kelsi jumps on her feet before I say anything.

"Sir, he is the one disturbing us! Why don't you ask him to leave?"

"He isn't disturbing my class, unlike you two!"

Ugh, I want to puke. This is just messed up herd mentality. Once again, Kelsi reacts faster than me and furiously packs her things, pulling the sleeve of my sweatshirt, furious.

"Come on, Mara. This class is shit anyway. They don't deserve you wasting your fire on them."

"That's right. Fuck off, witches!"

I light up my full hand, showing off my fire, making him shut up. I'm really tempted to burn down at least his desk or something, but then, I wouldn't be able to attend this university anymore. Let's not get kicked out before I decide if I actually want to keep studying or not...

We finally leave that class and Kelsi loudly slams the door behind her.

"What the heck?!" she grumbles.

"Sorry, Kelsi. You tried to convince me not to come back and I–"

"No, boo, you were right. You deserve the right to study like anyone else and you can't control what the crowd thinks. I mean, I knew you wouldn't be in danger or anything, but still, this is so fucked up. This is the fucking twenty-first century and we are all adults. How can freaking adults act like this? They don't know the first thing about you!"

"They are just scared of me," I sigh as we start walking in the corridors. "Werewolves are already a different species that humans have to deal with, and now they have me. They have seen what I can do. I just need to be extra patient and show them I'm not dangerous."

"Yeah, well, I won't blame you if you burn some asses until then. That guy deserves to eat some gravel for breakfast!"

I chuckle, and we find a ladies bathroom. The girl inside leaves as soon as we enter, and Kelsi even checks all the stalls to be really sure we're alone. Then, she drops her bag and looks for her makeup pouch.

"Anyways," she sighs, "did you tell Ben?"

"Yeah, he knows. He said he'll leave me with Liam, anyway. I don't think the werewolves are really watching me anymore now. After what happened recently, I'm probably not at the top of the dangerous people list anymore..."

Kelsi nods and gets up, opening up her pouch and taking everything out. She's got so many tubes of different colors, I'm getting a bit worried. Moreover, why does she have so much when she barely puts on any herself? I did notice she began putting a bit more effort into her appearance since her past as a model was revealed, though.

"Any preference?"

"As long as I don't look like I raided a makeup store..."

She rolls her eyes, but picks a palette, and has me close my eyes. I feel her put some light brush strokes on my eyes.

"What have you decided, by the way? About your classes?"

"Nothing for now, except that Clarissa picked the most boring classes in the world. If I'm still studying here next semester, it will be nothing like that."

"From what you told me, it sounds like your sister does want you to keep studying, anyway..."

"Yeah, she sounded sort of... motherly."

"You don't sound like you hated it, though. Open your eyes?"

I open my eyes, and she's frowning, checking what she did, and grabs something else.

"No, I didn't. It was kind of... nice. I guess it's going to be a messed up family relationship, anyway..."

"Close your eyes again. No, not that hard. Alright... Yeah, I guess that's the best she knows how to do. Plus, I think it's good you have at least one decent parental figure. I mean, if you need, you know she'll be there, so..."

Kelsi's right, it does feel good. I wasn't even that nervous when we talked last night, unlike all the previous times. She keeps going with my makeup, and I'm a bit curious to see what she'll do. I'm almost glad we got kicked out of class, it won't look like I took some time for this before going to see Liam... Crap, now I'm nervous again about seeing him. Will he come on his bike? I hope he does. ...Will it be awkward? Probably. I mean, we still have nothing saying Mara isn't his half-sister, and that's one issue we need to clear up soon...

"Mara?"

"Hm?"

"What was that thing you kept scribbling earlier? It looked like witchcraft symbols."

"Oh..."

Without thinking, I grab one of the lipsticks and draw them on the mirror.

"Hey! That's expensive lipstick!"

"Whatever, I'll buy you another one."

"Plus you have a pen and a notepad in your bag!"

"Kelsi, this," I say, ignoring her plea. "What do those mean? I've had these things on my mind since this morning."

"Huh... The three-moon one means Moon Goddess, the second is the Blessing, I think. The spiral... I don't remember which way which is which, but one is for Rebirth, the other for Spirituality, so either of those."

"Okay..."

"Why am I the one who knows these things better than you, by the way? You're the witch, start studying your basics!"

"Yes, yes... I'll get to learning them. I wonder why these three stuck to me, though."

"You did say you checked the book again this morning, maybe you remembered the prettiest or easiest ones."

"Maybe..."

"Anyway," she says, "do you like your makeup? Should I do more?"

I lift my eyes up, from the symbols to my reflection. However, I don't recognize myself.

Because I'm not staring at myself, not even with the change of makeup. It's that silhouette again, the one with paler skin. I gasp, shocked, and Kelsi chuckles.

"Not bad, huh? You've got pretty skin to begin with, so..."

Kelsi sends a glance toward the mirror, but it looks like she doesn't notice the difference. ...Am I the only one seeing this? It's... disturbing. That reflection is mimicking the slightest of my movements, even the way my chest goes up and down under my breathing, but unlike me, she has a smile on, and a confident look. Who the heck is that... She's even wearing my clothes. Skinny jeans, an asymmetric top with embroidered patterns, and a large dark denim jacket.

"Yeah... Thanks, Kelsi."

"You okay?"

"Yeah, I'm just surprised."

Just surprised to see someone else staring right back at me as if she's my reflection. I try to control my breathing, but this is so disturbing. I want to pinch myself, verify this is real, but I don't want to alert Kelsi. She obviously doesn't see that other girl in the mirror, and I am not sure what I'm seeing, either. Why is this happening? The only time I caught a glimpse of her before was when I used the magic circle! I glance down. ...Is it the symbols? Because I drew them on the mirror?

"Alright! Can you wait for me?" asks Kelsi. "I'll just go to the bathroom quickly and then let's leave before we get in the midst of another angry student mob..."

She disappears inside one of the bathroom stalls, and I'm left alone to stare at that strange reflection of myself. No, not myself. Who the hell is she?

I have no idea what to do. I keep staring at her, trying to get a clue. Is this Mara? Or Clarissa? Why does she feel so familiar? I raise my hand, slowly, and she does just the same. She's not me, but she has to follow my movements? Her skin tone is different, she has no scars. Her hair is not black, but dark brown, and... her eyes are blue, or dark gray, something like that. She had thin lips and a larger nose. The more I stare at her, the more her features get clearer, but she still looks... a lot like me. Who the heck is she?

Suddenly, her lips move, and I can clearly read what she's saying.

"*...Missed me?*"

What the heck is going on...? Missed her?

I glance back at the stall, but Kelsi is still busy. I take a deep breath and whisper, as quietly as possible, making sure my lips are clear.

"Who are you?"

She smiles.

"*...I'm dead.*"

Shit, this is the next level of creepy. I close my eyes a second, trying not to freak out. Maybe I'm not cut out to be a witch because I'm sweating, unsure what I'm doing and seriously creeped out. Yet, when I reopen my eyes, she's still there, smiling.

"*Going for a swim again, Clarissa?*"

Oh, shit. She thinks I'm Clarissa? Does that mean she's... Mara? The other Mara? For real? What the hell is going on? I can't even tell if she's a memory, an illusion, a dream... or a nightmare. I lift my hand, and put it against the mirror. That reflection's hand does the same. She smiles even more. It's a strange smile, as if she was twitching her lips, unable to control her movements properly.

"*I missed you too,*" she whispers.

Moon Goddess...

"Mara? Are you listening?"

I turn around. Seriously, why does she try to talk when she's doing her... stuff? I sigh.

"What did you say?" I ask.

"If you're happy with the makeup! We should buy you some. I think olive really suits you, you should try one of those looks I saw in that magazine last week..."

She keeps talking, but I'm only half listening. I'm more disturbed by what's going on in front of me. I don't know what to ask, but before I can come up with something, her lips move again. I can't catch the first part, but it's easy to read after that.

"*...To swim again.*"

Behind me, Kelsi flushes the toilet and comes out, so I hurriedly take my hand back. As if she could see it, I grab some paper to erase those symbols on the mirror while she washes her hand. As soon as I erase them, the reflection disappears, going back to my normal self. I can now properly admire the indeed very pretty makeup I have on, but unfortunately, my mind is elsewhere at the moment.

"Kelsi?"

"Hm?"

"...Is there a pool somewhere in the area?"

"Uh, yeah, the university has a public pool, a few streets away, but I've never gone there. ...Why are you asking all of a sudden?"

"Do you think... Clarissa went to swim there?"

"Uh... I have no idea, boo."

I open my mouth without thinking. Shit, I just realized, I still have that key thing I had found, with all the money. Could it be one of the pool's locker keys? It's worth checking... I glance at the mirror again. That other girl is gone, but it's as if I could still see her. Is she... showing me how to get answers?

"Why are you asking about the pool all of a sudden?" Kelsi asks again.

"I... uh... I just thought, since Clarissa should have been a Water Witch, it might be a lead."

"Oh... Well, I must say, that might be a better location for a date than a cemetery!"

I chuckle and we both grab our bags, ready to leave. I try to avoid glancing at the mirror, but I'm suddenly excited. I'm sure someone's giving me a hand, and this is exactly what I needed to find. I can't even believe I had almost forgotten about that key, and the bundle of money I found! I don't have it on me at the moment, but it doesn't really matter. I just need to drop by the pool and ask if anyone recognizes me, first.

We leave the bathroom, and I'm still trying to convince Kelsi to interact with Ben.

"You should ask him out," I say.

"Me? Mara, Ben is just a friend, I don't think he sees me like that..."

"Do you wear those glasses just for show, Kelsi? Seriously? Come on, I won't be there tonight, and Bonnie is working the night shift. Be a strong independent woman, ask him out. Take him somewhere."

"What if something happens to you?!" she protests.

I roll my eyes, pushing the exit door.

"Kelsi, I'm a grown ass witch, and I'll be with one of the strongest werewolves in the city. If anything does happen again, you or Ben won't be able to do much about it. Come on, just forget me for one night, have fun. You deserve it, and I feel like Ben could use it too."

"Really? Is something wrong with him?" she asks, suddenly all worried.

I laugh at her expression, but the familiar sound of a bike suddenly rises in the parking lot. Oh, Moon Goddess, the fire in my stomach is back again. I'm so nervous to see Liam again... Something inside me can feel him like a magnet I'm attracted to. I want to run across the parking lot to him. Instead, I take a deep breath and control my pace, barely hearing Kelsi who says goodbye and takes the other route. I wait on the side for him to come to me. He's got his helmet on, for once.

He stops the bike right in front of me and I'm so nervous, I could faint. My heart's threatening to burst out. Act cool, girl, you're a cool ass witch...

"Hi," I mutter.

He stopped the bike an inch away from my feet, and it's closer than I can take. His leather-gloved hands reach up for his helmet, and when he takes it off, shaking his wet hair, I don't think sweat has ever been that sexy.

"...Hi," he says, with those destructive sky-colored eyes.

Oh, I'm so done for.

Is it because we haven't seen each other in a while? I'm much more nervous than usual, and at the same time, I'm ridiculously happy. Liam, coming to get me in the university parking lot with his bike. I could get used to that. I can feel all the stares around us, and even some girls whispering. He's definitely attracting a lot of attention. Whatever their relationship to werewolves is, no one can say Liam Black isn't hot as hell. However, I'm the only one he's looking at. Yeah, I could totally get used to this...

"...I missed you," he suddenly mutters.

I blush even more if possible, completely taken by surprise. How can he be that straightforward? I wasn't ready for that! Breathe, Mara, breathe...

"...Same," I hear myself mumble.

That's all I can come up with at the moment. There's just too many emotions at once. Shit, I can be the most badass witch against some jerks, but when it's Liam facing me, I'm reduced to a shy teenage girl unable to come up with a full sentence. Moon Goddess, there should be some adaptation period or training when you get paired with a guy like this...

306

I take a discreet deep breath and try to calm down.

"Thank you for coming," I say.

"I didn't think your class would end early."

I don't want to tell him it ended early because I got kicked out, that's still something I have to work on. I simply nod, realizing he would have been fine waiting for me. I'm actually a bit glad he didn't, I don't think I could endure all those girls staring at him. Wait, am I really the jealous type?

"So, uh... how were your classes?" he asks, a bit awkward.

"Boring."

My short and honest answer isn't helping. He nods. We barely exchanged a couple of texts today, just enough to let him know when and where to get me. We stay silent for a long minute, both a bit unsure what to say. I'm happy to see him but... it feels a bit like we can't let go of what happened the last time we saw each other. I don't know where to begin though. How do we clear the air between us?

"Mara, can we... just go and talk somewhere?" he asks first, mirroring my thoughts.

I nod and glance around. Indeed, we're catching a bit too much attention around us. I don't know if it's Liam, his bike, or me... but a little crowd is gathering and from my previous experience, I really don't want to stick around.

I nod and he offers me the helmet. However, my eyes still go down on the bike.

"...Can I drive?"

"Heck no!"

I chuckle, amused by his offended expression, and finally take the helmet. As I can't help but smile, Liam seems to relax a little too. He suddenly grabs my hand, making me all nervous again, and gently pulls me closer. I feel the chills go up my spine, and sure enough, our lips finally meet for a kiss.

It's a very simple short kiss, but it sends some delicious heat waves throughout my whole body. Liam's leather glove around my neck is driving me crazy... When we part, I'm definitely blushing and hotter than I should be. However, seeing him smile softly is all that I need. I put on the helmet with my shaky fingers and hop on behind him in a hurry to hide my inner turmoil. I can't calm down just like that, though. Too close for comfort, as they say. Although I like being the one to drive, hugging Liam from behind isn't too bad...

"Where are we going?" he asks, suddenly bringing me back to reality.

"Oh, uh, the university pool."

He freezes and turns his head to me with a frown.

"The pool? ...Are you sure?"

"I know, but yeah. I'll explain once we get there."

He nods and starts his bike, apparently already knowing where to go. The powerful roar of the engine excites me a little, although we're not going far. Plus, holding on to Liam's leather jacket is a bit... enticing. I missed his warmth. As we ride across the campus, I'm shamelessly holding on to him as close as I can. Moon Goddess, I really missed him.

The ride is almost too short, and soon, he stops in front of some old white building.

Wow, the university pool is about as old as Kelsi had said. The blue letters are even fading a bit, and for a minute, I'm afraid it's going to be closed. A bit reluctantly, I get down from the bike as Liam turns the engine off.

"Haven't you had enough water already?" he asks with a sigh while I take the helmet off.

"I... got an unexpected clue earlier," I admit.

"...The voices again?"

His frown reminds me that I already told him about that too. I shake my head.

"No... I mean, I did hear them today, but it's okay, I think I can control them now. No, I think I found a way to get in contact with... Mara."

Liam doesn't hide his surprise. He stays speechless for a second, but then he gets off his bike and puts the chain on quickly before turning to me.

"You said, Mara?"

"The other Mara," I explain. "I think she's... still inside me somewhere."

"Ma-... I mean, you do understand how complicated and fucked up that is?" he sighs.

"Well, we can just add that to the list," I retort, pushing the helmet to him. "Liam, honestly, I still don't have all the answers and it may get weirder from here on out. So, if you don't feel ready for this shit..."

"No, no, Mara, wait."

He grabs my hand again, sending butterflies to my stomach. I look at his eyes, quite blue today. How does he ride a bike with one of them being blind...? I have a hundred stupid thoughts coming to my mind but really, I'm just crazy about the touch of his hand on mine. It's like I can't focus when he's this close.

He looks down at our hands touching, and takes a deep breath.

"I'm... sorry about how I reacted yesterday," he says. "I didn't mean to hurt you or anything. I... I'm just... My father was a fucking jerk, and to think that you're... maybe... another victim of his in some way, and... my..."

"Liam, I'm not your half-sister," I retort. "I know I'm not!"

"Alright, alright," he says.

He pulls me in for a hug, taking me by surprise again. Moon Goddess, he smells so alluring... I feel his strong arms wrap around me, and his large hand on my nape.

"I trust you, okay? I've decided, I... I'll trust you. It's just that I can't help being scared of the answers we'll find, how much dirt we're gonna have to dig up. I'm... I don't want to lose you, and I'm afraid one of us is going to regret it once we find the answers."

I take a deep breath and hug him back.

I understand his concerns, but I just... I don't know where I get this faith from. In Mara and in Clarissa. I don't really care about his father, I just need my answers, about everything.

"...It would make no sense that the Moon Goddess paired us, right?"

He takes a deep breath and we separate a bit, his hands lingering around me.

"Actually, I've thought about this a bit, and... what if I'm paired with... Clarissa?" he wonders. "And Mara, I mean, the other Mara is just a... passenger?"

I stay mute for a while. He even got that far? I chuckle nervously, but it's certainly not funny. I take a deep breath and put my hands on his cheeks.

"Well, I don't know for now, but I'm hoping to find some clues in there. About Clarissa or Mara, I don't know. I just have a feeling."

He slowly nods and we separate, although he immediately grabs my hand to hold, intertwining his fingers with mine.

"Alright. I'll... have to trust you on that one," he says.

Though I can tell he's about as unsure as I am, feeling his skin against mine gives me a bit of courage. I don't want to give up until we get to the bottom of this. And I am certainly not giving up on my bond with Liam. I need him.

We walk inside the building and immediately, the strong smell of chlorine annoys me. Liam makes a grimace too. I walk up to the welcome desk, and the old lady behind it brightens up when she sees me.

"Oh, it's been a while!" she says.

Liam's hand suddenly tightens around mine, I really wish I could do that mind-linking thing at this very moment. She knows me, she recognizes me!

"H-hi," I replied.

"Sorry, Clarissa, sweetie, the pool is being cleaned today..."

Liam and I exchange a glance.

"Th-that's too bad," I mumble, "but... um... I actually just came to get some things I forgot. Is that alright?"

"Oh, really? Well, you know the way. But it's only because it's you, darling! Is your boyfriend coming with you? He's handsome!"

I chuckle, and next to me, Liam's ears become a bit red too. The old lady opens up the door, and Liam and I walk into the pool. There's a long corridor with the changing rooms, but I ignore them and walk straight to the lockers. Careful not to slip on all the water spread out, I almost run to the first one I see, checking the lock.

"Mara? Are you going to explain?" asks Liam, a bit lost.

"Oh, sorry. I actually found a key, hidden in my bedroom a while ago, and... uh, Mara mentioned something about going for a swim, so I thought it might be a key to a locker here."

"Okay. So, does it match? You got the key?"

I grimace. I would have brought it, if I had known! I bite my thumb, nervous. How would I even know which locker it is? There wasn't a number or anything on that key! I take a deep breath and look around. What do I do now? Liam is waiting for me too. I glance to the side, and there's a mirror above the sinks. Should I try it? I put down my bag, but as I open it, I get another idea.

309

"Mara, is everything okay?" asks Liam, unsure.

I stand up.

"Yeah, uh… I'm going to try something a bit weird, don't freak out," I say.

"Okay…"

Well, I guess there isn't much that could freak him out anymore. I look around.

"Spark?" I call out. "Spark, if you want to make yourself useful, now is the time, lazy kitty."

I wait a bit, looking around. Liam doesn't say anything, but from his expression, I know he thinks I might have blown a fuse…

"Meow."

I jump and turn around. Moon Goddess! Spark is sitting right there, next to one of the lockers, and look at that, he has that damn key!

"Oh Moon Goddess, I can't believe this cat!" I exclaim.

"Where the hell did he come from?" asks Liam, frowning.

I chuckle and walk up to the cat. But to my surprise, Spark suddenly jumps higher, above the lockers. I frown.

"Spark, give me the key, please."

"Meow…"

I roll my eyes. Seriously? Now?

"Spark!"

I try to jump and get to him but that stupid cat is already too high! I sigh.

"Is it because I called you lazy?" I ask.

He stares at me from above, with that mighty look of his. Oh, seriously…

"Alright, I'm sorry, okay? I won't call you a lazy kitty again. You're a handsome, super useful kitty. Are we good now?"

Liam laughs.

"Mara, you don't seriously think that cat is…"

Before he finishes his sentence, Spark jumps down into my arms. I sigh and finally take the key.

"You were saying?" I ask with a little smile.

Liam's staring at me, his mouth open while I agitate the key and Spark climbs on my shoulder.

"My magic cat," I chuckle.

"You've got a… okay," he sighs. "Magic cat. Noted."

I smile and take another look at the key. There really isn't a number on it but there's a little sticky mark, it might have been torn off… I start looking around. Since the pool is closed, most of the lockers are open.

"You have to try all the locked ones?" asks Liam.

"I guess so."

We take a little look around, but there are only three, and actually, I already know which one it is. Of course, it has to be the thirteenth one… I feel a little nervous, but I don't wait a second before opening the locker.

To my surprise, it's almost empty. I mean, I don't know what I was expecting, but... there's only a little notebook. I grab it, realizing there are some signs on it. No, those are definitely witchcraft symbols, but I don't recognize them. Damn it, I should have studied more! An eye and arrows? I need to ask Kelsi later.

I open up the notebook, my heart beating like crazy. This was what Clarissa had tried to hide so hard... From just one glance at the first page, it's clearly a journal. The dates are on the upper left hand corner, and it starts a few days after Clarissa came here... Moon Goddess, this is really Clarissa's journal!

"It's blank?"

I turn to Liam, surprised. Blank? What does he mean, blank?

"...You don't see the handwriting?" I ask, surprised.

He frowns and shakes his head.

So this is what that glyph was for, others can't read this journal! Moon Goddess, I really need to read this. I can't wait, but we shouldn't really stay here.

"Liam, let's go," I say. "We should..."

I freeze, on my shoulder, Spark starts hissing too.

Snakes. Just like in the bathroom, snakes are appearing on the floor, emerging from the water. Spark jumps down from my shoulder to stand in front of me, his fur almost double its size as he hisses furiously.

"What the..."

Liam starts growling too, and grabs my arm to pull me behind him, but I resist him.

"Liam, no!"

He turns to me, surprised, but I step in front of him, immediately preparing my fireball, ready to attack. There are three snakes, the same size as the one Spark and I killed before in my bathroom. I fire immediately at the closest one and Spark jumps on another furiously. It's not a long fight. Just two more fireballs, and it's over, only dark burns left on the floor. I take a deep breath. Spark, perfectly calm, sits up to start grooming himself, getting rid of the dark ashes.

"What the fuck was that?" growls Liam. "How can there be another witch's magic in Silver City?!"

While Liam walks over to check out the burn marks on the floor, I'm lost in thought. I'm trying to think fast, to remember the recent events... the last time this happened. My eyes go down on the little notebook still in my hands.

"Liam..."

"What?"

"I don't think that's... another witch's doing."

He stands back up, confused.

"...What do you mean?" he mutters, walking up to me.

I take a deep breath, but the more I think about it, the more evident it seems.

311

"It happened before, in my apartment. I went to the bathroom after finding a magic circle hidden in Clarissa's room. Now, I've found her journal, and it happened again. In another area full of water. ...I don't think that's a coincidence, or another witch's doing."

"You mean…"

I nod.

"Yeah. Maybe Clarissa wasn't as powerless as I thought she was, after all."

Chapter 24

September 17

I'm still unsure why I decided to start this journal. Maybe it's the perspective that I'm bound to die soon, or about to do something crazy: survive.

If someone other than me ever reads this, then... Well, I guess it means I'm gone. I don't think anyone would be sad over it, so that's fine. Maybe Amy will be. I was surprised when my older sister agreed to help me. I never asked her for anything, she never asked me for anything, and that was our relationship for the last fifteen or so years. If I'm gone, she would be the only one I'd miss. I think she liked me a little. Probably.

I came to Silver City to find something about Mom. I have been researching witches for so long, but recently the first concrete proof I ever found about living witches led me here. It would have been easier if Father cared just a little to help me know more about Mom, but he doesn't. I won't miss him. I won't regret writing that either.

I have very few memories about my mom and the dreams I have about her tend to blur what I think I do remember. I can't tell what really happened from what I dreamed about. Maybe it's both. I try to do as much as I can to remember everything, because I don't have anything but my stupid brain to remember her by. Father threw away everything I had when I was taken to live with him. I only managed to save that one old picture that was in my backpack. I miss Mom. I miss our days together in that small house. We didn't have much, but we were happy. I even thought about going back, but I'm afraid that would only make me miss her more. Plus, Father could stop me from it.

At least now, I have something to focus on. I registered at the university and picked some courses randomly to throw Amy and my father off. If they know what my real aim is, they'll drag me home right away. I don't want that. The first class is tomorrow, I really hope that it's what I'm looking for.

September 20

It feels a bit strange to be in a city half-filled with werewolves when all I care about are witches. I tried to ask around and there definitely was a witch living in the area. However, it seems like she died... I really wish I could have met her and asked her if she knew anything about Mom. According to Mom, all witches are bound to each other. Unless they are some kind of failure like me, I guess.

October 3
I found a girl to come live with me. Her name is Kelsi. She's a bit of a weirdo, but she's nice and she doesn't seem to ask too much about me either. She keeps to herself, which I'm fine with. I think she did try to be friendlier, but hiding my state isn't compatible with getting closer to my roommate. I can't blame her for trying.

October 7
My health is strangely stable since I came to Silver City, which I'm really grateful for. I hope I can hold on for a while longer. I couldn't find anything about my mom, but the classes about paranormal manifestations are amazing and I feel more connected to her each time I learn more about witches overall. I just wish I can finish the year.

October 18
Professor Vutha helped me get some new books, they're fascinating. I couldn't stop reading, I almost forgot about this journal. I've been devouring each volume and spending nights reading them, learning witchcraft symbols, magic circles, names of demons, all the history of witches. I may not have any magic, but I'll be the most knowledgeable human about witches for miles around at this rate.

October 23
I think I might run out of time sooner than I planned. I coughed up a lot of blood last night. I'm glad Kelsi was out because it took forever to clean.

October 25
I don't know what to do. I'm feeling so sick this time. I almost called Amy, I don't know what to do. My lungs are literally killing me. I'm scared I'm going to die alone and someone will find me like this, in my bedroom. I don't want to die alone. I'm scared. I'm really scared.

October 26
I decided to write my will. I'm not sure what I own, but I want my sister to have it all. I wish we had been closer.

November 1
I don't know why I felt better this morning. Way better. Last night, I could have sworn I was going to die and I was going crazy but now it's stopped.
I almost did the unthinkable to stop suffering. The pain was just too much. My lungs were on fire, my head was spinning, I could barely walk. I was cold, so cold no one would believe it. I couldn't feel my body and yet, I'm sure I had

a crazy fever, because I was sweating like a pig. I barely remember what really happened. I went to the bathroom on all fours, threw up everything I had, and sat down in the bathtub. I remember I began filling it, thinking I'd rather die fast than in pain.

I must have passed out, but I have no idea what happened after that. When I woke up, I was still in the bathtub and it was full, but it had stopped before overflowing. I didn't even take the razor blade, so when did I think about stopping the tap? Maybe I hallucinated more than I thought...

November 5
There's definitely something weird going on. The pain is back, but now I'm hallucinating too. I thought it might be the meds, but nothing was changed and if anything, I've been taking less of them. So what the hell is wrong with me?

November 6
I heard it again. That voice in my head. I don't know what's going on. Am I going crazy?

November 9
I keep thinking about those circles I was drawing the other night. Could it be possible that I did something wrong with it? Or actually did some magic? Despite everything I know, I didn't think I could actually do this if it wasn't for the fact that I do have that voice in my head. It just comes and goes. I feel like I'm not alone. It's warm and not really scary. Just strange. Really strange.

November 16
I haven't heard that voice in a while and the pain is back. Is it strange to say I miss her? I don't know what I had done to get that voice in my head, but at least while she was there, I was feeling less pain.

I'm sure something happened last time while I was drawing those circles. I need to ask Professor Vutha and try again. I feel like this might change everything.

November 20
I don't understand what I'm doing wrong. Nothing happens anymore and I'm dying. I'm really dying.

November 25
I don't want to suffer like this anymore.

Mom, I'm so sorry. I know you told me to be strong, but I don't want to be sick. I'm tired of being sick, of being in pain. It hurts. It just hurts so much. No one cares about me dying. I'm just tired.

November 26

His Blazing Witch

I keep writing in this journal as if someone's going to care. As if my life ever mattered. Who will read this? Who will ever care about Clarissa, the freak? I don't want this pain. Why do I keep doing this to myself? I don't have anywhere to go, anyone who cares. I'm alone.

I've been alone since Mom died.

I should have just died with her.

November 27

I went to class like a robot today.

I held on until now. To the fact that maybe, something will happen. That you wouldn't want this. Mom, I miss you. I miss you so much. I miss you, I miss the way you used to hug me when I was scared, or when I was just tired. I miss your smile and your gentle hands. I don't even remember your face correctly. All I have left is your voice, your voice when you called me. I miss you so, so much. I just want to be where you are.

I don't want to fight anymore, Mom. I don't want to suffer. I don't want to live among all these other people who don't care. I feel lonely. The world could be destroyed tonight and I couldn't care less. This world is just meaningless, it keeps spinning without me and I can't keep up.

I don't want to be saved. I just want this to be done and over with. I want to go back to the past. I just want this to stop, I don't want all this pain. It's fucking painful to live, Mom. Why me? Why couldn't I be born normal? My body hurts, my lungs hurt, my head hurts. My body's failing me. Did you know this when you gave birth to me? That your baby would live with this much pain? Did you wish for a healthy baby?

My head is aching. I can barely see what I'm writing, yet I'm holding on to this pen and this notebook like I'll die if I let go. It's the middle of the night, and no one can feel lonelier than I am right now. I don't want to fight, why would I? No one cares, Mom. They live their lives without caring about people like us.

I'm scared. I'm scared of what comes next, once this is all over. Is it as peaceful as I think? If so, I'd let myself die right now... I'm just scared I won't find you once I open my eyes again. I don't want to be alone, even in death. It's so stupid. I've spent my whole life alone. I just wish someone would care, just enough. I just want someone to hug me, comfort me.

I don't want to disappear without anyone caring. I love you, Mom, I miss you. Was it painful when you left? I remember your face. Death doesn't look like death, it just looked like you went to sleep and didn't wake up. I wish you had woken up. They dressed you in white and they knew none of your favorite colors. I wanted to keep holding your hand.

I don't want some stranger to bury me. I don't want to be forgotten. I just wish everything would be alright... They'll talk and they'll make whatever they want of my death. I wish you'd do magic just once more, make me believe again. Now, I'm just all alone, both going crazy and lonely like crazy. I'm tired.

316

His Blazing Witch

I think I understand why people die now. It's not too hard to let go, it's just harder when no one holds you back. No one is holding me back, are they? I could die tonight. I've thought about death so many times, Mom. I wonder if she's gentler with witches.

November 29
I guess this is it. I don't want any more of these nights crying alone. I'm sorry, Mom. I tried, I really tried, but I just don't want to stay here and wait for death. The pain is just too much and meds won't help. It's okay. I'll be fine once the pain stops. There's no saving me, anyway. I'm just taking a head start, handing back the time I had left.

If I'm reborn, I wish I was a cat. I could lie in the sun and have people love me, hug me. Is it a strange thought? I want to believe there's another life waiting for me. I want another chance. One where I won't have a painful and lonely life. I just can't take being alone again.

It's alright, Mom. I'll just close my eyes and it will be as easy as going to sleep. I won't suffer again. I'll be fine.

I'm sorry, Mom. I just miss you too much and there's no one here for me. I'd rather go to the other side. If there's just the slightest chance I can find you, I'll come to you. I want to see your smile again. See you, Mom.

January 17
Mom, we're getting there.

She's with me. Mara appeared and she saved me. Do you know what she said? "If you don't want your life anymore, give it to me." I didn't die, Mom, I'll just survive a little longer. Mara's just like me. She's so much like me! She missed her mom so much too, and she stayed behind. She waited for an opportunity, for someone like me to help her. I can feel her all the time now. She's with me and when I need her, she helps me.

Together, we're stronger. We'll find the answers, we'll do what we can. I just want to help her, like she helped me. We will survive together. I know we can do this. I'm fighting, Mom, I'm fighting so hard, you'd be proud of me.

I'm learning witchcraft, I'm doing my best. I'm not a witch, but I'm your daughter. Mara's showing me all I can do, I never knew I could do so much! I'm feeling so much better now, Mom. I just want to hold on until we can finish this. I have a purpose, I want to help Mara before I go. I feel like I found my other half, Mom.

I don't know what she really is and sometimes, she even scares me a little. But she's my friend. She's with me when I need her and she shows me the way.

January 22
Mom, tonight I did real magic for the first time!

I cried, I was so happy it worked. Mara warned me it's dangerous, but that's okay, I can do this. It's not even real magic, just a little witch spell. Don't worry, I remember what you taught me. I'll be a good witch, no matter how weak I get.

Mara is doing her best to get stronger too. We are just trying to find a way. We'll be together and everything will be just great, Mom. I'll be fine. I know I will be fine.

January 29

I didn't want to write today, but... Things aren't going the way we wanted. I really want to believe we can make it, but... we're running out of time. My body is aching so much again, Mom. It's painful. I want to keep living. Mom, I want to survive. I don't want to die!

February 3

Mom, I wish you could help us. Mara is worried I'll die before we can find a way. I'm scared too. I really don't want to die yet, Mom, I'm so scared now. I can't believe I wanted to die.

Now I really have something I want to do. I want to be a real witch just like you, I want Mara's powers. Why is it so unfair? Why couldn't she simply be reborn? I'm trying things I didn't want to try, Mom, but I'm just terrified. Please forgive me. I just don't want to die. I don't want to die. Mom, help me, please. If you're watching over me, I hope you'll help me, we'll find a way. I just want to survive. I don't want to die. I promise I'll endure the pain, I just want to live a little longer.

February 6

Were you scared to die, Mom? I'm so scared. I don't want to give up on Mara. I wish our dream would come true, but it doesn't seem that way. I don't know how much longer I have left. It's getting harder to hide from my roommate. The only moment I feel fine is when I'm submerged in water... I've been spending all my time in the bathtub or the pool these days. The pain subsides a little when I'm in water, but... it kills Mara.

I don't want to kill her. Does it have to be her or me? I thought we could do it. I really thought it could work...

Why couldn't we have been born with the same sign? If she had been a Water Witch, it would have been so much simpler... My body can't take fire, her soul can't take water. We're like polar opposites, yet desperate to live together. She's my only friend, Mom, the only one I ever made. I don't want to give up on Mara. She's saved me so many times and there's so much she didn't get to do too. It's so unfair.

February 13

If anyone finds this journal... Please save Mara.

She didn't deserve what happened to her mother. She just needs someone to be with her. This is so unfair. She doesn't know her story. She didn't get to *meet her mom, to live her life. Why? Why did people do this to her? She doesn't deserve to be haunted like this. She just wanted to live.*

I probably won't be able to help her. I'm just so sorry. I wish I had done one good thing, in this short life of mine. What an idiot I've been. I wish I had found her earlier. I wish I hadn't written all those things, wish I hadn't done all of this. Why is it that we can't meet halfway? Why does one of us have to go? I don't want to die, but I don't want to lose Mara. I just can't. I wish we had found the solution.

Hopefully we find one before it's too late.

"Are you alright?"

I lift my eyes up from the journal to meet Liam's worried expression and realize I'm crying. I take a big breath, push a few strands of my hair away from my face, and nod.

"Yeah... Yeah, I just... reached the end of it. It wasn't a happy one..."

"...Can I?" he asks gently.

I nod, erase the glyphs, and hand him the journal. Liam grabs it and leans against his bike next to me, getting absorbed in it while I sniffle and try to calm down. We just left the pool and stayed in the parking lot; I couldn't wait any longer to read the journal. Shit, I didn't expect that... I barely got to the end of it. I look down at Spark purring against my ankle and I reach down to grab my cat, suddenly feeling the urge to hug him.

He seems all happy in my arms... Is he the manifestation of Clarissa's wish in some way? At least, this journal gives me the beginning of an answer to many, many things. Clarissa's train of thought was much more tragic than I'd imagined. How many times did she actually... consider killing herself but kept going? I can't fathom how much pain she must have been in. Some of her sentences were hard to read because her handwriting was so shaky, or blurred by the tears that spilled on it. You could feel her emotions engraved in the worn-out pages more deeply than on her actual words sometimes. I truly felt like for a few minutes, I was Clarissa, I was taking her spot, and experiencing a glimpse of her life.

I wished she had turned to Amy or Kelsi earlier.

Maybe it's easy for me to say but I have a feeling all she really needed was the support of at least one family member or a friend. I consider myself to trust people too easily and I've been mistaken sometimes, but... Clarissa probably needed this more than I do. I let out a long sigh and put my head on Liam's shoulder, feeling strangely tired after all this. I can't tell if it's from using my magic earlier or going through Clarissa's life but I suddenly feel like I'm exhausted. I'm glad Liam is with me, I don't know how much worse I would have felt if I had to read this alone.

"Wow," he says after he's done reading it. "That's... depressing."

"Yeah, I noticed that too. At least we learned a lot, though."

He nods.

"Do you think Clarissa is... I mean, you're obviously alive and well but..."

"I know what you mean. I think she... I think Clarissa did die in that fire. Whatever she was trying to do with... Mara, it didn't work or she didn't have the time to. Something happened in that hangar. The last entry to that journal was merely a few days before my accident, it's not a coincidence. Clarissa was running out of time. Either she tried something very dangerous and things went wrong or she was triggered to do that."

"You think she didn't intend that fire?"

"You read her journal, Liam. Clarissa didn't want to die. I don't think she would have lit that fire unless she had a very good reason to do so, or no choice. Actually... she probably wasn't even the one who did it. I think... I think Mara took over and while Clarissa did die, that Mara is still there."

"Wait, what do you mean, Mara is still there?" he frowns, turning to me. "...Is she the crazy voice?"

I hesitate. Is she?

No, I don't think so. The Mara I saw in that mirror and the way she spoke to me, it was different from the voices. She didn't have that strange, evil feeling in her. I mean, seeing a reflection other than mine in that mirror was creepy, for sure, but I didn't feel any evil from it, unlike that disturbing feeling when I get the voices.

I step away from the bike, still holding Spark, and glance at a little puddle a couple of steps away from us. Will I see the other Mara if I look at my reflection once more?

"No, she isn't. It's different from the voices I get. To be honest, I still don't really trust Mara, but... I don't think she has any ill intent."

"...You're speaking as if you can... talk to her," says Liam.

I nod.

"Sort of? She actually appeared... a couple of times in mirrors. She takes the place of my reflection. It only happened twice though and she only spoke during the latter. It didn't make much sense either. She just said she was dead and that she had missed me."

Liam remains quiet for a few seconds, looking baffled. I can't blame him, that's a lot... Is he freaked out or something? Maybe I shouldn't have told him so much, it's definitely too creepy...

After a while of me getting nervous and him not saying anything, he finally takes a deep breath, puts the journal down on his bike's seat, and turns to face me. I'm a little bit intimidated by his serious expression all of a sudden and a bit relieved that there's a cat between us. The sky is starting to clear up above us and Liam's eye is turning bluer with it... which intimidates me even more. I'm glad Spark is covering my chest because my heart's trying to thump out of there. Liam glances down at the cat, but he quickly puts his arms on my shoulders.

"Can I hug you?" he suddenly asks.

I'm so surprised by his question, I open my mouth like an idiot and don't know what to say. As if he had understood, Spark jumps on the bike leaving us alone and licking his fur. Traitor... I'm left defenseless and I find myself nodding, a bit unsure. What's wrong with me? Aren't we supposed to be beyond hugging? It's Liam's fault, why does he even ask and put me in that kind of heart-storm situation?

He sighs and steps forward, wrapping me in his arms. Moon Goddess, that feels great... He's all warm under his jacket and soon all my worries disappear as I curl up against his chest. Damn, I should ask Spark how to purr. We stay like this for a little while without moving and I wonder what's going on. Not that I'm complaining...

After a while, Liam steps away, leaving me all hot and confused.

"...What is it?" I ask.

"I just... felt the need to hug you all of a sudden."

"...I'm not Clarissa," I mutter.

"I know. It's not about Clarissa. It's not about that but... when you start talking about speaking to dead girls in mirrors and all that witch stuff, sometimes I feel... helpless. It's like you're going to disappear and leave me alone. The other Mara or Clarissa... I'm scared something is going to happen and the Mara I know is going to disappear in those flames or with some of that magic stuff going on."

Wow, I did not expect that... I glance at the journal. I guess it does come as something a bit heavy for a non-witch... or is it because of what happened to his ex? Is Liam scared he'll lose me too? I just... I'm happy he's still willing to be by my side, I didn't even expect him to have those insecurities. I thought he might grow afraid of me, not... afraid of losing me. I step forward and as brazen as I can be, I gather my courage to grab Liam's shirt. I hold on to it and pull him closer, putting on a little smile.

"Hey, don't worry. I'm not letting you go," I whisper.

After a second, I'm glad to see my cheekiness finally put a smile on his lips. His shoulders relax and soon, he wraps his hands around my waist. Oh, I'm in trouble now... A delicious hot shiver goes up my spine just from that. I had forgotten how large his torso is from up close, or how strong his arms are... Well, I'm definitely not going anywhere now.

Liam tilts his head.

"Oh, really? ...Going to hunt the big bad wolf?" he whispers, leaning a bit closer.

My heart's going for the rollercoaster ride again. I blush seeing his face coming so close.

"I'll put a spell on you," I chuckle.

"Please do..."

Just like that, we finally lose that awkward feeling between us and naturally reach for each other's lips. Liam gently kisses me and holds me a bit closer. It just feels so good to finally be able to properly kiss him again, after all of this. It's much more intense than the little peck from earlier. I missed that taste... I shamelessly let go of his collar to wrap my arms around his neck, holding him closer. Is it bad that I'm going crazy over his slightly wet hair?

His hands caress my lower back, making me blush more and more. The parking lot gets hotter all of a sudden... Thank Moon Goddess there's no one around because this kiss is probably barely legal. Is it because Liam is in his biker outfit? I just can't resist. We keep kissing for a while and that's all I want to think about. His hot breath, our hot skin, and the crazy sparks in my stomach.

"Meow."

We both jump and turn our heads toward Spark. My cat is giving us the death glare, sitting up on Liam's bike. I glare at him but Liam chuckles and kisses my neck.

"Alright, I think we'd better stop there."

"Do we have to?" I sigh, a bit disappointed.

Liam sighs and grabs my chin.

"You little witch," he mutters. "Stop tempting me."

I smile and bite my thumb, a bit excited. Liam clicks his tongue and grabs my hand to take it away from my mouth. Oh, that bad habit... I let out a long sigh.

"Actually, we really have to go," he says. "Selena's waiting for us at the cemetery."

"She's there? Why?"

"...She remembers where she saw your name, Mara."

"Oh..."

The hot atmosphere from before disappears all at once. I already had a hunch but... now I feel like this is going to be a hard one. I glance at the journal, but Liam gently pulls my chin and has me look at him instead.

"...Are you going to be alright?"

"Yeah. I... I figured it might be... I mean, it's a cemetery right? Moreover..."

I remember the signs I drew on the mirror earlier and nod.

"I think I know how to properly get in contact with the other Mara now. This isn't going to be as hard as it could have been. I almost have Clarissa's full story. It's time to get to know the other Mara. Plus I'm glad there wasn't anything bad between them. From reading Clarissa's journal those two just... genuinely loved each other. They wanted to help one another. I'm glad it's not some dark possession story or some Dark Witchcraft that went bad."

"...Well, we're not exactly sure it wasn't, right?"

"I'll get the answers soon." I nod, convinced. "Let's go?"

"Let's go." He nods, giving me another quick kiss.

I grab Spark to hold on my lap while Liam gets on his bike and starts the engine. The truth is, I didn't want to show it to him but I feel a bit sour. I just want this to be over and done with so I can go home and finally talk to Mara again. I hope that mirror thing will still work later.

I get behind Liam, hoping no one will say a thing about the cat I'm holding. I have no idea how I'm supposed to carry Spark otherwise and it's not like he's going to leave us. I guess magic cats don't mind a bike ride more than any other...?

We leave the pool's parking lot and while Liam takes us north, I'm thinking about Clarissa again.

I don't think I sympathized with her as much as I do now. From her memories, I had thought she was rather weak, but now I realize I just didn't know the real extent of her pain. She was more of a survivor than I am. Moreover, she could have not cared after Mara saved her life, but she still held onto the ghost like a lifeline desperate to save her. I can't even imagine how she must have felt, knowing she was condemned yet still hoping for a solution. I hope we find out about her real end soon, about how I got her body back to good health again.

At least, I now understand how she was able to do all of this. The magic circle in her bedroom, her contact with Mara, and the little snake traps. Clarissa studied witchcraft and did the most she could with what little magic she carried in her blood. She wasn't a full-fledged witch but she still managed to learn enough to do this much. It's impressive... I have full firepower and I'm handling it like a baby trying to stand up. In a way, the powerless Clarissa was much more experienced than I am. I shouldn't have underestimated all the books Kelsi handed me, that stuff is really for witches. Something as simple as three symbols on a mirror allowed me to get in contact with the other Mara... or at least, what was left of her soul. I wish I could know exactly who I was talking to, what she wants? Why wouldn't she be the one in this body? Why is she in the background? I'm starting to think Liam may have been right to worry about this...

We arrive at the cemetery and Selena is standing there, accompanied by a tawny wolf. Liam stops the bike right in front of them and I realize the White Moon Alpha has a really sour expression on.

"Hi, you two," she mutters.

"Hi," says Liam. "Hi Daniel."

The wolf growls briefly and I get off the bike, letting Spark down. Arms crossed, Selena walks up to me.

"Sorry it took me so long..." she sighs. "It only clicked when Liam mentioned you wanted to go to the cemetery. I... I come here from time to time, to see my parents. I once met with... Sylviana, here. She said she was visiting family..."

"Do you know where exactly?"

"I remember the direction she came from, I went there a couple of times after she died. I didn't know what to look for, though, so I... overlooked the name."

I nod.

"It's okay," I say.

She looks really uneasy about this, but I can't blame her. They probably feel worse than I do, to be really honest. I'm anxious, of course, but I'm more curious to find out what there is to see.

His Blazing Witch

Liam comes to my side and wraps an arm around my shoulder, giving me a quick kiss on the temple to comfort me. We silently walk into the cemetery. Spark scampers ahead of us, looking perfectly fine here. The black and gold cat even rubs his body against some of the little bushes. Or jumps on a tombstone to sniff it. I realize we're headed deeper into the cemetery, into what has to be the oldest part. This is probably why Selena isn't familiar with this area.

Strangely, the closer we get, the heavier my heart gets. I didn't think it would be like this, but my feelings get ahead of me and before long, my hands are shivering and I want to cry. I can't even fight it. I don't know which part of me is reacting, but I tear up involuntarily and feel the tears run down my cheeks for real. Liam gently rubs my shoulder. I'm not even sure why I'm crying, it's so silly but I can't stop.

We finally arrive in an area so old, most of the tombstones are covered with moss. Why is it here? Because of the Jones Family? We start looking around, Selena looking a bit unsure.

"Oh..."

She stops in front of a row of tombstones next to a very large tree. Leaving Liam's grasp, I get closer to check them. Most of those names are too old to be read. I keep looking and finally, I see it. It's a small one, with some ivy covering it. It's not old, but the flowers seem to have grown faster on that tombstone. Probably Sylviana's doing.

Mara.

My heart sinks when I read that name. I get down on my knees in front of it and my tears stop miraculously. I take deep breaths, trying to calm myself and ignore the stares behind me.

"Sorry..." I whisper. "Sorry it took me so long to find you."

I put my hand on the tombstone, mostly covered by the moss. My fingers follow the four carved letters. Did Sylviana do this? It would explain all the moss and flowers on it...

"...Are you okay?" gently asks Liam behind me.

I nod, but just as I do, something catches my attention.

Another letter, right under Mara. I didn't realize because moss was covering it. Don't tell me... Her last name? My heart starts beating like crazy. Oh Moon Goddess, maybe this is the answer we were looking for. Is this what Sylviana wanted us to find? Why did she cover it with moss? Maybe she didn't want us to find it? My breathing accelerates, and the adrenaline starts pumping. I need to know. I need to know now.

With my bare hands, I start scratching the moss furiously, trying to free that name.

"Mara, what are you doing?"

I'm on my knees in front of that tombstone and stubbornly scraping, letting the moss fall to the ground. My heart, Moon Goddess, my heart is going crazy as each letter is revealed.

B.... The first letter is a B. I keep going, hoping. I don't know what, I'm just hoping. The second letter is an L.

I stop, a bit worried. Maybe I shouldn't continue...

No, no, no, I ought to know. This can't be. It just can't be! I take a deep breath and light my fire, throwing it against that tombstone almost furiously. All the green covering disappears and the answer is right there. I hear them gasp behind me and I'm shocked too. This is definitely not what I had thought I'd find. Not Mara Black, but... Mara... Blue?

I stare at the tombstone for a few seconds, confused. Blue? Not Black, but Blue? This isn't what I had in mind... I turn around, and Liam and Selena look absolutely stunned, mouths open.

"You've got to be kidding me..." mutters Selena.

Liam frowns and turns to her.

"D-do you think it's... possible?"

She remains quiet, obviously shocked. What is going on, who are they thinking about?

Now that I think about it, I'm pretty sure Nora's last name was Bluemoon, but... Wait, is this related somehow? I go back to the tombstone and scrape off the moss that didn't burn with my fire earlier, just in case I missed something else. Mara Blue. I mutter it to myself, as if it'd make it more real, or something would happen. I almost want to laugh, because at least, I've got her real name. Not Jones, not Black, but Blue. I can't even say how relieved I am. This tombstone was made by Sylviana, right? This isn't a mistake. She definitely knew her niece's heritage. This is the answer we were looking for.

"We should go see Nora," suddenly declares Selena.

"Why?" I ask, getting up and wiping the dirt off my pants.

Selena hesitates and eventually sighs.

"...She'll explain."

I want to ask more, but next to Selena, Liam nods, making me feel like there's still a lot more I need to know... or be told. He extends his hand for me to take, and I step away from the grave, feeling a bit numb. Before we go, Selena quickly takes a picture of the tombstone with her phone, still frowning. She shakes her head.

"Now that's new," she sighs. "Alright, come on. Let's just go."

Liam grabs my hand and I follow them after another glance at that tombstone. To my surprise, Spark doesn't follow us. He walks up to the tombstone and rubs his back on it before lying down. Is he going to stay here? I don't really need to call him, I know he'll show up again soon when I need him... Maybe this is where he goes anytime he disappears? I mean, this cemetery must be a nice playground for bored magic cats.

We silently get back to the bike; Selena is driving a car, and we follow her back to Nora's house.

The trip back is very different. I hang on tightly to Liam, but for once, I don't really enjoy the ride. My mind is still in that cemetery and that vision of Mara's tombstone haunts me. I have a million questions popping up in my head.

I try to list them silently, but I feel like I'm about to learn a lot anyway. If Nephera really was Mara's mother, who is Blue? Who was her father? From their reactions, I feel like Liam and Selena definitely know already, but why did they seem so... shocked? I just hope the answer isn't going to be something worse...

We arrive in front of the now somewhat familiar house. Unlike before, there aren't any wolves in the garden, but it's also the middle of the week.

Selena or Liam must have warned Nora about our arrival because she opens the door right away with a large smile.

"Hi, everyone! Come in, I just made some fruit juice. Mara, would you like some?"

"Uh, yes, thanks."

As always, Nora is making me comfortable right away. I had seen their house briefly before, but now, I follow Liam inside a big living room. There's a big TV screen, but it's off, and instead, the children are playing on the carpet with the large brown wolf from before. Daniel actually walks up to him, and the two wolves greet each other before Daniel lies down with him, playing with the children.

It's funny to see such young kids so comfortable with those large wolves... The brown one wouldn't even pass for a family dog, more like some mix between a bear and a wolf. There's the young boy from before, sitting down and apparently reading a picture book, and the baby girl is lying against the brown wolf, making happy smiles at her older brother. Nora's children all have her black hair and blue eyes... little Will even has very curly black hair, but his skin is a little bit darker. If they take after their parents, they'll definitely grow to be handsome or beautiful.

"Hi, Will!" chuckles Liam, leaving me to go greet his nephew.

The little boy lifts his head toward him all curious, and I can't help but glance around.

"Your... husband isn't here?" I ask, a bit nervous.

Nora chuckles, bringing a tray from the kitchen with a large pitcher of fruit juice and some glasses.

"No, he's at work," she simply says while putting it all down on the coffee table.

"Thank Moon Goddess the girls are old enough to go to school," sighs Selena. "I thought Nate would never go back to work."

"Even your youngest?" I ask, confused.

"She's in kindergarten; Nate and I both work, and I'm busy with pack duties too. Otherwise, Nora or our friend takes care of her, but I wanted Aurora to be with other kids. Estelle had trouble adapting once she started school."

I guess it is pretty normal for a pack of werewolves to take care of the children together. I glance at Liam, already sitting on the carpet to play with Will and make faces at Lily. While the little boy seems shy, Lily is quite chatty and keeps making big smiles and moving her little fists around.

"Come on, let's take a seat," says Nora, going to the couch. "You have a lot to tell me."

I nod, but I don't know what Selena or Liam told her already.

I take a spot on the couch, sitting as close as I can to Liam. He's still playing with his nephew so I don't want to intrude. It's actually quite cute to see him act like a nice uncle...

With Liam's help, I succinctly explain everything that I have found out so far. From my relationship to the Witches' Ancestral Tree, to the Jones Family, and that newfound bond between Mara and Clarissa. Nora and Selena remain quiet the entire time. While I talk, Liam actually moves and leans his back against my legs. Neither Nora or Selena say a thing, but I'm pretty sure they noticed it.

I finish by talking about the cemetery and the tombstone we found. Nora looks really surprised and Selena, who has been standing to the side with a frown on all along, glances her way.

"...What do you think? Is it possible?"

Nora stays quiet for a moment.

"I... I honestly thought Nephera's... unborn baby was Judah Black's child. I mean, from what she had said that time, it sounded like... there wasn't another possible father. She said he wanted the child for himself too. I had thought it was because he was the father, but..."

"Maybe he just wanted another witch," said Liam. "Our father was... a junkie for magic power. I mean, for power, in general. It doesn't surprise me he would have targeted a child..."

They all make bitter expressions, and I already had quite the impression that Liam's father was the worst kind of scum. However, I really don't want to dwell on that fact any longer. The one I am curious about is Nephera and her story.

"So... do you have an idea who Mara's father was?" I ask.

Selena and Nora exchange a glance once again, and Nora sighs, crossing her arms.

"I never thought of that possibility, but... it might have been Alcott Blue."

I frown, confused. Now, that's a new name.

"Alcott Blue?"

"Do you know Nephera's story? With the... Blue Moon Clan?"

"Yes, Liam told me everything. About how Nephera was sent here by her mother, the Fire Witch, Danica..."

"Her adoptive mother, apparently," adds Liam.

I nod.

"Yeah, to help the Blue Moon Clan settle here and make sure your parents would be safe, your grandmother, Queen Diane, sent Nephera and members of her clan to Silver City."

"That's right, but things didn't go according to plan. The Blue Moon Clan was... killed, and only Selena and I survived. Sylviana saved me, and Selena was brought here by an older werewolf called Reagan."

"I understand all that, but what does that have to do with Nephera's partner? I mean, your... the Blue Moon Pack is the only one to use the name Blue, right? The other... part of the clan settled here is called the Sapphire Moon. I don't understand how it's related, your last name is Bluemoon too, not Blue..."

Nora takes a deep breath, and strangely, she now has a very sad expression on. She glances at her son, taking another deep breath.

"The name Bluemoon... in werewolves' families, only the leaders are allowed to use the names of their packs. For example, Selena's last name is Whitewood because she was adopted by the Alpha's family of her pack. In the case of Royals, though, Royal werewolves are always the leading Alphas, and as such, they take on the names of their pack. That's why my last name is Bluemoon. However, you remember Diane had a younger sister, right?"

My heart's speed increases a bit. I remember it all.

The story of the Blue Moon and Sapphire Moon Clans. Another pair of sisters separated young, who never saw each other again; I focused on the witches when Liam told me their story, like how Diane sent her younger sister here to Silver City...

"...Cynthia," I mutter.

Nora smiles gently, pushing a strand of hair behind her ear.

"That's right, Cynthia. Diane's younger sister, my grand-aunt, came here and established the Sapphire Moon Clan. She did a lot for her people, even without Nephera's help. It probably wasn't easy... Cynthia eventually established a family of her own, but she didn't want to take her older sister's name. Unlike Diane, Cynthia was born like a... regular Alpha werewolf."

For some reason, my heart is starting to thump like crazy in my chest. I don't like where this is going, but I need to hear it. I'm glad I can feel Liam's warmth against my legs, because I'm growing colder with each word Nora says. I don't like any of this...

"She took the name... Blue?" I ask.

Nora slowly nods.

"That's right. The group who had left the Blue Moon Clan established themselves as the Sapphire Moon Clan in Silver City, but Cynthia and her family kept their last names as simply Blue."

"So you're saying, Cynthia Blue could be my... I mean, Mara's grandmother?"

Once again, Nora and Selena exchange a glance.

"It could be," says Selena. "She had a son, a man named Alcott Blue. I never met him personally, but he was... old enough to have been Nephera's partner."

"...Actually, it would make sense," sighs Nora.

She gets up to grab Lily. I didn't even realize the baby girl was getting a little bit fussy. She calms down as soon as she's in her mother's arms and grabs one of Nora's black curls in her little fist, frowning and staring at it.

"Nephera mentioned briefly that... she was trying to get over Judah Black, wasn't she?" she says, looking at Selena.

Selena nods.

"She said something like she was moving on. She was getting a new life of her own... I never imagined she had actually found a new partner, though."

"Not just a new partner," says Nora. "Someone from the Sapphire Moon Clan. If... if all of this is true, Nephera really was trying to go back to the Sapphire Moon Clan. Cynthia was already dead then, but Nephera was going back to her position as the Sapphire Moon Clan's witch... Moon Goddess, it would have changed so many things."

They both look shocked by these revelations.

A part of me is a bit relieved about clearing Nephera's name. Is it Mara's spirit inside of me who's happy about this? I can't tell. I'm a messy, heavy bundle of emotions right now. I just want to have a definitive answer to this, to know who Nephera's new man was.

"So... Cynthia's son..." I ask, a bit unsure.

"His name was Alcott. The Alpha, Alcott Blue," declares Nora. "I only met him once, he was already... sick when I met him. Moreover, he hated Damian and his family, and wanted nothing to do with them. Back then, I thought it was because of how Judah Black had treated the Sapphire Moon Pack, but now, it's... His hatred was probably fueled by what happened to Nephera. Moon Goddess, I knew there had to be something else! I couldn't understand why Alcott loathed Damian and his father so much, but now... Moon Goddess, Damian's not going to like this..."

"He's not the only one," mumbles Liam.

While Liam's being all broody again, thinking about his father's misdeeds, my heart aches for Mara.

Once Nora mentioned the Sapphire Moon Clan and Cynthia, I had some hope that maybe there was still someone left from Mara's family, but... if this is true, Alcott Blue died even before Clarissa got to Silver City.

"Well, at least you and Liam aren't half-siblings," sighs Selena. "I mean, no offense, Liam, but it's really better that your father didn't have any other children somewhere."

"No offense taken," growls Liam. "Although, it does confirm that he was the lowest scum possible... Damn, now that explains why old man Blue hated us. Mom was probably pregnant with me around the same time..."

"Moon Goddess," mutters Nora. "I knew something was wrong about that whole half-sibling thing... Your parents were fated mates. Your father wouldn't have cheated on her..."

"Honestly, knowing Judah Black, even that wouldn't have surprised me," grumbles Selena.

"What about the Blue Family, then?" I ask.

They all turn their eyes to me. I don't really care about the Black Family matters, the fact that Liam's father was an asshole had already been established long ago, and I'm just glad Mara wasn't his daughter. However, now, I'm still waiting to uncover more of her story.

Nora takes a deep breath.

"Mara, there was... someone else."

"What? Who?"

Did Alcott Blue have a sibling? Is there someone else? My heart is beating like crazy, although Nora using past tense scares me. Is it going to be more bad news about Mara's family? Who did we miss?

"...Alcott had a son, who was the Alpha of the Sapphire Moon when I first met them," explains Nora. "...His name was William."

I immediately glance down at her son.

Will, William... Did she name her son after that man? Wait, if... if he was Alcott's son, wasn't he Mara's brother?

"William was our cousin," says Selena. "The grand-nephew of Queen Diane, although he wasn't a Royal, just an Alpha. A very good one too, he was strong."

"So he was... Mara's brother?" I ask, shocked.

"I... I wouldn't be able to say for sure if he was your... I mean, the other Mara's brother or half-brother," says Nora. "He... never mentioned his mother, I just assumed she died when he was young."

"Do you think he could be Nephera's son too?" asks Selena, frowning. "I mean, he was a boy, and he was older than us by, what, a few years?"

"I have no idea, but then, how would he have been fine without Judah chasing him too? Nephera did say he wanted to take her baby..."

"Wait, wait a second." I stop them. "You keep talking about him... about William Blue, in the past tense, but he was just a bit older than you are, right? Why... I mean, what happened to him? Was he sick?"

Nora's expression falls, and she slowly shakes her head.

"No, he... he died in the war, Mara, the one against Nephera, two years ago. On the same day Will was born."

I glance down at the innocent boy on her lap, with his big blue eyes.

"...Nephera killed him," says Selena.

My mind goes blank.

"...What do you mean, Nephera killed him?"

The two cousins exchange a glance, and Nora takes a deep breath.

"During the battle, our wolves were mind-linking everyone. We all just... felt William disappear."

"Reports coming in later confirmed that he had been killed by a water attack," adds Selena. "Nephera just... killed him among many other people."

My heart sinks. Oh, shit. Shit, shit, shit... Nephera killed her lover's son?

I don't even know how to react to this. It's just... so messed up. I can't believe it. I don't even know if I want to cry or scream in anger. Why was her whole life so fucked up? I know she did bad things, she was wrong, but the more I hear, the more Nephera's life just sounds like one damn tragedy after another.

"Are you okay?" asks Liam, putting his hand on my knee.

Am I? I don't know. I just found out the truth about Mara's family and it's not good. She doesn't have a family anymore, and even when they were alive, it sounds like what little she had was pretty wrecked...

I stand up and they all stare at me, but I just need some fresh air.

"Sorry," I mutter before leaving the room.

I walk out and go to the garden, which is empty this time. I just need to breathe. I take a few steps on the grass and take deep breaths, trying to calm down.

It doesn't work. Before I know it, I start crying, sobbing uncontrollably. This is so stupid! I try to wipe my tears, angry at myself for crying. Damn it, I don't even know why I'm crying! Yet, I can't stop; the tears take over me and it's strangely liberating. Is this what I needed? I don't know when I last cried like this, but Moon Goddess, it feels therapeutic to let it all out. I'm crying like a damn child in this garden. I couldn't keep my emotions bottled up anymore. It just hurts. Every answer I think I'm about to get turns into a brick wall that I run into every damn time.

"Mara..."

I shake my head. I don't want Liam's pity right now. Putting aside all my feelings for him, I'm strangely mad at werewolves right now. If it wasn't for Judah Black, Nephera's life and many others would have been different. Why does it feel like I missed the main villain of this story only to witness the trail of suffering he left behind him? I know Liam was a victim too, but right now, I just don't have the strength to share that pain. I can't.

"Mara, look at me."

"I don't want to look at you!" I retort. "Leave me alone, Liam, for just a minute. I want to be alone without anyone watching me for just a goddamn minute!"

"...Mara, you're growling at me."

"Enough! I said—"

"Mara, you're seriously growling! ...At me."

I calm down to focus on what he just said.

I realize only now. That... voice... I grab my shirt, in the middle of my chest, feeling strange. What is that? It's one of the voices I heard before. It's not a human voice, but it feels... animalistic. I never paid much attention to it before, but there's definitely something else. It's been drowned out because the other voice was so loud, but... it strangely echoes with my emotions right now. I turn to Liam, completely lost. He's standing a few feet away from me, looking cautious with his shoulders arched a little.

"If... if the other Mara was Alcott Blue's child, she ought to... be a werewolf," mutters Liam.

"Is that possible? A werewolf and a witch?"

"Well, I did just hear you growling," he says.

Moon Goddess, could it be? Is that how it's supposed to feel? There's something... odd about this. I don't... feel like there's a wolf inside. I always hear Ben or the others talk as if their wolf had a conscience of its own, but this feels different. I can't quite name it. Then again, I'm probably a different kind of werewolf anyway...

"Mara, it's okay."

I look up as Liam steps forward, suddenly remembering I was sobbing seconds ago. I try to wipe my eyes and arrange my poor appearance, but before I get to really fix the mess I am, he puts his hands on my cheeks gently. He's close, very close; I can only look at his devilishly handsome face and bright eyes. Right now, they have turned more blue, as the Silver City sky is more indulgent for once.

"Don't worry. Even if... the other Mara has lost her family, you have us, alright? You have me."

Is that what he thought I was so sad about? I nod, feeling a bit silly. His smile is... strangely disarming. How does he do that? I feel like a tiger who becomes a kitten every time he's in the room... However, I need this. I need Liam. This bond between us is the only thing that doesn't seem like it's about to disappear.

For once, I take the first step to hide my face on his shoulder. He gently caresses my neckline with his fingers. Moon Goddess, I love his strong arms around me, his smell surrounding my body. It's the most comfortable place in the world, and I'm not ready to leave it... I let Liam hug me, at least until I calm down, and it freaking works. I feel all my anger and frustration from before melt slowly as I lay myself in his arms. There's just... something so comforting about Liam being with me, as if all the weight I've been feeling on my shoulders had been lifted.

"...I want to speak to her," I mutter.

Liam eases his grip around me, just enough so that we can look at each other again. He frowns and wipes a tear left on my cheek, very gently.

"Speak to who?"

"To Mara... The other Mara."

"But..."

"She's... still here, Liam. She's been with me from the start, like the voices, like Spark. I just need to find out why, what she wants, what she can tell me. I'm not Clarissa, and I'm not Mara, either. I just need to find who I am, what I am. Why Mara was left behind and Clarissa is gone. I really need to talk to her."

He opens and shuts his mouth, looking at a loss. I take a deep breath.

"I... think I found out how I can do it. I just need a large mirror and a knife."

He grimaces.

"I'm not sure how I feel about that."

I chuckle nervously.

"I'm not about to slice my wrists open if that's what you fear."

He sighs and shakes his head before giving me a quick kiss on the cheek, making me blush and chuckle right away.

"I guess that's what I get for being a witch's boyfriend... Come on."

He takes my hand to pull me back inside, but before we go, I pull back, having him stop and turn to me with a confused expression. I smile and step forward to kiss him. I'm really becoming bolder now... This kiss is a bit salty, but it feels good. I just needed a way, once more, to confirm those feelings between us. I keep kissing his lips, and I feel Liam relax too, answering my lips just as much. He wraps his arms around me as we keep going, a bit bold.

Finally, though, we both remember where we are, and I retreat, hot and blushing. He smiles.

"What was that for?"

"To thank you..." I mumble.

I don't really know why I wanted to thank him. I left my brain somewhere out of those dangerous blue eyes' sight... Liam chuckles, and adds another quick kiss to that. Damn, I don't think I'll ever get enough of his kisses; that's dangerous.

This time, I follow him inside, where Nora and Selena are waiting for us. While Nora looks concerned, Selena smiles as soon as she sees us.

"Why are you two blushing?" she asks with a grin.

"Hey, don't start," grumbles Liam.

"You're the one who should know better than to act all sneaky in your brother's garden," chuckles Selena, visibly having a lot of fun.

Next to her, carrying her daughter, Nora has a smile on too, but she's obviously biting her lower lip to keep herself from laughing. Liam frowns.

"Stop making fun of me, you two! It's not like you and my brothers ever act so innocent, either!"

"Hey, I'm a mom now, I can't act all naughty in the open," laughs Selena.

"Really? What about that rooftop restaurant Nate rented out last month? He rented the whole place."

Selena blushes, and this time, Nora doesn't hold back and laughs. The blonde shrugs and turns around to go back in the living room with a sullen look. Nora and Liam watch her go. He has a victory smile on and puts his arm around my shoulders.

"You're still the sneaky one," says Nora. "You were a real pro at avoiding your brothers to go where you shouldn't."

"I'm a big boy now, Nora."

"Are you?" she chuckles, raising an eyebrow.

I feel a bit strange, witnessing their relationship first hand. How much does Nora know about Liam that I don't? Those two look close like siblings, even without their black hair and gleaming eyes. Moreover, Liam's blind eye is on the same side that Nora has her scar, although she probably isn't blind. I feel a bit awkward now, even with his arm around me.

"Nora?" I ask, a bit unsure. "Could I borrow a knife and... a large mirror, if you have one?"

She raises an eyebrow, looking surprised.

"Are you about to do something dangerous?" she asks.

"Probably not.... I mean, maybe for me? I'm not sure. I'll do it in the garden if it makes you feel better. I don't want to put your children in danger."

"...Alright. Liam, can you grab the mirror in the guest room upstairs?"

He nods and leaves us, and with a sigh, Nora walks to her kitchen to grab one of her knives.

"I just need a small one..." I grimace, seeing the size of that thing.

"Oh."

Was she thinking I was about to butcher someone or what? I swallow my saliva, a bit intimidated by her surprising collection of kitchen knives. I had noticed her kitchen was big and well-equipped, she probably cooks a lot... She brings me a smaller one.

"Here. I hope I get it back. Nate got me this set of kitchen knives last Christmas, I haven't gotten around to using it much yet."

"Yeah, I'll... be careful."

She nods, but to my surprise, she doesn't ask what I'm about to do with it. As we wait for Liam in the kitchen, I feel a bit awkward. I suddenly remember how I cried uncontrollably the first time we met... What happened then? Was it because we are related? Did the Mara inside me recognize Nora somehow? It didn't happen when I met Selena, though, and I met the blonde first. If I followed correctly, they should be equally related to me... I mean, to Mara. So why did I react to Nora more than I did to Selena?

Liam finally comes back with the mirror and Nora follows us outside, looking curious.

"What are you going to do with that?"

"Can you lay it down?"

He nods, and lays the mirror flat on the grass. It's just about my size and rectangular. It should be fine. I grab my phone and search for the pictures I took and added on the way there. I should beat myself up for not studying all that witch stuff earlier; I let Kelsi translate it all for me, not thinking about the fact that I was a witch and she wasn't. Of course nothing would happen if she studied or used those...

"Hey, Mara! What are you doing?"

Ignoring Liam and Nora's worries, I take the knife and cut my finger. Crap, that hurts... but at least there is enough blood. With a deep breath, I start drawing my circle on the lower half of the mirror. I need to check a thing or two on my phone, making sure it's a decent magic circle. Once I'm done, my blood having defined a clear enough shape, I add the three symbols above it from before. From Clarissa's journal and my previous experience, I'm starting to understand how this stuff works. I draw the witchcraft symbols, and with a deep breath, step inside the circle.

Immediately, I feel something happening, as if I was pulled inside the circle. I carefully sit down, Liam and Nora still staring at me in awe.

"Alright... Show me Mara."

As I'm sitting down, I see my reflection, sitting facing me. It slowly starts changing, wavering, turning into something else. My figure and face change.

It becomes leaner, paler, prettier. The hair too; the frizz changes into long curls that fall on her shoulders. She is smiling at me with a defiant expression like some naughty child. She tilts her head.

"Hi, Mara," I whisper.

She smiles even more, looking happy. It feels strange. I'm strangely calm, actually. I guess now that I'm getting the hang of it, I'm not afraid anymore... although I know this is dangerous.

"I need you to tell me your story," I say.

Her smile disappears and her expression changes into something sadder. She frowns, looking unsure.

"I want to know her story. Clarissa's story and yours."

"Clarissa..."

Her voice echoes mine strangely.

"That's right. You called me by her name earlier, but you know I'm not Clarissa, right?"

"You have... her face..."

"I know. But I'm not Clarissa, and I want to know why I... why I took her place now."

"You're the only one."

"What?"

The only one? The only one what? She closes her eyes, and suddenly, extends her hand against the mirror's surface. It's confusing, I feel like I could touch it. I raise my hand above it, and hesitate.

"Don't worry," she whispers. *"I'll show you..."*

I still hesitate. I can tell by instinct something's about to happen. I raise my eyes to look at Liam.

"If anything happens again, erase the circle," I say.

"O-okay..."

He exchanges a glance with Nora, visibly confused. I don't know if they can hear the other Mara, but from their lost expressions, I would say they can't. I turn to her again and put my hand on the surface, against hers.

Her fingers slide out of the mirror to grip mine, and before I can say a thing, I'm suddenly pulled to the other side.

It's a strange sensation, like a terrible cold taking over my body, or some ice being poured on me. For a second, I want to scream because the pain is so intense, but just as I'm about to, it's gone.

"Mara! Mara, are you alright?"

I try to look around me, but I'm in a circular room, very dark, with only one window at the end. I frown. Where is the other Mara? What happened? My body feels so strange. It's like swimming and being drunk at the same time; every movement is hard to make. I feel very strange...

"Are you hurt? Is it over already?"

Where the heck is Liam? I keep hearing his voice and Nora's, but from far away; what's going on? I glance back at the window, and suddenly, a fear grows in my heart. Oh, no, no...

I run toward it, with that growing feeling that there's something wrong, something very wrong. I run. Behind the window, I recognize Nora's garden, or a glimpse of it. I run faster.

"I'm alright, I think it just... didn't work like I expected."

I run faster. Was that my voice? How can it be my voice?! I arrive at the window, and I'm not in Nora's garden, I'm under it. I look up, and my own face is there, smiling at me. My heart sinks. Liam puts an arm around her, helping her up. I bang against the glass.

"Liam! Liam! Liam, I'm here! Liam Black, you damn idiot!"

I keep banging like an idiot against that glass, against that... window. Nora shakes her head.

"Let's get back inside and treat your wound, Mara."

The other Mara nods, holding her injured hand, and glances at me once more.

"Mara! Mara, stop!" I yell.

I know that bitch can hear me! I keep banging on the mirror, hoping one of them will notice, but both Liam and Nora look like they can't hear me. They barely glance at the mirror! My eyes meet the other Mara's. She's really... in my body. I see her wink, a glimpse of blue in her iris, and she bends down, grabbing the knife. Oh, Moon Goddess, no, no...

"Mara! Mara, fucking stop!" I yell, banging against the mirror, as loud as I can. "Stop! Stop, please! Don't hurt them! Leave them alone! Leave them and come back here, you damn ghost bitch!"

I start crying uncontrollably as she follows them inside.

I can't believe it. This is fucking nightmare! I keep crying, helpless, but nothing else happens, they're gone. They're gone and I'm fucking trapped in this mirror! What went wrong? Why, why did she suddenly turn like that? It can't be! The Mara Clarissa talked about in her diary was good. I know it. I didn't feel any evil from her until now, so what, what happened? I can't get out of my mind that spark of blue in her eyes at the last minute. ...Was that even really Mara?

More importantly, what the hell do I do now? How do I get out of here? Will they even realize there's something wrong before it's too late? She's not me, she just has my body. Won't they realize that? Even Liam, his bond is with me, not whoever is in that body!

...Or is that all there is? A physical relationship, some chemical reaction between us? Something damn... artificial. That can be changed with some damn body swapping witchery.

No, no, no, Mara, don't start being negative now. Your friends need you.

I look around, wondering if I can find something to help, but there's really nothing here. It's not even a room, it's just like a dark bubble, with no floor or walls. As if I was trapped in my own mind, which has got to be true somehow. What the hell can I do here? I glance down, realizing I'm still bleeding. The blood seems to fall into something like nowhere... Crap, this looks really bad...

"Spark! Spark!"

His Blazing Witch

My last resort is to call out to my cat, but I have no idea if he can hear me. I wait and try calling him a few more times, but nothing happens. Moon Goddess, I hope he's more useful wherever he is, because I could seriously use a clue right now... I glance around me once more, at a loss on what to do.

That's when something happens. On my left, something suddenly appears, a large oval emitting some bright light. I frown and get closer, until the brightness disappears to show what's going on outside. What the hell?! That's me! I mean, the other Mara! What's going on?

"*You really didn't manage to do anything?*" asks Liam's voice.

Wait, Liam is there too? I get closer and realize the other Mara's washing her hands, probably facing another mirror! So that's how it works... She glances up to glare at me briefly. I know you see me, you damn bitch... I violently bang against the mirror, as strongly as I can, but nothing happens. Maybe she's ignoring me, but behind her, Liam is standing there with his arms crossed and doesn't seem to be noticing anything either.

"Liam! Liam, I'm right here!" I yell.

"*I didn't. Why do you keep asking?*"

"*I don't know... Something feels different,*" he says, stepping back.

Moon Goddess, he knows. He can sense something is wrong! I can tell in the way he's standing away from her. Liam wouldn't leave me alone to wash an injury, he would be right there next to me. We can barely bear to be apart, yet now he won't make a move toward her.

Damn, that's my man. If only I could tell him I'm right here...

"*Are you alright?*" he asks, frowning.

I glance closer, down at what's going on in the sink. The other Mara glares at me, but I want to know what's happening. ...The injury? She keeps flushing the cut under the water, but the blood won't stop. Why? I look down at my own cut, still bleeding too. I couldn't care less because of my current situation and I did mistreat my fingers while banging against that mirror, but... wait, is that why? I grab my finger, and pinch it, forcing more blood out.

"*Ah!*"

Holy crap, that's it. If I'm bleeding, the wound on my body still bleeds; the volume of blood in the sink increases just as I pinched my wound. That's still my body, I'm still connected to it, and she can't heal if I'm not healed. Interesting.

I slap myself, and the other Mara opens her eyes wide, glaring at me and suddenly holding her cheek. So she does feel the pain if I'm feeling it... Well, you deserved that one for sure, you damn bitch.

"*Mara?*" Liam calls her.

"*I'm fine. Just... bring me a towel.*"

"*Okay...*"

Liam goes out of sight, and she glares at me.

"*You'd better stay still and behave,*" she hisses.

"Trust me, there's no way I'm going to let you mess with them, you bitch," I growl.

She clicks her tongue, and that makes me curious. Does that mean I can really mess with her? So, she can't do anything she wants, because this is my body. She won't be able to avoid staring at a mirror or seeing her reflection all the time. There's got to be something I can do about this messed up situation, I'm sure.

Liam comes back, wrapping her hand in a towel with a frown.

"*Liam...*"

I don't like the way she calls out his name. What is she going to...?

"*What?*"

"*Can you kiss me?*" she asks.

Freaking Moon Goddess, that damn bitch. How fucking dare she?! She glances at me in the mirror with a slight smile, but facing her, Liam isn't smiling. He chuckles nervously.

"*It's... a first that you're asking,*" he mumbles.

"*Please?*" she insists.

Oh fuck, I don't want to see this. Don't touch him. Don't touch Liam, don't touch my man, you damn bitch! I bang against the mirror, as hard as I can. Don't. Fucking. Touch. Him!

Liam hesitates, but he leans in closer, glancing at her lips. Damn it, Liam, it's not me! Liam!

When their lips touch, I feel a horrible pain scorching from inside. Something in me growls and whines furiously, upset with that scene. Don't touch our mate! He's ours, ours! Damn it!

I grab my injury and bite my wound furiously.

"*Ouch!*" she suddenly whines, stepping back while holding her hand.

"*Mara? Damn, your finger!*"

"*It's fine, just... just give me that damn towel!*"

She grabs it from his hand and leaves, sending me a death glare. That's right, you damn ghost witch, I swear I'll chop off all my fingers before I let you touch my mate!

Liam stays behind, and I can see him, standing alone in that bathroom with a baffled expression. He glances my way, but not at the mirror, in the sink full of blood. He frowns. Moon Goddess, did he get it? He has to know there's something wrong with that fake woman! He sighs and leaves, leaving my heart on a string. Damn it...

I step back and take a deep breath. I need to calm down. At least, it doesn't seem like she can attack them right away. I check my hand, but it's still full of blood; I bit it like a crazy dog. Well, I don't care about the pain if it can buy me some time. Still, I'm in trouble right now... What do I do?

"Spark! Spark, please..."

I sigh and keep calling him. I make sure to keep glancing all around me, in case the other Mara finds herself in front of another mirror. I can't believe I got myself in such a mess. Where did it go wrong? For once, I was so sure I was about to do something right, and I...

"Hi."

His Blazing Witch

I jump and turn around, only to face a little girl.

...What the hell is happening now? I look around, but she's alone, sitting down and looking up at me with big curious eyes. Big... blue eyes. What the...

"Mara?"

"Hi, Mara," she answers with a big smile.

Now I'm so confused. If she is... Mara Blue, then who the heck is in my body? In Clarissa's body?

I keep staring, but that child looks very young, something like, I don't know, six or seven? Although it feels like she could be older or younger, her physique is like going back and forth. Her long brown curls keep getting shorter or longer, and her face is like a baby at times too, and like a child's a few seconds later. However, her appearance stays the same, and I definitely see a resemblance to Nora. Her skin is a bit darker and her eyes are a different shade of blue, blue like the stormy ocean.

I sit down, confused.

"You're really Mara, aren't you?" I ask.

"Yes!" she exclaims, joyful.

"Wha-... I mean, what are you doing here?"

"Clarissa said I could stay, so I stayed. But now I'm very lonely..."

I'm trying to make sense of all of this. This is Mara, the real Mara Blue, Nephera's lost child. She's been here all this time! In... inside me. Her big blue eyes look at me with so much innocence, she's different from that reflection in the mirror, so... what happened?

"Mara, do you know who has our body? Clarissa's body?"

Mara suddenly looks scared and about to cry. She shakes her head, her dark brown locks flying all around.

"No, no, I can't say. She's going to be mad at me if I say..."

"Mara, that person is out there with my friends, and she could hurt them. You understand? She can really hurt my friends. Please, you have to tell me who it is."

Mara makes a pitiful face, as if she wanted to hide. She's pulling on... that blue tunic she's wearing, like a baby's shirt. What is that thing? I don't have time to analyze, though. She glances at the mirror.

"You won't tell her I told you?" she asks.

"I promise I won't tell her anything about you, Mara. I'll protect you if she gets mad."

"Please don't get mad at her... It's our fault... Mommy wasn't like this..."

Wait a second. Mommy?

My blood goes cold. Her mom? What the hell, is that... Nephera in there? Oh shit, shit...

"Mara, what happened?" I ask. "Why is Nephera here? Why is your mom still here?"

Mara starts sobbing pitifully, like a child caught doing something wrong.

"I'm sorry..." she sobs. "I didn't mean to... but I really missed Mom, and... and... Clarissa didn't want to, but I wanted to see Mommy just once..."

"Clarissa? What did Clarissa say?"

"Sh-she said mommy is too evil... but I didn't listen... I messed up..."

So Mara tried to call back her dead mother? The necromancy books Kelsi found flash into my mind. That's why!

"Mara, Clarissa wanted to see her mom too, right?"

"Yes, b-but... then... Clarissa said it's bad... and too dangerous... She said I couldn't use magic to bring Mommy back... That it would be too bad, but... but I didn't listen..."

That's why. They really were studying necromancy. Clarissa and Mara had a lot in common, but mostly, they had both lost their mothers when they were young. They found themselves longing for their mothers. However, Clarissa was almost a grown adult, she could see right from wrong. Mara couldn't.

"You lent your magic to Clarissa, didn't you?" I ask. "Clarissa didn't have magic, so you lent her yours?"

Mara nods.

"Clarissa is my best friend!" she says. "She found me when I was all alone... So I played with her, and we played with my magic. Clarissa is so smart, she taught me a lot of things! She taught me how to speak and use my magic! She really showed me a lot of things! But Clarissa was sick... I didn't want her to die... I didn't want her to die..."

She starts crying again, while I'm trying to untangle all this, with what I learned from Clarissa's journal.

So Clarissa somehow found Mara's... ghost, soul, or spirit whatever, while she was studying witches and magic. Somehow, Mara had the magic, but she was still an unborn child with no knowledge of the world. That's why Clarissa was in charge of everything, studying the magic, making decisions for them. However, Clarissa knew her own body was on the decline, and getting worse from using Mara's magic that was never meant for her. That's why she was saying Mara was dangerous. She was the one with the magic, but had no idea what she was doing!

Did Clarissa feel that Nephera could be involved too?

"Mara, we need to stop her. Are you sure it's Nephera... I mean, your mom?"

Mara grimaces.

"I... I don't know... Mommy is different now..."

"Different how?"

"She took... The Dark Magic..."

"What Dark Magic?" I ask, confused.

"The one that was in Clarissa's body... She... Mommy said she could bring Clarissa back if I gave it to her, but... but now I don't know... Mommy is very different..."

Damn it, something really went wrong here. What the heck really happened, and what Dark Magic was it? Inside Clarissa? Could it have been related to her disease somehow? I have so many questions, but for now, I need to be able to do something. I glance up at the two mirrors. It looks like they stay even if the other Mara isn't in sight anymore... So the more reflective surfaces she encounters, the more I'll be able to see.

"*You know how I always trust my instincts, right?*"

Selena! I run to the bathroom's mirror, only to see her walk in, frowning, and Nora closing the door behind them, still carrying Lily.

"*I feel it, in my gut,*" she continues. "*There's something wrong. What the hell happened with that mirror thing she did?*"

"*I don't know, it lasted merely a few seconds... Liam said he feels odd about her too. Moreover, I don't understand why she wants to speak to Damian and Nate. Wasn't she scared of them?*"

"*Yeah, I thought so too... It's weird how she insisted on seeing them. Tell Liam to be careful about Mara, I have a bad feeling. I already had that weird feeling about her before, but now it's like ten times worse.*"

"*I understand.*"

The two of them nod, and Selena leaves the bathroom, letting Nora rinse the bloodied sink. Lily is being all chatty in her arms, and I feel so bad. She's in danger, they all are. Thank Moon Goddess they already realized something was off! Did Selena always feel that part of... evil inside me? Not from me, but from Nephera?

The voices... Moon Goddess, that explains all the voices. I take a deep breath. At least, I may have a little bit of time before she wreaks havoc. She doesn't have magic, I do. She only has my body, and I can do whatever I want with it. I won't hesitate to break an arm or leg if it keeps her away from Liam and my friends... but I don't know enough yet.

I turn to the young Mara, who is watching me with her big blue eyes.

"Mara, do you want to help me?" I ask.

"I don't know... Help you do what?"

"To learn about magic, Mara. All of your magic. You said you taught Clarissa. I mean, Clarissa said it, right? You studied magic together. You're so good at it. Please, can you teach me more?"

Her eyes light up, and she stands up on her feet.

"Sure! I'm very good at magic, all the old ones taught me everything?"

"The old ones?"

"Yes! Mommy's mommy, the mommy of her mommy, all of them! They are so nice to me! Can't you see them?"

She points at something behind her, but to me, there's nothing. I shake my head.

"No, Mara, sorry. I think I... uh, I might not be good enough to see them yet."

...Or just not dead enough.

She chuckles.

"It's okay! Clarissa showed me how to talk to them, I didn't know before too! Now, what do you want to study? We can do magic glyphs, or cast fire spells! Or we can make magic circles!"

"How about you teach me how she took my body? Can I go back the same way?"

Mara glances at the mirror above us, frowning.

"Not from this side. Here, it's different... than on the other side."

Crap, I figured there might be some technicalities...

"Mara, look, look!" she says, pulling my arm.

She smiles, and extends her hands in front of her. A flame appears, and little Mara makes it dance on her fingers. I try to smile, and do the same, to show her. My flame appears, but I quickly realize it's just not as stable. Hers is extremely calm and controlled, while mine is just like any other wildfire... She chuckles, and to my surprise, her fire leaves her hand to come toward me! I step back, surprised, but her fire moves smoothly like a cat and comes to my fire, absorbing it and getting bigger. She stole my flame! It runs back to her, and I have no control over it.

"You're really bad," she chuckles.

I grimace. And here I thought I had mastered the thing...

"Your fire is a bit mean," she says.

"Mean? How mean?"

She points her fingers at my black scars.

"It burns you. Because it thinks you're not its master."

I stay speechless. Now that I think about it, she's controlling a lot of fire at once, but she doesn't have the slightest burn mark on her... How the hell does she do that? I take a deep breath.

"...Mara, you need to teach me that."

She smiles.

"Of course, I'll teach you everything! You'll see, it's so fun when you can play with fire!"

Oh right, I'll play with fire. And then, I'll burn that bad Mommy's damn ass out of our body.

#

Chapter 25

I take a deep breath and expand the circle. It grows unevenly and I have to focus hard to not let it get out of hand. This damn fire just won't listen to me. It grows unruly, like a dog running around in random circles. I try to focus, but the more I do, the wilder it gets. The flames get more intense and raging, and I feel the burn on my body. The dark scars appear, making me grimace.

"You're being too mean with it."

I sigh and stop, turning to young Mara. She's pouting, staring at me like I'm some... bully.

"What do you mean, I'm just trying to control it better," I say.

"You can't control fire, silly!"

I bite my thumb, completely at a loss. It's probably only been an hour or so, but I feel like the more I train with mini Mara, the worse my fire handling gets. I don't get it. She can just play around with it and use it however she wants, while I'm struggling to not get burned in the process.

"Look, just ask it to be your friend!"

She makes her own fire appear, and it starts dancing in perfect circles around her. Not only that, but she can split it in several circles, and I've even seen her make it change color. Is she much stronger because she's a spirit? I frown, still unable to get it. I feel like it's dangerous to let it loose, but the more I control it, the wilder my fire gets...

I don't have time for this. I need to get stronger, and fast, to get out of here. I get up, letting go of that pointless exercise, and walk up to the mirror.

"Are you worried?" asks little Mara.

"Of course, I am. Mara, your mother... She wants to hurt them, you understand? This is why I need to get out of here. Get stronger and fast!"

"Why do you want to get strong fast?"

"Well, I... I don't have time to lose," I sigh, turning to her.

She's crouching down, her arms wrapped around her knees, looking confused. She often takes that position. It actually looks like a fetal position, now that I think about it. It would make sense for her...

How long have I really been here? I just can't tell. The light in Nora's bathroom is only a light bulb that no one's turned on for a while, and the light above, in the garden, is my only clue. It somewhat starts to look like the evening up there... It makes me crazy to be stuck here, so helpless, with no idea what

343

the hell is going on outside with my friends. I tried breaking those mirrors, begging Mara, but it really looks useless. She can't do anything. It looks like she was right to say help has to come from the outside, but who the hell will be able to do this? How long will it take them to realize they have the wrong woman roaming around in my body?!

"...Are you sure she won't be able to use my magic?" I ask again, frowning.

"No. Mommy is a Water Witch," sighs little Mara, drawing circles on the floor with a pout. "She can't..."

Well, at least there's that. What is a witch without magic? No more than a human, I suppose, and I trust Liam and the other werewolves to be able to best her if she starts some trouble, but... what of Kelsi? Or the children? I keep seeing her with that knife in hand, over and over. At least, she seems to want to go after Damian Black first, but who knows what she's willing to do to get to the oldest Black brother? Who she'll attack? Moon Goddess, I'm going crazy in here, imagining the worst.

"Mara, you need to help me," I say. "I have to get out of here fast, learn fast. I don't have time for so many lessons."

"Why not?" she asks, tilting her head. "We have a lot of time in here!"

"No, no, you don't understand. Look, it's already dusk outside. Hours have passed since she forced me in here!"

She looks at the little frame of sky above us with a cute frown, then comes back to me, her big blue eyes looking surprised.

"Oh... So is it a problem? I can slow time for you, though?"

"Wait, what?"

She chuckles again at my baffled expression, and she nods proudly.

"Yes! You know, in here, it's magic! If you want, the magic will slow time for you!"

"You can really do that?"

"Of course! It's magic!"

I chuckle, nervous and happy at the same time. My heart is thumping wildly in my chest. Finally, Moon Goddess, if this is true, that's one good thing I could really use right now. The first one in a while, actually. I take a deep breath and nod.

"Alright, Mara. Let's slow down time so we can study, you and I. I mean... so you can teach me everything about magic."

"Everything, everything?" she asks, her eyes beamed up.

"Everything," I nod. "And please, slow time as much as you can. I'm going to need it."

"Of course!" she answers, excited.

To my own surprise, it really works. I didn't believe it at first, because nothing really happens right away or visibly. However, as I keep staring at the window, I do notice a little lonely cloud that doesn't move at all anymore, as if it was stuck in that purple-ish sky. The little branches on the trees in the corner aren't moving in the wind anymore. Moon Goddess, it actually works. I take a deep breath and look down at little Mara, finally seeing a bit of hope. With that settled, I'm ready. Oh, I'm so ready to learn what it takes to be a real witch.

One good thing about learning from a baby witch: she uses very simple language, no hard concepts like in those nightmarish magic books Kelsi had found. She is patient too. Everything is a game to her. If I ever had a childhood, this is probably what a young witch should have gone through. Little Mara waits until I've memorized all the witchcraft symbols she knows and gives me dozens of riddles to really master them all. All the runes and even the Gaelic and Hebrew languages? A new playground for strange conversation and charades. We also draw hundreds of magic circles, theorizing about new ones, chatting about everything we can do.

Moreover, we are literally playing with fire the whole time. Since we have no surface to write or draw on, we both have to use our fire to create the shapes we want. It's a nightmare for me to tame my flames enough for them to take the shape I want. It's like trying to draw with a string, I need to be careful, not only to draw well enough, but also to focus so everything stays as it is while I write more. I lose count of how many times my flames have run out and disappeared in a puff of smoke. It's a long exercise, but I do notice that I'm making some slow progress each time. It's like training a muscle, or learning to master a new weapon. I keep a cool head only by constantly reminding myself that I have time, and I really need to learn this. Mara makes anything out of fire in the blink of an eye, making me realize how big the gap is between us. At first, it takes me forever to master how to draw two symbols and keep them alive for a few seconds. My left hand is always the one to keep control the longest, whatever happens on my right is gone after just a few seconds of focusing elsewhere. It's nerve-wracking, but I keep going like I would keep writing to become ambidextrous. It slowly works and I feel like I'm forcing my brain to learn this new curve by sheer willpower. It is something exhilarating. My body and mind are not used to this, but every time I push them a bit further, I discover new doors that can't wait to be opened. It's exciting! I was probably only at five or ten percent of my abilities before. Like a girl playing with a stupid flame-thrower. Now, this is real Fire Magic. The one that makes me feel powerful and really in charge. I keep going, letting it flow through me.

By the time we get to magic circles, I start to get the hang of it. My control is much better, and the scars? No more appear when I create fire. My skin stays clear while my hands are dancing and moving to tame fire. I can feel it right down in my heart and stomach. I can focus on each circle, visualize it, and now, my hands and mind just know by heart what to do. Instead of simply drawing it, I can now produce the full circle at once, and being the stubborn Mara I always was, I keep working to make every single detail like I want.

Facing me, Mara has the innocence of a child playing with magic, but the knowledge of a timeless being. She's... incredible. I understand why Clarissa genuinely loved and treasured her so much. She wasn't born. She only knows of the world that Clarissa taught and showed her, whatever she saw through those mirrors. Everything fascinates her, and she celebrates my little victories even more than I do. It all amazes her; she has no idea about competition, frustration, or loss.

She never learned about good or evil, and I'm starting to understand why she wasn't able to tell how her mother used her, either... if it is Nephera. The more I learn from her about Light and Dark Magic, the more I realize little Mara didn't have the filter to see where things went wrong. However, I do. I'm learning fast, and I can tell, whatever has taken control of my... no, of our body, is most likely another entity. A bundle of Dark Magic that was left behind, both from Clarissa's sick body and Nephera's dark feelings she passed on to her child. Whatever Clarissa did, something went wrong, awfully wrong, allowing those entities to merge together and stay hidden here with the innocent young Mara...

"Look, look!"

I glance down, and indeed, the fire circle in my hands is much better than the one just before. It's crazy how much stronger and better my control has gotten. I really feel like I've found some new muscles, and I've been sharpening my senses enough. Now, I can feel my fire, control it perfectly to bend it to my will, but... strangely, it feels too calm. Before, there was like a willpower attached to it. Now it's just me playing with it. I sigh and stand up. This time, I try to expand my circle. It does exactly what I want, even when I add some more complex details. Why does this feel wrong? This is the kind of perfect control I was aiming for from the start! Why am I expecting my fire to... respond to me? Why does it feel like it's not... alive anymore?

I frown and keep forcing it. I want to provoke it, make it react. I need it stronger, bigger, fiercer! Why is it acting all shy now?!

"...Are you afraid?"

"Why would I be afraid of fire?!"

"Not the fire. The wolf."

"...What?"

I let the fire go, and turn around. What did she just say? A wolf? I keep squinting my eyes, but it's just... shadows. I try to look past the darkness, but I can't...

Suddenly, they appear. Two glowing eyes. One is of a sumptuous blue color, the other a mysterious glowing gold, almost orange. They are beautiful... but I can't ignore the beast hiding behind them. It's staring right at me, and there's... something in those eyes. Something fierce and powerful. I step back, cautious, and the wolf does exactly the same. No, it doesn't just mimic my movements, it's... like a perfect reflection. I take a deep breath, a bit nervous, and step forward this time. The wolf does the same.

Moon Goddess, it's...

"She's beautiful," I whisper, falling down on my knees.

This time, the wolf approaches, as my nervousness disappears. I even find myself chuckling nervously, taking the measure of what's happening. I keep staring, totally amazed. Moon Goddess, she's just so beautiful. I can feel... all of her. Her power, her savage, unruled power. My own heart is almost growing like a fire inside my chest, an echo of hers.

That's one unique wolf, I'll admit, but those colors on the fur are certainly more than familiar. Pitch black and gold... just like Spark. Is that even a thing for a wolf? It's definitely a wolf, though. My wolf. She looks like she's been through fire, a creature of ashes and embers. I am speechless.

Was that the other voice I was hearing all this time? In my fire and in my head? The animal, the one who growled for me when I was angry? The one who whimpered in my heart when I was sad? My smile slowly fades and instead, I... I want to cry. She was there, right? She was there, all this time, and I... I never realized there was so much more hidden inside me. I keep staring at the magnificent creature and, for the very first time, my heart suddenly feels complete.

"W-who... How?"

"It's our wolf," says the other Mara proudly. "I guess she was waiting too..."

"Waiting?" I ask, turning to her. "W-waiting for what?"

"For you, silly! She couldn't be born either, so... she was a good girl and waited with me all this time. With her and Clarissa, I wasn't too lonely, you know! But I think she didn't like Mom, so... she wasn't showing herself often... Now, she's gotten all better, thanks to you!"

I'm speechless. Is it because of... Nephera's dark aura? Was that why our wolf couldn't show herself? I take a few deep breaths, still shocked. I turn back to her, who's still waiting for me. I know she knows... and she was waiting for us. For me. Moon Goddess, that even explains why the voices were quieter when Liam was around... because that called her out. My wolf, his mate. That part of me who was... werewolf. Moon Goddess, this is real. I have a wolf. I... I do not know how this is possible, but... it's really my wolf. I can feel it in my core, as if she was both facing me and inside me. I guess it's the case, in a way? I need to take a deep breath to hold back my tears. I face her, still shook.

I'm not alone. I never was. I just... looked for the answer outside, when they were all inside. I slowly open my arms, and the wolf cautiously approaches. She feels so strong and big... she's powerful. I can feel her warmth. It's intense, but not to the point I'd get... burned. She's just there with me, standing tall and strong. She comes to me, and I can caress her. It's a strange feeling. I know she's in my mind, and this couldn't possibly be real, but I swear, I can feel the softness of her fur under my fingers, how far they dive in there.

I feel like I'm about to cry, and on the verge of bursting with happiness. It's crazy. I shouldn't have the mind to feel happy right now, but I swear, seeing my wolf here is just... amazing. She comes and rubs her head against my chest, and our warmth melts together. She slowly disappears, but I can feel her inside me. It's like... a stronger, bigger fire. I stand back up, filled with new confidence.

I light my fire.

This time, it's a real fire. So unruly, undisciplined, yet it's mine. A raging, savage fire, ready to heat up and burn. I smile uncontrollably. Yes, yes, now that's a real fire, and I can do whatever I want with it! I feel it burning, both in my hands and in my chest. My wolf growls, ready for action too. She's with me, she's sharing her strength with me, fueling that fire with her own power. Moon Goddess, even the scars on my body are slowly disappearing, retreating as if they were scared of the new strength in me. I've never felt so powerful!

"You're doing it!" says Mara, excited.

I think so too. I can feel my own heart beating wild with excitement. I grow the flames in my hands, bigger and bigger, until it feels like I'm ready to take the whole world down.

"*What... the...?*"

I turn around. In a new mirror, the Dark Mara, or Nephera's spirit, whatever this is, is facing me, and I recognize our apartment's bathroom. I smile and throw one of my enormous fires at her. She steps back, looking really scared this time. I get ready, and throw another one at her.

This time, a crack appears in the mirror. Her eyes grow wide in horror, but I smile and approach her.

"Get ready," I whisper to her. "Once I get out of here, it's game on."

I'm feeling so powerful right now; I'm more confident than ever and ready to take that bitch on. The only thing stopping me is that damn glass between us! She glances at the crack and the fear slowly disappears from her eyes. Instead, she puts on a smirk, and caresses the crack in the mirror. It slowly starts disappearing, leaving the glass as good as new. She smiles at my baffled expression, and like I had done before, grabs one of Kelsi's crayons to draw some witchcraft symbols on the mirror.

As I read them, I understand. That damn bitch is putting a reinforcing spell on the damn mirror! I try sending more of those new gigantic flames I have control over now, but this time, it doesn't flinch. There isn't even a single crack... Damn it.

"*You're not out yet,*" she chuckles. "*You'd better stay here and get a good look, because I'm going to burn this whole city down!*"

What did she say? What the fucking hell is she going to do?! She smiles again, and leaves the room. Damn it, damn it, damn it!

I knew she didn't have her Water Magic or my Fire Magic, but I forgot she could use basic witchcraft and runes. She might not be as powerful as she could be, but that doesn't mean she's powerless either. Shit, this is really some trouble coming right up our alley. ...And I am fucking trapped here!

"Are you mad?"

I turn around to the little Mara, who looks worried. I shake my head.

"Yes, a bit, but not at you. Don't worry. I'm just worried about what your mother is capable of doing."

Mara tears up, as if she is about to cry.

"B-but it's not really Mommy... I promise... Mommy is nice..."

I sigh and walk up to her.

"Don't worry, I... we will stop her, okay?" I try to comfort her. "We will stop her before your mommy does anything bad."

"You promise?"

I chuckle a bit nervously. The little Mara is so adorably cute, I can't handle it sometimes. I get how Clarissa was probably feeling all this time. Using her? Hell no. If anything, I think Mara gave her a reason to fight against her disease a bit longer. She is... just an innocent bundle of hope and joy, and it's contagious. No matter how frustrated I am, I can't stay upset when she is looking at me like that with those big blue eyes of hers.

"You must really miss your mom," I whisper gently.

"Yes... and Clarissa too..."

"Mara, is Clarissa really gone? What happened to her?"

"She... she told me not to watch... She was angry, but she said... you would be coming, so I will be alright. The bad men... they were really, really mean, and I was scared."

The bad men? Could it be the... Is she talking about the other corpses they found with our body? Wait, it sounds like Clarissa was attacked? Why? What did they want?

"Mara, those men, what do you know about them? Did they say anything?"

"No, uh... they said she should come with them... and they... called her really mean names. They said all witches are rotten... We are not rotten, right?"

"No, no, of course not," I say, caressing her hair gently.

Wait a minute.

How did these men know anything about Clarissa being a witch? She could only do the most basic witchcraft, and I am sure she stayed discreet at all times. She was desperate to hide her secret, even from her own sister and Kelsi. So how would those men have known? How could they know she was learning about witchcraft?

They had said those bodies were unidentified. Why? Silver City is a big place, very large, but this is the twenty-first century. With three people going missing, someone should have been able to find out who or why by now. Still, there wasn't the slightest clue about the three bodies. No missing person, nothing about someone looking for them. So where the hell did those men come from, and why target Clarissa specifically? And the way they talked... Witch hunters?

"Mara, can you remember more than that?"

She hesitates.

"I... I can show you?"

"Show me?"

Right, we both perfectly handle magic circles now, why didn't I think of this before? Moreover, I have Clarissa's body now. It's just going back in her memories, forcing this body to... rewind. Rewind all my five senses and experience what she experienced back then. It might not be a pleasant journey, but... I nod.

"Good idea, Mara. Can you help me draw it?"

"Yes!"

We both use our fire to create a new circle, adding some specific details to it, making sure we get exactly what we want. I... I'm amazed by everything I can do now. For the outside world, only a few hours have passed, but I feel like I've been in here for days...

We finally come up with a satisfying enough circle, and I turn to Mara.

"Alright, but it will be only me, okay? Clarissa said you shouldn't... watch this. So you wait for me, okay?"

Mara nods obediently.

"Okay, I understand."

She must have trusted Clarissa so much to not even try to insist...

I take a deep breath and step inside the circle. Maybe because we are already in a sort of magic zone, the area is extremely prone to help us. My magic circle starts spinning like crazy under my feet, and the surroundings change.

This is clearly the hangar from before.

I feel a horrible, cold chill... Oh, right, it happened sometime in the winter, right? I haven't experienced winter in Silver City yet, so I didn't expect so much snow. We are walking, with large burgundy boots digging into the snow, managing a path before us. I guess I'm just a passenger in Clarissa's body. It's a bit odd. I feel everything she's feeling, but I'm... unable to do anything. I feel the little hint of hunger in her stomach, her sore legs, the gentle feel of her scarf around her neck. All of her pain too. She's walking slowly, but it's a fight she's leading against her body. I can feel the throbbing pain in her lungs, her irritated throat that makes me want to cough, and that horrible headache. Moon Goddess, Clarissa, you really did your best until the end... Why is she outside in such weather, in her condition? She shouldn't be; she belongs in a freaking hospital bed at this point! Clarissa, what were you thinking...?

She keeps walking, looking around as if she's searching for something. Her eyes mostly go toward the sea, and she keeps looking for a long time at the waves each time. Her hands and lips shaking, she hurries up. I wish I could hear her thoughts too, but I'm just a passenger trapped in a front row seat.

After a few seconds, she glances at the numbers on the hangars.

"We're almost there, Mara," she whispers. "If I can just warn him... just... just in case..."

Warn who? Who is that "him"?

Before I get an answer to that, Clarissa suddenly stops. I heard that creaking from behind too. I don't like that... She glances over her shoulder, and sure enough, there are a couple of men coming from behind. Where did they even come from?! She gasps, something tells me she has the same bad feeling as me. I already know how this ends, I'm just scared to see it...

She tries to ignore them and hurry up, but just then, another silhouette appears. Another man wearing an ugly beanie and a big coat with a collar that covers most of his face. A single lady against three tall men. Moon Goddess, I really don't like the sight of this...

It's just instinct.

Your instinct, telling you something's wrong. Something primal inside you, that just knows your survival is at stake. Your instincts are telling you to leave this place, go somewhere safe. Walk away. Run. Do something, but get out of here. I can feel it just like Clarissa felt it. This dark shadow crawling in our minds, the fear that pours into poison.

Clarissa is smart enough to know she's in danger. She stops and looks around. It's nothing but the empty docks, snow, and those hangars there. Even the sea only has a couple ships at bay; all the others are spending the winter inside. Moon Goddess, I'm not sure I'm ready for what is coming. She retreats a few steps, but the sound of snow being crushed under heavy steps somewhere behind is not a good sign. Moon Goddess, please...

Clarissa swallows her saliva and suddenly turns around, heading to the closest hangar. That hangar. I feel so strange going back there in her memories. I thought it was all gray and rusty, but apparently, it was painted blue before it got scorched by flames... Clarissa gets to the door, but there's a heavy lock on it. She whispers something in Gaelic and I recognize the words for key and metal. Her finger quickly traces some runes on the frozen lock and sure enough, it magically unlocks just like that. She hurries to push the door open, hearing the men coming closer. Moon Goddess, I know all of this happened already, but it's hard to witness. I feel her terror, all this nightmare unraveling inexorably. I'm just glad Mara never witnessed this...

"Come here, little witch... Come here..."

Clarissa looks around and quickly finds a place to hide. This hangar is actually crowded with all kinds of stuff: mostly boxes, shelves, and random things. There are some fish nets hanging around, explaining that strange smell... This is so dark and creepy. Clarissa found herself a little corner between two shelves, but now, we can clearly hear the men walking in. She closes her eyes, so I can't see anything anymore; I only hear her whispers.

"Moon Goddess, please... I just needed more time..."

I feel her so strongly, I even want to cover my mouth to hide my breathing. This is just horrible. Hearing their steps, waiting as they get closer.

"Where did that damn bitch of a witch go?!"

"Keep searching, she can't be far. We can't go back empty-handed. As long as she's alive, it doesn't matter if we don't return her in one piece..."

One of them sneers.

"Yeah, I'm looking forward to that..."

What a bunch of assholes! Scum! Who the hell sent them, anyway?

While I'm thinking about this, Clarissa is already one step ahead. It looks like she's decided on something, because she left her hiding spot to go deeper inside the hangar, looking for something. Finally, she finds a piece of chalk and a large area in a corner. I easily recognize that spot... She starts scribbling on the floor, as fast as she can. Now that I know better, I can tell she's really good to be able to draw so fast and so accurately.

However, the sounds of the chalk on the floor alerts those men.

"There!"

I hear them coming, my heart going wild, panicked. How can Clarissa remain so calm in such a situation? She just keeps going, taking deep breaths and focusing on her magic circle. I have no idea how she can do that when the men's steps are coming dangerously close and fast. I want to tell her to run away, to find an exit, but she and I already know it's no use. There's no back door, nowhere to run. She can't hide indefinitely, either; they'd find her eventually. She doesn't even have anyone to help her...

I take in the full measure of how lonely Clarissa was. She didn't have anyone she trusted enough to call. Maybe she didn't want to let people get close, knowing she was going to die soon. Still, she was desperate to do one last good thing: to take care of Mara and make sure that child wouldn't be alone.

"It's okay," she suddenly whispers. "It's okay, Mara. I'll be gone, but... I won't leave you alone. All this... all that magic, my magic, I'll purify it. I know I can do this. I'll take that evil with me... We will be reborn, together. New and pure, again. It'll be fine, Mara, don't worry. We'll be stronger. It's just a little goodbye."

I want to cry, but Clarissa isn't crying. She's staying strong, drawing her circle so fast and carefully. Still, it's a damn complicated circle, and those steps are really coming closer. I can feel her fear, I wish I could look up and check our surroundings, but she's just stubbornly writing.

This is a real nightmare to witness...

"There you are, little bitch!"

Moon Goddess.

One of them draws out a knife, ready to stab her, and my blood goes cold. Still, Clarissa keeps an olympian calm. She glares at them and keeps scribbling, as fast as she can. She isn't going to make it. There's no way...

"Come here, I said!"

She's suddenly dragged by her hair and I grimace from the pain on her scalp. Those damn bastards! They try to drag her away, and Clarissa can only defend herself by grabbing his wrists.

"Look at this..."

"Not my style, but hey, a woman's a woman..."

"Is that okay, though? The other one said..."

"She said we can do whatever as long as she stays alive. It means what it means, right?"

Just then, Clarissa suddenly reopens her eyes, and with some weird movement, manages to free herself from his grip. Was that a self-defense move? She rolls away from him, and crawls back inside the circle, glaring at them.

"Hey, come back here!"

"You damn witch, do you think we..."

Before they can add a word, Clarissa starts chanting her spell. She's so loud, I can't hear what those men are saying anymore. A burst of flames suddenly appears from her circle, frightening them. They step back, but it's already too late. Clarissa keeps going, despite her unfinished circle. This can't be good, a magic circle can't work when it's not complete... The fire grows, clearly getting more dangerous, but Clarissa doesn't move.

Moon Goddess, I can't fathom the pain she's in. I don't want to stay here. It hurts! It burns! I feel the tears running down my face with that fire burning me.

"I'll be... reborn," she whispers. "We will be reborn, together, stronger... stronger..."

"Okay, Mara, that's enough!"

I'm suddenly pulled back, Clarissa and the fire are gone. Out of breath, sweaty, and still shivering from all those emotions, it takes me a minute to calm down and sit. What the hell...

Facing me, little Mara looks upset too, her arms wrapped around her legs with a sorry expression.

"It was very scary," she whispers, still looking afraid herself.

I nod, but I can't say a word. Moon Goddess... I can't believe Clarissa inflicted such a horrible death on herself. I know she didn't have much of a choice, but... that's just a horrible way to die. I look down at the old burns on my body. How much did she suffer until it was all over? What kind of nightmare did Clarissa have to go through for me to be here in her body?

It's so... horrible and infuriating that she had to undergo all this. How could she be so confident that it would work? Or was she just putting on a front to make little Mara not too scared? At a time like this...

I take a deep breath.

That's how I came to be. I'm not Clarissa Garnett. I'm not Mara Blue. I'm not even that wolf. I'm all three of them at the same time, a soul created by magic, the fusion of three fragmented souls. Stuck together imperfectly, but slowly adjusting. Clarissa knew her body would survive if only she got rid of the black magic that was tainting it, her disease. She sacrificed her memories in the process, and her being. I'm a bit of her too, the part of her that survived this. She wanted to merge with Mara, with her wolf. She wanted them to be reborn as one. ...I don't have amnesia, I don't have a memory to recover at all.

I chuckle at that realization.

I'm not even sad about it. Actually, I'm... grateful. I came to be because of their sacrifice. Clarissa's family is my family. Mara's magic is my magic. That wolf is... my wolf. Although it wasn't perfect and Clarissa couldn't do a perfect spell in the end, she still succeeded. She just left me more work and less clues than she thought.

"*No, no, Benny, wait! No, really, stop!*"

...Benny? I turn around, glancing at the window in the bathroom of our flat. I frown. What's going on there? Kelsi and Ben just walked in, and he's all over her while she's locking the door behind them with a frown. Moon

Goddess, I'm suddenly so happy to see those two, even though they can't see or hear me... although I did not expect them to be kissing and flirting with each other. Seriously? I was gone for what, a few hours? How the hell did they progress this fast? Ben keeps trying to kiss Kelsi, but she slaps his arms with her strength akin to that of a kitten.

"*Why?*" he asks, still trying to kiss her neck and cheeks, trying to get her attention. "*Isn't this why you wanted us to have privacy?*"

"*No! No, stop, stop, bad wolf!*" she keeps repeating, slapping his shoulders. "*Ben, focus! Didn't you feel something was wrong there?*"

He frowns and shrugs.

"*I... Uh, no... I mean... Mara was in a bad mood, but–*"

"*A bad mood? She was totally bizarre!*" retorts Kelsi. "*Something's odd, I can feel it. First, she barely talked to us, she glared at you, and she looked at me as if I was a flea! Second, she went and locked herself in her room right away.*"

"*Maybe she had a spat with Liam...?*"

"*A spat? Mara is the type who'd fire his ass if he annoyed her, not the type to go cry in her bedroom!*"

Oh, thanks, Kelsi.

"*O-okay, but... what do you mean, it feels wrong...?*"

"*Spark freaking hissed at her, Ben. That cat never, ever, hisses at Mara! It's her magic cat, for fuck's sake! He doesn't even hiss at me or you, but now, he's clearly got something against her, and he won't even go near her! No, no, there's something weird. She's acting super weird. That's... not the Mara I know, and I really don't like this. Call Liam Black.*"

"*Wait what? I can't call Liam Black just like that!*"

"*Then Selena Whitewood or Nora Black, whoever! I just want to check if there's something wrong, because I have a really bad feeling.*"

"*...Are you sure?*" he asks after a sigh.

Kelsi glares at him.

"*You know, there's a lot of things I'll never understand about Mara. I'm not a witch, I'm not even a werewolf like you guys. I know I'm probably some annoying sidekick. But if there's one thing I'm sure of, it's that this stubborn fire chick is my best friend. I know her. I've been with her for months, before and after the incident. When there's something wrong with her, I just know, and this time, I'm not going to stand aside. Not again.*"

I don't think I've ever been so proud to have Kelsi as my friend. How did she catch that something was wrong so fast? She'd make one hell of a detective. Or is it that she really feels bad about not noticing that Clarissa wasn't doing well before the accident, and now she's being extra careful? Still, I'm proud as hell that she's harassing Ben to make him ask the other werewolves about me. He's reluctant, but finally starts mind-linking Selena.

While he and Kelsi wait silently as he's busy mind-linking his Alpha, I realize they have been speaking softly the whole time. Is the other Mara next door? Damn, I don't know if I'd rather know where she is or keep her away from my friends!

"*What did she say?*" finally asks Kelsi, looking worried.

"*Yeah, apparently Mara tried to do some weird thing with a mirror in Nora Black's garden, but it didn't work. She just felt sick or weird after that, so Liam Black brought her back here right away.*"

"*That's it?*"

"*Uh, yeah. Oh, and apparently she cut herself to do that... magic thing with her mirror and she just kept bleeding like crazy, so that's why they asked my sister to drop by.*"

"*Your sister?*" Kelsi and I exclaim at the same time.

What the hell, I don't need more people to come and check on that crazy bitch right now!

Thank Moon Goddess, Kelsi looks just as worried as I am. She suddenly glances at the mirror. Finally! She probably made the link. She comes closer, her eyes falling on the symbols.

"*...Mara was in here just a minute ago, right?*"

"*Yep. ...Why?*"

Kelsi points at the witchcraft symbols on the mirror, whispering even lower than before.

"*These! Mara sucks at remembering these kinds of things and she can barely draw one correctly!*"

...Wow, thanks for the honesty, Kelsi.

Well, I can't say she's wrong, but at least I've graduated from being that bad now. She keeps staring at the symbols, very careful not to touch them. Behind her, Ben looks lost, but he grabs his phone and seems to be typing something very quickly. What is he doing? Texting Liam, perhaps?

"*Ben, that...*"

He suddenly covers her mouth with his hand, and as she's frowning, shows her his phone screen. What does it say? Was he typing to show Kelsi? She makes a very surprised and worried look that I don't like. What is it, I can't see! Then, Kelsi proceeds to nod, and shows him the mirror and the witchcraft symbols again. Ben makes a grimace and nods. I have no idea what their silent conversation is about, but suddenly, they both jump, their heads turned toward the door.

"*Did she...*"

"*Just leave?*" says Ben. "*Yeah, I think so.*"

"*Oh no...*"

"*Don't worry, I'll follow and keep an eye on her. You should stay, okay, and... watch over whatever it is she did here.*"

He's about to turn around, but Kelsi grabs his sleeve, looking worried.

"*Are you crazy?! She's been acting weird and we don't know what happened to her! Why would you go with her alone? What if something happens?!*"

He chuckles.

"I'm a werewolf, babe, I can take it..."

"Werewolf, my butt!" she shouts back. *"Even if you were a weretiger or a werebear, I wouldn't let you go! You're not fireproof, Ben!"*

He sighs and turns to her, suddenly wrapping her tightly in a hug. Although Kelsi is tall, Ben is rather muscular, and suddenly, she looks tiny in his arms. I see him smile over her shoulder, gently hugging her.

"Don't worry," he says. *"I'm a Beta; I'm tougher than I look."*

"But still... Babe..."

He unlocks their hug and gives her a kiss on the cheek, putting his hands on her shoulders as if to comfort her. He has a confident smile on and it breaks my heart. Moon Goddess, Ben, Ben, no...

"Relax, Kelsi. It's Mara, and it's my job to protect her, remember? I'll make sure nothing happens to her while you look into this."

"Ben, I'm not sure that person is even our Mara," mumbles Kelsi.

I feel her worry. I don't like Ben being alone with a crazy Dark Witch that's in my body! Can't I do anything? I try to slam against the mirror, but it seems like it doesn't even flinch on their side. Damn it!

Ben smiles and grabs her for a long kiss. Even as a bystander, it breaks my heart to see those two like this. They are so cute together, and now he has to go watch some crazy bitch who's stolen my damn body! I take a deep breath, looking away for a few seconds to give them their privacy, although they have no idea I'm here witnessing this. After a little while, they finally separate, and Ben gives Kelsi another big hug.

"I love you, babe," he whispers in her ear.

She blushes and nods, and he gives her another quick kiss before leaving the room. I take a deep breath. Damn it, they are just such an adorable pair of dorks. I really hope nothing goes wrong on his side. Stay away from the other me, Ben, for Moon Goddess' sake...

Then, Kelsi turns to the mirror, looking so angry I even step back, surprised. Her eyes go down to the signs again, and she keeps frowning while staring at them.

"What were you doing, Mara...?"

She suddenly leaves the room, leaving me flustered, but comes back just as quickly with an enormous book, a pen, and a notebook. She starts scribbling on her notebook, and I realize she's copying those symbols. She doesn't know these? Or is it to check later? Then, she opens the enormous book, and I recognize that witchcraft volume she was showing me last time. She compares the recorded symbols in it to the ones on the mirror.

"They are for... blocking... spirits? What the heck?"

She hesitates, but finally pulls on the sleeve of her sweater and starts trying to wipe it.

To my surprise, it doesn't move an inch. What the hell? Kelsi keeps trying to erase it, with a real tissue next, and even water, but it doesn't go away. Crap, is it because she's not a witch? Or did the evil witch do something to prevent

her from erasing it? Kelsi grumbles something in a foreign language I don't recognize, probably Korean.

"*What evil spirit?!*" she grumbles.

Suddenly, she stops frowning, her eyes lighting up as if she had just thought of something. She glances up at the signs again.

"*I'm such an idiot!*" she exclaims.

She leaves the room again, leaving me here, completely at a loss. I've never experienced something as nerve-wracking as having to watch her find a solution by herself. Did she think of something? I have no idea how to help her from here; this damn glass just won't move unless she erases that crap on the mirror first.

Finally, Kelsi comes back, and to my surprise, she's got a box of matches. Oh, Moon Goddess, she might be right! I mean... in a wrong way, but right. Fire is my magic element, that might be the only way to stop a Water Witch's spell. Although Kelsi was probably thinking the other way around, but nevermind. She breaks two matches with her trembling fingers before she can finally light one, and brings it toward the mirror.

"*I hope I'm not about to blow the place...*" I hear her grumble.

No, no, Kelsi, you're doing great! The fire approaches the symbols and as soon as it touches it, it starts burning right away. Moon Goddess, yes! She's a genius! The symbols disappear in a sudden crackle and Kelsi retreats, a bit scared. On the other side, I prepare my fire, ready to break that damn mirror open. I start firing as soon as I can, sending the huge fireballs against the oval mirror one after another.

Cracks appear, and while Kelsi screams in fear on the other side, I just keep going.

"*M-Mara?*"

I stop, and through the cracks, Kelsi approaches, looking half-terrorized, half-shocked. The mirror is half-wrecked now, with pieces broken apart like complex spider webs all across it, but at least it looks like she can see me.

"*Oh, shit, this is creepy...*"

"Can you see me?" I ask, my heart beating like crazy.

She slowly nods, swallowing her saliva.

"*Y-yeah, but uh... This is so weird. In some parts, it's me, in the others, it's you... I swear this is like one of those horror movies. What the heck is going on? You just left the place, and–*"

"It's not me!" I exclaim. "Kelsi, you were right, girl, that other... I mean, the other Mara you saw wasn't me, okay? It's an evil witch; she took my body and fucking trapped me in here!"

Kelsi goes white instantly, staring at me in shock.

"*Wait, what? For real?*" she gasps. "*An evil witch, my God, Mara, are you serious?!*"

"Y-yeah..."

"*Are you serious?!*" she repeats. "*You're telling me we're playing with possessions now? Mara, this is so creepy! And my Benny just went after her*"

too! He's gonna be sliced and diced by some crazy witch who stole your body? Mara, are you kidding me? This is insane! What... What the... Oh my God, I should never have let him leave with her! If something really happens to Ben–"

"Kelsi, Kelsi, calm down!" I yell. "Kelsi, stop! Ben is fine, okay? He's a grown werewolf, and I'm sure he's stronger than he lets on, okay? Plus, that other witch doesn't have any power, at the moment..."

"I just spent ten minutes understanding what she did to our bathroom mirror, and now you're talking to me! Isn't that enough?"

"It's just some basic witchcraft, Kelsi, even you can do it, okay? I promise she's probably powerless right now. She's a Water Witch in my body, a body made for a Fire Witch..."

"Wasn't Clarissa a Water Witch? Girl, this is so confusing..."

"It's fine, it's fine, it... Clarissa changed it before I took over; it's a Fire Witch body now, I promise. You'll see when I get out of here. I'm... I'm much stronger now."

She glares at me, crossing her arms. She'd be a bit persuasive if she wasn't half crying and pouting.

"Stronger? You're the idiot who got trapped in a mirror by some evil spirit! Now the not-witch human me has to free your ass! How the hell did you even get yourself in there?!"

"Not by choice," I sigh.

She sighs and unlocks her arms, looking at the edges of the mirror, shaking her head.

"Can you even get out this way? I mean, where are you, anyway?"

"Uh... It's complicated to explain. But yeah, no, I probably can't get out from here now that we have... wrecked this one. Kelsi, I need you to get to the other mirror, the one she used to trap me. The one at Nora's place. Please. You can do the same thing: erase the symbols and I will be free."

"Are you sure? Why did you wreck this one?"

"This one she had traced to keep me in. The others I drew myself and... got absorbed in that mirror. You can erase it just fine yourself."

"So you're in some sort of... mirror dimension?" she sighs, wiping her tears clumsily. *"God, Mara... What did you get yourself into again...?"*

She starts crying for real, and I'm feeling really sorry. I know it's probably just her nerves breaking down from all the anger from earlier, and how scared she is for Ben.

"I'm done with all this witch stuff," she grumbles. *"I swear, this is so tiring, all this crap... Can't it just stay in the books and a stupid Ouija board...?"*

"I-I promise things will be better soon, okay? But Kelsi, please, can you go free me?"

She glares at me.

"I swear, as soon as you're out of there, I'm kicking your stupid witch butt!"

I chuckle, but she storms out of the room before I can reply, grabbing all the books and matches. I hear a lot of rummaging in the apartment, probably as she's getting ready and taking her bag to leave. When I hear the front door slam and a new silence fills the air, I let out a long sigh, a bit relieved.

"...Is your friend coming to get you?"

I turn around, and smile at little Mara.

"Yes, she is coming to free me."

"Oh..."

Mara looks a bit sad, looking down with a pout. I smile and walk up to her, getting down on my knees to be at her height.

"...I have to apologize to you," I say.

"Oh? Why?"

"Because I forgot you and left you alone. I didn't mean to, Mara, but I had lost my memory. I didn't know you were here with my wolf. I promise I won't forget you two are here from now on."

Her eyes suddenly beam up.

"Really?" she asks, excited.

"I promise. You'll be with me all the time now; I'll think of you every time I use my magic. I'll make sure to... come visit you often."

"Thank you! I didn't want to be alone, but I'm happy now!"

I smile and she gets all excited by herself.

The truth is, I'm dying to get out of here and be back in the real world. I don't even know what is going to happen when I get out. Will I get my body back instantly? Or will I have to fight for it? I'm not sure, and to be honest, I'm a bit worried about what is going to happen next. I've never dived this far into magic before. I don't even know what I'm really about to face; however, I've never felt so powerful either. I have learned to tame my fire, and I have learned how to use my wolf. Even little Mara is here to help me. She's just a little voice in my head, but now, I'll learn to listen to her. Her voice was drowned out before, but things are going to be different now. I'm not a girl playing around with fire and second-guessing everything now, I'm... I'm a real witch.

Finally, I see lights appear above. It's night time already, and I see the flashes of a flashlight in the mirror. I have to cover my eyes because it's blinding, but I get closer to the mirror to listen.

"...*Left it here?*"

"*Yes, I just wasn't sure it was alright to move it since Mara left,*" says Nora's voice

"*Wait, is that blood? Oh, what the hell did she do...?*"

"*Are you sure she's trapped in there? But Mara is...?*"

"*Whoever that is, it isn't Mara,*" retorts Kelsi. "*Our Mara is trapped in that thing, and I need to get her out of there. Shit, I know I probably sound crazy, but... it's real.*"

"*Don't worry,*" says Nora. "*I'm not surprised by anything anymore when it comes to magic... Moreover, Liam also said something felt wrong, and I think so too. After she did that thing, she... Mara felt different. I thought she made a*"

mistake with her magic and that was why something felt wrong, but... I feel like you're probably right. Moreover, the timing of those fires..."

Fires? What fires is she talking about? I'm trapped in here and that evil spirit can't use my Fire Magic, why would there be freaking fires?!

"Shit, Mara really did make a mistake... Mara, if you can hear me in there, you're an idiot!"

I grimace. Yeah, I can hear that...

"What did she do? Is it bad?"

"It's a stupid mistake," sighs Kelsi. *"That symbol means rebirth, but if it's drawn the other way, it means spirituality... or spirit, apparently.... and because our Mara is a clueless idiot who can't bother to study her basics, she made the mistake of drawing a double-edged symbol on a mirror!"*

I roll my eyes. I get it, Kelsi, I get it... How could I have known there was another symbol the other way, and that it mattered to write it backwards on a mirror? Damn it. I guess this is the kind of stupid mistake that gets your body stolen.

I wait, a bit anxious if this is actually going to work or not. Kelsi grabs the towel Nora gave her, and starts wiping my blood off. Thank the Moon Goddess, it does start to disappear. I suddenly feel my body being drawn to the surface. Finally! My heartbeat accelerates, and I wonder if this is going to work. What about my body?

"Is this okay?" I ask the other Mara, who's watching too, with big curious blue eyes.

"What?"

"I... She took my body. What am I going to resurface as?"

Mara tilts her head, looking amused.

"Don't you have another body? It's going to be fun!"

"What?"

Before I can understand what she is talking about, I suddenly cross the surface, and find myself lying on the cold glass of the mirror.

Someone screams, and I hear rummaging around me. I'm a bit... numb. Oh crap, what the hell is going on?

"M-M-M-Mara?"

I raise my head, and thank the Moon Goddess, Kelsi is there, looking at me with a confused expression. One step behind her, Nora is there too, looking just as surprised. Yeah, I guess they didn't expect to really see me come out of a mirror.

"Oh... wow," chuckles Nora, covering her smile.

"I-is it her?" asks Kelsi. "Is that our Mara?"

"Oh, Moon Goddess, yes, it is," says Nora with a large smile. "This time, it's our Mara..."

What is going on? Kelsi should be the first one to be happy to see me. A bit angry if she wants, but at least looking relieved. Now, she's staring at me with big shocked eyes, as if she couldn't recognize me. Oh, what the hell, what happened? My body, what did Mara mean about my body?

His Blazing Witch

I try to stand up, and now, I realize something's really wrong... and odd. My body feels weird. I can move my head fine, but my... legs... I finally glance down, and immediately jump away from the mirror, panicked. What. The. Absolute. Hell! I hesitate and go back to the mirror to check again. Oh, Moon Goddess, this is real... I'm not in my body. As Mara said, I'm in the... other body. I'm a wolf.

Chapter 26

I'm a wolf.

Moon Goddess, I'm a freaking wolf! ...Damn, I did not expect that one.

"*Mara, can you... hear me?*"

I raise my head at Nora, a bit unsure. It's definitely her voice in my head, but... she didn't use her actual voice, did she? It's that thing they all do. The mind-linking thing. It's different from what I expected, and disturbing. I hear her like an echo in my head, very clear but as if she was standing farther away than that. Oh Moon Goddess, this is new...

I try to get up, getting used to the four legs, a bit unsteady. They are pretty strong, and once I've figured how to balance my body, it's fine to stand up. I check myself in the mirror again. Well, at least I'm a very pretty wolf... I look exactly like my inner wolf, even the heterochromia. One golden eye and a blue one. Between that and the gold and black fur, it's really unique... pretty and unique. However, I don't have much time to get used to this.

I take a deep breath and try to talk, but a growl comes out of my mouth. Oh shit, I'm really a wolf. How do I mind-link her back? I try to formulate a thought, but it's just... in my mind, not sounding like anything. I glance up at Nora, and hear myself whining, distressed. It's funny how easily my thinking translates into actions without me realizing. She smiles and comes closer, talking to me softly.

"*It's alright,*" she says. "*Just calm down, focus on my voice.*"

I try to, but... I'm a freaking wolf! I've never been a wolf! They all grew up with that ability, but I just learned I could even be a wolf half a minute ago, and there isn't some speed lesson on how to be a fucking werewolf.

Calm down, Mara, you got this. If you can make fire with your hand and create magic circles, mind-linking should be a piece of cake.... I try to focus on what Nora said, and hang on to her voice in my head rather than the fact that she's right here in front of me. I try several times, and end up growling, until finally, I think I grasp it.

"*L-like this? Nora?*"

"*Yes! Exactly, Mara! You'll see, it's a piece of cake once you know how to do it, you can't forget. It's going to be as easy as simply talking.*"

"*Yeah... Y-yeah, I think I got it now.*"

Between us, Kelsi keeps frowning and glancing back and forth between me and Nora.

"Th-this is really Mara?" she asks.

"Yes it is," says Nora with a confident smile. "I think she just... awoke a new side of her, since her body is taken."

"O-okay..."

Kelsi looks at me with an unsure expression. I can't blame her, neither of us expected this was even possible. I'm a bit sorry that I can't even talk with her like this, say something. Apologize for my mistake, to begin with. If only I had put in the effort I should have into studying about witches sooner instead of being so absorbed in my identity, my past, I wouldn't have made so many mistakes.

"Mara, are you alright? Anything that hurts?"

"No, I'm good, and quite fired up actually. But what were you guys saying about fires? What fires?"

Nora's smile disappears, and she glances Kelsi's way before talking.

"There are a lot of buildings on fire throughout Silver City right now. All the packs are mobilized to go and help, and... the humans are freaking out... All their firefighters are deployed but it might not be enough. Moreover..."

She hesitates, and I'm really getting worried about what she could possibly be reluctant to say. However, Kelsi decides to be more blunt and turns to me, frowning.

"Mara, they are all saying you did it. I get it's the other... bad witch that has taken your body..."

What?

Oh crap, that's what that bitch was after. Now she's using the fact that she's in my body to make me look like I'm the psychopath witch bitch they all feared me to be! Damn it!

"We are trying to hold her back, but... she's a Fire Witch," says Nora.

I growl, annoyed. Oh, it does work when I'm angry... Growling feels a bit good, at least to vent. However, growling's not going to be nearly enough, I need to stop her.

"What can we do?" mumbles Kelsi. "Mara's just a wolf right now... How can she beat a witch...?"

...Am I just a wolf, though? I still feel the same, at least inside. No, if I'm being honest, I feel even better than before. I feel stronger, more powerful. I begin growling even louder, but that's not what I meant to do.

I trained. I trained like hell with mini Mara, and a werewolf appearance is not going to stop me, hell no. I take a deep breath and try to feel my fire inside. Like my core, that big flame in my heart that's constantly burning. I feel a huge fireball in my chest, fierce and strong. I know that flame, I know it perfectly. Come on. My body has changed, not how this works. The limbs are just a bit different, that's all.

"Oh... Whoa, Mara!"

His Blazing Witch

I keep focusing, and flames appear at my feet. They don't burn the grass, they are white, so tame and gentle. They'll do what I want. I increase them, making Kelsi and Nora step back, but there is no danger, I got this. The fire spreads on my body and takes my colors. A black and gold fire, enveloping my body like some mane. I exercise a bit more, manipulating as I wish, growing it and making sure I completely master this in my new body.

"Oh God, Mara, if the situation wasn't so strange and scary, I'd say I'm super proud of you and impressed," squeals Kelsi, biting her fingers.

"Quite... impressive," whispers Nora, looking surprised too.

"I'm a werewolf witch, I guess. Shall we get going now? I can't wait to kick that damn bitch out of my body!"

"O-okay, let's go," says Nora.

We rush inside her house. Although it's obvious my flames won't burn them, they both stay at a safe distance from me, even inside. We run through the house, and I realize Nora's children aren't there. Did she leave them with someone? Nathaniel, or the brown wolf, perhaps? It doesn't matter.

We get out once again, on the other side this time, and I finally see it.

Flames.

It's even more obvious against the dark night sky. Towers of flames are growing in big yellow and red stripes, with dark smoke covering the area. It's like hell broke loose all over Silver City. Moon Goddess, that's a lot of fires to put out. Next to me, Nora looks devastated too, and from the way she frowns, I bet she's getting mind-links from all sides.

She turns to me.

"The barrier..."

I nod. We both think the same thing at the same time, and start running toward Sylviana's tree.

I have a bad feeling. I can't believe I've been such an idiot! How long was that Dark Magic waiting in the shadows to do this? To escape and destroy Silver City from the inside? We run as fast as we can to get to the tree, but even before we get there, I already know it's going to be too late. The fires are too big, and growing too fast. It's not like someone simply played around with matches. That Dark Witch used black magic to do this. Probably some magic circles, some runes, for those fires to already be this bad in the span of less than an hour. Moon Goddess.

We arrive, but as I feared, Sylviana's tree is in... a poor state. She's gone dark from the inside, and most of the leaves have fallen, the branches looking sad and limp. The bark is growing darker and darker by the second, looking frail and about to crumble, to rot. Nora runs to it, looking like she's about to cry.

"No, no, Sylviana... Mara, can you do something?"

I shake my head.

This isn't my tree, nor my magic. I can't simply reinforce it. Moreover, my element is fire, I'm at risk of damaging it even more if I try something. I've made enough mistakes for today.

"*I can't help the tree,*" I growl, "*but I can stop the bitch that's damaging it!*"

I turn around and run.

I run, like the wind, rushed by anger. I'm going to ruin that witch. She trapped me in a fucking mirror, she tricked little Mara, and she damaged Sylviana's tree! She's going to have to give me back my body and pay for it, now!

I growl, like a furious wolf, and keep running through the streets. Humans and wolves are running in the opposite direction, fleeing the fires. They don't even have time to be scared of me, I see their eyes open wide, and then they're gone. There are one too many monsters in this city right now. One too many witches. I hear screams, people yelling and panicking. I hear them cry about the witch, curse her, hate her. Somebody stop the Fire Witch. Someone kill the witch.

I ignore them and accelerate. I try to tame the fear in my heart. Yes, this is not going to end well for me...

I reach the first fires after just a few more minutes. I'm out of breath, but I'm probably the only one in the area who can even breathe! There's smoke, too much smoke, and black ashes everywhere. Two shops are on fire and a building behind them. Moon Goddess, I hope as many people as possible left the area. I take a deep breath, and slowly, pull my own fire toward those flames. I know the trick now. They can't hurt me. I'm a fire master, I can bend it to my will. I let my own flames melt into those, connecting to that fire as if pouring mine was a wave hitting the sea. I grasp it, hold on to it and start pulling. I take them all in. The fire, the big flames, they all come to me. There's so much... I need to keep focusing to not burn myself this time. That fire becomes mine. I'm charged like a monstrous fire beast, some stored inside, some enveloping me.

The fire is absorbed by my body, bit by bit, and I suddenly realize there's a group of firefighters nearby. They are wearing masks, and using something like large extinguishers, but they must have realized I was doing a quicker job, because they stopped to stare in surprise. After a few seconds, though, they cheer and resume, helping me put out the last flames.

As soon as I feel they can handle whatever's left, I run again toward the next scorched area. Where is she? Where is that damn witch?!

"*Mara, Liam's looking for you!*" suddenly yells Nora's voice in my head.

"*What? Where is he?*"

"*On your left, farther north!*"

He's on his way then. Is he with the other witch? Moon Goddess, I hope she hasn't done anything to him or Ben!

I take out two more fires on my way up, but this isn't enough. The damage is just terrible. How could she do so much in such a limited amount of time? No matter what, something's wrong here. There are too many different buildings burning. With the time it takes to draw a proper rune or magic circle, and the fires to grow this big, she ought to have had a head start of some sort!

"M-Mara? Is that y...you?"

365

I turn my head. Oh, Moon Goddess, Ben!

He's lying against a wall, holding a bloody wound on his stomach with a grimace. I rush to him. What the hell happened to him?!

"Oh... So it's... true," he chuckles despite the pain. "You're a wolf."

"Ben, you idiot! What happened to you?!"

I hear my whimpers, but he doesn't get my wolf voice. Still, he shakes his head.

"D-... don't worry about me. I don't think she... stabbed any vitals... I... I'll wait for the others, but... you have to stop her. She was... searching for the B- Black Brothers."

Oh, no, no, Liam!

"Go, girl," he says. "I'm happy you... weren't the one who stabbed me."

Shit, what do I do? I don't want to leave him here! I try to focus. Selena's my family too, right? I should be able to find her. The mind-link works between people of the same family! I have not experimented enough.

"Selena! Selena!"

"You're very loud... Who are you?"

What? Why am I mind-linking a child right now?! I already have one little girl in my head, I don't need another one!

"Sorry sweetie, I'll answer you later! Selena! SELENA!"

"Moon Goddess, Mara, shut it!" she finally answers. *"You're mind-linking like a freaking siren!"*

"Ben! Ben is—"

"I know! I'm running to him now! Just go stop that bitch!"

As soon as she confirms she's coming, I nod to Ben and start running again. She's so going to pay for this!

When a sudden new torch lights up the sky, a few meters away, I rush there, growling like a fucking beast.

It's a sea of flames over here, but I jump in anyway. I'm stronger now, this is nothing to me. I own fire, I am fire! I jump amidst the flames, trying to find my way across the ashes. It's a tall building with glass walls, but the first floor is completely overtaken by the fire, and growing fast toward the upper floors. The few people who managed to evacuate tell me this fire caught everyone inside by surprise. I rush in and find the first stairs I can. She has to be at the center of the fire.

"Mara, you have to stop her quickly. Selena and the others are trying to evacuate the people, but there are people trapped in the buildings. Damian and Nathaniel are upstairs too..."

Shit, is this the Black Corporation building? Now that makes fucking sense. She was wreaking havoc to get here! She intends to get back at the brothers! Of course. It makes sense with Nephera's history, but this isn't Nephera. Nephera died two years ago, whatever's possessing my body is much, much more dangerous, and crazy...

"Look who's here..."

His Blazing Witch

I stop after a new row of stairs, and turn my head. Amongst the flames, a woman is standing, on top of some bodies. The flames haven't completely caught up to this floor, but it's starting to look bad, really bad. Moreover, there's a black young wolf to the side, his left side covered in blood.

Liam!

"Did you lose something?" she chuckles.

I growl back at that bitch. Damn, I never thought I'd ever get to live this kind of experience, even being a witch. She has my body. It's my face, my body, my gold eyes, but I'm watching her laugh in a creepy way from a few steps away. On the side, Liam shape-shifts back into his human form, covered in dust and ashes, looking like he's been through hell and back.

"M-Mara?" he asks, looking at me.

I growl at him, annoyed. I'm mad at him, to be honest. I still haven't forgotten that kiss, and as we've already stated, I'm jealous as hell. Couldn't he tell the difference?!

He grimaces at my growl, looking sorry. Yeah, I'll settle that later... How did he even get here, anyway? Did he try to catch up to her while saving his brothers? I turn back to the witch and growl, showing off my flames.

"Oh? Are you sure you want more flames? The building is about to collapse... This body too."

Oh, Moon Goddess, I didn't think of that. If I'm in my wolf appearance, what protects my human body from the flames without magic? Nothing. That bitch is enjoying torturing my body, I bet she doesn't care about the damn pain! I growl furiously. I'm going to stop her. I'm going to stop that bitch, get my body back, and beat the crap out of that Dark Magic.

A loud creaking resonates and the ceiling shakes above us. Shit, the structure... How much longer can it endure? Can I take the flames back soon enough?

"The Fire Witch is scared?" chuckles the Dark Witch. "Humans are so weak, aren't they? You'll probably survive the fire, but if this building collapses, you'll be dead... and you'll stay dead this time."

"*Mara, Sylviana's tree is getting weaker by the minute. If it really dies...*"

We will be without a barrier around Silver City. ...And that will mean a lot more trouble than one Dark Witch in a fake body.

The heat is terrible, even for me. The flames are quickly catching up. Is Liam even okay in the middle of this mess? I try to control my fire, but it's a grain of sand in the middle of the desert. There's too much black smoke already, and I just wish he'd get out of here and let me settle this!

However, it's not just Liam. There are a lot more people upstairs, their future pending on this building about to collapse. This is a nightmare scenario...

The witch is in front of me, still smiling from ear to ear. I had no idea I could even make that kind of expression, but I do not like it. I want to slap that bitch and make her stop that stupid smirking.

"Any idea on how to get my body back?" I ask the other Mara, the one still carefully hidden inside.

"I-I don't know... It scares me..."

Yeah, it would scare anyone. What is that thing? I growl as a warning, and move closer, slowly putting myself between her and Liam. We circle around each other, but she just seems amused. That's not a smile of someone who is sane, that woman is crazy...

"A little witch got lost," she chuckles. "How many times can one get lost? Poor, poor little Mara... You're so weak! We can do better; we are the power you need!"

That voice isn't normal, and it's certainly not mine. It sounds like... like she's not alone in there. Is it even a she? Mara talked about a bundle of black magic, intertwined together. How do I undo this, and get my body back?

I growl furiously in warning. I need to remember that I control these flames, she doesn't. She can only do the most basic spells while she's in my body, but I can't because I'm in wolf form. Talk about a fucking mess!

"Mara, get out of here!" suddenly yells Liam.

I jump and dive just in time to avoid something falling from the ceiling, burning. I growl and realize those flames... I can tame them. I try to focus and like before, I shape my own flames to attract the others. Slowly, they are vacuumed up by my power, and those I can't simply digest, I add to the flames on my body. My wolf ought to be shining like a golden statue right now, the other witch is covering her eyes and squinting.

"You damn Fire Witch!" she yells. "You Cursed One!"

Cursed One that scares her, I'd say. I keep absorbing more flames, and getting closer to her. She starts tracing symbols in the ashes and I'm cautious. Is it a protection of some sort, a barrier? No, those symbols... Moon Goddess, a bombing spell? I start running toward her, I can't let her finish this! I growl furiously, warning her to stop.

"We are all going to die, you crazy bitch!"

She raises her eyes to me with a smirk.

"I won't die," she chuckles. "My wrath will survive, my wrath will always survive. Just like Nephera's anger, her pain. The curse will continue, the curse will always survive all those bodies, until all the werewolves pay for my pain!"

What the hell is she rambling on about?!

I can't stop. I need to stop her. I run and she starts retreating, the flames getting crazier around her. How do I stop that insane woman? How do I get my body back?!

No, Mara, calm down. Think. You're a real witch, regardless of which body you're in. This is just a problem that needs a solution, like any other. I need to ignore the body issue. What would I do to get my body back? She was able to do this with a stupid mirror and three symbols.

"Nora!" I shout. *"Nora, ask Kelsi if she knows how to reverse the spell! I can't trace the symbols with my body like this, but she can!"*

"Moon Goddess, Mara, you don't need to shout when you're mind-linking!" growls Selena. *"Nate is taking care of the people upstairs, making them all go toward the roof. Damian is..."*

He's here.

I feel his sinister aura rushing in like a hurricane even before his black figure appears. The huge dark wolf literally storms in, growling so furiously even I step back. The Dark Witch screeches and retreats, but Damian rushes to his younger brother's side first, and without even looking at Liam, stands just like I was seconds ago, between the witch and him. What the hell, we're supposed to... fight together? I glance at my body, standing a few steps away. I don't actually want him to get near her, he'd snap my limbs with one freaking bite!

"Nora, can you ask your husband not to... chew me?"

"Don't worry, Damian is just there for support and to keep her from going upstairs. He'll fight to help you but he knows it's your body, he won't hurt you."

"Great..."

Moon Goddess, I hope so. And at the same time, it's infuriating. I have a powerful Alpha next to me, but we can't do anything because that's my freaking body! Plus, we are running out of time. I know Sylviana's tree is being impacted by all the Dark Magic that witch is releasing here. The tree was made to contain the magic coming from the outside, not to act like an air filter inside! I need to stop it.

Suddenly, a horrible squeaking resonates, and the ground shakes under our feet... I mean, paws. Damian Black and I exchange a glance. He growls, and even without the mind-linking, I got that one.

Yeah, I know, we've got to hurry.

I leave him there, and start running toward my body again. She frowns, and runs away through the building. The rooms are too narrow and too burnt now, it's just a mess of smoke and flames everywhere.

"You'll die!" she screams. "I'll keep this body and kill you!"

I growl furiously and accelerate to catch up. I have to catch her. It's my body, my fire, my responsibility. I was the careless one, now it's my job to get her. As I run, I don't just pursue her, I try to grab as many flames as I can in my body. The smoke, the flames, everything, I absorb with my magic. It's hard, but I keep going. I am stronger now, I know I can take those flames.

"Selena, Nora, tell the brothers to have the people evacuate. I'll free the area around the emergency stairs as much as I can, but they really have to go, I don't know how much longer the building will hold!"

"Got it!"

I don't lose sight of the witch, but I have to slow down and try to get those flames. I am a Fire Witch, what's the point if I can't stop this?! My wolf keeps growling, and it's exhilarating. The feeling of my fur, fueled by hundreds of flames, so hot and warm even the sun would be less blinding. I'm shining, burning, and this power is like a new wave of adrenaline. My heart is beating so fast, I'm afraid something's going to burst.

"You can't catch me!" she laughs at the other end of the room we just barged in.

It's a large conference room with a bay window and an amazing view over the closest streets. Needless to say, I don't have time to admire my surroundings. Most of those windows have burst open, and there's glass on the floor. The witch catches a piece of glass, her–rather, my hand bleeding from how tight she's holding it.

"You'll see," she smiles. "I'll bleed you bit by bit, until this body dies from a slow agony..."

I growl at her, and suddenly I know what I have to do. All of her attitude, that anger, that craziness... I can't give in to her provocation. I keep walking around her, circling her carefully. I just need to keep her there while everyone else evacuates.

"*And then?*" I ask, sure she can hear me. "*You'll have a dead body you can't use. How many other witches in Silver City can you use to have fun? What's the point?*"

"I will always find another," she hisses. "My hatred won't die. My hatred will continue to pass on to generations of witches..."

"*Your hatred? What for? Nephera couldn't even see her child's spirit was still alive, and she died, leaving her alone! But you're not Nephera, are you? You're that evil thing that was inside her, and inside Clarissa too. What the hell are you?*"

She smirks, amused.

"I'm much older than that, I am the anger of all the witches before. I am the original one, the curse the werewolves can never get out of! I won't stop! I won't stop until all the werewolves are dead!"

...A curse? She talked about this too. What was that thing about a curse? I thought it was about Nephera, but now, she clarified this is something much, much older.

"You're an abomination," she continues. "You Cursed Ones should have never seen the light of the day!"

Cursed Ones. Again.

I growl. Cursed One or not, she is going to give me back my body, since she hates it so much. I start drawing circles closer and closer. She notices.

"What are you going to do? Kill me? This is your body, once it's gone–"

"*I won't have another. Yeah, I got that the first time. However, I need that body back, so I really suggest you freaking step aside and give it back to me now!*"

I growl and jump to attack her.

Even if it's my body, I'm not the one in it right now; I'll worry about the pain later, I suppose. All I need to do is make sure she stays alive and in a good enough state to be healed.

The Dark Witch screeches as I jump over her. The flames move to trap her, and she rolls on the ground, trying to get away. Moon Goddess, chasing my own body is the weirdest experience ever. She jumps back on her feet as I

370

stay away, cautious not to burn her completely. She grabs a chair, throwing it at me. I dive just in time to avoid it, but the next second, another one slams my flank violently. Shit...

I'm sure I felt something break on my left side. Damn, it hurts for real... but I don't have time to whine. I'm pretty sure if she kills me in my werewolf body, it's going to be game over.

I growl and bite back as soon as I see her arm, extended above my head as she's about to hit me again with that damn chair. I bite down for the first time, as hard as I can, and she screams. Moon Goddess, I officially hate my voice.

"Let go! Let go you damn beast!"

"I'll let go when you let go of my body, you bitch!"

She tries to kick me, but I'm stubborn enough to keep holding on nevertheless. The taste of my own blood quickly fills my mouth. Gross.

She keeps screaming furiously and suddenly her voice changes, she begins reciting something in an ancient language. Oh, shit. I let go and jump to the side, just in time to avoid a large bang, and what looked like a lightning bolt. What the hell, how did she do that?

"Mara, if you have any idea how I can retrieve my body..."

"A spell could work! But you'll probably have to knock her out first..."

I've never knocked someone out! What if I smash my own head instead? I don't want to be trapped in a wolf's body forever! Just as I try to get a hold of her again, she finds a long object to hit me with. I take the hit on the shoulder this time, enough to make me bow down. I growl and try to bite at anything that comes within my fangs' grasp. My canine teeth make contact with an ankle. She screeches again, and soon enough, I get kicked in the face by her heel. Damn it, I need to be more conscious of my body size, I'm super exposed at each attack!

Just as I shake my head, trying to ignore the growing pain on my forehead, the Dark Witch screeches and tries to run away again. However, at the opposite door, the one she was looking to escape through, a black wolf appeared, framed in the doorway. It's not Damian Black, I realize, it's Liam! He's a bit smaller than his brother, with a leaner body, blue-gray eyes, and that scar over the left one. He growls, warning her from approaching.

"Liam..." she says. "Liam, babe, it's me! Please let me through! Our bodies were exchanged!"

Moon Goddess, if he believes that crap for one second, I swear I'll...

However, Liam furiously growls clearly at her, not me. Moon Goddess, thank you! He probably can tell the difference with our bond now that I have a proper, physical body. We walk slowly, cornering the Dark Witch against the window. The flames and smoke are low now, allowing Liam to be here without coughing his lungs out. I do hope it will be enough for the structure to hold on a little while longer...

I growl, and she glares at me the most, holding her bleeding arm against her, retreating.

371

"You can't..." she hissed. "I'll haunt this body forever. You, all the Cursed Ones, you're mine. I'll unleash my wrath, at all the werewolves... forever."

"What the hell is wrong with you?!" I growl, furious. *"Who the heck are you?! Nephera is dead, and you used her mother's voice to trick the other Mara, didn't you? You..."*

Suddenly, I realize.

This isn't just about Mara. Why would these two have been brought together, to begin with? I know enough about them and their magic now. They were lured in, to get together and create more magic. Clarissa was afraid of the Dark Magic that was growing inside them. It couldn't have been Nephera, Clarissa was sick long before she ever came across Mara's spirit!

"You were in Clarissa's body too, harassing her! Why? Why are you doing all of this to them?!"

She laughs.

"Didn't you hear? I have to get revenge. I have an anger to appease!"

"Your anger should have been appeased when Judah Black died! Clarissa died! How many more bodies do you need?"

She laughs hysterically, and suddenly grabs another piece of glass, ready to attack us. Both Liam and I begin growling at the same time.

"Never," she hisses. "It will never be enough. I will spill the blood of hundreds of werewolves with these hands and it still won't be enough."

"I say it's enough," I growl furiously, stepping forward. *"Look at me! I am a witch and a werewolf! You're so blind you can't even see you've turned against your own kind!"*

"No!" she screams. "You Cursed Ones are damned! Damned!"

She throws some of the glass at me, and I feel a sharp piece graze my foreleg. Liam growls furiously, stepping closer to her, but I growl back at him. I'm fine!

She retreats toward the window, with nowhere left to go. Her eyes are somewhere behind me, and I glance quickly. Damian Black! Does that mean the evacuation is over already? Or was he worried about us? I want to rejoice, but I can't confirm anything for now. Beneath us, the building quakes again. Not a good sign... I really hope everyone else left!

However, I still have a problem.

We need to take her down. We need to leave this building as soon as possible, and leave with her knocked out. Sylviana's tree is in serious danger, and that's the last barrier between Silver City and those other witches out there; we can't afford to lose it. Liam and Damian can attack, but they don't want to injure my body. Kelsi can do the spell, she's smart and knows enough. She's seen the other symbols I used on the mirror. I growl and start getting closer.

"D-don't approach me!" she yells.

It's my body. I know how much it can take, I know how strong I am. I growl and jump on her, to attack her for real this time. I bite her shoulder furiously, and then dive to attack another part of her body. I keep jumping at her, biting, growling, attacking like a savage beast. I feel my own pain. She stabs me with a piece of glass, and there's a piercing pain in my stomach.

Suddenly, I hear something loudly creaking beneath us. Oh, no, no, not the ground...

Damian and Liam both retreat away from the large cracks that have appeared behind me. Is it about to collapse? They have to leave, now!

"*Mara! Get out of there!*"

I can't. If I let go, it will be another game of chase... and who knows what havoc she'll wreak in the meantime? I keep pushing, hearing something creak again behind her. The window! The glass window is about to crack.

"Mara!" suddenly yells Liam's voice behind me. "Are you crazy, you'll both die!"

Maybe, but she won't let go until we're both out. The window behind her vibrates strangely, and I get another idea. It's maybe even crazier than the original plan, but... I bite furiously, and push her again, her body against the window. We hear and feel the glass breaking behind her, and I jump still biting her. Her eyes, my eyes, open wide as we both fall from the building.

This fall feels strangely long. I feel the wind blowing up my limbs, and I try to focus on my fire. I need to slow down our fall, or both my bodies are going to be literally smashed against the ground. We are too high, way too high. If we crash from this height, at this speed, I'll die for real. I'm not too fond of the idea of dying now.

That damn Dark Witch is screaming and holding on to me for dear life. So she won't give up? Well, she's in for a fucking ride anyway... Damn it, I'm going to regret this later. But for now...

I focus as hard as I can on my fire, and summon all of it to me. I only have a couple of seconds, and Moon Goddess I wish I could extend it like the other Mara. This isn't my mind, this is the real world and it doesn't wait for me. I need fire, more fire, more... I growl furiously, summoning all of my power underneath us. This goes at the top of the list of crazy ideas I've had, but I've watched so many movies with Kelsi, it gave me that one crazy idea that might save my life... and my body.

The fire grows like a huge fireball under us, and I try to use it, like a propeller underneath us, to fight gravity. I summon all the fire I can find, inside me and outside. I even absorb more of the building's fire, like the most dangerous and hottest magnet around. The witch keeps screaming. With her inside, my body can't take it. It's hot, too hot, and burning the defenseless human skin she's wearing. If it was me inside, things would be different, but for now, I'm only glad I'm not inside and living that nightmare. I need to use that fire.

Finally, it happens.

Our fall slows down as the insane fireball beneath us propels us higher. Moon Goddess, the movies lied, you need a hell of a lot of fire to propulse a human... We are still falling, but I'm just gaining a few seconds and slowing our fall. I'm just desperate to fight as much as I can against gravity, against the ground that is coming closer and closer, dangerously fast. Holy shit.

The shock is horrible. It's not just the asphalt. I feel so many random pieces of debris that fell from the building brutally piercing my skin, scratching me, violently hitting me. I groan in pain, but Moon Goddess, it's a real scream in my head. The pain is just... horrible, echoing through my whole body in waves. Shit... I'm sure I don't have enough fingers to count my broken bones.

It's a miracle I'm still conscious. I move my head, and next to me, of course, I find my body. Unlike me, it's inanimate, eyes closed and unconscious. There's a mean blood stain on her face... Oh, Moon Goddess, that can't be good... I try to move, but it's too painful to even breathe. I move my eyes, very slowly, to glance above. The Black Corporation building is standing tall, covering us in its shadow. I almost feel like it's looking down on me now... Thank Moon Goddess, it still seems stable. Most of the smoke is gone... Thank Moon Goddess. At least the fire should be... contained...

No, no, stay awake, Mara, you're not done here. You have to help them find you... Did Liam see my fall? Then they'll surely find me... I hope sooner than later. I'm scared.

I'm scared they'll arrive too late, and my body will die. This one, or the other. Witchcraft... I should really stop messing up. It sucks to clean up my own mess...

"Mara! Mara!"

I hear my name like a far away echo. I'm not sure if it's in my head or in the real world. It sounds like Kelsi, though, so... I hear some rummaging around us. Is it really messy out there? Moon Goddess, I'm laying down on a pile of mess, I'm glad I can't sit... Lying down is still pretty painful in itself, though...

"She's here! She's really here! Oh, crap, crap, Mara..."

She swears a lot, and I'd chuckle if I could. A shadow comes over us, and I feel several presences around me. Who is there? Oh, did I close my eyes? I struggle to open them back up, and look around at the shadows hovering above me.

"Moon Goddess, she's alive, and even conscious. I can't believe it... With that fall..."

Nora's voice. So she found me, too?

I growl softly. I meant to tell them I'm okay, but really, a growl isn't very talkative. I feel a gentle hand over my head.

"Try using your mind-link, Mara. Don't talk, you'll hurt yourself even more... Moon Goddess, all that blood..."

"*The symbols... Tell Kelsi... The glass...*"

"Kelsi, she wants you to do that spell, now. Quickly!"

"What? But... If I do it now..."

"Find some glass to use around here, something big enough. I'll try to heal Mara's body as much as I can meanwhile. Let's hurry!"

Thank Moon Goddess for the mind-link. I never knew how handy it was, when everything is too painful to use... I hear them moving around. Steps going

374

away, and someone moving around. I still can hear Kelsi's voice, complaining a lot, half-crying, telling herself not to panic, but clearly panicking still. That's my Kelsi... Meanwhile, Nora suddenly appears in my line of vision, leaning over my other body. She exchanges a glance with me.

"I'll do what I can," she promises.

She leans over it, and her long raven curls hide whatever is going on from me. Good... I have no idea how bad my other body looks, but I saw that blood on my head. Damn, I hope that damn Dark Witch didn't wreck it. I like that body.

"Mara! Mara!"

I hear Liam's voice screaming over, and Nora suddenly sits up.

"Liam, over here! She's here!"

"Oh, Moon Goddess, Mara, Mara..."

I wish I could turn around to see him. His breathing is so uneven, I'm wondering if he's injured too. Did something else happen? Suddenly, Liam is next to me, and I feel his hand in my fur. Oh, Moon Goddess, I missed him... I really missed him. Nora moves a little, and Liam gets between my bodies. His eyes go to the other one first, the human one, and his eyes grow wide in shock. Yeah, probably not good... He looks at Nora.

"Please tell me you can do something..."

"I'll try," she answers. "They called an ambulance. If only Mara can hold on until then... Her friend Kelsi is trying to find a piece of glass large enough to do the spell back... if... her body can take it..."

Liam's lips tremble, and he turns back to me, the wolf me this time. Our eyes meet, and he looks like he's about to break down.

"Oh, fuck, Mara, I'm so sorry... I'm so sorry..." he whimpers. "I should have known sooner... I knew something was wrong, but I didn't want to doubt you again..."

Yeah, I haven't forgotten about that... I'm so going to whoop his ass if I survive this.

I growl a bit and he shakes his head. His hand on my fur is the best feeling in the world. He gently caresses me, right under my ear, fingers grabbing my hair as if to hold me back. He leans closer, and puts his face against mine, very gently.

"You have to hold on, just a bit longer, Mara... just a bit longer. I promise, I'm never, ever going to let you down again. But, please, don't leave me... Not like this."

I growl back, the only thing I can do. He stays with me a little, and I close my eyes. He smells like ashes and a ton of other burnt things, but it's my Liam. My mate. I can still feel him. Maybe it's even more intense because I'm in wolf form, but... I feel connected to him more deeply than any touch.

He leans back a little to look at me, his eyes watery. He keeps caressing me, and chuckles nervously a bit.

"You're beautiful," he whispers. "Moon Goddess, you're so damn beautiful... My tiger. My Mara... Just hold on, love. Just a bit longer..."

I try. I really try to. It's painful, and I want to give in to the sweet sensation of Liam caressing me, and that warmth that's about to envelope me. He keeps talking to me gently, softly, but I can tell his eyes are worried I'll pass out and give up. He keeps glancing at my body too, the one Nora's desperately trying to heal. What the hell, I don't want to die yet... not now... I need to protect them. Protect Sylviana's tree and the magic of Silver City. They all need me.

Shit, it hurts. I can feel my own heart now, beating in my ears, struggling to keep up. It's not good...

"I got it!"

Kelsi comes back with a large piece of glass that probably came from one of the burst windows. She sits next to us, her knees scratched against the debris, but she doesn't care.

Her fingers are covered in blood too...

"Is it going to work?" asks Liam, frowning.

"Well, I'm not a witch, but I am somewhat of an expert by now, and it's just about reversing the curse..."

"What will happen to the wolf?"

"I... I don't know. However, unless Mara gets back into her real body, I mean, her human body, something else can happen to it. I think I've had enough fake Mara for today."

Nora and Liam exchange a glance and nod.

"Alright, Kelsi, do it then. But quick. Mara is not in a good state..."

"Your healing didn't work?"

"It did, but she's... Liam, you know I can't heal everything. She needs real doctors, probably surgery."

"Fuck. Kelsi, hurry."

"Yes, yes... First, you move and put that thing between the two... Yes, like this. Now give me Mara's finger. Did she bleed somewhere... Ah, here, perfect; she has to be the one tracing them. It's not perfect, but... I don't want to risk doing it myself, I'm not a real witch, after all..."

What are they doing? I feel Liam getting behind me, although he keeps a hand over my body. I'm suddenly faced with my human self as they roll it over to face me, from beneath the glass. Wow... I really look like crap... It's probably going to be painful as hell to get back in there... at least the Dark Witch will be gone. That's one thing done, I suppose...

Signs in blood appear on the glass, Kelsi tracing them with my hand. My brain is too numb to read them, but I'm sure she knows what she's doing. The non-witch expert on witchcraft...

"Alright, that should be it."

"What now?"

"I guess they just need to both touch the glass, it should do the trick."

"Okay, then let's..."

"Wait!" suddenly exclaims Liam, as both girls were about to roll my human body over to me.

"What?!"

"W-what if... she doesn't survive? Look at her, Nora, her human body is... really damaged. What if we put her back inside, and she doesn't survive?"

"Liam, every second we discuss this is time lost for Mara! What do you suggest? She can't remain a wolf!"

"Maybe she can? She... she has better chances of surviving that way, doesn't she?"

Nora seems to hesitate, looking down at me. What are they talking about...? Meanwhile, Kelsi suddenly glares at Liam.

"You know, I thought you swore you'd believe Mara, but it looks like you still don't," she says. "She's a witch! She's not just a werewolf, or just your mate! She's a damn powerful witch, okay? She'll make it. I know she will. Mara just found herself, you can't do that to her. She's a fighter, I know she'll survive this. We have to trust her."

They hesitate again, and I feel Liam's fingers tightening on my fur. Oh, Moon Goddess, I love him, but really... I growl, as hard as I can. He sighs.

"Sorry, Mara. ...See you soon, my love."

I feel him lean over me, and his lips kiss my cheek. Then, he pushes me against the glass, and I suddenly bump into my human body on the other side.

Pain.

Pain, pain everywhere. It's horrible. My whole body is numb, yet still painful. I feel my heart, so, so slow. I hear voices around me, panicking, yelling orders. Someone's calling out my name. They all sound too much alike... I can't tell what's going on.

...Are you dying?

"Oh, little Mara."

I don't want you to die... I don't want to be alone again.

"I don't want to go, either. I want to see Liam and the others again. I want to help them, and all of Silver City."

I really like you as a friend. You are really, really nice. Like Clarissa. But you know, I still miss her a lot. She was my first real friend... and now, Mommy is gone too... Everyone is going before me, without me...

"I don't want to abandon you. I promised I'd stay with you, but... I don't know if I can keep that promise now. My body has suffered a lot. It's hard to fight. Human bodies aren't like astral bodies, you know. They have their own rules, and I can't cheat indefinitely. Clarissa already did a lot to help me get a healthy one. Now it's all damaged because of my mistake... I'm sorry."

No... she cries. I'm sorry... I know Mommy wasn't really Mommy, but... I thought... I thought she'd stay with me this time... I should have listened to Clarissa... It's all my fault...

"It's not your fault... You missed your mom. Clarissa missed her's too. It's fine. I understand."

The little girl from before... Do you think she misses someone too?

"I don't know who that girl was..."

I'm sure she's lonely... I felt her. And... they will all be lonely if you go... and very sad... I don't want people to be sad... They love you all a lot... I'm happy you had new friends... I'm happy you're happy...

"I know. I was happy too, happy with you. I'm sorry it's all ending now."

No... I don't want you to die. It'll be really sad if you die too. Can you stay a bit longer? For them?

"I wish... but I don't have the strength. I guess it was really stupid to fall..."

It's alright. Don't die yet. I will give you mine. You know, I thought about it a lot. I miss Clarissa, and maybe she is waiting for me, with all the others. I really want to see her...

"No, no, you can't do that. You'll die!"

I know, but it's okay. I'm not really scared. I was never really alive, you know. So, I'll just die a little. Just a little. And I am happy we met. You're my new friend. I really, really love you too.

"I love you too, little Mara..."

I hope you won't be lonely if I go, but you have a lot of friends now. It will be okay... I just hope you won't forget me?

"I won't..."

Hey, don't go yet! I said I'm the one going! You have to wait a bit. Just... promise you won't forget me.

"Yeah... I promise."

Okay. And keep my name too! This way, Clarissa said I'll really have lived. Like the other Mara, but the one with a life. Oh, it really is a bit complicated... but you have to live and be happy for two—no, for three, Mara. For me and everyone else. You really have to be really happy, okay?

"Yeah... I... I think I can... do that..."

Oh, good then! We will all be happy! And... help the others, please. I don't want others to live what Mommy lived... It is really too sad, that mean curse. It should stop now. You have to stop it, okay?

"Y-yeah..."

Alright, I guess it's time to go now... Oh, it's really a bit sad... I'll miss you... I love you, other Mara. Please be really happy, and when you're very old and very tired, you can come with us. You'll meet Clarissa!

"..."

Oh, I have to go first, you won't wait... Good night, Mara.... Bye-bye... Remember me.

#

Chapter 27

I'm heavy. Heavy, tired, and in a lot of pain.

I hear voices around, and some regular beeping. I'm uncomfortable... and Moon Goddess, so thirsty and hungry. Yeah, I'm literally starving, but my throat hurts. Wait, I really need to... wake up. I try to move, remember how I'm supposed to use this body. Something feels weird, I can't quite name it. I'm in pain everywhere, yet it feels like a big weight's been lifted off my chest. I feel remarkably better than before, but I can't explain it. I'm just tired and in pain, but strangely fine. What happened to me? I feel I'm... alone. No one else in my head. No strange echo, no little voice waiting. No more voices at all; just me and my wolf, patiently waiting...

"...Mara?"

Liam's voice. I hold on to it like a lifeline, and feel a gentle pressure on my hand. Is he holding it? I try to focus, and take control of my body again. Oh, the human body is so complicated... I already miss being a wolf. Yet, I slowly get back to my senses, and somehow manage to open my eyes.

A white ceiling above me, and some orange skylights... I take a deep breath that fills my lungs.

"Mara!"

"I'll call the nurse!"

I hear a lot of movement around me. Why is it so noisy…?

I take a second to try and come back to reality. I'm lying in a hospital bed, aren't I? This feels all too familiar. The gentle pressure on my hand returns, and I slowly turn my head. Shit, my neck is so painful... I finally meet Liam's eyes as he leans over me with a worried expression.

"Don't move too much," he whispers gently. "Your cervical spine is damaged..."

What isn't? I want to ask. My neck is painful, my ribs are painful, my arms, even my butt, and Moon Goddess, I have the worst headache possible. I take deep breaths, trying to ignore that stupid pain and focus on what I can. Well, I'm alive, that's good news. Very alive, and... lonely.

I had never realized it before, but... I never felt alone while little Mara and the voices were there. Regardless of if it was a good thing or not, there was always that presence at the back of my mind that didn't let me feel alone. Now I... I do feel alone. It is so strange. There's relief, but also, something sad about it. I feel abandoned. I feel so lonely, I want to cry. I start to weep, realizing little Mara is really gone, I'm on my own now. Just me, the new Mara, with all that pain.

"Hey, hey, babe... it's okay..." whispers Liam, visibly worried by my sudden crying.

I feel him gently caress my arm, and he leans over to hug me the best he can without crushing me. I wish I could hug him back. His presence and warmth makes me feel a lot better. I slowly stop crying, taking deep breaths.

Bonnie and Kelsi both barge in at the same time.

"Mara!"

Bonnie, very professionally, walks up to my side to check my vitals.

"How do you feel?" she asks.

"Like crap," I sigh, "but alive."

"You should be dead," she retorts. "Do you even know how many floors you fell? That was crazy, even for you! If Nora Black hadn't been there to help you, or if you weren't a witch–"

"I'd be dead. Yeah, my body agrees..." I grimace.

"Are you really in a lot of pain?" asks Kelsi, on the verge of tears. "You slept for a full night and day, but you cried a lot in your sleep..."

"Wait... It's been that long?"

I force my poor neck to turn again and look out the window behind Liam. Crap, it's really dusk.

"What about Sylviana's tree?" I ask him.

He slowly shakes his head.

"...It died this morning, Mara. The barrier is slowly fading. But don't worry, we can contain the witches for now. You should focus on your healing."

I frown, not happy with that response. The tree is really dead? How can they contain the other witches by themselves? It doesn't sound good to me. How can he ask me to rest when the situation has become like this?! I turn to Bonnie.

"How bad is it?"

"You mean your state? Quite bad," she sighs, grabbing a notepad, "or at least, it was."

"What do you mean?"

"You came in yesterday, and most critically, you had a severe traumatic brain injury with lesions and severe swelling. However, that wasn't the case twelve hours later. No more swelling, and your brain looked... almost normal. Just a bruise, as if you had simply knocked yourself against a wall. Believe it or not, it actually healed itself between the two scans you got. Same for everything else. A lot of internal injuries, including your perforated kidney and the bleeding that ensued. Then again, your blood replenished itself, and your organs seem fine after the surgery you had. Broken bones... Yeah, you fractured your rib cage, head, spine, and both legs. Seeing how you seem fine, I'll bet you're almost healed now too. You should be in an excruciating amount of pain right now, Mara, and certainly not awake!"

380

Well, I like how she put it, but I don't feel that fine right now. It does hurt like hell, and it's not like I'm going to run a marathon yet. However, it does explain all the pain and that horrendous headache I'm fighting against...

"It's... You're healing really fast," added Kelsi.

"Fast? How fast exactly?" I ask, sensing something wrong in her voice.

Bonnie and Kelsi exchange a look, and the nurse sighs, going back to her notes.

"Certainly faster than before," immediately says Bonnie. "Much faster, it's actually... remarkable. First, like I said, you shouldn't be awake so soon, so I do want to take you for a full checkup. I don't know what happened, but your healing process is totally different now. It's absolutely insane and quite impressive. I think... You're probably healing even faster than a common werewolf, Mara."

I chuckle a bit nervously.

"...Faster?"

Bonnie nods.

"Yes. I don't know what happened to you, but... well, it saved your life."

"...It's my wolf," I whisper.

I turn to Liam.

"Isn't it? I... unlocked something when I changed into my wolf."

He nods.

"I think so too. You feel... different. Not just to me, but to the other werewolves too. Selena said your aura had changed when she dropped by to visit you, she can't sense that evil she used to feel anymore."

"It's all gone," I whisper.

Along with little Mara, that evil thing that had been with me, all those voices, are now all gone. Damn, it feels really strange, but... I'm relieved. I'm the only pilot now, there is no more room for possession and Dark Witchcraft anymore. I rest my head on the pillow, and let out a long sigh.

"Do you feel okay?" asks Kelsi

I nod.

I'm probably feeling a lot better than I should, I realize that after Bonnie's words from earlier. Still, I can't rest with what's to come. With Sylviana's tree really gone, there will be no barrier left to protect Silver City against those witches that were itching to get inside. It's going to be up to me and the werewolves to defend it. I'm worried that, no matter how fast my recovery is, I'll be too late...

"You should focus on getting some rest for now," says Liam, as if he had read my thoughts. "We can hold on for a little longer, don't worry."

Suddenly, I remember all the crap that happened, and that I was mad at him. I turn my head and glare at him, making him all surprised. He retreats a little, lost, and glances over at Bonnie and Kelsi.

"Bonnie, Kelsi, can I get a minute with Liam before you do whatever checkup you want on me?" I ask, my burning eyes still on Liam.

"O-okay," says Kelsi.

They both leave, and Liam stares at me, dumbfounded.

"Mara, are you alr–"

"Alright?" I retort. "I don't know. My boyfriend kissed some strange evil spirit while I was trapped in some stupid mirror! How should I be?"

He opens his mouth, completely shocked.

"S-seriously? You s-saw that? ...Wait, that's what you're thinking of right now? That was just some stupid mistake!"

Some stupid mistake? Damn I want to burn that idiot down! I use whatever strength I have, which is not much, let's face it, and slap his shoulder, making him barely frown. I keep slapping, like a pup trying to impress a wall.

"You! Damn! Idiot!" I swear with each slap. "How dare you mistake your freaking fated mate?! You kissed her! You dared to kiss that bitch!"

"Mara, calm down, you're going to re-break your wrist, for Moon Goddess' sake!" He grimaces, grabbing my wrist to stop me.

"I don't care! I'll break all my fingers if it's enough to have you stop kissing strangers!"

"Come on, she had your body!" He rolls his eyes. "I felt something was wrong but she... uh... Well, she basically jumped on me."

"She did what?!"

What? What happened while they were together? What did I miss? Don't tell me they went further than a stupid, dirty kiss!

"Liam Black, I swear if you slept with my body while I wasn't in it, I'm going to–"

"Calm down, calm down! No, no, we just kissed, I swear to the Moon Goddess! And... Oh crap, why are we even having this fight to begin with?"

"Because, you dirty, dirty wolf! You kissed some evil, witch bitch!" I hiss, still furious.

"Well, technically, they were still your lips..."

Seeing my expression, he quickly steps away from the bed.

"I'm going to burn your–!"

"Oh, Mara! Mara!" suddenly yells Bonnie, coming back into the room and dropping her notepad to run to me. "What the hell is wrong with you two?! You should be resting, not assaulting your boyfriend!"

"If that idiot hadn't kissed an evil witch, I wouldn't have to!" I retort.

Bonnie and Kelsi immediately both glare at Liam in support of me. He's retreated all the way to the wall right now, and stares at the three of us in fear.

"Are you serious? That was an honest mistake! And I dropped her off at the flat as soon as I felt something was off too!"

"Liam, do you mind waiting in the hallway?" sighs Bonnie. "I don't really care if you two fight, but I'm not sure we have enough fire extinguishers around."

I'm still frowning when Liam leaves, rolling his eyes. Bonnie sighs, and starts checking me all over again with her doctor colleague, who acts very professional despite the scene before. On the other side of the bed, Kelsi chuckles.

"He really stayed by your side the whole time, you know," she whispers to me.

"I'm still mad," I sigh. "You have no idea how frustrating it was to be on the other side of that stupid mirror and see my... my fated mate kissing someone else."

"Yeah, I probably would have been mad too... Just don't be mad too long, okay? He really missed you, boo."

"I know. Don't worry. By the way, you and Ben...?"

Kelsi suddenly gets red all the way to her scalp.

"W-w-what d-do you m-mean, B-B-Ben and I? W-we... I-I mean w-we are not, not..."

She keeps glancing at Bonnie in complete panic mode, but the nurse is focused on discussing my state with her colleague, and knowing her, Bonnie probably doesn't even care that much. However, I don't really care about all their exams, while they are touching me all over, checking on my bruises, vitals and what-not, I can't help but tease Kelsi some more.

"I did see some interesting things from that mirror..." I wink at her.

She goes from tomato-red to almost eggplant.

"Mara! Are you sure you aren't still evil?!" she protests in a whisper.

I chuckle, but this makes my ribs hurt like hell.

"Yeah, it's probably not completely healed," sighs Bonnie. "I know you're somewhat fine but you shouldn't be playing around in your state, Mara. I want you to get a complete exam right away."

"Do you think I can leave tonight?" I ask.

"Tonight? Are you insane?! Didn't you hear me earlier?"

"Yes, and I clearly heard the part where you said I was healing crazy fast. So, I'm wondering if I'm healing fast enough to be released tonight. I promise I won't do anything crazy, but I still want to leave the hospital, Bonnie. I need to check where things are at with Nora, and a bunch of witches attacking is more important than a couple of broken ribs..."

Bonnie rolls her eyes at me.

"You're so stubborn, I don't even know why I would try convincing you otherwise. You still need a full array of exams, Mara. I am not releasing you otherwise."

"And then I can leave?"

"You can leave if you're in a state to, and with medical approval."

I growl a bit, but I can't really oppose Bonnie, she is the expert after all. So, I patiently go along with all of the exams they make me do, although it takes a lot longer than I had hoped. Bonnie keeps being amazed by my results, but to me, it just means I can get out of here faster. I'm taken in my bed from floor to floor, and I start to miss Liam again. Maybe I shouldn't have acted so harshly toward him... I was really mad, though. But I still miss him a lot. Damn it...

In the meantime, Kelsi left to get me some new clothes from our apartment. When I finally get back to my room to wait for some of those medical results, Liam is there alone. Not only him, but a delicious smell with him.

"Food?" frowns Bonnie, pushing my bed back in its spot.

"I figured she might be hungry..."

She sighs.

"Fine, but don't let the other nurses catch you with that!"

Liam nods with a smile and Bonnie leaves, closing the door after herself.

He and I are left alone in the room, and his cheeky smile gradually disappears.

"Hi..." he mutters, careful of my reaction.

"...What did you bring?" I ask.

"Barbecue. I figured you'd be hungry..."

"Moon Goddess, I am," I sigh. "Can you help me sit up?"

He nods and immediately jumps to help me put my bed in a seated position.

We keep exchanging looks as he's suddenly close, and we both blush a little. Liam is extra cautious of my reactions, but I'm just happy he's here... with me. He grabs the little tray and puts it between us, laying out all of the food. It smells heavenly to my grumbling and empty stomach. He's not even done putting everything on the table before I grab a piece of chicken to eat.

"...You like it?"

I nod, my mouth full. He smiles, and we both start eating, Liam sitting on the bed next to my legs. For a while, there is no sound besides our chewing and the ruffling of the wrapping paper. After a little while, Liam sighs.

"I'm really sorry, Mara..."

"It's okay," I sigh. "I can't blame you, anyone would have been confused."

"No, you were right. I should have trusted our bond more. I should have realized, right away, that something was wrong. After that... mirror thing you did, I was just worried about your hand bleeding. It took me a little while to realize something was wrong. The... kiss is what actually made me realize. It... wasn't like before."

I raise my eyes to look at him, and suddenly realize we are very close. I blush even more as Liam's eyes stare so deeply into mine.

"...Really?" I whisper, a bit shy.

He smiles.

"Yeah. When we kiss, you... tend to attack my lower lip more. You are more raw and your lips are warm. Your fingers too. I like how you brush my hair with your fingers."

Gently, he raises his hand and pushes some of my hair behind my ear, his fingers giving me chills as they slowly slide down my skin. They go down, until he reaches my neck, holding me softly in his warm hand. We get a little bit closer, and it gets hotter in here.

"Your... smell changes a bit when we kiss," he continued. "It's like hot wood, and crackling fire. There's something a bit spicier too, like... I don't know. Just your lips."

I chuckle, and slowly, grab a gentle kiss from him.

"Just my lips?" I whisper.

He nods.

"Yeah. Just your lips... and I love whatever they taste like."

He smiles, and leans forward a bit more, hooking his hand around my neck to pull us closer.

Our lips meet again, for a longer, deeper kiss. Moon Goddess, his lips... I'm melting. I feel my heartbeat going crazy and all of my skin warming up again. A chill rolls down my spine, and his hot hand on my neck is terrifyingly nice too. We keep kissing, very gently. Perhaps he's afraid of hurting me. I do feel a little cut inside my lower lip, but I don't care. I just want Liam. More of Liam. More of my man. I missed him so much. I push the tray out of the way, and wrap my arms around his shoulders to lock him in with me. He is careful about each of his movements, and I do feel he's a bit stiffer than before. Finally, he pulls me onto his lap, and we resume our kiss, gently holding each other.

I don't care about any witches, any wolves, or any battles for now. I just want a few more minutes, just him and I kissing and bathing in the warm light of the evening...

#

Chapter 28

As expected, it's not that easy to convince Bonnie and the whole staff to let me out. I feel like a lab rat, they keep wanting to do more and more tests to study the amazing speed of my recovery.

I suspect the extra life little Mara gave me is also playing a part... I'd surely be dead if it wasn't for her. I already miss her, but I just hope she's in a better place now. Moreover, I'm happy to be back to myself. I can still feel my wolf inside, but it's... different from the witches' voices. She's just there, like a presence waiting in the shadows. I will probably never be like the other werewolves. Clarissa wasn't one, although she probably had some werewolf blood and our wolf is only here because of little Mara, a survivor like me.

While we wait for my medical exams to be over, I take some time to explain everything to Liam. I'll have to tell Kelsi and Bonnie too when I get a chance later. I tell him all about little Mara, all the voices, how I trained during those hours I was trapped, and about my fight too, although he did see a lot of it.

"I need to know more about that curse thing," I explain, sitting on my bed. "There was something much darker than what Nephera could have conjured. For some reason, it was targeting me, little Mara, and Clarissa too."

"You're thinking that it's about witches? An ancient spell of some sort?"

I nod. Liam is sitting right by my side, his hand on my knee, gently caressing my leg with his fingers, although he's very serious and focused on our discussion.

"Very ancient," I nod again. "Little Mara talked about it as if it was... really, really old, and would be tough to undo."

Liam nods slowly, but I do realize that's really... not much to go on. We have no idea where to start, I feel like we've exhausted all our leads. Little Mara isn't here to help me anymore either... It's going to be very complicated. I sigh, looking down on our locked fingers, but just then, Liam chuckles and kisses my cheek.

"Don't worry," he whispers gently. "We'll be looking for answers together this time, okay? I'm sure we will find the truth soon..."

"Yeah."

I do hope so too, and the fact that we are now together, and nowhere near ready to leave each other, is a huge help. I manage to smile.

"If you can leave tonight," he resumes, "let's go to Nora and Damian's. You want to see the tree too, don't you?"

"Yes..."

It might be painful for the both of us, but I do want to see what happened to Sylviana's tree. Maybe I can do something about it, and Moon Goddess, I hope so because otherwise, it's going to be very, very complicated from now on... Seeing my frown, Liam gently rubs my leg.

"Don't worry," he whispers. "That tree probably wasn't meant to last anyway. I think Sylviana waited for the next witch to come... if she had seen you coming, which wouldn't surprise me either. We can just go see it later."

"Wait, so you haven't seen it either?"

He chuckles and shakes his head, holding my hand tighter.

"Moon Goddess, no. Mara, do you think I would have left your side for a single minute?"

I blush uncontrollably with just those words and that confident look of his. Oh crap, I have to remind myself we are still in a hospital room because otherwise, I'd definitely do something very inappropriate for the time and place... I focus on our intertwined fingers, trying to keep my crazy-beating heart in check. Keep it for later, Mara, later...

Instead, I satisfy myself with a quick kiss on his lips. Liam smiles automatically.

"Thanks," I mutter, clearly embarrassed.

"Oh no," he retorts. "I'll simply ask that you don't do something that crazy ever again. Do you have any idea what I went through, seeing you jump? Not just that, but both your bodies! Damian almost had to make sure I didn't follow right after you, I couldn't bear to think you had just died in front of me! Don't you ever, ever do such a crazy thing again, Mara! I can handle a lot of the witchcraft and crazy magic stuff, but please, your body isn't... replaceable, okay?"

I was not expecting to get scolded too... so I stay mute a long while. Not only do I find this surprising, I hadn't thought Liam would even think of jumping after me, but I didn't even take his feelings into account at all until now. No, I suppose I didn't even realize how much he already... cared for me. Moon Goddess, he's too cute...

I lean in to kiss him again, but he retreats, frowning.

"Mara, I'm serious!" he insists.

"Sorry," I mumble. "I mean, sorry I almost killed myself very recklessly... and left you behind."

"Not doing that again, are we clear?"

He looks like his older brother when he is all serious and mad like that. I nod like an obedient girl, I just want him to let me kiss him and stop frowning.

"Crystal clear," I chuckle, still a bit amused.

He sighs, staring at me as if I was some lost cause.

"And I always made fun of my older brothers for finding women more stubborn than them..."

"Maybe it's in your genes," I chuckle, leaning in to give him another kiss.

This time, he gives in, and returns my kiss without restraint. I can even feel his gentle smile against my lips, making me smile too. Moon Goddess, I missed him so much... Now I feel like we could be stuck together and I wouldn't mind at all. Perhaps the fact that I can now feel my wolf plays out in my undying desire for him too. It is a rather unique sensation, like I can feel him all the time, regardless of where he is, and I'm pulled toward him like a magnet of feelings I can't control. The only time we don't have a choice but to stop is when Bonnie comes back in the room and chases Liam out to finish my medical exams.

"Can I go?" I ask, surprised it actually worked.

"Yes," she sighs. "As unbelievable as it is, you're fine. I mean, I still wouldn't recommend too much exercise as you didn't eat for a full day, but other than that, I'd say you're... almost as good as new."

"Awesome," I nod.

Kelsi brought me some clothes earlier, and I'm happy to get into them. I don't think I'll ever get used to wearing one of these stupid paper robes they call a hospital gown... As I slowly undo it to change my underwear, I realize a lot of my scars are gone... Is that another gift from little Mara? Even on my arms, my skin is as smooth as any young adult woman's, and as I keep looking, I realize the only ones I have left are on my legs. It begins on my thighs, but as expected, the lower parts of my legs are still the most damaged. I guess it would have been too simple to wipe everything that happened in that first accident, the one that got me to replace Clarissa...

Damn, I'm going to have to tell the truth to Amy someday. I forgot about my half-sister... whom I still consider my sibling, I realize now. I guess the best part about taking over is that, unlike Clarissa, I get to pick what I still want in my life and what I don't... I'd probably be fine never meeting that shitty father of hers, or the brother I've only ever heard about... Do I really have to tell Amy, though? I don't know how she would react to all of this. Maybe I'm a bit scared she wouldn't consider me as her half-sister anymore, since I'm not exactly Clarissa... I try not to think about this too much as I put on the overalls and top Kelsi got for me. It feels a bit odd, after everything that happened, to simply walk out of the hospital. I should be dead, but instead, I'm very much alive, and mentally gearing up for more battles...

I try to chase away all the bad thoughts and instead, take this opportunity, maybe my last night of quietness, to take a little more care of myself than usual. I don't have any makeup or anything, and I regret I didn't ask for Kelsi's. I feel like making myself prettier, for any occasion I have to be with Liam... plus, he did say it looked somewhat good on me last time. Should I text Kelsi?

I walk out of the little bathroom, still mindful about my untamable hair. Maybe I should change my hairdo or something sometime... Just as I'm going through my stuff to find my phone, I realize I'm not alone anymore. I freeze, and look over my shoulder, to find a little girl standing there.

His Blazing Witch

She's just standing at the doorstep, looking a bit shy. She's biting her lower lip while staring at me, with big curious blue eyes. Her little hands are pulling on her dress, and she's slowly rocking her body upward and backward.

"Hi..." I say, a bit lost.

"Hi," she mutters, still very shy.

I take a glance, but I can barely peek at a portion of the corridor behind her. Moon Goddess, she isn't an illusion, is she? I've had my share of crazy stuff lately, even for a witch... However, that kid looks very real. She's cute too, but she feels strangely familiar to me.

"Uh... are you alone?" I ask softly. "Where are your parents?"

I turn around and slowly walk up to her, but she doesn't seem scared. Instead, she keeps staring at me with those big eyes, her lips a little open.

"Mommy is upstairs," she says.

So she isn't lost, is she? I smile and crouch down to be at her height. How old is she? Crap, I'm really bad at this, but she seems about the age of Nora's oldest child... Is it alright for a kid to wander alone in a hospital? Moreover, there's a little something bothering me. It's the way she looks at me, how she feels very familiar. Her blue eyes too. I feel like my inner wolf is just as curious as I am. I feel a... connection. Is that alright? I feel like my wolf knows this little girl, and we know her. I'm sure I've never seen her before, though.

"Did you come here to see me?" I ask.

She nods, and smiles shyly.

"Yes... are you still hurt?" she asks, her cute little brows frowning.

"I'm all healed up now," I explain. "See?"

I show off my perfectly fine arms, and she nods, looking satisfied. I tilt my head, and suddenly realize why she feels so familiar, after hearing her little voice.

"...You're the one who talked to me during the fight, didn't you?"

"Yes... I heard you were in danger. I'm sorry."

"No, it's fine. I'm sorry I couldn't really talk back then."

She nods, looking a little relieved.

Just then, Liam comes back, and his eyes go down to the little girl. He immediately smiles and lifts her up.

"Hey, Rosie! How are you, girl? Came to see Mommy?"

"Yes," says Rose with a little nod.

Just then, she stares at me again, and we exchange a little smile. Liam's eyes travel from me to her.

"Oh... uh, Rosie, this is Mara. Mara, meet Rose."

"Nice to meet you," I chuckle with a little wink for her.

Rose smiles, and hugs Liam quickly.

"I will go back to see Mommy now."

"Okay, girl. Be careful."

"Yes!"

Just like that, she shyly waves at me and runs back, a smile on her lips. Liam lets out a long sigh and comes inside, grabbing both my bag and my hand.

"Um, about Rose... How did you...?"

"She just came to my room like that. But, we actually mind-linked during the fight. It means she's... family, isn't she?"

"Yeah... Rose is William Blue's only child. She... didn't get to spend a lot of time with her dad, unfortunately."

"What about her mom?"

"Oh, she's actually hospitalized upstairs for a chronic disease. She's not in a bad condition, but Nora is helping her take care of her pack, and Rosie comes often too. She's really close to her cousins."

"That's good," I nod.

Strangely, I feel very close to that child I just met. She isn't even technically my niece, but... I guess the werewolf ties are stronger than actual blood, in a way. My werewolf has all the protective instincts over that little girl already. I know the timing is bad, but... I hope I can meet her again later.

Liam leaves a little kiss on my cheek.

"Let's go. You're all cleared up? To be honest, even if you aren't, I strongly suggest we abandon your paperwork-crazy friend and run away from here."

"I agree one hundred percent," I chuckle.

Despite us bragging about evading the hospital, I still meet Kelsi, Bonnie, and even Ben in the hall. Bonnie still has to complete her shift, but the new couple agrees to come with us over to Nora's house, taking the car. Thank Moon Goddess, Liam has his bike waiting for us right in the hospital parking lot.

"That pretty baby," I squeal, happy to see her again.

"I'm thinking you like my bike more than me," Liam chuckles.

"Will you let me ride it?"

"Why aren't you answering?"

"I asked a question. Yours wasn't!"

He rolls his eyes but to my surprise, instead of a straight rebuttal, he takes out a package from the back seat, and hands it to me.

"...What is that?"

"A present to my girlfriend for surviving one crazy hell and her own suicidal move."

"...I think I could have guessed the present part," I chuckle, giving him a quick kiss as a thanks.

I open the present, a bit excited. A present from Liam... What could it be? It's strangely heavy too! I unwrap it carefully, and soon, see some brick red leather in my hands. Moon Goddess!

"You got me a badass biker jacket?" I exclaim, checking out the marvelous clothing.

"Yep. I figured it could come in handy if I want to keep my crazy witch alive a bit longer..."

I almost jump on him before he finishes his sentence, and kiss him wildly.

Instantly, Liam wraps his arms around my waist, and I feel the bike slightly waver as Liam has to rest his butt against it while I assault him. I love him... We just kiss for a while, completely shameless, in the hospital parking lot. This is crazy, I feel like a love junkie. I can barely keep myself in check, and we slowly separate, although I can't tell who pulled back first. Liam chuckles, adding another kiss on my cheek. I'm blushing even more when he leaves his hands on my butt...

"I take it that you like it?"

"I love it!" I exclaim, raising the jacket in my hand.

He helps me put it on, and it's a perfect fit. Even a bit tight, which isn't a bad thing as it enhances my shoulders and waist. I love that he picked a red one too. Once I'm perfectly suited and zipped up, he nods, visibly satisfied.

"Good," he nods.

"Wait, when did you get this?" I ask, pouting as if I was suddenly suspicious of him. "Didn't you say you stayed by my side the whole time?"

"I ordered it online and asked Ben to go get it for me!" he protests.

I chuckle and return his kiss. Liam sighs.

"Moon Goddess, I want to keep you right where I can see you. I feel like the second I take my eyes off you, you're going to run into danger again."

"Well... I can't say it won't be happening again..." I grimace.

"Mhm. I know. Which is why..."

He swallows his saliva, blushing a little. Wait. Liam Black, blushing?

"I was wondering if you'd... like to sleep at my place again tonight."

This time, I'm the one blushing.

"Y-y-you're asking that now?" I mumble, embarrassed to death by his sudden bluntness.

"Well, we're going to Nora's, and there are a lot of ears there, so–"

Suddenly, a honking sound makes us both jump. Kelsi and Ben pull up in his car and the werewolf stops it right in front of us, smiling from ear to ear.

"I heard that!" exclaims Ben, smiling like an idiot.

"You..." growls Liam.

"Ben," I say, "I like you, but if you don't get out of here, I swear I'll turn your car into a two-wheeler."

He goes white and immediately drives off. Liam and I watch them leave the parking lot, and I turn back to Liam, realizing I have a few seconds left before I die of embarrassment.

"I... Yes," I stutter.

He turns to me, and after a second of remembering what I'm saying yes to, he smiles, and gives me another quick kiss. Ah, I need a million more of these, at least...

"Awesome," he whispers. "Let's go."

"...Can I d–"

"No, Mara, no."

Damn it.

His Blazing Witch

I don't think I'll ever get tired of riding this bike with Liam. For a little while, we just have fun, taking the highway and speeding between the cars to get to Nora's house. I can see where the sun has gone down on my left between the buildings as the sky takes gorgeous shades of pink and orange. I missed a sunny day, but I'm glad I didn't miss this. I hang on tight to the leather of Liam's jacket, and lean my head on his back. We're like a two-headed creature on his bike, enjoying the ride together, feeling each movement.

I wonder how our relationship would have been if it wasn't for all of this. The witchcraft, the danger, the mysteries. Perhaps we would have had a cute encounter in the parking lot of the university. A little crush, or love at first sight. Maybe we would have met during a wild college student party, waiting for our drinks at the bar, dancing together, and starting as friends. Or I would have walked into his favorite diner on the docks, and I would have fallen right away for that crazy sexy biker guy in his leather jacket.

I find myself smiling like an idiot, and create a million movies in my mind. I should really try to get a motorcycle license, so we can go on long rides together. ...Could we even leave Silver City?

Sometimes, I feel like this place is like a bubble. An amazing city, with all sorts of neighborhoods, humans, and werewolves. Buzzing with life, its nightlights and downpours, the seashore and the highways, the skyscrapers, the graffiti on the walls, the university, and the pretty family houses. The forest all around... Sometimes, I wonder what's outside. I know Clarissa had a life outside of here. She grew up in another city, with another lifestyle. But I am not her anymore. I am not little Mara, either. This is the first time I realize, I want... more. I want to study what I like, and I want to see more of this world I don't know anything about.

The world outside of Silver City.

However, when Liam parks his bike in front of the house, joking with Ben about his old rundown car being so late despite our detour, I keep all those feelings to myself.

They need me here, don't they? The Witch of Silver City. To protect them, to take over what Sylviana left behind. I let out a long sigh, taking off the helmet and shaking my hair out of the way. Not now, Mara. I guess we have more pressing matters right now.

This time, Nora's husband comes to greet us instead of his wife.

Damian Black is still as intimidating as ever to me, but strangely, I feel something has changed as he approaches me. He feels a bit... less threatening. At first, I wonder if that's because I can now feel my wolf, but no, his attitude really seems to have changed. He actually greets me first, although in a rather quiet way, a simple nod, before the others and lets us in. I wish I could mind-link Liam to ask him about this...

However, before I get any chance to whisper my question, Liam, holding my hand, guides me through the house and as expected, they are all outside again. Nora is trying to calm down her son as the little boy is crying silently in her arms.

"Sorry," she whispers as we come close. "Will tends to be a bit sensitive..."

Selena and Nathaniel are there too, but like Nora's other children, their daughters are not in sight.

"Who got babysitting duty?" asks Liam, curious too.

"All the big kids are at the movies with Isaac and his wife," chuckles Selena. "The babies are sleeping upstairs with Boyan. Danny's on night shift again, so he was lonely."

It looks like the huge brown wolf is the official babysitter of the family...

Once again, Nora prepared a feast, although it sounds like Nathaniel helped. However, we didn't come here just to eat. Quickly promising we'll be back soon, Liam and I leave them to get to Sylviana's tree. Liam's holding my hand a bit tighter, and I don't let go the entire way there.

I can feel it long before we approach the tree's location. No, to be precise, I feel what is missing. Everything I could feel before from that tree... It's gone, or going. So thin and barely palpable, like a mist just about to scatter. Strangely, the place around it still feels eerie, though. We slowly come closer, and the tree appears. I don't know if I was expecting to see it in... such bad shape. In the span of a few days, maybe a few hours, that tree has suddenly turned into a very pitiful thing. There aren't many leaves left on it, and the branches themselves look like they're about to collapse. The trunk seems so weak, just a rub would turn the bark to dust.

Suddenly, I remember Liam next to me, and look at him, a bit worried. However, he looks fine, just staring at the tree with a calm expression.

"It really doesn't look good..." he says.

"Are you okay?"

"Hm?" He turns to me. "Oh, yes. Don't worry, I know it's not... really Sylviana. I accepted that a long time ago."

"It's still a part of her."

"I know. Maybe I'm a bit too detached, but... I think I managed to say my goodbyes my own way, some time after we met... No, maybe even before that. I don't know. I was just used to her strange ways and always being a step ahead. I loved that tree, but it was more of a... a symbol."

I nod.

I get what he means, in a way. It's no use holding on to someone who's already gone... even if more of them is fading away in front of our eyes. Maybe Liam hurts more than he lets on too. His hand is still tightly locked with mine.

We stare at the tree for a very long time, just standing together like this. It isn't... completely dead yet. I can tell the barrier around it is about to fade away as well, but even if the tree is decaying fast, there's still a little bit of life hanging on. I spot a trail of ants walking down that bark. A bird comes to briefly sit on one of the higher branches too.

"...Let's go back?" he asks.

"Do you mind if I... stay here a little longer?" I whisper.

Liam gives me a surprised look, but he slowly nods, putting a quick kiss on my forehead.

"Okay."

"I'll be back soon," I promise.

I watch him go, stepping farther and farther away, back to Nora's house.

I turn to the tree, a bit lost. Why did I feel like staying? Am I the one not ready to say goodbye? I wish I had the chance to say hello... to even meet her. I take a deep breath, and come closer to the tree, putting my hand on it. The bark is lukewarm and rough.

"I wish I had met you," I whisper.

I just feel like I've been waiting for ages to say this... to get this out of my heart. I take a deep breath. I guess now is my last chance to let it out. Not that I think she may be listening to me. This is more of a prayer for myself, like one would whisper in secret at a loved one's grave.

"I wish you had been there to tell me all the truth, to teach me... to guide me."

I feel my throat choking up a little, but I ignore it.

"It's strange that we never even got a chance to meet, but... there is so much we have in common. Our magic, our lost loved ones... and Liam too. ...Please don't resent me for loving him. You probably knew better than I did how... These things work. I am just..."

What am I even trying to say? I shake my head, and take another deep breath.

"Anyway... I hope you'll be okay, in whatever next life you move on to. I sincerely pray you'll be happy, Sylviana. You spent... so much time, if not all your life, protecting others. I... I hope I can do it too. I might be more selfish than you are. I don't... I think you might have chosen your successor wrong, you know. I don't... feel so tied to this place. There's another family for me, out there. It might not be perfect, but... I just don't think I can be like you, Sylviana. I've always... gazed further than Silver City. You know, I used to watch those tall skyscrapers, from that hospital room, but... I wasn't really interested in the buildings themselves. I was curious about how far people could see from up there."

I turn my head, toward where I know all those buildings to be. I smile. It's strange to think that now, I'd probably be allowed in those buildings if I asked... I mean, aside from the ones the fires damaged. I turn to the tree again.

"I hope... you can understand my heart a little. I know you tried to protect them. I understand, and I promise I'll protect them too. I just wish..."

I don't end that sentence.

What... was I going to wish for? I sigh, and take one step back. I glance one last time at that tree, and this time, I have no words left. I nod slowly, and turn back, feeling a bit... empty.

A few steps away, I suddenly spot Liam, waiting for me. He waited instead of returning? I smile a little, and walk up to him, as he extends his hand. Instead of taking it, I just speed up my pace until I can hug him. He chuckles and hugs me back. Mm, he really is a bit bigger than I am... I like that. That old leather and gasoline smell is still floating around him too.

"Feeling better?" he asks.

I just nod, but I insist on keeping my arms around him for a little while longer.

"Mara! Liam! Are you coming to eat, you two?!"

We both chuckle like teenagers caught by their parents. Liam frowns.

"Hm... You think we can run away?" he whispers.

"Not without our bike."

"My bike, Mara. It's my bike."

"Um..."

He rolls his eyes, and I chuckle, grabbing his hand and taking him back to Nora and the others.

It feels like the calm before the storm.

The eight of us, eating around a table in the shade, enjoying a simple meal and friendly discussions. Of course, all our topics are light-hearted. I have to give a precise explanation of what happened to me during what we apparently now call the mirror curse, and the Black Brothers and I alternate to explain about the fight inside the building too. Nora and Selena keep grimacing as we explain.

"What about you?" I ask Ben, suddenly remembering. "You were in bad shape last time I saw you..."

The werewolf boy nods, and lifts his shirt to show me the large bandage around where I remember his wound to be, with a bit of a blood stain, even.

"I'm fine," he winks at me. "It stings a bit, but I'll heal soon with a badass scar!"

"It's not badass to have scars all over!" protests Kelsi, upset. "You should have been careful, you knew it wasn't our Mara..."

"Sorry," he chuckles, still blushing a bit.

Damn, they are so cute together. All the couples are sitting next to each other, but Kelsi and Ben look almost as if they are on a bench together, so close and acting so cute.

It feels a bit strange for me too to simply be here, holding hands with Liam in front of his brothers. Moreover, neither of them seem to care anymore. Actually, I think I know why now. It's just like Selena's change of attitude. I think they felt the... bad I was still carrying inside until now. With the Dark Magic gone, it feels as if they have no reason not to trust me anymore. Plus, I more or less saved Liam's life too, and Damian Black mentioned it himself. Which makes me think he also changed his mind about me because of that, and his brother too.

"...I still think it was strange," says Selena. "She set so many buildings on fire in record time. It's not like Mara was late to the party, but that bitch basically started all those fires simultaneously."

"Maybe not so simultaneously if she had help," says Nathaniel. "However, no one reported another arsonist in the area. They all think it was Mara."

"You mean the Dark Witch," says Nora.

"No," her brother-in-law retorts, "they think it was Mara. Nora, those people don't know what we know. For now, most humans in town will think she is a Fire Witch out of control."

"They are wrong," growls Liam.

"...It's okay."

They all turn to me, surprised. I let out a long sigh.

"To be honest, the humans are the least of my problems, for now," I continue. "It's not like they ever loved me, anyway. What I am most worried about are the other witches."

"I'm curious about that too..." says Selena. "I expected them to attack right away now that Sylviana's barrier is down. Why don't they?"

"Either they don't know the barrier is fading away, or... I sent a strong enough message already."

"That fire was pretty big," nods Liam. "It was probably seen way farther than Silver City."

I shake my head.

"Not just the fire. If they felt the barrier disappear, they must have felt me beating that Dark Witch too. Witches are... connected in a more complex way than werewolves, but we feel... when things happen to magic itself. When my body was possessed, the Dark Witch mentioned a curse. A curse much older than the hatred Nephera had. Something darker, something I felt too, and that killed Clarissa. ...Nora, Selena, you don't have any idea what it could be?"

The two of them exchange a long look, but eventually, shake their heads before turning to me again.

"No... we told you the truth exactly as we know it. I don't believe either of us has ever heard of a curse whatsoever. If anything, we've heard more about blessings, like what our grandmother Queen Diane got, reborn as the Moon Goddess reincarnate."

"Even with that, we aren't sure of anything," sighs Selena. "We haven't... we've got no memories of that. And the only people who know more are dead now."

I sigh and we all stay silent for a long time. I feel like this curse is going to be my next problem... unless the other witches come first. As none of us have any idea of what more to do, we just agree that, at least, my little showdown from yesterday bought us some time. It is more than likely that I scared those witches away. We resume eating, but I take a second to breathe in deeply and try to extend my senses further.

Now, I can do this much. Not only because Mara transferred her knowledge and powers fully to me, but my wolf is there too. It's like getting a sixth sense. It's something I can feel, but not quite see. I feel the barrier, even more precisely than before, without touching it. I feel my own magic, burning like a fire, one vivid spot in the circle the barrier put around Silver City. Bright like a headlight.

I feel... the others too. It's not precise, because they are too far, but I really do. One in the sea. Is the Water Witch hiding under water? Or did she find a boat or something?

Two more. One is definitely Ravena. Strangely, I recognize her earthly magic, as if it was a... force. The more I focus on it, the more I can feel it. It's almost as if the smell of soil and grass got stronger as I keep focusing on her. There's another one... A Fire Witch. She's close to the border... and I don't like that. She's staying just within a reasonable distance, though. Moreover, I feel her better than the others. Is it because she's a Fire Witch too? It's as if she is resonating with me. Now I understand why elements are so important. While the Fire Witch is like an echo of my own magic, Ravena feels less significant. She's there, but I can't feel much of a threat from her. She did mention she was the weaker one too... unlike the Water Witch and her wave. If she can cause so much damage from outside the barrier, she's going to be a pain to fight off for real if we go head-to-head...

"Are you alright?" whispers Liam.

While I was caught up in my thoughts, Nora brought the dessert, and is trying to keep her son away from it. I nod.

"Yeah, I'm just... thinking I might need to see Ravena."

Liam opens his eyes wide, surprised.

"Rav-... The Earth Witch? Why? I don't trust that b–!"

I put my finger on his lips with a quick growl, reminding him his nephew is right there. He frowns and pouts against my index finger, making me chuckle.

"I don't trust her either," I chuckle, "but she played Miss Know-It-All, so it might be worth a shot to ask her what she knows about that curse before doing anything stupid or waiting for the others to come to us first."

"Hm..."

He still looks unhappy with my idea, but it doesn't matter. I need to know, and that's my best option for now.

"Mara? What's on your hand?" suddenly asks Selena, frowning at me.

My hand?

I glance down, and suddenly notice it. Something appeared on my hand. It takes me a couple of seconds to realize it's another spell. What the heck? What did I do now? I quickly stand up and stand away from Liam, but it seems like an... inoffensive one. Kelsi stands up too and comes next to me to check on it.

"...Girls?" asks Ben.

"I don't know this one..." mumbles Kelsi.

"I do," I immediately say. "That's an astral projection spell."

"An astral projection?" repeats Kelsi, panicked. "Please don't tell me you're going to switch your body again!"

"No, I don't think so. This one looks more like a... key, or some sort of guide..."

How did it appear, though? I only tried to use my magic a little earlier, but it couldn't have provoked such a complex and delicate spell. Suddenly, after fixating on my palm for a long time, I realize. That's the hand I touched the dying tree with.

I smile and close my fist. Thanks, Sylviana.

Chapter 29

"Are you sure that thing won't hurt you? Or be dangerous?" Liam whispers.

I nod and put the dishes in the sink. He and I offered to do the dishes for Nora, but I know he was just looking for an opportunity for us to be alone and far enough from everyone else's ears. I wish we could mind-link already... Dinner was nice, but it is a bit strange to sit with werewolves. I could tell there was a lot more going on than what was said out loud. Selena and her husband in particular stayed quiet for a long time, but I'm sure they had to be arguing about something, because she seemed a bit mad and glared at him all of a sudden. Nora and her husband too suddenly switched who was carrying Will as if they had decided it together, without a word. I don't mind as it is part of their ways, but I'm a bit jealous. I wish I could do the same with Liam. Who knows what kind of things we could have said to each other if we had our own private little channel. For now, I can only mind-link Nora and Selena, but I still feel too shy to do so. Despite our bond, I'm not quite... familiar with using my wolf instead of my own voice yet.

"Don't worry," I say, showing the mark on my hand. "I'm pretty sure I know what this is. It will probably stay as it is until I do something to activate it. It's like magic circles which need a witch's blood."

"You think it needs blood?" he asks, his concerned eyes still on my marking.

It's taken over most of my hand and even a bit of my wrist now, but it stopped. It looks like a brown tattoo with a lot of complicated symbols, as if I had dipped my hand into something and taken it out before it dried. Nothing is changing anymore, so I suppose whatever was to be transferred from Sylviana's tree to me, it's done now. I'm curious to discover what she wants me to see... I wonder why I didn't get it earlier. Was it waiting for the protection to disappear? Or for me to become a full witch? Or awaken my werewolf part? Too many things have changed since I first saw the tree, now that I think about it, so I wouldn't be able to tell...

"Mara?" Liam calls me.

"Oh, sorry, I got lost in my thoughts... No, don't worry, probably no blood needed as it's already on my body. I guess I'll find out later. I'm pretty sure it just needs me to be unconscious or sleeping."

He stays quiet for a little while, then turns to me. What's that expression of his? He looks a bit flustered, and approaches me with a flirtatious smile.

"Does that mean you... want to go straight to sleep when we get... back?"

I want to bite my thumb, but I'll settle for my lower lip. Gosh... Liam Black is afraid I'll ditch him for some witchcraft? Or is he just trying to be playful now? Hm... this is too tempting, isn't it? I sigh.

"Well, you know, it's important to find out what this spell is about, so–"

"Mara!"

His offended expression, oh Moon Goddess, he's too cute! I can't take it anymore and laugh. He frowns.

"You're having fun, aren't you?"

"Terribly," I admit.

He seems a bit offended by my childishness, and I put my arms around him, a bit amused. However, we are alone in the kitchen, and seeing Liam act all possessive over me... it's just too sexy. I can't resist it. I put a quick kiss on his lips, but he's pouting and doesn't respond, just staring at me with an accusatory look. Damn, I think pouting Liam might be cuter than smiling Liam. What do I do now? I tilt my head, unable to hide that smile...

"Don't worry," I chuckle, "I probably don't need to go to bed right away..."

"Good," he retorts, still a bit sulky, "because I'm not letting you. I don't care about all that witchy stuff anymore, I just want you all to myself for a little while."

"I agree," I smile.

He nods, finally satisfied, and this time, comes to put a deeper kiss on my lips. I totally give in, of course. This has become so natural between us, yet I still always feel a bit shy... I wrap my arms around his neck, all possessive. I love those kisses, Moon Goddess. I feel like we've always been together, this is just so natural between us. I'm happy. My wolf is freaking delighted and totally enjoying this too.... Our lips get more playful and more demanding too. I love this. I hear him chuckle as we keep going like teenagers caught in a fiery love.

"You two..."

We freeze, and turn our heads to find Selena standing there with a raised eyebrow and two empty bottles. She sighs.

"If you were looking for some private time, you could have just said you wanted to leave instead of making out in the kitchen..."

Liam and I exchange a look, both embarrassed.

"Sorry..." I mutter.

Despite his red ears, Liam grabs my hand and guides me outside, the two of us basically with our tail between our legs as we walk by Selena's amused eyes...

I'm a bit ashamed, but I can't help but laugh when we get out of there, and Liam puts a kiss on my temple.

"Shall we leave?" he suggests.

"Did you want dessert?"

"Not really."

"Alright, let's go, then," I nod.

We quickly make our way back to the garden to say our goodbyes. I think no one is blind but Nora wishes us good night, with Ben and Kelsi announcing they will be going back to the apartment. To my surprise, Damian Black tells us to be careful on our way back which seems a bit... fatherly for him to say. I'm tempted to think this is his way to say welcome to the family...?

The four of us leave the house, Ben and Kelsi hand in hand, while Liam has his arm around my shoulders.

"Alright, I guess we will see you guys tomorrow?" asks Ben with a wink.

"First thing in the morning," I chuckle, not so embarrassed. "Liam has nothing to eat at his place. Expect us for breakfast."

"I'll make pancakes!" promises Kelsi with a huge smile.

I'm glad to see her so happy too. I was worried she wouldn't find her place in a world full of werewolves and witchcraft, but she's amazing at blending in and it's like she and Ben have found their perfect match. They could barely keep their hands off each other tonight, he's crazy about her, obviously. I smile and nod.

"Good night, you two."

They walk to the car and leave the driveway first while Liam and I put on our helmets and jackets.

"Hm... Should I drive since you drank alcohol?" I ask.

"No, Mara. Werewolves aren't as sensitive to alcohol, I'm as good as sober. But nice try, babe."

Damn it.

We get on his bike, and once again, I forget about not being the one driving it as I get to watch the amazing scenery. After dusk, we now have Silver City by night. I hug Liam tight and just enjoy this, visor open, a huge smile on my face. I love this city. It's a strange feeling. I think Silver City is beautiful and amazing, yet a part of me wants... more. Would Liam understand if I told him so? I'm probably the only living being here that should stay here and be sort of irreplaceable, yet a little part of me is dying to see more, get out of here. Still, it'd be difficult. There's only one of me, and because of my relationship to Silver City, to Sylviana, to Nora and Selena, I can't really leave... although my heart isn't sure about staying either.

I keep staring at the tall buildings, the neon lights, and the glowing halo of the moon overseeing all this. There aren't many cars, Liam easily weaves between them, driving his bike at a good speed. It's a strangely peaceful evening after everything that happened these last few days. Just a little, quiet break before a storm...

We finally arrive in the parking lot.

Strangely, I'm a bit sad to get off this bike. We could ride for hours and I wouldn't get tired of it. I really need to look into getting a license. How expensive would a bike be? Should I ask Amy for a loan or something?

His Blazing Witch

I take off my helmet and shake my hair while Liam puts the security on.
"You okay?" he asks.

"Great."

He smiles, and we walk inside the building, our fingers intertwined, the other hand carrying each of our helmets.

We start kissing as soon as the elevator door closes. It's as if with just his lips, Liam could take away all my worries and all the fatigue. It's so soft and gentle, yet sexy and enticing. I feel my temperature on the rise, and the she-wolf in me awakens to her mate's calling. This is just perfect and amazing. He gently caresses my cheek as we keep kissing, until we hear a ding.

I start to get out when an old lady steps in. Oh, not our floor yet... Liam and I exchange a look, a bit embarrassed.

"Good evening, young people!" says the granny.

"Evening..." we mumble, a bit embarrassed.

I want to ask if she's sure she's going up, but she hits the gym button with her cane. Oh, okay...

Liam and I retreat to the back of the elevator, and he keeps sending me glances. I know he's impatient and a bit annoyed. I smile. Just a few seconds... Our fingers are linked, and our hands couldn't be tighter. Our hips are even touching from standing so close. The floors pass so slowly on the little screen, and I can feel Liam fidgeting a bit. Oh, Moon Goddess... I am getting a bit hot too but there's an old lady with us! This is just too funny.

Finally, the door opens, and Liam and I step outside with a polite word to the granny. She smiles and waves at us.

As soon as the elevator door closes, I laugh, but Liam wraps his arms around me.

"Moon Goddess," he sighs. "I thought it was never going to arrive..."

He comes in closer to kiss me, but I back away.

"We're not inside yet!" I chuckle. "Open the damn door already, you hungry wolf!"

He growls and rolls his eyes in frustration, but almost runs to his door to obey. I swear I've never seen him unlock a door so fast. A second later, I'm pulled inside, our helmets fall on the wooden floor and I'm pushed against a wall, Liam's hands on me.

"Now, you're so not going away," he whispers.

"Who said I had any p–"

His lips are stuck on mine before I can finish that.

Oh, Moon Goddess... This is wild. Liam is hungry, and our kiss immediately becomes very wild, our lips frantically searching for each other, so eager it's almost indecent. His hands are on me, caressing my skin, sneaking under my clothes, and the temperature goes up fast. I'm hot, I'm really hot. I can barely catch a breath, but damn, that desire... I want him too. My wolf is crazy, I'm going crazy. I want him, I absolutely want all of him.

We just kiss, kiss, and kiss, over and over, regardless of any need for air. I just need his lips. I just want his taste, his tongue against mine, our lips colliding and melting. This is no tame kiss, but one full of passion, fueled by desire.

Our jackets come off in the blink of an eye, and we almost stumble over the leather as we slowly move toward his bedroom, trying to move together yet not interrupt our kiss. He pushes me against a wall, kisses me wildly and I do the same a few steps further, until one of us decides to move again and we progress inside the apartment. I want him, I want him bad. Is that bad? It has to be, but I don't care. I grab his hair, his skin, any inch of him I can put my hands on.

Finally, we get to the bed, and I fall back on the mattress, Liam over me. This time, we take a breath, as if falling horizontally had woken us up. We gasp for air, our chests moving up and down, our bodies so close and our clothes a total mess. He chuckles.

"...What happened to going slow?" he pants.

"Shut up."

I grab his collar, and pull him on the bed with me before rolling over to get on top. He smiles and I unbutton my overalls to take my top off, exposing my bra, totally shameless. It's strange that I don't feel an ounce of embarrassment, but I'm way beyond that. Liam takes off his shirt to expose his oh-so-well-sculpted torso, and my desire flares up again. Oh, the abs. I almost forgot his abs...

"Enjoying the view?" he smiles.

"I could ask the same to you."

He nods, his eyes going down on my breasts without any shame. Then, his expression changes a bit, into something more... sexy. His hands caress my waist, and sneakily go up behind my back, as he looks for a way to undo my bra. I smile and go down to kiss him, letting him take it off. He actually struggles for a few seconds but I don't really care, and just kiss him some more in the meantime. Then, it finally comes off and to my surprise, Liam immediately leaves my lips to kiss me... there.

I gasp. Moon Goddess, it's good... I breathe a bit louder, but Liam's tongue there and his hand on the other side are... doing things to me. I feel my temperature increase again, and my voice comes out unexpectedly. Fuck, I didn't think I'd like something like this so much... He keeps going and I grab his hair tighter, a bit more excited. He's so passionate, I feel chills going from my breasts to all my extremities... and I like it. I try to control myself, and wriggle around to get the bottom of my overalls off. They slide off the bed easily, and I'm now in my panties over him. Liam's hand suddenly changes targets, going south. Oh, shit... With both his hands on me and his mouth sucking too, I'm going nuts. Shit, I really, really like him touching me. Every inch of my body is on fire, but... the parts he touches are seriously making me crazy.

"Liam, Liam, wait..." I groan.

"You okay?"

"No, not okay, you're driving me crazy..."

He chuckles, but I use that tiny window to jump on his pants, and help him get out of them. He helps me and much to my pleasure, he's rather... ready once we free him. I smile uncontrollably, and Liam grimaces.

"Sorry, I don't think I can wait... much."

"I'm not asking you to," I retort.

He sighs and adjusts our position a little so we're really in the middle of his bed and both sitting, me still straddling him. I take a deep breath, and remove my last piece of clothing, while Liam showers my neck with kisses. He's so... eager and gentle at the same time. I'm a bit hot, but Moon Goddess, it's a good type of heat. He caresses my hips, my waist, my back, my breasts without stopping. Once I'm totally naked, I turn my head back to him, and we resume our deep kisses. I caress his back, his nape, and, much to my pleasure, I go a bit down to touch his butt. He clicks his tongue.

"...Where are you touching?" he chuckles.

"Just curious."

"Hm..."

While he's still staring at me with suspicious eyes, I slowly move my hand to caress his front. His smile disappears, and instead, he looks a bit flustered for a second. I'm not really sure what I'm doing, but I guess the mechanics are rather... simple. I slowly carry my fingers over his tumescent end, up and down, and Liam starts breathing a bit louder. His eyes turn a slightly darker shade, and he keeps staring at me. He's really reacting... and it excites me. I can feel my wolf, just as excited and eager as I am, but this is a new thing. I want to explore... Yet, as I keep going, Liam's fingers venture between my legs again. I gasp, but suddenly, I'm done with the foreplay. I bring my body closer to his, clearly showing what I want. Liam shudders too, and goes onto my neck to kiss some more. I direct him, and he lets me do this.

"Mara, slowly..."

I obey, and slowly slide down onto him.

I thought it was going well at first, but I suddenly freeze because of the pain. Liam caresses me gently, but... oh, fuck. I guess the good news is, this is really my first. Liam patiently waits for me, and I'm so thankful for that. He caresses me, whispers into my ear, kisses my neck and my lips for a very, very long time until I can get used to this. It's not better, but it gets... bearable. I'm a bit mad at myself for being so bold, but... I still want this. I start moving over him, careful about my own body. I can feel he's barely containing himself, but he does. I kiss him, to focus on something else and we both move slowly, carefully. Despite the pain, I'm strangely content. Just to feel him moving inside me, to feel his warmth inside, I try to focus on the good sensation, and occult the bad ones. I don't know if some of my magic does something, but it does become easier after a little while. I breathe a bit better and accelerate a bit. Liam looks like he's at his limit too. We move, not so fast, but finding our own pace, with many, many kisses along the way. It does get better, I get better, and we keep going, me a bit proud of myself for enduring, and Liam looking at his wits end. He accelerates as soon as he feels he can, and I move along with him, happy to let him lead. He suddenly groans, and I moan along with him, feeling him harden and freeze inside. I let him finish, my whole body trembling along for some reason.

I'm out of breath, and grimace when he slowly pulls out. Liam lets out a long sigh but right after that, our kissing resumes, and we both lie on the bed, still in each other's arms, our bodies entangled. Liam chuckles.

"...We'll get better," he smiles.

"Hm..."

I do hope so, because I want to do more of this with him...

"Mara, turn around."

I obey without thinking too much. I feel him cuddle me from behind and kiss my nape when he suddenly bites me The sharp pain goes through my whole body, so violent, I freeze, but it only lasts a couple of seconds.

"Moon Goddess, that hurts!" I grimace.

"Sorry, sorry," he whispers. "Don't burn me, I'll heal it... but I know you wanted it too, so..."

"Yes, but... you could have warned me... Didn't have to bite like a savage..." I grumble.

Liam keeps whispering apologies and starts licking my neck, but I'm set on pouting for a bit. It really hurts, and I'm mad at myself for not realizing what he was doing until he actually bit me... Thankfully, the worst of the pain has already subsided considerably. He gently keeps licking my neck for a little while and the pain disappears, but I feel my wolf reacting favorably to it. I like his hot breath on my neck...

"*...You hear me now?*"

Oh, Moon Goddess. I can! I smile uncontrollably. This is amazing... Liam is lying right behind me, but I've never felt him so close. It's like I have a direct line to his wolf, it's the best I can describe it. This is so unique and it feels so good to be so connected to him this way... After a little while, he stops licking and kisses my neck instead.

"Damn, you're already healed... except for your scar. Yep, you really do heal a bit faster than us."

"Warn me next time you plan to go all bitey, still."

"Sorry..."

He chuckles and kisses my shoulder. Hm... I should learn not to forgive him so fast. I turn around to face him, and Liam smiles, kissing me on my lips next. Yeah, I like that a lot. We keep kissing a little more, simply lying in bed, and I don't feel like doing anything else. I do feel a bit... dirty, but I'm super sluggish for some reason. I'm not even tired. Why would I be? I slept most of the day. I just don't want to move for now...

"...Aren't you going to bite me?"

I growl.

"No," I retort.

"No? Mara, why not?!" he protests, propping himself on his arms.

"That's your punishment for biting me like a savage, you bad boy."

"But..."

He's freaking cute when he pouts, I just want to keep going for a little while. I sigh and struggle to sit up next to him. Hm, I don't feel too well... and I'm feeling a bit dirty.

"I want to take a shower," I say.

Liam blinks a couple of times as I get out of his bed.

"S-seriously...? Mara, you aren't going to mark me?"

"Nope."

"But you can't mind-link me then! What's the point of me marking you one-way?!"

"Well, at least now, you can't mark anyone else," I chuckle.

"Mara!"

Oh, this is just too fun... So this is one-way, huh? So interesting. Although that explains why they can mark even human partners, although there's no use in their human partners marking werewolves; they have no wolf to mind-link with.

Things are different for me, of course. I can feel my wolf dying to bite Liam, and she's a bit mad at me too. Is it strange the wolf in me experiences her own set of emotions? I guess this is more like an underlying side of my own thoughts. Like when I go against my own desires, and take a different path. Well, I guess we'll be on a different path for a little while. I don't feel like forgiving this bad wolf so easily after he bit me without warning, and so savagely too...

Despite feeling odd, I make my way to his bathroom, purposely leaving the door unlocked. I need to pee and then take a shower... I can't remember what expectations I had of sex, but the real thing is really... I don't know, more down to earth than expected. Not in a necessarily bad way, though. I feel like I've learned more about my own body... and Liam's. I could learn some more for sure...

I get the water running above me. It feels good, to calm down my hot skin and wash off all of... this. My legs are a bit weak, though, for some reason. To be precise, all of my lower body is. I sigh and sit down in the shower, enjoying that it's a rather large one, although my butt doesn't appreciate the hard floor.

"Mara...?" Liam calls me, with a little knock.

"Come in."

I hear him carefully step inside and smile. He's surprisingly cute and cautious when he thinks I'm mad... I like this.

"I brought you something to change into. ...Can I shower with you? Hey, you ok?"

"Yeah," I answer, as he steps in. "I just felt like sitting down. My lower half is a bit... numb."

"Oh, okay. I thought you were feeling faint or something. ...Should I help you wash, then?"

"I'd like that," I chuckle.

His Blazing Witch

He seems to finally understand that I'm not that mad, and with a sigh of relief, he gives me a quick kiss on the cheek before grabbing the soap and a body sponge. I hear him sit behind me, and his knees appear by my sides. I really like the size of this shower...

Liam gently starts taking care of my back and arms with the foamy soap, and Moon Goddess, it feels good to just let him rub all the soreness out of me. I really like his hands... He's gentle, and I can close my eyes and let the smell of the soap and steam get to me. A few minutes, that is all I need and I just enjoy this quietly. This feels good, after everything I've been through... in the last forty-eight hours. Moon Goddess, I was falling from a building yesterday, and lying in a hospital bed just this morning. Now I just had sex for the first time with my werewolf boyfriend. Do witches ever get a break from craziness? I feel like I've been on a rollercoaster lately... which is why this little break with Liam feels amazing. I probably needed this without knowing I did. Just me and him, teasing each other, having sex like a normal young couple, and bickering a bit to make up later. This is just... freaking awesome.

I keep my eyes closed and wrap my knees in my arms, leaning my head on them, just to get some rest and enjoy this.

"I... realized we didn't use protection," he suddenly says.

"I realized too," I smile without opening my eyes.

His hands on my back stop.

"...Sorry. I was a bit impatient. I'll be more careful next time, but uh... what do you want to do about it?"

"I won't be pregnant just from that," I chuckle.

"Hey, are you underestimating my–"

"Liam, I'm talking about my cycle. Chances are extremely low at the moment if I'm not wrong, and I know I'm not. Moreover, I'm a witch, I know how to take care of myself and my body. Don't worry... I'm just surprised you didn't know better yourself."

"W-well, it's not exactly as if I was prepared. I mean I should have, but–"

"It's not all on you. But don't worry, I'll find some spell for it without trouble, so I don't risk getting pregnant every time we get naughty. I don't want children at the moment, and neither do you, I suppose?"

"Not really. Maybe later. Damn, I didn't think we'd have this conversation about having kids already."

I chuckle,and agree. Are we really already talking about possible future kids when we were as reckless as teenagers just minutes ago? We still have a long way to go, though.

"...Isn't it better for you to use medicine?"

"What do you mean?"

"As opposed to your magic... you know, for contraception. Wouldn't it be safer to use actual medicine rather than... witch stuff?"

I chuckle and turn around to face him, a bit amused.

"Aren't you supposed to be the expert on witches? Of course my magic is safe to use on my own body! It's just about creating a simple spell, and I'm sure dozens of witches have done the same before that. Are you telling me Sylviana didn't?"

To my surprise, he rolls his eyes, looking elsewhere and obviously a bit annoyed too.

"Why do you have to ask about my ex now...?" he sighs.

"Because your ex was a witch too. Come on, don't tell me you never had this discussion with her before?"

He remains quiet, and certainly avoids my eyes.

...Wait a minute. I feel like I'm missing something. There's no way an accomplished witch like Sylviana valued human medicine over our magic and witches' knowledge. I've learned enough from my training with little Mara to know the oldest witches were midwives! There is nothing we don't know about women's bodies, and certainly about not making babies at random. So why would Sylviana not have had that talk with Liam?

"Liam... don't tell me you and Sylviana never...?"

"Moon Goddess, that is private!" he suddenly exclaims.

He gets up and backs away from me, but I can tell he is embarrassed. I'm so shocked I chuckle nervously.

"Are you serious? Liam?"

"First, it's nothing funny," he retorts. "It's very private. Secondly, I'm not completely ignorant! It's not like nothing happened, we did... stuff. We just never went that far. Sylviana was older than me, and she... uh, kept..."

I did not expect that. I don't know what teenage Liam was like, but I'll definitely say Sylviana was a saint for resisting him. Or just not... into that? Damn, I have a lot of questions I do not want to think about right now. I slap my cheeks and try to organize those thoughts that are popping up.

"So this was also your..."

"First. Yes."

I stay speechless, and barely remember to close my mouth. I hear him sigh.

"Fine, laugh if you want."

I stand up to face him, a bit annoyed now.

"Why would I laugh?" I retort. "I'm not going to make fun of you, there's nothing to laugh about!"

"But earlier–"

"I was surprised, Liam!" I exclaim. "My boyfriend is a walking sex bomb who had a past with another woman, older than him, to boot! I never imagined you'd be a virgin like me! Well, I wasn't even sure I was, but... anyways. I don't find this funny, okay? I promise. Actually, I wish you'd told me. I would have felt less... I don't know. Inexperienced."

"I still have more experience than you."

I slap his shoulder.

"I won't make fun of you, but don't you start boasting!" I growl.

He finally laughs. I want to stay mad at him a bit longer, but I can't. He's just too cute, too sexy, and too much for me to handle. I cross my arms, but Liam is quick to wrap his around my waist, binding me in his embrace. I try to pretend to pout, but my lips are twitching and not convincing enough. He leans in to give me a kiss, and this time, I really can't resist. I wrap my arms around his neck for more caresses. He gently pushes me toward the wall, getting the two of us under the hot shower.

We begin a wild game of trying to kiss between the water, chuckling and letting our lips and faces get wet. I play with Liam's hair, pushing it back and forth, even sideways, anything I want. While he lets me do that, his hands go to my lower back, grabbing and patting my butt. ...Does he really like my bottom? To my surprise, he keeps fondling my butt cheeks for a while, and suddenly, uses his grip to lift me up. I laugh from suddenly being taller than him, and wrap my legs around his waist. Holding me, he resumes our kisses, and I realize I might like kissing him from above...

Our kissing gets a bit less playful and more sensual. Mm... I just want to keep kissing those lips forever. Liam's thin lips are not giving me any rest. We keep going, and my hands go down his back and up his neck, caressing his large back... Damn, I wish I could grab his butt too. I chuckle at that thought and keep kissing him, until he gently bites my tongue.

"What are you laughing about?" he mutters against my lips.

Should I tell him? Hm... I'm not sure I want to. I shake my head, and just insist on some more kissing before letting my lips drift to his face. I kiss his cheeks, with the little spikes of his beard sticking out. He's better without it, though. I like a clean shaven Liam... I keep going, to his cute nose, and switch to his eyes. He closes them, and I want to kiss his eyelids, but... His scar appears, and even when it's closed, that white layer over it bothers me.

"Liam... don't move."

"What?"

Thankfully, the mark from Sylviana's spell is on my other hand. But this side, I can take care of with my other hand. I apply my fingers against his scar. This scar was caused by magic, but Nora couldn't heal it... I see. This isn't just a scar, as expected. A curse... Whoever did this intended to kill him, and it left traces.

"Mara..." he sighs.

"I said, don't move."

My serious tone gets him to obey, and I do hope I'm not too heavy, but I really need to focus right now. I can feel it. It's very small and insidious, but... there's definitely Dark Magic contained in that wound. No wonder Nora was unable to do anything. It is small, well hidden, and a more complex curse than it seems. Now, I'm even more glad I spent time finally learning proper witchcraft with little Mara.

"Do you trust me?" I ask, a bit worried.

"A hundred percent, Mara."

"Alright... Seriously, don't move, okay?"

409

He doesn't answer, but I feel him freeze like a stone. I take a deep breath, and light my fire. I do my best to control it, so the fire is a fully magic one. It can't hurt Liam. I slowly bring it closer, and sure enough, I feel the Dark Magic inside react. It's like a worm trying to stick to a rock, resisting my magic and squirming. Damn it, we'll see if you can stay in my mate's head any longer. Liam still doesn't move, but I can tell he wants to. I feel his jaw clenched. Is he in pain?

I try to go faster, and my fire fully covers the area around his eye, going inside. It's not the kind of fire Liam could feel, but that curse isn't dying without a fight, probably struggling. Don't you resist me, you little piece of sh-...

Suddenly, I feel it. It's gone, completely disintegrated under my fire, erased. I gasp, a bit unsure. I get rid of my fire, and stare at Liam's eye, my throat in a knot. The scar is still there, but...

"Liam? O-open your eyes..."

He obeys, his eyelids slowly go up.

Oh, shit. His eye. I want to bawl like a baby. For the first time, both his eyes stare at me with the same color. I see the shock, his irises widen, and he suddenly puts me down, out of breath.

"W-what the..."

"I figured I should try," I chuckle, grabbing his face in my hands. "Can you really see me? Is your eye okay? Does it hurt?"

"I-I can. Moon Goddess, Mara, I see you perfectly!"

Holy shit, I'm so happy! We both laugh and smile like crazy, and Liam hugs me, ecstatic.

"Damn, Mara, you're... amazing," he chuckles against my ear.

"Thanks," I reply a bit nervously.

He suddenly retreats to unlock this hug, but puts his hands on my buttocks and lifts me up again, picking up right where we stopped. We kiss like crazy love junkies, half-laughing and playfully biting each other's lips gently. This time, we quickly move on to something a lot more sensual. Our hands start grabbing every piece of flesh we can, and our breath accelerates at the same rhythm. We both get the same signals, the urge to do more. Liam suddenly shifts to kiss my neck, driving me crazy.

"Are. You. Sure?" he asks between each kiss.

"Yeah... I think I'm... healed already," I gasp.

"Damn."

Yeah, I think I'm going to love that super healing ability of mine too... Liam swiftly moves, and once again, I feel him between my legs, the heat spiking like crazy in my stomach. Oh, Moon Goddess, are we in a rut or something? I can't stop. He can't stop. Maybe the hot water helps too. The steam, and everything. I just... I want more; I'm okay with being lewd as long as it's with Liam. I mean, Liam's just my type of hot....

He begins moving, fast, and I have to take deep breaths. Body healed, yes, but not used to this yet. Oh Moon Goddess, it's already... so much better. I feel it. I feel him ramming inside me, driving me crazy. He's excited, and I don't think it'll be long before we both get there. We keep kissing and moving, so excited, nothing else matters. I'm impressed by his strength, I have to hold one wall of the shower. He keeps going and going, driving me fucking crazy. I hear my own voice echoing in this glass cage, and I just might love the sounds of my own pleasure mixed with his manly groans. Oh, this is really, really good... and somewhat addictive. I try to control my pleasure, focus on my breathing. Deep breaths, Mara... breathe...

"...Mara?"

I open my eyes, a bit confused. I hear Liam chuckle.

"Sorry, tiger... Too much. I think you passed out."

"You think...?"

"Sorry," he sighs.

He leans in to kiss my forehead.

"You were, uh... mumbling some weird stuff. And, that spell thing on your hand too, it began to move."

I panic, and suddenly sit up on the bed. Liam dressed me in one of his shirts, but that's the only change. The spell on my hand is back to exactly how I remember it. He sighs, and lies down next to me.

"It stopped doing weird stuff as soon as you woke up," he explains.

"...It probably needs me to sleep for real," I say.

I woke up too soon. I let out a long sigh, and lie back down next to Liam, who chuckles, and wraps his arm around me. I notice he's only wearing his boxers... Damn, I can't believe I missed the end of our action. I swear next time I'll be in top shape... He chuckles.

"What are you thinking about that's making you frown?"

"Not telling you. Good night."

I close my eyes, a bit stubborn, and curl up on the mattress. I hear him chuckle and turn off the lights before coming back to hug me. Hm... Time for some sleep, dreams, and magic.

I didn't think I was that tired, but Liam's warmth behind me quickly soothes me. I breathe slowly, waiting for the darkness to come... and some answers.

Strangely, I'm aware I'm dreaming from the start. It is an odd sensation, like I'm in a place I'm not supposed to be. I look down, but I can barely control myself. I'm... floating, but my body feels too heavy to move. I manage to lift my hand. As expected, the spell is still there... It looks more like some key, though, and parts of it are now strangely glowing on my skin. Or, my dream representation of my skin. I need to keep in mind this isn't real...

Am I supposed to do something? I look around once again and finally, the landscape changes. I'm back in Nora's garden, a few steps away from Sylviana's tree. Except that the tree looks very different. It's full of leaves, its bark is as good as new, and there's no trace left of that tree's decay I saw today. However, those leaves are strangely white and glowing. I approach, a bit at a loss. What is this...?

Suddenly, something moves from behind the tree. I step back, wary of it.

A snake. I frown. A large, thick snake with green skin slithers along the tree's roots, hissing and coming my way. Oh, no, no, no, how am I supposed to flee that thing? It looks about as tall as me! I try to light my fire, but in a dream, I have no idea how to, nothing responds the same. Moreover, I soon stop trying; what if I set Liam's bed on fire without knowing? No, I can't be careless with magic, not again. But then, how do I deal with that thing?

Perhaps it's not that dangerous? I try to step forward, but it suddenly hisses and shows two pointy fangs. Okay, nevermind. We are not going to be friends, not today. Then what?

To my surprise, something suddenly jumps in front of me. It's so large I'm scared at first, until I recognize the large tiger on fire.

"...Spark?"

He growls loudly at the snake in a defensive stance. Moon Goddess, is my cat defending me? I didn't expect magic cats to be sidekicks even in dreams... although this is a magic dream.

Spark keeps growling furiously at the snake, standing between it and me like a wall of fire. I quickly understand he's defending me, making sure that snake can't get near me. I carefully stay behind him, unsure what to do. The snake tries to get past Spark to attack me, but every time, he's met with a violent bite, or a swipe of Spark's gigantic paw. It lasts only a few seconds, but after a while, my cat seems to have had enough of this. He growls furiously once again and jumps on the snake, claws out.

Something happens.

The snake vanishes in some dark smoke, and by instinct, I grab Spark to pull him back. I don't like this... The smoke keeps growing, darker and thicker. My tiger cat growls, curling up his giant body around me, and I don't like this either. This thick, dark cloud keeps spinning and surrounding us, like the eye of a hurricane. I'm... getting cold. Like, very cold, which makes no sense when a fire tiger is literally standing next to me. Yet, it's real. I'm shaking, and my breathing goes crazy. What do I do?!

I look at my hand, and more of those symbols are glowing. If it is some sort of key, it should be helping me, not sending me to some trap! Or is this some sort of security? I step forward, despite Spark's growling. I have a feeling we won't get a second chance if I don't solve this now.

Putting my marked hand forward, I literally dive it into the wall of black smoke.

Moon Goddess, it's ice cold... Still, I keep going, I know there's got to be something about that spell on my hand. The ice crawls on my hand like hundreds of small little needles. Damn, that hurts... I keep going, despite Spark and my inner wolf both growling to warn me. I know I can do this. ...Just a little more...

Suddenly, the dark smoke vanishes.

I stumble a couple of steps back, exhausted. My hand hurts, but when I look, the spell is glowing again... almost all of it this time. Good... So I was right. What was that black smoke, some sort of security check? Damn it, witches do know how to keep their secrets. My hand is going to be numb for hours...

Spark comes up to me, gently rubbing his large face against my arm. I think I like his big cat form, he's even bigger than I am... We both finally look up as the dark fog disappears. We are back, or still at the tree, but the snake is gone. Instead, a large blue butterfly is there. It's on the tree, immobile against the bark. With that kind of size, it has to be another manifestation of magic... It suddenly flies up to me and, unsure, I extend my arm to it. The butterfly gently comes to me and as soon as it lands on the spell, the scene changes again.

I'm in a small house that feels... familiar. It's not Sylviana or Nora's house, it's... Clarissa's. I keep looking around but I'm pretty sure. I recognize some details that she had put in that particular sketch. Everything is exactly how she remembered it... The little windows with their blue curtains. The empty vases, and the piles of books on a table. I observe a bit more, intrigued. There's a strange necklace with a large, blue bead with what looks like an eye in the middle.... It takes me a few seconds to find the answer in my witch knowledge. It's an evil eye, the Turkish Nazar. A protection against evil charms, envy, and jealousy...

Suddenly, a little girl comes running in. It's a bit strange because I can only focus on a few things at once, as if my field of vision was narrow, with everything else blurry or disappearing as I move. Still, I focus on the little girl and immediately, I recognize her. It's *us*. Clarissa, the young little girl. She's wearing a bracelet with the same beads as the large one hung on the wall and a white dress. She smiles and runs toward a fireplace.

"Mommy, Mommy!"

The young woman sitting by the fire turns to her. I didn't realize how young her mother was... She has white skin, and long, curly black hair. She's very pretty with her blue eyes, but she looks... tired. Very tired. There are marks on her arms too, like witch marks. Like a witch that has exhausted a lot of her magic.

I glance at the butterfly flying around me, and it gently goes toward them. This is obviously a memory, but to my surprise, the woman smiles, and welcomes the butterfly on her finger.

"Mommy, it's so pretty!"

"Yes, Clarissa, but it is sacred. You shall not keep it."

The little girl nods, and puts her hands behind her back, well-behaved. The butterfly gently lands in that woman's hair, and for a second, she looks up, and I think our eyes meet.

It only lasts a very brief moment, but I'm... almost sure she actually *saw* me. I try to control my breathing and hold Spark a bit closer to me. Is it even possible? This scene is a memory, she shouldn't be able to... see me. Or is it something else?

The woman sighs, and focuses on her daughter again, gently caressing her hair.

"Mommy, could you tell me another story? I love to hear your stories..."

"Of course, my baby. Come here."

Clarissa smiles wide and sits on her mother's lap. The woman kisses her forehead very gently, and begins to brush her hair with her fingers as she starts talking.

"Once upon a time, there was a little girl. The little girl was a witch, and she lived alone, far from the humans who feared her. She had no friends and no family."

"Oh, she must have been lonely..." says Clarissa, frowning.

"Yes, Clarissa. She lived alone, and practiced magic every day. She couldn't help the humans who lived in sickness, but she helped the nature around her. She healed the trees and fed their dry roots. She cleaned the rivers, and made their waters blue. She tamed the fire, and fed it wood. She was loved by animals. The one who loved her was a young wolf."

"A wolf?"

Her mother nods.

"Yes. The young wolf saw how lonely the witch was, and came to visit her every day. The witch and the wolf became friends, and soon, a unique bond formed between them. The little witch grew into a beautiful young maiden, and the wolf grew up. However, the wolf wasn't strong enough. The wolf had a pack, but the pack was constantly hunted down by the humans. The pack needed a strong leader. So, to help the wolf, the witch made him stronger. She used her powers, and she gave him a human appearance, so he could talk with the humans. She made him a werewolf.

"The first werewolf began talking to humans. He learned their ways, and he learned how to live with them. He taught the other wolves to stay away from humans. He became the powerful Alpha of his pack, loved by all, but no one loved him more than the witch. As her beloved wolf now had a human appearance, the witch began to love and love him more. She fell deeply in love, and as he treasured her greatly, she thought the wolf loved her too. The wolf came to visit her every day, bringing her gifts and affection. However, the wolf's love was different. The wolf already had a partner, a young she-wolf he loved greatly."

"Oh, no..." mutters Clarissa.

"Once the witch learned of this, she got angry," resumed her mother. "The wolf had betrayed her, she thought. He never loved her, and only used her for her powers. She had lost her only friend, and her only love. The pain and anger drove her mad. She couldn't get over her heartbreak. She cried for days because of this pain, and felt the loneliest a being can feel. Her magic tried to help her, but instead, the heartbroken witch did something very bad. Guided by her feelings, the witch put a curse on the werewolf and all of his descendants. If one was to ever betray a witch, they would have to suffer a curse. After that curse was cast, the witch isolated herself. She hated the humans and the wolves.

She wanted to be alone again, and not suffer anymore. Once her anger had been put into that curse, she felt very empty and very lonely, but she couldn't trust anyone anymore, for no one could understand her pain, she thought."

"What did the curse do, Mommy?"

Her mom shakes her head.

"Something terrible, Clarissa. The witch never saw the werewolf she loved again."

"...Is it the end of the story, then?"

"No," smiles her mom. "When she thought things were over, the young she-wolf who loved the same wolf came to the witch's door. The witch thought this one had come to take revenge on her lost loved one, and she prepared herself to fight. However, she was wrong. The female wolf had come to apologize to the witch."

"To apologize?" repeated Clarissa, raising her eyebrows.

"Yes. 'I'm sorry,' she said to the witch, 'because my love with the wolf you loved has caused you a lot of pain. I came to apologize for your pain, for now, I am very lonely too without my mate. I understand your anger, but please, accept me by your side now. I know you longed for a companion, and my mate was by your side for a long while. Now, please let it be me. I cannot bear to remain lonely, and I cannot bear for you to be lonely, either. My children have grown and gone. I won't have anymore, but I do not want to remain alone anymore. Please, witch, keep me by your side.'"

"What did the witch do then?"

"The witch was very confused, of course. After she had put such a terrible curse on their family, the she-wolf had come to ask for her forgiveness, and to keep her company too? It was very hard for the witch to understand. So, she decided to let the she-wolf stay by her side so she could wait and see. To her surprise, the she-wolf had spoken the truth. She became the witch's friend, her only friend. The witch understood her mistake. She had taken the wolf's love for granted, and when she had turned him into half a man, she had thought that man was hers. Humans are selfish creatures, but wolves are not. The she-wolf had a pure heart, and so, she did not envy or resent the witch. So, when she realized her mistake and the terrible curse she had put on innocents, the witch was terribly sorry."

"I feel sorry for her too, Mommy. Did she undo the curse, then?"

Her mom sighed.

"No, Clarissa. Once a curse is created, it is stronger than its creator. That is why no witch should ever cast a curse mindlessly."

"I understand, Mommy. Then, what happened to the witch and her friend?"

Her mother smiled.

"The witch said the truth to her she-wolf friend, and she apologized a lot. Sadly, it was too late. She couldn't undo the curse. So, instead, the witch tried to protect her friend. First, she gave her name to that she-wolf who didn't have one, so they could share that burden and weaken the curse. Then, she turned her into a werewolf too, so she could teach her magic."

"But... wolves can't learn magic!"

"They can, my love. This is a very old story from a very long time ago, a story from the first witches who were much, much stronger than us."

"So the she-wolf became a werewolf... and a witch?"

"Not exactly. She became something a little bit different. She wasn't a witch, but she had strong powers to protect herself and her descendants. She only practiced the whitest, purest magic. She taught that magic to her daughters, and their daughters, so they could all protect their families from witches' Dark Magic."

"So... what happened to the curse?"

Her mother sighs, and her expression got a little darker. To my surprise, she lifts her eyes, staring directly at me.

"That curse is still there. It comes back to poison the minds of witches betrayed by their werewolf lovers, and poison their children. It is a very Dark Magic that is very, very old..."

"Can we break it?" I hear myself say at the same time as Clarissa.

"Of course, my love. When a stronger witch appears and breaks the curse, it will be over."

Clarissa suddenly jumps down from her mother's lap.

"Then, I want to be very strong, Mommy, so I can help all the nice werewolves!"

"You like werewolves?" chuckles our mother.

"Um... I think so. I like the nice she-wolf, Mommy, she was so nice to the witch! I want to be strong like her, and only do the white magic like her!"

"You're right, my baby. She was very strong. She was the strongest of all. Do you know? That she-wolf and the witch's friendship is still considered sacred to us and to the werewolves. That is why the witches always try to protect werewolves, if they can. We are friends."

"I will be friends with all the werewolves!" nods Clarissa, her eyes sparkling. "I love the she-wolf, Mommy. She is the best!"

"Yes, my baby. She was so beautiful, strong, and loved that all werewolves still remember her name. They forgot the witch who gave her that name, but they never forgot the she-wolf's name. They have kept it sacred, it is a name given only to the most beautiful and strongest of them. They become loved by the Alpha wolf, and they are the mother of their pack. And when us witches meet a werewolf with that name, we know she is our friend..."

"Really? Mommy, Mommy, what was the name of the witch and the she-wolf, then? What was it?!"

Her mother smiles.

"You will remember it, Clarissa. ...Her name was Luna."

Her name was Luna...? It suddenly comes back to me. The Witches' Ancestral Tree! One of the oldest witches had a name like that. Is that... the witch from the story, the one who began the curse? I have a million questions flooding through my mind, but more importantly... I have this answer. Moon Goddess, this explains so much.

I look at Clarissa's mother, gently caressing her daughter's hair. It looks like she forgot about me now. This story... she told Clarissa on purpose, didn't she? Some witches can foresee the future, like Sylviana. I haven't been able to use that ability other than in action, as a self-defense reflex, but... at least I can see the past when it matters. I should try to work on that too. It is the only thing little Mara couldn't help me with, I guess.

"Mommy, have you seen werewolves before?"

Clarissa keeps chatting with her mother but they are simply just talking to each other, I guess there's... nothing left for me to learn here.

How do I get out of this? The butterfly is still with Clarissa's mother, fooling around in her hair and I suddenly understand it's no stranger to her. I thought this was Sylviana's, but... what if this was her magic creature instead? She was an Earth Witch just like Sylviana was, it wouldn't be strange if they have the same pet...

"...*Are you envious?*"

I turn around.

Standing there in the darkness is a young woman. She's... beautiful, but also scary. She has bright green eyes, and crimson red hair floating around her face. Her dress too, looks like it has black embroideries at first, but... eventually, I realize it's not fabric at all, but sheer darkness, floating around and covering her arms and body.

Even without her appearance, I can tell. There's something evil about her, something that puts me on edge. Spark circles his body around me too and starts growling again. She smiles at me, but there isn't an ounce of happiness in that smile. It's just straight creepy.

"Who are you?" I ask, spreading my fingers as if to start a fire.

"*Don't you envy me too?*" she smirks.

It suddenly hits me. Red hair, green eyes, looking about in her thirties, and a witch too... Sylviana?

No, this can't be right? Sylviana wasn't a Dark Witch and she's dead. She's been dead for a long time. Why would she appear now? I mean, she obviously put that spell in her tree, but...

I glance back, and the scene behind me with little Clarissa and her mother is gone. There's nothing but darkness... Damn it, what now? I don't like this. Moreover, the air is starting to get colder. I feel it, like a chill going down to my bones. I try to ignore it. I know it's not real. I have to remember this is just a dream. A dream that looks like it's about to turn into a damn nightmare...

"*What is it?*" she chuckles. "*Is the little witch scared?*"

"I'm not scared of you," I hiss, "and I am no longer a little witch. I can control my powers and—"

"Your *powers?*" she suddenly says, louder. "*Those aren't your powers, are they? Didn't Clarissa Garnett give them to you? You don't have any powers.*"

417

I stay speechless. What the... What the hell is going on? She steps closer to me. I want to step back, but my feet feel like they are suddenly glued to the ground. What the actual hell, there is no ground, this is a dream! Yet, I feel them freeze. I can't move, it does literally nothing when I try. It's the cold, taking over my feet. It's not even... cold anymore. It's ice cold and making me feel more numb each second.

"You don't have powers, you're just a replacement... Nothing you have is yours, is it? That family. Those werewolves... None of them really like you, do they?"

"Shut up," I growl. "You don't know anything."

"Oh, I know," she chuckles. *"You're nothing but a broken soul... A patchwork made of random broken pieces. You take what you get and you survive, thinking you're legit... Aren't you scared?"*

The cold crawls up my legs as I try to fight it. I need to get out of this. I need to get out of here. She comes closer, but I don't want her any closer. I try to get mad, to look for my inner flame. Yet, my fire is surprisingly small now, as if this cold was affecting it too. Why? Why can't I get out of here? I'm getting really nervous now and this sense of danger is scaring me.

"You're not Sylviana," I hiss. "You're that curse."

She chuckles, and her appearance changes. Damn, I knew it. Now that I've uncovered her, she doesn't care about playing around and it will just get worse... I see her shift until she takes the traits of a similar woman with darker hair, blue eyes... I would swear this has to be Nephera. She tilts her head.

"Mara, Mara," she sings. *"Even your name isn't really yours. You stole their body... their powers... little nameless thief... Mara, the thief with a fake name..."*

"Stop it. You know nothing about me, you're just a curse. All those dark feelings those other witches had."

"And you? You think you can escape them?"

Right now, I'm not sure I can. The closer she comes, the colder I get. I don't feel well. I'm shivering like crazy, and I can't feel my legs anymore. The damn irony. I've known the pain of getting burnt, now I'm going through the opposite... I look around but Spark is gone. I'm suddenly hit by a new wave of cold, and I'm really not feeling well.

"Even Liam..." she suddenly whispers, changing back into Sylviana. *"You stole what wasn't yours... Your mate? You think you deserve a mate that wasn't intended for you? Something else you stole from someone... like a scavenger..."*

"Get the fuck off me," I growl. "Liam is mine. Not yours, not anyone else's. Mine."

Hearing her talk about my mate fuels my anger and my fire. I don't want her to talk about him. I struggle more. I need to get out of here now!

"You're a liar... You're nothing but–"

"I'm a fucking witch, you damn bitch of a curse. So now, you get *OFF ME*!"

I focus on my flame, getting ready to let it all out. It's now or never. She has to go. I'm cold, I'm so cold that I can't feel my legs, my chest, and soon, my hands... I can't let my flame die out. I can't keep listening to her. I prepare my fire, growing like a storm inside of me, and I'm about to spit it out when she suddenly disappears.

An earthquake takes over, my body is shaking.

"Mara!"

I finally open my eyes.

"Moon Goddess," says Liam. "Mara, can you hear me? Are you okay?"

W-where...? How...?

I nod instinctively, but I'm not okay. It takes me a few seconds to realize where I am. Liam's bed. Liam's arms. He's holding me, looking panicked. I'm still confused, but Liam keeps shaking me and rubbing my arms to keep me awake, until he's sure I am. I'm shivering like crazy and still feeling cold as hell.

"W-wha-...?"

"Mara, are you okay?" he asks again.

"I... I'm cold," I finally blurt out.

"Cold? O-okay."

Before I realize, Liam carries me out of the bed in one move, and I just desperately hold on to him. I'm letting him take me wherever he wants. I'm as strengthless as a doll right now, I can't move a single muscle. With just my finger on his skin, I focus on his warmth. He takes me to the bathroom and back into the shower. Damn, how many showers will I take today...?

He puts me down on the shower floor and has the hot water running immediately. We are both still in pajamas and getting soaked in them, but we don't care. I just need to breathe. I don't feel so well, I'm nauseous. I'm scared and that sensation of ice covering my limbs won't go away. I rub them frantically, hoping it will fade soon. I need to calm down. It was just a nightmare, just a nightmare...

"Are you feeling better?" asks Liam.

He rubs my arms and stays close, his gray eyes not leaving me. I nod and just stay as close as I can to him, letting the hot water wash over me. I need to calm down. I breathe slowly and inhale Liam's scent to calm me down. His hands don't leave me for one second. He's gently rubbing my back, my arms, my neck, without asking anything, just waiting for me. Moon Goddess, that's all I need right now. To focus on his hands, on him. He's here. He's my mate and he's here.

The shivering slows down, and he gently rubs some water over my forehead. I didn't even realize how much I was sweating until now... That was one really bad dream.

"Thank you..." I mutter.

"It's alright," he sighs. "As long as you feel better soon... Damn, I don't think I've ever felt your skin this cold... or even seen you shivering crazy like that."

I weakly nod a bit, and put my forehead on my knees. Damn it, now I'm exhausted... again. I move my toes, as if to make sure they're back. The ice is gone... I'm still shivering a bit, but it's nothing compared to before. I feel like my whole body went out of whack. What the hell...

I'm glad Liam keeps hugging me. He's drenched too but he just stays there under the shower with me, caressing my shoulders, massaging my nape to make me feel better. After a little while, he slowly turns off the water and wraps me in a gigantic bath towel, the softest one too, and takes me out of the shower.

"Damn it, you're still cold..." he frowns. "Uh... How about a hot drink? Hot chocolate?"

"Sounds good," I mutter.

"Okay then, hot cocoa it is. If this doesn't warm you up... I don't know what will."

He carries me to the kitchen and, in a familiar position, gently puts me on the kitchen counter before running to the kettle and cupboards.

"While I do this, want to update me on the latest crazy witch stuff?"

"It was the curse," I grumble.

"The... You mean *that* curse? I thought that spell was–"

"I'm not sure what happened, it hid inside the spell and tried to trick me... I'm not sure why. Or even what happened at all, to be honest. Everything was going okay for a while and it... appeared at the end."

I sigh and wrap the towel tighter around me. Liam pours the hot water on the cocoa mix and brings it to me.

"Here."

"Thanks..."

I immediately take small sips, ignoring that it's burning my tongue. It feels good. The sweetness is even more efficient than the hotness of the drink itself. I feel it go down my throat and into my stomach, finally warming me up from the inside. Liam sips a bit from his too, and comes back to me, gently rubbing my arms again.

"Better?"

I nod and let out a long sigh.

"Thank Moon Goddess for hot chocolate," I whisper.

"I know, right? Best thing ever."

I chuckle, and Liam leaves a quick kiss on my forehead. I lean on his shoulder. Damn, I'm a bit better now, but I'm tired again. Still, I need to let it out. I don't think I'll be able to close my eyes after this.

"...There was a good part and a bad part. Which one should I start with?"

"Hm... the bad part? I feel like I'll need something to calm me down afterwards."

"I saw your ex."

He opens his mouth, shocked.

"Sylviana?"

"...Do you have other exes I should know about?" I frown.

He closes his mouth right away.

"Nope. But... what... I mean how...?"

"It wasn't really her, to be honest. The curse took her appearance to confuse me..."

"Mara, what happened?"

He puts his hand around my nape, he can tell I'm not okay. Oh, what the hell, why do I feel like crying now? I've been crying so much these days, but shit, she really got to me. As soon as I'm about to open my mouth, I feel the tears coming. I try to take several deep breaths, I don't want to cry, I don't want to cry...

"Hey, babe, it's me, okay?" he whispers gently. "Just me. Let it out. I'll listen."

Liam gently kisses my forehead, my temples, my cheek, and the wall breaks. I start crying. I'm exhausted, I feel like crap, and I'm completely messed up inside. I've had two fucking rough days and I just need a break from this whole mess. I hate that I'm letting everything she said go to my head. I don't want to. I thought I was stronger, but... damn, I have insecurities too.

"She... I mean the curse, it just... called me a thief..."

"A thief?"

I nod, sobbing silently.

"That I don't... have anything that's really mine, or... me... Clarissa's body, her f-family... l-little Mara's powers... even you... You're not really my mate, and—"

"Okay, okay, Mara, stop right there. Babe, look at me."

I make an effort to raise my eyes from my cup, and look Liam right in the eyes. This time, he looks dead serious and cups my cheeks in his hands.

"Mara, you're my mate," he says. "Alright? Don't let any curse or any bullshit magic tell you otherwise. I don't give a damn about your body, your family, your magic, or whatever. You're my mate, my Mara."

"But—"

"No buts," he growls. "Mara, it's not about *any* of those things, okay? I love this Mara, the one that's right in front of me right now. The Mara that is one hell of a badass witch one day, and a sexy student chick I can pick up after her classes the next. I love how you are with your friends, with my family... our family, and even how you care for your weird magic cat. I like that you're fine with my stupid noodles and hot chocolates. I like that you can threaten to burn my ass when you're jealous, and when you're a brat who tries to steal my bike... Okay? I love this Mara, the girl I saw on the dance floor, who chased me to the border and got trapped in a downpour with me."

I smile. I didn't realize how many memories we already have together... Liam smiles too, and kisses my cheek quickly.

"I love how cute you are when you cry, when you smile, and even that stupid habit of yours to bite your thumb when you're hesitating or stressed. When you make efforts to dress up or try makeup, and when you're as dorky as your friend too. That's my Mara. You're stubborn and reckless as hell, you always have so many questions, no one can keep up with you, and you're crazy enough to jump from a building to save everybody but yourself."

Now I'm getting shy, but Liam isn't done. He smiles again, and kisses my other cheek.

"There's no other Mara like that, okay? I don't care about what name you want to use, or how you came to be, okay? I... like the parts of you that make you Mara. Your crazy magic stuff I can't keep up with, but that's fine with me. Your body too, I don't care if it's borrowed or whatever, I'm glad you got one that functions well. I could tell when it wasn't you, couldn't I?"

"It took you long enough..."

"Hey, that body is still hot, for the record, and I didn't know there was a soul-swapping option on it."

This time, I can't help but chuckle at his half-offended, half-annoyed expression. However, he soon sighs and puts his forehead against mine.

"Mara, if there's only one thing in this world you can trust, it's me, remember? You said you needed our fated mate bond. I need it too. You healed something in me, Mara. I didn't think I could bounce back after what happened two years ago, but... you happened, and things changed again."

"...Really?" I mumble.

"Yes, babe."

He comes in to kiss me. It's one very sweet kiss, with a chocolate taste, and it's so good. Our lips are so gentle, it's almost too tame compared to our usual kisses. Still, it makes me feel a lot better. Liam is being extra gentle on purpose, and rubbing my wet cheek with his thumb. When we separate, I'm done crying and have a bit of a smile on, while his goes from ear to ear.

"That's right," he chuckles. "My Mara. My feisty tiger."

I chuckle back, and lean in to steal another quick kiss from him.

"Thank you..." I whisper. "...I love you."

"I love you," he repeats almost instantly.

Liam gently takes my mug out of my hands, places it next to us on the counter, and hugs me tightly. I'm warm now. I'm warm and feeling much better than before. I can't believe I let her use my insecurities like that... I really fell deep for it. I take deep breaths against Liam's neck, his scent calming me down. We almost smell the same now. I wrap my hands around his waist, and realize his pants are still soaking wet.

"You're..."

"I know," he sighs. "It's okay. Plus, maybe it will dry while you tell me the good part of that shit dream you had."

"Oh, right..."

I take a deep breath, and as we separate, Liam hands me my mug back. He sips some of his too. Yeah, I'm going to need more hot chocolate while I tell him everything...

Maybe because it was a magic one, this dream is still so vivid in my mind, so I have no problem reciting each detail to Liam. He doesn't say a word while

I tell him everything, simply sipping his hot cocoa and gently rubbing my leg, worried that I might still be too cold. I'm good, though. Actually, telling him about that horrible dream, or nightmare, is like pouring out all that angst I got from it. The more I share with him, the more relieved and detached from it I finally feel.

I had to start all over with the story told by Clarissa's mom, but Liam gets really angry when I get to the curse taking Sylviana and Nephera's appearances to trick me.

"Damn it," he growls. "Well, at least now we know what that shit was all about..."

"Yeah... It really was much older than Nephera herself. Even I almost gave in to it. This... bundle of dark feelings, it has probably grown from all those it affected, witch after witch."

Liam sighs and nods.

"Damn, I wonder how many witches were... betrayed by werewolves before."

"Liam, I have a theory, but... it's a bit... crazy."

He chuckles and caresses my hair gently.

"Babe, if I had ever stopped at crazy... I wouldn't be crazy about a witch."

I smile and blush, but this is serious.

"Liam, Nephera was... betrayed by your father, right?"

"Yeah, I mean... yeah."

"...So the curse was activated with her, and it fueled her anger. But it didn't really... affect you and your brothers, right?"

He hesitates, frowning, and from his expression, he's probably looking through his memories as well.

"I mean, it's not like we had a... good childhood. Our dad was crazy, to begin with, and not the good kind of crazy. Our mother spent all the time I knew her in a hospital, so..."

"Yes, I mean, I know, but it's... Look at little Mara, who wasn't even able to be born, and Clarissa, born with a sick body. I think they lived the same thing."

"You think Clarissa's father betrayed her mother?"

"Either him, or her mother's father betrayed her mother," I nod, thinking. "...I don't know... I mean, I don't think Clarissa's dad is a werewolf, Amy would have told me. Or maybe she doesn't know herself... I'm really not sure. But, even if he wasn't the one to betray her, I think Clarissa's mother could have been a cursed child herself. If her own mother was abandoned herself by a man, unfortunately, it passed on to her own daughter, and to Clarissa after... Clarissa did mention that her mom was always weak too, and she... died young, of disease. It sounds odd for a witch, especially a good witch. I think Clarissa's mom struggled her whole life to buy them time, and it was some miracle in itself that Clarissa was born at all. Maybe she gave her life to extend Clarissa's, just like she and little Mara were later able to survive on each other's strength.

423

I think the curse just... doesn't let go like that at once. But I think... you and your brothers were protected."

"What do you mean?"

I don't answer yet. I have all my gears spinning like crazy right now, I feel like my brain is going to explode, but... damn, thanks to that dream, all the pieces are slowly coming into place. Not just Liam and his brothers, but even Selena and Nora's story. Moon Goddess, if... if I look at it from a witch's perspective, everything makes sense.

I take a deep breath and look up at Liam again.

"Liam, the story repeated itself, not just once, but twice. Nephera was betrayed by your father, and he went... insane, right?

"Y-yeah..."

"But you and your brothers were fine. I mean, you... endured his madness, but you were all born healthy, even long after your father had betrayed Nephera. The curse didn't pass onto you."

"Okay... I mean, yeah, I suppose that's true. So how do you explain the curse didn't work? Plus, you said it happened twice...?"

"Yeah, the other time is with Queen Diane."

"Q-Queen Diane? Nora and Selena's ancestor? ...I don't follow, babe. I mean, even if there was a man, Queen Diane wasn't a witch, she was–"

"A Luna. A Royal, and the reincarnation of the Moon Goddess," I finish. "The most powerful werewolf ever known, right? In that dream, Luna, the werewolf Luna, had powers akin to a witch, but she wasn't a witch herself. She was a powerful werewolf, the first female of her kind. I know this sounds insane, but... what if three generations ago, the story had been repeated? And the descendants of Luna had awakened this power she had?"

"I mean... I can totally understand that Nora and Selena are basically descendants of the first Luna through Diane, but why would they have anything to do with the curse?"

"Liam, a woman with power akin to the Moon Goddess didn't just appear out of the blue! ...If you look at it from the witch's perspective, it all makes sense! I mean, we know there's magic, and it has its own rules, but the Royals are basically magic werewolves! Nora and Selena have powers the others don't have because of their parents, right? Because Queen Diane was their grandmother, she was the powerful Royal Luna. That curse doesn't work on them, and I'm sure they protect their partners too."

He stays quiet for a long moment, frowning and thinking about my words.

Liam takes a deep breath, and grabs his hot cocoa to empty it in one go.

"Let me sum it up," he says. "The first Luna was the first female werewolf, but she was created as... the first Royal, to counter a very, very old curse created by that other Luna, the witch on the Witches' Ancestral Tree. Since that... story, every time a witch was betrayed by a male werewolf..."

"The curse grew stronger, poisoning her descendants, and driving the male werewolf to insanity."

424

"But my brothers and I weren't... poisoned."

"Because your mother protected you, Liam. I think she and Queen Diane were able to defeat the curse. Queen Diane was even stronger because she basically awoke the powers of the First Luna."

"Queen Diane wasn't betrayed!"

"She wasn't the one that was betrayed, Liam! Think about the story, for the curse to happen, Diane wasn't the one betrayed, a witch was!"

He stays mute for several long seconds.

"Wait... you mean... Danica? Sylviana's... mother?"

I nod.

"Liam, think about it. Do you seriously think Diane had children out of the blue? No matter what powers she had, even witches can't have children by themselves!"

He stares at me, completely dumbfounded for a while.

"So your theory is... the twins' father..."

"Betrayed Danica, the witch. Or, another witch, if there was one around. Maybe Nephera's father...? Well, I don't know, but in any case, if Diane forgave that witch, and they got over their hatred..."

"The curse would have been weakened again," Liam whispers.

"Exactly."

"Holy Moon Goddess, Mara, that's... a lot," he let out.

"I know, it's a lot of supposition, but it all makes sense. Diane was stronger because she made exactly the same decisions as her ancestor, Luna. She awoke the strongest part of her bloodline, the one that made her a stronger werewolf with some magic powers, and protected her children at the same time. The twins were born fine. Unfortunately, the curse probably hit her back using Nephera, but... that explains why Nora and Selena are so strong. They get their bloodline almost from the First Luna herself."

"...What about my mother, then? I don't believe she... forgave Nephera."

"Did she resent her?"

He stays quiet for a moment.

"...Not really. She didn't even blame her..."

"Then that's the same, Liam. Your mother unknowingly protected you three by not holding it against Nephera, so the curse only worked on Nephera, who couldn't forgive, and your father. If you think about it, all the curse's victims were people who couldn't forgive. Clarissa's mother, or grandmother, and Nephera. Your father. The people who were fine or stronger are the ones who did. Your mother and Queen Diane. Both forgave and thus, protected their descendants, just like Luna did by forgiving the witch."

He stays silent for a long time. From all the frowning and pouting, I can tell he is definitely thinking about everything I said, trying to make sense out of my crazy theories.

I do admit it's far-fetched, but I believe that story. I believe in it like I believe in the curse, and I know for such a bad thing to ever be created, there ought to be some strong sentiments behind it. Resentment, hatred, but also the pain and jealousy of a broken-hearted witch. I felt echoes of that pain and that hatred during my first fight against the curse when it was possessing my body. The saddest thing is... there is no real culprit, to begin with. That wolf didn't purposely break the witch's heart, but it also couldn't control the strength of her love either. She was a lonely woman who fell for someone who gave her attention. It's so similar to Nephera's story, it's obvious in my eyes, the curse found the perfect vessel through her, but it also feared its enemies: the Lunas who forgave. The people who cared about those witches, like Sylviana who was the only one to feel sorry for her own sister...

"...Liam, say something please," I sigh after a long time has passed. "...Do you think I'm wrong somewhere?"

He slowly shakes his head, and grabs my hands, rubbing them with his fingers.

"No... I mean, everything you said does make sense. It's just that there are too many gray areas. I mean... I do get the thing about the curse using Nephera. It totally makes sense with what happened. I don't know about Queen Diane, to be honest, like Nora said, anyone who knew about her is dead now. I do believe it would be... more believable to think she had a man, secretly, rather than that she conceived the twins out of the blue. That part was odd from the start. Moreover, she was said to have powers of healing, divination, and the likes, which are basically witch powers. So the whole... super Luna part, I get that, and it fits Nora and Selena too. What I don't understand is the part about the children. Clarissa and little Mara too, Nephera's daughter. What did they have to do with this? They were witches' daughters, why did they have to be cursed as well?"

...Liam has a good point.

I'm trying to remember what the Water Witch had said. She didn't see Clarissa and little Mara as the same, did she...? She called Clarissa a Cursed One, but considered Nephera's daughter a real little witch, although she was unborn. So what was the difference...?

"...Their father," I finally realize. "Nephera's daughter was the child of another wolf, one who hadn't betrayed her mother. While... Clarissa, or her mom, was the child of whoever had betrayed her. It would have explained why Clarissa and her mom were cursed as well. The curse wasn't... purged. It simply moved on to the next vessel that came its way. From the moment I woke up in Clarissa's body, the voices were there. The voices of all the witches from the curse, all those who had hated men and werewolves before. She mentioned it in her journal too, it was driving her crazy. Clarissa was constantly depressed and pushed into the darkness by those voices. Those voices were the curse's doing. Mara never had those voices, because her mother didn't pass the curse on to her. She was... unborn, and Nephera died still prey to the curse."

"It does... explain a lot," Liam nods, "even why the other witches don't like you in particular."

"Of course. Like the curse said, I'm basically a... patchwork of whatever survived it. Like we said, Clarissa wasn't even supposed to survive this far with what she was carrying. It's no wonder she wasn't born a witch, the curse probably took everything from her. Without her magic, her body struggled until the end..."

"...Until it was replaced with little Mara's Fire Magic."

"Exactly. There's absolutely no darkness in an unborn witch's magic, the curse couldn't do anything as soon as those two got together. Clarissa got a lot better as soon as she and Mara got together, and the curse even almost disappeared when I took over. It tried to attack me... psychologically. It reacted to male werewolves, in particular, or simply men trying to harm me. It reacted to feelings like anger, loneliness..."

"Basically all the components for a good curse," sighs Liam.

I nod.

He grabs my mug, and takes a gulp of my hot chocolate. When he lowers it, he has a little brown mustache above his lips... I can't resist, I lean in to kiss and lick it away. Liam looks at me with a little smile once I'm done, licking my own lips.

"...Miss Witch, I thought we were having a serious discussion right now?"

"We are," I chuckle, taking my half-empty mug from him.

Liam chuckles.

"Okay... Well, at least we definitely see clearer about that whole curse now, and even what was... wrong with you, if you don't mind the shitty wording."

"I get it."

"But the curse is completely gone from your body now, right?"

I hesitate. ...Is it?

"It's not... I mean, the more time I spent with you, the weaker the voices were. I haven't heard them in a while since we actually got together, so I think... getting a male partner helped a lot. But... it still surfaced through the mirror, and in that dream Sylviana gave me too."

"So what, it's just hanging around and waiting to do shit whenever it gets a chance?"

I sigh.

"Well, it's still there, one way or another. Remember the tale? The curse was stronger than the witch who had created it. If it got stronger with each witch that was betrayed by a male werewolf ever since, maybe now it's... trying to come back."

"Why would it come back? Anyone who... defeated it died. Queen Diane died, Nephera died, my mom too... I don't know what that curse is after. Why would it have clung on to you, of all witches? We already know there are Dark Witches out there, so why you? Does it have a grudge because of your rebirth of something?"

"Maybe it's just not so easy to transfer...?"

"Mara, you kicked the hell out of it just yesterday. For Moon Goddess' sake, you almost killed yourself just to get your body back! Why would that curse still hold on to you? There are at least three witches nearby!"

"...I guess I don't have all the answers yet," I sigh.

I put down my mug and grab Liam's torso, hugging and clinging on to him. I just need his presence, for him to comfort me right now. I feel a lot better thanks to the hot shower and the hot cocoa, but I'm still a bit... angsty from that dream. I hear him chuckle, and he hugs me back, putting a kiss on my head.

"...I like when you get all clingy," he whispers.

"You'd better not say you're tired of it anytime soon," I grumble on his shoulder.

"Nope."

We stay like this for a long time, simply hugging each other. Thank Moon Goddess I have Liam... I don't know where I'd be at if it wasn't for him. I feel sorry for all the witches who got let down by a werewolf. I don't know how I'd feel if Liam broke up with me. I already felt the worst when I had to watch him kiss a body I wasn't in...

"...Do you feel like going back to bed?" he whispers.

"Not really," I admit.

I feel like if I go back to bed now, I'll dream again, and I'm not ready for another round of that crap. I'm exhausted mentally but not physically, it's a strange sensation.

"...What time is it?"

"Uh... too late for delivery, too early for pancakes," he sighs.

"Your stomach is your clock?"

"Pretty much. It's hungry o'clock right now."

I chuckle into his shoulder. My big hungry wolf...

"...I really don't wanna go back to bed," I confess.

"What do you want, then?"

"Hm... A late night ride. Just you, me, your bike. We can find fast food or something for your hungry stomach... and mine. I'm hungry too, actually. I think magic consumes calories."

"Damn," he chuckles. "You're really my girl. Come on, then."

He grabs me by the waist and lets me down on the kitchen floor with a smile, hugging me again.

"Alright, let's go get changed," he smiles. "I think I'm going to love the idea of a late-night date with you."

We ride around for a very long time without a specific destination in mind. It's so late in the night that there aren't many other vehicles. Liam can easily weave and speed on the highway, both of us enjoying the ride as one. I love the sensation. I could ride for hours with him, even if I'm just sitting behind him. This just feels amazing. No one but us, the star speckled sky, the howling wind, and the dark asphalt firm beneath us.

His Blazing Witch

Liam takes the highway all around Silver City, and we do a full tour of it. It's amazing how each neighborhood's been marked by its inhabitants. The lights of the Arts District, with the colorful walls and their creative graffiti. The Hispanic neighborhood in the north and the few nightclubs still thumping with music. The business center is vast, with its skyscrapers and neon lights. The green outskirts, where the habitations are more scarce and the forest begins. The rural jungle of the Purple Moon Clan is amazing and after that, the white houses of the Sapphire Moon territory emerge. Traveling back down to the south, there are large green fields again. Probably hunting grounds for the majority of the wolves... We go by the university campus, covering much more land than I could have ever possibly visited by foot. I still don't want to give up on my studies. I'll need to look into that, after all of this is over...

As expected, our course brings us back to the seashore. I think this might be my favorite part of Silver City, which is strange for a Fire Witch, I'll admit. Yet, there's something about the tranquil waves and humid air that calms me. I lift my face shield and take deep breaths, the saltiness washing away the remnants of that nightmare from earlier. I notice Liam slow down a little around this area too. Maybe he feels the same. After all, he did used to spend a lot of time here...

We decide to go back downtown after maybe an hour or so. Liam is cautious not to make his bike any noisier than necessary, courteous to the people most likely sleeping in the buildings around us. He finally stops in a street with several little shops and a few bars still open. It must be close to closing time, though. Liam stops in the middle, and we attract the attention of a few young people standing outside. Hm...

"I'm starving," he grumbles while taking his helmet off.

"Me too. Damn, and it smells like food in the air too."

"I know, right? I used to come here when I craved a midnight snack..."

"You didn't come for the nightclubs?" I chuckle, putting my helmet down.

"I was never fond of dancing, or crowded places... That's more Nate's stuff. I just like to drink, so I'd accompany him from time to time, but nah..."

I smile, and as soon as we are both down from the bike, I step closer to him.

"Really?" I say, using my most seductive voice. "That's too bad, I was looking forward to a few nights out dancing with you... I think we missed our chance last time."

Liam gulps down, his eyes going down on me.

"I-I guess I can make an effort," he smiles. "Plus, I like it when you... dress up."

I raise an eyebrow, surprised.

"Really?"

"Yeah..."

I chuckle. It does make me want to dress up just to see his reaction. I am not fond of makeup, though, nor am I good at it yet, but I do feel like I could always experiment more clothing-wise... I have to get Kelsi on it. I wrap my arms around his neck and give him a quick kiss.

"That's a deal then," I say. "We need to have a date night out, I want to see you dance..."

"Ugh. Don't expect too much."

"I promise I won't."

However, we'll have to save that for another time. Neither of us is dressed up to go to the club, it's late, and besides, our stomachs quickly make themselves remembered with loud grumblings.

"Alright," I say. "What do you want?"

"As long as there's meat," shrugs Liam, taking out his wallet. "Can you go get it? I'll watch the bike, and then we can find a nice spot to eat at."

"Deal."

I walk into the closest little shop, and quickly place an order. Now that I'm smelling all the greasy food from up close, I realize I'm literally starving. I do seem to have a big appetite after using magic... when it doesn't make me sick. I order the most meaty thing I can find on the menu for Liam, a cheeseburger for me, some fries for us to share, and two drinks. I pay and wait a couple of minutes for the food. I hope we can find somewhere nearby to eat, neither of us brought a bag to carry all of this...

Just when I'm about to leave, I glance up at Liam outside, who is... not alone anymore. I frown. What the heck? I was gone for less than five minutes but there's already two chicks standing next to him, giving him all smiles and acting way too clingy for my taste. Seriously? I step outside silently, a bit annoyed. Well, not just a bit.

"S-sorry, no..." he's saying, trying to take his arm back from the girl who's clinging to it.

"Oh, come on! Just a dance or two!"

"No, I want to go for a ride!" laughs her friend, giving him some extra winks.

"I told you, I have a girlfriend!" he growls, annoyed.

Neither of the girls are intimidated by his growling, or maybe they are too drunk. I cross my arms, waiting to see how this is going to turn out. I don't know whose ass I want to burn the most...

"She isn't here right now!"

"Isn't it just an excuse?" one of the girls giggles. "Oh, come on, hot stuff!"

"Hey, hands off the hot stuff," I call out.

The two girls turn around, alerted by my voice. They scowl and check me out from head to toe with annoyed expressions.

"Who is that?" asks one of them, still staring at me.

"The hot stuff's girlfriend," I smile.

Between them, Liam sighs, visibly annoyed.

"Mara, please don't get mad..."

"I'm not mad."

"You're mad."

"I'm not mad. Look, I'm smiling."

"Your smile is scary..."

"I'll keep the scary smile on until they take their hands off you, then."

The girls look confused by our exchange, and Liam tries to free his arm once more.

"Okay girls, you really better go now. This is my girlfriend and she can be scary when she's mad. Plus, she's got my food and I'm hungry, so please..."

"That's your girlfriend?" asks one of them with a smirk.

"Why don't you stay with us instead? Look, we're sexier, and you can come eat with us! You can get two instead of one!"

"Thank you for the offer, but I'm a one-gal type of guy. I just want my girlfriend and she is seriously going to fry your asses if you don't go. Now."

"Well... you can fry my ass anytime!" giggles drunk girl number two.

Well, I can arrange that.

Liam must have read my mind, because he makes a grimace and shakes his head. He then moves to seriously get them off of him and steps aside, even away from his own bike. The girl that was clinging on to him pouts, but the other one suddenly lands her eyes on his bike.

"Hey! Look!"

She starts to climb on the bike.

Oh. Fuck. No.

"Get off my damn bike!" growls Liam.

"You get off the bike right now or I swear I'm frying your asses," I hiss too, shoving the bag of food into Liam's arms.

"Very funny, you can just–Ah!"

I light up my hand as a warning, and the flames dancing on my palm finally get their attention. The girl almost jumps off the bike, landing ungracefully on her knees, while the other makes a horrified expression.

"Y-you're the witch!"

"Told ya I could fry you. Now, get off the bike, away from the hot stuff, and go back inside."

One of the girls runs to her friend, grabbing her arm to pull her away.

"Come on, let's go. That bitch's just crazy..."

"I'm not scared of a witch!" yells the other. "Your magic can't hurt me!"

I raise an eyebrow. Seriously? I have literal fire in my hands and she's still acting arrogant? I guess it's true when they say alcohol makes people feel invincible... However, before I can say a word, she suddenly raises her top, showing off a weird tattoo on her belly. What the heck...?

"See? I have a protection spell on me!"

"...Mara?"

I feel hesitation in Liam's voice, and I know why. He's seen enough magic to recognize a genuine spell, even tattooed on a drunk human girl. My expression must be a dead give away too. ...This is so wrong. Why the hell is there a real magic spell tattooed on her skin?

"...Where did you get that done?" I ask.

"Ha!" she exclaims with a victorious smile. "See? You can't do anything to me! I've got protection!"

"You don't even know what this is, you idiot!" I yell at her.

I approach her, grab her wrist, and look at her stomach from up close, but her friend freaks out.

"Hey! Let her go, you crazy witch! Don't touch us!" she yells.

"I wouldn't be touching her if you didn't play with witchcraft yourselves, you idiots!" I shout back. "Answer me! Where did you get this?!"

The one whose wrist I'm holding just keeps complaining and trying to free herself from my grip, but she's too drunk to do anything for real. Liam steps up next to me, just as concerned. Her friend, probably not as intoxicated, is getting whiter and whiter, realizing I'm dead serious.

"I-I don't know," she mumbles. "She said a lot of our friends just got the same thing... I-it's popular..."

"What do you mean, they got it too? From where?"

"Is this dangerous?" she asks, starting to tear up. "I didn't think that was real! Is it dangerous? She won't die, will she?"

"You idiots got stuff tattooed and you didn't know what it was?" growls Liam.

"I just thought it was a joke! Like those stupid challenges we always do..."

She keeps trying to explain herself, but she doesn't seem to know much more, and her friend just keeps trying to free herself from my grasp. I let her go, and she swears, but it's more a weird mumbling than anything very insulting. Her friend grabs her arm.

"I-is it dangerous?"

"I'm not sure," I answer. "How many people have this tattooed? Who started it?"

"I don't know! I think it came from some post on the university blog... No one took it seriously, but because there's... I mean, since you're a real witch, it just became the next cool thing to do..."

"You idiots got tattoos for a challenge?" frowns Liam.

"Not all are real tattoos! Most are just temporary ones... but... I-I think since some people did it for real, it became like the next step to get it... a-and since it is pretty..."

Moon Goddess, I just want to gather those people and smack some sense into them. How many of them have this on them now? And most importantly, who the hell cast that spell on the humans? Why? I have a really, really bad feeling the more I think about this...

"Mara?" asks Liam.

"I don't know what this is," I admit. "That's a symbol I've never seen before. I... I think it's a new spell, made by someone else. It would be the only reason I can't recognize it, if it's... custom. I recognize some bits, but... it's too complex."

The more I stare, the less I like this. This isn't just some random spell the next idiot could come up with from a book about witches or some internet research. This one is so complex, even for me, it would take hours to come up with that sort of thing...

"Hold her," I suddenly decide.

Her friend hesitates, but Liam goes to grab the girl's wrists, and he's stronger when it comes to holding her where she is.

"W-what are you doing?"

"I'm going to take this off her. Unless you want your friend to keep showing off this spell not knowing what it is or what it'll do to her?"

"N-no..."

"Then help us hold her."

She nods, a bit hesitant, and tries to calm her friend down while I light up my fire very carefully.

"H-hey! You're not seriously going to burn her, are you?"

"No, just the spell, don't worry."

"Don't worry? You burned down buildings just two days ago! Why should we trust you?!"

I glare at her.

"If I planned to hurt you, I wouldn't need my boyfriend to hold your stupid friend who can't make one smart decision for herself!"

The girl glares back, but she has nothing to say. I better make this quick, the other one keeps wriggling and protesting, and I don't want to cause a scene here. I very carefully approach with my fire, and it turns a somber blue as soon as it reaches her belly.

"It stings! Stop it!"

"It will do a lot more than sting if I leave it there," I retort, focusing on this.

The spell doesn't like me trying to rip it off that girl's body. I insist and it slowly disappears, but not without a fight. Damn it... it comes off because a witch didn't personally put it there, but it's still strong enough to resist me. Holy shit, I didn't think that kind of crap could happen...

After a few more seconds of struggling, the spell is finally off of her body and the girl starts crying out of the blue.

"You okay?" asks her friend.

"No... I think I'm going to puke..."

She gives us a sorry nod, and pulls her friend toward whichever street she's going to throw up in. Ugh... I roll my eyes and turn to Liam, shaking the fire off my hand.

"...It's not good, is it?" he sighs, grabbing our bag of food he had left on the ground.

"Nope... but there isn't much I can do now," I sigh. "I don't know what the heck that spell was, where she got it from, or what it was for..."

"She mentioned the university blog. Let's get out of here before someone gets nosey, find a place to eat, and you can check my phone."

433

I nod to that, and we get back on the bike, riding away from there. Luckily, I don't think anyone noticed what I did back there. It's still late enough that there aren't many people outside. Liam rides only a few streets away, and we settle for a spot by the river that splits Silver City. He secures his bike, and we sit on the grass. He's so hungry, he jumps on the food first, but I want to check online before I get my hands all greasy...

It takes me a few minutes, and I'm starving, but I finally find it. I want to roll my eyes.

"Found it?"

"Yeah... Moon Goddess, this is just plain stupid. Someone posted this symbol online, saying it's an efficient way to protect one against a witch's magic... Well, my magic, I guess. It was posted a few days ago. There are a bunch of stupid answers, people joking, and then the idiots who did get it posted pictures online."

"Damn, people are really *that* stupid."

"...I think it boomed because of what happened yester-... I mean, two days ago. Damn, there are pictures of me too."

"Wait, what?"

I give him back his phone. It's nothing big, but I don't like it. People took pictures and videos from afar of me setting fire to the buildings... no, the Dark Witch doing this. It wasn't even me! I grab my cheeseburger, too hungry to care anymore. This isn't even on the top of my shit pile...

"What the heck," growls Liam. "Who posted that shit?"

"Students in need of something interesting in their life," I grumble, my mouth half-full.

"Mara, it's not okay! I'm pretty sure that's illegal."

"Liam, I'll settle my privacy issue later," I sigh. "I'm sure Amy and her army of lawyers can do something about this. For now, I want to know who put that spell online and how. The original creator of the post used an anonymous account, but they also posted some of the videos. That wasn't innocent at all."

"You think they are working with one of the witches? Or the curse?"

"Probably," I sigh.

Liam growls a bit, but I just eat some fries mindlessly. Why does this feel like the calm before the storm? We really can't catch a break... I hope Kelsi can help me on this one, she's much better at technology than I am, and probably more familiar with the university blog too. After a little while, I take Liam's phone away so he can focus on his food, as he keeps grumbling about the pictures of me. His sandwich is soon gone, though, and I realize another one wouldn't have been too much for him. Note to self: never underestimate a werewolf's appetite. Even I'm left unsatisfied after that cheeseburger, somehow...

"Damn..." suddenly sighs Liam. "Sometimes I really wish you weren't a witch."

"It's okay," I shrug.

"It's not, Mara. I read some of those posts. You don't deserve that crap...
"

"I'm fine, Liam. For real. I don't care, honestly. I'm fine with being the freak of the town, as long as I got the people I need by my side, okay? I've got my family, my friends... and my hot stuff too."

He suddenly blushes slightly.

"...Oh Moon Goddess, you're not going to forget that one, are you?"

"Certainly not!" I laugh.

He rolls his eyes, but after watching me mock him for a minute, he takes me by surprise and leans in for a quick kiss. I stop laughing, and now I'm the one blushing.

"Damn it," he whispers. "You're so cute when you laugh like this. Now I want my hot stuff too."

Oh... the way he said that doesn't leave much room for interpretation. I lick the mayo off my fingers, and give him another quick kiss back.

"Hm... Now that we're... sated, shall we go back?" I suggest, with a little smile.

"...Are you sure?"

"Yeah. Plus, there is something else we need to settle."

"What's that?" he asks.

"Well, I didn't think it would be an issue if I didn't mark you right away, but it looks like I can't leave my boyfriend alone for five minutes before he attracts chicks like moths to a flame, so..."

Liam opens his mouth, but then he closes it.

"To be honest, I was going to protest, but I'll attract all the drunk girls you need if that convinces you to finally mark me."

"...I don't know if I want to mark you, smack you, or kiss you right now."

"You can do all three if you want," he chuckles. "Come on, let's go."

Oh, Moon Goddess...

Chapter 30

"Babe... I'm sorry..."

I hear him grumble, although it's muffled in the pillow. He's really upset... My eyes go down on the ugly bite mark on his neck. Okay, maybe I did go a bit overboard. It's a red mess, and probably painful too, though he won't even let me lick it. Liam's decided to sulk, but even that is too cute. I chuckle, and caress his exposed back gently. We did go home, but we didn't end up sleeping much... Maybe four or five hours? I can't say I'm very tired, though. I chuckle and lean over, kissing his back, the sheets still wrapped around my body. The sun just got up a little while ago, and we now have full rays of sunshine on us, which I love... the smell of the sheets in the morning.

Liam's lying on his tummy, his face in the pillow in a weird position. Can he even breathe like that? I know he's not sleeping, but still. I smile; although the first part didn't go so well, the rest of the night was quite... interesting. Werewolf endurance really is quite something.

"You bit me meanly too, for the record."

"Mh-didn't-mumfumgrumbmemuf...."

"Babe, I can't understand a thing."

He growls. Uh, I'm not sure I got that. I bite my lower lip, and kiss his shoulder again. He's trying to hide it, but I know he's reacting to it... I keep spreading kisses on his back, going lower and lower.

"Don't go there..." he grumbles again.

I smile and put a kiss on his buttcheek, amused. This time, he lifts his head from the pillow.

"I said don't..."

"Done sulking?" I chuckle, putting my head in my hand with a smile.

"...You're a mean witch..."

Moon Goddess, he's so cute when he pouts, I just can't resist. I smile more, and lean over him, very conscious I'm naked too. He sighs and finally turns around, letting me lay on his chest. We exchange a kiss, although he tries to act reluctantly.

"...You're not tired?" I ask.

"I'm good. Just hungry, as usual... You?"

"I'm good. I think I've still got our midnight snack in my stomach."

He nods, and we exchange another quick kiss before I grab my phone to check my texts.

"Kelsi's up and making those pancakes... We're on coffee duty."

"Roger that."

"...Do you want me to do something about your neck?" I chuckle.

He grimaces.

"Your teeth are not allowed anywhere near my neck for a while. Moon Goddess, I can't believe you made a bigger mess than me."

I shrug, because unlike his, my neck is completely fine already. I can feel the scar of his bite when I touch it, but pain-wise, there's nothing left. Unlike that ugly thing I left on Liam's nape... I chuckle, and lean over him for a kiss on his lips.

"I'm sorry," I mutter. "...Are you sure you don't want me to heal it?"

"Nope, I'll be a big boy and endure it."

"Okay," I chuckle. "Well then, big boy, shower time?"

"You can go first," he laughs. "I feel like my water bill isn't going to go any lower with you..."

Thirty minutes and a shower later, we are both dressed and ready to go. On a side note, if I spend more time at his place, I'm really going to need to bring some clothes over. I'll probably change once we get there, although I do like wearing Liam's shirts. We finally get downstairs, but once we are back on the bike, I can't help but remember the events of last night... I mean, the serious ones. It doesn't feel good at all, it feels like the calm before the storm.

I try to enjoy the ride with Liam, but this time, I just really need to get my head back into business. I feel like from now on, things are just going to get more and more serious... Only stopping to grab coffee for everyone, we finally get to the apartment, where indeed, Kelsi is cooking and acting all playful with Ben.

Ben's actually half-naked, and I realize once again he's tall, but not as muscular or big as I thought. Moreover, I see the large wound on his stomach, still bandaged.

"Hey, you two!" he greets us once we get inside.

"Hi, Ben..."

To my surprise, he comes and hugs me quickly, a large smile on his face. I'm a bit taken aback. What was that? Liam gives me a little glance to the side too, but I don't dare say anything. Moreover, as soon as he's done, Ben runs back to the kitchen to hug Kelsi from behind.

"Ben!" she protests. "I told you not to do that without warning, you're making me all jumpy..."

"We watched a show that was a bit scary last night," he chuckles. "Kelsi's so cute when she's spooked!"

"I'm not spooked! I-it's just that I'm cooking and you're all over me..."

Ben chuckles, but adds another kiss on her rosy cheek before turning to us.

"Coffee?" asks Liam, raising the tray we just grabbed from downstairs.

"Hell yes!"

I let the boys get their noses into the coffees and walk over to Kelsi, who's making those pancakes, although her eyes are more on Ben than her pan...

"Someone had a good night?" I chuckle.

"You're one to talk! Did Liam get attacked by a bear?"

"Ah... We got a bit... bitey."

Kelsi laughs.

"My boo getting all territorial! I'm happy for you, Mara, really. I feel like you've... opened up a lot more now."

"Thanks," I blush a bit. "You too, actually. I mean, I was rooting for you and Ben for a while, but..."

Kelsi nods, probably blushing even more than I am. She's actually not wearing one of her ugly sweaters today, but instead, a really pretty burgundy dress of mid-thigh length, with an off-the-shoulder white top underneath and tights. She doesn't have her huge glasses on, either. I always knew she was really pretty, but she's definitely shining right now. I smile and decide to hug her. I am so happy she's been by my side from the start, ready to act as my friend and be supportive as hell...

It's so sudden, she freezes, and it takes two seconds before she hugs me back. My goodness... I can almost feel her trembling, and when we separate, she has cute tears in her eyes.

"I-I-I'm not crying!" she immediately mumbles.

"I didn't say a thing!"

Moon Goddess, she's so cute, it's hard to repress a laugh. She takes a deep breath and blinks to chase them away.

"I-it's just I know you're not a hugger, so... uh... It makes me really happy you acknowledge we're really close friends, okay?"

"Kelsi, it's okay. You really don't need to explain a hug to make me feel comfortable!"

She pouts.

"O-okay, but... uh... I appreciate it."

"Okay," I chuckle.

I take a deep breath, and before this gets any more awkward, I let her go back to those pancakes.

"Actually, I needed your help and opinion on something, boo."

"What? What is it?"

I take out my phone, and quickly show her the university forum with everything Liam and I witnessed last night. The tattoo, but also pictures and short clips of me. There's something new, though; it looks like one of the girls from last night posted about me removing her friend's tattoo, and warning her friend. Kelsi's eyes open wider and wider, until we switch and she takes my phone while I watch the pancakes. She frowns, looking angrier and angrier as she keeps scrolling through the posts.

"What a bunch of... idiots!" she suddenly shouts. "I can't believe there are so many pictures of you too! And those tattoos... My God, for real?"

"Some are temporary, but some are real," nods Liam, coming to lean on the counter.

Kelsi is still mad, but Ben takes the phone from her to check out the posts while she turns to me.

"Mara, that is so serious! This is really witchcraft, isn't it? Do you have any idea what it is...?"

"Some high-level witch's work," I sigh. "The problem is, this is so... unique, I'm not sure what it does exactly. I'll need to study it longer to find out."

"There are so many runes and details..." sighs Kelsi. "Wait, I'll go grab the books! I actually got some new ones..."

She runs off to her bedroom, but at the same time, Ben gets off his seat and runs over to his computer, my phone still in hand.

"Ben...?"

"I think someone from the university did this."

"Obviously, but—"

"No, I meant... someone really from the university, Mara, not a student. Don't you think it's super odd how this got onto the university forum? Those are the kind of sites you can't get on without some sort of identification. The security for these kinds of forums have been increased to protect the students. Anonymous account, my butt..."

Liam and I exchange a look, but for a few minutes, Ben gets fully absorbed into typing furiously on his laptop, while Kelsi is taking out every book about witchcraft we've got in the place. She really got even more since last time... I need to be careful she doesn't get a bit too obsessed with them. I let her get a head start and walk into my bedroom for a few minutes, just to change into clothes that are actually my size. With a little smile, I remember Liam's comment, and go for a pair of black leather pants. It's true I have rather nice legs... I pair it with a simple gray T-shirt, but add a little touch of makeup, borrowing Kelsi's once again. I need to ask her for more advice when we finally get a break from all this.

When I get back to our living room, Kelsi is bending over the witchcraft books and taking notes, while Liam has apparently been delegated to making pancakes. He raises an eyebrow once I walk in, though his eyes go down to my tight pants... I send him a little smile, but go over to Kelsi, giving her a hand in helping decipher this new spell. She's already made good progress, actually. It's scary how she almost knows those books by heart... There is some very dark stuff little Mara didn't cover with me that Kelsi actually found, and is surprisingly helpful too.

After a while, Liam brings the pile of pancakes over and we finally take our seats, the four of us eating and sipping our coffees, but most importantly, comparing our finds.

"As we thought, those tattoos are bound to humans to make them some sort of vessel," I explain, checking those details again.

"Did you determine which of the... other witches did that?" asks Liam.

439

"From the types of runes, I'd say the Water Witch?" mutters Kelsi, spinning her fork in her hand.

"No... the Fire Witch," I mutter.

"What? Are you sure, Mara? But those–"

"I think she used a water-type spell to reduce my efficiency against it. I struggled a lot just to remove one last night. If it had been a type of Fire Magic, it wouldn't have been able to resist me so much. Fire attracts fire, it would have come off almost naturally. This one repelled my magic... but in the end, it wasn't strong enough. The Water Witch we met looks like she would have done a much better job. I think this spell was made by a Fire Witch, using a water-type."

"Is that even possible?" asks Liam, frowning.

"I took the body of a Water Witch," I shrug. "That's why I struggled so much too, the body wasn't prepared to handle fire to begin with, but it adapted. The elements... They are meant to cohabitate, in the first place. Just because one isn't our main doesn't mean it's completely inaccessible to us, I think... although it does mean whichever witch did this, she was powerful as hell."

His mouth half full, Ben grumbles.

"Ah, this is getting too complicated for a stupid wolf like me. Anyway, can you take it off all those idiots?"

"One by one? It would take a while, and a lot of my energy. Plus, it will be a while before we find them all..."

"The humans still don't trust Mara, either," adds Kelsi. "Just look at all those posts on the forum... The Dark Witch, I mean, the curse made sure the humans are scared of her. They think she lit several buildings on fire."

"Actually... there's that too," I grumble.

"What?"

I grab my cup of coffee, making the liquid swirl inside the cup.

"Those fires spread too fast, to too many buildings. Think about it. That witch couldn't possibly handle my power well, she could barely fight me. The only reason she overpowered Liam was because she was in my body."

"...Which I care about..." he sighs.

I chuckle, and put my hand on his shoulder.

"Right? The curse needs a powerful and willing host. It won't use a human, but I have a bad feeling about all of this..."

"Why are those witches all after Silver City, anyway?" sighs Kelsi. "There are tons of other places to go! Why do we have three of them roaming around?"

"...They probably think I'm not legit," I sigh. "They want to take Sylviana's spot, probably thinking she should have left it empty..."

"The Royals are power magnets too," adds Liam. "We've had issues with vampires, werewolves, and witches since Nora was revealed to be a Royal."

...Is that all there is, though? Now that Liam mentions it, I do feel like I'm still missing a piece of the puzzle here...

"So, we have three witches at the border looking for a fight, someone who probably isn't on our side either and in the university, and that curse lurking around for a reason to attack?"

I think Ben summed that up well.

"...I think the Fire Witch has an insider at the university," I mutter. "I think I know who too..."

Kelsi and I exchange a look and nod.

"Professor Vutha?" exclaims Ben, his eyes suddenly perking up.

"She was the one who knew a bunch about witches," says Kelsi, counting on her fingers. "Mara had issues with students right after she met her, and she is someone with a position to make an anonymous account on the university forum. She did say some of the books you... borrowed from her came from her personal collection too. I mean, I know weird people, but that teacher had demonology and necromancy books!"

"We should confront her," nods Ben. "If we go to the university and report those posts as a... an attack on Mara's privacy, I'm sure they can find who was behind it. I already looked it up, but there's no way they can't find who made that post, even if they tried to create a private account. People have to use university identification; I double-checked."

I nod and turn to Kelsi.

"Can you go and confront her with Ben? She's just a human, she won't be able to do any magic or harm you with it. We need to know which of the witches she works for, and if she was the one who set the fires."

"Sure!" nods Ben with a large smile.

"Of course, boo. But what about you? Don't you want to come?"

"...There's someone else I should have asked long ago," I sigh.

Liam grabs another pancake with a sigh.

"The Earth Witch?"

"Yes. She definitely knows more than she said, and now that I am powerful enough, she won't be able to avoid me or try to play any tricks on me."

"What if one of the other two attacks?" frowns Kelsi. "I don't mean to underestimate you, but if you have to take on two witches by yourself... Mara, you just came out of the hospital, again!"

I grimace.

"I know. First, I don't think Ravena would attack me now. She's an Earth Witch, and she was already reluctant to attack the first time. The Fire Witch... she hasn't shown herself yet, so I can't really tell. The Water Witch is the one I am worried about, but she stays south, probably in the sea. I don't think she'll show herself if I meet Ravena in the north."

"Okay," she sighs.

I smile. She's clearly still worried about me, but for once, I'm rather confident in what I'm doing.

"Spark!"

441

They all turn heads, but as expected, my cat just hops onto my lap as I call him, rubbing his gold and black head against my chest.

"...I swear he had more black last time I saw him," grumbles Kelsi.

"Kelsi, Spark will be coming with you," I state.

"What?" she exclaims.

Ben scoffs on his pancake.

"He's my magic cat," I chuckle. "He'll help you if you're in trouble, and I'll know right away too."

"What trouble?! You're the one about to get in trouble, why do I get to take the cat? I already have Benny–!"

"Please?" I insist. "I'll feel better sending you to a witch specialist if you take him with you."

She keeps frowning, but I grab Spark and put him on her lap. Kelsi glances down at the cat, unsure.

"...Okay, but first, the cat better behave. Spark, I do tolerate you, but no biting or claws, okay?"

"Meow..."

As if he knew exactly what to do to pacify her, Spark acts all cute and quietly lets her pet his head. Kelsi has a bit of a sullen look on, but I know they do like each other... like two cats would, somehow. She then turns to me, looking really serious.

"Also, she is not the best witch specialist in Silver City, okay? I'm pretty sure *I* am!"

I chuckle and nod, totally fine with acknowledging that Kelsi is definitely a walking library when it comes to witches... and a bit too passionate about the matter too. Still, I know if anyone can give me a hand, it's definitely her. I don't doubt she can corner Professor Vutha and make her confess everything she knows. I just hope that the professor doesn't have more tricks up her sleeve than Kelsi would be prepared for, which is why I'm sending her with Ben and Spark. Regardless of her knowledge, that professor is a human woman. At least those two will be able to protect Kelsi if anything happens.

"Will you be fine?" I ask Ben.

He sighs.

"I'm good, Mara. I may be injured but I'm healing fast. Plus, I'm a Beta, protecting someone is my specialty. Especially if it's my girl!"

"Ben!" Kelsi protests, blushing.

We all chuckle, but it's a bit late to act shy. Ben gives her a quick kiss on the cheek, and we resume eating while they flirt. Even Spark is in a playful mood, his big eyes on our food.

"What about you, Mara? You've never fought with a real witch face to face yet..."

"I'll be fine," I nod. "I've unlocked my full power now, I know probably as much as any witch out there, if not more, and Ravena is an Earth Witch, so she'll be at a disadvantage."

"What if the Fire Witch gets involved?" asks Ben, frowning. "Will you be at a disadvantage?"

"...I don't think so? It would be hard to tell, though, I guess I'll see if it happens."

"You're too laid back about this," he growls.

"We'll be fine," interrupts Liam. "Don't worry, I'm going with her. Plus, we will be near the White Moon Pack. If anything happens, we can always call Selena for reinforcements."

I nod, but I sure hope it won't go that way. I'm rather confident as a witch now, it's a bit of a matter of pride, but I don't want to have to ask the werewolves for help aside from Liam. This is definitely something that has to be settled witch to witch, which is why I'm even madder that one of them involved the humans, to begin with...

Since nothing is really urgent for once, the four of us enjoy this breakfast together, changing the subject to Kelsi and Ben's movie and Liam and I talking about our night ride. I notice Liam's smiling a lot, and I like it. This really feels like... home. I like this feeling. Just the four of us, chatting like any group of friends, regardless of our differences, whatever's going on outside or inside Silver City. We chat about university too, and I realize I don't really know what Liam actually does for a living, other than being a werewolf and being one of the Black Brothers. Still, I have this strange feeling of wanting to go back to those ordinary days, although there weren't many; just living here, going to university during the day, and maybe enjoying a double date at night. That'd be nice...

Unfortunately, enjoying a break does mean there's still a lot to do once we're done with the pancakes, and the coffees are gone too. With everyone ready, we leave, Kelsi carrying poor Spark like a potato sack in her arms... I'm shocked he doesn't even complain with his lower half hanging like that.

"Alright," says Ben, playing with his car keys. "Try to stay alive until lunch, everyone?"

Kelsi slaps his shoulder.

"Ben, that's not funny! Mara, be careful, okay? I know you're more powerful now, but those witches are..."

"More experienced. I know. Don't worry, just focus on the professor, and text me when you're done at the university, okay? I will update Selena and Nora too. Ben, don't hesitate to ask for reinforcements if things look bad. We've already seen what can happen even with witches outside of the barrier..."

"Gotcha."

I quickly hug Kelsi, and we go our separate ways, Liam and I riding north while Ben, Kelsi, and Spark head toward the direction of the university to find out the truth.

"Did you update Nora and Selena?"

I almost jump, hearing Liam's voice in my head while we're on the highway. Damn, I need to get used to this.

"I will."

443

I do so right away. As expected, it's as easy as picking a name on a list... I feel my connection to the two young women, and grab it to hold on. They are more used to it, so they are perfectly calm and probably continuing whatever they're doing while I coolly explain everything that's happened so far.

"*Wait, so you're headed north now? Alone with Liam? Mara, you should have asked for more back-up!*" protests Selena.

"*You just got out of the hospital too...*"

"*Don't worry, I'm perfectly fine. Moreover, I just need to ask Ravena what she knows about the curse. More than confronting those witches, I think this should be our priority now.*"

"*Are you sure? Those witches want to get inside Silver City, and the barrier is almost gone...*"

"*I... I have a feeling it's all connected actually. The witches' interest in Silver City, the curse, and me. Even your presence in Silver City... I'm sure there's something bigger we haven't grasped yet. But my gut tells me it's all linked, and maybe those other witches know more too.*"

"*If you manage to make them talk, that is.*"

"*I know, Selena, but I should at least try. It's obvious they aren't fond of werewolves. They don't like me either, but... maybe I'll find common ground for us to exchange info.*"

"*Oh, whatever. You're the witch, and it's not like you'll let us stop you anyway.*"

"*Alright, but stay with Liam, okay? ...I feel your new bond, I'm so happy for you two!*"

"*Thank you, Nora,*" I blush.

"*We'll celebrate when those two come back alive from the border! I can't believe Liam found a more stubborn mate than him... You're the most reckless pair I know, and that's saying a lot.*"

I chuckle, but basically, they gave me all their support, if I needed any. We keep chatting about the curse, what I found out, and how it correlates to their story. Nora agrees with my theory that Diane's children probably weren't as miraculous as having no father at all, but Selena is skeptical of Danica's role.

"*In my opinion, it would have made even more sense that the betrayed one was Nephera's birth mother. She left her daughter to Danica, didn't she? I don't believe Danica would have raised a child that wasn't hers if something big hadn't happened. Moreover, she almost sent her away as soon as she could.*"

"*She sent her to Silver City,*" adds Nora. "*It would all come back around... and she would have sent Nephera away so she wasn't cursed by staying around?*"

"*That's a lot of ifs once again, but at least with that curse, a lot of things make more sense!*"

"*Even for my parents...*"

"*Nora?*"

"Nothing, Mara, don't worry. Thank you for sharing this information, though. I'll think on it a little, I feel like it might explain more than we think!"

"Don't think too much, Nora, I'd rather think about it in a more practical way. Let's see how it goes for Mara at the border before we agonize over a legend, okay?"

"I know, I know..."

The two of them agree on asking me to be careful, but that's a given. I can't help but smile throughout our conversation. I feel like I've gained two more older sisters, and it's rather nice... In the end, Selena still insists that she will put some of her wolves on standby near the northern border, and asks some to go to the university, just to accompany Kelsi and Ben if they need more backup. Strangely, I feel like there isn't an ounce of animosity left in her behavior toward me. Since the curse left my body, or at least hasn't made itself heard at all in my head, Selena seems to be ready to fully trust me. I feel it in her voice, she doesn't talk to me like a child, but more like a... younger sister. The same way Liam's older brothers address him, in a way, and I do understand we are the "young ones" of their pack.

Still, I'm the only witch in Silver City right now. I am glad for the werewolf in me that links me to everyone else, but by now, I've learned that this isn't the only thing I need. No, even if I wasn't a werewolf... it probably wouldn't matter much. I was Liam's mate before we even had any idea I might also be part werewolf. I felt a connection to Nora before that, and we didn't wait for my inner wolf before getting into some trouble either...

Liam finally brings us close to the border, and I realize there isn't much of a border anymore. It's like a spider web, full of holes and so fragile too. I could probably break it, with a lot of time and energy. Which makes me wonder why Ravena and the other witches haven't done so yet.

We get off the bike, and I feel a little boost of adrenaline kick in out of the blue. I hope Kelsi does well at the university, but I'm feeling pretty confident here... not overestimating myself, hopefully. I can feel the other witches too, and to my surprise, they are close, but not together. Do they not get along, or is it meant to be some sort of trap? Liam glances behind us, and I can tell some werewolves are hiding nearby, as Selena promised. Good, because I may not have time to worry much about my mate if things get bad...

We leave our helmets and jackets with the bike, and both start walking silently, getting past the border without any trouble. What a difference... It didn't feel much more than a tingle on my skin this time. It's nothing to be glad about, unfortunately. It just means trouble has gotten a lot closer...

"There she is!"

I glance to the side, and sure enough, Ravena appears, her arms crossed, a haughty smile on her lips.

"Someone has gotten a lot stronger without my guidance," she chuckles, tilting her head.

Once again, her appearance is atypical. She's wearing a different, long patterned dress, and her hair is held up by some wooden hair pins too. Her makeup is still as horrible, a thick dark burgundy layer on her lips and some dark eyeshadow that would make Kelsi cringe.

"I did my research," I retort.

It's so different from our first meeting. I feel my inner wolf growling and even without looking, I can tell exactly where Liam is standing, ready to shape-shift at any moment. Even Ravena looks different to me. Not just physically, but I can gauge her and... she's definitely weaker than I am. She doesn't let it show though. She has the mighty attitude of a witch who knows her spells and curses.

"That's too bad," she sighs. "I would have loved to groom a promising student like you..."

"That's funny. The other witch I met wasn't too fond of me or my power."

"Oh, I noticed her too. I don't know her, honestly, and I didn't feel like going near, she's been staying... out of reach."

I'm pretty sure Ravena knows more than she lets on about the other witch, but this is the least of the things I'm curious about right now. I step closer and to my surprise, she retreats, her smile fading a little. So I was right, she is cautious of me, more than before. She knows I'm no longer a child she can play around with. I haven't shown my flames yet, but she can probably tell... That's a good thing for me. She probably won't risk attacking, especially when I have a werewolf with me, but I could very likely handle her by myself. Even last time, she wasn't too keen on the idea of fighting directly... She's wary of me.

The one thing I'm worried about, though, is that the other witch is coming closer. Maybe that's also why Ravena is getting more tense, but the Fire Witch is in the area and, from the way I can feel her, getting closer.

"I still have some questions for you," I explain, hoping it won't be too long before I get my answers.

"Oh? Let me hear them."

"What do you know about the curse?"

Her smile falters for a second. She definitely knows... She knows something about it. She clears her throat, and regains her composure quickly.

"I wonder. What curse are you talking about?"

"You know exactly which one," I growl. "The curse that affects witches and their descendants. You even mentioned it, actually, didn't you? You said witches and wolves used to work together, but witches were now used to getting betrayed by werewolves."

Her eyes quickly go to Liam, who's begun growling softly behind me.

"I also mentioned I hate wolves. Did you have to bring that one? No... Oh, so my former hunch was actually right on the spot, was it? You're not just a witch..."

"I'm also a werewolf," I nod.

"Oh... You're even more interesting than I thought. Do I take it that you will not be claiming Silver City, then?"

"I am."

"You can't own a city dominated by werewolves, young lady."

"Why not? I am a werewolf too."

"Until they only remember you're a witch, and turn their backs on you. Trust me, this isn't just some old hag's saying. Do you have any idea how many times witches have been betrayed by werewolves?"

"Enough to make that curse stronger and stronger over the years," I growl. "I know. However, things are different for me. I am a werewolf and his fated mate. He cannot betray me now."

Ravena rolls her eyes.

"Lucky you, darling. However, what of our sisters and mothers? You're one exception, for sure. Still, it doesn't mean we should all be jumping and cheering for werewolves. Do you know why girls like you grow up without a mother to guide them? You should know Silver City's story by now, surely?"

"So you knew about Nephera..."

"Of course I knew. You have to do your homework before you take on a city like this. However, Nephera–"

"She was my mother."

She leaves her mouth open, staring at me, dumbfounded.

"I'm surprised you didn't know," I chuckle. "The other witch is the one who had done her homework the best then. Mara was the name Nephera's stillborn child was given. I have her soul in me."

"You're... a Cursed One?"

"Yes. I am a Cursed One. An unborn girl's soul in a Cursed One's body. Mara wasn't born, but her soul wandered until it found a cursed girl and together, they fought off the curse, and I was born. So now, I want to know about this curse I was born upon, which attacked me no more than two days ago."

This time, Ravena is done smiling. She just stares at me, looking upset. I guess witches really can't stand Cursed Ones... even when they know the tragedy behind their birth. A patchwork of souls, and moreover, I am part werewolf too. I guess there is nothing a regular witch should like about this.

"I wondered why you were so powerful already... You foolish girl," she growls. "That curse is just going to wait until it consumes you slowly, like all the others!"

"No," I growl back. "I fought it once. It took over my body, but thanks to my werewolf side, I managed to fight it off! I–"

She chuckles.

"You're so naive, aren't you? Do you think you can simply fight something like a curse? Without using your magic? It may be gone now, but it will come back. A Cursed One paired with a werewolf. There is no way this curse will let you off easy, child. You just wait. It will slowly consume you..."

Suddenly, I remember the nightmare. ...She's right. The curse did come back. I thought I'd be safe from it, but that nightmare was just plain horrible. I would have rather kept the voices. Don't tell me... It will happen again? How many times? I'm glad Liam was by my side to help me dissipate my doubts, but...

"I see," she chuckles. "It has begun already, hasn't it? ...See? This is what strong curses do, and why they are so powerful. They are as insidious as poison. They consume your mind before you even realize it's there, and slowly, we all go insane... It can take any form, but I'm sure you're not free from it yet, young girl."

"H-how do I fight this curse?" I growl, getting madder as she may be right.

She shrugs.

"I wonder. You're still bent on being with werewolves, so it won't be easy for you. It's a thousand-year-old curse, how would I know how to break it? However, if I were you, I'd have started working seriously on that question, girl. Your time is limited..."

"Enough!" growls Liam. "Tell us what you know!"

Ravena's eyes immediately shift to Liam, and she glares at him.

"Don't talk to me, dog!"

"You're the one who should watch your tongue while talking to my mate," I growl.

"See? You're their slave already, little girl! Did this wolf make you feel special? You're so foolish, like all the others. Just you wait. Werewolves and witches aren't meant to be together..."

"We are!" I retort, annoyed. "I am his fated mate, chosen by the Moon Goddess herself to be his pair. You may not like werewolves, but you should know enough about the Moon Goddess if you're any kind of witch!"

This time, I'm the one to be glared at by her angry green eyes, but Moon Goddess, I don't give a damn. I won't stand back, and I won't let her ridicule my bond with Liam or use it against me. We are both marked now, we just can't be separated. I don't know how I'd stand if I wasn't so sure of that fact, but I certainly feel stronger than before. I'm almost thankful for that nightmare, as it made Liam confirm our feelings for each other.

Ravena scoffs.

"There you go again... Don't you understand yet? If you keep going against the curse, it will consume you even faster! You were bound to be a victim; as a Cursed One, there is no escaping this. Struggle all you want, child, you are just going to try and buy some time. You may not even have much left before it consumes you. You'll never be free simply because you have this wolf, and we won't leave you alone either! A witch and a werewolf? This is one lame joke."

It's impossible that there haven't been any other cases of witches also being werewolves before. It can't be that the curse acted every single time...

"Tell me what you know about the curse before I get really mad," I growl.

This time, I'm done chit-chatting, and I'm done begging for answers. I light my fire in both my hands, letting her know I'm damn serious and she's going to get roasted if she doesn't spill the beans quickly. Her eyes go down to my hands, and she puts on a sour expression.

"Don't play with me, little witch. You may be uneducated like one of those dogs, but you should at least respect your elders..."

"The elder better start talking," I retort.

Liam growls too, and steps closer. Earth Witch or not, she probably won't like having to face both me and an Alpha werewolf much. She hesitates, slowly stepping back, keeping her eyes on the two of us.

"You're one annoying little... What do you want to know, anyway? You've already unveiled quite enough by yourself, haven't you?"

"I know of the original tale. The one about Luna, the witch and the werewolf..."

"Ah, that. Another example of how those annoying beasts claimed something that wasn't theirs, isn't it? They conveniently worshiped that she-wolf, and they let our ancestor fall into oblivion. This is why we need our magic: to remember. We keep our daughters and sisters close and teach them what we know, or what we can hold on to from the past. Yet, witches are bound to disappear because of them. Because of werewolves, growing in numbers like ants!"

I squint my eyes. I understand what she means, but... more than that, I can almost feel that fear in her eyes. Witches are scared to disappear, to be forgotten. They keep their enemies at bay, but they also keep themselves from the world. That's why they want to be in cities without any werewolves who can recognize them. Humans are generally clueless, and witches don't like to mingle with them, aside from making children...

"So you knew well about the curse and its origins."

"Of course I know," she retorts. "If you had been raised or taught by a real witch, you'd know too, and you would have kept away from werewolves..."

So this is also why witches don't want to associate themselves with wolves in the first place. To avoid the risk of being cursed like their ancestors... Moon Goddess, is that why even Sylviana was careful about Liam? I try not to glance his way, but... that would make sense. Maybe that's another reason why things never actually got serious between them.

"Well, too late for me," I sigh. "However, since we have now established that, can we move on? How do I undo this curse for real? You mentioned it before, but there's no way that thing is unbreakable, is it?"

She scoffs.

"Hear yourself, child. You're talking about a thousand-year-old curse. Do you think you're the first one to try? Or is it because you won a battle, you think you can win this war?"

"It would already be easier if you stopped acting like a conceited bitch and gave me some actual answers!" I shout, getting seriously annoyed at her attitude.

"...Let's see if the child can beat it."

I freeze and glance to the side just as Liam begins growling furiously.

Another witch appeared. The Fire Witch.

I increase the flames in my hands. She isn't like Ravena, this one is definitely stronger. She's already looking dead serious too, and quite intimidating at that. She's surprisingly young too. I had imagined her to be older, but she looks like she could be my age, definitely no older than thirty, unless she's using magic or something.

She's wearing a thick but cropped fur coat, and flashy clothes that show off her curves. Her hair is split into dozens of small little multicolored braids, and her skin is as dark as it can be. She looks like she just walked out of some fancy rapper music video, but from the mud on her shoes, probably not...

"A Fire Witch," she chuckles. "It's been a while since I have fought one of my peers..."

So she fights other witches for sport? What the hell? I steal a glance toward Ravena, but from her expression, she isn't fond of that woman either. She stepped farther away, and I can't blame her. Not only does the new one look really strong, but with two Fire Witches in the forest, this is not looking good at all...

"Maybe now would be time to call reinforcements..." mutters Liam in my head.

"Not yet. If more people get involved between us, it will make things worse. Ask them to wait nearby, but no one should approach, Liam."

This is definitely about to get nasty. I wish I could tell whether the new witch is friendly and very willing to talk, but just like me, she immediately lights up her fire. Hers is strangely purple-ish, and from the way she's moving it around her fingers, she definitely knows how to wield it...

"Liam, stay behind me."

"I don't think we've been introduced yet," I tell her loudly.

"I'm Ayesha," she scoffs. "I don't really care about your name, though."

"...What is it you want, then?"

She smiles.

"Just a bit of fun. And to teach you manners as well. After that, I'll happily train your dog too. He looks rather cute to me, he could be my new toy..."

Liam and I furiously growl in unison. Who the hell does that bitch think she is?! As if I was going to let her lay a single finger on my mate! I know she's deliberately trying to provoke me, but Moon Goddess, she succeeded! I increase the fire from my fists, and she raises a thin eyebrow.

"Oh, someone wants to play with fire. Feisty, of course. That's a Fire Witch thing..."

"Rather than trying so hard to piss me off, you could get the fuck away from here," I hiss.

"I don't think so. See, that old hag here isn't the only one interested in Silver City... I could use a new place to settle too. I don't think a little girl like you can really stop me, either, so I'll just..."

She steps forward, but this time, I'm not playing anymore. I increase the fire in my hands, and throw one fireball right to her face. I didn't curve it or anything, it flies in a straight arrow toward her.

However, she stops it. It happens so fast, I don't even breathe. She extends her hand, and opens it, as if she was receiving a mere ball. She chuckles at my baffled expression, and closes her fist, making my fireball vanish. That easily. Oh, Moon Goddess, that can't be easy...

"Here comes a little witch who knows nothing about fights between witches," she laughs. "Really? Attacking me with a simple fireball? What is this, kindergarten?"

"You should go easy on her," says Ravena. "She's basically self-taught..."

To my surprise, Ayesha glares at her.

"I don't like you either, old hag. You should just fuck off before I get on your case!"

So they don't work together... no, more than that, they don't get along. Ravena had mentioned the other two witches were probably not going to be as "nice" as she was, but I didn't suspect they would actually hate her as well... That's good to know, though. I turn to Ayesha.

"Fine, I don't know much about fighting another witch," I shout back, "however, shouldn't you learn to talk before attacking me?"

"I didn't come here to get a drink and become besties with ya, dearie."

"Well, I have questions anyway. What do you know about the curse? And what was that tattoo your lackey spread?"

She rolls her eyes.

"I have no idea what you're talking about."

"Don't play pretend," chuckles Ravena. "Someone's been trying to play naughty ahead of us..."

This time, Ayesha prepares another fireball in a split second, and I get ready. Can I receive it like she just did with mine? However, much to my surprise, she actually pivots her upper body at the last second, and sends it flying without any restraint or hesitation toward Ravena. The Earth Witch has to jump to the side to avoid it, and when she raises her head, her confident expression is definitely gone.

"How dare you...!" she yells.

"I did warn you to fuck off," shrugs Ayesha.

She has another fireball dancing on her fingers, and she's obviously ready to hit again. Ravena glares at her, then at me, but we all know she won't win anything by staying around. She starts stepping back, cautious, and quickly disappears between the trees. I frown, and glare at Ayesha.

"I wasn't done talking with her," I growl.

"Oh, as if she was going to reveal anything. That selfish bitch is only good at playing around and using others' weaknesses, she can't do shit upfront... You, cutie pie, look like more of a straight-forward kind of gal."

This time, she puts her hands close together, and increases her fire.

"What's your problem?!" I growl, already annoyed at this crazy one.

"Oh, come on, I just want to play a little. Test how good my new little witch sister is..."

She should find another playmate, I don't want to play with her! However, I don't have a choice. Ayesha's about to send another damn purple fireball, and if I don't stop it, it might really cause some serious damage. She plays with it like a ball in her hands, smiling. She's really testing me.

"Mara..."

"Stay back, and run if I tell you to."

Liam doesn't have time to protest. The purple ball flies my way and I have just enough time to use my hands to receive it, as she did. I didn't even think. I extended my hand, and with all my might, lit another fireball to receive it. The two make an awful crackling noise as soon as they meet. It lasts for a few seconds, then her fire disappears, and I can breathe. I wasn't as efficient as her, but I still managed to stop her attack, somehow...

I'm far from okay, though. I may have gotten better, but I did not expect to have to fight a witch now, not so soon. My heartbeat increases, the adrenaline rushing through my veins. This isn't just a friendly match, I know she's probably just waiting to get rid of me to take Silver City. I can't afford to lose or even be injured, there are two more lurking around!

She chuckles, and lights up her hands.

"Alright, someone's a fast learner!"

Right after that, she sends more purple-ish fires, and I have to stop them once again using mine. It's nerve-wracking. I have to find out where they will land, act fast, and yet stay as composed as possible to keep control over my own fire, making sure it will be big enough to withstand hers. It's like trying to stop balls while juggling with my own. Moreover, she doesn't just stop there. Right after I've blocked those, she sends another two, and another, and another. She keeps sending them, in pairs, making me completely follow her rhythm. The speed at which she produces them is terrifying. The whole forest could be burnt down if I wasn't there to receive it!

"Come on, show me what you got!"

Instead of two, she suddenly joins her hands again to send another fireball, even bigger than the previous two. Moreover, this one takes a dramatic blue color, and gets larger and larger. What the heck is that?!

I prepare myself, but I can't grow my fire that much or fast enough, and I don't even know what I'm about to block! She smiles like a demon, her black eyes shining with confidence. Suddenly, she throws it, and I change at the last minute. I split my fire, and instead of blocking it with my own fireball, I cover my hands with my fire, and receive it like a cannonball.

My feet slide in the mud, but I hold on. I feel the heat on my fingers, but I don't waver. I'm holding my fingers like hooks to stop it, and add some pressure to crush it. I keep pushing and pushing, until it explodes in my hands.

"...Not bad, for a young one," she chuckles. "Let's see how you do when it's not so simple..."

What the hell does she mean, not so simple? My wolf growls and wants me to shape-shift, but now's not the time. Ayesha smiles and moves her finger. A magic circle appears in the air, slowly and steadily getting bigger and more complex. The runes are appearing in the air so fast, traced by her fire, I can't even keep up. My eyes go left and right, trying to decipher her circle, but she keeps smiling.

"Come on... Are you going to let me finish?"

I glare at her and forget that stupid circle, preparing my fire instead. If I can just give her one big blow, just one... I make it bigger and bigger between my hands, ready to strike.

"Mara, let me attack her!"

"No, Liam, stay behind me, I don't know what she's preparing!"

Ayesha isn't looking, she's smiling and focusing on her magic circle. I don't like that look in her eyes, it can't mean anything good! I hurry to prepare my fire. It doesn't need to be precise, I just need one blow...

"You're so slow," she laughs as she glances up.

That's it. I growl furiously and throw it.

She raises her magic circle like a shield in front of her, and just from the look in her eyes, I immediately know. She tricked me. I fucked up. I just feel it.

My fire hits her magic circle at an impressive speed, but it doesn't do any damage. Nothing at all. I frown, confused, as her magic circle vanishes with my fire. She chuckles again.

"Nice little fire, baby witch. However, you should be careful where you aim, right?"

I know from her expression. It's...

A loud ruckus breaks behind us. I blink, as a huge fireball suddenly hits Silver City. I see her magic circle appear in the sky above the tall buildings, and my very own fireball, with red and pink, suddenly shoots down in a flash of light.

"Holy shit..."

"Nice shot," she chuckles. "Oh, sorry, did you mean that for me?"

I can't even believe this is happening. My own fire attacking Silver City, my city, the one place I wanted to protect! This is a nightmare! I can't swallow what just happened... She redirected my fire above the buildings, and I didn't have time to do a thing about it. I gasp, unable to control the damage that has already been done. I didn't even have a chance to react, let alone stop it!

"Mara, it landed in one of the already burnt areas, there were probably no victims..."

"You can't be sure of that!" I yell, forgetting to use the mind-link.

Liam seems shocked by my reaction, but I'm so furious right now, to the point that I'm even crying. These aren't tears of sorrow, but of frustration. I turn to Ayesha, with that naughty smile on her lips as if she had just taken a toy from a four-year-old. She shrugs.

"You should stop it if you don't like it, little sister."

"Don't you fucking call me that," I growl.

"So?" she asks, warming up another ball of fire in her hands.

I prepare mine, but this time, I don't restrain myself; I shoot right away, one after the other. I'm so furious that I don't dare to slow down for a second. Ayesha drops her smile. She has to focus to keep up, and either catches my fireballs or sends hers back. I see her step back, again and again, overwhelmed. I keep firing, my anger fueling each of my fireballs.

"Careful," she yells between two catches.

Careful? Careful of what, is she going to fucking burn my city down in flames if I don't stop? I have no plans to stop until I get rid of that arrogant bitch! I keep firing, literally, stepping closer and winning more ground on her. Ayesha tries to keep up, and at some point, it looks like she gets used to my frantic rhythm. She stops grimacing and instead of stopping them, starts grabbing my fireballs one after another and adds them to a much larger one she's building. I don't like that either! The fire in her hands is clearly a mix of mine and hers now! I stop sending fireballs, as it's obvious that one's going to come in my direction sooner or later...

"What?" she smiles. "Aren't you going to try and catch it?"

Moon Goddess, does she think she's training some dog or something?! However, to my surprise, she glances at the sky. It's very brief, but it gives me a second to realize what she's about to do. I'm not her target!

She chuckles, and just as our eyes meet again, she suddenly throws it into the air. I see the fireball start to make an arch above us, but this time, I won't let it hit my home. I raise my arms, and with all my focus, I work my inner fire to call my fire back to me. All of it, as much as I can. It's a new sensation, like claws in my stomach, trying to pull toward that gigantic new fireball. It's calling it back, but I'm pulled toward it too. My inner flame gets more and more unstable, growing to answer the strength of the pull. I keep my arms in the air, my fingers so tense it hurts, and I don't stop trying to call it back. It's tiring, horribly tiring, as it calls for all the strength I can gather, physically and mentally. I didn't even take a step, but I feel my feet dragging in the mud as my whole body simply moves toward the fireball like a damn magnet.

"Mara!" yells Liam.

"I... can... do this..." I growl, pearls of sweat running down my temples and my chin.

I close my eyes, and try to pull harder, but I hear a sudden burst behind me. Something hits my back, and a weight falls right behind my legs. Oh, Moon Goddess, no, no... I dare to glance over my shoulder, and I see Liam. Liam, on the ground, his wolf form reeking of something burnt.

"Liam!" I scream.

"*I'm... okay...*"

Yeah, right, he's obviously not! He tries to get up, but he's burnt, he's severely burnt! I can smell his burnt fur all over, it's horrible. I feel my tears start again, but I can't let go. Not until I've finished absorbing that fireball...

"Damn, I liked that wolf. Why did he have to do that? Does he really like you or what?"

I glare at Ayesha over my shoulder. I want to slap the hell out of her face for the look she is giving Liam. I'm so going to end her once I'm done here! I close my eyes, and mobilize all of my inner fire to get that flame back. This is my fire she used, my magic, my powers. You'd better come down, you damn flames!

Finally, it obeys. Her share of purple fire seems to evaporate, and I see the red flames coming back to me.

"Oh... You're really a fast learner..." she whispers.

I don't care about the impressed tone in her voice. I'd rather have her scared and get the hell out of here! I finish dragging the humongous fireball close to me, but I have to take a step over Liam to protect him.

"Stay behind me, Liam, and down!"

"I'm okay!"

Moon Goddess, I hate that he says he's fine when I can literally smell his injury, the smell of burnt flesh and fur, from where I stand. I know my mate's about as stubborn as I am, but I won't have it. This is my fight, my responsibility! Ayesha smiles, and prepares her fire again, her hands glowing with purple flames. She's ready, and I don't care either way. I just throw my large fireball at her, and she barely stops it with her hands, her feet sliding in the mud from the force of it. However, she still manages to completely dissipate it in her hands, and once again, we go back to exchanging fireballs for several minutes.

After a little while, though, my anger lessens a bit, enough to realize that she's merely toying with me. From her skills earlier, she shouldn't just be playing with fireballs. We haven't even used magic circles, or is it that neither of us have given the other the time? I can't tell. This is my first time fighting another witch, and it's so obvious I'm a damn newbie... I keep holding my ground, though, and the fact that Liam is lying down right behind me gives me more strength. I am not letting her get any closer to him, or to Silver City. In fact, we've moved a few steps deeper into the forest, and more trees have gotten burn marks from our exchanges. It's a miracle of some sort that we're not in the middle of a complete forest fire yet.

"Alright," she sighs. "You're really starting to get annoying, little one. I didn't plan to spend that much time on you..."

What does that mean? Does she have something else planned? Is it related to her accomplice Professor Vutha? Moon Goddess, I hope I didn't send Kelsi and Ben into something even more dangerous... I throw another fireball, and I'm now getting very confident with them, I can curve my shots, and call them back too. I throw another one; however, I miss her head by at least two inches. She smiles, but I did it on purpose. Just as she gets ready to fire, I call back my fireball, and it suddenly hits her from behind.

Ayesha is thrown forward, and shouts in anger or pain.

"You bitch! That hurts!"

"Does it?" I growl.

Damn, she deserved that one. She glares at me and gets back on her feet just as quickly. She seems really furious now, her eyes glaring at me, and her fire strangely changes to bluer shade.

"You little pest..."

She starts preparing more fire, it seems she's done with mere training or whatever the reason she was going easy on me for. I get ready to receive it, but to my surprise, I see runes appearing in her fireball right before she throws it. Wait, how does she...?

I don't have time to wonder. I receive the first fireball, and it literally explodes as it reaches my hand. I scream. It hurts so fucking much! The flames exploded like a hundred little shards, and my hand gets burned for real by her fire. I learned my lesson. When the next one arrives, I dodge it, and it explodes right above me. Holy Moon Goddess!

"Lesson number two," she chuckles. "A surprise is always nice!"

She throws more of her trapped fireballs, but I won't stand by. If I don't put everything I learned with little Mara into practice now, I may as well have learned absolutely nothing. I move my hands symmetrically, quickly, and when she launches the next ones, I raise my magic circle like a shield in front of me. Her fireball explodes, but this time, I stopped it. Moreover, I won't just stand still. I erase the circle, and move immediately to create my own fireballs, and just like Ayesha did, I incorporate some runes before throwing them. Her eyes grow wide, but just like me, she uses a quick magic circle like a shield, and they almost explode in her face, forcing her to retreat a bit.

"So you are really that good..." she chuckles behind her shield.

I glare. I'm not playing, and I don't need her validation either.

"Get the hell out of my city."

"No," she retorts immediately.

Then I won't restrain myself. Not that I was before, but...

We keep exchanging fireballs, most containing runes that make them explode or are made to weaken the other's magic circle, but as of now, I realize I've gotten to her level. Ayesha looks annoyed, but she isn't bragging, so I guess there isn't anything else she can come up with to stop me. I knew it... She looks too young to know a lot of tricks.

However, I won't settle with a status quo. I relentlessly attack her, and make her retreat farther and farther away from Liam and Silver City.

"You little pest..." she finally groans after a particularly violent attack of mine that weakened her shield and injured her forearm.

"You can go find another city!" I yell, sending another fireball.

However, this time, she decides to use the same magic circle, and my fire rebounds on it, coming back to me. I didn't even realize we had gotten so close, with me pushing constantly for more ground and her unwilling to back off. I see my own fire coming back, and cover my eyes, but the blow throws me back a few steps, and I fall on all fours. Damn it, I think I sprained my wrist...

"You stubborn little one..." she sighs.

His Blazing Witch

This stubborn little one isn't done, far from it. Even down on my knees, I prepare another fireball and send it her way, preventing her from approaching me. From the smell, I suddenly realize a nearby tree may have caught fire. Shit. I get back up, trying not to show that my wrist is injured.

"You should stay down," she warns me.

There's no smile in her eyes anymore, we're done playing. I chuckle.

"You can dream on."

I prepare another magic circle. I'm... tired. I didn't realize before how fast and recklessly I was depleting my magic. I should have shape-shifted earlier. Now it's too late, and my wolf is furious. I wanted to fight as a wolf, but she left me no time to shape-shift, and I'm not even familiar with that yet. I was just so focused on Liam and protecting Silver City... She throws one fireball after another, and I feel my shield painfully taking the hits. It's like a violent shock each time one hits, and she's set on not leaving me any type of rest. She manages her power better than me, and when I try to prepare another fireball, I just end up with one that's no bigger than an egg.

"That's it?" She laughs. "Someone's out of magic?"

I glare at her. She may be laughing, but she can't have that much left either. We've been at it for a very long time, and neither of us are in our best element, either, surrounded by trees and humidity. If it was dry and hot, things may have been different, but for now...

I take a deep breath. I do have one crazy idea, but... I step closer to her, and she tilts her head.

"What? You're going to throw one last?" she chuckles.

I smile. Oh, no, I'm somewhat crazier than that... I suddenly charge, running like crazy her way, and I hit her hard with my magic circle; I see the shock in her eyes as we both fall on the ground. The fall is rough as we roll on the mud and grass down a little hill. Ayesha didn't expect a physical attack, and that was my best shot... I try to get back up as fast as I can, but I'm... not well. I don't know if I hit my head, but I just... I get on all fours, but I don't feel like my body will get up. I hear her chuckle.

"What is it? The little witch has given all she can? You're too young. You should have—"

She suddenly stops, and I hear it too.

The sound of a deep, furious, and threatening growl. Just as Ayesha turns her head, her eyes wide open in panic, something black jumps on her. I hear her scream and for a few seconds, it's a violent scene of fighting in front of me. Furious growls, the sound of bones breaking, and the witch trying to fight the wolves off in despair.

"Mara!"

I turn my head, confused, and Nora runs to me, hugging me out of the blue.

"W-what...?"

"It's alright, it's alright. Are you hurt? Oh, you are... Okay, breathe. Let me do this..."

457

I don't know what's happening. Nora helps me lie back down on the grass, and all I can hear is the furious fight right next to us. Ayesha screams again, but those have to be the most terrifying growls ever, even for me. However, surprisingly, the wolves suddenly retreat, and as Nora helps me sit up gently, Selena walks onto the scene.

"P-please..." whimpers Ayesha, terrified of her.

Yet, Selena is in her human form, in a denim outfit, and she crouches down to the witch's height. She grabs her coat and her wrist.

"She may be young," she says, "however, she's certainly not alone."

Then, I hear the sound of a bone breaking, but a hand gets in front of my eyes. Ayesha screams again.

"Stop! Stop!"

"This way, you won't try to pull another one of your fucking spells on us. If you heal those wrists back I'll break them again. Are we clear?"

"W-w-who are you...?"

Selena smiles.

"Let's just say you're not our first witch. I understand you need to move your arms and hands or whatever to do any kind of spells, so unless you want us to damage yours some more, you'd better stay down and answer our questions."

As if to add to her words, the two black wolves on either side of her growl loudly as a warning. I know who those two are, but...

"Liam?" I mutter to Nora. "Where is Liam...?"

"He's fine. Don't you feel him? Mara, calm down, he's alright. I healed him before I came to you."

I nod. Indeed, I... I can feel him. He's coming this way. Thank Moon Goddess... Nora smiles, and caresses my cheek gently.

"You've done great," she whispered. "We didn't want to let you fight alone, so we waited until we could intervene... You did great, Mara."

I chuckle nervously. Moon Goddess, why do those words feel so good...? I nod, and before I can resist, I start crying again. A few steps behind Nora's shoulder, Selena's golden eyes are on me too and she nods.

"That's right, witchy. I'm proud of you too. But remember, no matter how strong of a fighter you are, you need to trust your friends, okay? We are no good without backup. Moreover... you're part of the pack now. Remember that. You're a witch, but you're also one of us, okay?"

I nod between my tears, but my throat is too tight to answer. Selena sighs.

"And next time you go head first into a fight without warning us, I'm kicking your ass. So remember that too."

I laugh nervously and Nora chuckles, grabbing my wrist. She uses this... strange white halo thing that I can't even see clearly between my tears. Meanwhile, though, Selena goes back to being serious, and still crouching down, she pulls Ayesha forward. The Fire Witch has lost all of her previous arrogance, visibly terrified of Selena and the two black wolves.

"Now," she says, "I strongly suggest you start talking because I'm tired of watching Mara run around for answers and not getting any. So, what the hell is wrong with you guys? Why Silver City, why us? Is it about the Royals' power again?"

Ayesha grimaces, but the three-legged wolf next to Selena growls in warning.

"I-I wouldn't care for your city... It rains all the damn time here, why would a Fire Witch care?!"

Selena slams the back of her head, pissed at her attitude, but... she does have a point.

"So?" I ask, frowning. "Why the hell are you here if you don't care about Silver City?"

Ayesha rolls her eyes.

"You... You said you wanted to break that curse, didn't you? Well, you're not the only one! Isn't that why we're all here in the first place?"

"...What?"

"The curse... Wait, you really don't know?"

She stares at me, looking surprised, as if she had just understood something. Then, she glances at Selena before turning back to me.

"The curse, you have to break it where it first started! Here, in Silver City!"

Nora and I exchange a glance. I did not see that one coming...

"The curse began... in Silver City?" I repeat, baffled. "The whole... the tale of the witch and Luna, it was... here?"

"Yes," says Ayesha, rolling her eyes. "Damn, I thought you were just trying to keep it all to yourself, but you seriously didn't have a clue? Everything leads us here. Witches have been trying to break this curse since... well, ages."

"So Silver City was the starting point?"

"Girl, that's what I've been saying. You think we like knowing that there's a curse waiting to drive us nuts? I don't care much about the werewolves or the humans, but no witch wants to let that damn curse go on. We try to protect the few children we can have."

It makes sense... Witches are becoming rarer and rarer, and that curse probably hasn't been helping with that. If they couldn't even fall in love with a werewolf without risking the possibility of their partner going crazy, then this ought to be a real issue for any witch. Even those who don't care about werewolves, they might have tried to break it just to protect the future generations.

"Generations of witches have tried to find a way to break it," she continues. "Eventually, we narrowed it down to Silver City. From what we know, this is most definitely where it all began."

"...Ravena mentioned that to undo a curse, you have to take it back to its very start."

"Yup," she sighs. "It's like a knot, you need to find the beginning and the end to undo it. Otherwise, you'd risk making more of a mess. So we had to find where it happened, and why. Unfortunately, Silver City has been a bit of an... occupied territory."

She said that while glancing at the werewolves, and Selena growls back as a warning. Still, Ayesha can't do anything now. Both of her wrists are broken, and probably more bones in her hands too, judging by how she keeps them in a weird position against her chest, almost in a cross.

"Wait... it's not like Silver City has been completely barred to witches," says Nora with a little frown. "There were witches here. Even long before us werewolves came..."

I gasp. Something suddenly clicks in my mind. Pieces all coming together, everything that was said, and now, with what Ayesha just revealed... I keep playing it over and over in my mind, but...

"Moon Goddess... It all makes sense!" I exclaim, turning to Selena. "You guys mentioned that Danica, the Fire Witch that was Queen Diane's friend, sent her adoptive daughter Nephera here. You said it was because her ancestors were originally from Silver City, right? That was Danica's reason, but what if..."

"Nephera was one of Luna's descendants...?" whispers Nora, finishing my sentence.

We exchange a long look, and she slowly nods.

"That would explain a lot," she gasps. "She would have been a target of choice for the curse, but also, one of its biggest threats."

"She could have broken it," I nod, excited. "If it wasn't for her fateful meeting with Judah Black... Nephera was the one who could re-enact the curse, or break it!"

"They said she was sent here to find a powerful source of magic, something that was linked to her ancestors," adds Nora, completely shocked but excited too. "She never found it, but somehow, Danica knew there was something here in Silver City that Nephera had to find!"

We all stay quiet for a few seconds, completely shocked by these revelations.

Moon Goddess... The mysterious source of magic was the origin of the curse. Nephera was completely overtaken by it, but the curse must have felt she was there to end it. She was the prey of choice, a young witch left by herself in a city full of werewolves. The curse acted in the most cruel way. She forgot her mission, got lost in her tragic love for Judah Black, and eventually lost both her man and her child to that horrible curse...

"There you go," sighs Ayesha. "I'm sorry to break it to you, but Silver City isn't just a city all of us witches want for the view or whatever. I mean, there are plenty of cities to choose from, but we purposefully come to this one because of all of the magic power it probably hides. You really think we like to go head to head against werewolves?"

Selena growls at Ayesha's attitude, but... she has a point. This place is complicated for witches to come to from the start. Regardless of Sylviana occupying it before I came, there are tons of werewolves and humans. Why would lone witches purposefully come to such a place? Even more so a Fire Witch, considering how much it rains over here...

I thought it was because of the Royals' presence, but... it's probably not worth all the risks they took. The war from two years ago is the best proof thinking about it. Nephera was strong, probably full of the curse's power, but she still got killed in the end, even after gathering an army of vampires. Moreover, now, there are Nora and Selena, and the Black Brothers too. I remember how scared of them I was... I still am. Why would witches be so obsessed with this place? There had to be a very good and meaningful reason for it, and that reason was the curse.

"So you're saying the curse is actually hiding a lot of magic?"

"The curse *is* magic, girl," says Ayesha. "Very Dark Magic, but still magic. Breaking a curse is like opening a big box with a lot of gold inside. It's dangerous, but imagine transferring something as powerful as this curse to yourself... let alone the will to actually break it just to save our future daughters, this is the kind of perspective that would make any smart witch greedy for that power. Not even ten Royal werewolves could measure up to that... although they probably come from the same witch to begin with."

I hate to admit it, but I understand her point. Considering how old and powerful that curse is, I can totally get why it would make some... greedy. I've experienced its power first hand. If this is the power of one of the first witches, the one who created the Royals, it couldn't even be measured!

"Mara!"

I turn my head, and Liam, still in his wolf form, runs to me. I immediately hug the huge black wolf, glad to feel him. Moon Goddess, I was so worried for him... He's standing on his four paws, and looking alright. I don't know how much work he gave Nora, but there's nothing left of that burnt fur smell and no visible injury either. He just looks dirty, but damn, I couldn't care less. I hug him strongly, feeling a lot better now that he's there.

"I'm so sorry," I mumble. "I'm sorry I got mad at you and all..."

"It's okay, Mara. I promise it's okay. I get it. And I'm fine, too..."

I nod in his fur. Thank Moon Goddess, he's fine. I don't know what I would have done if something happened to Liam, even more so if it came from my fight. I already feel so bad that he got injured...

"She okay?"

It takes me a few seconds to realize he's talking about none other than me, but to Nora. He probably just let me hear that out of politeness.

"She's just tired," smiles Nora, gently patting my shoulder.

Moon Goddess, I am. I was alright until a while ago, but that fight literally emptied me. I'm tired, hungry, and still an emotional wreck after all that. My life these last few days has been one hell of a rollercoaster...

I turn to Ayesha, still held by Selena. She isn't going anywhere, but if I had to be honest, I wouldn't consider her much of a threat anymore. I probably depleted a lot of her magic too in that fight, and with both hands broken, she's pretty much as harmless as a human.

"So we're sure the curse has to be broken here, in Silver City?" asks Selena, glancing our way.

Nora and I both nod.

"Everything points that way," she says. "I don't think so many witches would be wrong either. Moreover, we were all gathered here... Although our reasons were different, it's probably no coincidence that both you and I ended up here, and Mara too, is it?"

Selena nods. Indeed. Although those two are of the same blood, if they were brought here by people unaware of Silver City being such a special place, it is one interesting point... plus Nephera's history, and myself.

"Told ya..." sighs Ayesha.

"Next time, you state your intentions more clearly," I growl.

She shrugs.

"It's every witch for herself out there, girl. We don't all have a full pack of werewolves ready to back us up, okay? Moreover, a witch can't trust another witch. We mess with each other more often than not. It's hard enough to survive by ourselves, now we have to look out for those other greedy bitches."

I frown. So none of those three were probably working together. They were all brought here by their common interest in the curse, but because of the barrier, the werewolves, and myself, they couldn't do anything.

"What about the tattoos?" I ask.

Selena and Nora must have received an explanation from Liam, because neither of them seems surprised to hear me asking. Ayesha, however, rolls her eyes.

"Once again, I have no idea what you're talking about."

"Stop playing dumb!" I growl. "You had that professor from the university post all the–"

"Mara," suddenly says Selena. "You should call your friend Kelsi."

I frown, confused for a second, but just then, my phone vibrates. I forgot Selena's actually Ben's Alpha... she must have mind-linked him... I struggle to get it out of my pocket, with all the damn mud on it. Leather pants, not such a good idea for fights...

"Kelsi," I sigh.

"Mara! I have good and bad news," she begins immediately, talking fast and out of breath. "First, Professor Vutha vanished from the university. So, when Benny and I got there, we looked around and got a hold of someone from the university's IT department, managed to convince him to check for us and all. Very nice guy, by the way, but a bit too interested in me, so Benny was a little upset. Anyways! We confirmed that it was her behind the blog post and all, but when we ran her identification information, it all turned out to be fake! I could tell at a glance that her identification papers were completely photoshopped, the phone number didn't work, her address was a house that's been up for sale for the last three years, and even her emergency contact was a stupid manicure shop!"

"Okay. ...And the good news?"

462

"Oh, uh... I guess I m-miscalculated, or that was probably the good news... Well, the better one of the two."

Crap, I don't like this... I hear a lot of noise in the background, as if someone was rummaging through a lot of stuff, papers, and wooden furniture. Kelsi's moving non-stop too, as if she's running around, yet she still manages to speak and breathe.

"Okay," she resumes, "so, basically, after Benny and I convinced the IT guy to shut down the full post about the pattern for the tattoos thing, Benny asked the nice IT guy to run a full check, and it turns out that wasn't the only creepy witch thing she put out there. He's still with him, trying to compile everything, but she was super active. The last time Benny updated me, there were over a hundred, so we're going to have to sort out whatever she did. Of course the IT guy is shutting it all down, just in case, but it's probably for the better. While Benny was doing that, I found a security guy and managed to convince him to let me in her office..."

"You've been busy," I chuckle nervously.

"Yes," I hear her sigh. "Well, I'm still here and going through all this stuff. I really found a bunch of things in her office, boo, and it's not good. Really, really not good. A lot of witch stuff, of course, but there are even some curses and magic circles I've never seen before, and you'll probably be the only one able to decipher them. I'm trying to take as many pictures as I can and gather them..."

I hear a loud meow in the background.

"Oh, and Spark's been helping me too. Did you know he can unlock some locked drawers? Saved me a lot of time and a couple of hairpins."

"Yeah, he does that from time to time."

"I kind of love him now, I promise I'll be nice to him from now on... Right, Spark? Yeah, good kitty... Oh, anyways! I found more of that same pattern that was tattooed everywhere, as if she had been distributing them to the students or something."

"Okay, so more tattooed idiots than we thought, probably..."

"Yep, sounds like it. Nothing seems to have happened so far, though. I've been checking the university social media, nothing creepy or slightly witchy to mention. How are things on your side, by the way?"

"Uh... Okay, I guess...?"

While Nora helps me up, I try to recount the events on my end to Kelsi. Aside from my fight, there isn't much to mention. Selena forces Ayesha to stand up, closely guarded by the two black wolves. She must have injured herself too during our fall or been bit because she's limping a little.

"Oh, goodness, boo, are you okay?"

"Yeah, don't worry, Nora healed me already, and I got... reinforcements."

"What do you want to do?" suddenly asks Selena.

I pause for a second, surprised. She's... letting me decide our next move? I hesitate, but all eyes are on me, indeed waiting for my decision. I even find myself blushing a little. I've always felt like I was under their care, so it feels a bit strange that she's... suddenly letting me lead. Not just them two, but even all three of the Black Brothers...

"Mara, you're the Silver City witch," chuckles Nora. "You're the expert. What do you want us to do now?"

I nod, a bit ashamed I'm just standing here.

"Let's bring Ayesha in," I decide first.

"Are you sure?" frowns Selena.

Even the other Fire Witch raises her eyebrows.

"Yeah, it's probably better to have her where I can see her... where we can all watch her. I need to ask her more about the curse too, and also, I can't keep running north and south around Silver City. If the Water Witch attacks, I'd rather make sure this one is under control."

"Fair enough. I can break more fingers if needed..."

Ayesha grimaces and glares at Selena, but at least she probably won't risk anything more today. Liam comes to rub his furry body against my legs, regardless of the dirt on both of us. I grip his fur with my fingers without thinking; I'm just glad to feel him close to me...

"Kelsi?"

"I'm still here and listening, boo," she answers over the phone.

"Stay at the university, I'll come right there to join you, okay? I–"

"Mara," interrupts Nora. "I know you want to know more, but... you've been fighting a lot, and despite my healing, I think you could use a little break... okay? Kelsi can join us at my house."

I hesitate, but... Nora's not wrong. I'm fine mentally, but my body is exhausted. I thought I'd be fine not sleeping much, but I didn't think I'd have to go all out against another witch, either... or have my magic supply drop to a new low. Moreover, Nora's house is around the midpoint of Silver City, so it's not a bad position for me to be at the moment... I've lost track of Ravena's whereabouts and I'm too tired to try and track her with my magic right now. Moreover, Liam must be exhausted as well. I don't want to push him, even if I know he won't say a thing. Going to Nora's house could be a good way to gather all the information we have, ask Ayesha more, and prepare something of a plan... I take a deep breath and nod.

"Okay. Kelsi, can you join us at Nora's house?"

"No problem. I'll send you what I found so far if you want to get a head start, boo! I'll join you as soon as Sparky and I are done opening all these drawers..."

Sparky? I smile, and she's already back to opening and closing things, probably going through every nook and cranny. When she's got something in mind, Kelsi certainly doesn't know how to hold back... I can imagine the absolute mess that office has got to be right now. I turn to Nora.

"Let's go, then."

Luckily, they brought cars, so I can actually sit in the back and relax on the way there. Since he stayed in his wolf form and probably didn't want to dirty the sexy engine, Selena took Liam's bike to ride it to the house.

His Blazing Witch

I'm in the car, Nora driving while Liam's in the passenger seat, and I guess I'm supposed to guard Ayesha in the back, but she's just staring outside, looking completely out of it. I suppose I'm not the only witch that's exhausted. I'm more worried about the pictures Kelsi sent to me, and just after studying the professor's documents some more, I sigh and close my eyes.

"Told ya," chuckles Ayesha.

Kelsi and I were both wrong.

The pattern and all those things found in the professor's office were the work of an Earth Witch. Ravena.

Chapter 31

"Boo!"

I open my eyes, getting out of the half-asleep state I was in just seconds ago. Damn it, I really tried not to fall asleep. I wanted to at least wait until Kelsi was here, but after we got to Nora's house, I was pushed to the bathroom for a much needed hot shower with Liam. He and I were so dirty and tired, we didn't even think of doing anything... naughty. He just changed back into his human form, taking some of his brother's clothes, while I also changed into a tank top and a pair of jeans, probably Selena's, judging by the size. Sadly, the leather pants went straight into the laundry pile...

Once we got back to the living room, it was apparently around lunchtime already, and Nora had magically gotten food ready for everyone. On the table, several plates were displayed like a buffet, including a large pan with an impressive quantity of bolognese pasta, a pyramid of burritos, and some cold slices of beef. I can only imagine how full their fridge must be to be ready to welcome werewolves at any moment...

However, I was almost too tired to even eat. I set myself in one corner of a couch with the plate I managed to fill up before the others got to it, and I just ate mindlessly, fighting the urge to sleep. With Ayesha still in the room with us, I really didn't want to give in, but it looks like I lost the fight...

Kelsi runs to me, while behind her, Ben's got both eyes on the table.

"Hey, can I get some?" he asks, his hand already reaching for a burrito.

Spark jumps on my lap, while Kelsi takes a seat next to me. She places a huge pile of papers and some books on her lap, probably everything she didn't have time to check or copy. However, she crosses her arms on it and looks at me with a frown.

"Boo, you look terrible... Are you alright?"

Liam comes to sit on my other side with his second serving of burrito. Like me, he seems tired, and just leans against my shoulder while he eats.

"Sorry, Kelsi, I'm just... exhausted. Can you update me on what you found?"

"You could take a nap," she suggests.

I look around. Yeah, maybe I could. Nora and her husband are chatting in one corner, busy catering to their guests. Selena is with Ayesha, who actually begged to get some food too. I can't blame her, if she used as much energy as I did... Now she's trying to eat with her injured hands, but I suspect she must be healing already, judging by how she can already hold a burrito. At least, I don't think she's dangerous anymore. She's seated in one corner, and with the house filled with werewolves, I don't believe there's any risk... Selena's husband took over the bathroom, and more wolves arrived inside and outside of the house. It's an almost continuous flow of werewolves, in their human or wolf form, coming in quietly to grab some food and go back out. It looks like Nora's cooking is the official roll call of the pack...

"...I promise I'll take one later, but I really need to hear what you found."

"Okay."

She grabs Spark to switch his position with all the documents that were on her lap for mine. The cat protests, but still curls himself in a ball of fur to get petted by Kelsi, while I have to open the documents and books. She already marked a lot of them with folded corners and some sticky notes she found Moon Goddess knows where. Next to me, Liam grabs some to help me look through the pile, checking the contents as well.

"Can someone translate these for me?" he asks.

"Those are necromancy rituals," I say out loud.

I know a lot of ears in the room are listening, although the discussion may seem to be going on only between me and Kelsi. She nods, and grabs a page to show me a new pattern.

"This is the most similar one I found to that of the tattoo. I don't think that professor was only spreading it, I think she actually may have helped create that tattoo for... whichever witch she worked for. I found a lot of different sketches she had done, and a ton more of them in those creepy necromancy books."

The necromancy books she mentioned are actually filled with dust, very old, and even stink a bit. I need to manipulate them carefully for the pages not to fall apart in my hands. Kelsi grimaces while petting the purring kitty.

"Yeah, they were hidden... Sparky found them in some secret panel under the rug. I think those are real witch's books, they don't have any information about a publisher or an author..."

I raise the book for Ayesha, sitting across the room, to see.

"Ring a bell?" I ask her, raising an eyebrow.

She shakes her head.

"Nope... but have you seen those runes?"

I nod. The runes on the cover... They are very thin, but to a witch, they are hard to miss. I put my finger on it. Those are a bit more complex than the key Clarissa had on her journal. An older witch, then? It would match the... dust.

"I'll bet that professor collects witches' possessions to study them," I sigh, still looking through the pages.

The handwriting inside seemed like it had been printed at first glance because of how regular the letters were without having lines, but the more I look, the more this was done with fresh ink. There are even some stains on the paper. It's written in a foreign but modern language I don't understand.

"Selena, is that Spanish?" asks Liam.

She frowns and comes over.

"...Portuguese," she says after just a few seconds of looking at it. "I don't think I can translate it, but I can find someone if it's urgent."

"...Maybe, but I don't think we have time," I shake my head, putting that book aside.

I go through the other documents, massaging my sore neck while reading. As Kelsi had said, it's a lot of random research, more sketches of what eventually became the tattoo design, and tons of notes... There are even parts of the genealogy of some witches. Not the full tree we saw, more like just a few branches of it.

"It's strange; can't all witches see the tree?"

"Maybe that professor was doing some digging of her own," says Kelsi. "I found a lot of research on witches, and for all three elements too. I think she was fascinated."

That's a very plausible theory based on everything Kelsi found... The one part I'm worried about though is that there's still a lot of necromancy involved. It's in the choice of runes for the patterns, the two history books, and even those rebirth symbols that keep coming up.

"...It looks like she was digging for some very ancient magic," I declare after a while. "It looks a bit like the revival circle that was used for me..."

"The one in the hangar?" asks Ben, coming to stand next to Kelsi.

"Yeah. However, this one was meant to call back something much more ancient and powerful... I think they tried to climb up the genealogy of the Witches' Ancestral Tree to find the best way to get to the original Luna."

"Wait, what?"

Ayesha suddenly stands up, abandoning her food, and walks up to me before Selena can stop her. She doesn't want to harm us though, she comes over to glance at the document lined up in front of me.

"Those bitches..." she mutters, visibly upset.

"Are you willing to cooperate now?" I ask, raising an eyebrow.

"Hey, I'm the kindergarten representative compared to these crazy bitches," she retorts. "You see all this? This is not what I would come up with, I'm more of the upfront attack kind of gal."

"I noticed."

"The one you should be worried about is Ravena. I had told you she was a schemer! You know this has to be her work, right? Look at this! This crazy bi–"

"Hey, no swearing in this house," growls Nora.

Ayesha glances at her, probably shocked this is the kind of thing the mistress of the house cares about at the moment, but she is met with all the werewolves present glaring right back at her. She makes a sour expression, but comes back to me with a sigh.

"That crazy hag doesn't want to end the curse. From these, you should be able to tell too, right?"

I nod, my eyes going back down on the documents. Kelsi leans toward me, visibly worried.

"Really, Mara? What is she looking for, then...?"

"...I think she wants the Dark Magic stored in that curse," I say, looking for Ayesha's reaction.

"Wait, what? Is that even possible?" asks Liam.

I shrug, grabbing the sketches of the tattoo to study again.

"...She seems to think it is... This curse is basically a huge bundle of dark, untamed magic. I felt it too, while it was... inside me, and active. That thing contains a lot of power, enough to even have its own conscience. It is powerful, for real, but a single witch should have issues controlling it... especially if she's the only host."

"Oh, goodness," says Kelsi. "Is that what the tattoos are for? To get... more hosts?"

"...Maybe. I don't think humans are normally affected by the curse, which is why she might force it inside them. It won't come to them naturally, but if Ravena forces so many humans to attract the curse, it will be spread between them, while the Dark Magic will resonate with hers..."

"Okay, I'm completely lost now," sighs Ben.

"Basically, Benny, that Earth Witch Mara had met before wants to share the curse with the humans because they are not affected, but the curse will have to fight their minds. Meanwhile, she will be free to focus on the Dark Magic of the curse and control it. That magic won't go to a human since they can't host it, you know? Like... I can't shape-shift into a werewolf even if I really wanted to. It just won't work. Only the... the bad feelings involved in the curse can affect humans."

"Exactly," I nod, since Kelsi summed it up well. "I had those... voices in my head, and all that anger and jealousy long before I mastered my magic properly."

"So, will the humans be in danger, or not...?" asks Ben, frowning.

We all turn our heads to him. Really?

Kelsi grabs his ear lobe and pulls, annoyed.

"Benny, a witch is about to use humans as vessels to host a dark curse! What do you think?!"

"Ah... Okay, okay, I got it... Stop pulling..."

Kelsi lets go, and turns back to Ayesha and me. From the way she glances at the other Fire Witch, she still doesn't trust her, but Ayesha just grabs her burrito to finish it, her eyes still going over the documents spread on my lap, Liam's, and the little corner of the table in front of us.

"What about the Water Witch?" asks Selena.

"I think she and Ravena have different objectives."

"Of course they do," sighs Ayesha. "A lot of witches have tried to end and destroy that damn curse. I mean, a lot, a lot. As you already know, everyone failed."

"What happened to them?" asks Kelsi, looking worried again.

The witch shrugs.

"Either the curse killed them, cursed them, or they got away, I suppose. The only sure thing is that everyone failed, since it's still here... It's strange, though."

I agree.

"By now, someone should have found the solution... especially if there have always been witches in Silver City. How come none of... Nephera's ancestors were able to undo it?"

"How do you undo a curse like that, exactly?" asks Nora.

Licking her fingers, Ayesha turns to her.

"Most curses are born from strong negative feelings. Hatred, anger, jealousy, wrath, sadness, pain. Most curses are created during wars or after a crime was committed, because it asks for a very, very strong resentment and a Dark Witch to do it, but none I've seen before are as popular as this one... Actually, it might be the oldest and strongest curse ever."

It probably is, indeed. If it is as old as its tale, dating back to the oldest of witches and the first werewolf Luna... I sigh and pile all the documents back together while Ayesha resumes talking.

"Breaking a curse usually asks for a Light Witch to solve the feelings that created it in the first place. All witches are sisters. It takes one of us to undo what another witch has done."

"There has to be some sort of trick to it," says Liam, shaking his head.

He puts an arm around me.

"If," Liam continues, "as you said, many witches have tried and failed, although you all seem to know the tale and its origins... There must be something that goes wrong every time, right?"

Ayesha gives him a strange look, checking out my mate from head to toe... Can she stop leering at him like that? I growl, bringing her attention back to me.

"Indeed..." she says. "First, this isn't just your witch next door who created this curse. I guess that would be the first and main issue... like I said, it will take a strong witch to undo this. Second, the location. No one was sure until a while ago, either. If some knew, they probably didn't share it too much either for fear young witches would run here and get caught while playing with fire... Moreover, witches are territorial, yes? Let alone the fact that you werewolves are all over the place, and the previous local witches didn't let many of us in..."

Indeed, the barrier was keeping those three out until recently. I suppose now it's going to be more than two or three witches flocking to Silver City like moths drawn to a flame. They will try their luck at undoing the curse and, at the same time, gaining control of such a big place.

"Finally, the curse itself. As you already know, it's growing, and powerful. Over the years, it probably grew until it became pretty much unstoppable. Not all of us are in a hurry to get killed, either. Each time a witch loses to that curse, she adds fuel to the fire, the curse taking her magic. Who wants to fight a few-centuries-old curse now, risking their lives and their magic? Nope, I'd rather stay away from it."

"You were rather close for someone who meant to stay away," says Selena.

"Well, things changed recently, didn't they?" shrugs Ayesha. "Two witches dying. A new one came out of literally nowhere. A pair of Royals showing up in the area too. That's enough to appeal to a few power-hungry and curious witches like me."

I don't really care about Ayesha's motives at the moment. From what I've experienced so far, she was at least the most honest about it... I keep staring at that paper, and finally grab one of the sketches, and take Kelsi's purse to rummage around for a pen.

"...Mara?"

"We need a new plan of action," I mutter.

I start to write things on the paper, aware that I have at least three pairs of eyes above me trying to read it.

"...Oh, not bad," chuckles Ayesha.

"Mara, what are you doing?" asks Liam, confused.

"Like Ayesha said, the curse has grown too strong. For now, our best chance is if we can weaken it, and find where all the other witches before us failed. We already know where that curse started: here, in Silver City. I mean, it would be great if we could narrow that some more, but... first, we need to find as much information as possible about the people related to that curse."

"You mean the two Lunas?"

"Those two, and the male werewolf too. That professor was probably researching who their blood descendants are to weaken that curse too."

"Well, aren't you... one?" says Kelsi. "That would explain why that... Ravena witch was so interested in you, and the other one so... upset about your history, as well."

I nod, tracing the most basic organigram to symbolize that triangle, between the original trio, and now... between their descendants in this time.

"Exactly. Well, I'm very likely a descendant of that first witch, from my relationship to Nephera, while Nora and Selena are... descendants of the first Luna."

The two cousins exchange a look.

"So now, we'd need to find who are the descendants of the first... male werewolf in the tale? The one both Lunas fell in love with?"

I nod. This is probably harder, though. I mean, unlike in the first story, we have literally no clue... Kelsi makes a sour expression too, and grabs one of the papers to read it over again to try and find another clue.

Suddenly, though, Ben scoffs loudly, almost coughing out his mouthful of rice. Kelsi grimaces, but hands him a napkin.

"Benny, what is it...?"

However, he starts laughing, while we're all waiting for him to finish his mouthful and calm down without choking. Nathaniel Black walks back into the room, changed into clean and casual clothes, still drying his hair with a towel. Ben starts laughing again as if he had seen something funny. Nathaniel exchanges a glance with his wife.

"For Moon Goddess' sake, Ben, explain yourself!" yells Selena, finally annoyed.

"S-sorry," he chuckles, barely able to contain himself, "but... isn't it obvious who the descendants are? I mean..."

He stares at all of us, but I'm as lost as the others. Ben rolls his eyes.

"Seriously, guys? You can't tell me no one realized that *all three* of you fell for a trio of *siblings*! All three descendant chicks from the story, both the witch and the she-wolf, each one falling for one of the Black Brothers? I mean, seriously? What other proof do you need?!"

We all turn to our partners, the three brothers pretty much as baffled as us. Liam opens his mouth, but soon closes it with a little embarrassed smile. I glance at Nora and Damian, Selena and Nathaniel. ...Okay, maybe he's got a point.

"You think... Nate, Damian, and Liam are the descendants of that male werewolf from the story?"

"Don't you think so?" chuckles Ben. "I mean, I always thought it was a huge coincidence that you and Nora fell for... two of the Black Brothers when you're actually cousins, but now, Mara is Liam's fated mate too? That's rather... big, isn't it?"

He isn't wrong. I mean, what were the chances of that happening? Even if Selena isn't actually Nathaniel's fated mate, she still ended up with him regardless. Plus, Nora and I did get paired up with Damian and Liam. Like Ben says, it would be a pretty huge coincidence if the Moon Goddess had just chosen to pair us with those three like that.

"Wait a second," says Kelsi with a frown, "I may have missed something but... weren't the children of the first Luna and that werewolf the same... children? Why are Nora and Selena Royals while the... Black misters are just normal werewolves?"

I chuckle. Black misters... I'm glad to see I'm not the only one impressed by the Black Brothers.

"Blood and genetics among werewolves don't exactly work like other characteristics," explains Nathaniel Black. "We inherit mostly from our fathers if the werewolf is male, and mostly from their mother for she-wolves. I'm not talking about our physical traits, but our werewolf ones."

"That's why I'm not as powerful of a Royal as Nora is," nods Selena. "Although my dad and her mom were twins, my mother was human. Hence, I inherited more human characteristics, and my father probably didn't give me as

472

much... Royal power as what Nora received from her mom either. It's true for our children too, Nora's sons have less Royal characteristics than their sister and cousins because they take mostly after their fathers' Alpha genes."

Oh, now that I think about it, I did notice that even if he kept his blue eyes, Nora's son's fur was pitch black like his dad, not white like Royals... Whereas Selena's daughters had white fur.

"That probably explains why there are no... male witches," I suddenly realize out loud.

"The witch gene is female-only," nods Ayesha. "Witches can have sons, but they'll be human."

"I get it," says Kelsi. "So, although the parents were the same, the genes of that Alpha male werewolf was passed along to his male descendants, while the Luna gene went to the female descendants..."

Everyone nods.

Aside from the history and biology lesson, it does also explain a few more things. Why the Black Brothers are so powerful, for one. If those three are directly descended from the first male werewolf, they probably have some of the purest Alpha genes too.... The rest were probably diluted by having children with humans, or simply meeting other werewolves that were created differently. Maybe there are more stories like this, of witches creating werewolves. We don't even know exactly how much of that tale is true. She may not have actually created a werewolf, but just made him stronger or something... Oh, I don't know. That's too much thinking for me right now.

"Alright," I state. "So, we do happen to have... the descendants of those three key characters right here."

"Will that help?" asks Nora.

"I believe so. The curse becomes stronger each time a witch gets betrayed by a werewolf, right? But here, the curse has three examples of werewolves who did not betray their mates..."

My voice goes down once I realize the glare Selena is sending her mate, her arms crossed. Nora makes a little grimace too, while Nathaniel has no choice but to stand there.

"Oh, really?" she says.

"I thought you'd forgiven me?" sighs her husband. "It's been years now, I have no intention of leaving you..."

Selena growls, but she doesn't say anything. Alright, maybe just a little bit of bad blood left between those two, but I don't think he betrayed her for a witch... The only witch known in the area was with Liam, so I'd be very surprised. Once again, from what I know, Damian and Nora have always been solid, and Liam and I... Well, despite a rocky start, he chose the werewolf and the witch, so I guess that works.

I clear my throat, trying to ease or ignore the tension in the room.

"A-anyway, the point is, the curse will probably be weaker against any of us three."

"What else can we do?" asks Nora.

473

"...We can try and narrow down the actual location where that curse began. There was always a mention of a powerful source of magic in Silver City, so... we don't have to wait for one of those witches to act for us to try and find it. If we can get to it first and fight that curse before they meddle, even better."

"How do we find that?" frowns Selena. "From what you said, no one else has been able to find it yet, right?"

I massage my temples, trying to think of the actual solution to this.

"I'm not sure... I could use a location spell of some sort, but I'm probably not the first witch who tried that..."

"Nope," nods Ayesha.

"What else?"

I bite my thumb, but Liam immediately grabs my wrist to take it away from me. Well, I'm still nervous and I really have no idea...

"Don't worry, boo," says Kelsi, putting a hand on my knee. "I'll try to think of something too. Who knows, so far, all witches have failed, but I'd be the first human to try!"

"Our witch specialist," chuckles Ben, giving her a little wink.

"Good idea. We can help you too," adds Nora.

I can't help but smile, feeling a lot better. It's true, I don't have to be the only one to look... and they are not pressuring me either. It doesn't mean there's nothing I can do, though. I don't want to sit on the sidelines while they do all the research, I have to be more prepared than that. I grab the list.

"Another thing is try to understand the curse."

"Didn't we know that already?" frowns Liam.

"Well, I thought so too, but if everyone knows exactly the same story, why have so many witches failed? I believe there is more to it, and I plan to dig deeper."

"How?"

"W-well, it may be quiet for now, but the curse is still inside me..."

"Oh, no, Mara," he growls. "No, no, no."

"What is it?" asks Nora, stepping forward, visibly worried.

"The curse is still inside Mara," says Liam, although he's still frowning my way. "She wants to seek it out and have a little chit-chat with it. Mara, do you realize how sick it made you, no later than last night? You were shivering!"

"Shivering?" repeats Kelsi, visibly shocked too. "Mara can...?"

"Yes, she can, and I'm not letting her do that again, I've had enough boiling hot showers for one lifetime!"

"Liam, I know, but just how are we going to fight that curse if I can't even understand what's wrong with it? I can't just let it dominate me like last time, I need to overcome it. I'll be just as useless if I can't even calm down the part that's inside me!"

"No, Mara," he growls. "I'm a hundred percent against this crazy idea. The mere thought that this stupid curse is still inside you already makes me worried sick. Now you actually want to go and wake up all that crazy and risk making yourself sick again? I know you're strong as hell, tiger, but that thing messes with your head! It just did last night, Mara! You're already tired as hell because you couldn't even go back to bed, now you want to do that all over again?"

I let out a long sigh, but I don't know what to say to that. I know Liam's right to be worried, and as my mate, he knows better than anyone how risky this is for me. However, I just can't sit still. It's not like me to give up, but I also don't want to make the mistake of provoking that curse on whichever birth place it's hiding if I can't even contain the darkness inside me.

"Mara," says Nora, "I think Liam is right... I know you really want to do well, but... there's been a lot happening these past few days, and honestly, there's probably more to come. You should rest a little."

Just as Nora said that, I feel a wave of fatigue suddenly come over me. It's not as if I hadn't felt it before, but... it was like a little thing in the back of my mind until Nora mentioned it. Plus, we just had lunch, and the digestion coma might be kicking in too. Liam wraps his arm around my shoulders again and pulls me in to gently kiss my forehead. I nod.

"Okay..."

Nora smiles gently.

"You can take one of the rooms upstairs and have a good nap. I promise we will wake you up if anything happens, alright?"

"Get a good rest," nods Kelsi. "I'll just keep studying this stuff and see if I can find more clues!"

"You're just impatient to dig into all that old witch stuff some more, eh?" chuckles Ben, teasing her.

Kelsi blushes, but we all know he's right. Ayesha suddenly lets out a long sigh.

"Finally! I'll help the human chick too."

I stare at her, giving her a clear warning.

"Ayesha, if anything happens..."

"Hey, I'm out of magic, alright? I'm not stupid enough to do anything when I have this many Alpha werewolves around and plus? I am actually interested in all this stuff too. Also, you guys fed me and no one actually killed me, so I guess I can behave for a few hours."

"We'll watch her." Selena nods behind her.

I know she and the others actually have enough power to keep Ayesha contained if anything happens... I guess I just feel a bit nervous about leaving her alone with Kelsi, but she won't be. Moreover, Kelsi happens to know a lot about witches. She might even be the first one to notice if anything is wrong, but I hope it won't get there. Ayesha even takes another burrito before sitting on the other side of the table, already grabbing one of the old, dusty books with a grimace.

Selena sighs and leans against the mantel. Meanwhile, Nathaniel and Damian Black keep exchanging glances, but whatever it is they are mind-linking about, they don't want to share. Nora smiles again, and gestures for us to go upstairs.

I am a bit embarrassed that Liam and I are taking a room with all his family here, but he guides me so naturally to the stairs, we leave the room in just a few seconds.

He picks an empty bedroom, probably one of Nora's guestrooms. I didn't realize how big the house is from the outside, but they do have several guest rooms on top of theirs and one for each child... Now that I have a bed right in front of me, I'm just dying to get in there and close my eyes. I take off my pants to be more comfortable, and climb on it, Liam chuckling behind me.

"That's... cheating," he says.

I chuckle.

"Stop being a pervert and come here."

"I'm not a pervert," he protests, climbing on the bed too. "My girlfriend is in panties right in front of me and I'm supposed to lie down and be a good wolf..."

"You can sleep on the floor if you want."

He makes a vexed expression, but he knows I wouldn't make him. He shakes his head, and comes to lie next to me. He takes off his top, but not his bottoms. Hm... afraid to lose control, perhaps? I smile a little and curl up against him. I can't help but cheat a bit, and put my fingers on his pecs, following the lines of his muscles.

"Hey..." he growls a bit.

"Don't move," I protest.

"Oh, you're a sadist..." he grumbles, closing his eyes.

I chuckle, but really, I'm... too tired for that. Maybe when we wake up? This is still his brother's house, though, and with everyone downstairs, I'm not sure I'd dare... I lazily trace circles on his chest, feeling my eyes wanting to close. Liam is already breathing slowly too, not reacting to my movements. He puts an arm around my waist, and I like his heat against mine... The smell of his skin too. We smell like the same soap, but it's still Liam's smell underneath... my mate's smell. My wolf is content, and she lies down like a good girl too.

I have trouble actually giving myself up to that deserved rest though. I really hope Kelsi can find a solution or a clue to help us... I'm glad we made some breakthroughs together, but I have this lingering feeling of fear and angst that won't go away... Is it the curse playing with me, like Ravena said? She did mention it would try to make me mad. I won't go mad. I don't want to be the crazy witch again...

"Mara, sleep."

Liam's slow and deep voice takes me by surprise. How did he know? His eyes are still closed... He sighs slowly, and snuggles up closer to me. He wraps me in his arms, and after another kiss on my forehead, he leaves his face against my hair. I can tell he's taking slow and deep breaths, as if he's content with my smell too.

"No witch stuff, okay?" he whispers. "Just try to sleep."

"Mhm," I nod.

He's right... I won't be able to do anything if I'm exhausted. I've been at this for hours, and it hasn't been that long since I left the hospital, either. I try to calm down, and instead of all those thoughts coming to my mind, I focus on my wolf and his. Is it because this is the less witch part of me? I suddenly feel a lot better, and lean into that, letting the sleepiness take over for real this time...

I fell into a deep slumber. I must have been really tired, because I really fell heavy into that nap. It takes me a while to really wake up, and remember where I am. Oh... Nora's guestroom. I smile automatically upon recognizing Liam's smell next to mine. Unlike the cute position we fell asleep in, he's now rolled onto his belly, his face half-engulfed in the pillow. I smile and watch him sleep for a little while. Moon Goddess, he's so... adorable. He seems younger when he's like this. I realized before how much he's like his older brothers when he frowns, but now, he's just Liam... I really, really want to brush his short hair, but it might wake him up. He only has an arm around my waist now.

How tired was he that he didn't even feel me waking up? I can tell even his wolf is in a very deep slumber. Well, the big wolf had two rough nights because of me, and after eating, he probably deserved that nap... I chuckle. Moon Goddess, thank you for putting him by my side... I really love Liam.

He's kind, gentle, funny, and caring. He's a powerful, imposing werewolf when he needs to be, but he is also incredibly human at times. He reminds me that I am human too. Not just a crazy Fire Witch. He helps me to keep both feet on the ground, and think about... who I am. Who I want to be, the Mara he's known since the beginning. Liam never met Clarissa or little Mara. He didn't have any expectations of me. If anything, he was the only one who didn't judge me because I was a witch, but because I was this mate that suddenly attracted him when he hadn't asked for it. It probably was hard for him, but he didn't reject me... He protected me, and trusted me when I needed him to.

What would I have done, or become, if it wasn't for Liam? Even more reckless, probably. I smile like an idiot, but I'm just... happy. I don't really care what will befall us later. I don't want to think about witches, curses, and fights right now. I need to enjoy the quiet while I can... while we can still have this little bit of happiness. This room is like a little bubble. Once we step out, I'll have to become Silver City's witch again, and Liam will be a Black brother. Now, it's just Liam and Mara. A pair of fated mates like any other... or maybe not.

"Mara?"

I raise my head slowly.

"Nora?"

"I hope I'm not disturbing you... I felt that you were awake, and Liam's still sleeping. I wanted to offer you something... My help, actually."

"With...?"

His Blazing Witch

"The curse that's still inside you. I felt it earlier, when I was healing you. How about... we try to do something about it, but together this time?"
I smile. Now, that sounds like something we can try.

I move very slowly to get out of Liam's embrace, and off of the bed. My man must have been really tired because he doesn't react, and instead, his snoring intensifies. I smile and pinch my lips together so as not to laugh. Moon Goddess, he's way too cute for me to handle. Once I'm up, I stretch slowly. How long did I sleep for? I feel a lot better and rested already...

Grabbing my pants, I sneak out of the bedroom, ready to join Nora. I quickly put my pants back on, hoping no one is going to show up at the end of the hallway. It's actually quite quiet... Where is everyone? I thought it was because we were upstairs, but as I go downstairs, I realize the house is really quiet. I walk past the living room, and Kelsi doesn't even notice me passing by. She is frowning while staring at a book, her glasses sliding down her nose. Curled up on her legs, Ben's big brown wolf is sleeping, and she has an arm around his neck, as he covers most of her legs. They really are a good pair... Across from her, Ayesha is sitting on the floor, legs crossed and also studying a piece of paper. She's the only one to notice my presence and glances up, giving me a little nod. Looks like that's another Fire Witch tamed...

I leave those three to their study, or nap, and keep walking, heading for the kitchen. As suspected, Nora is there, just putting something in the oven.

"Did you sleep well?" she asks with a soft voice.

"Like a baby," I nod.

"Oh, I wish my baby slept that quietly."

"Where are they... I mean, where's everyone?"

Nora chuckles and takes off her apron, undoing her ponytail too.

"Well, Damian is watching the children in the garden, and Selena and Nate went to... reconcile."

I lift an eyebrow.

"I hope I didn't get anyone in trouble..."

"Oh, no," she chuckles. "Don't worry about that. Those two love to fight, I think. It's their way of expressing their feelings better... They both went through a lot, so it's always better when they talk it out. Trust me, they must already be happily reconciled by now."

Oh. Well, I guess, if it works for them...

"How is it going, by the way?" she asks. "Between... you and Liam?"

I blush. Oh, damn, are we on the love topic now? I wasn't ready for that... I nod.

"Y-yeah, I guess we're good. We... pretty much sorted out our feelings recently, so... it's a lot easier for me."

Nora smiles, making me even more embarrassed. Why do I feel like a teenager sharing her love life with her mom or her big sister?

She picks up a couple of mugs, and starts boiling some water, nodding with that satisfied smile on her lips.

"I'm glad he found you, Mara. That you're his mate."

"Don't you think it would have been easier for everyone if... I was just a normal werewolf?"

"I never thought of that," she shrugged. "Liam is someone who needs... motivation. He's always tried to protect everyone, and he's pretty stubborn too. He grew up looking up to Damian and Nate. After what happened, I was worried about him... He kept dissociating himself from us, and I feel like we weren't there enough for him. Those three brothers, they all do that same thing where they don't share when something is bothering them."

She hands me a cup of hot cocoa, and turns to me. We both walk to the little kitchen counter to sit at.

"I guess it's part of how they grew up, but... they have a hard time trusting people and they put others before themselves, all of the time. I was afraid Liam would be alone, or find someone that wouldn't suit him."

"You think I... suit Liam?" I ask, surprised.

Nora chuckles and nods.

"I think you do so perfectly, Mara," she chuckles. "You don't realize how much you've helped him since you arrived. This Liam is the Liam I knew when we were younger. The spunky, curious, will-driven Liam. Moreover, you're not just a girl in need of saving, are you? You're even more stubborn than he is, which is pretty amazing in itself. You constantly challenge Liam, you motivate him without knowing. You went and sought him out when he didn't want to be found. Now, every time I see you two together... I just wish he had met you sooner, Mara."

That's it, I'm officially as red as a tomato... I blush, and hide in my hot drink as if it could help justify the heat. Nora's striking blue eyes look like they can see right through me, and they are just making me more and more shy...

"You're cute together," she chuckles behind her cup.

"Th-thanks..." I mutter, dead embarrassed.

Are we really? I keep seeing those couples of wolves together as if they'd always been, and Liam and I might be a bit of... an odd pair, in the midst of that group. Yet, Nora makes it look so easy.

"...I don't think his brothers like me, though..." I finally mutter.

Nora looks surprised, and she puts her cup down.

"Mara, he's their little brother. You're a witch we knew nothing about until recently... Those two just have their big brother instincts kicking in. Don't worry about it. Nate and Damian are like that to pretty much everyone... Elena too."

"You mean Selena?"

"She was known as Elena for a long time. I still call her that from time to time... Anyways. Don't worry too much about first impressions, Mara. You're family to us all now. You're part of the pack. They might be big grumpy Alphas but I swear to the Moon Goddess, Nate and Damian would never let you fend for yourself. Not with everything you did for their little brother, really. Those two are just... grumpy around the edges."

"Grumpy around the edges?" I chuckle.

"You know what I mean," she says with a little wink.

I nod. The truth is, I can't forget how the two older Black Brothers jumped in against Ayesha, just this morning. Their position was very clear. They weren't just defending Liam, they were between me and her too. I touch the mark on my neck, brushing the scar. It's true. I'm part of their pack now... Maybe I've just been too shy to act on it. Unlike them, this wasn't my world to begin with...

"Alright," she smiles, "I know you were worried about that darkness, that part of the curse still inside you."

I nod and put my cup down, licking the chocolate off of my lips quickly.

"Do you think you can help?"

She smiles.

"I may be nicknamed the Black Luna, but my specialty is more about light..."

Suddenly, her hair begins to... glow. Not just glow, but it turns white slowly, from her roots, going all the way down to the curls on her shoulders and below. I gasp. This is... amazing. It's not just the new hair color, but the way her aura moves with it. It's like a river of light around her, an aura so calm and peaceful, I can barely believe it. It feels so smooth, pretty and cooling, just like snow.

"That's... impressive," I whisper.

"It's a Royal power," she smiles. "I used to only be able to use it from time to time, mostly at night... I've been practicing, and now, I can use it during the day too if I channel my energy. It's a bit hard to explain, but you should be able to understand."

I nod. I'm probably some sort of aura expert, I know most werewolves can't see it like I do. I'm absolutely impressed with Nora's, though. I almost feel like I can touch it, but I wouldn't dare lift a finger. There's definitely something that feels... sacred, or holy, about it. I feel like I'm drinking a cup of hot cocoa with a half-deity right now. I think I finally grasp why all the werewolves react like they do around Nora. It's not just because she's their Luna, or a mother figure. It has nothing to do with her mate either, she's just... like the moon herself. A power so pure and innocent.

"That's amazing," I insist. "This... It's magic, but it's also different. As if you were nothing but... Light Magic, as opposed to the dark one harnessed by the curse. And you can control that?"

"Not fully," she tilts her head. "To be honest, I only began working on it because my baby would cry when he saw my hair white... I think he couldn't recognize me. I dyed it at first, but it made me wonder if I couldn't control it somehow, and once I did, I decided to just keep my hair black all the time. It came just like that, but basically, if I try to control my healing and purifying power, my hair turns white, and I'm much more efficient..."

480

I nod. I finally understand why Nora thought she could help me. With her like this, I don't see how the darkness could be able to control me... But then again, I've never tried. She takes my hand gently, her pale skin making a nice contrast with mine.

"So, do you want to try?" she asks.

"Definitely," I nod.

"I said I'd help, but you're the witch," she says. "I can lend you my power but this curse is still inside you, right? You'll have to do the hardest part."

"Don't worry, I think I know what to do now," I smile confidently.

I hold her hand a bit tighter, and Nora just nods assuredly.

"I'm going to... try and dig it out," I say. "If anything happens, don't react. I'll just hold your hand and try to rely on it. If Liam wakes up, tell him I'm sorry too."

"Roger that. Anything else?"

"No... Please, just don't let go of my hand, alright?"

"I promise," she smiles gently.

Well, now... It's a bit embarrassing, but I lay my head on my other arm, like a student about to take a nap at her desk. It's a bit hard to try to take a nap in Nora's kitchen, with her holding my hand, but this isn't just about me falling asleep this time. I have learned enough to actually know how to dive in my subconscious state...

It's much faster than trying to fall asleep. I find myself jumping and crossing an invisible barrier, like I'm floating. I'm in that strange state again...

This time, I am back in the strange, dark room. However, I feel a pinch of sadness, as little Mara isn't there anymore... It feels so big and empty without her. I feel like it was ages ago since she taught me all about my magic, the runes, and magic circles. So many things happened in such a short time. I wonder when I'll be able to take a break and feel all of this. At least my wolf appears. She slowly comes up to me, staring with her blue and gold eyes. I smile and caress her fur... What's on my hand? There's a strange white glow coming from my left hand... Oh, is that Nora's power? It's... nice. I didn't realize before that this white glow was still following me. It's covering the hand she's probably still holding, giving me that gentle, cool effect. I feel so incredibly calm thanks to it.

I look around. Now... How do I do this? Before, the curse always came to me. Through the voices, through those hallucinations, it always tried to get to me first. Now, this place is just so... quiet. I know the curse isn't gone. It's just biding its time, isn't it? Just like Ravena said. It will stay in the shadows, look for a way to drive me mad, very slowly. I won't let it do that.

"Are you that sure?"

There you are. I turn around, and facing me, the curse took my appearance once again... with a few different details, though. It isn't an exact copy, the curse won't mimic some of my features. On this version of me, my skin is perfect, all the little defects are gone, even the thinnest wrinkles. This Mara's hair is perfectly combed too, not a frizzy mess like usual. The one thing that

481

bothers me most though are the eyes. The eyes are blue, once again. Why always blue? Was the first witch a Water Witch?

"Yeah," I respond. "I decided it was either time you pay rent, or get out of my body."

"*I like it here,*" she chuckles, "*in your head. Your little head, always so full of thoughts. Of doubt...*"

I don't give a damn how small my head actually is, but I hate her preying on my thoughts like that. She smirks, and starts walking in circles around me. She's really trying to mess with my head. She's wearing a very sexy black dress for some reason, heels, and she is confident like a queen. I keep my fist closed, trying to stay calm. I know she's going to try and mess with me again. I've been here before. I have Liam's words with me, Nora's words too. It won't be as easy as the last time.

"*What is it?*" she giggles. "*Mara has decided to get rid of me?*"

"If you already know, time to take the way out," I growl.

My wolf growls in unison with me, but she ignores her.

"*There you go again... Fighting me... Fighting the darkness inside you. Because that's what you're afraid of the most, Mara, aren't you? You're not afraid of me. Of course, you wouldn't be. What really scares you is what you so desperately want to ignore...*"

"Liam loves me," I retort. "Don't you even bother to hint at anything regarding my mate. He knows exactly who I am, and he loves that part of me. Not Sylviana. Not Clarissa. Me, the me who is broken."

She starts laughing hysterically. Alright, I guess that's all my speech does to her... I knew this wouldn't be easy. I look down at my hand. Nora's white glow is still there. I'm still there.

"*Oh, Mara, Mara...*" she sighs. "*You don't even realize. Liam doesn't love the broken you. He loves you because he doesn't know the wreck you are inside.*"

I freeze, and glare at her. The way she's walking in circles around me, like a predator playing with its prey, annoys me. Why is she doing that?

"*You're so broken, Mara, you don't want to know who you are.*"

"I already know plenty."

"*No, you don't. Because you're just ignoring the real answer, the one you had from the start... The witch inside of you, Mara.*"

"Oh, so now I'm not witch enough? That's new..."

She chuckles.

"*Oh, no, Mara, that's not it... You're a witch. You just haven't realized you're a Dark Witch.*"

I feel my blood suddenly go colder.

"Shut up with this nonsense."

"*This isn't nonsense, it's the truth. You were born by feeding on two other lives... You were born with a curse already engraved inside you. Don't you even see? You were born a Dark Witch, Mara. You were born powerful. Yet, you're constantly trying to tame your power, to tone it down. You're so scared Mara,*" *all the time. You're scared your mate will realize how dangerous you are. You're scared you'll hurt someone... Aren't you?"*

I'm about to answer, but something appears. A vision.

It's my fight from earlier, with Ayesha. I see us fighting, as if I were someone else watching. The fireballs exchanged at an incredible speed. I'm... I'm quite amazed by myself. I look so confident, standing there, sending back each blow. And then, this attack... I grimace, witnessing that scene again. My most powerful fire, thrown right into Ayesha's circle. Her smile, just as it enters... and then, unleashed over Silver City. I feel a knot in my throat.

"See what you can do, Mara. You could erase that city off the map anytime if you wanted. You could kill all those witches who roam around your territory... Aren't they so annoying?"

"Enough of this," I growl. "I'm not like you. It's true I'm cursed, it's true I was born out of Dark Magic, but it's no use. You won't possess me."

Then again, she smiles and suddenly stops walking around to come up to me.

"Do you know why you can't chase me?" she chuckles. *"You can't, because I am you. I belong here, just like she does. We are both you."*

I follow her finger, pointing at my wolf. My wolf stares, but she doesn't dare to growl again. The other Mara smiles and, to my surprise, she grabs the wrist of my hand covered with the white glow. She raises it to my eye level, and I feel the glow disappearing, without me able to do anything about it.

"This Light Magic? It won't be of any use to a Dark Witch like you, Mara. She is pure and you're cursed. You will never be able to wield this Light Magic. In the end, your fate is to be consumed by the curse. By me. By us."

"You don't make any sense... I was able to defeat you once already!"

She laughs.

"No, Mara. You merely shut the door. I'll destroy the wall if you do that again. Just watch, Mara. Unless you finally accept who we are, you won't be able to beat me. You're too weak, and you're too scared."

She takes a couple of steps back, going back into the darkness.

"Don't worry, Mara. It isn't so dark once you stop focusing on the light..."

Chapter 32

I slowly open my eyes. There's this strange sensation of heaviness, both in my head and my heart, but I don't fight it. I just take my time to slowly come back to my senses. Nora's cool hand on mine is my guide. Her touch is so soft on my skin, she's even gently rubbing it with her thumb as if to comfort me. I take deep breaths and slowly sit back up.

"Are you alright?" she asks.

"I think so... I didn't manage to beat her, though," I sigh.

"Did you have an actual... fight?"

"Not really," I confess. "More of a... talk."

Not a pleasant one, either, but it still left me pretty... confused. What was that, exactly? I try to explain it to Nora, or at least, to the best I remember. I feel like this short meeting with the curse inside me was like a dream, so fleeting I am already about to forget everything she said. Recounting it to Nora word for word actually helps me to remember even better, and she just nods, listening to my words carefully. She only gets up to refill our mugs with more hot cocoa, and I didn't realize how much I needed it until I felt the warmth between my hands. When I'm finally done explaining everything, I take a breath and taste it, so sweet on my tongue.

"So this is why you snuck away?"

I almost spit out my cocoa, and turn around to see an unhappy Liam standing at the entrance of the kitchen. Uh oh, I forgot I had my back to the door... He's frowning, his arms crossed, and, much to my delight, still half-naked. I exchange a glance with Nora, who looks a little sorry. This is entirely my fault anyway... I should have woken him up. I sigh and turn to him, although I don't get up; I'm afraid I'll feel dizzy.

"Hi..." I mutter, a bit embarrassed. "Sorry, how much did you... hear?"

"Pretty much everything about my girlfriend trying to provoke a witchy curse hidden inside her body with my sister-in-law's help. What were you both thinking?"

"I wasn't at risk," I sigh. "Nora's light... magic kept it at bay, the curse didn't even try approaching me."

"Mara, it doesn't need to; that thing is inside you!" he protests, walking up to me. "Why are you always so reckless?! Without telling me too!"

"I'm sorry I didn't warn you," I sigh. "I don't think I was reckless, though. Liam, I really wasn't at much risk this time, okay? I had Nora and–"

"Mara, I know I'm not grasping everything about the Light and Dark Magic stuff, the curse, and all the witch stuff. I thought I was the expert in Silver City, but since I met you, I'm just dragged behind and just hoping to understand whatever's going on before you get yourself killed. You can't..."

To my surprise, he closes his eyes, and lets out a long sigh. Before I can say a thing, Liam puts one knee down in front of me, leaving me totally speechless. I glance toward Nora, but she's leaning against her kitchen counter and smiling behind her cup. I focus again on Liam.

He takes my hands gently, and his eyes, bluer than usual, hold me hostage.

"Tiger, I know you're damn strong, but... please, please, don't do things without me."

"Liam, I just didn't want to wake you..."

"Mara, I don't care. Wake me up. Kick me if you need, but don't... do things like that again without me. I don't want to wake up and have two minutes of panic wondering where you are. I'm done seeing you in danger, half-dead, or fighting for your life and others, okay? I just–"

He interrupts himself, and glances to the side at his sister-in-law, who's still smiling.

"Nora, can we have five minutes alone, please? I can literally feel you staring at me."

"Sorry," she chuckles, before stepping out.

We both wait until Nora has left the kitchen, a bit embarrassed. I don't know if I should find this funny or cute that he's embarrassed to be heard after what he said... and he isn't even done yet. Liam lets out another long sigh, grabbing my hand again, a bit more relaxed this time.

"Do you have to be on one knee...?" I ask, a bit awkward.

He chuckles and, taking me by surprise, suddenly lifts me off my chair as he gets up. Before I can even protest, I'm put down on the counter this time, and I even almost spill my hot cocoa. Liam chuckles and gives me a quick peck on the lips.

"Alright. Are you listening now?"

"I'm all ears..." I mutter, embarrassed.

Do we really have to be in this position, though? He's leaning forward and dangerously trapping me, my legs on either side of his hips, the wall a few inches behind me. I make myself tiny in front of him, trying to pull away, slightly intimidated by his sudden male Alpha position. ...Does he realize he's half-naked? Because I do, I really do, and his bare torso in front of me does a damn good job of grabbing all of my attention. I need to remember to breathe. He's dangerous when he makes his big bad wolf gaze like that...

"You don't leave me alone," he says.

"Okay..."

Is it me or did his voice get a bit deeper? We are so close, I don't even get to shy away from his striking blue-gray eyes. We're just a breath away too, and I really want to kiss him, but doing so while he's scolding me might not be the best idea...

"Mara, you better stop being such a reckless witch, because I'm going to get really mad at some point. I'm serious."

Just as he says he's serious, I smile nervously. I think I like serious Liam... He frowns and I have to pinch my lips together, but it doesn't really help.

"You think I'm funny?"

"N-no..." I try hard not to laugh.

I take a deep breath and put a quick kiss on his lips.

"...But I think you're really cute when you're mad at me," I confess.

He growls.

"That is not the effect I was looking for. Can't you take your boyfriend seriously?"

"You're the one underestimating me, and provoking me too," I retort, my eyes going down to the pairs of abs lined up right in front of me.

Liam grabs my chin between his fingers, making me raise my head.

"Look here," he says. "Mara, I am really, really serious. I was really worried just a couple of minutes ago. Don't you disappear on me again, please."

"Sorry... I didn't disappear, though, I was just downstairs..."

"Downstairs doing dangerous witch stuff. What does it take for you to understand I worry about you? My girlfriend is a walking bomb, she loves to get herself in trouble and with nobody to help. You need to have me tag along, Mara. I am your mate. I may not be a witch, but I am your mate. Don't leave me on the sidelines. Please."

I let out a long sigh. I know where he's coming from, and... I just can't blame him. He has watched me go through hell and back, all in just a matter of days. I can understand he doesn't trust me, in many ways... I put my arms around his neck, only too happy to caress his skin. Damn, he's sexy with his post-nap hairstyle... I just want to brush it forever, but for now, we're having a serious talk.

"Alright, I'm sorry," I whisper. "I know I should have... probably woken you up."

"Not probably," he growls. "You should have. That's it. Mara, I'm never going through that shit I went through again. If I have to put my witch on a leash, I will."

I smile and tilt my head.

"We might just try that sometime," I whisper into his ear.

Liam raises both eyebrows, and I swear I almost saw his wolf ears perking up.

"That might be–Hey, are you trying to change the subject right now?"

I shake my head, and give him another quick kiss to have him drop that frown.

"No, we're right on topic. I get it, Liam, I promise. No more leaving you. Or at least, not without telling you where I'm going and so on. ...But once again, for the record, I was literally just downstairs."

"Downstairs doing witch stuff with Nora. What was that, by the way?"

Although the conversation took a more serious tone, he wraps his arms around my waist, not letting me go at all. Not that I mind, but we are still in someone else's kitchen... Oh, well. I guess Nora must be used to half-naked brother-in-laws. Lucky her...

"I thought that with Nora's help, we... I could get rid of the curse inside me, for good. Nora's power is basically nothing but pure Light Magic. She was trying to help me clean the curse out of my body, to make it short."

"So... it didn't work, from what I understood?"

I grimace a bit.

"Not really... I don't feel like... I lost, though. It's a strange sensation, but I think the curse wasn't as... aggressive as before."

"You mean it didn't try to completely take you over?" says Liam, raising an eyebrow. "I hope we're never doing the body swap thing ever again, because that was really disturbing."

"No," I chuckle. "I think we're good on that one. No, I just think... The curse was actually trying to tell me something."

"I heard the part where it said you were a Dark Witch. Are you going to tell me that isn't complete bullshit?"

I grimace, hesitating a bit.

...Is it, though? In some ways, the curse wasn't completely wrong... Moreover, it's a very ancient being, it probably knows loads more about Light and Dark Magic than I do. I just feel like it was trying to teach me something. I've been seeing all of this as a... a bit of a black or white situation, so far. Light Magic against Dark Magic. Good witches against evil ones. Is it really that simple, though...? I keep trying to think about it, but something was off today. Really off, in the curse's attitude. I just can't pinpoint why. It wasn't as aggressive as before, and I thought it might have been because of Nora's doing, but... No, I feel like something really changed. Did I trigger something? Or is it because little Mara is gone?

Liam kisses my forehead, reminding me where I am and with whom.

"Sorry," I mutter. "I was thinking..."

"I could tell. You ignored me and my abs for almost a full minute straight. I'm vexed."

I chuckle and, just to play, I lean forward to kiss him, while running my fingers down those abs... Liam shivers and grabs my wrist.

"Oh, no, no, no, you bad witch... Hands off that area, please."

Bad witch.

...Am I really a Dark Witch? Is it about my magic or my body? Or my actions? I can't begin to understand what that curse was trying to say, but I feel like there's something very important about it. Why has it changed so much since the last time?

"...And there she goes again," sighs Liam.

"Sorry," I sigh, kissing him quickly again as an apology. "That curse just gave me a lot of... food for thought."

"Anything I can help with?"

I hesitate... Well, we do need more honesty, so...

"Liam, do you think I could be a Dark Witch?"

To my surprise, after raising an eyebrow, he clearly hesitates. I see him making little movements with his lips, seriously pondering over the subject. I wait. I know he wouldn't lie just to comfort me, and seeing his reaction, I'm even more curious now...

"To be honest, I'm... not really sure what you are. I always thought you had a totally different vibe from the other witches I've met. I thought it was because we were mates, or because you are half-werewolf... You're kind of a lot of different things, so it's hard to compare with anything I've known, but..."

"But?"

"I don't know," he shrugs. "Mara, you're really... different. You might be the first witch she-wolf in a while too, and you had kind of... an unusual story."

That's for sure. I was basically born from... a curse myself, wasn't I? Clarissa and little Mara converted the energy of their dark curse to create me. At first, I wanted to tell myself they had used Light Magic and created something good out of something bad, but... isn't that too simple? Or just my wishful thinking?

There is no... right or wrong in magic circles. The curse is undoubtedly dark because it is nothing but a bundle of dark feelings, that's a fact. However, what about everything else? Witches aren't born evil, they turn to the darkness because of resentment, anger, envy. They do bad things and use magic in a wrong way, using it to torment others, but... would it make sense that magic itself was evil?

"Mara, Sylviana had mentioned that... Dark Witches use other people's energy to feed their magic. Good witches use their own, and that's how they get the dark markings. They use their own life force, and they sacrifice their lives for it..."

"...I haven't been getting dark markings," I whisper.

"What?"

"During my fight with Ayesha. I mean... since little Mara is gone, there has been no trace of those dark markings, that would say I use my own energy."

Liam gasps, realizing what I'm saying.

Shit, I didn't even realize. I had become so powerful all of a sudden, I didn't even notice I wasn't getting marked by my use of magic anymore. I felt powerful, and tired when I used too much, but something in my body definitely changed. How? What did I do, what happened? More importantly, where have I been getting all that energy I have...?

"Mara!"

We both turn our heads and Kelsi runs in, but she makes a brutal stop once she witnesses our position, and Liam's naked torso. She becomes red and turns around, just as Ben, still in his wolf form, walks in too.

"S-sorry!"

"You're good, Kelsi," I chuckle.

"If you're going to date a werewolf, you might want to get used to that," laughs Liam.

I punch his torso, making him groan.

"Don't tell my best friend to get used to you being naked!"

"What, it's the truth! We're all always half-naked, it's easier to shape-shift... Ben too..."

I keep glaring at Liam, but turn to Kelsi, as she can't hear our exchange.

"Did you find something?" I ask.

"Y-yeah! I mean, I might have found something... I'm not a hundred percent sure, but it's a solid theory..."

"That's my girl," I smile.

I turn back to Liam, and push him away from me to get off the counter. He steps back, but still sends playful glances my way. We will settle this later...

"Go get a T-shirt," I whisper to him, before walking off.

I hear him chuckle, but he goes back upstairs while I walk up to Kelsi. She's holding a huge book again, full with little sticky notes she probably put everywhere. When we walk inside the living room, Nora's there with Ayesha, still in the position we left her. They are looking over the impressive stacks of papers and notes that cover the coffee table, which is saying a lot considering that table takes up the entire area in front of the large couch.

"You've been busy... How long did I sleep?" I chuckle, grabbing one of the papers.

She really did go through everything. Judging by how Ben yawns and stretches, I'd say there wasn't much surveillance needed for Ayesha either. I glance at the other Fire Witch. I can't tell if she has any markings, her body is actually mostly covered by her clothes... Now that I think about it, is that why all the witches we've met were so covered? I'm always kind of hot so I got into the habit of wearing rather short clothes, but Ravena's dress was covering a lot of her body, same with the Water Witch and now Ayesha too.

"What?" she asks, noticing I've been staring for a while.

"...Where are your markings?" I ask.

She grins.

"Show me yours and I'll show you mine..."

I make a sullen expression. I don't have any to show, that's my issue... I decide to ignore her and turn to Kelsi instead.

"So?"

"I think I found where the curse is. Or at least, places it could be."

"...How so?"

Kelsi smiles.

489

"Actually, I think it was... simpler to think the other way around. The curse is where no one else is."

"What?" asks Liam, walking in, T-shirt on.

"Well, it's a bit far-fetched, but I think the curse is where... there are no werewolves."

"This is Silver City," I say. "There are wolves everywhere. Every place is werewolf territory!"

"Well, I thought—"

"No, Kelsi might be onto something," says Nora. "There is one place in Silver City that is not a part of any territory."

"Really?"

"Oh yes," she smiles, crossing her arms. "A place that sure brings back some memories..."

"East Point Ground?"

We turn around as Selena just walked in. She's wearing a new set of clothes, an off-the-shoulder white top that shows off her tan and denim shorts. I can't help but remember what Nora mentioned. Yep, they went to reconcile...

Nora smiles and nods.

"It makes sense, doesn't it? The stadium is still being rebuilt, and it used to be on the Blood Moon territory before Damian let it be for everyone. Historically, the only place I can think of that always remained completely neutral was East Point Ground."

"True..." mutters Selena.

"Why did it remain neutral?" I ask, surprised. "I thought all areas of Silver City were divided between the different werewolves packs..."

"I'm not really sure," says Nora, tilting her head. "It's a bit of an... odd place. It was always used as some crossroad between territories too, so I guess no one ever really thought of claiming it. It's a rather large area, though. Because it remained neutral for all the werewolves, we use it for duels, mostly. The humans don't go there because it's a fighting spot too..."

"This is still just a theory, though," says Liam.

Kelsi makes an apologetic expression, putting her book down on the table.

"Sorry, that's really the only one I could think of, and I did try to come up with the best ones I could. In any case, I think a witch would have eventually... found something if they were always with a wolf pack. Nephera spent her childhood with the Sapphire Moon Pack. Sylviana was with the Purple Moon Pack. At first, I thought that since both the witch and the female werewolf from this story are obviously related to those packs, it could be somewhere on their territories, but then, Sylviana or Nephera would have eventually found it, right? Moreover, if we take Nora and Selena's history into account too, it's almost all of Silver City that would have been covered!"

"...I don't follow," frowns Liam.

"With the abilities we have now, Nora or myself should have been able to detect something," Selena explains.

He nods.

I am a bit unsure with that theory as well, but I have never been to East Point Ground, so it's hard to say. The only place I ever felt a big amount of magic was Sylviana's tree and the hangar where Clarissa had made that magic circle. Other than being filled with werewolves, Silver City was a rather... normal city to me so far.

"Plan B would be to search the old fashioned way," shrugs Kelsi. "I haven't found anything else that could help find the curse's original location in all those books, boo, sorry..."

I smile. How can she look so sorry when she's done so much? I walk over to her and put an arm around her shoulders.

"Kelsi, you're a witch genius. Don't worry, it's not like we have to find it this minute, either..."

"Easy to say," retorts Ayesha. "You don't know when that old wench Ravena will find it..."

"Well, judging by all of her stuff we got, she might be at the same point as we are," I retort. "What else could she do now? Her lackey fled and there are now two Fire Witches in Silver City."

"Wait a second. Since when were we on the same team?" frowns Ayesha, crossing her arms.

I glare at her.

"We'd better be on the same team," I retort. "Otherwise, you're trespassing, and I'll happily kick you out."

Selena starts growling to support me and Liam too, glaring at the Fire Witch. Clearly outnumbered, Ayesha uncrosses her arms with a sour expression.

"Fine, fine, I get it... It's not like I have much of a choice, anyway."

"Right. So you might as well help us," I say. "Anything you want to tell us that could help?"

She rolls her eyes.

"I'm not a bookworm like you guys. I see danger, I throw fire. I'm a very blunt kind of witch, for the record. Honestly, I shouldn't even be here after witnessing the kind of crazy you are. I've never seen a witch like you, and that's not a compliment!"

I shrug. Indeed, there's no one like me, but I can live with that. I'm born from a curse, haunted by another one, half-werewolf, the reincarnated cousin to a pair of girls with Royal blood, mated to an Alpha male, and with half a soul keeping me alive. Oh, and a magic cat. Can't forget my poor Spark...

I sigh, and actually walk up to the couch to grab the bundle of gold and black fur. I still can't believe how relaxed he is in a house full of werewolves...

"What about Ravena's spell, then?" I say. "Did you find anything about those tattoos?"

"Nothing more than we already did. I already alerted the people at the university so those who can get rid of it will, but... not everyone has come forward, I think."

Damn it, and we don't know when Ravena will actually strike... I nervously bite my thumb, upset. Is there really nothing we can do?

"Alright," says Nora, suddenly clapping her hands together, "I'm going to start making dinner, everyone should be here soon."

"Dinner already?" Kelsi whispers to me with a frown.

"Werewolf stomachs," I chuckle.

I have to admit, I'm hungry myself... again. Damn, do we really burn that many calories? Is it because I used magic to visit the curse earlier? I actually don't know what time it is, I didn't check when I woke up... Moreover, Nora probably has to prepare for a lot of people.

"Ben, Liam, can you get some wood for the firepit? We should have a barbecue," says Nora, happily. "Mara, Kelsi, you two can help me in the kitchen."

"It's not that I don't want to help," says Kelsi, "but I thought I could do more research..."

"You've already spent the whole afternoon reading all that stuff," protests Selena, taking her book out of her hands. "You and Mara need to learn to take a break from all that stuff. We can go visit East Point Ground after dinner to see if we find anything, but for now? You both stop it."

Just like that, Kelsi and I are not given any choice, and pushed into the kitchen to help. Is that really alright? Just like Kelsi, I feel guilty for not looking more into this curse, especially after I already napped this afternoon! Yet, Nora doesn't listen to anything we say, and before we can find something else to protest with, Kelsi and I are suddenly peeling potatoes and helping Nora prepare several dishes.

Meanwhile, Selena and Ayesha are apparently tidying the living room, piling up all the papers and books Kelsi was working on. I can see Liam and Ben outside, more playing than actually getting the wood ready. I suddenly realize, Liam has been putting up with all my crazy for several days too. He probably deserves this break even more than me... even Ben is still healing from that stab wound. I'm glad Nora was able to help him, but still. He got involved because of me. Kelsi too. Now, she's silently trying to figure out how to cut the vegetables without losing a finger, but would she have become so knowledgeable about witchcraft if it wasn't for me?

A strange wave of gratefulness pours into my heart. Damn, I'm really... not alone.

Despite the situation, I feel very calm and happy, all of a sudden. No, not happy, just... content. This is the kind of thing I could see happen over and over again. Having dinner at Nora's house, with the family and friends. Kelsi and I, being ridiculously bad at helping her out but laughing about it. The boys outside, showing off their strength and bickering. Nora's gentle humming.

Suddenly, a huge ruckus comes from the entrance of the house. Nora smiles.

"Here they come..."

"Mama!"

A little boy just ran in to grab the bottom of her skirt.

"Hi, my baby," she smiles.

She takes off her oven mitts and apron to lift her son up and hug him. Damian Black walks in right after, barely glancing at us before going to kiss his wife. Kelsi and I, intimidated by his silver irises, look down automatically and do our best to make those squares very, very even...

With the children back inside the house, it's a lot livelier all of a sudden. I don't think I'm much of a kid person, but Selena's daughter, Estelle, is incredibly polite and easy to be with. She's rather mature for a girl who is... what, about seven or eight years old? I'm not sure, all the werewolf kids look rather big to me. She helps Kelsi and I cook, and James too is happy to sneak around to get whatever he can... Now I know where he gets those plump cheeks from! There's a lot of noise in the living room, probably more people, but Kelsi and I stay in the kitchen to help out, neither of us too confident in mixing with the werewolves. Moreover, from the way Ayesha went outside to take care of the fire pit while everyone came inside, I feel like this is sort of a daily werewolves meeting thing. I hear Damian, Nora, Nathaniel, and Selena talk a lot. They might be updating everyone who missed anything on our current situation...

I let out a long sigh, realizing how my situation has become everyone's...

"What are you sighing for?"

I get a delicious chill from the two arms surrounding me from behind. I smile and turn around, putting a quick peck on his lips.

"Why aren't you with them?"

"Adult stuff," he pouts. "I got kicked out."

Hm, more like he didn't want to handle it... Still, I'm happy he came to us. Ben comes into the kitchen too and walks up to Kelsi, much to the pleasure of the children, who run to play with the big wolf.

"That guy is going to be even bigger than Boyan if he keeps going like this," frowns Liam.

I smile, but I think he's still not that big, though. I can't forget the sight of the enormous werewolf I saw. That guy definitely has werebear blood, I don't understand how he can be that huge... Then again, I have yet to see him in human form, though I'm definitely curious.

"Damn, I could get used to you cooking," chuckles Liam.

"That's easy to say when everything's already almost done!"

"We are both no good compared to Nora," pouts Kelsi across the kitchen counter. "I really want to steal her recipe book. I barely have enough skills to make us breakfast..."

Liam and I chuckle, but Kelsi's baking skills are plenty enough for us. Liam and I are useless in the kitchen... although I feel I could definitely learn from his sister-in-law.

"Mara?"

I turn my head, and to my surprise, Nathaniel Black is standing in the doorway, looking as serious as ever.

"Daddy!"

His blue eyes suddenly soften when his daughter runs to him. She really is his copy... They have the same striking blue eyes, and even her blonde hair is closer to her father's shade. They chat for a couple of minutes, but apparently, they already saw each other today, so Estelle quickly comes back to finish her mix with the flour. I hesitate, and Liam tightens his arms around me too.

"Can I speak to Mara... alone?" Nathaniel insists.

Liam and I exchange a glance, but he reluctantly lets me go to his brother.

"If he's rude, you can burn his eyebrows!"

I chuckle, but I'm still very nervous. Without saying anything else, Nathaniel walks out to the garden, toward the firepit. Ayesha seems to be simply meditating and to my surprise, she's got a sort of big dark lizard with large scales and a strange head on her shoulder... Her familiar?

Nathaniel briefly growls as a warning, probably not happy with yet another witch invited... however, he ignores her, and we walk even further past the firepit. I suddenly realize, he doesn't want the others to hear what he's about to say. I glance over my shoulder, and indeed, Liam is at the kitchen's window, staring our way.

"Tell me if he says something nasty."

"No eavesdropping, hot stuff."

With that, I cut off our mind-link. I hope I'm not going to regret being alone with his older brother... If Damian Black is a hurricane, Nathaniel is like a snowstorm. That guy has the aura of a cold-blooded murderer. I don't know if it's my werewolf instinct or my witch senses speaking, but I'm not fond of being alone with him. Are Nora and Selena immune to his aura or something? I can almost see it, the black cloud around him... I blink several times to ignore it, and he turns to me once we're far enough.

He takes a deep breath, and to my surprise, simply puts his hand in his pants' pocket, looking relaxed.

"I think our last meeting wasn't the best," he simply says.

"Uh... yeah, I guess."

When he found me in his brother's apartment acting all lovey-dovey? Yeah, not the best memory I have either...

He lets out a long sigh, and nods.

"I won't apologize for that. I have always done my best to protect my brothers, especially Liam. He tends to be reckless, and with our history, I didn't think him seeing a witch was the best thing either."

Yep, I definitely got the message about that...

"The truth is, Liam was hurting a lot after what happened during the war; Damian and I had... a lot of other things to focus on, and we felt sorry neither of us could really help. Even Nora tried her best, but Liam ignored us for a while. He was at a low point, and none of us were able to help him. He became almost like a rogue."

I nod. I'm not sure where he's going with this, but I'm kind of glad it isn't the he's-too-good-for-you kind of talk... It's not, right?

"Anyway... When you came along, I was rather surprised he was finally learning to be more... open toward others. I didn't think he'd accept another witch into his life so easily."

I cough a bit, unable to hold it in. So easily? I have memories of me running after some stubborn guy in the rain that doesn't match Nathaniel's words. He makes it sound like Liam literally fell for me on day one. Not that I would have hated it, but there's more to our story than that...

"Then again, I suppose I can be quite... stubborn, in my own right. I also tend to rely on my wife's opinions a lot, and as you know, Selena wasn't fond of you, either, at the beginning."

"Truthfully, she was right not to be," I sigh. "Selena was able to tell a part of me was... still containing some darkness."

Nathaniel nods, but without looking my way. Actually, I realize he's probably keeping an eye on Ayesha, somewhere behind me. Ever the watchdog, I guess... He takes a deep breath.

"Anyway. Time has passed, and... I have to admit, you've proven yourself to be more than what we thought you to be. I acted rude too, that time at Liam's apartment. Not only to you, but I didn't trust my brother with his... choice, either. I am probably the worst in this family, in terms of being able to judge people."

"It's... alright," I nod. "I wouldn't have trusted myself either. Moreover, I... I am happy that Liam has older brothers like you to count on. ...In case he meets the wrong witch."

Nathaniel smirks.

"Indeed. Anyway, this is my... apology, for before. From both me and Damian, actually. Don't expect this kind of talk from our older brother, though, so I'm just saying this for the both of us."

"Oh... uh, thanks... I mean, cool."

Great, Mara. Awesome. Speech of the year to the stiffest guy you know handing you an apology we wouldn't even have dreamed of. Let's just be glad no one else is listening...

Nathaniel suddenly lifts his hand, and taps his eye.

"Thank you for healing him too. Liam quickly explained to us what you had done for him. It was something that was weighing on our minds for a while, and normal medicine couldn't do anything for him no matter what we tried. I think this injury was what made him somehow... darker too. So, thank you."

"You're welcome," I mutter. "It was... a remnant of Dark Magic, so.... if it makes you feel any better, there really was nothing human medicine could have done."

He nods, and as his hand goes down, I can't help but stare at... his missing one. I bite my lower lip.

"I... I wish I could do something for you too," I mutter.

He glances briefly that way, but shrugs.

"It's not important. I already knew it was too late after the battle when we couldn't recover my arm. I spent a long time convincing Selena it was okay, and I really am. I've learned to live with this. But... thank you for mentioning it."

I nod, a bit embarrassed. I guess that's... it, right?

"Nate!"

We turn and Selena is walking up to us, while Liam is standing a few steps away in the garden. She smiles as she approaches Nathaniel.

"Liam asked me to save his girlfriend from you... What are you guys doing?"

Nathaniel and I exchange a glance, but as neither of us comes up with an answer, she laughs.

"Don't tell me, he gave you the brother-in-law speech?"

I blush, while Nathaniel rolls his eyes.

"I'm going to go back," I mutter. "Thanks for the pep talk!"

I turn around and walk away, as fast as I can without running.

Why the hell did I say that...? We were almost done, Liam, you idiot!

Chapter 33

"You're really not going to tell me?" he insists.

"No!" I chuckle, amused by his pout.

Liam's been asking all evening now, but I won't tell him what his brother and I discussed. I feel like this should stay between me and Nathaniel Black. There's nothing really secret, but... I just don't feel like Liam ought to know either. I smile at his grumpy expression and put a quick kiss on his cheek, snuggling a bit more in his arms.

It's been a quiet evening, despite the dozens of wolves present in Nora's garden. Kelsi and I clearly underestimated how much food needed to be prepared to feed a group of werewolves... I feel like I peeled enough vegetables for a lifetime. Still, I'm happy we contributed a bit to the large meal in front of us. Because a lot of them are still in their wolf form, the dinner was served like a buffet on a large table, everyone coming and going to grab whatever they pleased. It's cute seeing the kids happy to hand large slices of meat to big hungry wolves... and a bit odd too when they start fighting for them.

Liam and I took a seat a bit away from the group, to be just the two of us for a little while. I love being part of a pack, but I think he and I are still more like a pair of loners... He sighs and gently rubs his nose against my neck, making me shiver a little. I'm shamelessly sitting on his lap, my hands around his neck as we've been cuddling since we finished eating. The firepit has all the wolves, humans, and couples gathered around, but we are almost the farthest away, watching the nice scene from afar. Kelsi went for a walk hand in hand with Ben a while ago, and I'm happy those two are spending some more time together without any witchcraft books.

I'm keeping an eye on Ayesha, but she's been silently eating against a tree for a while, staying away from all the wolves. I get a witch probably wouldn't be comfortable in the midst of all this... Selena was chatting with her earlier, though, and I don't think she's that uncomfortable. Maybe just a bit uneasy, given the situation. It's a strangely quiet night, despite our current situation. Once again, I have a feeling that this is the calm before the storm...

"We should make plans," suddenly says Liam.

"...Like a battle plan?"

"No, plans as a couple. Stuff we want to do after all this crap is over..."

I smile.

"Hm... Mr. Liam Black, I really like this romantic side of yours. What do you have in mind?"

"I don't know. The usual stuff? Maybe a few dates would be good, for starters."

"I want to go back to eat that cheeseburger," I immediately state.

He chuckles, and puts a quick kiss on my cheek.

"Okay. I want to go back there with you for a real date this time too. What else?"

"More bike rides. Time for just the two of us..."

I lean in and gently kiss him. His beard is growing out a little, just a few spikes on his chin, but it's nice to brush it with my fingers, just this once. Liam answers my kiss without hesitation, and I feel his lips turn into a smile. His hands get a little bit more adventurous on my body too. I feel his fingers under my tank top, caressing my waist. His other hand is on my butt, and I wonder why I don't wear skirts more often so we could get a bit naughty like this...

I have more ground to play with; I caress his back, my fingers brushing down his spine and up to his hairline. I like his broad shoulders I can lean on, and the smell of his skin. Funny enough, he's the one to smell a bit like bark and firewood this time, and I don't hate it. Underneath this, it's still his smell, my Liam and my mate. Something reassuring, something that completes my senses. There's also a hint of salt in our kisses, and something sweet and sour. It makes me a little bit hungry again, but I'd rather have some more of him. Liam must have tasted it too, because he gets even more playful, biting my lower lip, groaning a little as we get a bit more savage.

"You do know there are kids around, right?"

We both stop, a bit guilty, and raise our heads to see Selena, staring at us with a little smile. Liam rolls his eyes.

"Not you, please. With all the times you and Nate asked me to watch the girls so you could get some time off..."

"Hey, there's a time and place for that," she chuckles, "and you two don't even have kids."

Liam and I exchange a look. Hm... We may have been a bit too naughty, indeed. I chuckle, and he sighs, brushing his hair back.

"Fine, we'll... watch it."

As he says that, he still wraps his arms a bit tighter around me like some grumpy kid, making me chuckle. I turn to Selena, though. I don't think she came here just to make sure we stayed kid-friendly...

"Everything okay?" I ask.

She sighs, and comes over to watch the firepit and the others with us, although she crosses her arms.

"I don't know. You know, I always thought of myself as a warrior. I'm definitely a fighter, maybe one of the best in Silver City, those guys included. But... You know, Mara, we already had a war two years ago. Although we survived and defeated the enemy... I mean, Nephera and then all those vampires, it didn't feel like we won it either. We lost a lot of people, Mara. Both humans and werewolves. Sylviana too... I lost one of my best friends. I almost lost Nate. I'm not sure I can say I'm over it yet, and now, we may have more of that shit coming at us. I just don't know how I feel about it, honestly."

I get where she's coming from... Maybe it's easier for me because I wasn't here for their previous fight. To me, it feels like something I'd read in a book, but for them, it was very real, and they still bear the scars today. Not only the physical ones, but emotional ones too. I just need to look long enough to notice it. The way all the wolves move, as if they were constantly establishing some perimeter. The glances Ayesha gets at every move, as do I. How Damian Black keeps his wife and children close. How all the wolves are actually watching the kids. There's never one out of sight, or too far they couldn't reach them. If one of the pups wanders off, another wolf gets up and brings them back to the rest of them. They look out for each other, but not simply in a familial way.

I think I finally get why Nora's house is always so full of people. It isn't just because it's the Alpha and Luna's house. The wolves need to feel their family is there, the pack needs to stick together. Silver City is such a large place, yet they are all moving around together, no one is ever really left alone.

"...I know this isn't my area of expertise. I think your human friend might be even more prepared than we are, but... I don't know how many of us can endure another fight, Mara. If there is one, I'm not sure how much the Alphas will be able to guide them either."

I take a deep breath.

"...I'm not an Alpha."

She turns to me with a frown, looking confused. I chuckle, still staring at the bonfire.

"It's funny. I spent so much time trying to figure out who I was... No, what I was. And now that I know, and I've come to terms with it, I realize... well, it just might not really matter anymore."

I smile, a sudden boost of confidence taking over, and brush Liam's hair gently with my fingers again.

"I'm an Omega, Selena," I declare with a smile. "I know I also have the aura of an Alpha wolf, but... truthfully, I'll never fully belong to the pack, no matter how much you welcome me. That's a fact, and that's... that's completely fine with me. I don't really need that. I'm fine with whatever I have now. I'm okay with being a freak, and I am okay with not picking a side. I'm a witch and a werewolf. I am Liam's mate."

"For sure," he smiles with a quick kiss on my shoulder.

I smile back at him, but quickly turn to Selena. Her amber eyes are more serious than ever, but now, they just feel so familiar to me. I can see the bonfire dancing in them, and I imagine she sees the same thing I do...

"The packs need someone like you and Nora to guide them, most of the time. You're the Lunas, you're the Royals. You're the perfect leaders for your people. But me? I'm... not really anything like you guys. I'm the freak who will handle the witches and the Dark Magic. I don't want... I don't want to be someone's Alpha. However, I'll come forward and lead anytime you need me.

I'll protect this place, these people, whatever it takes. I swear, I'll be there, but I'll be free too. I just have... so much more to find, Selena, and I don't think... not all of it is in Silver City."

They both stay silent, probably a bit surprised by my words, but I've never been so sure of anything. This is all coming to me now, so clear and bright like the future. I've tried so much to find a reason to be, a role to fill, and I never came to realize... I could be whatever I wanted in the first place. Clarissa and little Mara left me this gift. If I'm a funny mix between two worlds, why shouldn't I simply be the best of the two?

After what seems like a while, Selena chuckles and pushes her blonde hair back with a long sigh.

"Oh, Moon Goddess... You're one surprising gal, Mara."

"Thanks," I smile.

She stares at the firepit for a while, but I know this isn't really what her eyes are saying. There's a veil of nostalgia in her eyes, I can tell. She chuckles.

"...You remind me of someone," she says. "An annoying old hag... and my mentor. I didn't want to admit it at first, but... you're an awful lot like her. Stubborn, unapologetic, and at times, a huge pain in the ass."

"Okay...?"

She takes a deep breath.

"...But that someone was probably the woman I admired the most," she finally confesses. "She was an Omega wolf too, simply by choice. She had the heart of a Beta, the strength of an Alpha, but she was still an Omega. For a long time, I wondered why she hadn't... settled for a pack. Why she simply didn't pick one, or come to the same one as me, instead of always going back and forth. I even resented her for not staying."

"...Did you ever get to know why?"

She laughs and turns to me.

"I think I finally understand now, because of one stubborn Fire Witch."

Liam and I exchange a glance, a little bit confused. Selena shakes her head with a smile.

"...I think you can't settle your heart in a pack. You just leave it with someone."

I smile.

Yeah, I really like the sound of that, and it does feel like... me. Liam sighs and rests his chin on my shoulder while I'm left with my thoughts to ponder Selena's words and mine. I think she's right on point. It's not about Silver City itself. It's not about a city, its buildings, or where it is. It's about the people I met here. The ones I come back to. I think Liam, Kelsi, Ben, Nora, Selena, everyone... They were the ones that made Silver City my home. I find myself smiling uncontrollably, but for once, I know exactly where I need my heart to be. I know exactly what I want, who I am.

Still...there's something that bothers me, just a little. It feels so easy, almost too easy. I don't have the responsibility of a pack. Truthfully, being an Omega means I won't take any responsibility as a wolf... I'll just be a werewolf among many. I'm fine with staying on the sidelines until they need me. Until they need the witch me. It bothers me a little...

"...Don't you think it's a bit selfish of me?" I ask Selena.

She chuckles and shrugs. Her amber eyes are following a young white wolf who's playing with her younger cousins and her dad.

"We're all selfish, Mara. Humans and werewolves alike. You can't be selfless all the time, happiness does come with selfishness, at times. I know a lot about it, to be honest. I've made some choices that were selfish of me, but at that time, if I had chosen any other way, I would have imploded. There are times where you have to do what you want, and put yourself first. Don't feel sorry about that. You're super young too. Technically, you're even younger than any of us. How could we chain you to Silver City when you've literally known nothing else? Nora and I are fine with our current roles, we're happy as Lunas. But you? Like you said, you've got the heart of a rogue wolf. You don't keep a wolf on a leash, girl."

I smile, happy that she understands my thought process. I turn to Liam, a bit worried, but he just smiles, brushing his lips against my skin.

"Don't look at me like that," he says. "Wherever you go, I'll go. No leash for me, either."

"As if we were ever able to put a leash on you," Selena laughs. "You're the most rogue of all of us! What a pair, you two... I think we will just have to sit back and see what kind of mess you'll bring home next..."

"Hey, we're not that bad of troublemakers!" protests Liam.

"Oh, really? How many buildings have gone up in flames since you two got together, again?"

Liam gasps.

"Hey, you know that's not true! That was Mara all by herself..."

"Thanks for the support," I growl.

"Sorry, babe, but you're real trouble. Always happy to help, though..."

"Yeah," chuckles Selena. "At least, Mara is–"

She suddenly interrupts herself, and from the way she's frowning, I get a bad feeling. What's going on? She turns around, and stares somewhere behind us, looking concerned. I get off Liam's lap and on my feet too. It can't be one of the witches, I would have felt it...

"Mara, something's happening to your friend," she mutters.

What...? Holy Moon Goddess, Kelsi!

I start running in the direction she and Ben walked off to, the same direction Selena was staring at. I hear Selena and Liam running behind me, but the fear of something happening to my best friend is making me faster than ever. Fuck, not Kelsi!

I spot them just a couple of minutes later on the sidewalk, and something's definitely wrong. Kelsi is bent over in a weird position, with a panicked Ben next to her, and she's... puking on the grass. What the hell? I accelerate to get to her side, and from Ben's expression when he spots me, this isn't just food poisoning.

501

"Mara! I don't know what's going on, she felt sick all of a sudden, and she began... puking..."

She isn't just puking; there's a weird dark liquid coming out of her mouth, and I'm pretty sure I haven't seen Kelsi drink anything but some beer tonight. What the hell?! Ben is holding her hair back, and Kelsi is trying to calm down, but she shakes her head.

"I'm... okay..."

"Shut up, boo, you're not okay at all," I growl. "Ben, help her sit down."

He nods and immediately obeys, helping her sit down on the grass before Kelsi pukes again in an impressive waterfall of a thick liquid. I realize whatever's coming out is not just black; there's a lot of worrying dark red too.

"Someone call Ayesha," I yell over my shoulder. "Ben, did anything else happen?"

"I swear, nothing," he says. "We were talking about one of our movies, and all of a sudden, she went super white, and she said she was going to vomit..."

Just as he says that word, Kelsi makes a sour expression, and I have to step aside as she pukes some more... Damn, how much came out already? There's literally a pond of it right next to us! If this goes on, Kelsi won't–

I light my fire. What is that stuff? I approach my hand to try to burn it, and as I expected, it reacts, the liquid suddenly boiling and making smoke under us. I frown and try burning it some more.

Spark appears next to me, hissing at that stuff. Yeah, I thought so too...

"Oh, gross!"

I turn to Ayesha, who just arrived, making a disgusted face.

"You've seen something like this before?"

"What do you think?" she sighs. "This is clearly Dark Magic, and a stupid curse. Your friend is human; she played all afternoon with witchcraft books, she probably got this from opening something she shouldn't have..."

Damn it. This is really not what I needed. Kelsi being cursed too! I glance over at the dark red pool and quickly move my fingers and hands again, creating a magic circle. I'm a fucking witch too and if I want to save my friend, I will. I focus until my circle is strong enough, and send it onto the little pool of blood.

The liquid fumes and makes disgusting sounds as it slowly boils on the grass, leaving the area barren. However, it doesn't just disappear. Underneath it, engraved in the soil, new runes appear, not the ones that I made myself. I wanted to find how to undo that curse, but it looks like I found its maker instead. I decipher them in less than a minute. Those are geographical coordinates, and it's close; I can already guess where they lead... Ayesha sighs.

"Well, looks like you got yourself an invitation..."

"Mara, what do we do?" asks Ben, visibly worried for his girlfriend. "Can you do something?"

I put my hands on Kelsi's forehead and stomach. I don't even feel the curse... Damn it, how could I let such a thing happen?! I'm a fucking idiot! Ayesha stays carefully away with a grimace on.

"That bitch Ravena..."

"I told you to be careful of that cursed bitch of a raven," says Ayesha. "I wondered how you guys had gotten your hands on all her lackey's stuff, I guess she did put some sort of trap on it..."

I hope no one else is getting sick like Kelsi. She was the one who spent the most time on those things, and Moon Goddess knows where this curse was or how many more people it can affect; I'm very worried about her. Even without my magic, I can tell she has one hell of a fever, and whatever it is she's puking, it can't be good. Not when there's this much non-identified crap coming out of her mouth...

"Ben, carry her. We're going to take her to the closest hospital for now."

"You can't do anything?" asks Liam with a sorry expression.

"This is an Earth Witch's magic, and clearly, I'll have to go meet her, she wants us to settle this directly. All I can do is buy us some time... We have to resort to the good old human way... and ask Nora."

Liam nods, and while he's probably mind-linking her, I ought to try and do something. I trace runes in the air, as fast as I can, trying to focus only on making Kelsi feel better. Thank Moon Goddess I paid attention to little Mara's explanations on Light Magic and Dark Magic balance... I finish my circle, making it as complete, thorough, and efficient as I can, but this won't be enough. I can only buy us time for now. Ravena wouldn't have come up with something to attack my friend if she knew I'd get it out easily...

I put my magic circle toward Kelsi's stomach, and it shines vividly before disappearing. My magic is inside her now, though, which is already better than nothing, surely...

"What did you do?" asks Ben.

"This is Light Magic to protect her, and it should help bring her fever down too. I still think she needs to see Nora and be taken to a hospital. She threw up too much, it can't be good..."

Just as I finish my sentence, Nora arrives with the two other Black Brothers, looking concerned. Liam must have updated them all already because she immediately puts her hands above Kelsi, and her hair starts glowing white. We wait a little bit while she tries to heal her. I can feel Nora's aura coming over to wrap Kelsi around like a cocoon... Moon Goddess, I hope this can make her feel better. She looks really sick... I take Kelsi's hand and hold it. I really hope she's alright, but she looks half-unconscious already... Her eyes are fighting to stay open. She has a thin layer of sweat on her forehead, and with such a fever, it must be hard for her. She isn't a werewolf or a witch, either, Kelsi is just a human... Despite the fact that he's very still as he's carrying her, Ben looks panicked, his eyes going from Kelsi to us non-stop.

"Nora, she's going to be okay, right?" he asks.

"I feel the Dark... Magic inside her," sighs the Luna. "It's fighting me off, though. Dark Magic resists my power much more than normal injuries. It's like Liam's eye, I can't do much about this. I can help with the fever and make it less painful, but... Kelsi was attacked by Dark Magic, the remedy has to come from magic too..."

They all turn their eyes to me, but I can only nod.

"Sorry," I mutter. "This is my fault..."

"Mara, I couldn't care less about finding who to blame right now," frowns Ben. "Girl, you have to do something."

"I will. I promise I will. Can I entrust you with Kelsi for now?"

"What are you going to do?" asks Nora, worried.

"Exactly what Ravena wants of me," I growl. "She's looking for a fight, she's fucking going to have one..."

She can attack me if she wants, but harming my best friend? That witch bitch just crossed the damn line.

However, to my surprise, Ben puts Kelsi into Nora's arms and takes off his shirt, immediately followed by Liam.

"Wha–"

"I'm coming with you," he says. "I won't be able to do anything even if I stay with Kelsi, and Bonnie's already on her way. Plus, I want to be with you if we can get to that damn witch."

"But Kelsi–"

"Kelsi would tell me to do exactly the same thing, Mara. She trusts you a hundred percent, and she's going to kick my furry butt if she learns I did nothing while you fought in her stead. I'm coming."

Before I can add a word, he shape-shifts into his huge brown wolf.

"Mara, go," says Nora. "I'll take Kelsi to the hospital and join you guys when I can."

"We're coming with you," adds Selena.

The next minute, I have three more wolves shape-shifting to follow me: one cream golden-eyed one, and the two older Black Brothers. Only Liam doesn't shape-shift, but he's half-naked and ready to go.

There's no time to argue anymore. Kelsi's life is on the line, and I know I can trust Nora with it. I nod and turn around, and our little group begins to run fast, heading southwest. Liam is the only one running on his feet next to me, but we don't have any issue keeping up with the werewolves. The fact that we are running across Silver City means we have to slow down to cross streets, take sharp turns, and avoid the crowds. People move away from us quickly, though. The appearance of our group, full of Alphas and bigger-than-the-norm wolves, is enough to get everyone out of the way as soon as they spot us. Moreover, everyone knows something's happening. Wolf howls are echoing throughout the city, and it's an incredible feeling. It comes from everywhere, other wolves letting us know where they are if we need reinforcements. I never realized how werewolves were literally everywhere. The full moon is shining bright over us, and its light is illuminating all the buildings, giving Silver City that unique glow that fits its name perfectly.

"Mara, you have to let everyone mind-link you," suddenly yells Liam next to me.

I frown. I'm blocking them? I take a deep breath, and realize I've barely called out my inner wolf... It's a strange feeling, like two versions of me overlapping, and I have to focus on intensifying either. The witch side of me is naturally dominating, and on the other hand, my wolf will gladly take a mental nap unless I need her. I focus, and begin growling without thinking. I feel it. Oh, Moon Goddess, yeah, I feel that.

My wolf's the one running, and she's excited as hell. We accelerate, the adrenaline rushing through our veins. It's amazing. Although I'm on two feet, it feels as if I'm on four, and getting faster. I accelerate ahead of the group, ignoring the flames I feel behind me. The wind's rushing behind me, but my legs have never felt so fast, so great. I'm almost flying. I run, faster, faster, like I'm winning a race.

"Get it, girl!"

Selena's laugh echoes in my mind, and I smile at the cream wolf running beside me. The excitement is contagious, and for a while, it almost turns into a race between us. Liam has a dangerous smile on too, and he won't lose.

Moreover, it's not like we forget what we're headed into. We're going to fight, and this is not going to be a pleasant journey. I'm not sure what to expect, but I know I owe Ravena a fucking lesson after what she did to Kelsi. I feel guilty too. I shouldn't have let my best friend handle all those witchcraft books without at least checking them myself. I thought things would be fine because they were handled by a human before and I couldn't feel anything wrong from them, but I really should have known better. This crap is my fault too, and I'm not forgetting that; I just don't have time to blame myself yet, I need to settle this with the culprit first...

A new howl echoes, and we take a sharp turn to the left.

The docks... I don't like that Ravena brought us here, but at least that's a good sign that she doesn't know where the curse originated from, either.

"Mara, it smells of humans... a lot."

We don't see them, though? The Black Brothers all begin growling, and I glance around. Some nasty clouds have decided to mess up our arrival and hide the moon... It's dark on the docks at this hour, and I'm grateful for my night vision, but that might not be enough to see all the threats lurking in the dark. I ignite my fire to give us more light and see what's going on around us.

There's no sign of Ravena, but there aren't any signs of the humans we can smell, either... What the heck is going on? We slow down and progress carefully between the hangars. Seriously, out of all the places she could decide to provoke me, she chooses the seashore? Why? As an Earth Witch, shouldn't she have tried to kill me in her own element, the forest? For once, it hasn't rained in a while, either! What is she playing at? I keep walking, watching out for any threats. I don't know if we have too many wolves or not enough, but I have a feeling we'll find out soon...

"What about the wolves from this area?"

"They are on standby. They said nothing has happened so far, but they noticed more humans than usual on their territory."

"Humans? ...Like students?"

"Yeah."

Oh, I don't like that. I turn my head to the hangars, but all of them are closed... or so it seems. No, it's too quiet. Liam and I exchange a look. He's staying close, and he's still in his human form too. He doesn't want me to be the only one on two feet, and he knows I'll have to stay like this to use my magic.

"Good evening, Mara."

I stop and glare ahead.

Ravena appears from behind one of the hangars, a malicious smile on her lips. She's changed her clothes again from the last time we saw her, but it's not any better. She's wearing a very flowery top and a long, slit leather skirt, her hair held up in an oversized bun, only a few strands near her face. Let's not even talk about her awful gaudy makeup...

"Do you seriously have a death wish?" I growl. "I didn't think Ayesha was right when she mentioned you're one hell of a snake."

"Oh, are you mad?" she chuckles, tilting her head. "You can't blame me. You're the one who sent your little thief to steal my books..."

"Your books? Don't lie to me, those books weren't yours to begin with!"

"They're still not for a human to take."

I frown. What, so she has something against humans, now?

We suddenly hear a ruckus coming from all the closed hangars. What the hell does she have in there? It sounds like at least three or four of those are packed with... Moon Goddess knows what. I don't like the fact that we still have yet to spot any humans, either.

"Babe, you may want to have more people ready to help us..."

"Roger that. I have a bad feeling too."

It's not just a bad feeling, this is more like the minute before all hell breaks loose. I intensify my flames.

"So what now? I'm past your offer to become your disciple, by the way."

She rolls her eyes and crosses her arms in an elegant manner, almost theatrical.

"That's something about you, Fire Witches. You tend to be arrogant. I can't blame you, as that's a trait of your element. It doesn't make it any less annoying, though. Well, I'm not interested anymore in having you as a student. I'm not fond of that... dog side of yours."

I growl even louder, as if to prove her right. Right now, my wolf side would gladly take a bite or two off that evil mouth of hers!

"Take your curse back from my best friend's body. Right. Now."

"I don't want to," she retorts. "Why should I?"

"Well, I'm about to fry you to the bone if you don't," I growl, showing the large flame on my hand.

"Oh, so you think you can threaten me now? Mara, little one, you haven't quite realized what we're doing here yet, have you?"

I frown.

What is she talking about? Now I really, really have a bad feeling... I glance toward the hangars, but I quickly realize, it's the other side that we ought to be careful of. The sea.

We see the sea suddenly getting a lot more agitated, and those waves get a whole lot bigger, very quickly. I take a step back, wary of it. Oh, this is seriously not my favorite playground... Nausea hits before I can control it, and I bend over, almost ready to throw up.

"Mara! You okay?" asks Liam, grabbing my shoulder.

I nod. I'm not going to puke. The air is just humid, and I should be able to ignore it. I take a deep breath, and glare at the waves. Now I know what she was trying to do. Ravena wanted to call me to this side so I'd be weaker. I should have known as soon as I saw the sea, but I had almost forgotten how fucking much it affects me.

However, it doesn't mean I can't do anything about it. Humidity is nothing but water in the air, and I'm still a Fire Witch. A powerful one.

"Liam, everyone, step back. Don't stand close to me."

They all obey right away, moving like one wolf. I take another deep breath, and intensify my fire. More and more; not just in my hands, but on my whole body. I need to warm up the air around me, I need to make it dry as a desert. I keep going. I feel the flames dancing on my neck, on my collar bone, on my arms. My body is so hot right now, and my skin is almost glowing. I feel the hotness myself, and around me, it's like a layer of heat fighting off the humidity. It may not make a huge difference in our environment, but at least my nausea goes down.

Ravena looks like she did not expect that. She steps back with a sour expression on.

"I have to admit... You're one powerful and annoying little witch..."

"Thanks. Now, take your damn curse back before I put my threat into action," I hiss. "I'm not joking, and I'm not just going to be a nice little witch, either."

"...I won't."

This time, I'm not holding back. I prepare a massive fireball, one as big as my head, and I throw it Ravena's way. She prepares a magic circle in just a few movements, but we both already know it won't be enough. When she puts it in front of her, it's clearly too small, and when my fireball hits, not only she is thrown a few steps back, but my fire burns her hands, making her scream.

"I told you I wasn't playing," I state, stepping forward.

"Good job, Mara," says Selena.

"No, something's wrong," retorts Liam. *"This is too easy..."*

I agree. From what I've seen of her, Ravena is too smart to face me directly in petty games like this. She managed to get me where she wanted. It can't be as simple as her underestimating me a little...

As if she had heard our thoughts, Ravena suddenly starts laughing and rubs her hands together, healing them with her magic.

"Oh, Mara, you think you can play with the big girls now? Well, well, it's time to play, indeed."

I feel a weight fall down in my stomach, and as the sea intensifies its ruckus on my right, I hear an even louder ruckus on my left. All the hangars' doors fall down, one after another, as we finally see what they were hiding. Oh, that can't be good. A young woman comes out, and another. Slowly, the hangars start spitting out dozens of young women, a lot of them wearing that stupid tattoo on a visible patch of their skin. Not only that, but they look... possessed. Their eyes are completely inexpressive, as if they were just sleeping, half-awake. They put one foot in front of the other like puppets on a string. Still, they are coming toward us, a large circle slowly forming.

"Now we know what she wanted humans for..."

"We can't attack humans!"

"Yeah, want to guess if those chicks will feel the same about us? They're being controlled!"

"Mara, can you stop this?"

I slowly shake my head, but I'm thinking. I'm thinking, fast. Can I? It took me a while to erase just one of those damn tattoos, and now, there are dozens of them!

Before I even have time to process what's going on, something else happens. On the other side, the waves I wasn't watching anymore just got a whole lot bigger. Not only that, but now, a vaguely familiar silhouette is standing on top of them, perfectly still as she's riding them. Her waves are tall above us, and she's looking down with one intense glare I'm not sure I like...

"See?" chuckles Ravena. "I knew I needed an alliance. I guess I had picked the wrong witch..."

Oh, for fuck's sake...

Chapter 34

Two witches and an army of human women ready to get to us. It doesn't look like they have any weapons, but it doesn't feel like this is going to be easy, either... However, right now, I'm more worried about that Water Witch than Ravena or those women. She controls a stronger element than mine, and without the barrier anymore, she will now be free to attack us at full strength...

"Why are you helping Ravena?!" I shout at her.

This isn't about simply understanding her intentions, but helping us gain time. If we have more werewolves around, we might be able to rally them to stop the human women from attacking us. I have no idea what's going to happen next, and I don't like it. It feels like we're dancing in Ravena's palm, and I'm not having it.

The Water Witch glares at me in a familiar stance. She really can't stand the sight of me...

"You damn Cursed One," she hisses. "You still have the guts to stand here..."

"This is my home and my city," I growl. "I don't care if you have a problem with Cursed Ones, but if you have an issue with me, at least leave the werewolves alone!"

"I don't owe you anything, and I don't care about your dogs, either. It's so typical of Cursed Ones to hide behind others... You're really the worst of us!"

"What the hell is your issue with Cursed Ones?!" I yell back, fed up. "You think I chose to be cursed? You think any witch chose to be betrayed?"

"They chose to lay with dogs! They betrayed their own blood when they gave in to those greedy dogs!"

So that's her problem, huh? She doesn't give a damn about the curse or its victims. She resents the witches who made the same mistake of falling for werewolf men in the first place... However, something doesn't sit quite right with her earlier words.

"But you didn't hate Nephera, did you?" I retort. "You knew she was Mara's mother, and you blamed me for the curse that took the first Mara, her unborn child. Still, you knew Nephera fell for a werewolf man twice, didn't you?! So why do you hate me so much when you know what she went through?!"

She suddenly looks like I slapped her. Yeah, I hit a nerve, didn't I?

509

I can't help but glance at Ravena, still waiting on the side. She doesn't look so arrogant anymore, and she's glaring at the Water Witch, her eyes full of doubt. It looks like their alliance is paper thin, isn't it? What deal did Ravena strike with her for them to be on the same side? Something's not right here. Ravena is after the curse's Dark Magic, but what is the Water Witch after? She loathes that curse and whatever it created. So, why would she agree to help Ravena? Why would she stay so close to Silver City too? She's not powerless, she could have picked any other place, but she stayed around... simply to attack me? No, it doesn't feel as simple as that.

"Mara..."

I glance over my shoulder. The human women are coming forward.

"Are they armed?"

"I don't know..."

I don't like this. If Ravena really wanted to make a mess, she would have given them some weapons or something... but I feel like that cunning bitch of a witch would have an even more twisted plan in mind, and I don't like this at all... I turn back to the Water Witch and that imposing wave still threatening to fall over us. I need to sort this out. If I can maybe reason with her, we could get ourselves in a better position, perhaps...

"You really hate me because I'm a Cursed One? What of the other Mara, then?"

"You are not Nephera's daughter!" she shouts.

"So it's about every Cursed One but Nephera? I wouldn't exist if it wasn't for her!"

"You insolent little witch!"

She waves her arm as if to slap me, but from the distance and her stance, it won't be as nice and easy. As I feared, the movement has the water move instead, and a portion of the huge wave comes right at us. All the wolves growl, but it's not going to change things. It washes over us and we roll on the asphalt. That thing hit us like a huge wall, much heavier than I anticipated. If we take more of those, she's going to smash us on the ground like ants!

"Mara, you may not want to anger her," Selena growls.

"Sorry."

However, I know she's pissed because I touched a nerve. That Water Witch isn't motivated by greed like Ravena. If I can find out what she's really here for and what her deal is with Nephera, maybe I can turn things around...

Suddenly, a growl behind me gets our attention. One of the women just jumped at Ben with a little knife in hand. Oh, shit... He bites her wrist without being too brutal, just enough to make her drop it, and pushes her back, but I feel like this isn't over. Quickly, another one moves, and begins doing the same, attacking Nathaniel's flank. He growls and easily steps away.

"Don't injure the humans."

"I know!"

The bantering between the Black Brothers is echoed by several growls. The human women are all moving forward, but... strangely, they seem to

510

mostly want to attack the male werewolves of our group. Ravena definitely used a portion of the curse to misguide them...

The women are closing in on us, and I don't like how we're cornered by the edge of the water.

"Mara," says Selena, *"we can handle the human chicks, but you have to do something about the witches."*

I know. I increase my fire, slowly and steadily, but enough to hold back a second wave, I think. The Water Witch is still glaring at me from above. What do I do? I know I have to provoke her to make her talk, but that might not be the wisest move either if I want to avoid getting all of us killed...

"What do you have to gain by allying yourself with Ravena?" I growl. "She wants the curse's Dark Magic! How is that better than me being a Cursed One?! At least I didn't choose it!"

"I do not care about that witch's ambitions," she retorts. "That curse has to disappear!"

"And what's your genius plan, then? Killing me, and then what? You think you can break the curse by yourself?"

"I'm closer than anyone else!" she retorts.

"Yeah, that's why you've been hanging around Silver City, in the same waters for weeks? Face it, you don't know any more than we do! Ravena is just using you and you're too blinded by anger to even realize!"

"Enough!"

This time, she moves both arms, and the waves grow much bigger. My blood leaves my face. If we're hit by that...!

"Mara!"

I prepare my fire, growing it as big and as fast as I can. Just like I learned earlier, I add runes, the best I can think of. I need to protect us, but if I don't control this, she'll hit the human women too, and I'm not okay with that. I need to stop her! I increase my flames, channeling all of my inner energy, animating my fire furiously. No more restraints.

When the wave appears above us, covering the sky, I take a deep breath, and extend my fire like a wall in front of us. It's large, but not broad enough...

"You're one stubborn little..."

I extend my arms, and to my surprise, my wall of fire is much larger than I thought. I keep it up, and feel the water hit against it. I intensify the heat, and an impressive cloud of steam appears above, but nothing hits us.

I stand my ground, and the pressure continues, but I know we've made it. How...? I glance to the side, and to my surprise, Ayesha is standing a few steps from me, in a similar stance. She's fueling my fire with hers, helping me stand against the wave. She's groaning, frowning and visibly having a hard time, but she stays there.

"You're really a whole bunch of trouble, aren't you...?"

"Ayesha! Why...?"

"You haven't killed me yet and the wolves gave me food too. I'm many things but not an ungrateful bitch."

I can't help but smile despite the situation. I don't know if it's because we're both Fire Witches, but I do feel we have a few things in common... including stubbornness and too much sense of pride. She helps me withstand the wave until it's over, and although my arms are aching once we're done, I feel relieved. Both wolves and humans only felt a few harmless droplets, and the air is filled with steam, but at least no harm was done.

"*Mara!*"

I turn around just in time to see the wooden spike flying our way. I react quickly and create a magic circle just fast enough to stop it. The wood explodes against my circle, and a few shards hit me. I growl and lose my focus. I hear furious growling, and my inner wolf echoes them angrily. Another spike is coming at me, but I realize it too late. For a second, I'm sure it will hit me, but a dark shadow suddenly appears in front of me.

Damian Black lands on all fours, the spike in his fangs, and growls while breaking it with a snap. We both glare at Ravena, looking upset.

"You're really one cunning bitch..." I hiss.

She purposely waited for me to be focused elsewhere to strike. Ayesha lights up her fire next to me too, ready to send her blue fire Ravena's way.

"How about we do this face to face, you damn raven?" she says with a smirk.

"You should have stayed out of this," Ravena shouts back at her. "Nothing here is of any concern to you!"

"Too bad for you, I've kind of grown attached here. Their witch is a promising one, and the wolves make some mean barbecue..."

As if this was some funny pun, she chuckles and increases her fire with a smirk. Ravena doesn't look so happy.

"Well, then, I guess we'll have to get rid of you too!"

She moves her arms, and since I've learned from the last attack, I prepare a new magic circle, ready for her attack. We must have upset her because she doesn't wait to strike. New wooden spikes fly our way. She's not just targeting me now, but the wolves as well. I quickly prepare several fireballs, and Ayesha imitates me. We manage to break those wooden peaks before more reach us, and our werewolf allies only have to jump to avoid those we couldn't get rid of in time. I feel a bit better knowing we can easily avoid her attacks, but it doesn't change the fact we're stuck sandwiched between two angry witches, a group of innocent women very willing to attack us, and the sea...

"Stop being so tame, little witch!" laughs Ayesha. "You think you're still in kindergarten?"

Before I can say a thing, she prepares a new fire ball of her own, and angrily throws it at Ravena. It makes me wonder if she doesn't have more against the Earth Witch, but she's right; I can't simply stand still and take attack after attack. Ayesha doesn't ease her fire at Ravena, forcing the Earth Witch to retreat. I guess she can handle Ravena for now, but I'm more worried about the water one...

I turn around, and sure enough, she's still there, surfing strangely on that wave above the sea. It surprises me she hasn't attacked again, but she's still glaring at us like we're some ants...

"I want to solve that curse too!" I yell at her. "What is wrong with you? You're just going to attack me, get rid of me, then what? This is still a city of werewolves! And that curse? You won't be able to get rid of it so easily, either! You think you're the first witch to want to get rid of this? Hundreds of witches have tried, and you know what? I'm sure you'll fail too, because you're already so angry and blind!"

"Shut it!"

She sends another wave my way, but it's not as strong as before; I use my fire and stop it just before it hits me. She looks furious, and sends another one, but I won't back down. Her blows are not as powerful; is it because she's doubtful now? I even have time to glance to the side. Ayesha is doing just fine, and she's obviously trying to make Ravena step farther away from us. It would be good to separate her from that Water Witch indeed... She's probably the one who convinced her to attack us. If we can ruin that alliance between them, that would be a good thing for us...

I'm more worried about the werewolves. It would be a piece of cake if they could seriously attack the human women attacking them, but for now, they can only avoid and try to scatter them while not being hit. Thankfully, those women look haggard, and they don't throw any big blows or seem to attack seriously. Compared to the werewolves' speed, this is more like them attacking blindly and slowly, waving their blades around with a low chance of hitting anything... So far, only Selena and Ben have small cuts, nothing too big. But there are too many of those women. They keep forcing the werewolves to retreat toward the sea, and I don't like how we're getting more and more cornered...

"Naptera, stop playing around!" suddenly shouts Ravena from the other side. "Just get rid of the wolves!"

Naptera...?

The Water Witch glares at me, a new wave of anger rising. She sends another wave of water my way, much stronger this time. I take a deep breath and block it the best I can, ready for the blow. I can barely stand my ground, but I push it, focusing on her water.

A Water Witch named Naptera. She hates the curse, she hates me, but she was even more furious about the fact that I took over little Mara's power. She got absolutely furious when I mentioned Nephera. Why didn't I see it before? Even angrier, I send a fireball back, making the wave disperse.

"Don't you think you forgot to mention something?!" I shout at her, pissed. "This isn't about Ravena or beating the curse, is it? You're so mad at me because of what happened to Nephera! She was raised by Danica, but Danica wasn't her mother, was she? Her mother was no witch, but a descendant of that witch named Sadia Jones... I bet if I looked at the Witches' Ancestral Tree again, your name wouldn't be so far from them!"

513

"Enough!"

This time, I don't have much time to avoid the new wave that hits me. It comes so fast, and much slimmer than before, but I manage to prepare a fireball just in time... and then, I get a furious hit in the stomach. I hear myself shouting in pain, like an echo from far away.

"*Mara!*"

Before I can do a thing, a new wave hits me at full strength, and I get swept off the ground. I don't control anything, I'm thrown in all directions. I try to fight it, do something, anything, but the pressure is too intense. I try to ignore the pain and gasp for air, but before I can, I swallow a huge amount of salty water, and I feel myself dropping in the sea. Something that tastes like iron on my tongue, and red in the water above me. I want to throw up furiously, and my body feels terribly heavy. Damn it... She got me. I try to swim back to the surface, fight the pressure, but as I open my eyes, Naptera is angrily facing me in the water.

Oh, f-...

"I told you," she says, speaking despite the two of us being underwater, "you should have known better..."

This is the worst. I'm completely defenseless in the worst environment possible for a Fire Witch. Underwater. How could I be so stupid to let myself get sunk so easily?! I shouldn't have underestimated Naptera. I'm a fucking idiot.

"*...ara! Mara, are you okay?*"

Half a dozen voices suddenly echo in my mind, and although they're ringing quite annoyingly, at least they're helping me stay awake and focused. I have to fight this hellish nausea coming up, but my whole body is shivering like crazy.

"*Yeah, I'm... still alive for now.*"

I can't guarantee how long that'll be the case, though. Not when my enemy is facing me just a few strokes away, glaringly obvious that she's got a much larger hand in this fight now. Can I even get out of here or defend myself? I try to light my fire, but underwater, it's a bit depressing... I insist. This is magic fire, I should at least be able to do something! I got sick when it was raining, but I wasn't completely powerless. It can't be that simple. Elements can work together, can't they? It has to work somehow. I'm not stupidly dying here, hell no.

I look around, hoping to find a clue, a solution, but Moon Goddess, it would take something akin to a freaking miracle now.

"*Liam, don't!*" suddenly yells Nathaniel's voice.

"*Mara, hold on, I'm coming!*"

"*Liam, stay out of here!*" I shout back mentally.

"*I'm fine, I can swim!*"

"*I don't doubt that, babe, but I wouldn't bet on you saving me while avoiding getting killed by an angry Water Witch! Stay the hell out of here! I'll manage!*"

514

That's one big fat lie, but I really don't want to have to worry about my mate on top of everything else. I can't, I already need to focus on saving my own ass first. Oh hell, why can't Spark come out when I really need a huge clue...?

"You're such a big mouth," says Naptera, with visibly no issue talking underwater. "Now you'll finally shut up!"

I growl. I can't talk, but I can certainly growl, although it would be more convincing if I didn't continuously feel like throwing up... I feel weird. This isn't just about this nausea, but my whole body is going nuts, making me feel like I'm going to pass out, yet feeling electrified at the same time. There's something completely weird going on with me, and I have no idea what it is, where it comes from, or how to handle it. It's driving me crazy.

Naptera moves her hand, and I'm suddenly blown away by a new wave. Is it bad if I throw up now? Because I sure feel like I'm about to, and I think it would help.

"You're right," she continues. "Sadia was my closest friend, and she chose to give her daughter a name close to mine... It was before she was betrayed by one of those bastard wolves though!"

Is she really going to tell her story now? Couldn't it have been done when I was above the surface and not when I am trying not to drown?!

"She was so in love, and when that man left, she was so broken... She knew of the curse, of course. So many of us have fallen to it, and we keep making those mistakes, over and over again like pitiful dolls. Yet, Sadia wanted to believe in love more. She thought she and her partner could break it once and for all. She had meant to find its origin, which she thought belonged with her ancestors."

She wasn't wrong. Nephera came from the line of the original witch that was the first one betrayed... I wonder how Sadia failed? She ought to know where her family was from, wouldn't she? If she belonged to the Purple Moon Clan, to the Jones family, she should have belonged here in Silver City. How did she fail? Then again, we always meet a dead end. Even witches who knew of the location didn't succeed in breaking that wretched curse. So, how...?

"When she arrived at my door, she was exhausted and a wreck. Even worse, she was weeping at the thought of her daughter being cursed as well. Sadia wanted to try and save her baby at all costs, so she thought she ought to send her to another witch, to perhaps break that fate of hers."

So that's why Nephera was sent into Danica's care. Because her mother was cursed, and while looking for a way to break that curse, she had to keep her baby away... This is just too sad to think about. I feel bad for Sadia. Judging by how Naptera speaks and her expression, Sadia couldn't have been very old when she passed.

"She died before she could accomplish anything. Such a foolish girl... I tried to persuade her to give up, but she was obsessed with saving herself and her daughter. Sadia had always been a dreamer, and she believed too much, once again."

515

I can't blame her. I wouldn't be able to sit still, either, if I knew a curse was threatening my life and that of my child's as well... I feel pity for Sadia, but now, at least, that part of the story is clearer. Naptera's links to Silver City, that curse, and myself too. She isn't here for Silver City itself, or the curse's Dark Magic like Ravena, she just wants to end it. She probably didn't expect me to be here too, someone born from Sadia's blood and even more of that damn curse... I wish I could reply to that monologue of hers, though! Thanks for the explanation, but can we get back to what really matters? Her issue isn't with me, it's with that curse, we should be on the same page, not taking a swim!

I growl again, and to my surprise, my wolf seems just fine. She's not feeling that hellish nausea? Is she a wolf or a freaking fish?! I try to focus on her instead and stop fighting. I can't come up with fire and I feel like the more I try to channel my inner fire, the sicker I'll get, so let's just think smart for once and stop. Damn, Selena was right, I'm so obnoxiously stubborn...

I'm running out of oxygen, though, and quickly. I struggled too much to fight off those waves. I'm surprised Naptera isn't attacking me more. I'm underwater, I should already be dead if she had any serious intention to kill me... Maybe she cooled down because she spoke, but I won't complain. It gives me a few seconds to think of a plan... or at least how I'm going to save my ass in this situation.

What's the deal with my inner wolf? I'm usually in witch mode, I didn't even think about her much. Okay, maybe I was leaning too much toward my firepower, but it's still pretty nice to have that much firepower in hand for fights! I decide to close my eyes and focus on her only. Strangely, I feel a bit relieved as soon as I reach inside... I manage to align with her calm, and the lack of oxygen isn't so pressing anymore. What are you trying to tell me?

"Mara, we have more humans attacking!"

I'm sorry, but I have to ignore the others for a while. Why have I never looked deeper into my own aura when I'm so good at reading others? I can't tell, but now, I notice, my wolf's aura is slowly shifting. How the heck are we doing that, I wouldn't be able to come up with the beginning of an explanation. It's like seeing two different colored inks mixing. From a bright orange, my aura is slowly getting tainted by a dim, quiet blue. Where is that blue aura coming from? Where was it all this time? I'd know if I had two different auras! However, the more I let it in and accept it, the more obvious it gets: my wolf is the one.

I try to look into my subconscious, where I met little Mara and my wolf... Of course now, my wolf is alone in there. She greets me with her blue and gold eyes, but once again, I feel like we're two separate entities. It's like right before I realized she was there, we're not in perfect sync. I may be a badass witch, but I'm obviously one poor excuse of a werewolf... Alright, girl, let's ponder on the why later and act now before we die.

I focus, and let that blue aura of hers come to me. Although I said I wouldn't look into it, it definitely has Clarissa's signature... I smile without thinking. Of course. Why didn't I realize sooner? This is the body of a Water

Witch, to begin with! It went through a lot of shit to adapt to little Mara's soul as she was a Fire Witch, but this is still a body meant for a Water Witch! How did I not think of that?

I'm sorry, girl. My inner wolf growls a bit, but I don't think we have time for grudges anyway. I try to calm down. This is the body of a Water Witch. No matter how much it adapted to little Mara's fire, it can't have completely erased Clarissa's original body's capabilities, right? I may not be able to bend water, but I should at least...

Oh, Moon Goddess, it works! I stopped blocking my nose and mouth, and somehow, I can freaking breathe underwater. It's a bit... scary, but although I breathe water in and out, I'm not suffocating or anything. No need for gills, my lungs are just fine with getting a water influx, apparently. This is crazy... and I absolutely love it. I get an adrenaline rush as well as an awesome confidence boost. Compared to the I'm-about-to-die from earlier, this is fucking awesome. With my heat kept inside and my body doing what it knows on the outside, I'm feeling good. I'm feeling great, even. Knowing that I'm not about to die drowning is kind of awesome.

"How are you...?"

Naptera looks shocked, and I can't keep myself from grinning. Yeah, I know. Who would expect a newbie Fire Witch to be just fine underwater? I can't believe my nausea is gone as soon as I shut my inner Fire Witch down too. I wish I had listened to my inner wolf earlier. Sorry, Clarissa. I promise I'll do better from now on with what you left me. This is crazy, insane, and awesome. I may not be able to use Water Magic, if that's even possible, but I know what to do. I take a deep breath and move my legs around. I try going left, I try going right. I can swim, alright. Moon Goddess... The others are going to add this to my list of crazy stuff, right at the top of the pile.

"Surprise," I say. "Cursed Ones are full of surprises, don't you think?"

Okay, maybe I'm enjoying this a bit too much, but let's face it, I'm a total cheat in my own way.

"Now, want to hear what I think about your whole speech from earlier?" I resume, losing the grin. "Well, I'm really sorry about what happened to Sadia. I really am, Naptera. I'm sorry about what happened to Nephera, and I'm sorry for everyone else who got cursed, including the two amazing young witches who gave birth to me. Yes, I'm a Cursed One, but I didn't choose to be born from someone else's ashes. I don't have a childhood of my own because of that, and Nephera's baby didn't even get to see the light of day with her own body! I'm really, really sorry about all that, but guess what? As much as it sucks, killing me and the werewolves isn't going to solve anything or bring anyone back!"

"Enough!"

This time, I'm prepared. I tame my inner fire, having it be faint and quiet for once, and let Naptera throw me across the water. What else can she do now? I can swim and breathe just fine. I don't think she's got anything to slam me against either, or so I hope. It's pretty dark in here... Alright. She can have me spin a hundred times if she wants, she'll still have to listen to what I have to say to her!

As soon as she stops swinging me around, I right myself and growl with my inner wolf.

"You know what? Yes, I'm cursed, and you can suck it! I'm a Fire Witch in a Water Witch's body, so if anything, I may even be the craziest and yet most positive thing to have ever been born of that curse! I didn't sign up for any of this, but I'd freaking work to stop it if you'd calm down and listen!"

"You're nothing but a child, you know nothing!" she shouts back.

"I fucking know enough!" I growl. "You can call me a child, a brat, a Cursed One, even a dog if you will, I don't give a damn! By the Moon Goddess, I am what I am, and I'll fight that damn curse until it finally ends! I'm sick of you witches trying to kill me or use me for whatever! Can't we work together for once? You think I'm a brat? You think you're better than Sadia? You're an old wench controlled by your emotions too!"

This time, she closes her mouth, visibly shocked by my words. I was expecting another mean blow of anger, but it's clearly not coming... Well, it was high time I finally talked some sense into her. She doesn't try to swing me around again, although I prepared myself for it. I focus on my inner wolf, and she's still there, fierce as ever, ready for a fight. Naptera doesn't try again. She's glaring as if she could kill me with her eyes, but she won't move, visibly stuck by anger.

This isn't our fight here, though, and we don't have that much time to lose either. Now that I'm alright, I'm more worried about whatever's going on at the surface.

"Liam, is everyone okay?"

"Don't you ever ignore me again!" he immediately shouts back, his wolf furious at me.

"Okay, okay, I'm sorry... Are you alright, babe?"

"We're... managing. It's getting tense here. Ravena disappeared and Ayesha came to help us out, there are too many humans, and since we don't want to hurt them... What about you? We haven't seen you come out, how are you...?"

"Bonus power from Clarissa, I'll explain later. I'll try to get out of here as soon as I can, so please hold on until then!"

"I will, but please stay safe and come back to the pack soon, babe."

"Gotcha."

I know Liam tried not to worry me, but from his words, the situation must not be ideal up there, and seeing how Ayesha had to stay behind to help, it's probably getting worse. I don't like the fact that Ravena escaped either. I'm not comfortable with the thought that this witch with a capital B is roaming free in my city...

"If you're done tossing me around..." I start, but Naptera's not having it.

"Shut up!"

She suddenly starts moving her hands around, and oh, Moon Goddess, I don't like what's going on. Water gathers in her hand, but it's... cold. Very, very cold. I've never seen this before. The water gathers like ice in her hands, and I suddenly don't feel as confident about this anymore. The water takes a sharp shape, something that looks rather long, a bit too big, and too pointy as well. My wolf whines upon seeing this and I'm not feeling great either. My confidence from before melts like snow. What the...? An ice spike!

Oh, Mara, why did you have to open that big stupid mouth of yours...? Think, think, Mara, think... Ice. Of course she could manipulate ice, she's a fucking Water Witch! Come on, Mara, use your brain. What can I do? Even if I have Water Magic at my disposal, I'm way too fresh of a newbie to use it already. I just need to escape a damn ice spike for now, so let's just focus on what I can do!

My wolf. I need to listen to her. Stop thinking so much and simply trust her. Something I'm not used to, but it's never too late for a change, is it? I try to calm down, despite the threat, and channel her all I can. No, I don't just channel her; I give her complete control. I feel it coming like a sudden wave building from the inside. She jumps up, filling my limbs and using her instincts to take over my body. In a split second, she comes in, I step back; I'm a she-wolf. I'm an animal, and my human self disappears under the female wolf guiding my body. I hear us growl as a warning, and with a disgusted look, Naptera launches her weapon right at us. She's even better than I imagined, aiming right at us, but now that she's in control, my wolf is much stronger and more confident. No more whining. She growls, and just as the spike seems like it's about to hit us, she jumps to the side.

I can't believe how well she's moving in the water. How good we are. It's the two of us now, but her influence is amazing. I thought I was doing okay earlier, but the truth would be more like I was just glad to not be drowning. Now, we're just swimming around, my wolf moves so fluidly, so easily. It almost feels like... like the water's my natural environment. I can't believe how uneasy I was before compared to this amazing feeling. My wolf is definitely in her element. She moves swiftly, as if the water is her playground. Naptera's weapons fly past us, and I barely feel it above our shoulder. It's truly a strange and yet amazing sensation. The water gently caresses our fur, offering no resistance to her strong paddling. I smile, a boost of confidence coming in again. I'm hot, yet cold, the adrenaline kicking in. I know we can do this. We're good. We growl as one at Naptera, a clear warning.

As we swim, I notice our paw... it's white. Since when did we have any white fur at all? After a bit more paddling, it's clear only one is, though. The other one is still black and gold... I'm curious to see what happened yet again with my appearance. Surprise after surprise, really... Will I ever get used to this?

Alright, I'll worry about my looks later. I need to get out of the water first. It's been a nice little swim around, but they are waiting for me at the harbor, and I can't let Naptera play around with me like a cat with a mouse any longer.

She doesn't look in a hurry to attack again, and I've had enough. Each time, it's the same. She attacks because she's angry, but I don't feel any murderous intent, so what? I growl, and start to swim away from her. I can't lose any more time with her. Either she attacks me seriously and we finish this, or she can finish her stupid tantrum alone. My friends are in danger, I don't have any time to lose here!

I start swimming, as fast as I can, feeling almost more fish than wolf. I'm fast, and although I can feel Naptera behind me, I'm careful just in case she'll attack again... I may have gotten more comfortable and less vulnerable underwater, but this is her ground, not mine. I have to get out of here before something I can't avoid happens...

"We're not done!"

I jump to the side just in time to avoid another one of her damn ice spikes. Seriously? I turn around and growl, but her eyes have... darkened. Oh, Moon Goddess, that can't be good. Not just that, but the water is getting colder too. I mean, really cold. Like ice-cold, and I don't fucking like it. I growl and swim, but I can feel the chill crawling closer all around me. The water gets more white and shiny, and although it's pretty, it's not the time to admire this. I'm going to be trapped like a freaking ice cube if I don't do something soon!

"...Perhaps you should thank me," she said. "You won't die. You'll stay here, child, trapped until someone else frees you... Your friends might find you, but at least, I'll take care of the curse meanwhile..."

I growl. Take care of the curse, my butt! And calling me a child as if she sort of likes me now? What the hell is wrong with this witch, is she that freaking stubborn that she won't admit she's wrong and headed for a dead end?

I keep paddling as fast as I can, both to get away and get myself out of here, but that won't work. Naptera's now somehow decided on keeping me underwater. Damn it, does she ever give up? She's not an enemy, but she's still a freaking pain! I'm not even that far from the shore, but I still need to get as close as I can, I won't even be able to get out of here by myself. The cold around me is just terrible. I feel like I'm taking a swim in some frozen lake, and when I glance up, it looks like some ice is appearing. I can't believe she's fucking serious about this!

Alright, we have to stop playing defense. I growl, looking all around for a solution, an idea. There's no miracle coming, though, just the two of us under the ice... Think, Mara.

I try to take deep breaths and stop swimming away; I need to focus on myself. I always find the answers inside, not outside. I need to stop running around blindly.

...I'm a Fire Witch. A Fire Witch, and also... a bit of a Water Witch? Damn, this whole thing is getting confusing, isn't it? I decide to close my eyes. Keeping them open or not doesn't matter as I can feel Naptera's attack coming at me through the water movements, but it helps me focus on my wolf and my inner flame. They are both a part of me. I had to shut down the latter to let the Water Witch inside me take over, but... Come on, this is my body. This is me.

I knew it from the start. I am no ordinary witch, I'm... a patchwork. A freaking Frankenstein's monster of a witch, something that shouldn't have existed in the first place.

...I am something impossible. How about we test that now, Clarissa, little Mara?

I open my eyes and shape-shift into my human form in a breath, an arrogant smile on my lips.

I stare right at Naptera, and my newfound burst of confidence stops her. She even retreats a bit, looking unsure. She's not just looking at me, but looking around me. That's right, Naptera, just you watch. I should thank her for allowing me to unlock so much of these abilities I didn't know I had, but... time to go to the next level. It's time I stop thinking of what I should be able to do or not. No more rules, Mara. Let's just be as impossible as hell.

I open my arms and take deep breaths. I ignore the cold, the ice, and instead, I channel my inner fire again. This time, I try to control it very, very precisely. The tame flame that had almost been extinguished opens up, but it's... chilly. I direct it not inside, but toward my hands, as if I was trying to keep it there. It's as if before, it was running wild anywhere it wanted, but now, I'm only letting it out through my hands, but big, hot, and strong. Very, very hot... and cold. My heartbeat accelerates, my blood rushes through my veins. It's insane, but it's happening. My wolf growls, I smile. I can't tell if I'm human or wolf anymore. Fire or water.

I'm... both.

It's a new fire that emerges in my hands. An ice-cold, blue flame. Something between fire and ice, something so hot or so cold, it's impossible to tell, but it's mine. I smile uncontrollably. A chill runs over my skin, both hot and cold, just exciting and thrilling.

Horror appears on Naptera's face, as she retreats again.

"Y-you... How... It can't be..."

"I told you," I say. "I'm not like any other."

I sound arrogant, and I can't say I hate it. Let's face it, I feel more powerful than I've ever been. My flames have ignited into a mysterious new shade, the deep blue that appears at the heart of a flame. How I'm able to generate fire underwater, I don't know. Is it even fire? Or ice? I don't know. It's magic, and it feels amazing at the end of my arms, glowing like a light in the darkness of the deep sea. I increase it.

"Stop!" she shouts. "You can't control two elements, you're going to kill yourself!"

Just you watch, then.

I keep increasing my flames, the fire and ice fighting to maintain that perfect balance on my hands. Two corridors of bubbles appear around my arms, as if the water is boiling around me. Steam? I feel my heart accelerate again. Silver sparks appear all around my body, and I realize it's the ice breaking under the pressure of my flames. I look up at the ceiling of ice that has been getting thicker and thicker all this time.

"Don't you...!"

As Naptera starts preparing another attack, two more ice spikes, I make my decision. I'm done playing, and she's been slowing me down for too long already. It may have been just a handful of minutes, but those precious minutes are those my friends have been missing me for this fight. I can't stay here and entertain her any longer!

Still focusing on balancing my Water and Fire Magic perfectly, I let her spikes come to me, and this time, I simply blow them away with my hand. It's like twigs brushed away by a breeze, and this time, Naptera's look means she's been defeated for real.

"...Told ya."

I turn around, and swim away, leaving her there. I already lost enough time, and I need to use this newfound magic to get out of here and help everyone. I make sure not to slow down until I reach the shore.

"*Liam!*"

I wait and tame my magic, the cold surrounding me quickly again. Thankfully, he doesn't make me wait too long. A human hand appears in the water, and he pulls me up. My body lands on the wet asphalt, and I take some deep breaths. Moon Goddess, that feels good...

"Mara! You okay, babe?"

His hand is on my neck, patting me, and, as crazy as it may sound at that very moment, I'm suddenly hit by the fact that I'm... completely naked. Oh, the joys of being a werewolf... I curl up and look at Liam, his dark silhouette hovering over me.

"Hi..." I let out, with a hoarse voice I don't recognize myself.

"What happened? Damn, you're... cold as ice!"

"Yeah, I don't recommend a swim now... How's the... fight?"

Oh, damn, I'm tired. With his help, I struggle to get back on my feet, my whole body a bit numb because of the cold. The sensation of the wind on my cold skin has to be something akin to hell. I try to focus on my fire and warm myself up as fast as I can, and Liam hands me a bundle of black fabric. I unfold it. It's a very simple black tank top and shorts outfit, but I won't complain now. I put it on as fast as I can. Is that why he stayed human, in case I needed to change back? Once I'm dressed, I can forget about myself and look around. Liam stays close to me, holding me as if he was afraid I'd go back into the sea or fall.

"What happened?" he insists, ignoring my question. "What about the Water Witch?"

"I beat her... I think. At least for now. H-how about you guys?"

"We're doing okay, but we're a bit stuck. We were waiting for you to come out to move..."

That's what I can see. The werewolves look tired, but fine, aside from a few injuries here and there. Probably those they couldn't avoid... Although, the situation isn't exactly fine. They are now completely surrounded by the human women, and... damn it, how many are there? The number has at least doubled

522

since earlier! How long was I actually underwater? It looks like every female student has been made into some weird witch zombie! At one end of the group, Ayesha is standing there, putting up firewalls behind the human women, making sure they don't escape either. So she also agreed not to injure them...

However, as I start to go to them to join the fight, Liam grabs my hand and gently puts his other one on my cheek. Only then do I notice how panicked he looks... and exhausted too. He's been fighting in his human form all this time? Just so he could wait for me, to pull me out of the water? I suddenly feel very sorry for my mate. I pull him into all sorts of things just because we're so different. I want to say something, but before I do, he pushes some of my wet hair out of my face with a frown. He looks very worried and is staring at me with... a confused expression. What now?

"Mara, are you sure you're okay?"

"Yeah, I'm alright. Liam, I promise. I've never felt... so powerful. Listen, underwater, something new happened! I didn't think it was possible, but..."

"...Yeah, uh... I think I can see that..."

"You can see it?" I repeat, confused.

Liam grimaces, realizing we were not talking about the same thing. I mean, how would he know about my new ability? And why is he staring at me like that?

"Uh... babe, you're aware one of your eyes has turned... I mean, that it turned blue... right?"

Wait, what? It did? I lift my hand to touch my eyelid by reflex, but as expected, I can't see it, of course... I can only guess which eye it is following Liam's gaze... It seriously turned blue? He keeps staring at me with a confused expression. Oh, alright. We really don't have time for that, and I guess that's not the weirdest thing that happened today, after all...

"It's nothing," I say. "Liam, I'm a Water Witch too."

"...A what now?"

"A Water Witch, Liam. I know how weird that sounds, but... I can use both water and fire. I can't really explain it yet, but... I did. I used it against Naptera. I can combine both Clarissa's and little Mara's powers."

I smile like an idiot. I know this is the weirdest timing ever, but now that I've managed to get out of the water and out of Naptera's clutches, I had to say it. It's just too big, too amazing, and I need to share this with someone. Seeing Liam still stunned and visibly at a loss, I nod and give him a quick kiss to wake him up.

"For real!"

Liam nods, obviously still a bit shocked. Well, I can't blame him... He's got no choice but to learn to adapt pretty fast with me, I suppose... After a while, he sighs.

"Alright, I'm going to skip the whole it's-not-possible thing because, well, you're Mara, so I guess nothing normal applies to you, like, ever..."

"Thanks..." I say with a little sorry smile.

Moon Goddess, I love him and how fast he adjusts to all of my crazy.

"...But also because we actually have to move and we need your help, babe. We have wolves reporting about some movement at East Point Ground, and I really don't like that."

My smile disappears, and I focus again.

"Ravena. She found the spot..."

"She may have spied on us or something," nods Liam. "Her goal is apparently to keep us here while she... tries to take over the curse's Dark Magic."

"You shouldn't have waited for me!" I protest. "Why didn't Ayesha go already? What of the other wolves?"

I look around, and although I can't see them, I can tell many more wolves are waiting in the shadows... Why didn't they get involved yet? What's wrong?

"They can't," says Liam, shaking his head. "We tried to send people toward East Point Ground, or at least, for someone to get out of here, but as soon as they pass some invisible border... Look."

I look in the direction he's pointing at, and after a furious growl, a black wolf tries to jump over a group of young women. He's fast, and careful to stay far enough from their blades. He will be able to pass, somehow, no?

However, I promptly realize, he's not the one in danger. As soon as he's past the first rows of female students, something happens. All the ones remaining between him and East Point Ground, suddenly... put the blades against their own throats. Not only that, I can already see some drops of blood rolling down their necks! That bitch really ordered them to commit suicide if they can't stop us!

"See? Selena tried to get out of there earlier, and... six girls died. The same thing happens if the other wolves try to join our group. We ordered the others not to get near East Point Ground, who knows what Ravena will do to them..."

"She won't do anything," I growl.

I open up my hands and focus on my sensations from earlier to bring back my blue, ice-cold flames. You're done cheating, Ravena. Now you've really done it. And I won't let you get away with this...

Chapter 35

There are at least a hundred young women all around us, like a wall between us and the other wolves, cornering our little group on one end of the harbor. They keep trying to attack with their knives, but the truth is, their numbers are too great and only the first lines are fighting the wolves. I glance further away, and as Liam said, it's no better on the other side. The other wolves aren't moving, blocked by all those chicks threatening to either attack or commit suicide.

I have to put an end to this, we can't simply lose time here while Ravena is on the other side! I start walking toward those women, and as I thought, they instantly attack me too. No, it would even be fair to say they focus more on me than the wolves. I move my body to avoid the first attack and grab a wrist coming my way to dodge another blade. Selena's training is coming in handy... I don't simply avoid them or dodge them, though. I grab their wrists and freeze or break them. Whatever works to stop them.

"We have to take them all down," I say.

"We will injure them!"

"You don't need to kill them," I retort, out of breath, before dodging another one. "Just make sure they can't attack you or injure themselves more! Moreover, they obey some sort of rule about you not going past them, right? All we have to do is make sure they can't tell when we are out of their way..."

He frowns, but I have an idea. Taking a deep breath, I put my hands together, and focus. Fire and water. It's ironic that Naptera herself is the one who gave me the hint I needed to get out of this situation. I make sure to control my powers the best I can and activate both parts of me. My inner fire burns inside, while the water gently runs along my veins, like a flow that's ready to get as big as a waterfall if I need. I can't help but smile, a bit excited. I opened a new door once again, but I feel this last one I opened is the hardest to take control of. Fire and water aren't really a pair, they're opposites. It takes all of my focus to balance them, as if I was pulling both sides and keeping them from fighting. They want to dominate the other, I can feel it. I manage to keep them in control by keeping them away from each other, but this is a complex exercise. Still, the thrill sends shivers down my skin. It's like holding back two giant beasts ready to attack...

I freeze one hand and heat up the other. Soon enough, and with all of my focus to keep it going, steam starts appearing around me. A strong, thick, white fog that spreads to my surroundings.

"Mara..."

I don't have time to look at Liam's baffled expression. I focus even more to get one hand colder and colder, and the other hotter and hotter. The two beasts are roaring, ready to fight, but I need to keep them in check and just an inch apart to do what I want. It's draining, but exciting. Even more so because I've been used to controlling my fire for a while now, but the water is new, and I need to learn how to control that stream. They are so different, I can't even re-use what I know about my fire. Water is much easier to tame, I know I can stop the flow anytime. It's harder to control, though. It's like the difference between a feisty cat and a vicious snake... They're so different, and I need to learn and adapt fast.

Using my fog, the wolves start attacking again and make their way through. They understood right away; unlike the humans, they can use their sense of smell and their enhanced vision to find the targets, even in this situation. I can even hear them all mind-linking each other, making sure no one gets isolated or separated from the pack. I smile as they figure it out pretty quickly and progress. From the bits I can see through the white steam, they are careful not to permanently injure the girls, but it's harder when they have to hold back... Still, we are finally moving. As I extend my fog, I can hear the sounds of fights coming from all sides, even opposite to us.

As soon as I feel I can, I stop creating more fog and join the fight to help us make our way through. The wolves I can still see have apparently agreed to knock over the girls, and bite their wrists until they let go of their weapons. They are basically harmless once they're disarmed, and with the white curtain I've created all around us, they can't tell where the wolves are, either, so they're not trying to kill themselves.

"Mara, it's working!" exclaims Liam, excited.

"Yeah, it's–"

Before I can finish my sentence, I feel dizzy all of a sudden. Oh, I did not expect that...

"I warned you," suddenly says a voice behind me.

I glance over my shoulder, only to guess that it's Naptera's silhouette in the fog. So she decided to get out of the water... I glare at her, but ignore her, coming to my senses and resuming the fight. It looks like she's given up on attacking me, but I don't like having her behind me...

"You're going to kill yourself," she hisses. "No witch was made to handle two elements!"

Oh, can't she stop fucking talking...?

I realize I'm asking a lot of my body. I used to get very tired and... damaged when I used my firepower the first few times. Now, I am dealing not only with that, but with an extra new power as well, and those two won't even cooperate. Of course I'll get tired twice as fast...

However, I'm far from done, and far from giving up. I've learned my own limits by now, I can handle this much.

"If you're not going to help, you can leave!" I retort.

She's lost her animosity from before, so I don't think she'll attack me again, but I don't like the idea of leaving her here with the rest of the wolves... She glares, but I glare back, and that's the last time I look at her before I continue fighting my way out of this crowd.

Ignoring the Water Witch, Liam and I keep going, heading northeast. Because our group is staying close, we progress fast and smoothly while the rest of the werewolves are attacking the humans more slowly from the other side.

"Mara, here!"

Selena found a way out, at last! We run through the opening, ladies first while the Black Brothers make sure none of the human girls can attack us or something. It feels good to finally move toward where we're actually supposed to go! Like last time, I run alongside the werewolves, but I'm not as joyous as before. I had hoped they'd do okay while I was underwater, but Ben's got more blood on his fur, and Nathaniel Black is limping a bit...

We don't have time for a checkup, though. We get closer to East Point Ground, and there's a strange feeling in the air. I don't like this... We meet with some other wolves, maybe about a few dozen or so, but as per the Alphas' orders, they remained at a safe distance, so I'm not sure how many are really waiting in the area. Our two groups meet, and to my surprise, Lysandra Jones is standing there, the only one in her human form, a smirk on her face as we approach.

"...Took you long enough," she says.

"We were held back by another witch... How's the situation here?"

"Boring, at best. We stayed at a distance as you recommended. The witch arrived half an hour ago, but all she's been doing since is tracing circles and weird symbols on the ground. I warned everyone to stay away, and keep the humans at bay too. If there was–"

Before she can finish her sentence, a terrible noise shakes the whole area. It's violent, sudden, and deafening. Even worse, it sounds like an explosion. I block my ears by reflex, and a lot of the wolves crouch down. Liam jumps in front of me, covering me with his body, and for a few seconds, I'm completely unable to tell what's happening. It's just so strong and powerful, I have no idea what's going on.

Slowly, after that first loud bang, the noise dissipates, but there's an odd feeling lingering in the air... Shit, I don't like this at all. I'm very uneasy, and I stay close to my mate. I need to know what's going on. I finally look over Liam's shoulder, and it's clear no one understands what happened. It's not over, though.

Right after that, the ground literally starts trembling under our feet. Not just a little wave, but more like a violent rumble. The sound is almost as bad as the first explosion. We fall down, on all fours or on our knees, completely at a loss. I see wolves rolling down some hill or on top of one another, unable to keep standing. What the heck is going on?!

"Witchy, do something!" yells Lysandra.

I glare at her, but while the ground is still shaking like crazy under us, I grab Liam's shoulder to try and steady myself, and look toward the center of that plaza.

The chaos is even worse down there. The wolves that were close try to crawl away and retreat carefully as the vibrations are even worse at the center of that area. Of course, that's exactly where Ravena is. I need to control the feeling of sheer panic growing inside to try and see what's going on. Is she doing this herself? Or is something worse happening? I can't tell from this distance. All I know is that those symbols Lysandra mentioned were definitely witchcraft, and whatever she was trying to do, Ravena may have succeeded. I can barely believe my eyes, but the ground is opening all around her. This is clearly no normal earthquake. This is her doing, but there's no telling if she's actually aware of what she's unleashing. Long and deep cracks are running all around, and despite all the soil flying left and right, I can tell those cracks are positioned exactly where the lines of her magic circles were. This is the work of an Earth Witch at full power...

I wouldn't say Ravena looks alright, though. I keep staring, and I don't like what I'm seeing. I don't like that at all... Fucking hell. Something strange is happening to her, but it looks way too familiar to me. Long black lines are running on her skin, even up to her face. She is in a weird position too, her face turned toward the sky and her mouth open as if she was screaming. Even weirder, her eyes have turned entirely white, and her hair is floating all around her... Oh, Moon Goddess, I don't like that. It has to be the curse trying to take over her body. I see the movements of a dark aura all around her, growing like a roaring storm ready to unleash. I can see this earthquake is the work of Ravena fighting at full power, but this is definitely not a good sign. I don't know how she thought she could endure the curse, but she was wrong. Things are looking really bad, and if I don't stop this madness soon...

Mara, what the hell is going on?!" yells Selena in my head.

"It's Ravena! She's trying to overtake the curse!"

I really don't think things are going well for her, though. Her state is odd, to say the least, and I can see that dark cloud of magic growing stronger and thicker all around her. She definitely awakened that curse, but it might have been a really, really bad idea... I didn't expect it would be this bad. I don't know much of what's going on from where I am, but the ground is shaking more and more, and she's alone at the center of this earthquake. This is not going to end well. Those cracks are getting larger and larger, and I even spot actual chunks of the ground falling inside those large gaps.

"Oh, she really is that crazy!"

Somewhere behind us, Ayesha just arrived, and she's barely standing up, fighting the terrible shockwaves underneath like the rest of us. She has no choice but to fall on her knees with a grimace. Yeah, welcome to hell... Ignoring all the wolves that growl at her, she lifts her head up to me.

"What's the plan?" she yells over the noise.

"I need to get closer and stop her! If this goes on, she'll destroy all of Silver City and us with it!"

"*Mara, you can't!*" shouts Nora. "*This is too dangerous, we can't even get close! We can barely stand, and the ground is full of holes everywhere! If you fall into one of those, we can't tell where you'll end up!*"

"Nora, if I don't stop her, this is going to get much worse! Ravena is currently fighting the curse, and once she loses, it will be free to do much worse! This is an earthquake, this is Ravena's doing! She might not even be controlling it!"

"How about we let the curse kill her, and join the fun after that?!" shouts Ayesha.

"The curse won't wait! It's already getting stronger each second! Can't you see it?!"

Ayesha frowns and glances beyond, but she seems at a loss. What, she seriously can't see that crazy dark cloud? It's almost big enough to be over our heads now!

"I only see that old bitch's aura, and it's going freaking crazy!" she yells over the ruckus.

"*No, I see it too, Mara!*"

I turn around, and Selena's golden eyes are turned toward the sky, as she's growling toward the dark cloud.

"*Me too...*" says Nora.

What, so only those two can see the curse's dark aura...? And Ayesha can't? What the hell is wrong with that curse?! However, I need to save my questions for later. For now, I need to get to Ravena and stop this madness somehow...

"Mara, what do we do?!" asks Liam.

"Remember when the curse was possessing me?"

"You think I'd forget?!"

"It has to be the same kind of thing!" I shout, making sure our allies hear me. "We have to knock her out, so at least the curse lets go of Ravena! I'm sure she is fighting it from the inside as well, so if we can force it out of her as we did for me..."

"...We can stop all this craziness," nods Liam.

We both stare at the large field of ground between us and Ravena. This isn't going to be easy; there's a long way to go, and the closer to Ravena, the crazier it gets... The cracks are opening wider and wider too, so we can't even predict if one spot isn't going to crumble next!

"...I'll do it," says Liam.

"Liam!" I protest.

I don't want to see him of all people run into that battlefield! It would be almost suicide! However, he grabs my shoulders, forcing me to look at him, looking more determined than ever. It's strange how clearly I can hear his voice despite everything going on around me. It's as if we were alone in a room, not in the middle of dozens of growling wolves and an earthquake.

"I'm the fastest wolf around," he says, his eyes shining. "You said I just have to knock her out, right? If I can get there, this whole crazy earthquake thing will stop, and you can get to her."

"Liam, don't. I'll do it! I'm fast too, and I'm a witch! If I get hurt or trapped, I can get myself out of there, but you–"

"Mara, enough!"

I turn around, and Selena fights the shaking to come closer.

"We know the risks. Liam won't go in alone, wolves attack as a pack. If several of us go, at least one of us will make it. We pick our fastest wolves, and as soon as one of us makes it, you can do your part."

"No, no," I shake my head, "this is my fight, this–"

"Mara, enough! I know what you're feeling, but you have to stop that. I know the curse is your fight, but it's targeting all of Silver City!" she shouts back. *"You're not alone, you're one of us. You're a wolf, and we are your pack. We attack as a pack, whether you like it or not. You're not the Luna, so don't discuss. Everyone works together."*

I slowly nod. I understand her words, her reasoning, but my heart isn't happy with that. Not just Liam, but the idea of so many of us running to Ravena, toward death and danger, is terrifying. I'm not afraid of getting injured, even killed, but if something happens to someone else because of me...

"Think of Kelsi," adds Nora, as if she'd read my thoughts. *"The faster this is over, the more chances she has. Come on, Mara, get ready. You're running with us."*

I take a deep breath and nod.

Right, we're one pack, and they all know what's at stake. I can't protect everyone, but I can do my very best to end this fight as soon as possible. They are all fighters, better ones than me. All I need to do is to focus on the fight, not on them. This is more important, for now. I turn to Liam, determined. He gives me a proud smile and quickly kisses my forehead.

"Get ready, tiger," he whispers. "This might be the run of our lives..."

I nod, and he gets up with me. We're now used to the ground shaking, enough so we can somehow stand up and face the mess in front of us. I look around and see several other wolves get in position. Ben looks ready to go, growling already, his fangs turned toward Ravena.

Selena looks ready to go too, but her husband and Nora stay back. Damian Black is the one to come forward a few steps away from her after a quick lick from the white wolf next to him... I feel my throat tighten again, seeing wolves I don't even recognize about to run with us toward danger. Lysandra, who had fallen down like all of us, rolls over and gets back up on all fours in the form of a dark brown wolf.

"Mara, you stay behind me," says Liam

"But–"

"No buts, babe."

Before I can retort anything, Liam turns into his black wolf and growls softly. Oh, Moon Goddess... I better not lose that furry black butt of his.

"Alright," I sigh, with a quick kiss on his muzzle. "Don't worry about me, I'm not leaving you for one second."

"*Everyone get ready!*" shouts Selena in our head. "*The goal is to get to the witch and knock her out! You get there as fast as you can! If you can't make it, keep running until you get out of there, and watch out for those gaps!*"

Those large openings on the ground are what worries me the most. I haven't looked at one from up close, but I can guess I'm not going to like whatever's down there. There's a strong smell of fresh, labored soil in the air, and something more bitter, like soot... That might be me, though. For a split second, I consider shape-shifting into my wolf form, but I'm pretty sure I can keep up as is. Moreover, I'll be more efficient with my powers if I can move my hands.

"Ayesha, stay here with them!"

"You're a crazy witch," she grumbles. "Crazy but brave, I'll give you that..."

From the way she stares at the path in front of us, she wouldn't have risked going there anyway. I can understand her. This wasn't her fight in the first place... I'm just glad she somehow managed to stay, keep up, and help us. I wish I had time to check where Naptera's at, but I don't. That's one too many witches for me to watch, and there's only one I can afford to focus on right now.

"*Boyan, Lysandra, Tonya, you take the left side. Isaac, Ben, Johnny, on the right. Everyone else, follow your Alpha or Beta! Go!*"

We start running, fast as the wind, despite the violent quakes breaking all around.

It's even worse once we actually get close to the East Point Ground plaza. It's in the shape of a convex sphere, but Ravena's attack has completely changed the area. I see stones turned upside down, torn out of the ground, and thrown away. I actually see one literally spit out by the soil a few steps away from us as we sprint our way in. If we get hit by one of those... it's going to hurt, bad. Damn it...

We run as fast as we can. Because we're focused on speed rather than staying upright, our feet barely touch the ground before we jump again, and we're not as bothered by the uneven ground moving under us. It's more about finding the next place to land on, and making sure we don't trip over one of those endless crevices. I try to focus all I can on Liam, but I'm scared for literally every wolf who followed us. They are all behind; as Liam said, he's definitely the fastest. I can barely stay with him, and I feel my fire behind me, reacting to my need for speed and propelling me like a comet. The only ones fast enough to keep up with us are Damian and Selena. The black wolf seems to shorten the distance at each jump with his monstrous size and dark aura. He's like a dark shadow, landing where he wants with no regards for the state of the ground underneath him. A couple of times, I fear he's about to disappear in one of the gaps, but he immediately pulls himself up and keeps running as if it was nothing.

Meanwhile, Selena's just as impressive. She's like a white bolt, light as a feather and fast as the wind. I'm amazed at her graceful run, and how she lands swiftly everywhere as if she weighed nothing. Moreover, I can feel her golden aura extending all around us as if she was lending her strength to everyone. I bet she's mind-linking them all, coordinating this attack and ensuring we don't lose anyone...

Right. I need to focus and do my best too.

We can do this. We're already halfway there, and I can now see the details of Ravena's expression. The crevices are long and deep indeed, but if we focus on the land that's been spared, we can do this. It just gets harder and harder as we get closer to the epicenter... I hear one wolf howl, trapped, with nowhere left to land. She has to go back and find another path. Another one, a gray male, almost falls before his friend comes and bites his nape to pull him up. The situation is definitely getting more and more difficult as we get closer...

Suddenly, I feel the ground fall under my foot. I barely realize what's going on, but the landslide gets worse, and without a chance to react, I feel myself getting pulled down.

"*Mara!*"

Selena's call got Liam's attention, and I see my mate turning back, but it's too late. I feel the void underneath me, and I just know I'm going to fall. Panicked, I move my arms around, trying to find somewhere to grab. Everything's going too fast for me to have time to use my magic. I'm going to fall...

My feet suddenly hit the water. ...Wait, the water? I glance down, and before I know it, it's up to my waist. I look back, but it's a real stream coming my way, flowing through the crack and probably spreading to the others. A brutal flow of water slowed down my fall. What the hell is going on?! I swim up to make sure I stay at the surface, but the water is quickly filling up this gap, and I'm pushed up, back toward Liam...

"*Mara, you okay?!*"

I grab his fur as soon as I can, and he bites my top to pull me out of there, the two of us out of breath. I'm soaked, but Moon Goddess, I'm alive... I look down at the large crack that almost killed me seconds ago, but the water level is already going back down. That was salt water, wasn't it? I glance around, looking for an answer, until my eyes land on a silhouette standing far away from us.

"Naptera..."

She doesn't move or try to say anything. Even if she did, she'd probably be too far for me to hear. All I can get is her sullen expression, but she looks... resigned. So she decided to lend a hand, after all?

"*Mara, let's go!*"

I nod and get back up on my feet behind Liam, and we resume running like crazy. I'm still soaked from my dive just then, and my head... full of questions. Naptera took our side? Or was she just helping me once? She stayed afar, does that mean she isn't going to help in the fight? As long as she doesn't cause more trouble.

I keep running while I'm torn between hundreds of questions. Suddenly, I feel something coming. I slow down. I can't see it, but all my senses are alert, like a force coming from right in front of us.

"Liam, stop!"

My mate brutally brakes, and jumps out of the way as something, indeed, seems to emerge from the ground. It's a little hill at first, but it keeps growing and growing in front of our eyes, until it stands as tall as a man. Liam and I growl, but we also slowly retreat, careful where we step. What the heck now...?

The strange hill suddenly makes a very, very weird sound and breaks into two. It's almost like an egg opening, and before I can even worry about what's coming, a silhouette emerges out of that muddy mess.

"Holy Moon Goddess, what the fuck is that thing?!"

I have no idea. It looks somewhat human, but a human made of clay by a four-year-old! That thing has no face, just a rough shape of four limbs and a head, and it steps out of its shell, a moving bundle of fresh soil and mud. What the hell are we looking at...?

"Golems!" Liam's voice echoes in everyone's minds. *"Watch out!"*

Just as he says that, I hear a furious growl somewhere behind me. I glance back, and a silver-gray wolf is already pinned on the ground by a golem that has overpowered him.

"Johnny!"

Two wolves that were behind him jump in to attack and bite that thing, but... it's just freaking mud! I turn around, and as I expected, it's Ravena's doing. Her head is now turned toward us, her face distorted by a horrible rictus that doesn't even look human. Her eyes have gone completely dark... What the hell has the curse done to her?!

"Mara! Do something, we can't bite these things!"

Indeed, Johnny Seaver and his wolves keep attacking the bundle of soil and trying to get it off him, but it's like fighting against a mudslide! I turn around, and the one in front of us is big and menacing too. It launches its large fist toward Liam, who dodges it with a jump to the side. Still, if he gets hit or trapped by that thing... I step back, careful to stay out of reach, and look around, but those things have appeared all over East Point Ground, ready to guard their maker. They are attacking the wolves closest to them, everyone that came to attack with us. Selena and Damian Black have no issue dodging theirs, but the bigger wolves like Boyan, Ben, and Tonya are in trouble. They are too big, and they don't have enough safe ground where they are to dodge that thing without risking falling into a crack!

How do I help them? There are yards between us!

"Lysandra!"

His Blazing Witch

A scream pierces the air, and I see one of the wolves about to get swallowed by those gaps. From a distance, I can only see her silhouette, trapped between the two edges and desperate to get back to the surface. There are two golems on her, and they are pulling her into the crack! Her paws on the edge, she's trying to pull herself up, but there's too much weight on her, dragging her down. Shit, I'm too far!

"*Mara, go!*" Selena urges me.

"*But—*"

"*Just go, you stubborn witch! We will save her, you stick to the plan!*"

I can't go, they are all about to get killed right where they are! The two gigantic brown wolves jump to help pull Lysandra Jones up. They are too far away, I can't tell which is Boyan and which is Tonya. They are just two gigantic bundles of brown fur, battling on the edge and trying to bite her where they can pull her up, or crush the soil around her. As soon as they do, though, we see two more silhouettes of clay emerge from the ground behind them. Oh, hell, no... The two golems grab the brown wolves, either trying to pin them down or push them to the edge too. With horror, I see the ground tremble and crack under their feet, looking about to crumble. No, Moon Goddess, no!

"It's fucking mud, you idiot!" suddenly roars Ayesha.

I see her run toward us to the closest group of wolves. She charges up her fists with fire, and suddenly, shoots it right at the mountain of soil trying to suffocate Johnny Seaver. The gray wolf has to turn his head to protect himself, but as soon as the witch's fire hits the mud, it suddenly stops moving. Of course! Heat solidifies it! That thing stops moving, and the wolves attack it. It's slow, but they can get rid of all that soil and move away from it now that it's not moving anymore.

I focus on my inner fire, and turn around, shooting a large blast toward the one attacking Liam. It was high time. That thing had just about trapped him under its arm, a grip of mud around his waist, but as soon as it's solid, Liam growls furiously and gets out of there. I turn back, but the brown wolves are still struggling, and I have to hold my fire. I can't shoot! If I solidify the clay around Lysandra, it's going to get heavier, and that ground is already on the verge of collapsing with all that weight... Shit! What do I do? I turn to try and find Naptera, but she's nowhere to be seen. Where the hell did that fucking witch go?! I try to look around us, but there's no way I'll be able to fill the cracks with enough water until it gets all the way to the one under Lysandra...

Suddenly, as I'm desperate for a solution, my eyes meet with Lysandra's. We lock eyes for a second, in a weird moment that seems to just stop in time. It's strange. Although she's so far from me, and in her wolf form, I could swear she's smiling at me...

"*Go, Mara fucking Jones.*"

It hits me violently. The reality of what's going on, of what's at stake, and what I simply can't do. I'm trembling, but those words push me away from them. I take a step back, and another. Still locking eyes with her, until I have no choice but to look away, my heart ripped in two. I don't watch what happens.

I just hear the ground that collapses, and the terrible ruckus that follows the earthquake on the other side of the area. I hear voices of dozens of wolves screaming in my mind, calling their names in despair. Each voice hurts a bit more than the other. I hear some yelling orders, but I run. I cry, and I keep running. Someone yells at me to keep running again, and I have no other intention.

I run to put an end to this madness, as soon as possible. I'm furious, I'm broken, and I'm ready for this fucking fight. I gather my inner fire like a volcano prepares its lava, and I suddenly shoot it ahead of me, bursting that clay monster in front of us. The mud sprays all around, but I don't stop, and run past it as if I was flying. The black wolf runs just as fast, now staying right next to me, ready for our next opponent.

They keep coming. One golem after the other, and I can hear the fights going on behind us. Those monsters of clay are trying to slow the wolves down and throw us into the gaps. I'm not powerful enough to produce enough water and fill the cracks like Naptera did, but I burst my fire at each one I can. As soon as I spot a wolf or more fighting one of those monsters, I launch my flames to burn it. Some wolves even have to dodge my violent firepower, but I have no time and no patience left for self control right now. I hear Nora's cries and Selena's anger. I feel them as if they were right next to me, and I can only hear them right now and Liam. They are like a voice overpowering everyone else, like my soul sisters following me where I'm going. I feel their pain and anger like mine, but I don't even have time to check on the others. I just have to keep running, I have to put an end to this. You damn curse, you're going to pay for this...

I accelerate, my heart beating as loud as the earthquakes all around us. The sky above us is getting darker and darker, and I can't even tell if those are clouds or the curse. It's just horribly loud, above and below. Liam and I keep running, trying to make our way past the hills of mud and the monsters emerging out of them. Each time a golem comes out, I use my fire to burn it, and Liam tears it apart as soon as it's dry enough for him to bite into.

Although we found an efficient way to get rid of them, I feel like we're not making enough progress at all. At least, not fast enough. The ground keeps moving around us, and twice already, we had to go back to find another way before we reached a dangerous edge. I'm even more panicked that I feel the fights happening everywhere behind us. I try to shoot a fireball each time I can, but it's not enough. I'm too far from most of the wolves, and I can't help out everyone while also running away from them... If only I had even more firepower! I have to control it so I won't also injure a wolf, but those things are emerging non-stop now; nowhere is safe.

"*Mara!*"

I stop, and look behind me.

The situation isn't looking great. I hadn't realized as Liam and I kept tearing those things apart before they could get big, but... the golems are just getting bigger and bigger. They are bigger than the wolves now, no longer human-sized... This is really not good. Aside from the Alphas making their way through, most wolves are overwhelmed or stopped right where they are and pushing their fight. Ben and another wolf team up against one golem, and despite their big size, they are in trouble too. I arm my fist with a gigantic fireball, and shoot it their way, bursting through that thing's back. That's enough for them to jump and attack what's left, but... this is just one out of so many.

"Mara! You have to keep going alone!" roars Selena.

I turn around, but... there's still a long way until I get there. While I run to Ravena, what will become of the others? I already had to watch three of them fall!

"Mara...?" calls out Liam, waiting for me a couple of steps away.

I glance at my mate, but I can't decide. I know I should keep going and not stop to worry about them, but... I can't. My inner wolf hates leaving her pack behind, and I agree with her. This isn't who we are. This isn't what I do. I am not just a witch, I'm also a wolf.

...And a wolf stands with her pack.

"Stay close to me," I tell Liam, before rushing back.

"Mara, what are you doing?!"

"You're not going to make it alone, and neither am I!" I shout back.

I speed up, going back, and powering my fists as much as I can. I have to keep them down to control the fire, and at each new step, I'm almost jumping in the air from the power bursting out of my fists. I feel as if I could almost take off and fly! I smile, but there are many fights that need me. I start attacking the first golems, one after the other. The wolves quickly understand and jump away from my fireballs, but I'm not stopping. I send one after the other, like a catapult attacking all over the ground. Liam joins me, and runs to help the closest group of wolves defeat their opponent.

"Mara, you're just wasting time!"

No, I'm not. I'm trying to think, how can I help them without being everywhere on the ground. I see Ayesha, and she is busy maintaining a barrier at the rear... A barrier against whom? Suddenly, I see them. The human chicks are gathered on the other side and fighting with another pack again. Did the fight from the seashore get all the way here? Already? The Fire Witch is busy containing them, so she can't help me in this situation... I'm on my own...

I keep powering my inner fire, so strong, it feels as if it's enveloping my whole body. The flames are, at least. I'm like a human torch, spreading my power all over the area, unable to contain it. Even Liam has to stay away from me and my fire... but it's not enough. The more I keep fueling that fire, the stronger it gets, even... thicker. I feel as if it's a body about to come out of mine, and... suddenly, I realize. I smile and step back. Forgetting all of the golems for a handful of seconds, I just focus on my inner fire, and keep it growing. I shoot right at my feet this time. I don't just burn the area, I maintain it, more and more, focusing all of my strength on it, growing that gigantic thing like a bonfire right in front of me.

"...Spark!" I shout.

A deafening roar shakes the area.

From the fire, a gigantic cat jumps out. No, the cat is the fire; I laugh, unable to contain my excitement. It's really Spark! The enormous feline I had seen from the witch circle is standing there, twice as big, and he has those magical golden eyes of my cat. He roars again, gathering everyone's attention, and turns his enormous head to me. It's as if all of the fire I had created before is now assembled to make up his body, the soot and flames battling all over like black and golden fur... I smile and caress his face, although my hand meets nothing but the warmth of that fire. He purrs, and the ground shakes under us.

"Go get them," I whisper.

A golden spark appears in his eyes, and he roars again before jumping across the field. The force of that jump has me step back and Liam crouch down. In just one jump, he's on the other side of the area, and ferociously attacks a bundle of golems that was over a dark gray wolf. It's a strange sensation, as if my inner fire had been taken out of me, and was now moving independently with its own will... Spark the giant fire cat jumps again, smashing two golems with his paws like a cat would hunt a mouse. Selena, who was the closest, lifts her golden eyes to the cat, the two of them staring at each other before Spark jumps again.

"Nice move, Mara..." she gasps in my mind. *"I'll give you that one."*

With my fire cat helping the werewolves all across the area, I can move again, my heart a bit lighter. A part of me is fighting at the back, and I can run again with Liam.

"Are you alright?" asks Liam.

I nod without thinking. In truth, I can feel Spark as if he was pulling on my inner fire, and it's tiring, but... I'm alright for now. We resume running, and thanks to the new ally, more wolves are able to catch up to us. Selena and Damian Black are behind us again, each of them finding their own path toward the Earth Witch. We're finally getting closer!

A loud ruckus suddenly shakes the ground beneath us. Liam and I both jump to the side out of reflex, but it's not enough. That hill is growing, growing much bigger than any golem we've encountered already... The ground beneath us starts rising, too fast. Before we get to jump away again, we both lose balance and roll down that new hill. I feel my body rolling down and hitting the ground, again and again, as if I was falling all the way down a huge mountain. It just doesn't stop. I try to catch the ground, something, but I'm swallowed by a wave of soil and dirt, and my vision darkens. I can't...

"I got you."

A strong grip suddenly pulls me out of there. I feel my body flying above ground, and I suddenly hit a more stable one under me. I'm exhausted, but I struggle right away to get back on my knees, and find out what's going on. I grab the black fur in front of me without thinking. I realize just then the wolf standing in front of me in a protective stance isn't Liam... it's Damian. He doesn't care, though. He growls at the gigantic thing finally emerging from that mountain in front of us. Oh, Moon Goddess... not only do we have a giant hill now separating us from Ravena, but there's something just as big coming out of it. Two clawed paws emerge first, digging through the dirt, and Damian Black growls even more. Oh, what the hell, that thing is... a bear?

"Mara! You okay?"

Liam arrives at my side, followed by Selena. He looks like he's been through hell, his fur is as dirty as can be... I nod, but I'm much more preoccupied by that thing before us... Selena growls too.

"I take it this one's not a golem..."

"It must be her familiar," I gasp.

That bear isn't made of clay, but of soil. Just like I had materialized a gigantic fire cat... Oh, shit, how are we going to beat that thing and get past the hill to get to Ravena? I get back up, and the two black wolves move simultaneously to get between that thing and me and Selena.

"Liam?"

"You go," he says. *"Damian and I will take care of that thing..."*

"Selena, you should go with her."

I see the cream-white wolf hesitate too. She glances my way, but before I can say a word, another wolf suddenly jumps in. A third black one.

"Nate!"

"I can't let my brothers have all the fun, can I...?"

Indeed, he comes to stand in between his brothers, growling just as furiously.

That gigantic bear doesn't flinch in front of the trio. It's growling too, and frankly, it's at least three times bigger than them! I can feel its hot breath from where I stand... Can they really handle that thing? I stare at Selena, and she's unsure as well.

"Selena," says Nathaniel, *"this was your idea. You follow the plan. Go with her."*

"Nate, no," she growls. *"You're–"*

"I've still got three limbs and my fangs; I'm still a fighter, Elena."

She freezes. I feel something happens between them, but... unfortunately, there isn't much time for this. After a couple of seconds, without a word, Selena gently rubs her face against his flank, then she turns to me.

"Let's go."

She jumps first to take a detour around that giant bear. Probably not liking that the white wolf ignored him to take the long way around, that giant thing growls loudly. Just then, the biggest of the black wolves attacks, followed by the three-legged one. Liam glances back at me.

"Stay safe, tiger."

"You too, hot stuff."

With a heavy heart, I turn away and resume running, following the white wolf that's running past. As soon as I've turned away, I hear the raging growls of the battle behind us. The three black wolves are furiously and relentlessly attacking the magic bear, making sure it won't follow us. Selena and I keep running, as fast as we can.

"Are they going to be okay?" I can't help but ask.

"They're fighters. They'll be fine."

I can hear the anger in her voice, but I know it isn't directed at me. It's probably more the whole situation. Maybe she's mad at herself too, but I don't know why. I just keep running. I don't have the energy to be mad right now, I'm just worried about Liam, about his brothers, about everyone.

"Nora!" I call out. *"How's the situation on your side?"*

"Your giant cat is helping us a lot... and some humans came to help us on the other side too! They are trying to stop the girls from attacking or injuring themselves."

"...What about Lysandra, Boyan, and... Tonya?"

"...I'm not sure; they haven't reappeared..."

I can hear the sadness in her voice, and I'm choking up a little too..

"...There are wolves trying to dig the ground where they disappeared," she continues, *"but... I don't know, Mara. The golems and the ground are trying to bury us alive. I have to help those who make it, but... it's not stopping, and the rest of the wolves are trapped on the other side of the fire barrier. I don't think it would be any better if they were here, though. The number doesn't seem to matter much..."*

"Nora, perhaps you should come over here then," says Selena. *"I have a feeling we're going to need a lot of your Light Magic here..."*

I agree.

I don't like the area we just arrived in. The sky is so dark, it's as if night has already fallen. We just got past the giant hill that emerged, and we can see Ravena again, but... I have a feeling the Earth Witch is in a much more dangerous situation than we are. Actually, she's on her knees, her body strangely bent backwards, her face turned toward the sky with a horrifying expression. The dark lines are all over the visible parts of her body, even on her face... I realize she's not the one that's been attacking us all over the battlefield. It's the curse, using her powers. Or maybe they're using each other, but either way, it's clear Ravena is losing control. The whole area is shrouded in the darkness, and Selena and I slow down, cautious. We can both tell there's nothing good going on here...

"Stay close."

I nod, and get as close to the wolf as I can. I don't even dare light up my fist with my fire. I can feel Spark using a lot of energy back there, and I might have to leave him that source for a while...

Something suddenly shines in front of us, and I jump in front of Selena, putting up a magic circle to defend ourselves. The rock breaks violently against my last-minute shield.

"Nice one, Mara."

"Stay behind me," I nod.

As soon as I've ended that sentence, more rocks are lifted from the ground and fly our way. I have to move quickly to block them, and widen my magic circle in front of us. Oh, fuck... Each of them bursts violently against my shield, the strength making me step back with a groan. Damn it... She's not happy we're here.

"Ravena!" I shout.

A few steps ahead of us, her body twitches bizarrely, and her head spins, like a doll, to turn toward us. A strange grin appears on her face, one that has nothing human about it. Oh, hell... I'm not sure there's a Ravena left in there. Selena growls louder.

More rocks are lifted from the ground... This time, they are shrouded by some of that weird dark fog... I get ready nonetheless. When they hit, though, it's much more powerful than before. I feel my magic circle violently hit, once, twice, and a crack appears. How can there even be a crack in a...?! The next one breaks it apart, and I'm forcefully hit right in my chest. I gasp, out of air, and fall back.

"Mara!"

I feel Selena jump in above me, but she's not going to be more resistant than me, it can't be! I try to stand back up, but I'm still in a shit load of pain. Moreover, to my surprise, the dark rocks don't seem to... hit her? What's going on? I crawl back, and Selena stays right in front of me, stopping those things from coming near us. It's like there's some sort of... shield.

"Are you alright, Mara?"

I turn my head, and to my surprise, Nora is there. Her blue eyes look filled with worry, she puts herself under my arm and helps me up. Her white fur is covered in mud, but still strangely shining underneath... She and Selena both stand by my side as I painfully get back up. Oh, I can still feel that hit right in the middle of my chest... Damn it.

"You were fast," says Selena.

"I was worried... and some of our wolves managed to come in and help. I figured I'd be more useful with you two, with all that... that Dark Magic..."

She might be right. The darkness surrounding Ravena's body is somehow getting thicker as her expression transforms into a grimace.

"You..." her voice comes out like a strange rattle out of her body. "Cursed..."

"Apparently, attacks meant for Cursed Ones are useless against Royals like us," says Selena. *"It might be our turn to protect you this time, Mara..."*

"Perhaps, but I can't stay hidden behind you two. I need to get to her."

"Do you know how to break the curse yet?" asks Nora, sounding worried.

"...I think I got a clue. No, several, actually. I think I know why everyone else failed..."

"Does that mean you can succeed?"

I chuckle, massaging my chest.

"Actually," I sigh, "I think I might be the only one who can put an end to this..."

His Blazing Witch

I hope I'm not mistaken, but the more I think about it, the more it all makes sense. That curse, and why so many witches failed over the years... Selena and Nora exchange a glance.

"*Alright, if you think so... How do we proceed, though?*"

"First, we need to get to Ravena and somehow knock her out, then have the curse focus on me instead."

"*Looks to me she's pretty out of it already,*" growls Selena, her head turned toward the Earth Witch's scary state.

"I don't think so. I don't think the curse could use her powers like this if she was... It's probably more like she's being used like some vessel. Ravena thought she could control the curse, but now it's controlling her instead. I need to take her place and be the one to fight it off. I–"

A loud ruckus comes from behind. We all freeze and look back as the furious growl of the bear echoes all the way here. In the darkness, the sky above us suddenly seems to rumble like a storm, and the shadow of that monstrous thing appears briefly in the sky. Moon Goddess, it looks even bigger... We hear several wolves howl, a heart-breaking sound that can't be good...

"*Liam!*" I scream, just as Nora and Selena call out to their mates as well.

The seconds pass, and I try to feel my mate. I'm so panicked; it's a real mess. I desperately search for him, my wolf and I united as one. There are so many wolves scattered all around, and I'm so panicked I can't even focus properly. I'm a mental and emotional wreck until I finally feel him reaching out to me.

"*I'm fine... I'm fine, babe! You... focus on your own fight, Mara! Don't worry about–!*"

He can't finish his sentence; another loud bang like an explosion resonates. We see soil flying from behind that hill. Oh, Moon Goddess... I can even hear Damian and Nathaniel's furious growls. That must be some fight from hell going on over there, but all we can witness are the ferocious growls and shadows moving. I hope they will be alright... Next to me, Selena growls.

"*Let's focus here. The big boys know how to take care of themselves. Mara, are you sure we only have to get you to her?*"

"I'm not sure of anything, but that's... that's the first thing."

Although I can tell we're not quite there yet. There's only a stone's throw distance between us and Ravena, but from the way her scary expression is still turned toward us, I'm sure those last few steps are not going to be easy.

Selena growls again, and she's the first to start running toward the witch, as expected. I get right behind her, ready to prepare any fire or magic circle, and I feel Nora running right behind me too. For a second, I hope this will happen much quicker than I imagined, with just us running over. Of course, it doesn't happen like that.

We hear a loud rumbling beneath us and, right at the last second, Selena jumps out of the way as a sudden gap opens under her feet. It's just a hole, but it suddenly pulls in everything that was around like quicksand. It happens so fast, but I can feel the monstrous volume of pressure under there. She's going to try to pull us in and kill us... We can't rest. Nora and I split apart when another crack appears on the ground between us, and this time, a new golem emerges. Before we can react, that thing grabs Nora's back leg, and she growls furiously, struggling to get out of there.

"Don't move!" I shout.

I prepare my fire, a smaller one this time, and throw it right away, just enough to harden the mud around her feet and let Nora break away from that thing. She runs as fast as she can farther away, but we're all split up already, and Ravena isn't done with us yet. Stones slowly rise from the ground and, as I step back to prepare for this, they fly our way, too fast, way too fast. I raise my arms, trying to conjure a circle, but it hits it so violently, I'm thrown back on my ass in the mud. Oh, shit. The ground immediately starts trying to grab me, but I won't let it. I take a deep breath and invoke my inner fire for the nth time today. I know Spark needs it, but I may need it more right now! I set as much of my body on fire as I can, burning all the damn soil until I have enough strength to get back on my feet and get away from that mess.

I glance to the side, but Selena and Nora are already battling a new golem while trying not to get swallowed by the ground. Damn it! She's trying to slow us down and keep us away from her... I run to help them out, and other rumblings echo in the sky above us. There's really a storm coming! Now, seriously? Or is that the curse acting out? I feel the humidity in the air, but it doesn't stop me. I'm already trying to make my way despite the mud, and anyway, I've extinguished the fire within to let Spark have most of it...

Instead, I prepare another magic circle and, like a shield in front of me, I run into that golem to try and push it with brute force. A bit unconventional for a witch, but that thing bursts as soon as I hit it.

"Nice one, Mara..."

"We're not done yet."

Indeed, that golem is already reconstituting itself. This can't go on. Ravena has an endless supply of soil under our feet, while my inner fire is being pumped to Spark on the other side of the battlefield. I do not want to leave my magic cat without any source of power, either, as I know he's protecting all the other werewolves... Another round of rumbling resonates above our heads. The storm is already above us and getting louder. The perfect setting for a battle... While the golem builds itself back up, more stones are gathered around it. A lot of rocks, actually... Is that thing making itself armor? Before I can even realize, it suddenly moves and punches our way, hitting my circle.

The shock is violent. I feel the strength of it resonate through my whole body, and my magic circle shatters as I realize I'm about to get hit. That fist appears right in front of my eyes.

I feel the hit before the pain. A bundle of rock suddenly hitting my body, something breaking. I'm sent flying away, and the pain starts as my body violently hits the ground. It's almost an out-of-body experience, as if there was an echo in the pain that engulfs me. I hear my own groan of pain and their voices calling me in sheer panic. Damn, that... hurts...

"Mara! Mara, are you okay?!"

I groan, the only answer I can formulate out loud. It feels like all the bones in my upper body are shattered... Maybe they are. The pain is... of a hellish level. I taste the iron in my blood, filling my mouth, and I spit it out by reflex. Oh, damn... My head is spinning just from the pain. I have a vague impression I'm lying down, but... I'm so numb for a second, I can't feel anything but that pain.

"Hold on, Mara..."

A wave of ice suddenly envelops my body. I can breathe again as it gently caresses me, numbing the pain a bit. I see Nora's white fur in my field of vision, and I can feel her aura, like a white coat over me. It's like a cold shower washing the pain away, and Moon Goddess, that feels so good and relieving. I can move again without everything hurting like hell... I'm a bit sore, but I quickly manage to move and try to get back on my feet. Nora heals me as fast as she can.

"S-sorry..." I grumble.

"Don't apologize; it's okay... Thank Moon Goddess you survived that hit..."

I just realize what happened, and indeed, I'm not going to take another one like that. I underestimated that golem thing because I thought it would be slow with all those rocks... It's clearly not. As I get back up, still in pain but on a manageable level, I see Selena battling that thing. The cream-white wolf is more like bouncing, jumping, and running all around that stone-reinforced golem. She's making it move all around and run after her without giving it a chance to hit her. I really acknowledge she's one of the best fighters around. She's incredibly fast, quick-witted, and she doesn't give that thing a single chance to catch or hit her. However, she's also stuck; how the hell are we supposed to attack that thing? It's like a mountain between us and Ravena!

Next to me, Nora growls too, but I don't see how we're going to get rid of that thing... The sky above us is growling loudly too, and I feel the air getting more and more humid. I don't like this. If it starts raining, the soil under us will become mud, and it will be even harder to move around and get out of there. I don't even want to imagine the mess it's going to be on the other side. I just hope everyone's holding on...

I prepare a new magic circle, but this time, I prepare it well. I make that thing much more resistant, much more robust so it won't be shattered in one hit. Or at least, I hope so...

Nora and I run back toward Selena. I'm still in pain, but I can manage this much. Nora's power is fantastic, I still feel as if there is some ice numbing the most painful areas, and I think it's still healing me somehow. Her white aura is surrounding my torso and working to heal my broken ribs. Strangely, I also feel... lighter. It's not about the pain, but having that white, calm aura around me makes me feel a lot more relaxed, as if a weight I wasn't aware of had been weighing on me all this time. What is this? Selena's golden halo seems a bit different from before too...

Then I realize.

I didn't pay attention because of the fight, but the dark aura isn't just around Ravena anymore; it's... everywhere around us. I can't believe I didn't notice it before! It's like a dark fog, so transparent and absolutely everywhere, I have to focus to really see it. It's engulfed everything around us, and me too. When I really look at the two Royals, I can see they are immune. Not just that, but it's as if this dark thing is avoiding them. Their auras are protecting them from that dark fog but... not me. It's even the opposite. It looks like it's almost drawn to me, and melding with my own aura. Darkness attracts darkness, I guess...

"Mara, any plan to get rid of that thing?!" shouts Selena.

Even her inner voice sounds out of breath, and it's understandable with the crazy speed she's been at for a while now. I look at the golem once again. The rocks are gathered so tight around its body, I don't know what could get inside. Even if I tried to burn it, it would take a while for the fire to penetrate... I take a few deep breaths and try to summon the water this time.

Just like before... I try to tame the fire in me and channel the water instead. It's so much harder to do this when I have to focus on that golem attacking us, and the damn ground trying to swallow us wherever we step! Moreover, the area is dry as hell... Moon Goddess, I changed my mind, I wish it'd freaking rain so I could use the water. I'm a total newbie at trying to conjure some! I can't give up, though, or next time, Selena or Nora might be the ones sent flying!

I focus and call out the inner Water Witch in me. I beg my wolf for help, and she's right there with me, focusing as well. There's water... There's always water somewhere. I direct my fingers toward the ground, trying to pull as much as I can. I feel it... I feel the rumbling, the small, minuscule drops getting attracted to my position like magnets. Come on, come here...

"Mara, watch out!"

I jump to the side out of reflex, barely avoiding a new throw of stones. Damn it, I'm trying to focus here! However, that wretched thing isn't going to wait for me to finish. The sky loudly thunders above us, and this time, the dark clouds gathering above us are definitely real... Wait.

I may be wrong or crazy, but... I try to ignite my inner fire again. I know how to balance the two now, don't I? I roll on the ground to get away from the golem, letting Nora jump over me, fangs out, and I glance up at the sky. It's full of hot air up there; that storm is right above us. I take deep breaths. I'm not a science nerd, but the inner witch in me knows...

"Selena, get ready to jump as fast as you can out of there when I tell you!"

"What? Mara, what are you planning?!"

"Trust me! Just... please keep that thing busy, and get ready when I tell you to run! Get as far away from that thing as possible!"

I'm not even sure myself this is going to work, but... it's definitely worth a try... I think. Moon Goddess, for a crazy witch, this might be my craziest idea yet...

I let the two wolves run toward the golem to distract it while I prepare myself. This might hurt me a lot, now that I think about it, but... Oh, what the hell, I'll see to that later if I survive it. I glance toward the dark, dark sky, my heart thumping like crazy. The rumbling, again. I hear the howls and growls of dozens of wolves behind us. They are all waiting for me to end this fight and trying to survive in the meantime. I have to stop that thing...

I close my eyes and focus. The ground beneath me slowly tries to swallow my feet, but I ignore it. I have to focus on what's happening above, not below. I gently call out my inner fire, and tame that water flow inside of me. That's right, a perfect balance. I can control both if I stay in that quiet, calm balance inside. I ignore everything else. I'm a witch of two elements, and I can master both at the same time. I know I can. My wolf is there, helping me, sharing her inner strength with me to make this work. Her quiet but powerful stance helps me, like a strong backup I can rely on. That's right, girl. We are two, but also one.

Fire and water. I got this. I smile, my breathing getting more intense. I take a deep breath, and once I feel like I've channeled both elements, I slowly raise my hands toward the sky. I'm buried down to my ankles now, but I don't care. That damn golem is about to get meanly stoned...

I feel the hot air above, and I focus on this. The heat is my thing. My palms toward the sky, I feel it until I'm strong enough to control it. I got this. I make that heat mine. I focus even more, until I can feel it like invisible strings channeled to my fingers... The rumbling in the sky answers me. I take another deep breath, and while still holding this mass of hot air, I find the water stocked above. If there are clouds, there has to be some... Yes, I can feel it. I don't need to control these, I just need to make it cooler... and cooler... It's exhausting, exhilarating. I feel the power of both worlds, both elements, channeled through my hands, and yet it's all happening in the sky. I'm controlling so much of what's going on above our heads, I've never felt so powerful. A shot of adrenaline runs through my body, delicious hot and cold chills as if to motivate me even more.

"Now!" I shout.

Both wolves jump out of the way, running as fast as they can away from the golem, as instructed.

Left alone, that stone giant seems to look my way, and advances forward, aiming right at me. The thunder resonates in the distance, and I smile. I prepare to channel all that energy, and suddenly, guided by my fingers, the air starts crackling and sparking between us. The golem takes another step, and I make my move; A gigantic lightning bolt rips the sky apart and violently strikes that thing down.

It's amazing and terrifying. I feel the electric current literally bursting through me, the sparks running on my skin. It's... electrifying. Literally. The power blast travels throughout my body. I feel as if I'm about to explode, but I keep my arms like antennas directed at the golem. I'm absolutely frying that thing. It's just a matter of seconds, as long as I can hold it. The golem vibrates, a bright light coming from all the gaps between the rocks. It's working! Suddenly, that thing implodes from the inside, wrecked apart by my lightning bolt. I let go at the last second to protect my eyes. Mud flies everywhere, spilling on us and all around, but so do the rocks. Several of them hit me, but I barely feel them. I'm still high from the strength of that lightning bolt, and my whole body is kind of numb too...

"Holy Moon Goddess, Mara, that was fucking epic!"

I smile, still a bit excited, but I stumble back. Wow... My body feels strange, I guess the electric shock didn't leave me completely fine, after all. I feel tingling all over, and there are white dots in my eyes when I blink. I need to close and open them several times to make sure I'm not about to go completely blind.

"Mara, are you alright?" asks Nora, sounding worried.

I nod, but I might need a moment to get back to reality. That was... brutal. Did I seriously just conjure a lightning bolt? That was awesome! I chuckle, still in that strange thrill, but I know I also need to get back to the fight. I focus on my breathing, and on what I see to get back there. The golem has been simply blasted apart, the remnants of its legs still standing there, a bit of dark smoke coming out... Well, that's done. I wipe the mud off of me, and the girls shake themselves too. Selena carefully approaches that thing to sniff it, but just from the burnt smell, I'm sure that thing is done, at least for now.

"Well, looks like you literally fried that thing..."

"Yeah... I might need some time before doing that again, though," I confess.

"Don't overdo it, Mara," says Nora.

Just as Nora said that, a terrible rumbling resonates under our feet. Again? I crouch down, ready for anything, but the ground just keeps vibrating, and I have no idea what's going to happen this time. Another golem? The two wolves come closer to me, Selena growling loudly, ready to attack whatever comes at us. I try to calm down, but my body is still feeling strange from the previous attack. I try to focus on my inner fire, but... it's sort of extinguished right now. Shit, did I really overdo it?

"Mara, watch out!"

I jump to the side as Nora yells, rolling down in the mud just in time to avoid the large gap that opened right where I stood a second ago. I feel another rumbling under me, and I have to roll again to ignore a large fist of clay emerging from the ground. What the heck now...? All over, the ground is starting to open and close like giant mouths trying to swallow us whole. I can't be trapped now! I'm tired as hell, but I still try to keep moving. This is the only way to avoid those things and the giant fists that emerge from the ground all around us.

I glance to the side, but Nora and Selena are doing much better. Their wolves are quick and using their instincts to know where to jump next. It might finally be time I shape-shift... However, something feels strange. I glance up as the thunder is seriously picking up, but the dark aura is still just as thick and getting larger. It's spreading like a mist all around us, and I don't like that at all...

"What's the situation on the other side?" I ask Selena after another jump to safety.

She glances my way, and jumps again to avoid another hole trying to grab her. We can't seem to get closer to Ravena, those things are keeping us at bay...

"Apparently, not getting any better. Your witch friend had to pull her fire back as the human chicks began acting crazy and trying to actually burn themselves. There are more wolves in the area, though, so it's turning into an all-out war on the other side..."

"The guys are doing okay," adds Nora. *"Damian said they are winning over that bear, for now..."*

She and Selena exchange a glance, but I already know what they are thinking. Even if they suffered real damages, their husbands would probably keep quiet about it for as long as they can. They don't want to worry each other, we just all need to focus on our fight... I'm dying to mind-link Liam, but I'm scared I'll distract him at the wrong moment, and I can't afford that. I have to stay focused and finish this fight right here.

...How, though? She's managed to keep all three of us at bay, and although one of us manages to get closer at times, she gets twice as violent in that zone until we have no choice but to back away. We haven't been able to get closer than an arm's length, and that's not enough... While I'm still thinking, something violently hits me from behind. A rock. Damn it!

"Mara, don't stay there, keep moving!"

"I know, I know..."

I run before another gap opens under me, and manage to avoid another rock flying my way. Oh, for Moon Goddess' sake! I can't think and focus on the ground and my surroundings at the same time! I jump again, and glance at Ravena. Oh, hell... She's losing blood. From her eyes, nose, mouth. This really can't be good... I don't like this at all. The curse is going to kill her at this rate!

"Selena, Nora, I need to get there now!"

"What the hell do you think we've been trying to do?!"

I want to roll my eyes, but Selena's right. However, this is not working. We can't keep running around like this; the longer the curse keeps using Ravena as a vessel, the faster she'll die. She may be one bitch of a witch, but she doesn't deserve to be killed like that. I can always make her pay for all that crap later... I keep running, trying to think of another plan. What do I have left? My fire is practically exhausted, and I won't be able to replenish it anytime soon. There isn't enough water for me to control, and I'll definitely kill myself if I try summoning another lightning bolt. Unless....

"Nora, Selena, I think I'm going to do something really, really risky."

"If you say it like that..."

I'm not lying, though. This might be one rather suicidal move, but... it might also be the only one that will work right now. I take a deep breath, and at the next move, I jump into my wolf form. It's so easy, I land on all fours, running to get away from the next gap trying to swallow me. I growl, a bit excited, and shake my body. Well, my wolf seems in good shape... I use her inner strength and summon my power again. Come on, get back at it. We have conjured much more fire than that before... A warm feeling invades my stomach, and I feel it. That blue flame perking up in the darkness. It's small, but very excited, like a spark ready to get much bigger and explosive. I run again, excited. I need to charge up more... I keep running, fast. I don't stop anymore to be careful of the ground. I just keep running and jumping, fast, faster. I only focus on my inner fire, the adrenaline and those little sparks now running through my whole body. They are still blue, but such an intense light that they could also be white and blinding. Hard to tell. I don't stop to analyze it, though. I just focus even more to get that feeling rushing through my whole body.

"Mara...?"

"I'm going to make a run for it," I say, *"and I'm not going to stop!"*

"You're going to get yourself killed!"

"No. I won't stop. I'll charge and use my power to destroy any obstacle."

"Mara, you can't! You're going to get hit!"

"I won't stop."

This fight has to end, and soon. I can't stay back and be careful not to get injured anymore. I'm already injured, and all three of us will get more hurt if I don't act now. There are humans and werewolves dying on the other side of that mountain Ravena created, I can feel it. I feel the sorrow and anger of all the werewolves. I hear yells, screams, and the faraway sounds of a raging battle. I hear the black wolves fighting a giant bear on the other side, our mates fighting like beasts for our survival. Everything is happening here. That curse is driving us crazy, and building fear in us. Even more so in the minds of the humans. They are making both groups fight each other, and I won't stand for it. It has to stop. Now.

"Get ready," I say, even my inner voice is out of breath.

I feel it. The electricity, charging up all around me. It's like I'm burning inside and outside. Flames are now surrounding my entire body, flying behind me as I don't slow down. I hear the crackling all over my body, as if it was getting ready to break or explode. My blood's burning and rushing. The speed helps me focus as I summon the hot air, both above my head and inside my stomach. I'm a wolf, but I'm also a witch. I can control the magic regardless of the body I'm in. I'm a Fire Witch, a powerful witch. I can do anything. This is my fire, this is my power. I'll summon the sky's wrath to this ground if I have to. I've never felt this powerful, as if it was all coming together. Fire Magic and Water Magic. The two reluctantly mixing, fighting, and melting inside to make something much more powerful, more dangerous. The electricity starts crackling and hissing along my fur. I'm charging up like a lightning bolt, and the heat starts to devour me from the inside.

"Mara!"

His Blazing Witch

I ignore them, and keep running. More. I need more. I need to be unstoppable. I ignore the pain, I muzzle it. I'm not suffering, I don't feel a thing. My whole body's about to burst, I'm nothing but power. The crackling gets louder in my ears, a monster taking over my body with hisses and high-pitched screams. Series of blinding flashes blink before my eyes, making everything else dark and almost monochromatic. I stop seeing with my eyes; I have to trust my senses to not get completely blinded by the random flashes. I feel the lightning forking all around my body, violently ripping and streaking the ground. I hear the furious rumbling of the sky above. The thunderous booms echoing my race, as if trying to get back ownership of that running lightning power. But it's not the sky this time. It's me, just me. The thunderous power coming from my guts, from my growling wolf like a beast of electricity and fire.

"*Now!*" I shout.

I change direction and this time, aim right at Ravena. The wind flies in my ears. I keep running, charged with electricity like a thunderous bolt ready to strike. The ground is ripped apart all around me, nothing can stop me. I jump past a gap that opened too late, and another one, and dodge a clay fist that emerged from the ground. My wolf only relies on her instincts, we're almost flying above the ground. I'm blind, but I know exactly what to dodge, where to step. The crackling increases like a ticking time bomb above, ready to explode. The bird screeches around me are deafening. I just keep running toward the mass of darkness in front, like one would run inside a thunderstorm. I feel its power, I feel its fear. Something tall appears in front of me, but a white wolf-shaped form jumps on it to get it right out of my way with furious growls. I lost sight of Nora and Selena, only to hear them furiously fighting those new obstacles. I feel something hitting me, again and again, but it's blasted against the electricity running throughout my body. I feel like a lion, all my senses on edge, my hair standing up to the last bit. My whole body is electrified, I'm summoning this tremendous power like a goddess would summon thunder. I only borrow it for a minute, but for that minute, I'm beyond all the magic power I could have imagined...

I finally get inside the hurricane, right beyond the dark cloak. I see a human body. Ravena's body. I'm there! ...I jump right on it.

The thunderous boom explodes right above my head. I hear the sky break, and the lightning violently strikes my body. I feel as if my whole being is exploding in a thousand pieces. I fall, and I hit another body under me.

Voices call my name, but I'm... really out this time. I can hear faint crackling, remnants of the electric power summoned in this place. I try to open my eyes, but either I'm blind, or... they refuse to open. I can't tell. My body is heavy, and some parts I can't feel... at all. I just know for certain I'm not dead yet. I'm in a tremendous amount of pain, but that pain comes as if it was from behind a glass wall. I'm... numb. I feel cold, all of a sudden. I feel... the darkness. The cold, scary, and swallowing darkness surrounding me. I can only feel that. What is this...? It comes to me slowly, like a scared creature. I feel its power, though. Like shadows, ready to engulf everything, a hungry and blind beast ready to swallow me... I feel it circling around me, coming closer and closer, sensing me.

"...Yes, come. Come to me. I came for you, after all..."

The darkness touches me. It feels as cold as ice over my skin, my fingers, my nape. It's penetrating through all of my pores, getting inside and taking over like a demon looking for a host... I feel the darkness filling me... it's taking a hold of my body, trying to swallow everything it touches. To taint it, to corrupt it. It wants it all... my fire, my wolf, my power. My magic, all of my magic, to devour it...

"You can't have me."

I don't know where I find the strength to speak. That thing hesitates, and like millions of small little black snakes, it scatters all around, trying to get away from my fire. Oh, no. You got close, now you're going to get burned... I can't feel my body, but I channel all the power I can. If you want it, come and take it, you damn curse.

I grow my fire, I make my wolf growl and my water flow. My inner self is gearing up for battle against that thing, and the shadows react. Like a dark cloud, it gets thicker, almost hissing back at me, ready for a fight. Come here... Let's get to a common ground where we can talk. If you want my power, come and get it... I tease it with my flame, taunting it, making that thing approach until I can get a hold of it for real. It knows of my power... It knows I know who they are. Who it really is behind the shadows, lurking, waiting for hundreds of years. Waiting for revenge, poisoning minds, and growing in the darkness.

"...I see you."

A shy white light appears, and I let myself be pulled toward it. I know who you are. You can't run from me like you hid from all the others... I know you... You and I are the same. We are the same... The same darkness. You can take my power. I'll give you what you want, what you've always wanted. I'll free you from your madness... and then, you'll be free.

Free to unleash your wrath.

Chapter 36

The light and the darkness are both there, slowly coming closer, surrounding me in this strange place of silence. The light is shining, so bright and pure, yet so shy in front of me. It's brightening the darkness around like a small window. I feel myself slowly, naturally, pulled toward it, and I do not fight it... I'm not scared. I know where I am, who is there.

I feel myself slowly drown, like coming out the other side of the water. Moon Goddess, it's so cold over there... so lonely too. The silence is echoing within itself, making everything sound so small in the middle of something so vast. I try to focus on the little, vivid flame in my stomach, holding on to it like the only source of warmth around. I really feel like I'm going to freeze to the bone if I forget it's there to warm me up...

I hear wailing, somewhere on my left. I try to remember how to even see anything, and a shape slowly appears. It's a woman, and she smells of... fresh grass and soil... Ravena!

She's curled up on what ought to be some sort of ground. She's obviously in pain... I hear her wailing, but I can't... go anywhere near her. I can't even pull myself there. I'm like a tiny speck of dust, thrown left or right on a breeze's whim, while she's a rock, abandoned there and left to her pain. Her sobbing is so genuine, I feel sorry for her. I can't see the details of her face in the darkness, only her silhouette shaking, following the rhythm of her cries. Damn it... She smells like death. I have no idea how to save her. I don't even know how I can regain control of my body.

"Help... me..."

I hear her muted plea, making me even sadder for her. ...Can I do something for her? I want to reach out, but... I'm so powerless right now.

"Ravena...?"

I can barely recognize my own voice, as if it was coming from very far, like an echo... but she hears it. Her silhouette stops shaking, and I can finally distinguish the traits of her face. The blood I saw earlier, coming down from her eyes, nose, mouth, and ears is still there... She's not going to make it. I can almost see the veil of death in her expression: her empty eyes, the way she looks so tired...

"...Ravena."

It takes me a lot of strength to manage to call her, but she hears it. Her gaze that was so blank and aimless before settles on me. For a strange second, we stare at each other, enemies stranded in the same nightmare. She gasps, a new stream of blood coming out of her mouth.

"You... Please..."

She's struggling to speak, out of breath and out of time. I'm watching her die... I'm watching her die, and I can't do anything about it. Ravena is just at her end, the curse took all it could from her, and left her to die. This is so horrible... Regardless of her wrongdoings, she didn't deserve this.

"Stop... Save..."

Each word looks awfully painful to her, yet she's pleading to me all she can. The red is filling her mouth and running down her lips, her cheek, while her raspy breathing is painful even to listen to. I take a deep breath, and try to regain my body's control. I struggle, in the darkness, to move a single muscle. I know it's way too late to save Ravena, but... if I can at least offer her some... peace...

"I will," I mutter. "I promise I will stop this... I'll save them."

Ravena keeps staring at me, her eyes so empty, I have no idea if she heard me. The darkness looks about to swallow her. It's getting thicker and dark all around her, as if the shadows were about to engulf her... Right before it engulfs her, I see her lips exhale one last breath, and she closes her eyes. The next second, she disappears, the shadow grabbing her away.

Moon Goddess... I need to stop that thing. How many witches have died and suffered unfairly like this...? I need to move. I can't let it swallow me like this too, I don't want to disappear without even a fight... I look up at the white aura, and begin moving my body to get there. I feel like each of my limbs is heavy as hell, but I keep going, I keep fighting to evade that darkness. The darkness isn't what I'm worried about. It's about losing all my strength here... It may look like it's not doing anything, but I know this curse is sucking my strength and lifeforce to get stronger. Well, you won't have it. I'll destroy you first.

I hear a growl next to me. A wolf...? No, it's bigger. I frown. I know it's not my wolf, so what is... Suddenly, something pushes me with incredible strength. I try to look back. ...A bear! Ravena's bear? It's definitely a bear, and it looks like... soil? This one looks friendlier than the bear that's fighting the Black Brothers outside. It must be her spirit or something. She's trying to help me... I guess she doesn't hold it against me now.

With the magic bear's help, I somehow manage to lift my body enough to be on my own two feet, but the area is really much darker now. I take one step after another, until I face that large white door thing. It's shining so brightly, but it's also very cold... I take a deep breath. I think I already know what happened... The truth behind the curse. We were wrong from the start, and for so many years. I fall on my knees in front of it, I glance toward the bear.

"I should be fine now... Thanks."

It leaves with a low growl, and rubs its head against my arm. It feels like warm soil rather than fur, but it's not bad... Right after that, it vanishes, returning to the darkness. I glance down, realizing I can see my arms... or most of them. The dark markings are all over me again, in a familiar pattern. I can't even see the tips of my fingers, they are slowly devoured by the darkness. Oh, Moon Goddess, I might really disappear here. Even more intriguing, though, is the pattern that appeared on my arm. It's not a dark stripe this time but a real magic circle, although I'm unfamiliar with it. The writing is clearly an Earth Witch's doing... One last bit of help from Ravena, perhaps...?

I don't have time to wonder any more. With the bear gone, the cold is getting even worse, and the shadows darker, more menacing... It's time to go. I take a deep breath, and open the white door.

A wave of snow hits me in the face right away.

It's alright; I love snow! I keep running, on all fours, in the dense, magnificent white coat of snow lying before us. My entire pack is running with me. Our group is enjoying itself, progressing like one in the vast area of land. I see the pine trees far ahead, the bright blue sky above. The pups are having fun and trying to keep up with us too. The older wolves are somewhere behind, closing the group... I'm young, and I only care about running, having fun. The snow flies all around us, and we scare a few birds away. The very tall rock far ahead has become our goal, our destination, but we have time before we get there. The sun is high in the sky, and we should hunt by the river first.

I run with my fellow wolves, the young male next to me is the one I like most... No, I love him. I can feel he is my mate... He is a bit different than the others, sometimes wandering around, but I don't really care. He is an Alpha, and perhaps someday he will leave to have his own pack... Will he choose me as his partner? I sure hope so... I am the fastest and largest female of our pack. The other males have tried mating with me, but I'm only interested in one wolf...

Night comes.

I'm tired from our run today, and my belly is full with the results of our hunt. The pups are being nosy a bit farther away... I wish I could have my own someday. Will he let me carry his offspring? Our young ones would be so strong if they are both of ours... I look around, but he's gone off somewhere again... He has been leaving more and more often lately... I can't help but be a bit worried. What if a bear attacks him? Or a human hunter? I get up, and silently leave our group, going to look for him. I miss his smell, but I'm sure I'll find him soon...

I stray through the tall pine trees. The forest is quiet in the darkness of night, and I'm walking silently in the snow... I walk deeper into the forest, looking for my loved one. I hesitate when I smell some human activity. Wood burning... It has to be a human... I also pick up my mate's smell, though.

Suddenly, he appears, alone and safe. Oh, so he is fine... He has that strange smell on him, though, I do not like it... He reunites with me, and we sniff each other, lick each other, checking and exchanging our smell. Oh... we are alone now. Shall I invite him to be just the two of us...? He follows me deeper into the night... So this is it...

I wake up, alone again.

Where is he off to again? Should we stay hidden? Are the humans gone yet? I need to hunt, our pups are hungry... I should go hunt while waiting for him. I go out, this winter is colder than the others... Those human hunters are so scary. I hope they finally leave us alone... I hope my mate returns soon. I bring a rabbit back for our little ones. They are so young and yet so strong already, I am proud of our pups. Soon we will be able to have our own pack and raise them with everyone, far from those scary humans. ...I wonder where my mate is. Did he go to the house with the human female again? I know he likes her, but she smells odd, even for a human one... Is she hoping to tame my mate like men tame dogs? I hope not... I don't like how he acts so submissive with her. He is an Alpha, yet he is so obedient to a human woman...

I silently follow him again. I am just curious... My mate has been smelling so funny lately, even our children have a hard time recognizing their father. He has been bringing more food, but... I wonder why he feels so different now. He knows how to avoid the humans, and where to hunt safely. But I don't recognize my mate, and it pains me so much... I just want to understand what it is he likes so much about that female woman... Is she the one providing him with all that food? It makes my babies happy and safe, but...

He said she is too lonely, so he keeps her company every day... Doesn't that female have a pack of humans with her? Why is she living alone? Is she an Omega...? I keep following my mate, my head full of questions. I have so many questions, and so much worry in my heart.

I hide among the trees, watching them from afar. The woman, and my wolf... They play together, and she looks happy like a young female in love... Is she in love with my mate? She acts like she is... like he's hers. My heart hurts. I step back, a bit scared. I do not understand... We should stay away from humans, so why is he acting like this with that one...?

Suddenly, I see my mate change. Something is so strange with him... He became a human! My mate turned into a human male! What is this…? I'm so scared!

My mate is trying to bring me food, to apologize for making me scared. I am still scared... I am scared for our babies. Why did my mate become a human, and now he is a wolf again? I am so scared... He still goes to the woman, he can't leave her. Why doesn't she have a pack? Why doesn't she have her own mate? What is she doing to my mate…?

My mate is gone, and now he's not coming back.

I have waited many mornings. I looked for him, and I went to the female human's house, but he was gone. Something strange happened to him... I don't know what happened to him. Did he go to the humans forever? Or did a bear kill him? Did the hunters get him? I've waited for so, so long... I'm so scared and lonely. My babies have grown and are all gone now, and my mate is gone too, I am alone... so sad and alone.

This evening, I decide to go and see that woman.

I wonder if she is as lonely as I am... I wanted to just look from afar, but I hear her wailing and I see her tears. She is as sad as me... Wolves howl like wind, and humans cry like rivers when they are sad. I've howled a lot, and she has cried a lot. We are the same, that woman and I... I go a bit closer, to see if her pain is the same as mine, and it is. She has lost her mate too, she has lost her love like I did. We loved the same, and we feel the same sadness now...

I go up to her door, because we are both lonely.

She is scared and angry, at first. She cries and she yells at me, but I'm not scared of that female. I know she was different from the human hunters, from the males. So, I lie down in front of her, and I wait. She talks a lot, human words I cannot understand. I can only understand her sadness and her pain. So, I can only lie here and wait. I have no pups to return to this time, and my mate is gone. Where else would I go...?

She opens and closes the door to her lair several times, speaking to me as if she hopes I'd understand. After a while, though, she calms down. I step forward, and she lets me into her lair, so I go and lie down in the warmest spot, wondering if my mate had once done so.

"...Why are you here?" she says. "You're his mate... Why would you come to me, after what I did? I thought you had come to kill me. ...Aren't you mad? You should be hating me, so why are you... here…?"

I wonder what that human is talking about. I hope she understands. We are both lonely females who once loved the same wolf... Ah... I miss you so much, my dear mate. You and I were fated, weren't we? I hope I can dream of you again tonight. I want to dream about our races in the snow, back when we were young pups in one pack.

I try to sleep, but I am not used to this lair. The woman stops talking, but she gives me some nice food... It must be good if she agrees to share with me. I didn't even hunt for it. Was she the one who provided food to my mate to feed our babies, all this time? I thought we were lucky he was such a good hunter, even in the coldest winters, or when the humans were out hunting too... I hear her sob again, but I just eat and go back to my sleep. She's a peculiar human... Her house smells like the forest, and so does she. The trees come to her when she moves her hand, and they bloom when she wants. I do not understand everything, but she doesn't try to harm me, so I stay here and ignore what she's doing. It's her lair, after all. I only want to get some sleep, and perhaps, tomorrow we shall hunt together.

After a while, I feel her watching me again. I keep my eyes closed, but I can feel her stare on me. I hear her sob again. How do humans cry so much…? Don't they need that water?

"You're really a strange one... Are you lonely too, now?" she whispers. "I don't deserve another companion... or are wolves such pure creatures that you've already forgiven me for what I did? I don't understand you, wolf..."

That woman is really strange. She's lonelier than I am... I know she didn't have a pack before, but I don't understand how she really doesn't see any humans at all. She seems like a young and strong female. Do human males have no need for her? She is able to feed herself too, although I don't see her hunt. I leave to hunt for myself, but I never see her get any meat for herself, and she doesn't try to take mine.

I know she doesn't trust me. She never shows me her back, and she always looks out for where I am in her lair. She talks a lot too, but I've gotten used to it by now. ...Did she turn my mate into a man so he could understand her? Unless we are old, wolves are not meant to be alone for long. So are humans, I suppose... Yet, this female is always alone. No human ever visits her, which I cannot really understand. Was my mate her only companion? Why doesn't she look for a pack at all? Or does she like her territory too much, perhaps? How peculiar...

Perhaps because I am no longer a young wolf, those quiet days by her side, trying to understand this strange human, are going by faster than I realize. Winter comes back already, the first dashes of snow taking me by surprise. The woman is still wary of me, but she's grown accustomed to my presence. She even shares her food with me, a strange thing as she knows I'm capable of hunting for my own. I think she is trying in her own way to befriend me, but I still can't make up my mind about her. Curiosity about the one my mate seemed so fond of led me here, but after all this time, I still cannot understand. He was the best Alpha of our pack, and yet, he was so strangely drawn to her. What trick did she use to have him stay so long by her side every day? Does she know where he has gone off to?

I still look for him sometimes... I hope he will come back, although there's no sign of him. No trace, no scent, nothing. It breaks my heart over and over that I can't even find a trace of him. Did he become a coat on a human's strange skin like so many other wolves? The humans have been targeting more and more of us.

I follow that woman when she leaves her house each time, with the hope she will guide me to my mate. I know I should have abandoned it by now, but... I don't see what else to do. I long for the sight of his black fur, for his warmth and his beautiful eyes, his strong teeth, his superb figure. He was so strong and fierce... Oh, I miss him so much.

Each time, the woman stops in front of a strange little stone that makes me feel... odd. I do not understand the way of humans. Why does she need to cry over a stone? She talks a lot too, each time we're there, but she goes silent when we go back to her warm and large lair. I wish I could understand what she says... She's begun talking more and more to me now, with a lot less crying. Her eyes don't seem so fearful or defiant when she looks at me now; we are not enemies, and I don't have a reason to attack her. She hasn't harmed me, she just acts like a lone wolf. I just don't want her to touch me. I am no dog, I shall not let a human pet me. I only growled once, as a warning, when I felt her hands on my fur, and she's kept off of it since. At least she understands the wolves, it seems, better than I understand her human ways...

"...What is it you want, by staying here?"

There she goes again... It's late, and I just want to fall asleep by this nice, warm, burning fire she set up. That woman gets a lot more chatty once the sun sets, for some reason. During the day, she just does thing after thing, merely saying a few words once in a while, and I go hunting, but when I come back and I just want to enjoy my meal by the fire, she starts. Again.

"I do not understand you, wolf... You don't seem to hate me or fear me. What is it you're here for? ...Don't you hold any resentment, after what I did to you and your mate? To your children..."

Sigh. I know she'll just stop after a while and go to bed once she starts crying a little...

Not today, though. What is she doing? She stands up so quickly, it takes me by surprise, and she starts doing things, moving her stuff around and making a lot of that strangeness that characterizes her. Things appear in the air, and I don't like this. Birds don't come out of nowhere, but this woman has things appearing all over her house! Plus, there's all this strange noise too, a rumbling as if dozens of sneaky moles were running under us! What is it...

"...You're doing?"

Wha-...?

I look down, and there are... human legs underneath me. Did a human appear out of nowhere? I try to step back, but I fall down instead! What is going on? I can't... control my body properly!

"What is... human..."

"Calm down."

I look up at that woman staring down at me. Did I just... understand what she said? Not just that, I... actually understand her words.

"What is this? That?"

Is that me talking like a human? What a strange thing! I feel my throat and mouth so different, and every part of my body too, it... doesn't move like it used to.

"You... turned me human?"

I can't believe I am talking like a human, and... with the body of a human! Oh, why are they furless if they are so cold and their skin so strange?! I feel like a dead fish! I keep moving around, trying to find some sort of balance, falling, and falling again. This is so annoying! I put my paws... hands down, and look up at that woman.

"What is this?!"

"I needed to talk to you directly, and this is much more efficient," she says. "...Are you alright?"

"No! I'm... a human, how could that be alright?!"

She rolls her eyes, a gesture that I know means she is unhappy. I don't care if she's unhappy, she is the one who turned me into a human! She moves and hands me a blanket.

"What is that for?"

"To cover yourself! You're naked."

"Well, bring my fur back, then! I'm cold!"

"The blanket is for that. I promise I'll teach you how to turn back into a wolf once you answer my questions."

Oh, so she did this to me because she has questions to ask? This human woman is impossible! I didn't ask for her questions, but she turned me into a human just so she could ask them! What odd human way of thinking is that?!

I grab the blanket and cover myself with it anyway, because I am cold and I miss my pretty, comfortable fur. Where did it even go, and how did she do that? I've seen her do that thing to my mate before, but I didn't realize how strange it is! I really feel terrible in another skin, why did my mate do this?

"What are you doing here?"

"I came here after my hunt and I sat here."

"No, I mean, why are you in my house, with me?"

"You opened the door for me!"

"That's not what I... Why do you always come back here, to be with me? Why do you spend time with me, why... don't you hate me?"

Now she has tons of questions! I liked it better when I couldn't understand her at all! She was noisy before but it's worse when I know why she makes all those noises...

"I do not hate you," I say. "I don't hate you. I don't understand why you want me to hate you. I don't hate, I'm a wolf."

"You must hold some sort of resentment!"

Resentment, what is that now? I try to think, and this... strange new human mind translates for me. Ah, anger, hatred. So many negative emotions... How do humans even come up with such thoughts? I feel like my whole head has expanded to many things I just didn't need, and now they are all annoyingly filling my head.

I have anger at the rabbit that manages to escape me, but it doesn't last. If it's gone, it's gone, what is the point of resentment? It's better to move on to the next prey. I still don't understand humans... I shake my head, and something moves on my shoulder... Oh, hair. Well, I still have some, then... It is the same color as my fur... I push it out of the way, a bit disturbed that it's so long and in one place rather than well distributed all around my body.

"Answer me!"

I growl back. Don't shout at me, or I'll bite you, human woman! She acts like an Omega trying to pass as an Alpha, even dogs have a better attitude than that!

"I don't know what this resentment thing is," I say. "Your human ways are too complicated. I came here because we are two females alone. I came to look for my mate, but he is not with you. I don't know where he is, so I stayed. I don't have a reason to leave. You shared your food with me."

Oh, all those words come out flowing without me having to think much, which is new. The thinking, I mean, not all that loud words thing. I'm sure howling and growling is much more efficient, but now, I have so many words coming out, and so many thoughts... How do humans deal with all of this? I feel like all my usual basic needs have been... surrounded by dozens of others! How do they take care of all that? I thought humans were strange, but it turns out they have a lot of different needs to them, perhaps why they do so many strange things all day!

"You... don't know?" she mutters.

"Don't know what?"

Now that I am the one asking, she goes silent. Oh, humans, always so complicated! Nevermind. I look down on this strange body... Should I try to stand like her? I feel like a pup trying to find her balance, but this cannot be so complicated if they walk on two legs all day... Oh, indeed, it comes rather naturally. How funny, and... how tall! So this is how humans see the world, is it? Even the objects around me have changed... or is it because of my eyes? I feel like I see more colors than before, but... how do they watch for enemies? I can only look forward and I have to turn my head so many times! So annoying... Do they not fear to be hunted at all?

"Then... why... why are you here, staying with me?" she asks again. "Don't you have a... pack, or pups?"

"No. I wanted to have a new pack with my mate, but he is gone. My pups have all grown and gone too. I don't need to mother them anymore."

It is strange, though, how I suddenly miss my children. They should be all grown up and fine, but... I feel the need to see them again. Is that why female humans mother their offspring for so long? I had noticed they keep them for several winters, and their little ones are slow to grow too!

"What did my mate like about being human?" I ask, struggling to formulate my thoughts.

Mara!

"What?"

"What?"

She stares at me oddly.

What did I just... Did I hear something? It didn't come from this woman, but I felt like... Did I forget something? I feel like I... or, maybe I... I can't tell... What was that again? Did it... say something? What was that strange... word...?

No, it must be this strange human body again. I need to adapt to it better...

"He liked that we could... discuss," she says. "He was curious about us, humans. About my powers as a witch. Your mate wanted to find ways to understand humans, to protect you... to protect the wolves."

"What is a witch? Is that a hunter?"

Oh, no, the words don't match. It's strange having a vocabulary, yet a lot of words just come out as I think, not because I actually understand them... So, so strange. She sighs, and gets up, crossing her arms.

"I am a witch, a human with... special abilities. I was born with it, and it makes me stronger than the humans."

"Why aren't you the Alpha of your pack then? Why don't you have a pack?"

"Human packs are different from wolf packs. They fear the stronger ones, so they... cast them out of their packs. I've never been with a human group for long; they avoid me."

"Humans are truly too strange and illogical. Did he succeed?"

"What?"

"My mate. Did he find a way to protect the wolves from the human hunters? Is that why he left? Don't you know where he went?"

Her strange skin suddenly changes color, going whiter. She looks down like a wolf showing submission. I haven't tried to attack her, though. She slowly shakes her head, another gesture I don't really understand.

"N-no, he... he couldn't. I... I made him change into a man, a human man so he could... see and understand humans better, but he... he wanted to be stronger and find ways to fight hunters off your territory. He... he didn't succeed."

I feel sad. Did my mate leave to find another way, then? Did he find another human, and decide to stay with them instead? I don't think so... I've seen a lot of human groups and he wasn't with them. Everything brings me back here instead. I don't understand.

"...Do you want me to teach you?"

"Teach me?"

"How to be powerful... how to be a witch. If I can... give you my powers, you'll be stronger, like your mate wanted. This way, you can... do what he wanted, and we can stay together."

"I don't understand. You said my mate didn't succeed."

"I can make you a witch! Witches are only... females, that's why your mate didn't succeed in what he wanted to do."

"...Will my mate come back if I become a witch?"

She takes a deep breath.

"We... we can try," she says. "If... if you become a witch like me, and we are both powerful enough, then... perhaps... perhaps we can make your mate come back."

Mara!

I turn my head. ...Who is calling me? No, they're not calling me, that's not my... What is my name? Oh, I'm a wolf. I don't have a name. Why did I think this was my name...?

"What's my name?" I ask the human.

"I don't know. I mean, you're a wolf... You probably don't have one."

"I see... What is your name then? Humans have names?"

"Yes... My name is Luna."

"Alright, then, I like it."

"What?"

"That name. You can call me that."

She makes a strange sound with her mouth.

"That's my name, you can't take it!"

"Why not? I don't have one and you do. It doesn't leave you, either. If you can share your food, you can share your name. So I'll be Luna too."

She lets out a long sigh.

"I feel like you'll have a long way to understand being a human before being a witch..."

"You're the one who made me one, aren't you? So now, teach me so we can make my mate come back, Luna."

"I understand... Luna."

Chapter 37

Being a human is strangely complicated.

They do a lot of unnecessary things and act as if their own bodies are too weak. Their skin is not enough, so they wear other animals' skin or fur. They don't use their hands to eat; they use things that touch their food instead. They clean themselves with water rather than their tongue, and they do that every day, for some reason. They burn their food before they eat it, but they don't even eat all of the meat. They are very particular about where they sleep, where they sit, where they eat, where they pee, and for a reason I don't understand, they hate the ground for all of that. They have bad eyes, bad sense of smell, and their body is not comfortable with anything either.

Aside from the physical side of it, being a human is a lot of trouble. My head is always filled with many more things than before, and I think about things I didn't know I could think about. Everything I feel, and even the emotions I knew before, are so much stronger. Now, I know anger is much more complicated from a human's point of view. There are different forms of anger, more or less powerful, and it can last longer than I thought... which is what Luna calls resentment, when anger lasts for a long time over something that's already done. I never thought that could happen before... I'd forget about anger as soon as the next emotion came up, but it turns out humans handle many emotions at once and they can't easily ignore them. They stay sad for a long time, and very sad too. All day long, and even more at night. I've become sadder because of Luna's sadness. When they are happy, though, it just doesn't last long. Humans are never just content. They get easily irritated, nervous, or upset, but they aren't easily content or satisfied. There's always something that flies into their mind to distract that happiness.

I am thankful I can go back to being a wolf when I want. Being a human is just way too complicated, and at times, I just want to be a wolf like any wolf, without all those annoying thoughts, and with my comfortable body too. My human body is a lot of trouble! Each time I feel there's something wrong with it, it turns out this is part of the human's norm...

Luna is not very patient with me, either. It can't be helped; like she says, witches are more human than humans. She feels every emotion deeply, and she even feels the emotions of others. That's way too much for me. I'd rather stay a wolf and not care much about all of this.

His Blazing Witch

I miss my mate even more when I am a human, and it hurts. It hurts like it never hurt before, and I can hardly take it. How do humans endure such pain? I understand that they cry to let the pain out, but the pain just doesn't go away with all those tears we spill! It makes the chest lighter, but the pain is still there, like a thorn I can't get out of my heart, no matter what I do. Even worse, now that I've experienced it, I can't even make this pain go away when I return to my wolf appearance. I don't know why, but of all the emotions, sadness is the one that afflicts me the most and ignores the bit of relief I try to get whenever I change back. I have almost given up by now, and I only shape-shift when I want to be alone, or when I am tired of Luna's lessons.

She wants to make me a witch, and I understand we can get closer to my mate this way, but she's too impatient sometimes. Like a human, she gets angry and mad too fast. I don't want her anger and her pain too, so I ignore her when she gets frustrated with me. I am barely just learning to be a human, but she wants me to be a witch too, as fast as possible. She wants me to learn everything like one who'd force a pup out into the sunlight too soon. She's impatient like a hungry cub, and it's annoying. I've almost bitten her a few times, but I try to be nice, so I growl a lot instead...

Being a witch is more interesting than being a human. I learn a lot about our environment, nature, plants, water, and the ground we walk on. About fire too, that stingy little thing that acts so feisty. Witchcraft is that strange thing that makes me connect deeper with all those things. Actually, it's not like anything about it is too difficult. I understand they work even more simply than a wolf does; nothing is as complicated as humans. What is complicated is understanding that strange language the witches have come up with to name things, those runes as Luna calls it, and mastering it to do even more complex magic. ...Although, at times, I don't like magic.

It's rude, and it forces all those elements to bend to its will. I do not like it. Luna is strong, but if I was fire or water, I'd get mad at how she manipulates it so brutally. I'm glad witches can't direct wolves like that; I'd fight back... Perhaps that's why she finds I'm so good at being a witch. I understand those elements better than her. Water is composed and calm like me. The fire is so playful, yet capricious like a young cub. It's strong, but it doesn't like to be tamed, and only wants to grow. Nature is even easier to manipulate. I know the soil beneath my feet, I know the sounds of trees, and the smells of all those good, nice things. I find Luna selfish when she imposes her magic on it.

I still don't really understand why my mate was so adamant about coming to see this witch every day, but she is indeed very lonely. Sometimes, she looks very sad, and I don't understand why. She often stops talking about what bothers her rather than stating it fully, which is frustrating to me.

If only I could find my mate to ask him... I still look for him, whenever I can. Sometimes at night, when Luna sleeps and I can't seem to find the same peace. I have seen no trace of him, but I still have that little hope in my heart. I've spotted a few of my children with their new packs from afar, but no sign of their father. Perhaps being a human at times exacerbates my longing, but it's becoming more and more painful every day.

"...Don't you go there anymore?"

"Go where?" asks Luna, as we are eating.

"To the stone. You used to go all the time before."

She stops eating and moving. She does that when she is surprised, so I wonder what is surprising about what I said. Did I make her upset again? She looks upset. What was upsetting about my question? Is it that intrusion thing she talked about before? Humans are strangely very picky with that thing they call intimacy; there are some invisible walls, things we're not allowed to see, and things we can't say or ask. Luna gets very fussy over such things, so I have learned to read the signs.

"Can't I ask that?"

"...I don't go anymore," she replies.

So strange. She went all the time before, but now she doesn't go anymore. I wonder what was so special about that rock anyway. I think there was something written on it, but back then, I saw it as a wolf and couldn't read it. I wonder what I would be able to read if I went now. Why do humans carve words into rocks anyway...?

"Alright, enough talking," she says, suddenly standing up. "Let's resume training, you're getting better."

"Better than you, Luna?" I ask, a bit excited.

Luna glares back at me. She doesn't like when I act prideful, but it won't stop me. Wolves are prideful, after all, and just because I live with a human doesn't mean I'll stop being an Alpha. I like being strong. I am strong with magic.

As soon as we resume training, Luna forgets about being angry, and goes back to explaining things in words I can understand. She makes me draw magic circles and play with nature, water, or fire. I do everything she says effortlessly. She teaches me about Dark and Light Magic, although that is a bit unclear to me still. She explains how witches have to be careful about their emotions, but... to me, their emotions aren't the issue. Luna and the humans are just too riddled with all those emotions... The emotions control them already. I don't understand why she's so scared I'll be overwhelmed by mine, when I'm better than her at controlling my anger or my sadness.

"You don't understand," she says again. "Magic is powerful, especially your magic. Because I've created you, you were not made to handle magic in the first place. I am only able to because I am a powerful witch."

"I'm more powerful than you, though."

"No. Being more capable of manipulating the elements or magic doesn't make you more powerful, Luna. You have to understand the real nature of magic, how it flows through our emotions, and how it guides us."

"Are all witches like you, then?"

"...I'm not sure. I haven't met anyone else like me but my own mother. And she learned everything she knew from her mother before her, and our ancestors before that. We receive magic through our blood, and we have to be careful with our gift."

"I understand... So you're the only one who can make someone like me, then?"

"...Yes. But there are others like you, though. Not witches, but wolves that turn human. I was able to do so because you, like your mate, carry that blood in you. I only... awoke a very old, dormant power."

"Really?"

There are more changing wolves? I wonder where... I believe that if I had met one like us, I'd know. Would this be where my mate went, then? To look for more people able to change, like us? Indeed, I don't feel like a mere wolf anymore. Although I can change back, my human self will still be there, from now on. Its birth cannot be taken back, just like I can never really forget, even as I revert to being a wolf, what it is like to feel so many emotions.

"Do you know more changing wolves, then?" I ask.

"No... I have only heard about it, and found the rest in your blood. Let's just go back to training now, *Mara.*"

"...What did you call me?"

"Luna. What else would I call you? Come on, focus."

No, I heard that other name, again... Mara. Who is Mara? It's odd... I feel like I've forgotten something very important, something I want to remember, but I can't. That name has been haunting me for days now. I hear it at random times, calling me, always calling me... Why would that name be in my head? I've never had a name before; I am a wolf. Still, it feels like... it's truly mine. So... how?

"Luna, focus!"

I growl, annoyed to have her irritated with me. So impatient. Even if she were an Alpha, I wouldn't allow her to disrespect me like this! I try to focus again, but I'm too distracted by the name haunting me, but that's not the only thing.

I glance to the side while playing with the fire, and sure enough, it's there. This strange butterfly... It's always near, but for some unknown reason, Luna can't see it. She didn't trust me when I mentioned it. I don't think the butterfly minds her, either. It follows me all the time, even when I leave the cabin. I have no idea what that thing wants, or why Luna can't see it. It's just there, like an annoying little bug. I've tried chasing it, but it ignores me and flies away like any butterfly would, so I've decided to leave it alone.

Mara!

I ignore it again and focus on my magic. Luna will get mad at me if I am distracted; she's just impatient to have the two of us achieve what she wants. She said it is dangerous magic, so I ought to grow stronger, much stronger, or else this spell might kill us both. I have never understood why this spell would kill us, but I understand danger and death, so I just follow her orders, like a wolf following the lead.

"Almost there... We're almost there!"

The circle expands beneath us, but... I feel sick. Those menacing black marks are growing on my body, making me suffer more and more. It's painful! I let go, the circle disappearing, and me falling down on my knees.

"Almost!" grunts Luna, her black markings disappearing too. "We were almost there..."

"Why is it so... painful?" I ask, out of breath. "Why can't we just bring my mate back? This thing... Each time we grow it, it becomes so painful!"

"...He's just too far; we can't get him back yet with our current power. He's in... a place that's very hard to reach, Luna, but you and I, we are strong, we can get there... Come on, let's try again!"

"No," I protest. "I am tired, I want to rest. I don't want to suffer again to make my mate come back."

"Don't you want to see him again?!" she yells, mad. "You can't give up!"

There she goes again... I growl as a warning, but she ignores me and gets back into position.

"Come on, Luna, again!"

I growl, but I ought to help her. Perhaps, this time...

I take a deep breath and extend my hands to prepare. She starts the circle, and we articulate each element like a limb. We need all of them. Soil, water, fire... It's hard to move them all, and incredibly tiring, but we still do, relying on each other. The circle expands, and the pain grows, but finally, I feel something happening inside. That sensation, gripping my guts, that something is pulling from the inside...

A horrible stench appears. So strong, so fast, I'm about to let go and throw up. I feel horribly sick, and that thing makes me want to vomit. Not only that, but... something appears inside the circle. Something unnatural and scary. It... looks like bones... No, I must be wrong. Yet, that thing is moving, and Luna looks... happy. She keeps holding on, but I can't. Something's wrong, and I don't like that. I let go and step back, completely hit by the pain. What was that? Human bones? What happened?!

"Why did you stop?!" she screams, crying out of the blue. "We were almost there!"

"We weren't! That was... death," I scoff, shocked. "What happened?!"

She shakes her head, furious at me.

"It's part of the process, Luna! If you hadn't stopped... Oh, Moon Goddess! I can't believe we were almost there!"

"No, I'm not doing that again. That thing is dangerous and scary. Let's not call it back."

"You're... Ugh!" she screams in frustration, but I change back, and leave her there.

I can't handle it when she's like that, it just makes me uneasy. She's going to cry and scream, get mad for one of those strange reasons humans find when they're unhappy. I won't be there for it. I walk away. I need a walk, I need to get away from that crazy woman...

His Blazing Witch

I wander aimlessly in the forest, relieved to finally find some peace of mind. In the quietness of nature, I can rest my mind. Both wolf and woman, beast and witch, I can find a gentle balance here. I don't feel as uneasy, as torn by my two identities as before. I like my white human hair almost as much as my white fur. With magic, I feel the nature around me even more intensely, as if it was greeting me, so soothing.

My steps push me toward a part of the forest I recognize. It should be around here... I find it. From afar, I recognize the rock Luna acted so strange about. I must have made a detour from the house. A bit curious, I approach that thing. I wonder what word made her cry so much. What would make a witch so sad? She only ever cries about that rock or my mate. I can understand her crying over my mate being gone, but why a rock? Is that another one of the humans' strange customs? I step closer, hoping to finally get an answer to a question that was lying around my mind for quite a while now...

I shift back into a human so I can read it and understand. I stop in front of the rock. It takes me a little while to read, this time. Is it because it's carved in stone? It feels like the letters are moving, dancing and confusing my eyes. I force them to read. It's just one word, so why is it so hard to figure out...?

Liam.

...What is Liam? It's odd. Why does that name feel so familiar... Liam. I know Liam. Liam is a... It's my... my mate? No, it doesn't make sense. My mate doesn't have a human name... My mate is... No, wait, why am I so sure? My mate is Liam. Liam... Liam Black. What is this? That truth is engraved in my mind, so set in stone I can't shake it off or ignore it, not even for a second. Like a hammer pounding in my head. Liam, Liam Black is my mate. Each time I think about his name, about him a little more, my heart races. Liam, Liam, Liam... What... Who is Liam?! Why can't I remember him...? Who... Why... Why would my mate's name be there? What is that... What is that stone? What's going on...?

As if to echo the storm in my head, a headache breaks in, and I stumble back, utterly lost. I don't understand. The name on that tombstone, it... it's almost glitching, like something's wrong. No, something is definitely off about that thing. My mate... My mate is dead. Liam is... Liam is not dead. If Liam was dead, I... Oh, Moon Goddess, it hurts so much just to think about it! I can't! I can't, I can't imagine for a second that Liam is gone, no. It's impossible, I wouldn't... Oh, how could I...?

"What is it?"

I turn around. The witch is there, staring at me with that cold look in her eyes... Something's off. She's standing at a careful distance, and there's something odd about her, something different from before. My heart accelerates a bit, wary. I feel danger, restless. I look around. The forest is still the same, but my gut tells me something is off about all of this as well, all my surroundings shouldn't be trusted. What does that mean? Why did that tombstone... make me feel like this?

She steps forward, but I growl, as a warning. I don't want her near me, or near my mate. ...Wait, what am I saying? My mate is dead, so why would I think...?

"What is it, Luna?" she asks, tilting her head. "You look confused."

"Don't... call me that."

"It's your name. Luna. You chose to take my name, remember? You're Luna."

"No."

I growl, pissed for some reason. This isn't my name, this isn't... true.

Mara!

Who the hell is calling me?! This voice just keeps coming to my ears, again and again, like some distant echo I can't ignore. I feel so drawn to that male voice, to this... feeling. This thing in my heart, that feels just so warm and so good. I want to see you. I want to see my mate, find my mate. I need you...

"We will find him, together," says the witch, gently.

No. I don't trust her. Something's off about her, and I just trust my instincts, the instincts that warn me to stay away from that woman... I growl again, warning her not to approach. I know something is off, and I won't let myself get trapped in this lie. I just... want my mate. I step back again, closer to that tombstone, but... that's not my mate, I know it in my heart. My mate is alive, I haven't lost him. My mate... My Liam.

"Enough, Luna, let's go back."

I don't trust her, and I know she lies.

"What have you done to me?" I growl.

"Nothing. You're like me now. There is nothing here."

"What is that?" I ask, glancing at the tombstone.

This time, she stops and chuckles.

"This? Don't you already know, Luna? It's your mate's. You know it, right? He is dead. I killed him."

Those words hit me like a dagger in my heart. No, no, no, Liam isn't dead. I don't believe her. I can't believe her. Liam isn't... I can still feel him! There's no way my mate is gone. I need to ignore her words. Each time she speaks, her voice... I even forget that other name each time she calls me Luna. I'm not Luna...

Mara! Mara, answer, please!

I smile, keeping my eyes closed. That's right. That's my name. Mara. My name, so bright and so warm, like... like a flame. That's right. I'm Liam's mate, Mara. I'm not Luna.

"Enough," hisses the witch. "You're coming back with me. I killed your mate."

"No, you're lying."

"It's the truth," she continues. "I killed your mate, Luna. I killed the wolf you loved so much, I killed the one you loved the most."

I feel my heart aching, my throat tightening, the tears coming up to my eyes. No, no, I can't believe her. I can't give in. This... This isn't my pain, she's just trying to make me feel like it is, to confuse me. I need to get out of here...

Mara, wake up, please! Mara!

How do I wake up? I'm not asleep! I'm awake, and trapped here!

"...Liam?"

Mara! It's me, babe. Come on, come back to us, please. Wake up! Mara, wake up!

How do I wake up? How do I get back to him? I ought to remember. I keep my eyes closed, trying to ignore what I hear, what I feel. That snow under my feet isn't real. This cold isn't real, neither is the sound of the leaves rustling in the trees, or the sounds of the forest. I can't trust any of this.

Liam... I need to focus on Liam's voice. I feel him. Moon Goddess, it's so strange, but also... so warm. I smile without thinking, absorbed by our bond. I can feel him... His warmth, his presence by my side. He's here, he's alive, and he's with me. I am alright. I feel... his hand on my shoulder. I smile and grab it. It's faint, but I can feel his large hand, his gentle fingers grabbing mine back. Moon Goddess, I'm so relieved. He's really there... I can feel him, my inner wolf feels him too, like we're complete again. Oh, I feel like crying...

"Stop it!" she screeches. "Your mate is dead, and I–"

"Stop lying!"

I finally open my eyes, and this time, I'm sure. The snow, the forest, none of this is real. Whatever she did to me, I can see through it now. Perhaps because I know, everything now feels... so fake. I can see her illusion wavering. Everything turns into some weird shades, like an image unable to settle in my eye. The only thing that doesn't change is the butterfly. I see it fly and land on the tombstone. It flaps its wings a couple of times, and I stare at it, like my only point of focus.

"Stop your stupid illusion trick," I growl.

This time, she just stares, but... the witch. She's not real either, is she? I can see through her lies, now. This is all... fake. I take a deep breath.

I am Mara Jones, Liam Black's mate. It all comes back to me now. Moon Goddess, how long... have I been here? I was really in the she-wolf Luna's place. All this time I spent here, in this illusion... I've been here for years! No, no, it can't be. As the panic rises, the hand on my shoulder seems to fade away. I try to hold on to it, but the anger, the pain comes back to haunt me. I didn't leave them behind. I couldn't have. I didn't... I look around, hope to see a sign, something, anything to help me out of this nightmare. I want to see my mate, I want to know he isn't dead, that everything's alright. This is a dream, but doubt creeps in, to make me waver, and I can't stand it.

My eyes finally land on the butterfly. That blue, mesmerizing butterfly, that looks so peaceful and pretty inside this nightmare. I take a deep breath.

"...Help me," I whisper.

It flaps its wings, just once, and suddenly takes off, flying to me. I put my hand forward and, as soon as it lands on my finger, a wave of relief comes over me. Not just that, but all of my memories come back too.

Silver City. Kelsi, Ben. Nora, Selena, the Black Brothers... and Liam.

"I'm here, tiger."

I glance over my shoulder, and he's here.

Moon Goddess, he's really here. It's Liam. I suddenly lose all my strength and fall back, right into his embrace. I chuckle nervously, half-crying and half-laughing, just so glad to see him. I feel his torso against my back, protecting me... For a while, I get lost in his blue-gray eyes above me, darkened by the storm raging above us, as if those were the only things I ought to see for the rest of my life. They probably are.

He's a mess, he looks panicked and stares at me as if I was about to disappear at any moment, but no doubt, that's my man. I chuckle again, and he sighs, hugging me tightly.

"Moon Goddess, Mara... Thank Moon Goddess you're back... Damn it..."

I nod, but the truth is, I'm still not... completely back. It's like one universe is trying to overtake the other. I see the forest around us, but I also see the raging flames of a fire, wolves fighting golems, and in front, Luna still standing there and watching us. Above us, there's a clear day, but, somewhere behind, like a strange filter, also the raging clouds of a thunderstorm.

I'm still being pulled toward that other place. She wants to keep me trapped there, to keep me in that forest, with the sorrow of a loss that isn't mine. I feel Liam, but he's the only tangible thing that I can hold on to. Everything else around me is wavering, as if I was on the verge of falling into one world or another... I look down at the butterfly on my finger. It starts... melting there, and I watch as it literally imprints itself onto my finger. It's now stuck there like a very vivid tattoo... I feel a slight pressure, but that's it. Is this what's helping me stay awake? I hold on to Liam's arms a bit tighter. I need him, otherwise, I'll go back into that horrible nightmare where I think my mate is dead...

"Enough, Luna!" I growl, warning her.

"What is it?" she chuckles. "You're dreaming, Luna. Your mate is dead, and I killed him... Don't you hate me?"

I close my eyes again, for a second. I'm not going to give in to her lies. This is probably how she got them all, all those witches. Make them see that nightmare, make them feel the loss of their mate, and then, have them give in to the hatred. But I won't. My mate is right here, I haven't lost him.

"Mara, who are you talking to?" he whispers, sounding worried.

"...You can't see her?"

"What? Her? ...No, I only see... some sort of dark hurricane. It's like the black aura you always mentioned..."

So this is really happening all in my head.

It's the same mind spell as the one I was stuck in when I trained with little Mara. Somewhere out of time. I stayed there for years indeed, taking the female wolf's place, but outside, probably a lot less time has passed. Thank Moon Goddess...

"Liam, how long was I... out?"

"A bit over an hour. You... got in the same state as Ravena, with the dark eyes, so we thought you had been taken too, but Nora said she could still feel your spirit, and the white aura in it... Selena too, she was sure you were still fighting. I could still feel our bond, but it was... very faint. So we just kept fighting to get to you."

Over an hour? Moon Goddess, I can't believe I abandoned them for so long... I knew I had to walk in Ravena's stead, into this trap, but still... I hope everyone's alright.

Something suddenly makes an awful noise on our right, and Liam growls, but to me, there's nothing but the forest!

"Liam, what's going on?!"

"The golems are coming closer," he whispers quickly. "Don't worry, we won't let them get to you... So you can't see them, huh?"

"N-no, I have to focus," I mutter. "I'm still trapped in her curse, just... more awake, now."

"I figured so. Your eyes... One of your irises is blue, and the other turned gold again. Are you going to be okay...?"

I chuckle. I hope so...

"Can you kiss me? Now?"

"Anytime."

I feel his lips on mine, but it's very faint. Moon Goddess, his lips... They are so warm...

"NO!"

Luna's scream pierces my ears, and everything around fades back into the forest again. This time, she isn't pretending anymore. A magic circle has appeared under us. I growl. I can feel Liam, but he's gone from my vision. She's blinding me somehow, but I don't care. She can win the visual battle, but my mind is where I need it to be, and crystal clear.

"Stop it, Luna," I growl.

"You think you can beat the curse? She's like you," she hisses. "You're just like her, and once you experience her pain, you'll give in too. You're a wolf, like her, and once your mate is gone..."

"Like you, you mean?"

She freezes, and I snicker. I knew it. I struggle to stand back up, but I feel Liam's hands helping me get back on my feet. Although I can't see him, his strong embrace is all I need. I know he'll never let go as long as I need him. I swallow my tears. I am not giving in to her charade.

"Enough..." she hisses.

"No, you're the one who should have enough," I retort. "Enough of your lies. You know, I knew there was something wrong about that whole curse thing from the start, Luna."

"Shut up!"

"It didn't hit me at first, when I heard the tale for the first time. The wolf and the witch, it fit with everything we knew about the curse, the witches, the Royals. Except that... there was something that didn't make sense. I can't believe I missed it."

She stays silent, but her eyes are glaring at me. The black markings on her body are shining.

"Why would the witches be the one to suffer?" I continue. "It was Nephera's story that made me realize it. If you look at the picture, she was the main victim of that curse. She lost her child, she suffered the most, and went insane until she attacked her own sister. Sure, the man she had once loved went crazy, but... why did the Black Brothers' mom not get affected by the curse? At first, I bought the whole motherly protection thing. Perhaps there is some truth in it... but even if it was true, why would Nephera have been the one driven crazy by the curse, consumed by it? If the Witch Luna had placed the curse, it should have attacked the male werewolves, but not the witches. Why would she have cursed her own daughters? Why would my mother have been cursed, and Clarissa too? Nephera, and all the other witches, just for falling in love with a wolf? Only to be abandoned and suffer more when they would meet their mate. Why?"

She steps back, looking defiant, and I step forward, ignoring all the fatigue and pain. I know I have the pieces to all of this. I can see the doubt in her eyes. She even has trouble keeping up appearances. The witch from before had long red hair, but now, that hair is getting brighter and clearer. I can see behind her mask, behind her spell. I'm breaking free from her magic, and she knows it. The spell is being lifted, and the forest is slowly disappearing. I see the dark sky, the thunderstorm, the fire, the golems. I feel Liam even closer, I see his arms wrapped around me.

"There were two witches in that tale," I continue, determined. "Luna, the original witch, and Luna, the original werewolf, who received magic powers. ...This is the real reason all the witches before me have failed, isn't it? They tried to stop a curse created by a witch, they thought they could reason with her, stop her, that they would be able to relate to the witch. They had no idea what they were really dealing with, and they were all wrong."

I chuckle. Moon Goddess, finally... finally, I'm getting to her. I don't feel sad, nor do I feel happy about it. I'm just... so calm. It's even weird how calm and composed I am right now. I understand, and I see the truth. I take another step, and once again, she retreats. She's almost acting as if she's scared of me now.

"That's right," I whisper. "I know who you really are, why I am the one you couldn't stop. You did this whole charade to try and stop me, but it won't work, not on me. Because I'm not just a witch. We're the same, aren't we? Both werewolf and witch. You're not Luna the Witch, you're the other one in the story. You made me feel your pain. ...Luna the Wolf's pain."

I see the shock in her eyes. She stares at me, completely stunned, her disguise slowly falling in front of my eyes. It's as if while she is recovering her appearance, she finally leaves me, and I feel like Mara again, without any confusion. I'm still half trapped in that strange forest, but at least I see my body for what it is. I glance to the side, and Liam's name is gone from the tombstone, replaced by letters in a language unknown to me... Although I already knew, I can't help but feel relieved seeing that it's gone. I hold Liam's hand a bit tighter, knowing he won't let go of me.

"Luna... you have to stop all of this now," I mutter.

"Don't call me that!" she suddenly yells.

Her scream throws a monstrous blow at us, like a gigantic slap that burns our faces and forces us to step back. For me, it's like a gigantic wave of that dark aura, but Liam's groan lets me know that he felt it too. Still, we manage to keep standing, and I take another deep breath. I need to have more time, save enough energy to fuel up my magic again... I feel drained for now, and I probably used too much during that illusion without even knowing...

"But it is your name, isn't it," I resume, determined. "The only name you knew, the one she gave you. You can take mine or anyone's you want, it won't change a thing, it won't change the past. No matter whose name you put on that tombstone, it can't change the truth, Luna. You can change your name, but you can't really give that pain to anyone."

"You know nothing," she hisses, pushing her white hair back. "You know nothing of the pain I went through. Should I make you lose your mate too so you understand?!"

I growl furiously, warning her. If she touches one hair on Liam's head... I step to make sure I'm still standing between him and her, just in case.

"What?" she smirks. "Are you scared now, brave Mara? Don't you think you could withstand the pain that I felt?"

"You have to stop that stupid lie of yours! You wanted all the wolves to put the blame on Luna the Witch so you could feel fucking sorry for yourself and have them pity you and hate witches on top of that!"

"That's all she deserves!"

Another blow, and this time, I feel Liam holding and pushing me to stay standing, his growls in my ears. I'm glad he's supporting me, because I don't think I'd have the strength to fight this otherwise. I can endure the pain it blows at my face, but it burns, and I'm too tired to keep standing for now. I hope I can win more time and make her talk, because otherwise, she'll kill us both right here before I can reason with her...

I try to look around, and my vision is starting to adjust and ignore the fake vision of snow around me. I can see the darker, muddy ground underneath, and more importantly, the silhouettes of all the fights happening not far from us. I think I see more of their auras rather than the actual people, though, in particular the bright white and gold ones next to me.

"Nora and Selena?" I mutter.

"You can't see them?" worries Liam.

"Sort of..."

"We're right by your side, Mara," says Nora's voice in my head, comforting as ever.

"We're not leaving you, witchy."

I nod, feeling a lot better with them by my side. I can almost feel Nora's gentle white aura surrounding me, probably shielding me while also trying to heal my body. I see Selena and the two other scary dark auras jumping all around us, probably defeating enemies invisible to my eyes... You're a poor excuse of a witch, Mara.

I turn my eyes back to Luna. I'm the only one who can see her, aren't I? She doesn't look bothered at all by everything going on around us, and I think she might be an illusion herself. After all, Luna the Wolf died centuries ago, this is merely her curse playing out and carrying her memory, her spirit... I need to get to the root of the curse and stop it. I probably already weakened it by revealing its true nature, but she's still standing like a hurricane in front of me, ready to strike again and blow us all away.

"You have to stop your curse, Luna," I insist. "It's been centuries now. It has to stop!"

"It won't," she says, looking strangely calm. "You've seen it. My curse will continue, and keep haunting the witches for all the harm they have caused our kind with their wretched greed... Once I kill you and your mate, I'll get stronger again, and the next generation will feel my wrath just like all the ones before!"

"For Moon Goddess' sake, killing me won't solve it! Snap out of it! You think you can survive eternally? If the curse lives on, so will the wolves and witches! There will be more love between them, even if you hate it! Wretched greed? It's just love, whether you'll admit it or not! You think you can stop people's feelings? You think you can love and replace it with fear or anger? With that stupid curse? Even if you keep cursing the witches, they won't stop trying to stop your madness, Luna. Another one like me will be born someday. And she will say the same thing to you, Luna. No... perhaps I am not the first?"

She frowns and glares at me, making me realize. I can't be the first witch-werewolf. This... This whole charade of hers, it's way too well done. I wonder how far the witches who tried to stop her got into her illusion, but I'll bet she showed them Luna the Witch's side, or she didn't even bother to enchant them at all. Like Ravena, she probably just used them like vessels and got rid of them as soon as she was done.

That whole number she did on me, though, it felt like she knew. She knew to put my mate's name on the tombstone, she wanted to let me feel what she felt...

"So that's right, Luna, isn't it?" I scoff, glad I made another point. "I am not the first to try and get to you, to stand before you like this. You've seen other witch-werewolf mixed girls like me. Did you make them go through it all as well, Luna? They had different names, different mates whose names you put on that tombstone. How did it go? Some failed, but some saw through it. I tell you, Luna. I understand why I was born now–"

574

"Enough! You're cursed, an abomination!"

"I'm a result you should have expected long ago!" I shout back. "Wolves and witches will keep falling in love, even if you kill me and my mate! Even if you get rid of me, you'll see many more Cursed Ones like me! We will bear the mark you put on us, and we will be the only ones to see through you, because we are just like you!"

"You know nothing!"

This time, the blast hits us right away. I barely see it before I'm thrown across the ground, feeling my body fly like dead weight. I hear growls and voices calling us, and my body violently hits the ground. Oh, shit... I grimace and roll on the other side, holding my painful ribs.

"Mara! Mara, are you alright, babe? Babe, talk to me!"

I feel his hands all over me, and he touches my flank, making it painful again without knowing. I growl.

"Liam, don't... Oh, Moon Goddess, give me a second... and hands off, I think my ribs are broken..."

"Oh, shit, sorry..."

I feel his hand move gently to my shoulder instead, the other under my head. I spit out some blood that was stuck in my mouth, and he helps me sit back up gently.

"Are you alright?" I ask, knowing he got blasted away too.

"Yeah, I landed upright..."

Better than me, then. He helps me up, gently holding me where he thinks it doesn't hurt. I hear him sigh before he gently kisses my temple. More like licks it, actually, and I turn to him, a bit confused.

"Sorry, but you got... blood..." he grimaces. "Damn, babe, you look ugly..."

I roll my eyes. Yeah, I mean I feel the blood dripping down at least five different spots on my head, and I feel like I just got run over by a truck, so I can imagine...

"Call me ugly again and I'll burn your ass..." I sigh.

"Noted. At least you still have some good burns... Is she still there?"

I look over his shoulder. Luna is still standing there indeed, but there is now a large space between us, and violent winds sweeping across the battlefield. I take a minute to look around, and the illusion is finally gone.

The battle has moved to be centered around us, with wolves everywhere fighting golems. It seems like the cracks in the ground don't break anymore; with the heavy rain that began pouring Moon Goddess knows when, we now have a wide mat of mud under our feet... No wonder I look like crap, after I rolled in that... Liam rubs his face with the back of his hand too, only spreading more mud. Is it a wolf thing that I don't find it that gross? It might even be a tad sexy to see him with that mess on his torso... I notice he's not completely fine and just dirty, though. There's blood clotted with the mud in some parts, and I feel bad for complaining when he visibly has tons of bruises too... I approach my hands to try and heal him, but he grabs my wrists.

575

"No touching and no healing, Mara, you need that magic!"

"What happened to you?" I grimace.

"The bear disappeared right after you got into that... weird state," he sighs, turning his head to where Luna stands. "We didn't defeat it, so we figured... something had happened. Once we got here, though, you were blocked inside this weird tornado thing, and... havoc ensued."

"Wait, what?"

"*You heard him,*" says Selena, a few steps away. "*She used your powers to attack us... It was a nice relief not worrying about where to stand at first, but I have to admit, running from flames and water is harder than it seems...*"

"Was anyone injured?"

They both exchange a look. Wait, what does that mean? Someone got hurt for real?

"Don't worry, babe, it wasn't your doing..."

"Liam, it was still my power! And I stayed stuck inside that... illusion for about an hour!"

"*Trust me, it felt longer than that for us...*"

"Selena!"

Well, it felt a lot longer than that for me too, but at least I was out of danger, aside from her sucking out my powers! I can't believe I attacked my friends, and I have no fucking memory of it! I look around, but I'm so panicked, I can't even focus to find out who is missing. With the downpour around us, the mud flying and covering everybody's fur, I can barely recognize the wolves I actually do know.

"Liam, who did I harm?"

"Mara–"

"Tell me," I retort before he can protest.

He sighs, grimacing.

"Ben was... forced to leave the fight. We lost contact with some other wolves, and my brother got burned a bit..."

I look around, quickly spotting the big, black wolf, the one with the silver eyes. Moon Goddess, it's true. He's seriously limping on one side, and there's a long, bloody, pink patch of exposed flesh on his flank...

"Moon Goddess, I... burned him?"

"Mara, Mara, no!" protests Liam, forcing me to look at him. "Babe, we know it wasn't you. Look at me. Babe, look at me."

He grabs my face in his hands, forcing me to look at him. His eyes are dark gray like the storm above us, only hiding a faint hint of blue in them... Oh, Moon Goddess, I feel like I really hadn't seen him in years. Now that I can properly look at my mate, my Liam, I feel like bawling. I sniff it back down, probably making a horrible expression, because he chuckles.

"Mara, this isn't your fault, tiger. You probably saved us a ton more than that, I'm sure of it. I don't know what happened to you during all that time, but don't worry about anything. We're your family, your pack, and we trust you a hundred percent."

"Ninety-nine. You tend to be reckless at times."

I chuckle, but Liam probably didn't hear that... He still smiles back at me.

"You're Silver City's witch, Mara, nobody here will change that, alright? We know she's trying to use you, and we don't care, we know you. You're our Mara, our crazy Fire Witch, alright?"

He smiles a bit more and steps forward, igniting the fire inside me again. I feel my wolf wake up too, reacting to the closeness of our mate, as if she had been put into a deep sleep until now. Despite the cold rain pouring on us, I feel his warmth, his skin close to mine, and his gentle hands on my body. It feels like the whole fight around us slowed down to give us a little break, this break I really needed with him. Liam takes a deep breath and kisses my lips, a slight taste of iron between us. It's a bitter, ugly kiss, but it is real, and imperfect, and raw, and Moon Goddess, I need it. We don't have time for more, but that precious second between us is all I needed. I nod silently.

"...I love you, Mara," he whispers.

"I love you too..."

He nods.

"It's good that you know. Now, you're in charge. You tell us what to do, we will follow you no matter what, okay?"

"If you have a plan, I'd love to hear it," growls Selena. *"Since you were in that no-coverage zone, it's been hell here. We tried to get to her, but we had no way to get into that hurricane thing. How did you stop her?"*

"Because I'm a werewolf-witch. The culprit behind the curse isn't the witch, but Luna, the werewolf-witch..."

"The first Royal?" gasps Nora.

"Exactly. She's the one who created that curse, and that's why the witches couldn't stop it. The normal witches, that is. They called people like me Cursed Ones because we were the only ones who were both witch and werewolf like her, the only ones who could get to her..."

"How did you get out of there?"

"I'm... not entirely sure. But I think the key is inside that hurricane. I need to get back to Luna and make her stop."

"You're not going back in there!" shouts Liam. "Look at yourself, she almost killed you! You can barely stand!"

"You're really weak, Mara," adds Nora. *"I can barely feel your life force... let alone your magic."*

I take a deep breath and stare at Liam. I know what I might be about to do is dangerous... but I need to stop this curse, at any cost. Otherwise, she will use me to unleash herself all over Silver City, and start haunting witches all over again. I look at the fight all around me, knowing I ought to stop them all.

"I'll be fine," I shake my head, "as long as I can convince–"

"Oh, cut it out, Mara," suddenly growls Selena. *"That witch has been having her tantrum for centuries, she's not going to listen to you so easily, not without you having your magic fully charged back up at least."*

"Selena is right. We need to help you get back to a state you can fight–"

"Nora, no! We're losing time, and it's not like I'll suddenly charge up or heal so easily!"

"Don't underestimate me! I'm still the Luna of Silver City, if I say I'm healing you, I'll heal you!"

I don't dare to say a word after hearing Nora get mad. She's usually so calm, it genuinely took me by surprise. Facing me, Liam chuckles, but moves and stretches his shoulders as if ready to go back to fight.

"What about your magic?" he asks. "Luna must have used a whole bunch, right?"

How do I charge it back up...? Before I can even think, I feel it. A flame, a powerful one, moving away from me, yet it's mine...

"Spark," I gasp. "If I can get back to him, I'm sure I'll be able to transfer the magic he drew back to me."

"Alright. Let's get you to Nora, to the cat, and then you can play with that crazy curse..."

"But it's going to take too long," I mutter. "By the time I'll be ready–"

"She doesn't control you anymore, Mara," says Liam. "Look around. No new golems coming out of the ground, we're only dealing with the ones she had already made. She doesn't control your magic or Ravena's, as long as she doesn't get her hands on another witch, I think we will manage..."

Moon Goddess, I hope so... I take a deep breath and try to focus, but when I open my hand, only a very small flame appears. Alright, time to run and get back in shape...

"Ready, hot stuff?" Liam winks at me, ready to run too.

"Ready when you are, babe," I smile.

#

Chapter 38

We keep running, away from Luna's shadows this time, and back onto the battlefield. We are searching for Spark, but I actually know exactly where to go. Each time I focus a bit more on that flame inside of me, I can feel its echo on the other side. I feel my cat, fighting and roaring against his enemies. That's my Sparky... I guess I'll owe him tons of treats and pets later.

We're not anywhere near him yet, though. The truth is, the battle has intensified all around us, and the rain is acting against the werewolves, trapping them in the mud and slowing down their movements. Running is fucking difficult too, and I'm out of breath in a matter of minutes. Not to mention I just went through hell and back, being suddenly thrown back into the reality of this fight is... hard. I'm grateful I can reach out to my friends, my pack, to share their strength and ignore the sore muscles and heavy body. Using our mind-link, I update them on everything I went through while Luna had trapped me. The illusion, the truth behind the curse, the real past she went through, how she did... everything. The only thing I try not to mention is that tombstone thing. I don't know why but it... haunts me. The vision of Liam's name there, it's just scary, and I don't want to think about it. I know he's aware I'm skipping parts of the story from the looks he gives me. After all, he did hear me mention the grave earlier, but I just... I don't want to talk about it now.

Thankfully, there's a lot more to discuss than that.

"*So... the curse was started by Luna the Wolf, the first... Royal?*" says Selena.

"*Exactly,*" I nod. "*She wasn't the first female werewolf, from what I understood, but she was the first Royal, the one who got pure, Light Magic to make her more powerful. Her mate couldn't receive magic since he was male, so it makes sense that the Royal bloodline was a... girl-only thing. Witches are only women.*"

"*It partially explains why my dad was a bit less of a Royal than Nora's mom, his twin...*" agrees Selena.

"*So the targets of the curse were... witches falling in love with werewolves from the beginning? The whole thing about us being able to protect our children... Was that fake?*"

"*I'm not sure, Nora, but that's what it looks like. If you look at each time the curse appeared, Cursed Ones were the child of a witch and a werewolf, just like Nephera's baby and myself. I bet Clarissa's dad had werewolf blood too,*

579

but that's a question I'll solve later. The witch went insane, and the child only survived if... Dark Magic was used."

Now that I think about it... it might explain why Clarissa ended up in her father's care instead. If her mother knew she was going to be sick, or losing sanity, perhaps she decided to protect her daughter by sending her to her dad... Perhaps that's even why Nephera didn't stay in Silver City at first. Other than Judah Black trying to kill her and going insane, she may have known she'd be a danger for her new mate, and perhaps their children...

"There's one thing I don't understand. If that's the key to the curse, why did she let you see all this?"

"Because she is actually the same thing as the ones she despises! Luna is half-werewolf and half-witch! From what I saw, she was trained in both Light and Dark Magic by the witch, but look at us. Nora, your Royal blood only kept the Light Magic, although it's very tame and more of a purification power now. But it's you using your own life energy to protect and heal others, right? That's the definition of Light Magic. Meanwhile, I'm a Dark Witch."

"Mara..."

"No, don't worry. It's a pain in the ass, but it's the truth. I'm a fucking Dark Witch, we don't need to pretend anymore. I was born using the life force of two others, Clarissa and little Mara. I'm a Dark Witch whether I like it or not... perhaps more of a mix of both actually, now that they are gone. But that's why Luna has no choice but to actually resonate with me. Her illusion shows me her point of view, not the other Luna's. She's just the same as I am, and that's why she loathes Cursed Ones the most. Because we are what she tried to stop, and now, we are the ones who can stop the curse."

I jump over a hill and roll down to avoid a golem trying to grab me, Liam jumping on his back right after to give him a monstrous kick. When did he find the time to put on a pair of jeans, by the way? I don't have time to dwell on that for long. I get back up, and start running again. We are not just rushing through the area; each time one of us can, we help other wolves defeat the golems. It's not a waste of time, seeing that the curse can't create more. She still had plenty of time to create a nightmarish amount of them, though...

"What about the humans?" I ask, suddenly remembering the possessed girls.

"You'll see," says Selena, with what sounds like a smirk in her voice.

Is that good or bad? We keep running, everyone strangely silent, probably focused on not getting killed. The closer we get to Spark, though, the better I feel. Moreover, the rain around me isn't affecting me like it used to anymore. I feel... fine with it. I know I could channel all this rain and use my water element instead, but for some reason, I still feel fire is supposed to be my main power. It's the one I'm most comfortable with, and I am missing it at the moment.

Our group slowly makes its way back to Spark, and finally, I catch sight of my giant blazing cat, who turns his big head to me as soon as I appear, his ears perking up. He definitely made a huge difference in the fight here. The field is unrecognizable; East Point Ground is completely turned all upside down. All the hills around him smelling like burnt soil are most definitely his doing... Still, there are a ton of golems around, and I understand what Selena meant. The humans. The girls that were possessed before are now all collapsed on the ground, and some people are actually trying to grab them and evacuate the battlefield. Spark, some wolves, and some human men are forming a wall between the golems left and the defenseless women, fighting back, while the rest are trying to get them out of there quickly. Spark is at the front, jumping from one golem to another while trying to stay away from his allies and not burn anyone. Now that he's seen me, though, the large cat jumps in my direction.

"Spark!"

He immediately starts purring, the sound so loud it's almost an echo to the thunder above. He rubs his flank against me, and I smile, his warm flame immediately making me feel a hell of a lot better...

"Missed me much?" I chuckle, pushing my hands through his hair-like flames.

"What now?" asks Liam, arriving by my side.

With the arrival of the two Lunas and their mates, the line of humans and wolves were taken by surprise, but at least the path is getting cleared in front of them. I turn to the closest ones to us, who have their eyes on the strange witch petting her fire cat.

"Are you going to be fine without him?"

The two guys whose golem just got defeated by a simultaneous attack from Selena and another trio of wolves exchange a curious glance. They look like they have been through hell, and one's shoulder is covered in blood, but they turn to me and nod.

"Y-yeah. Can you... stop all this?" he asks, hesitant.

"I sure hope so..."

They nod and leave to get to the next golem already, their wolf allies following behind them. I take a deep breath, and turn to Spark, who's agitating his tail, irritated by a nearby golem.

"Spark!"

He turns his head to me again, and I extend my arms to touch his burning cheeks.

"No more play time for you, big tiger. Can you go and watch over Kelsi for me?"

He lets out one of his cute meows, deeper than usual because of his size, and rubs his forehead against mine. Moon Goddess, I love my magic cat.

"Good boy."

I pat and caress his head, but we need to get going now. I take a deep breath, and focus on those flames surrounding him. They are my fire, to begin with. I just need to take it back... Letting Liam and the others defend my position, I close my eyes and focus. I feel the black markings appear on my hands, but it's alright. As long as I focus on my flame, I'll gain more power than I lose. I take a deep breath and focus on cutting myself off from everything going on around me. I focus on my breathing, and at each inhale, I feel the fire inside burning bigger, as if I was eating those flames up. I can almost feel them streaming out of my mouth... I keep going, feeling the flames outside disappear while the one inside grows. Oh, it feels so good to have it burning again. I didn't realize how cold I was from that freaking illusion of hers... Not anymore. I feel my fire raging inside, the sparks electrifying each pore of my skin, the blood getting hotter and hotter in my veins. Yes... I'm back.

I open my eyes, feeling the golden, reddish halo in them. At my feet, little Spark is back, and the now completely black cat meows cutely.

"...Uh, wrong cat?" asks Liam, a bit amused.

"Just out of magic, he'll be fine. Spark, go!"

The black cat rubs his small body against my leg, and quickly runs away from the battle. With his small size, he has no issues avoiding the golems and jumping out of sight. The few people who do spot him seem surprised to find a cat lost on the battlefield, but they don't have time to focus on him. I smile and open my hand, feeling like I could take down a freaking volcano. Big, red flames immediately appear, making me beam.

"Now that feels good," I chuckle.

I turn around and quickly blast two nearby golems with my fire, the huge bundle of mud exploding and splattering the humans and wolves that were fighting it just before. Awesome. I look down and the black markings are still there, but more scarce; nothing to worry about, for now.

"*Mara?*" suddenly calls out Nora. "*I... I think Selena and I may have come up with some sort of crazy theory...*"

The white wolf approaches me, and I hear a chuckle from Selena in my head. A crazy theory? What did those two talk about that I didn't hear? I'm usually the one coming up with crazy plans, so I'm kind of excited Nora is the one with one now...

"*Luna the Wolf... You said the witch gave her the power of elements earlier, right? To control them like you do?*"

"*Yeah,*" I nod, wondering where she's going with this. "*She made her into a super powerful wolf by transferring some witches' power into her. In the illusion, she had all three of them. Water, fire, earth, and Luna the Wolf couldn't use them at full strength, but it was enough that the witch could use her for her crazy necromancy spell...*"

Nora and Selena exchange a look, and suddenly it hits me. Oh, Moon Goddess.

"*Are you guys... suggesting I give you... some magic?*"

"*It could work, right?*" says Selena, coming forward and visibly excited. "*You said it yourself. We are Royals, we aren't very different from Luna and you, right? If that witch managed to give her some powers, can't you do the same to us?*"

"*Wha-... You can't be serious! You guys aren't cursed, and even if you are full of Light Magic, if I give you elements, you will have to use your own life force to manipulate it! It means you could die!*"

His Blazing Witch

"Are you going to tell us this isn't what you've been doing all along?"

I can hear that tone of reproach in her voice, and almost see her raising a suspicious eyebrow... Oh, damn it. It's true I haven't been able to use little Mara or Clarissa's strength in a while, which is why I'm getting really tired, but... I shake my head.

"Still, this is super dangerous! I am not sure I can do it, and I was out of magic just a few seconds ago, remember? We just got me refueled, so to speak! I can't share it with you, I'll need it to fight. So, now, where I am going to get more magic!"

They exchange a look and nod. What, they already thought about that too?

"Well, it's not like you're the only witch around, are you?" says Selena, stepping forward.

They can't mean... Ayesha and Naptera?

I look up, and sure enough, I can spot the Fire Witch, not having the best time fighting. More than that, she's visibly hurt, from the way she's limping and grimacing. ...Could it work? I try to look through my memories, everything little Mara taught me, and... what I saw from that illusion. Perhaps it was a long-forgotten kind of magic, because it was nothing like I have ever seen before, but... now I can't forget it. I spent... actually several years watching an ancient witch practice her magic on a werewolf. It's still there, clearer than a dream, it's a memory, a memory Luna gave me. How ironic is it that Luna herself gave me the keys that might give us the victory...? It doesn't mean it will be without danger, though, even if I manage to reproduce that crazy spell.

I take a deep breath and start running to give assistance to my witch peer.

Ayesha sees me coming, and with a frown, steps back to watch me blast the golem that was giving her a hard time. She lost her coat and her arms are now exposed, full of markings, but she looks alright, just a bit... exhausted. She catches her breath while I get rid of her opponent, shaking her head. Once that thing is reduced to ashes between us, she stares at me with an odd expression.

"Looks like someone decided to come back from hell."

"Missed me?"

"Don't push it," she grins. "What happened in there?"

"A lot... but I think I have a chance to actually end this," I nod.

She slowly nods, looking relieved. If anything, I'm impressed she really stayed behind to fight. I have a feeling Naptera will be harder to convince to help us...

"How are you holdin' up?" she asks, massaging her neck.

"Better than you, by the looks of it."

"Hey, some of us were fighting while you were getting nap time."

"How about you get the nap now, then?"

"What?" she tilts her head.

I chuckle.

"You get a time out, Ayesha. We borrow your magic, and you get to sit the next round out."

She glances around at the fight raging around her. Now that I see her from up close, she does look tired, her lower lip covered in blood, and the markings appear on her neck too. She lets out a long sigh with a grimace right after, holding her shoulder. Next to me, Selena steps forward with her golden eyes staring at the Fire Witch, looking a bit excited. Ayesha's eyes go from her to me.

"I'm not sure what your idea is, but... deal."

"Thanks."

I look down at the wolf.

"Selena, ready?"

"I'm always ready for more firepower, witchy. Bring it on."

I try to focus as much as I can. I know the spell, but having seen it done once doesn't make me an expert at all... Still, I am one of the most powerful witches around, and I have the knowledge of dozens of generations in my mind now. I take a deep breath and face Ayesha, trying to feel her power inside. She's frowning and probably a bit anxious as to what I am preparing, but she's visibly too exhausted to protest now anyway. I only hope she's still got enough magic...

I find the core of her magic power, her source, and indeed, it feels a bit different than mine. I can't quite describe it, but it's as if... it has a different constitution. It makes sense, though. Ayesha comes from a different line of witches, her power was forged differently, as if her magic had its own fingerprint, very different from mine. Still, magic is magic, and fire is still my specialty... As soon as I get a hold of it, a large magic circle appears under her feet.

"Is this... harmless for them?" asks Nora, sounding a bit worried.

"Magic isn't like a limb or an organ, it's more akin to... a deep breath. I'll deplete her of most of what she has left, but afterwards, Ayesha's magic will still be there, she can produce more again once she's rested. Like emptying her lungs, but she can still breathe in. For Selena, though, I can't guarantee... It might feel a bit weird."

"I'm not a pup, Mara. Hurry up."

Indeed, it's not like we've got forever either. I have to focus on this spell, and if it wasn't for the Black Brothers forming a protective triangle around me, I'd be defenseless. Still, I trust them fully, and I don't have much of a choice anyway. I close my eyes and focus, reproducing the spell I saw, to the best of my ability. I feel the circle moving, from Ayesha to under Selena's feet, and I hear the witch gasp and fall on her knees. I need to focus on her fire, to keep it inside the circle, trapped outside of its owner. Fire is so... whimsical, I need to hold on tight and not let go. Still, I keep my grip on it, and gently, push it toward Selena's golden aura. I feel her hesitation, but I keep pushing, as if I was introducing her to the fire. Ayesha's blue flames slowly start to change, and they feel different too, as if they were adapting to the new owner. They turn a bright gold color, almost white, something strong and blinding.

"Wow... Now, I like that," chuckles Selena.

Looks like it's working... I take a few more seconds to make sure that magic is adapting to Selena's body, but there's obviously something going on with her aura that protects her, and that Ayesha's magic recognizes too. Light Magic. It just finds its way to take and convert that magic into Selena's. Once I make sure it's stable, I slowly open my eyes to find the cream-white wolf's body now dominated by large, white-gold flames. Wow, it's... even more impressive and beautiful than I imagined. Her mate approaches, visibly worried, but she's fine. She looks like a young sun on four paws burning bright, almost blinding.

"Nice," I chuckle.

"This feels... pretty awesome," she growls, moving her limbs as if to test it.

"You don't have a lot, though, and unlike *real* witches, you're not going to be able to replenish it easily, so be careful to not run out right away."

"Got it. We just need enough to get you back to that hurricane thingy anyway, right?"

"I guess... Nora, are you sure you want to do this too?"

She steps forward and nods. Meanwhile, Ayesha steps back with a grimace and a groan.

"I'm fine, thanks for asking the guinea pig... Also, who the hell are you going to get to do that crazy new spell?"

"...I was thinking Naptera?"

She scoffs, staring at me as if I was crazy for a couple of seconds.

"Wait, you're serious? You do know she tried to kill you, right? Also, she's been sitting the whole fight out!"

"She can keep sitting it out, but I don't care if she likes me or not. Last time I checked, she wants that curse gone and so do we. ...Do you know where she is?"

Ayesha grimaces.

"You really are a crazy one... Last time I spotted her, she was somewhere west..."

Right, I can actually feel her. It's faint, but... there's definitely the trace of a Water Witch in that position. I nod and turn back to Ayesha.

"Can you get yourself to the general hospital?"

"As long as I don't get bit on the way..." she mutters, looking down at the wolves.

"I promise no one will touch her," Selena nods.

"Yeah, you'll be fine."

"Nice. Also... I hope the wolves remember, when this is all over. That I helped..."

I nod, a bit thankful indeed. Looking back, Ayesha was certainly a huge help in all that mess. Perhaps she will ask for some sort of payback once this is all over, but I'm not too worried. I know now that Dark Witches aren't all bad, and some also stand in between with more complicated motivations... She quickly leaves the area, limping a bit, but at least she should be able to get out of here.

"Let me guess... The other one isn't going to be as easy to convince?"

"I don't want to force Naptera," I say, "but I think I can convince her, at least. After all, she may hate me for being a Cursed One, but she probably hates the curse more. She helped me earlier too, it must mean something."

All the wolves remain silent, but I know this isn't going to be as easy as I make it sound... Still, I ought to try. I start running again, in the direction I felt Naptera. Now charged up with flames and that Light Magic, Selena flies ahead like a lightning bolt, visibly enjoying her new powers. She was already strong before, but now she's scary powerful. The White Luna already figured out how to keep her flames brimming despite the rain, and she jumps on two golems on the way, frying them effortlessly like a thunder witch more than a fire one... At least I don't have to worry about Selena for now, she's obviously doing great without my guidance.

Meanwhile, Nora runs by my side, her snow white fur like a shooting star in the darkness, her blue eyes looking right ahead.

"Mara, I keep thinking... If we get rid of the curse, will you be alright? As a Cursed One..."

"I hope so. Perhaps something will change, I'm not sure. It's not really important for now, though, don't worry about me..."

"Stop saying things like that, we already told you a thousand times. You're family to us... you're like our little sister. Of course we worry."

I can't help but smile, her words warming my heart more than worrying me. I know. I know I found a new family here in Silver City, a real one.

The warm feelings are quickly cooled down by the never-ending pouring rain, though, and the sight of Naptera. As I suspected, she didn't leave the area, only watching the fight from the sidelines. She makes a sour expression as we approach, already glaring at the wolves. Only Nora and I dare approach at a distance, but the Black Brothers stay back, all growling as a warning.

"...So you did come out," she says.

"Naptera, I'm almost there. I found out the secret behind the curse, and I can end it. But we need your help."

"We?" she repeats, her eyes still defying the wolves.

"The curse is strong, and it was created by the first Royal," I quickly explain. "Not just a witch, but a werewolf witch, who had access to a very powerful magic, and carried very dark feelings inside. I can't get rid of all that darkness by myself. If I go inside again, she may consume me just like she did with Ravena. I know you felt it too."

There's no way she didn't feel the Earth Witch's passing. The curse used her, emptying her magic before it killed her. It was much more aggressive and reckless than the spell I used on Ayesha. Crossing her arms, Naptera glances toward the large tower of darkness on the side.

"...That arrogant Earth Witch brought her own demise."

"Are you going to stand there as more of us die, then?"

She stays silent. Oh, Moon Goddess, she's not making it easy, and it's not like I have a lot of time to argue with her, either... I take a deep breath, and try to remember everything she said earlier. Wait, there's something...

"...How old are you, Naptera?"

She glares at me, and although it could seem legitimate, I know it actually means I aimed just right.

"You're... much older than you look, aren't you? I didn't realize before, but... Nephera wasn't Sadia's daughter, she was her grand-daughter or something like that. Sadia gave birth to a human child first, didn't she? She had a son, a human son that didn't appear in the Witches' Ancestral Tree."

"There you go again, talking as if you know anything," hisses Naptera.

"You're the one playing charades. I've studied our family's ancestry, and Sadia was the daughter of a witch named Beatrice Jones, but Nephera couldn't have been her daughter."

"...There are still many things you need to learn about witches, little one. Nephera was Sadia's daughter, but to preserve her child, she tried to... delay her birth."

I frown, trying to understand. Wait, could it be a... reincarnation? That's the only thing that would make sense. Just like little Mara and I... Sadia tried to protect her child by waiting?

"She protected her soul?"

"...She tried. Sadia thought that by having her daughter be born later, after her own passing, she could protect her soul from the curse... but the curse found her anyway."

Now that solves one mystery... Also, I don't know how I should feel about witches actually playing around with unborn children's souls, but I guess I'm not one to speak, with my own history. I take a deep breath.

"But it didn't work out, anyway. You stayed alive all these years, Moon Goddess knows how long, just to see your friend's daughter be taken by that curse again. I understand you hate that curse, maybe more than anybody. Wouldn't it be time to stand up and fight now, though? Aren't you tired of being on the damn sidelines?"

"Says the child who came to steal my magic to give it to a wolf..." she hisses, her eyes going down to Nora.

"Borrow," I correct her. "Plus, if you're as old as you pretend, I'm sure you've got plenty to spare. And... and it's raining, for Moon Goddess' sake!"

She can't tell me she is going to run out of Water Magic anytime soon, we're literally almost swimming in a giant mud puddle! I step forward, deciding to end this quickly.

"Naptera, please. I don't care who you do it for, but this curse has to be stopped. You know Sadia wanted to protect her child, how much she sacrificed for it. If she was your friend, why would you stand back when you have a chance to help defeat what she tried to fight?!"

She glares at me, but this time, I see doubt in her eyes.

"...Do you even know what you're risking?" she asks.

I take a deep breath, and look inside to wake my Water Magic, taming my fire at the same time. It gently flows in like a river, and I feel my left eye changing, most likely turning back to that gentle blue again. Naptera looks stunned by my eye, and finally uncrosses her arms. After a while, she sighs.

"...And here I thought you didn't look like her. Freaking Jones... Fine, I'll help you. But if you fail to take down that curse–"

"I won't," I retort, showing how determined I am.

Naptera gives me one more doubtful look for the sake of it, but her eyes then go to Nora, checking the white wolf out. I'd rather act before she changes her mind. I take a deep breath and once again, activate the spell. Unlike Ayesha, Naptera is probably charged with Water Magic, so this will be a bit trickier for me...

"Ready, Nora?"

"Anytime."

I nod, and after a deep breath, begin the process. Once I reach out for Naptera's magic, I see the difference between a witch who has had several decades of experience and myself. Compared to her Water Magic, mine feels like a furious uncontrolled stream. The flow I touch is like a gentle river, spreading throughout her body like a perfectly controlled tide, so perfectly imbued in her it's as if I was looking at her veins rather than at a magic network. I am impressed, but I am also wondering if I can ever dream of achieving such perfect control over my magic...

I don't have time to gather more inspiration from Naptera's mastery, though. I slowly start pulling the strings of that water stream, trapping more and more of it in my spell, as much as I can entrust Nora with. I feel some resistance, but it's like undoing the knots in a complex network of water strings, and as soon as I manage to pull one little stream after another, more naturally follows. I try to save as much as I can since I don't want to completely deplete Naptera or give Nora more than she'd be able to handle. Soon enough, I reverse the spell, and slowly transfer all of the Water Magic I could gather into Nora's body. To my surprise, her body seems even more easily accepted as a new host by the Water Magic than Ayesha's fire in Selena's. Is it because she has more Royal blood? I am not sure, but her white aura is definitely quickly figuring out how to handle all of it, and the magic starts to resonate with her in a new way.

When I open up my eyes, Nora's body has changed again. Amongst the white fur, I now see very faint, tiny, white sparkles, like... like snow. Nora's white aura seems to have grown even more icy and stronger, as if her body was surrounded by a cloud of blizzard. The air around her really is colder, and I step back after a shiver.

"That's... interesting," she says, shaking down her body.

"...Ancient blood wakes ancient magic," says Naptera, looking down at the now truly snow white wolf. "Your kind may carry some of the witches' forgotten powers..."

"You mean... there might be more than the three elements of water, earth, and fire?"

"There are only three core elements," she says, "but who said they couldn't be used in different ways, to do... more? You did it before, didn't you?"

Now that she mentions it... I used lightning and even fog. This was only possible because I could combine both fire and water. Until now, I thought that witches were restricted to the use of only one element, but... in the illusion, weren't the two Lunas using all three of them? They were so much more powerful. Is it still possible we could one day achieve the same thing again? Even if it was centuries ago, as Naptera said, perhaps not all of those powers have been lost, just... locked.

Naptera lets out a long sigh, her eyes going beyond me to where Nora is.

"Perhaps you were right... Perhaps the new generation has more to teach us about ourselves than we thought. Even the ones we thought to be... broken."

Whoa, she's almost sounding nice now. At least she's let go of the whole "Cursed One" thing... I nod, and suddenly, my eyes land on my finger. The butterfly tattoo, it's still there. Now that I focus on it, I feel some sort of energy, but it's very tame, I'm not too sure what's hidden there.... Maybe it would be good to remember it for later, for the final assault. I feel like it's going to take everything we've got to defeat the curse for real this time. I take a deep breath, and look down at the newly powered wolves by my side. Both Lunas are absolutely... impressive. Selena looks like a lightning bolt, shining so bright it's hard to look for too long, while Nora is winter personified. I smile, and look inside for my own magic. I feel my inner fire, shining in all its full glory again, making my blood boil and ready. There's my Water Magic too, gently flowing like a slow stream inside. I think "touching" Naptera's has made me more conscious of my own, and I quite like the idea of gaining knowledge through other witches' magic...

Naptera slowly steps back, and I turn around, facing the two Lunas and the Black Brothers.

"*Ready, ladies?*"

"*Ready when you are, Mara.*"

Liam smiles and steps forwards, looking more confident than ever despite his ragged appearance.

"Let's take this curse down, tiger."

We all turn around and get ready.

The hurricane from before has grown much bigger, like a black storm taking over the battlefield. Perhaps because it felt our rise in power, the curse ought to have grown stronger too. If I am completely honest, it is scary to look at. The rain is still pouring down on us, the thunder growling above, and we're just about to run into much worse than that. The storm is loud and yet it doesn't fully cover the sounds of the raging battle all around us. The golems are like hellish silhouettes of mud scattered around the battlefield to slow the groups of wolves and men down. And many are down already. I feel a heavy weight on my heart as I take a second to notice the bodies, furs of all colors dirtied by blood, and the lifeless limbs sometimes sticking out of the ground...

"Let's go," I both say and mind-link.

Moving like one, the white and black wolves start running with me across the battleground, all of us aiming for the gigantic hurricane. Nathaniel and Damian each cover our flanks, and in front of me, Liam, now in wolf form, is running like a bullet shot right ahead, his black figure not slowed down at all by the slippery ground or heavy downpour. Seeing my mate run before me is like a lamplight in the darkness. I just need to follow him, trust him. I feel our mind-link, stronger than ever, like our minds are holding hands and not ready to let go at all. I feel his gentle strength pushing me, and I borrow some of his fearless confidence. I've never realized how perfect we are for each other until this very moment. How Liam is perfect to protect me against my fears, support my boldness, and feed the fire of my bravery. We truly are meant for each other. I feel his trust in me, and it's like another boost I can use. It fuels more of that fire in me, and appeases my heart.

I'm in a strange state during that last race to the end. I feel the pain of everyone around me, all the fights going on. I feel a wolf's body violently hitting the mud. The warm blood dripping, and their pain. The tired body, the fear, and the anger. But I can feel their bravery too as they stand back up. That's right. No wolf is running away, and they are all standing, next to the humans, to defeat the enemy as one. The heart of Silver City is beating right here with them, men and wolves, and I can almost feel its spirit. It's beautiful, powerful, and yet so fragile...

We keep running, nothing able to stop us in our race. I feel like my feet barely touch the ground, we're flying above the mud, the hills, and the traps on the way. Selena is like a flashing bolt, breaking the formation at times to dash through a golem, fry it, and come back, making reckless zigzags all around us. Nora is more careful and sticking to me, probably worried about my health and more cautious about what's coming next. I can't blame her; the closer we get to that thing, the scarier it clearly is...

This isn't about what we see. That hurricane is scary, but that monstrous aura is much, much darker and worse. It feels colder than death, scarier than hell itself, like a mountain ready to crush us at any second. Even just knowing the curse is going to try and instill fear into our minds, I can't help but shiver. I have to focus on my inner flame to get over it. I keep running, holding on to my fire and using it to spread that same feeling of warmth and courage to the others through the mind-link. I can hardly describe it, this strong sense of community between the six of us. Like one wolf, one family. One body with very different limbs, and me and Liam at the head. Even his brothers seem to finally let me in. I can't explain how, but I feel their wolf minds, and instead of scaring me as usual, I feel them like two strong beings I can rely on. Like... big brothers, really. That's kind of nice, especially when Damian Black glances his silver eyes at me, and I suddenly feel supported too.

His Blazing Witch

And I'm going to need their support, because we finally arrive at the base of that hurricane, and its strength is already trying to blow us all away. I dig my feet in the mud, and the wolves all do the same.

"*How are we going to get past that?!*" shouts Nathaniel in our heads.

"*I think I can get us through,*" I nod, "*but I'm going to need everyone to stick real close, and Nora, Selena, you two need to help me through...*"

"*We got you.*"

I nod, and right away, all the wolves get near or behind me, ready for it. I take a deep breath, and try to harness both my fire and water power together. This hurricane is made of a dark aura, some steam, and wind. I may not remember my school days, but I'm pretty sure wind is just cold or hot air... I try to calm down internally, and like before, split my fire and water power, one in each hand. It takes me a few seconds, but this time, I'm not alone. The fact that Selena has Fire Magic and Nora some Water Magic helps a ton. It's like trying to reach out for them, I know exactly where to direct my magic, on each hand. On my left one, I feel my fire, strong like a little brazier, and on the right one, water flowing gently in a small circle. Now, I need to use it all to get us a passage through.

I step forward, fighting against the strength of her hurricane, but at least Selena and Nora's presence near me are like shields against the dark aura. They don't erase it completely, but it's more like they fade it, allowing me to move without too much pressure. They make it so much more bearable for me... I hear the Black Brothers growling together, probably feeling the darkness more than they can see it. Liam's just one step ahead, next to my leg. I take another step, and so does he. If I move, he moves. I know he's not leaving me to face this alone, he's sharing his strength with me.

I start using my magic with all of them supporting me, each in their own way. I focus like never before and, stronger than ever, I push the winds away from us. It's like trying to undo a gigantic knot, pushing my cold Water Magic one way, the hot fire one the other, and struggling to let our group through. The hurricane resists, and increases its strength, but I won't let go. I extend my arms, one each way, and create a bubble of protection around our little group. I feel Nora and Selena too, understanding what I'm doing and sharing some of their magic, like vessels I can grab more power from. One step after another, we advance through the deafening noise of the winds bashing all around us, trying to crush us. The pressure is so terrible, I feel it in my arms and all of my body. If I let go of my focus for just one second, we will all die. I can't let go. I keep pushing and slowly advancing. I feel all of them, moving with me, like one body again. We are doing this, we're advancing and pushing our way into the eye of the hurricane.

"*You're doing great, Mara. Just a bit more...*"

I can't answer; I'm too focused on getting us through this. The pressure is burying my feet into the ground, and the pain in my shoulder is getting... too much. I'm sweaty, feeling gross, and like I'm getting squeezed from all sides. The wind is blowing in my ears, and I need to close my eyes to stay focused.

One foot after the other, I keep pushing, hoping we're getting close. It's worse that I don't know when we'll reach the middle of this, if there even is one... I feel Liam silently sending me encouragement, and I just focus on my inner fire, on the core, to find the strength to continue.

"Get ready, everyone. We're almost there..."

I keep going, silently praying I'm not going to empty my recently refilled magic on this. I just need to keep us alive, though. To make sure we make it inside...

"Mara!"

I'm suddenly grabbed and thrown forward on the floor. To my surprise, I land on dry, warm ground. Liam runs up to me, helping me up.

"Are you alright? Sorry, as soon as we saw the opening we figured we should rush in..."

"Thanks," I gasp.

I'm still feeling a bit tired from the effort before, but at least now, I can stretch my sore arms and shoulders a bit. Oh, I'm so going to feel that for the next few days. Once I'm up, I finally look around. The others are spread like a square around me, growling at all sides, to the hurricane still going on around us, but it's... strangely quiet in here. I feel the wind, but it's as if we're in some sort of a bubble. I can even see the sky far above, not blue but at least not as dark gray as before. So this is what it's like inside... if what we are seeing is real.

I feel some magic going on all around us. I do not like this...

"So you made it after all."

We turn around and surely, risen from the ground, is... Luna. How is that possible? It's really her, with long, white hair, blue eyes, and wearing a familiar black dress. Where have I seen that dress before...? Oh, Moon Goddess. She's using Ravena's dead body as her own. The Black Brothers growl, and I feel disgusted too. I didn't recognize her before because her traits are somehow superposed with the Earth Witch's, and she changed her eye and hair color somehow.

"...Necromancy," I whisper.

"That's right," she says, with a surprisingly gentle voice. "A true witch, who masters all three elements, can obtain power over life and death. Of course, Luna first omitted to mention this when she began training me. However, now I understand that magic was capable of bringing back my mate... of erasing her mistake."

"...Something feels off. And it stinks too."

"She's using a dead body, what would be surprising about a corpse stinking...?"

"No, Selena's right. The corpse can't be that rotten already, but it smells like a fucking cemetery. Something really is off."

I stay focused, but I can't ignore their conversation either. I look down and try to search for clues on the ground. I feel her magic, powerful and overwhelming, all around us, slightly beneath the ground, in the soil... Did she use Ravena's powers again? I look up, and stare at Luna, trying to understand her.

"...You were right," she finally says. "I can't expect witches to stop falling for wolves, for our mates."

"Great," I sigh, wondering if it really could be that easy. "Will you put an end to the curse now, then?"

"No. I won't have to if I get rid of all the witches first."

...Say what? Her eyes go down on Selena and Nora, and both of them growl, but before I can react, Luna's expression suddenly goes dark, and the ground beneath them moves. Damian is the first to react. The large black wolf jumps in to push his mate out of the way. On the other side, Selena felt it coming at the last second, and jumped back to avoid the wood spike that suddenly came out from the ground.

"You shouldn't have made them witches," says Luna. "Now I will have to kill them too."

"It's temporary, and it's to stop you," I retort.

"...You know, I never really liked fighting," she sighs. "Despite my Alpha blood, I'd always leave the fights to the males in our packs... I am much more fit to protect."

What is she getting at? She is so calm and ironically, it's making me nervous as hell. The others too, I can sense they are ready for her next attack, the next threat. Luna steps forward, and our group steps back as one. She chuckles.

"You think you have found a new pack... You think they can replace the family you lost," she whispers.

"They are not replacing anyone," I retort before she can spread any doubt.

However, Luna is not looking at me. Her eyes go to all my companions, one after the other, and a wry smile appears on her lips. The ground beneath our feet starts shaking again, and we all are on guard, ready for the next attack. What is it going to be this time? More golems?

"You think you're the good people. You think the Lunas are all powerful, and you have all the answers, but... what happens when the past comes back to haunt you?"

"*I have nothing to be afraid of,*" growls Selena.

"Really?" suddenly says Luna, turning her head to the golden-eyed wolf.

Fuck, she can hear our mind-links? We all exchange looks, but no one dares to use it anymore. If she can read our mind-link, this is one hell of an advantage lost to her... The ground gets louder beneath us, and I'm really starting to freak out about what the hell she'll throw at us next. A hill suddenly seems to climb up in front of Nora, and she backs away, Damian growling too right next to her.

The ground starts to form a new shape, just as it did when it was about to free the golem, but, instead of a humanoid shape, this time it's... a wolf. Oh Moon Goddess, and the smell is just horrible. The soil retires slowly, and I'm not sure what I'm looking at. It looks like a wolf, but... this thing is dead. It's standing on all fours, and growling loudly, but based on the exposed skull, the opened ribs, and that flesh almost gushing out, that thing is definitely, a hundred percent, supposed to be dead. Oh, I feel like throwing up. Even Ben's horror movies don't get that disgusting.

The one thing I'm worried about most, though, is Nora's reaction. She's stopped growling, and instead, she's slowly backing away, looking... in complete shock. Damian immediately takes a protective stance in front of her, growling furiously at that thing for a reason I don't understand.

"It can't be... It's... Vince..." mutters Nora.

"Can someone update me?" I growl.

"That guy abused Nora years ago. But he's also been dead for years!"

I turn to Luna, who has a smile on, visibly satisfied with that terrible joke of hers.

"See? Power over life and death," she says.

"You damn bitch," growls Selena. *"If you can hear me, note that I'm going to rip your–"*

"Rip my heart out?" finishes Luna, raising an eyebrow. "Like you did with your ex?"

Another dead wolf suddenly emerges from the ground, at least in a better state than the previous one, except for that very visible bullet hole in its head... Selena immediately starts growling at that thing instead, joined by her mate.

"Diego..."

Before I can say anything, both Damian and Nathaniel jump as one, each on the enemy facing them. The four wolves fight brutally, the already torn flesh being ripped apart under the furious growls of the Black Brothers. I can tell they are dead serious, and very, very mad. Without their wives having to move an inch, it's over. The remains on the ground clearly won't get back up for another round this time. I'm... surprised it was that easy, but when I look back at Luna, instead of looking surprised, she just smiles... As she's still staring, the ground suddenly swallows the remains, burying them deeper into the ground again. Nora suddenly throws up, and I can't blame her.

"That was fucking disgusting of you," I growl at Luna.

"Was it?" she smiles. "Well, it's easy when you have to fight against an enemy, but... what happens when you have to fight those who were once your loved ones?"

The ground starts shaking again, and more little hills appear, all around us this time. Oh, Moon Goddess, no, no... More wolves suddenly appear, and this time, the shock in the wolves' eyes is much worse. Nora is paralyzed in front of the black and white male wolf facing her.

"...William..."

Moon Goddess, that's... William Blue? My... half-sibling?

"Stop it!" I yell at Luna, realizing what's going on.

She just keeps smiling, and more bodies are unearthed. I'm getting really nervous and panicked this time. She's bringing back a lot of them. Liam gets closer to me, growling furiously. Another wolf appears in front of Selena, and this time, she doesn't growl, but backs away.

"*No, no, no...*" I hear her. "*Mara, I can't fucking fight Levi... Not him...*"

From the brown fur, I can already tell this is Ben and Bonnie's deceased older brother, who was once her best friend. I know he died in the previous war, but... he's standing in front of her right now, as impossible as it sounds. His eyes are... dead, but the wolves all around us are real and moving. Luna is bringing back fucking zombies of their friends, of everyone they lost before. Holy shit...

"Dad..." mutters Liam, and his older brothers are growling at the same huge, black wolf that looks like them.

What the... Even Judah Black? She can't! I turn to Luna, furious.

"Stop it!" I yell, trying to find the root of her necromancy spell beneath us. "Leave them alone!"

"Them?" she says. "Do you think I'll spare you?"

"Sorry to disappoint, but I have yet to lose anyone in Si–"

Before I can finish my sentence, the ground starts shaking in front of me, another hill forming. Oh, Moon Goddess, no, no... I see the ground opening again, and another wolf steps forward to face me, growling. I feel my heart sink, and everything else inside. No, no, no. I can't... I can't believe it. It's Lysandra Jones.

This has to be a freaking nightmare. I can barely believe what I am seeing, but this time, it's... real. Painfully real. Lysandra is dead, and facing me with a scary amount of dark aura surrounding her. Unlike the others, her body is looking almost... fine, as she hasn't been... dead for long. I feel my blood boiling with anger, and all around me, loud growls are echoing my feelings. I can't believe she went that low.

"Mara, tell me this isn't fucking real..." whispers Liam.

We are back to back, as he has to face his father with his brothers, and I can feel the anger, but also the fear, in his voice. Unfortunately, this isn't an illusion this time. It's very real. This Dark Magic is using the people we lost against us, and Luna is the one doing all of this.

Before I can even make a decision or answer Liam, they all start attacking at once. I hear Nora's voice scream in my head as William jumps at her, and Selena jumps to avoid an attack from Levi. The Black Brothers didn't wait, though. They all jumped as one to face the huge, angry, black wolf.

Lysandra jumps too. Perhaps because she was a warrior, she's much faster and precise than I anticipated. I roll down on the side, finding myself almost next to Nora, who jumped to my side just prior to facing her cousin.

"*Mara, we need a solution. We can't face them!*"

"*They are dead,*" suddenly says Nathaniel. "*Nora, Selena. They are dead. Those people aren't the ones you remember.*"

"*Easy to say for you...*" his wife growls.

"Selena, I'm sorry, but he's right. I can't... feel any life from them. They are just empty bodies moved by Dark Magic."

"Then do something about it, you're the magic specialist!"

She's stubborn in not wanting to fight her once best friend, and I can't blame her. I don't want to fight Lysandra or William. Only the Black Brothers are actively fighting the wolf that was once their father, but I guess the feeling has to be much, much different from ours. I feel Nora's pain, her distress so heavy, I almost feel my own heart sinking.

When Lysandra jumps on me again, I'm ready. I jump down, rolling under her, and get up right in time to blast a fireball at William. The body is thrown to the side with a terrible burnt smell, and my fire consumes it.

"Mara!"

"Nora, I know it's hard, but... Nathaniel is right. And while we are losing time here, Kelsi, Ben, and more are in danger. She didn't put her hands on Tonya and Bobo either, so perhaps..."

The mention of her best friend seems to be what helps Nora decide. With a furious growl, she suddenly increases the white aura around her, almost chilling the air with an icy cloud of steam. I see her turn around and jump on Lysandra, freezing that body as soon as she touches it. I fire up my hand and, without looking, send a fireball her way. I need to take a deep breath. I try to seem fine because they need me to lead here, but... I think I just can't process Lysandra's death yet. She was one of the closest people I had to an actual, living relative... I turn to Luna, even angrier now. She wouldn't have wanted that. I can almost hear her voice... Lysandra would have told me to stop being a crybaby and fucking move on. She was a warrior, and she knew I was too. She said our blood as Jones' made us strong women, and I need to hold on to that right now. If I let go, if I allow myself to be weak, it will be our downfall...

I turn to Luna, who has her eyes on Selena. The white wolf is jumping from one side to another, as quick as a lightning bolt, but she hasn't attacked yet. I can tell she's struggling internally. For Selena, the strongest of us to be so hesitant, I can't see what she's seeing, all the memories that are probably tormenting her right now. I can't even see this wolf as Ben and Bonnie's older brother. All I see is that dark mass around him, the darkness that animates this body... All around us, it's the same. Bodies animated by this Dark Magic are fighting their once allies. Some are emerging from the ground they had died in perhaps just minutes before. I'm angry, and also sad. Our enemy has turned into something much worse than damn mud golems, something much more difficult to face. It's as if all of Silver City's past had suddenly come back to life to haunt those trying to save it... Even with my short history here, I feel overwhelmed. I can't begin to imagine what everyone else is dealing with... The Black Brothers are facing their father with difficulty. I can't imagine the monster he must have been alive if he's that hard to kill now. Liam barely mentioned his father to me, but... I can see it.

The darkness is much more powerful around the dark wolf, so much I can barely tell if it's his fur or the darkness. He violently attacks his sons, one after the other, going for their injuries or weaknesses, or trying to take advantage of them. Nate is violently bitten on his flank, and Damian jumps right in to bite back. Liam is on the other side, trying to look for another angle to attack, and he jumps and shape-shifts with exactly the right timing to tear open the wolf's flank. Just as he does, Judah growls, and turns around to bite him violently.

"Liam!"

"Don't worry about us!"

With Damian's help, and Nathaniel who jumps back in to bite their father too, they manage to have him release his fangs on Liam, but I feel his pain. Unlike the three brothers, their father doesn't seem to feel any pain... Still, they take a second to step back, check their injuries, and then dive right back into this fight. They know where their fight is, and they know they need to defeat their former abuser. I take a deep breath. I need to trust Liam... I need to trust them.

My fists clenched in rage, I turn to Luna. She is the one to stop.

"See?" chuckles Luna. "You're going to tell me to forgive the witch, but... can you guys forgive someone who does such a thing to your loved ones?"

I look down as her hand is pointing at the remains of Lysandra... Then, she chuckles and glances to the side, to Selena, still struggling to face her deceased best friend. I take a deep breath.

"We aren't going to forgive you, Luna. And... I never asked you to forgive her."

This time, she loses her smile, and glares back at me.

"There's no way to forgive someone who does that to somebody you loved, is there? Especially someone like your mate. I would kill anybody who touches Liam, and he would do the same for me. I'd be even more ruthless toward someone who doesn't even respect his death..."

The memories from before all come back. The grave, with those unreadable words, and the spells. Luna's pain when she was missing her mate... I only felt a fragment of it, and she hadn't even realized the truth yet. I can't imagine what she went through. I take another deep breath.

"It was normal for you to hate the witch," I continue. "All that hatred... No one is a fucking saint, to forgive someone who does that to the one you loved the most... When I first heard the tale, I wondered... I wondered why the female wolf would forgive the witch, and be so kind to her. The truth is, the tale was embellished and distorted the truth. It ignored your feelings, and the pain you went through, Luna."

"Shut up..." she hisses. "Don't start talking like you understand my pain! You have no idea what I went through, the darkness that wretched witch put in my heart!"

As she says that, a violent blast suddenly hits me. I feel myself rolling on the ground, again and again, until someone traps me under four legs.

"Nora!"

"Don't move..."

She uses all of her weight to lay down on top of me, her claws in the ground as we are both trying to resist that strong wind. I feel her ice-cold fur, and how she's trying to shield the two of us with her magic. Suddenly, a deafening bang is heard and a scream. The wind that was blowing violently at us stops right away, and the scene appears in front of our eyes. Selena, growling and sending electric sparks all around and Luna, holding her burned hand.

"That's the thing when you start playing with bodies, you have to take their pain too!" growls Selena.

Despite her growling, I can hear the... cry in her voice. She's trembling. A few steps behind her, a burned body is on the ground, still smoking... So she overcame it, after all. Perhaps seeing Nora and I in danger made her decide. Now, her lightning magic is literally electrifying everything around her, and she's slowly stepping up to Luna, ready to fight.

"This damn witch magic..." hisses Luna. "If you want to play with it, you'd better be sure you can handle it."

The darkness around her grows again, and I get back on my feet right in time for the first attack. A rumbling starts under her feet, and she suddenly raises two enormous rocks from the ground. They levitate to eye height, and then, she suddenly throws them our way.

"Mara, Nora!"

This time, I'm the one to jump in front of Nora and use my Water Magic. I don't know where it comes from, but my thoughts are suddenly so clear, I know exactly what to do. I invoke the stream inside and, putting my hands in front of me, I suddenly erect a gigantic water wall in front of us, like a wave emerging just in time to block the rocks. As soon as they hit it, I know my water isn't going to be enough to stop them, but that's not my intention. Using the stream, I make those rocks follow its flow and, with one large movement of my arms, I send them like a curveball right back to Luna. The whole action lasted perhaps three seconds, but Moon Goddess, that felt good.

She sees it flying right back at her, and dives to avoid them. Selena uses the opportunity to strike. She jumps to a prodigious height, and dives like a lightning bolt right on Luna. With deafening thunderous booms, the ground is struck multiple times. *Bang, bang, bang.* The lightning forks down and rips the ground apart, sending burnt soil flying all around. Nora and I start running at the same moment, and I send two fireballs ahead. They disappear in a sudden cloak of dark fog surrounding Luna. Just like the hurricane from before, the darkness gets thicker and starts spinning all around her as she steps back to disappear into the shadows.

"Nora, stop her from using the ground!"

The white wolf nods, and suddenly stops running, burying her paws deeper instead. All around her, the cold suddenly spreads like a white fog. While she stopped behind me, I keep running, the ice gradually covering all the ground under my steps. The battle is raging all around us, but this is the epicenter. I just have time to dive as I see sudden dark fireball-like things fly at me. Is she using Fire Magic now too? We're pushing her to use more magic! She tries to expand the darkness as Selena is restlessly striking her from above. Nora's magic is covering all the ground in that area, and I have to be careful as I am half sliding on the mirror of ice beneath my feet. Her Light Magic is much more useful as it surrounds the area, trying to keep Luna's dark hurricane contained this time. Still, we have no idea where she is in that thing, now as big as a damn building. I keep running to get closer and sending fireballs as Selena keeps jumping or running to try and blindly send lightning bolts into it, hoping we will hit her.

Luna isn't just hiding, though, she's fighting back. All our powers combined are forcing her to stay where she is until we hit her, but she won't let us win so easily. The darkness is trying to scratch Nora's ice and fight the white mist to expand, and Selena and I have to constantly run and be on the move to avoid her attacks. She attacks us non-stop, no one can tell who is the prey and who is the attacker now. I'm trying to locate her in the darkness, but I have to jump and avoid all her attacks constantly.

"Girls..."

Nora is struggling to keep her contained. She's using a lot of magic to keep the ice as a barrier from the ground, and the white mist around us to prevent her from attacking; moreover, she's the one most exposed. The Black Brothers are now facing more undead wolves, all coming toward us, but they can't cover such a wide area to keep them all from attacking us, the dark hurricane is too wide and Selena and I keep moving around it. At this rate, we're going to get killed by another undead wolf, or Luna will use their attacks to get us first.

"Damn it!" suddenly roars Selena.

A wolf just jumped from behind to bite her, and although she managed to burn him right away, she got stuck on the ground for one too many seconds. A huge blast suddenly comes her way. I raise my hands, trying to prepare a defensive magic circle, but–

"Mara, watch out!"

I'm violently hit from the front just as I thought I had sent the magic circle to protect Selena. Something dark covers my vision, but the shock isn't as violent as it should have been. Something inside rings, like an alarm going crazy. Something's wrong. My inner wolf howls in pain, and I feel as if something inside just got... torn apart.

I painfully roll over and struggle to get on all fours. What just...?

"LIAM!"

That name wakes me up like a slap. I look to my right, and he's there. Liam, lying on the ground. Lying on the ground with... with a large hole in his stomach. My heart sinks. No, no, no, no...

"Liam? Liam!"

I grab his fur, any part of him I can, but he's not moving. He's... Liam's not moving. Not at all. His eyes and mouth are open, but he's not moving. He's... he's not responding. I grab his fur and try to shake him, but no. There's... nothing. I try to feel him with my inner wolf, but it's... faint. Our bond, it's... really... going away.

"LIAM!" I scream. "Liam! Liam, wake up! Liam, don't, don't... Li-... Nora! Nora, please!"

She turns her head to me, conflicted.

"*Mara,*" she cries in my head, "*if I let go here, sh-she will...*"

She seems almost stuck where she is, but I don't care. I don't care. My mate is dying! Liam is dying, he's leaving me, he's... I scream, as loud as I possibly can, because I just can't contain it anymore. I scream out all of my anger and frustration, all of my pain echoing on the whole battlefield like a mad woman. Because I am fucking mad, and I can't take it anymore. I won't. None of this.

"...I'll end this," I whisper, tears rushing down my face. "I'll end all of this now. Nora, please. Just... save Liam. I beg you."

She stares at me, her blue eyes so conflicted. I know. I know that if she lets go, Luna will have time to take us all into her hurricane, and Moon Goddess knows what worse. But right now, I can't. I can't even imagine Liam dying right here, like this. Nothing else matters to me.

"Go."

We turn heads, and suddenly, a new chill grows throughout the area. The white mist gets even more dense, and a new layer of ice expands quickly under our feet.

Naptera just appeared, and she's down on her knees, her palms against the icy ground, her eyes on the dark cloud.

"...I'll hold it for you, so you'd better end this, Mara."

Nora runs over as soon as she understands Naptera is taking her place, and gets to Liam right away.

"*Oh, Moon Goddess...*" she whimpers. "*M-Mara, I think it's... too la–*"

"Don't say it," I growl, shaking with anger. "Just... Just do whatever you can. I beg you."

I take a deep breath, and leave a kiss on Liam's cheek, caressing his fur gently. I just want to hold on to him, one last time. I hug his body, still warm. My hands are trembling in his fur, shaking so much I can barely hold on. I need to hold on to the little life left I feel in him, and... end this.

I slowly stand up and, determined like never before, walk right into this hurricane.

"*Mara, don't!*"

"I'm not scared of her damn darkness," I retort, my throat tight, carrying my anger and my pain with me. "She wanted to show me darkness, she's going to fucking get it."

I'm not scared at all. I was born from that darkness.

I am a damn Dark Witch.

Chapter 39

Hearing their voices behind me, I step into the darkness. This time, the winds won't stop me. I light up my fire, holding it around me like a halo. I ground my feet in the ice and keep going, despite the darkness blowing on me. I feel it, this horrible mix of anger, pain, frustration. All those dark feelings keep whooshing in my ears, on my body, so violently it starts to dig little cuts into my skin. I can't even tell if it's hers or mine. It's just pain, echoing mine over and over, and I ought to fight through it.

Right now, I don't fucking care about the physical pain. I feel it, ripping my flesh and slowly pressuring every inch of my body, but I don't give a flying fuck. This hurricane can break me, she can crush me with this. She can break all of my bones and cut all of my skin open, it will never hurt as much as the pain bleeding from my bond to my mate... I feel it. Even when I can't see him, I feel Liam, his pain, and our bond getting thinner and weaker every second. I don't have time.

I force my entry in, I keep going like a madwoman. Like a mad, angry witch. She can't scare me, this darkness doesn't scare me. If anything... this just fuels my dark emotions, and makes me even stronger.

"You don't know it," her voice says, echoing around me. "You don't know the pain yet, and that darkness. How it fills you up, eats you up until there's nothing left!"

I scoff. Really? She thinks she can intimidate me with this?

"You're so wrong. I'm not scared of your darkness. I was... born from the darkness. I am a Dark Witch, even more than you are; I already went through it all."

That's right. I experienced it all, through Clarissa. Her pain, her screams, so many emotions she shouldn't have gone through. I lived all of it, through her memories, her journal, and this body. She suffered a hundred times and tried to fight. She fought depression, loneliness, and the anger from the injustice of being born with a broken body.

"You think you're the only one who lost someone?" I growl, pissed. "You think you're the only woman who's ever suffered, who became jealous and bitter? Wake the fuck up! Everyone's got some darkness in them!"

"Oh, you think you can give me lessons on pain? You think you're better than me, perhaps? But... what happens when you actually lose your mate, Mara Jones?"

No, I can't let that happen!

I light up my fire, searching inside to find the strength, and throw some fireballs around. They disappear into the darkness, hitting nothing, apparently. Damn it...

"Oh, I feel your anger..." she whispers. "Of course, we are angry. We are sad and helpless. You're going to suffer through it too... and then, you'll know what this darkness truly is about."

I can already feel it.

The fear that crawls into my mind as I'm running out of options, and Liam is running out of time. That heavy weight in my heart, pulling me down to the point I want to fall on my knees and cry, break before it crushes me. That invisible hand that's choking me up, suppressing the words and thoughts until there's nothing left but the chaos, a bastard mix of fear and anguish. I want to cry, scream, howl. I don't want to feel this, I don't want to carry this burden, to even think that Liam might really... be gone.

I need him. I need my mate, I need his warmth, his gentle smiles, and the way he completes me perfectly. His blue-gray eyes that carry a million words, and the way his hands touch me. I love the way we are together, one and the same, he and I, and how we're different yet perfect as one. How many people get to find their perfect match? The right person for them, the one you know will hold on even if things get damaged a little, even if... you're the one that's been damaged already. Liam is my rock, the one who will hold on, be there, and support me when I need him. He's the one who makes me feel like... there's nothing we can't accomplish together. We could run to the moon and back together, and laugh like fucking teenagers getting high on our own kind of crazy.

But... Liam is going.

He's going to a place where I can't reach, where I can't follow. Somewhere I can't feel him anymore... Instead of our bond, a void is growing, huge, deep, and horrifying. That monster is sucking me in, filling my mind with despair, and that pain as if I'll never recover from it. Just... It's empty. It's fucking empty, where I felt him. I can't feel his wolf, I can't feel him. There's nothing left of him.

"Liam..." I cry, out of breath.

I close my eyes, forgetting everything else, and I try to search for him. I try to hold on to that faint, derisory hope that I'll find his light, somewhere inside, just if I look deep enough.

But there isn't one. I gasp, unable to stand anymore. He's... gone. No, no, no. I must be wrong, somehow. This must be an illusion, or I must be dreaming. I can't...

"Nora...?" I call out, my throat so tight I wouldn't be able to say this out loud.

"M-Mara... I... I'm so... so sorry, Mara... I..."

I feel it fall deep, deep inside.

It... hurts. Moon Goddess, it hurts so much. I feel the tears coming, but there's nothing worse than that huge pain in my chest. It grips me inside, it... wrecks everything. Sadness flows in, pours in, making me strangely... numb. I need to remind myself to breathe. I try to breathe, but, fuck, it... it hurts. So, so much.... I keep sobbing, my throat, head, and heart in pain. I can't hold it in. I cry like a child, like nothing else matters. I hear my loud crying resonate, my erratic breathing, the broken gasps, and my own wailing.

"See... You and I are the same..."

I wipe the tears from my face, even if more come running down it. I look around–no, I glare around.

"The same?" I repeat, so much anger built up in my voice. "...You think we're the same?"

"The loss of our mate is something only another can understand–"

"YOU HAVE NO IDEA HOW I FEEL RIGHT NOW!" I shout furiously. "Don't you fucking compare my pain to yours!"

"You're the same as I was," she whispers, almost gently. "This pain–"

"This pain is mine and mine alone! I don't give a damn about your pain, about you and your mate! Liam was my mate, and you have no idea how I feel! Don't compare me to you, don't compare my mate to yours! Liam and I had something no one else could understand!"

I light my flames, grown much larger by my fury. I spread them over my entire body, just like the havoc I feel inside.

"You know nothing!" I cry out. "You think I feel like you? There's no fucking way, Luna! My pain is mine alone! There's no fucking comparing it!"

I keep scorching my surroundings. My fire is burning bright, large, and unafraid to have everything go down in flames around us. I feel those flames all over my body, like a human torch, and I won't stop until I burn down every damn thing and have her come out. She wanted some darkness, she's going to be fed some fucking ashes!

"I felt the same anger when I understood."

She suddenly appears in front of me, and I calm down the flames that were pouring out my hands, bringing them back, close to my body. My eyes hurt from crying so much, tears still rolling down my face. The heat of my body carves long streams along my face, where those tears dry as far as they manage to roll down.

"It's not the same," I scoff, suddenly laughing nervously. "The same? For it to be the same, you would have to have known who Liam was, how much he mattered to me. He was my mate, not yours. You know nothing of Liam. The few but amazing memories we had together. The way he... smiled when he looked at me. You should have known the touch of his hands on my body, how he made every inch of my skin feel. There are no two Liams, and there aren't two Maras, either. There's only us. And I swear, you're not going to take any of that and claim it as yours."

A strange calm suddenly dominates me. Perhaps because I've let out all of my emotions, my mind is crystal clear at this very moment. I look down and quickly prepare a magic circle under our feet. She frowns, looking down, but takes another step closer to me.

"Mara, this darkness... You should know how it feels now. You and I went through the same experience... I can show you how to become more powerful than before."

"I only care about power if I can fucking blow you up," I hiss. "You were right, Luna. The darkness is alluring. It's powerful, and it's easy to give in. But you know what? It's no fucking answer."

I trigger my magic circle, and just as she realizes what's going on, I lock it, closing my fists and turning them as if I'm turning an invisible key underneath us. She gasps and stops moving. No, she can't move. She tries to fight it, grimacing, but I'm holding onto her. Now that she stole Ravena's physical envelope, she's much easier to catch and trap. And now that I am also using that Dark Magic, I don't fucking care about hurting a body that's already dead.

"Let me go!" she screams.

"Oh, I won't," I state, taking deep breaths. "You killed my mate. I don't feel the slightest bit like letting you go."

I tighten it. Like a gigantic claw around her, she makes a grimace, and I don't care. I just make it tighter and tighter, until I'm really sure she can't move, she can't escape. She probably can't breathe, either. I light the fire in my hand, leaving the other to lock that magic circle, keeping her where I want her.

Slowly, I finally step closer to her. I carry my pain and my anger with me, like huge weights I'm consciously taking in with me, swallowing it. With each breath I take, there's still this darkness, hammering me with the painful, bottomless realization that Liam is gone. It hurts, it hurts and it won't go away. Still, I keep going. I want her to see this.

As she sees me approaching, she smiles.

"You want to kill me, don't you? You want me to suffer, like I made your mate suffer and bleed."

I burn her. I didn't hesitate a moment before sending that fireball to hit her shoulder, and I don't regret it as she screams in pain, falling down on her knees and violently shaking. A bitter smile appears on my lips. I let the darkness come in, pouring its strength in me like a painless poison. That's right, I'm a Dark Witch. I won't think twice about giving back the pain she gave me... but, strangely, it doesn't give me any kind of satisfaction. Stranger is the fact that I already knew all that. Perhaps because I've already experienced so many negative emotions, I know there is nothing that will relieve the pain in my heart. Crying, screaming, hurting to the point where I'm physically in pain won't help. So, how could hurting her instead even do me any good?

I take a deep breath instead, aware of my heart feeling like a bottomless, dark hole, and get down on one knee to her height.

"If you're still here, why would I think any of what you did relieved your pain in any way, Luna?"

Her eyes open wide in shock this time. That's right; there's nothing she can teach me about the darkness. Little Mara may have taught me the higher levels of magic, but Clarissa was the one who gifted me with the understanding of what darkness, true darkness of the heart, is really like. It has the same color as fear, the same taste as despair.

"There's something you don't understand," I say. "No matter what I do to you, it won't alleviate the pain from the loss of my mate. I can swallow all of that darkness around us, to the very last bit of it, become the Darkest Witch the world has ever known, and it won't change the truth that makes me bleed inside. And you know who taught me that in the first place? ...You did."

She makes a sour grimace, but... I don't react to it at all. Instead, I close my eyes, and take a deep breath.

I open myself up and slowly, I use my sadness, this despair that overtakes everything else in my mind, and I take all of that darkness in. Everything. I absorb the whole hurricane, as if I was drinking it, letting it pour into that bottomless pit I feel, right where my bond to Liam was before. I take in as much as I can. All that sadness, that anger, that pain... It's so raw and painful, but I am in that strange state where... none of it matters. Nothing else can hurt me anymore.

"You don't understand..." she mutters painfully. "You... you're all the same. You can't understand my pain. You've never gone through the same..."

I ignore her and, while I keep that darkness coming to me, I know what it is I truly need right now. I focus as much as I can until I can reach out to them. Like a thin, shining thread through the fog. I find their inner voices, their inner selves, and I hold on to them, like someone would ring the alarm for help.

"Mara!"

They jump in at the same time, both crossing that fog like lights in the darkness. I open my eyes and see them. Selena, growling between me and Luna, and Nora, running toward us.

I finally let go and, just as she comes to me, I hug Nora's white fur. I feel her quiet, cold strength coming over me.

"I'm sorry..." she sobs. *"Mara, I am so sorry... I really tried..."*

I can't utter a word. As if Selena and Nora's return were making Liam's death twice as real, and twice as painful. I can't stop sobbing, and I can't let go of the white fur, of Nora's gentle embrace. The darkness I've taken all inside is like a dead weight dragging me down, and Nora is making that weight fade, grounding me there. I feel her sorrow and Selena's anger, both echoing mine.

Strangely, we share several minutes like this in silence, just my crying and Nora's, and Selena's faint growling, despite the pain I feel coming from her too. I just need... those two. I need their support. They have something Luna will never be able to have: a real, genuine bond with Liam. They both knew my mate, and thus, they are the ones able to understand even just a portion of my pain. Luna will never, ever have that.

After a while, I open my eyes again, ignoring how they burn from crying so much, how my inner powers of fire and water are slowly melting inside, fueling me with something new, something dangerous. I take a deep breath, my fingers still hanging on to Nora's fur. But I have to put an end to this. I swallow, trying to get something to pass down my tight throat, and I redirect my attention to Luna.

She's mad. Her glaring eyes are fueled with anger, directed at the three of us.

"You can't run away from this..." she mutters. "This pain will haunt you forever."

"Oh, I know," I retort. "However, unlike you, I'm prepared to let it haunt me, Luna. I won't give it to anyone else like you did, and I won't ignore it."

I take another deep breath and close my fist against my chest, right where the dark hole is.

"This is what you can't understand. This darkness is not an answer. It is no beginning, neither is it the end, Luna. It will stay there, and there's no getting rid of it so easily. There is no magic that can alleviate my pain, and I don't want it to, either. I won't give it to you, I'll suffer through every stage of it. ...Because if I don't face it, it will be as if what Liam and I had was never real in the first place."

"You can't!" she yells, furious. "I can give you the power to bring him back! You've seen my powers, you've seen what true magic is like! You can have him back, Mara Jones. Your mate. You can bring Liam back!"

"*...Mara, what is she saying?*" asks Selena.

"You know I'm telling the truth," laughs Luna. "You know I have the power to bring your mate back, Mara Jones. If I have the three powers, I have the power of life and death! I am the mightiest, most powerful witch and Luna you will ever meet. If you kill me, your only chance at bringing your mate back will go with me."

I take a deep breath and get up, stepping a bit away from Nora to ignite my fire. I have to put an end to this, now. I hold on to that bottomless pain inside, to the void in my heart. To my memories.

"No," I declare, calmer than I thought. "I already know what you are trying to do, Luna. If I give in, this curse will go on. It will go on through me, and through everyone else who will suffer that pain, again and again."

"But your mate–!"

"Liam was the most stubborn, reckless, and righteous wolf around," I shout back, "and as much as I'm dying to bring him back, I know he would give me fucking hell for that. I would have to give in to this Dark Magic and sacrifice myself. I would have to sacrifice the Mara Jones he knew, the one who stood against you. There is no way he'd ever accept me bringing him back like that, through your Dark Magic. So, the answer is a definite, painful, fucking no, Luna."

"*Mara...*"

I know.

His Blazing Witch

I know how insane I must sound right now, to pass on this opportunity, but this is exactly what I exist for, and why Liam had to die. This is exactly how this wretched curse wants to play out, and this is exactly what Luna has been aiming for. The more witches experience her pain and give in, the longer this curse will go on. Who would willingly let go of their mate when given the chance to bring them back?

There's only one way to stop this curse: go through the same journey as Luna and, unlike her, have the strength to make the right choice. It's not easy. I'm crying, bleeding, and screaming inside. I want to fall down on my knees, give up, and beg her to bring Liam back. I want him back so desperately. But, in a strange paradox, Liam's memory is exactly what keeps me from giving in. I'm holding on to those memories, to who he was, what he wanted. He was protected, shielded all his life, and he saw too many people die. He believed, deeply, in doing the right thing for others. If I brought him back, it would be the worst betrayal I could give to him, and I would break what was between us. I am not going to betray and fall out of the Mara that Liam Black loved. I won't.

"You foolish little–" groans Luna, struggling against my spell.

"Yeah, all that, and you haven't seen anything yet," I growl back.

I prepare my fire in one hand, the Water Magic in the other, and prepare to fire.

"*Now?*"

"Now," I nod. "We have to force her to stop everything!"

"Stop it!" screams Luna. "I am Luna! You can't stop me! You can't–!"

"*Oh, shut up,*" growls Selena.

She starts activating her lightning magic again, and Nora prepares her ice blizzard too.

This is it. This is the last attack, the one I need to break the curse, once and for all. I won't give in to her, and I won't stop my attack, either. I am not doing this for revenge, it would be meaningless. I am doing this for Liam. For Sylviana, Nephera, Lysandra, for all the witches and werewolves who suffered because of that curse. For generations of witches and wolves who couldn't love freely, or suffered through it.

"*We're with you, Mara.*"

Strangely, Nora's words bring me a sudden feeling of calmness and confidence. As if... my pain was slightly alienated. I extend my inner self as if to touch them, feeling them right by my side. Their auras gently come to me, almost as if they could melt into mine. They are so similar, yet different. One soft, cold, and soothing, the other bright, hot, and energizing. The White and Black Lunas. The Sun and Moon of Silver City. Yet, to me, they are so familiar, so much like myself. My new family, like... my big sisters. A bond stronger than blood, stronger than our genes. Something that binds the three of us together, tighter than fate, stronger than anything physical. They are here, with me, supporting me, and I know they always will be. I start crying again silently, but this time, it's different. Those are warm tears, bittersweet tears of gratitude. ...You were right, Liam. I'm not alone.

I won't ever be alone again.

I prepare, gathering all the magic I hold. Everything, burning, boiling, and building up inside, getting bigger, as I take all I have left inside. Dark and Light Magic, fire and water, everything that's been left inside. I feel Nora and Selena doing just the same, preparing to attack with everything they have left in them. This is the last attack.

Luna can probably feel it too. She's panicking and wriggling, trying to break herself free of my magic circle. I hear bones breaking, one after the other, as she doesn't care about hurting that stolen body. Sorry, Ravena...

"You can't!" she screams. "You can't! I'm eternal! My wrath has to continue, or the werewolves will–"

"The werewolves deserve to live in peace, and the witches deserve to love whoever they want," I retort with a broken voice. "You have done enough wrong, Luna. Time to end it."

I raise my arms, ignoring her screams of anger and fear. It's an enormous mass of magic that's now above my head. Fire and water are fighting each other, making a loud crackling noise, almost burning my fingers and provoking a lot of steam around me. The fog is flying around, but I make sure to look Luna's way, and her way alone. It drains all the energy inside me, everything I had left of my magic, to the last drop. I have to use all the strength I can to even keep it contained before it explodes. I look to Nora and Selena, also ready.

They launch their attack half a second before me. A blinding light and a thunderous boom as Selena strikes first. The bolt keeps forking and crackling as she hits Luna, again and again. Nora's ice comes right after, like a violent snowstorm taking over the area. Even I can feel the ice freezing me down to my bones. I'm next.

With a massive rage, I throw my gigantic magic fire and water ball right ahead, the blast so violent and sudden, the ground trembles under our feet. The explosion blows all of us backwards, thrown across the area like paper dolls. I hear the deafening mix of lightning cracking, the fire and water explosion, and the whooshing of that ice mist.

It's over. I can feel it. The darkness from before, it's... gone. Washed away like a wave, leaving a big, empty area under it. Something nude and bare, completely new and... fresh. I shiver. Moon Goddess, is it... over?

I open my eyes, feeling sore all over.

It's the snow again. Except, this time I'm not Luna. Luna is there, just a few steps away from us. She is completely different, all of that... dark aura is gone. She looks defenseless, weak and sad. She's crouched down in the snow, shivering and crying faintly. I look to both sides, and exchange surprised glances with Selena and Nora. The two wolves are as dumbfounded as I am...

"...Luna?" I call out gently.

"Leave me alone..."

Oh, I didn't expect to hear her in my head. I painfully get up, each muscle in my body protesting after what I just put them through... I let out a sigh, and slowly get back on my feet, trying to ignore all the aches.

"*Mara...*"

"*It's alright. She's different now. This... is the real Luna, the Luna from before. You can feel it too, right? There's no Dark Magic left in her. She's just... herself.*"

I make my way to the white wolf. She growls a bit as a warning, but I can tell she doesn't have the strength to fight.

"*Leave me alone,*" she repeats. "*I failed... I am not the Luna you thought I was.*"

"Honestly, I didn't expect you to be real in the first place," I retort, "but here we are, somewhere in a memory, to meet you."

"*...You don't need to meet me.*"

"*No. You needed to meet us,*" replies Nora, stepping up next to me.

I know she understood why we're here too. Selena comes after us, a bit more hesitant. The white wolf is still lying in the snow, and I realize, on our left, there's the tombstone.

"*Don't look at the grave.*"

"*Why?*"

"*Just... don't.*"

I'm not sure what can be triggered if we stare at that grave, but I wouldn't risk it. It's like... a gut feeling telling me not to. I glance around. It's the exact same scene I saw, except that there's nothing else around us. There's no sound, for starters. No wind pushing through the trees, not a bird singing, no sound of leaves rustling. Even the snow under our feet doesn't creak. It's as if everything had stopped, stuck in this precise moment in time, leaving only the four of us here.

We walk up to Luna, but she turns her head to the little wooden cabin. This Luna has... lost all of her will. She's just a bottomless pit of sadness and loneliness.

"*It's all over,*" she growls. "*You should go back. There won't be... anymore of that curse. He's really... not coming back.*"

"You can't stay here, either," I retort. "This place... you're still trapped in here, Luna."

"*I'm fine with being trapped.*"

"Why? You need to move on. There's nothing left by staying here, all alone."

"*I'm fine with being alone!*" she growls.

We all take a step back. Although she's lost her power, she's still a wolf, and all three of us are much too tired by the fight. I take a deep breath.

"This curse... it appeared in the first place because you didn't want to let go. You didn't want to... face the truth, Luna."

"*Nothing will change,*" she growls. "*Leave me be!*"

"No. Things need to change. You have to move on, Luna. Look around you. This memory... you're the one trapping yourself here. You had the power to end that curse long ago. Centuries ago, perhaps, but you chose not to. Not

609

only that, you left the room open for more witches and werewolves to suffer just like you did."

"Enough. You know nothing."

"Perhaps I don't," I retort. "You lost your mate, and the woman you even considered your only friend used you and betrayed you. She probably had her reasons and her own feelings for doing what she did, but... she shouldn't have forced you. Just like you shouldn't have forced this curse on the generations that came after you, Luna."

"This is my anger, my pain. I'm free to do whatever I want with it!"

"What about your children?"

She suddenly turns to Nora, who stepped forward.

"Your children lived on, didn't they? They grew up fine, they had their own children and that's how your blood was passed down, for many generations, until it came to us. Your mate's, and the witch's too. Why didn't you choose to focus on your children instead, Luna?"

"My children were wolves. They didn't need their mother once they were grown!"

"Perhaps not, but you needed them," growls Selena. *"You needed a family, and a pack, but you chose to stay alone."*

"Yes, and it was my choice!"

"You chose to bury yourself in your loneliness and anger, Luna, and it created a curse that affected everyone. The witch, and your mate... They are both long gone. There's no reason for you to stay behind."

I suddenly feel another wave of sadness and fear coming from her. She whimpers.

"I won't forgive," she says. *"Don't ask me to move on. That witch took everything from me!"*

"I am not asking you to forgive!" I retort. "Luna, even if you wanted to... there's no one left to forgive except yourself."

"...What?"

She stays silent this time, and finally gets on all fours, although she's growling. But we are also werewolves, and we can tell there isn't much animosity in her voice.

No, this is the growl of an animal that's afraid and trying to protect itself. Luna doesn't want us here, she isn't the one who chose to appear, raw like this. She truly wants to be left alone, but I have a feeling that if we do, nothing will truly and definitely be solved. This is necessary if we want to make sure that curse ends and doesn't come back...

"Luna, if you can't face the mistakes of the past, they will haunt you and keep you down."

"I made no mistake!" she growls. *"That witch was the one who used me!"*

"Really? Do you think she played around with necromancy spells out of anger or out of despair? It was necromancy, but... she didn't use Dark Magic, did she? ...She used her own life force."

I suddenly realized. We never heard how the other Luna disappeared, how the witch left. If Luna had killed her, if they had even fought, things would have been very different. However, there's... no one else here. Her mate never came back, and the witch is gone too. She's all on her own.

"Luna... I never got to see what happened after that spell was completed," I mutter.

She stops growling, glaring at me instead.

"*...I have nothing to tell you.*"

"*Luna, you can't move on with a heavy burden on your back,*" gently whispers Nora. "*This all happened... in the past. Like Mara said, a faraway past. You need to let it go now.*"

"*That witch didn't disappear on her own,*" growls Selena, "*and we already saw your little necromancy trick. You know it was possible, at least partially, to bring your mate back. Something went wrong with that spell, which is why you didn't want Mara to see that memory.*"

I see Luna step back this time. She glances at all three of us and growls a bit again, without much conviction this time.

"*You won't understand,*" she whimpers. "*You can't understand...*"

"Luna, we are not here to judge you or blame you. But there's something you've been hiding for way, way too long, and you have to let it go, now. You can hide the truth if you want. That's completely your call. But by doing so, you will also be burying any chance for change."

"*Any chance to let go of your pain,*" adds Nora with her gentle voice.

"*...I am Luna,*" she says. "*I made no mistake. I tried to protect my family, my mate, and I failed. That witch was responsible for everything.*"

"*For Moon Goddess' sake,*" growls Selena. "*Everyone makes damn mistakes! You're not the Moon Goddess and you're not perfect! What is wrong with you?!*"

"Selena..."

"*No, Mara, I'm growing tired of this shit! We are here extending our hands to this selfish bitch while our mates and our packs are still fighting Moon Goddess knows what out there! It's too damn late to play the innocent gentle Luna soul now, so just fucking spit it out!*"

Luna growls, furious, but... I can't say Selena is wrong. She may have said things a bit... too brutally, though. I take a deep breath and step forward, ignoring the loud growls coming from both sides.

"Luna, once you admit what truly happened, and face it... You'll be able to let go of all of this. I promise. I know it's probably... painful, and heart-wrenching enough that you would have rather held on to a centuries-old curse than to relive what happened here. But... once you learn to face the truth, no matter how painful it was, a lot of things can get better."

"*...You can learn to forgive those who hurt you,*" gently says Nora.

"*You can also get stronger from it,*" adds Selena. "*Everyone makes mistakes.*"

"...And from those mistakes, something better can be reborn," I finish. "...Luna, please. This curse has to end now. With the truth. We have made too many sacrifices already."

"...*Alright,*" she mutters, "*but... promise me after this, I will be free to go. For... real, this time.*"

"I promise," I say, standing back up, "but first, let Nora and Selena go, please."

"*Mara? What are you talking about?*"

"This is a time loop, just like the one I was in earlier. The concept of time is different here. If you don't get out quick enough... who knows how long we will really spend here? It might be days before we come back."

"*But—*"

"You have children," I say before they can protest. "You should go back to your mates, tell them we won. I will... stay here, and learn the truth. I'm the only one who can afford to stay."

They lower their heads, knowing exactly what I mean. My mate isn't waiting for me.

Chapter 40

The two wolves by my side exchange a look, and I can feel their hesitation. I take a deep breath, and nod.

"It's really alright, I promise. You two go back. There's no more danger now, nothing I can't handle alone. Go back to your mates and everyone. They need you."

"*...We need you too,*" whispers Nora. "*You have to come back, Mara.*"

"I know. It's okay."

"*We're serious,*" growls Selena. "*You'd better bring your ass back as soon as you can. We do need you, and I don't want to lose anyone else today.*"

"I promise I'll do all I can to come back... as soon as possible," I add as soon as she growls again.

I hear them sigh in my head, but I try to stay reassuring. I'm tired, but... at least, I feel like the final fight is over. This is... just part of the aftermath. We did it. Now, it's just up to me to get to the bottom of things and prevent it from ever happening again. Nora and Selena were a huge help, and I wouldn't have gone that far or even survived if it wasn't for them, but... this confrontation between me and Luna doesn't need to involve them. This is my cross to bear, and they don't need to shoulder that burden with me. I know they want to go back to their mates, and they deserve to. I turn back to Luna, still crouching in the snow blanket.

"Send them back. Please," I insist.

I may sound polite, but I make sure my voice is clear. She growls a bit, but soon, the snow under Selena and Nora begins moving. They get in a defensive position, but I can see them being pushed away, gently blown back into the real world. They disappear slowly, as if an eerie blizzard has taken over the spot where they were standing, and the last thing I see are two pairs of glowing eyes, one blue and the other golden.

I wait until they are fully gone, and I look inside for them... My inner wolf easily reaches out to those soulmates of ours. I smile, reassured by the relief they are both feeling right now. They definitely got back to their mates. A knot comes back to my throat, and my heart suddenly feels a lot heavier, just as I am reminded I lost mine. I take a deep breath, but a couple of tears still come out. Liam... I'll end this for you, babe.

"...It's just the two of us now," I tell Luna.

"*Indeed... The crazy ones.*"

"The werewolf witches," I chuckle. "You must have seen many of our kind in here."

I look around in this strangely vivid memory frozen in time. Luna slowly moves, but stays at a reasonable distance from me. I can feel her suspicion, her doubts. It's strange. Now I can... feel her, a bit. It's not as crystal clear as when I try to communicate with my pack, but there's definitely something familiar about it. She has a heart like Nora or Selena's. Something that shines brightly, vividly, but with a heaviness to it. The heaviness of her past.

"There weren't that many," she retorts in a cold tone. *"Not even ten... Our kind is too rare, and the curse took care of those who did live."*

"Like Clarissa and little Mara. But I was created by the same Dark Magic, so it couldn't kill me, right? The curse tried to get into my mind, but I was different from them all."

"Of course you are. You were created by Dark Magic, yet also imbued with Light Magic by your link to the Royals. There's something special about your existence... and your bond too."

Again, that knot that chokes me up. I take a deep breath, trying to control it.

Destiny or the Moon Goddess probably didn't pair all three of us with the Black Brothers by some haphazard mistake... No, it feels like something bigger was at stake, like the wheels of fate making sure every piece fell into the right spot. I take another deep breath and turn to the grave. ...I still see Liam's name, and it's painful as hell.

"...Tell me what happened, Luna."

She finally moves. Her paws silently dive into the snow as she walks up to the grave. She suddenly rubs her head against it, in a very canine-like way. I hear a faint whimper.

"I missed him so much... I would have given almost anything to bring him back. Perhaps a part of my wolf self had already known he was gone, but... every day I spent with Luna, I felt him grow a bit further. As if she was telling me."

"...Did you ever find out how he died?"

"Luna said it was the humans... Perhaps it was also the wolves. By trading half of his wolfhood with the witch, my mate had become a stranger to his own kind. He wanted to become stronger, for the packs, but... he lost them. He lost their trust, and he couldn't get the humans' either. Luna was too different from mankind."

"They hated witches."

"She hated humans just as much," scoffed Luna. *"She didn't just choose to live alone, she had no choice. She... scared them. She probably would have scared a wolf too if she hadn't been so close to nature itself."*

"But you befriended her."

"She befriended me. Luna wanted a companion, after she had lost my mate, I probably came at the right time... She introduced me to her world, and

began thinking that with my blood, as a pure werewolf, and magic, we could do the impossible together..."

"Bring him back."

Luna suddenly growls, and steps away from the stone, almost as if she was wary of it, or... scared.

"*She didn't bother to tell me the specifics, she... knew it was something forbidden by the laws of magic. She... didn't know what she was doing.*"

"Was the spell too powerful for her?" I ask.

"*Oh, no, the spell itself would have worked... if it hadn't included a clueless, eager wolf.*"

I frown. Luna is the one who caused the necromancy spell to... fail? I swallow my saliva. I feel like I'm standing in a sacred place hiding some terrible events. Actually, the whole place suddenly looks much more sinister. Luna keeps moving away, and she's now slowly walking toward the house. Once again, the completely still state of our environment is disturbing. The snow under my feet makes no noise, I step on it as if it was stable, thick ground. The trees, wind, and everything around is completely quiet...

Luna stops a few steps away from the house, and I know where we are. This is where the spell happened, right before I got out of that memory. This is where the two Lunas stood, above a magic circle. That thing is still carved in the ground, like a traumatic burn. Luna walks up to that thing, but she's careful not to step inside. She stops just a couple inches away from the border. Now that everything is much clearer and I'm using my own mind and eyes, I observe that thing with a strange feeling. It does feel very ominous...

"*When I understood what Luna had tried to do... When I saw the grave, it hit me. On that stone was the name she had given my mate. He was the only male she had ever cared about, her first companion, just like he had been mine. I understood what she was doing, what we... were about to achieve. I'm not sure how long I stayed there, while the truth hit me violently. I just remember running back, and yelling at her to start over. What I didn't know back then was that she had already used too much of her own energy in the first attempt.*"

I can imagine.

If Luna was on her own guiding the spell and using the she-wolf as a... battery, it must have required a crazy amount of focus from her. Moreover, she did it using her own life force. She was a good witch, a witch that used only Light Magic, not Dark. Which meant she used her own life force to try and bring him back. I can't even fathom how hard it must have been for her. Not just hard... she had to give up her own life force. How much of one's life was to be given to bring another one back from the dead? That's... frightening.

"*I insisted we try again,*" whispers Luna. "*Once I understood she was trying to bring my mate back, I became obsessed with it. I didn't care about anything else... about her. I'm still sure she was involved in his death. At the time, that was a good enough excuse to ease my conscience about using her.*"

"...So you resumed the necromancy spell?"

Luna slowly lowers her head, her blue eyes on the lines of the circle.

"...We did. This time, I was fully involved in it, and... blinded. So blind, I focused on the magic without realizing what I was doing to Luna. She had been the one to drive the spell, pour her life force into it. Now, I was taking it from her, more and more, desperately."

Her voice breaks on those last words. I feel... a bottomless sadness from her. She whimpers, and slowly crouches down on the circle. She looks at the other end of it, as if she was seeing something there, or someone. I feel her sadness melting with mine, adding to it like another weight on my heart.

"...She didn't tell me," mutters Luna. *"I kept going like a mad wolf, and she didn't tell me she was dying, or that I was using Dark Magic without realizing. I just chose to save my mate, and disregard everything else. No matter the price, I couldn't let go... I couldn't do what you did."*

I try to take it all in. All her sadness, but also the heavy truth behind this tragedy. Luna and I are different in one thing... She had no one else. For me, I could stop because there was Nora and Selena, Ben and Kelsi, and everyone else in Silver City. I could hold on to the fact that, even if... I lost Liam, I wouldn't be completely alone. I wouldn't be the only one to remember him, and I would be able to share my pain and that burden with someone.

Luna had no one like that but the same witch who had taken her mate from her. Actually, neither of them did. They had each other, but they could only hold on to the man they had both loved and were desperate to bring back. They couldn't trust each other enough to know they'd be there to support the other. They were desperate to regain the one they thought would be there...

"I would have been scared too," I mutter.

"Then why aren't you?" she suddenly growls and turns around. *"You didn't hesitate to give away a chance to be with your mate, and instead–"*

"I did hesitate!" I growl back. "This was perhaps the hardest choice I've ever made in my life!"

"Then how?!"

"Because I'm not scared to be alone," I suddenly drop.

I just realized that now. I scoff as it suddenly hits me, and shake my head, a bitter smile on my lips.

"You weren't... scared to lose your mate, Luna. You had already lost him. You were just... scared to be alone. Just like why you went to that witch in the first place. You couldn't stay alone, so you went to the only person that was probably lonelier than you."

"No, you don't know what you're talking about," she growls.

"Oh, no, I'm just understanding now," I retort, turning around.

I walk back to the cabin, and push the door to go in. It all stayed exactly the same as in my memory, except that now, I'm seeing things from a human's height. It's still all the same. There are no smells, but... it's the same bed, the same table, and the same stool. All for one person. One bowl, one... spoon, one meal that seems to be cooking in the little chimney. There isn't even a space for another human in here... I shake my head, and hear Luna barging in behind me.

"You were both frightened," I continue, looking around. "You were both terrified at the idea that you'd be alone again, after you had experienced being with your mate. You didn't want to go back to your children for fear their pack would reject you, so you went to the only woman who could understand you, and was as lonely as you were."

"What?"

"The curse didn't originate from a mistake in the spell," I declare, turning to her. "That spell was perfect, it was working. Even if you turned it to Dark Magic, you could have emptied all of Luna's strength and brought your mate back. But it failed. And instead, you got trapped in it. You don't know how Luna died, do you? You're not even sure how your mate died, and you didn't know how that spell ended either!"

"No! I–"

"You weren't just the creator of the curse, Luna," I say, stepping closer to her again. "You were also its first victim. Your Dark Magic realized how scared you were to be lonely, abandoned again, and fed on it. It pushed you to be alone again, and hate the only friend you ever had. It made you lonelier than ever, and yet constantly looking for a new host to experience your loneliness again. That's why it poisoned the minds of witches, forcing them to be alone again each time they had found a mate. Nephera ran from her second chance mate, although she was pregnant with his baby. Clarissa's mother was alone with her child too. All those women ended up alone because the curse pushed them to leave, somehow."

"Enough!" she growls. *"You're not making any sense! I killed Luna who tried to use me! I created the curse with my Dark Magic!"*

"...I don't believe you killed Luna," I mutter, turning around to look at the room. "I think you're the one who died trying to bring your mate back, and you didn't want to face the truth because you would have had to face your greatest fear to end that curse. Embrace the loneliness, and renounce your mate forever. That's why you endured all those years, and survived through the curse rather than to give up. It's like a... cursed loop. Making the wrong choice, over and over again, until someone could stop you. Until someone like me came along. Same story, same kind, and I was given the same choice. I can stop you because I'm not scared to be alone, Luna."

"No, no, no. She died. The witch died when we created that curse! Otherwise, why wouldn't she have stopped me?!"

"She couldn't," I shake my head. "I think... the curse you were trapped in was too strong for her to handle. She knew she didn't have the strength, as you took most of her life force. Moreover, it would have meant giving up on you forever... If I had been her, I wouldn't have wanted to make the same mistake twice."

I keep looking around the room, and I know what is missing. There's no Witches' Ancestral Tree here... Perhaps it didn't exist back then, or perhaps Luna herself invented it for the next generations to keep track. I chuckle, as the truth suddenly comes to me, so easily it's almost risible.

"She had children," I say. "I saw the Witches' Ancestral Tree, and... Luna, the first witch, had children. Back then I wondered which one of you the tree was referring to, but if it had been you, Selena, Nora, and their grandmother would have been on there. No, it was her, and she definitely had descendants, like Nephera. No, she lived. Luna lived, and she couldn't stop you, so... she did the next best thing she could. She made sure no one could ever use that spell again. I understand why there's only one curse now. Your friend Luna was the one who made sure no other witch could go through the same thing you did..."

"Wh-... How?" she gasps.

"...She made sure there would be no more witches with three elements. She split them into a cycle. In that tree, all witches had one element starting from a certain point, but there was none under the oldest witches' names. Now I know why, I think. Perhaps until someone would be strong enough to have all three again... or enough witches could come together against the curse."

A silence follows my words, and as I look over my shoulder, Luna steps back, almost as if she's scared. The truth is probably scary for her, but she needs to hear it. Perhaps she should have heard this long ago.

"Your friend couldn't save you, but she didn't want to lose you either. She just did her best to ensure your curse wouldn't affect too many witches, or be used again. I always wondered why witches were so wary of werewolves, but perhaps she was behind that too. Telling her descendants they should avoid the wolves... avoid falling in love with them, and triggering your curse. She made sure none would have all three elements again, and no witch would fall in love with another wolf, at least not too soon."

I fully turn to her this time and shrug.

"You said it. Children of a witch and a werewolf are scary rare... Both because of you, and Luna's warnings. I think she knew, Luna. She knew that... after a long time had passed, and both your children had grown, things would change. That Royals with your Light Magic would appear, and werewolf witches like me, full of Dark Magic, would come back too. Perhaps everything was written long, long ago, just for you, Luna, to save you."

"No, no," she whimpers. *"I killed her. I killed Luna, she wasn't my friend..."*

I let out a long sigh. Try thinking one way for centuries, resenting one person and hating them so much it becomes the fuel that consumes you, and this is how it ends... A huge, bitter lie. The one person she thought had betrayed her turned out to be her savior in the end. This is another side of the tragedy... She thought Luna the Witch had died because of that curse, but Luna the Wolf was the one who disappeared. If I had been that witch, I would have felt twice as sorry for my mistake, and given anything to repair it. The only two friends she had were killed, both because of her... Talk about a novice in befriending wolves. No wonder her loneliness became a family trait...

"Luna, it's okay. She was your friend, and she tried to save you. You were both... desperate, and dealing with something you couldn't handle, there's no one to blame."

"....I can't, Mara. I can't. She will never forgive me. After all these years, after all I've done."

"Luna... She won't forgive you. She can't. Your friend died a very, very long time ago, and I'm sure she regretted leaving you. I think her forgiveness isn't something that matters anymore. The only one you ought to forgive is... yourself."

I suddenly hear and see her break into tears, literally bursting into loud sobs. It takes me a few seconds to realize she's shape-shifting into her human form. She's not in Ravena's body this time, just... Luna's human self. With her long white hair, and her blue eyes drowned in tears. I never thought she'd be so... tiny. Her body frame is almost as small as a child's, and she seems frail now. She's curled up in front of me, her arms around her knees and letting it all out. That's right... Only humans cry and despair this much. I don't know how her wolf heart could handle this much. I sigh again, and get down on my knees to hug her. It's... odd, to console my enemy like this, but this Luna isn't the one who killed Liam, possessed by a curse. This one is a truly remorseful person, who regrets it all. I feel her sadness inside as much as I see it outside, and strangely, it puts some... ease in my own heart. As if it was a bit easier to forgive her myself.

"I'm so... so sorry," she cries, with a pretty but broken voice. "I can't believe... Oh, Moon Goddess, what have I done...? All of them... All those people... I... I really..."

She keeps crying. This, I can't do anything about, it's her own burden to carry. I can't erase the wrong she's done to other people and... I can't forget my own, either. After all this, I'll still have to return, and face the painful truth... I take a deep breath before it gets too tight, before I can't get any air in my lungs. It's painful, and it's hard, so hard. As if the echo I had been pushing to the back of my mind was coming back, louder and louder, to haunt me again. Perhaps because Luna is crying her heart out, and I'm not. I don't know. It's... as if I can't process anything right now. I just know I did what I had to, what I should have done, but Moon Goddess, it's hard.

"Mara..."

I'm surprised when she calls out my name, and suddenly raises her head. Even more surprising, she gently puts her hand against my cheek, staring at me with her eyes full of tears.

"Even you... Moon Goddess, I've hurt so many of my children, and Luna's..."

I hadn't realized until now, but... I'm actually a descendant of both of them, aren't I? As a werewolf of Royal blood, and a witch of Sadia's line... If Luna was the first werewolf whose Light Magic awoke with a witch's powers, was she the first Royal? Luna had said she awoke long dormant powers... Hard to tell. It doesn't really matter anymore. Some stories are perhaps better off as legends.

"I'm so sorry to you, Mara. I'm... sorry..."

She keeps crying and apologizing to me, but it just feels odd. Do I want her apology? Do I want to take it, and if I do, will it ease my pain just a little? I take another deep, erratic breath in. No, probably not. Apologies are never enough, they just... put the pain out there. It doesn't take it away, or make it less painful. I can't let it go, just like I can't forgive her like that, but... I can just let go of the hatred. Like forgiveness, it won't help much...

"I'll go," she whispers. "I... I'm so tired now. I don't know how... I did it, but I want to rest. Perhaps... I'll see them on the other side."

I nod faintly. I don't know if there's another side, and if there is, I don't want to know. I just hope... it's a peaceful, quiet place. I hope... No, I don't want to think about it.

"Mara, look at me."

I lift up my eyes, and behind the tears, she suddenly looks very determined.

"I understand what Luna did. She... tried to get rid of necromancy, and the Dark Magic I had made. The three powers should stay separated, Mara. You're strong, but I don't want to risk one of my daughters getting... trapped in a curse again. You need a very pure heart to resist that spell, Mara. Light Magic, Dark Magic... This world needs both, but never necromancy again. This is a world we should leave alone. The cycle of life and death can't be broken."

"I understand..." I mutter.

"Mara."

She forces me to look up again, and gently smiles.

"I... broke that cycle first. So, if you want to make things right again, just... one last time, and... the right way, you can. Do you understand?"

"...W-what?"

No, I don't understand. Make things right again? What does she mean by that? She gently smiles at me, and moves to hold my hands. She's stopped crying, and I realize I'm the one that's been sobbing. I just notice now how blurry my vision is, and the tears rolling down my cheeks, my own erratic breathing and the stupid hiccups in between.

"You're strong, Mara," she whispers. "You're... so, so much stronger than many of us. You need to guide them. All the witches, the ones that have been lost, like me. Teach them about how precious that balance is, teach them how to love wolves again, and to live in peace with the humans. Witches were never meant to wage war, Mara. We love all kinds. Humans, werewolves, animals. All of them. We are the healers, the protectors of this world. This is our most precious gift, and it comes in different shapes to each one of us. ...We shouldn't be afraid to love ever again."

Gently, she presses her forehead against mine, and I feel... something opening. For a second, I'm terrified that my own head is being split in two, but it's not. I just feel... as if my mind expanded all at once. So many things... no, even more magic than I had ever dreamed of suddenly comes to me, bursting inside like a tornado. I feel like I've just stepped into the most gigantic library in the world, or inside the head of a supercomputer full of knowledge. Moon Goddess, there's... so much!

"Teach it all," she whispers, "to our daughters, our sisters... teach them everything I'm giving you. Bring our kind to what it was always meant to be, and let them teach others next. You will be the last one to carry so much power, but we can start over, to bring a new generation the peace I never had, Mara."

"That's... kind of a lot of witches for me alone..." I mutter, a bit worried.

She chuckles.

"*...Who do you think taught the werewolves how to mind-link in the first place?*"

Oh... Oh. Now that she mentions it... that probably wasn't an animal trait. I chuckle nervously, in a bit of a weird state after all that crying. I guess I have a lot to... learn from that knowledge she gave me. I take a deep breath, and finally nod, my head full and my heart heavy.

Luna closes her eyes, holding my hands a bit tighter.

"...Moon Goddess, I can finally go," she whispers.

Suddenly, her eyes move to somewhere over my shoulder, and she gasps, her eyes filled with tears again. What is it? I glance back, but I see nothing but the wall... Yet, Luna keeps staring at something I can't see, and she slowly lets go of my hands, stepping away from me and turning back into her wolf form.

"*...Go back, Mara. Don't stay trapped here like I did. Go back to your family, to your pack. To your people. To... your mate.*"

She moves to walk past me, and... slowly, she disappears. W-... What just happened? I stand up, but she's really gone, I can't even feel her anymore. There's nothing where she stood a second ago, just... some traces of snow, melting on the ground. I look around, a bit lost. I'm alone in that cabin, but things around me start to change. Moss appears under my feet, covering the ground. The walls and wooden furniture all start to rot at an incredible speed, it decays. I have a bad feeling.

I run out of the cabin, and turn around, to see... ruins. Just ruins, where that old cabin stood a second ago. There's no roof, no walls, just a few... rotten planks left there. I look to the side, and the magic circle's gone too. I realize I hear... the birds. The birds, and the wind in the trees too. It's back. This place is back to normal, this is the real world.

Wait, if this is the real world, where am I? How the hell do I go back now?!

No, no, calm down, Mara. You're not clueless, you're a witch and you can do this. I take a deep breath. This is definitely the modern world, my time, just... the wrong place. Where the heck am I? Luna, you fucking old witch, you could have sent me back before you freaking left... No, no, no, focus, Mara. I take a deep breath and look inside, channeling my inner wolf to feel Nora and Selena. No matter the distance, I should be able to feel them...

I got them! It's very faint, but I can feel their position, like a compass inside me... Oh, well, now, time to get there. You're a witch, Mara, you got this. I look inside, searching for something to help. Wait... is that a teleportation spell? No, it can't... Oh, Moon Goddess, it really is! I take a deep breath, a bit nervous, and trace the circle in the ground beneath me. It's a bit scary how easily I can do this now, in... literally two seconds. Powerful witch, she said. No kidding... I take another deep breath and, as soon as that circle is done, I use my magic to activate it, bringing me back to Silver City. This better work...

"Moon Goddess, Mara!"

"Mara, where the heck did you come from?!"

I open my eyes. Wow... I'm back at the site of the battle, on the ravaged East Point Ground, but... it's later. Night has fallen, and... everyone around looks exhausted. Nora runs to me, in her human form, wearing some clothes but looking like she didn't get a shower or a nap. Her black hair is stuck to her temples from the mix of blood, mud, and sweat.

"Thank Moon Goddess you're back," she suddenly sighs before hugging me.

Selena arrives behind her, dressed too, with a sour expression.

"How long has it been...?" I mutter.

"We came back an hour ago, and... for them, a bit more than that," she sighs. "We're just... trying to... find the bodies. That makes it one less, I guess..."

After her sentence, I hear Nora letting out a cry next to me.

"Nora? What... Who did you... find?"

She sniffles and steps back.

"Many wolves," she mutters. "We just... we just found Tonia and Bobo. Tonia... She didn't make it, and... Bobo just left for the ER with... a lot of other people. I did what I could, but..."

She breaks down in tears again, and I hug her again, unable to say anything else. Oh, Moon Goddess... Selena looks restless too.

"Can you help?" she asks with a tired voice. "The whole... fight stopped as soon as we came back, but there's still a ton of people buried. Perhaps there are more we can find... and save."

I nod. Of course I'll help... Moon Goddess, I'm terrified, but we have to find all those bodies...

Suddenly, my finger hurts, as if a ring had just burned me. Moon Goddess, the butterfly tattoo! I let go of Nora, and look at it from up close. That thing is... glowing on my finger. Not only glowing, but moving and spinning around my finger. I can feel the magic imbued in it... Earth Magic!

"...What is this?" asks Nora, staring at it too. "...It looks like a butterfly?"

"Yeah... A present from Sylviana. I think. Step back a second, Nora."

She nods, and wipes her nose as she carefully steps away from me, standing next to Selena. Oh, Moon Goddess, could it be? Is that what Luna was referring to when she mentioned I could do... more, for the last time? I take a deep breath, and focus on that ring, unlocking the power inside. It suddenly bursts out.

I feel the ring explode, and a large mark appears on my hand, on my arm, spreading through my body with a strange sensation.

"Mara!" shouts Selena.

"I'm alright! These are different markings... Just stay back for a second."

I'm not sure I can handle this, but it's coming anyway. I feel it grow inside, like a new strength, a... large tree pushing my Fire and Water Magic aside to take up some space. Oh, Moon Goddess, that's a big bundle of Earth Magic. I need to take big gasps as I let it all in, feeling it grow inside. This is so different from what I'm used to, and it doesn't even leave me room to adjust to it. I feel my feet suddenly rooted deeper in the ground, and my whole body as if... torn in all directions, attracted to the ground like a magnet. I feel each tree around like an underground connection, from my feet to their roots... It's powerful, but it's not... me. I feel it. That thing isn't staying in me like the fire, not even like water.

"...What color are my eyes?" I ask Selena.

"...They're back to dark brown, maybe a bit golden. Not blue or anything else."

I nod. Alright, I guess I know now... This is limited. All of it. It's not part of me, just a little... borrowed. I get down on my knees, and bury my hands in the ground, closing my eyes.

I feel it... all of the ground around. The minerals, the soil... I can find a shy baby root in one area, or a buried stone there. I can find... what shouldn't be there. I take a deep breath and, using all my power, I start moving them, bringing them up. I move the ground above them, undigging the bodies and bringing them to the surface, one after another. I try to use the mind-link and, through Nora and Selena, find as many wolves as I can... I realize I can feel the humans too through Selena's mind-link. She's... connected to them too. I feel like I'm not breathing, this power is too big for me. I force myself to take another deep breath, and keep bringing them back. One after another, the bodies and those still holding on to life... I hear cries of joy or sadness around me, people shouting all around, but I don't have time to listen. I have to go on, bring them back as fast as I can. Perhaps some can still be saved... and the others can find a proper grave.

I stop only when I'm sure I can't find anybody else. I'm... out of breath, and I can't stand up for now. However, all the cries of joy around me makes it worth it. This was worth it. I nod, feeling a bit better.

...Liam.

I lift my head, knowing exactly where my mate is. ...Why did Luna say I should go back to him too? I... I look down at the markings on my arms. I still have that Earth Magic. I... I have the three powers. It's not for long, and I can't save anyone else, but... if it's my mate, perhaps...

No, I can't use Dark Magic. I can't do the same. I can't...

Wait a second. What if I use... Light Magic?

"...Mara?" Selena calls out.

I began stumbling toward him without thinking. I reach it, the cloak they covered him with. I fall on my knees next to Liam's body, unaware of his brothers on the other side. Moon Goddess, I'm shaking. I'm shaking so much.

I'm scared, and at the same time, I'm... feeling hope. This crazy, blazing flame of hope. I pull back the cloak, just a little, to see his face. I let out a gasp. Moon Goddess, Liam... Liam, Liam, Liam... Is it possible?

"Mara? Mara, are you alright?" gently asks Nora, putting a hand on my shoulder.

"No... Nora, I think I'm about to do something *really* crazy.

My heart is beating like crazy. I feel so insane, crazy, and excited. I shouldn't be, right? I... I am faced with the body of my mate, with... Liam's dead body. It's the worst vision ever. My Liam, lying there, just... nothing inside. I can't feel him at all. Not him, not his inner wolf, nothing. My eyes see him, but inside, I feel nothing, just that horrible void that eats me from the inside. I keep staring, and a part of me really wants a miracle. I don't want to see his... cold skin, his blue lips, or his body not even moving to breathe... Death looks horrible, and empty. It's Liam, but there's nothing there, I'm... just facing a body. I never thought it would be so hard. I'm fighting inside with the horrible urge to cry again, to bawl it all out, and yet, I have that crazy idea shining in my mind, like a flame that won't disappear. I must be going insane.

I can bring him back... Right, Luna?

"...What are you going to do? Mara, talk to us!" says Selena behind me.

"...I can use the same spell. The one Luna wanted to use to bring her mate back."

"*You can bring him back...?*" asks Nathaniel.

I nod.

"Mara, no!" protests Nora. "Isn't it the same Dark Magic that caused all of this in the first place?"

"It is, but the spell itself wasn't the cause. It turned into a curse because of the dark feelings that caused this spell, and because Luna used Dark Magic in the first place, not the other way around. I've seen the spell. It was perfect, and it would have worked if Luna hadn't been so inexperienced and dominated by her emotions. She knew nothing about the difference between Dark and Light Magic; only Luna the Witch did, but she couldn't stop her mistake."

"Wait a second," growls Selena, "isn't the difference between the two about... using your own life energy?"

I remain silent as an answer.

Yes, it is. That is one of the founding principles of magic. Witches need life force to make their spells, either their own or someone else's. Luna the Wolf was so desperate, she unconsciously used her friend's... and turned that spell into a dark one. However, Luna the Witch was about to do the right thing... She wanted to give her own life to bring the wolf she had killed back.

"Mara, no!" shouts Nora, falling on her knees next to me. "You want to sacrifice yourself? This isn't... Liam wouldn't want that!"

I take a deep breath and turn to her. It's strange, I want to cry, but... I'm also feeling stronger and calmer than ever. Nora's blue eyes show she's much more worried and panicked than I am, I can even see her lower lip twitching. She's cried a lot already today. Behind her, Selena is standing with a shocked expression too, but she doesn't say anything, her eyes going back and forth between her mate, Liam, and me.

"I know," I gasp, "but... Nora, this is my last chance to use the spell. I'm running out of Earth Magic, and... I'm sure Sylviana gave it to me for a reason in the first place. She loved him too. Moreover... I don't plan to die yet."

"B-but... then..."

I chuckle a bit nervously and exchange a look with his brothers. Damian and Nathaniel have been through hell too, and they stay silent. I know they probably miss their little brother so much too... I try to take a deep breath, but I realize how heavy my chest feels. I can barely fill my lungs, and I have this knot, still there and so painful.

"...I'll share with him, Nora. I have to use Light Magic, and willingly give Liam some of my own life force. I think I can handle that spell well enough to know when to stop."

"What does that mean?" asks Selena, frowning. "You'll be fine, then? You can heal afterwards, right?"

"I'll be fine," I nod, "but I won't heal, there will be nothing to heal. This is more of a... long-term thing. The life force I give Liam won't come back to me, ever. I will... probably sacrifice some of my own life span in the process. Maybe a few decades."

"...You're... going to give Liam years of your own life?" mutters Nora, shocked.

"...Yeah, in a way."

"Mara..."

A heavy silence follows my words, all of them looking conflicted, and I feel it inside too. I know what they are thinking. They don't want me to make that sacrifice, but... they all love Liam too much. They can't stop me knowing that it can bring him back. I turn to his brothers again.

"It... won't be the same," I warn them. "Liam will get more years, but... even if I give him an even share, he and I won't..."

"*...You won't live to grow old,*" mutters Damian.

"...No."

This is a hard decision to make, but this is why I am making it for them. This is my life and my mate. Compared to living and dying old alone, I would rather share what I have left with him. Even if we only get one or two decades together, it's okay.

"...I don't like this," cries Nora. "This is just... so unfair. I can't believe you will lose so much time, and... Liam too..."

"It wasn't fair for him to die either, Nora. But it's okay. A lot of people don't even get this chance, or as much time together as we will. This is... the last time this choice can be made. After that, I will no longer have all three powers, and no witch will be this powerful for a long while, either. Luna gifted me some of her Light Magic, and Sylviana left me some of hers too... just for this moment."

Nora is really crying now, and Selena has that conflicted expression on too. To my surprise, Damian is the one who turns to me next.

"Mara... I'm not sure Liam would be fine with this. He loved you."

"I know," I chuckle. "That's why I'm making this decision for his stubborn ass. He can get mad at me later, this is... about me, and my selfishness. I will... tell him the details later, and explain everything to him, I promise. But... I want to do this, both for him and myself. I know I would... be okay, but... if I can genuinely make this choice, I want to. Not just for my own selfishness, but this is also... for Luna. This is the one life she took that I can bring back."

Nora bites her lower lip, and Selena shakes her head, visibly frustrated. I know they are sorry for me, but this won't change my decision. I take a deep breath, and gently take Liam's hand. Moon Goddess, it's so cold...

"...Can't we help, somehow?" suddenly asks Selena. "We have Light Magic too, right? Can't we do anything to... help out?"

...I didn't think of that. Nora turns her big blue eyes to me, full of hope after hearing Selena's words. ...Can they? This wouldn't be like the two Lunas' mistake, if they are willingly helping me with this spell. But still, I don't think I can just say yes like that! I shake my head.

"No, you guys have children and everything. I can't ask you to do that, this is about our lifespan we're talking about. What if I take too much?"

"You were sure you could control what you'd give Liam just ten seconds ago!"

"When it only includes my own life as a margin for errors! I know the spell but I have never actually done it before!"

"You can just take a little!" says Nora, looking all hopeful again. "Just a bit of mine, and a bit of Selena's. She and I are only Light Magic, and full of it too! Mara, you can just tap into it and get yourself and Liam a few more years!"

"You guys are... No, no, this... this is very dangerous," I argue, turning to their mates, hoping they would stop them.

The two brothers exchange a quiet look.

"...We would do the same if we could," mutters Nathaniel.

I can't help but roll my eyes. Now this does sound insane! This is too much! I am grateful they want to help, but what if I seriously end up taking too many years off of them? It's not an exact science, we're talking about necromancy! It's dangerous and damn unpredictable! I could end up splitting their lifespan in half instead of just taking a couple of years!

Nora smiles, a bit bitter, and takes my other hand gently.

"Mara, please. You're not alone, remember? You and Liam are our family. I.... We are so grateful you're willing to give away some of your life for him, so please... let us do this for you. Just a bit, alright? You deserve this, Mara. You deserve as much time as you can get with Liam... I understand we won't know exactly how much time you guys have left, and anything could happen before that, but... at least, let us do our share. Let us help you a little, Mara. Please."

626

Shit, I feel like crying again... I can hardly believe this. Liam, can you imagine? They are all willing to give some of their lives for you... for us. I hold her hand a bit tighter. I feel her... I feel Nora and her wolf; here with me. I feel all of them and how close we are, like a family indeed. I take another deep breath, but it's hopeless, I burst into tears again. I can't, I'm just... Moon Goddess, it's been a hell of a day. Nora smiles and hugs me gently.

"...It's alright, Mara. Everything will be alright."

Just as she says that, something in my heart does feel relieved. I feel as if everything will be okay again. Just... I feel as if her words were a key. Something that soothes me, and gives me confidence. A bright, vivid, and warm flame shining in my heart. Yes, we will be alright.

Even if it's just a few years, one or two decades together. Liam and I are going to live young, die young, and be fucking happy in the meantime. We're going to be together, and that's all we need. Perhaps this was meant for us all along, and it feels perfect in a way. We're going to have to enjoy each day twice as much, live enough for the lifetime we should have had together. Life doesn't always play out the way we want it to, but... this is one hell of a second chance, and we can't waste a second of it. I want me and him to be happy every damn minute we are together. Live as if we were going to die tomorrow, or next week, or next year. I chuckle, feeling a bit silly and strange. Yeah, this is just like us. Restless, reckless, impatient wolves.

"...Alright," I mutter, trying to focus. "Get ready, then."

I take a deep breath and Selena comes to sit on my right side, putting her hand on my shoulder. Nora is still holding my hand, so now I can focus completely on Liam. I take one last look at him and close my eyes.

I keep the new flame in my heart close, and I summon my Earth and Water Magic at once. I feel Liam's body, where I need to intervene, what I need to do to bring him back. Humans are made of matter, and now I understand why a witch needs all three powers. The earth is for the body, the muscles, the skin, and water is for the blood, everything inside that flows and moves. I focus it on Liam, finding that horrendous gap, both in his body and in his soul. I feel the magic circle appearing beneath us, but I keep going, I know how it has to play out. The spell comes to me so easily, as if it had always been stored in my mind. The Earth Magic fixes the tissues, the Water Magic gets everything running and moving again. I work silently to focus my magic on healing his body. It's a long and draining process, but it's only the first and easiest part.

Now, this is where I bring his life back. I take another deep breath and, his body restored, I need to breathe life back in. I focus on my inner flame, and grow it, bigger, brighter, hotter. A fierce fire burning inside, channeling my own life energy. I feel it... it beats just like my heart. Gently, I convey it to Liam, placing it in his body. His wolf takes the energy, but the magic doesn't stay, and I have to continuously send some, return it to me, and send more again. It's difficult and really draining as I feel my flame diminish. I can almost feel... my body getting tired. It's not decaying, but I feel how it's getting tired inside, how I'm using several years' worth of energy. Like running several marathons in seconds, or crossing two oceans without breathing. I have to keep focusing, or I'll give too much, and pass out and die. We don't want that, right, babe? I take another deep breath and, just when I feel my fire about to give out, I stop, and gently pull some of Selena and Nora's. It is easy to find, I feel their hearts like little birds within my reach. I want to be careful, I just pick a little from them, and that's it. Maybe... Maybe not enough, but that's plenty already. I know you wouldn't agree to this either, babe, and I am with you on that one... I get their energy inside, and take another deep breath to close the bond.

I look for him. I look for Liam, his wolf, to see where I can wake him up, how to light the flame inside him with all that energy... I found it. I gasp, and rush all in at once. That's one hell of a lot of energy, and I burst in, like a spark in the darkness, praying that fire will take and grow.

"Moon Goddess!"

I try to stay focused despite the gasps and exclamations of joy around me; I just need to finish this properly... I give it all I have left of the Water and Earth Magic to make sure his body is fully healed. I search for anything that I may have missed, reinforcing each organ, each muscle. I give it all out, without an ounce of regret. This is the first and last time I'll perform this spell, so I might as well be sure... You wouldn't have wanted me to keep it either, right, Luna?

A couple more seconds later, I finally open my eyes. I can already see it. Liam's face has restored its colors, and... he's breathing. I let out a nervous chuckle, half laughter and half a cry. His brothers are frozen like ice on the other side, but Nora is crying next to me, and Selena gasps again.

"...Babe?" I call out, holding his hand a bit tighter. "Liam!"

Liam stays unconscious, but I take a deep breath and slap his torso, a bit annoyed. I didn't freaking fix you so you could take a nap here!

He opens his eyes and sits up all at once.

"Whoa!" he exclaims, out of breath. "Wh-... What the... hell...?"

"Liam!" I cry out, jumping to hold him.

Oh, Moon Goddess, thank... thank you for letting me bring him back... I keep sobbing loudly, Nora's echoing behind me. I just can't stop the waterfall, and I keep crying, hugging my mate tight. I hear him chuckling nervously, and he holds me back.

"Okay, uh... Did I miss something? You guys are... making faces... Mara, babe, you're killing me here..."

I chuckle, and pull back a bit to give him some space, and look at his face. It's really him. My Liam, with his blue-gray eyes I love, his confused expression, his warm skin, and half-smiling lips. Moon Goddess, I can hardly believe it really worked. He is back. My mate is back with me, for real.

He keeps staring at me and sending glances to his brothers and sister-in-laws, completely confused, with no idea what just happened.

"Wha-... Seriously, you guys are making such weird faces... Mara, you okay? And Nora... Guys, seriously, what did I miss?"

Nathaniel suddenly shakes his head and walks away, his shoulders low. I'm a bit worried for him, but Selena exchanges a smile with me, and goes to hug him a bit farther away, hiding his face onto her shoulder. Next to us, Damian Black chuckles too.

"*Welcome back, Liam.*"

"Thanks...?"

He sighs and hugs me.

"Okay, I guess you guys can explain to me later what happened while I passed out... Mara, you okay? You look very pale."

"I'm just a bit tired, babe," I chuckle, putting a kiss on his cheek. "I'm glad to see you... I love you."

He raises both eyebrows, and I see a dash of red appear on his cheeks, traveling all the way up to his ears.

"Th-thanks... I love you too, hot stuff."

I chuckle, and hug him again. Moon Goddess, it feels so good to feel Liam's warmth again, his arms around me, hear his voice ask again what did he miss. I hear Nora keep crying, tears of joy this time.

My head on Liam's shoulder, I keep looking around, and although my heart feels a lot better with my mate back, I can't help but see how many people we did lose in this battle... Everything around us is desolated, and no one else is able to cry of relief. There are still too many bodies, too many wounds. The rain has stopped, but the sky clearing doesn't match the atmosphere down here. Everything is... hard to process. I take a deep breath.

We will need to take care of our people. Heal the wounds, bury the bodies, see what we can save. The battle has left traces everywhere. There will be a lot to do, but... the worst has passed.

This battle is over. ...And it was the last one for Silver City.

#

Chapter 41

"...So you've really lost all of your Earth and Water Magic?" Kelsi asks with a sorry expression.

"Yep," I nod.

"And neither are coming back?"

I glance down at the burn on my finger. It's a bit odd how it burned my skin and stayed there as a reminder... It's not ugly, though. From up close, it looks vaguely like a butterfly, otherwise, it's just a brown triangle. I shrug.

"The Earth Magic, definitely not. The Water Magic... perhaps it will awake again later, if I try harder? I'm not sure, but I think I would rather not, though. I want to respect Luna's decision, for now. So, unless I really need it... I will stick to my good old Fire Magic only."

"I see..."

She looks down, her hand gently petting Ben's head. The big brown wolf is covering her leg and one half of the bed, but neither of them seems to care. I chuckle. It's actually his bed, although Kelsi still has an IV drip in her arm too, and is wearing a hospital gown. Ben has his own on the same hanger, and he's got a lot of bandages covering his body and his broken leg too. Our poor Ben even got half his tail amputated... Kelsi told him it was cute, though, so he's probably fine with it now. I wonder if there's going to be any damage on his human body, or if we will just have to get used to seeing a wolf with the tail of a pomeranian each time he shape-shifts... Still, I'm glad he's okay, that they both are, and together. The only reason the nurses accepted this arrangement is because of the lack of beds at the moment... and Ben refused to sleep anywhere other than by Kelsi's side. I feel a lot better knowing those two are fine... It's been a rough night, to say the least. It's probably sometime around 5:00 a.m. now...

After we evacuated those who could still be saved, everyone worked together to gather the bodies. Wolves and humans working together, helping each other through the hardest. I had to wait for a while before I could check on these two, so I'm a bit relieved now, and catching a break too. I think half my night has been fighting, the other bringing back bodies and transporting people... Kelsi looks tired too, but I'm glad she's alright. Apparently she got better as soon as we beat the curse, although she's still pretty weak. She doesn't remember much of the incident, either, which is good.

630

"...What will happen now?" she asks.

"The Alphas are checking on everyone, organizing the last rescues, and overseeing the packs... Selena has talked to the human leaders too, and Nora is here, helping with the healing for those she can. Everyone is pretty exhausted, but... you know."

"You do look tired," she mutters. "Your clothes too..."

I grimace. Yeah, I probably look like crap... I'm not the worst, though. The hospital lobby is full of blood and mud, despite the volunteers who tried to help keep it more or less clean...

"Mara?"

I glance over my shoulder, and Bonnie is there in the doorway, waving at us. She's the one who took care of Kelsi for the first half of the night, but then she got a lot more busy...

"See you later," I say to Kelsi, getting up.

"See you. Try to catch some real rest, okay?"

"I will. You watch over the big boy."

"Sure," she smiles, petting Ben's fur.

I turn around, hiding my sigh, and walk out to see Bonnie.

"How are you?" I ask as I step out.

"Not the best shift of my life, I'll admit that much," she sighs. "Oh, here."

She hands me a chocolate bar, and I'm more than glad to finally be able to eat something.

"Oh, thank Moon Goddess," I sigh, feeling the chocolate warm me up.

"You're welcome. I snuck some from the nurse's office, I figured you didn't get any time to eat... They are bringing in more food, though; apparently, the werewolves and humans that didn't fight are all trying to help and send us sandwiches soon."

I nod, but my mouth is too full for now. We walk through the hospital corridors, stepping aside when someone rushes by, or helping push a bed when we can. We're far from the war zone it was just a few hours ago, though. Now the most important surgeries have been done, the injured found beds or places to rest, those who could went home, and the emergency cases are lessening... We make sure not to hinder anyone and try to squeeze ourselves out of the way until we make it to the floor above.

"Boyan is still stable, all his vitals are improving, so he will be fine," she finally announces when we get to an empty examination room.

"Oh, that's awesome," I let out a long sigh. "I didn't dare ask..."

"Yeah, I know, everyone has been mind-linking like crazy, I've shut it out too... but his surgery went fine, and you know, Betas are strong, so I bet him and my brother will recover fast."

"Good... Anyone else I need to know about?"

"Nothing new... Werewolves are tough, so those who made it to the end of the battle will probably make it... Humans, probably not as much, but we are working on it. I'm glad a lot of people volunteered to help or donate blood. I have rarely seen so many people working together to help, it has been the best comfort all night... Did you get examined yet, Mara? You look like–"

"Crap, I know. No, I'm good, just tired. There were people who were much more urgent than me."

Bonnie chuckles and turns to me, shaking her head and turning on the little light.

"Well, I'm free now, and you have an opened brow ridge, both ears bleeding, many contusions, and from the way you're standing, at least a couple of broken ribs."

"What I need right now is a shower," I chuckle and step back as she brings her hands closer to my face. "I'm fine, Bonnie."

"At least let me stitch your brow ridge and check your cuts! Do you know how much bacteria you can get in there? You should get a full check up and some X-rays too."

"I'm still a witch, Bonnie, I'll heal myself just fine!"

"Don't give me the witch excuse. Didn't you just say you lost two of your types of magic? Plus the necromancy spell? What tells me you have any left and you aren't going to pass out the minute I look away?"

I sigh. She's giving me her schoolteacher mean look too, with her hands on her hips and the frown on.

"Wait... Did you eavesdrop on my discussion with Kelsi?" I realize.

"Mara, if my brother isn't snoring like an overfed pig, he isn't sleeping. I was looking for you, and he happened to be listening when I mind-linked, so if you want to blame anyone, blame Ben. Now, show me that cut."

"Bonnie–"

"Sit down," she orders, pushing me toward a stool on the side.

I sigh and surrender, sitting my butt down on that stool before she gets really mad. Bonnie puts on some gloves and starts touching my eyebrow, which does hurt. I grimace a bit, but it does feel good to sit down and let someone take care of me for a minute... I chuckle.

"What is it?" she asks. "And by the way, you really do need stitches. It's pretty deep."

"It's just... it reminds me of how we met. Like... both you and Kelsi, my first memories of you are in this hospital, and here we are again..."

She finally loses her frown and smiles too.

"True... Well, I do love my job, but if you could stop being so reckless..."

"Sorry, you're friends with a crazy witch... I don't think I'm going to stop the craziness anytime soon..."

"Moon Goddess. You should be grateful you have a nurse as a friend, then."

I chuckle, and for a little while, neither of us adds anything. It stings where she's disinfecting or stitching, but it does feel good to sit down, close my eyes, and think of nothing for a while, letting Bonnie take care of my wounds and patch me up the good old way. I let out a sigh and try to mind-link Nora quickly.

"Hey, how are you holding up?" I ask.

"Not too bad... A bit tired, but there are many in worse condition than us. Thankfully, we are getting to the end of it. I am proud of our wolves; a lot of them insist that the humans are taken care of first, since they don't have our regeneration abilities..."

"Sounds good. You should get some rest, Nora, you sound awfully tired."

"I know, but you too, Mara. Make sure you stay home for a while, okay? Get some sleep, you fought the hardest of us today."

"...Will do."

"Alright. Liam is still at East Point Ground, but take him home with you."

"Thank you, Nora."

"...We're the ones who should thank you."

She cuts the mind-link, probably still very busy too. I let out a bit of a sigh.

I'm not sure wolves and humans will think the same, though... All that mess was caused by a witch in the first place. I don't really know what Nora and Selena will tell them, but I doubt they will find the witches completely guilt-free. Naptera disappeared before the fight ended too, and only Ayesha stayed behind to help. Last thing I heard, she was on Selena's territory helping out. I guess I can check in on her later...

"... I'm so glad Bobo made it," suddenly sighs Bonnie. "I didn't want to lose another family member."

"Oh, I forgot he's your brother-in-law..."

"Yeah, but... you know, we're all a big family in the pack. I'm still... not really processing that more people died, I think I'm just glad it's over again. I love Silver City, but... I hope you're right and this was the last battle, Mara. Because I'm sick of trying to save people and watch them die."

"I know... I'm... sorry I couldn't save your brother."

She lets her arms down for a second, looking a bit sad.

"I... When I heard what had happened on the battlefield, I admit, for a second, I... wondered if you couldn't have brought more people back. But then, I heard your chat with Kelsi earlier, and... you sacrificed a lot. Your magic and... half your life. It made me think, and I realized I am not you, Mara. I'm not a witch, and I don't have a mate yet, so I'll never understand what it took for you to make that choice. I'm... glad for you and Liam, but... you know, as your friend, I'm also very sad you made that choice."

"...I know."

I just don't regret it, for now. I haven't told Kelsi the truth yet, so I suppose Bonnie heard it from Selena. Perhaps I'll wait a while before telling Kelsi what happened with that spell, and Liam... The consequences that I will face. A few more minutes pass in silence, with a couple more stitches and grimaces of pain for me.

"So... what's going to happen now?" asks Bonnie. "You know, since the barrier is gone and everything..."

"Silver City doesn't need a barrier anymore, I think. There's a new witch in town..."

"Look at you, acting all tough and what not... But seriously, so, no more borders, no more barrier? What about... I don't know, other threats? Other witches or vampires?"

"I don't think the vampires would have attacked if it wasn't for the curse and Nephera... and about the witch, not to brag, but I'm pretty sure I can handle any on my own. Moreover, I think Ayesha was hoping to stay around for a while too, so Silver City is good."

"...You say that as if you're not going to stay around yourself," she mutters, raising an eyebrow.

"Maybe not..."

I still kept in mind what Luna said to me about the other witches, the newer generation... I haven't really looked into this yet, but I do feel.... connected to more than just wolves right now. It's like new voices, on a different channel. They are rather quiet for now, but I know I could definitely strengthen that bond easily if I wanted to.

"Well, as long as you don't plan to come back to the hospital too soon," sighs Bonnie, "I'll be good with anything you want to do."

"Really?" I chuckle. "You're not going to... I don't know, warn me about dangers and stuff?"

"I think you've outgrown being an angry and trapped witch. And Moon Goddess, I'm done with it too; you're a pain when you're stubborn as hell."

I laugh a bit. I would probably miss Bonnie not being the angelic voice over my shoulder, though, now that the evil ones are all gone...

"How about you?" I ask. "Any... plans for a werewolf companion yet?"

"Seriously?" she rolls her eyes. "Now you're the one trying to give me dating advice?"

"Why not?" I laugh. "You're a single nurse, quite sexy, and pretty bossy too. I know some guys out there would love that. Oh, and a redhead. Do you have any idea how popular redheads are?"

"If you want me to kick you out, you win," she growls. "Get out of here before I kick your witchy butt."

I laugh still and get up, my eyebrow all stitched up and covered in smelly disinfectant. I'm still in need of a shower, but at least that's one less part of my poor body hurting... I turn to Bonnie who's gathering the dirty compress and cleaning up.

"...Thanks, Bonnie."

"Moon Goddess, don't do that. Get out!"

"Bye, Bonnie!" I chuckle, leaving the room with a smile on my lips.

I get back into the maze of white corridors, strangely silent despite all the activity going on behind doors. It's strange how different I feel compared to a few weeks ago. I was in such a hurry to leave this hospital and see Silver City, but now, I feel like... it doesn't really matter anymore. Here or outside, I belong to Silver City. It's not going anywhere, but it's not waiting for me either. This place will be here wherever I go...

His Blazing Witch

I slowly make my way out of the hospital, greeted by a few wolves on the way, thanking the medical staff I see, and buying myself a hot drink at the vending machine as soon as I'm outside. I pick a hot coffee, strong and bitter, just what I need to wake myself up. It's still a bit cold outside at this hour, and I don't even have a jacket... Still, I walk away from the hospital, enjoying the cold wind on my skin, and the first lines of purple in the sky. As soon as I'm a few streets away and I silence my inner wolf, there's nothing but silence... We're too far from the city center to hear the first cars, and there's nothing but some grass around. I cross the river, my eyes set on the horizon, in a strange but relieved mood. It's really over... It's over this time, isn't it, Luna? I really hope she got to a nice place, and saw her friend and mate again. Perhaps with Sylviana too. That would be nice...

"Hey, babe?" I call out, a smile on my lips.

"Morning, hot stuff!"

"How are you feeling?"

"Strangely fine. Still unsure what happened, I feel... reborn, if that makes any sense... How about you?"

"I'm okay. ....Wanna grab some breakfast?"

"I'm starving. I always am. What do you want?"

"...Cheeseburgers?"

"That's my girl. Cheeseburgers it is, then!"

"Let's meet at the apartment? Mine, not yours. I'm grabbing the coffees, you bring the food."

"I like the sound of that!"

I smile. Liam doesn't know yet how right he is... I'm still not sure if I should tell him. Whenever I do, it's going to be a long and painful conversation... I still ought to, though. I take another deep breath and glance at the sun, already rising behind the skyline. Well, good morning to you too, Silver City...

I keep walking, trying to sort my thoughts, what I am going to tell my mate and how. The more I walk, though, the more I realize how tired and sore I am. Each step sends a wave of pain to various areas of my body, making me grimace. I really could use a shower... I stop at the coffee place downstairs, glad that I found my jacket after the fight. I just have enough cash on me for our coffees, but from my poor state and the way I am ruining the entrance, the lady behind the counter must feel a bit sorry because she adds in a couple of cookies with a wink. I thank her with the best smile I can muster and leave. Perhaps she heard what happened at East Point Ground too by now... It's odd how life goes on no matter what. It doesn't really matter how injured Silver City is. People go to work, pour coffees, and resume their daily life. Some might be in the hospital with their loved ones, but... for the rest of the population, the world just has to keep spinning as it should.

I can't help myself and start nibbling on my cookie even before I reach the elevator. The chocolate bar from before wasn't enough, I'm starving... I hope he arrives quickly with those burgers.

I knew the apartment would be empty, but it still feels strange to come home alone, so early... I'm already missing Kelsi's positive energy and Ben's furry butt on the couch. I take a deep breath anyway, and leave the coffees on the kitchen counter, going to the bathroom while licking the leftovers of my cookie off my fingers. Liam was on the other side of Silver City, I should have some time to shower if he's getting those cheeseburgers... Will he find something open so early? I get rid of my clothes on the bathroom floor and grab some clean underwear before I dirty anything else. Damn, I'd better wash all this or throw it away before Kelsi sees it, she's not going to like this mess at all...

I step into the shower and turn the tap to the maximum pressure, using cold water only. Moon Goddess, that feels so good after the crazy night I just had. I stretch my neck and shoulders a little, but really, every single muscle of my body hates me right now. I take several deep breaths, watching the mud and blood run down the drain. I'm so tired, I could take a nap right here. Still, I try to simply wash everything away, the dirt and the fatigue. At least, I do feel refreshed after a few more minutes under the shower. I thoroughly wash my hair, my face, and my body, careful about my injuries. I can't help but grimace around my belly area... Bonnie was right, there's definitely a broken rib or two in there under those nasty dark bruises...

Suddenly, while I'm groaning and trying to wash my flank without straining something already injured, I feel someone behind me. I smile as I feel his arms gently come around my shoulders.

"Damn, I don't like to see you all hurt like this," he groans, putting his head against my neck.

I smile, and run my fingers through his hair. I can feel his slow breathing against my skin, as if to remind me he is really here, with me...

"Good morning, hot stuff," I chuckle.

"Mornin'..."

Moon Goddess, I love him but he stinks... I turn around to take a look at my mate. I've never been happier to see those clear eyes staring back at me, a candid spark in them. Liam leans forward to kiss me, but I back my head away a bit. He frowns.

"What?"

"I just spent half an hour trying to wash myself, and you're very dirty, Mr. Black. At least wash your face."

He rolls his eyes, but I put my arms around his neck and pull him under the shower. He growls.

"Moon Goddess, Mara, it's fucking cold!"

"Poor baby," I chuckle. "Come on, at least rinse your face, I want to kiss you too."

He still grimaces, but looks up, letting the water wash away a good portion of the dirt on his face. Moon Goddess, he really is hot from this angle. I brush his neck, and let my fingers climb up his jawline, caressing it playfully. Finally, I move on to gently rub the dirt off his cheeks, lips, chin, nose, and forehead. Liam lets me wash him like a kid, even pouting his lips and closing his eyes tight while I rub the dirt off. His skin's natural color finally reappears as I make all that mud come off bit by bit. After a while, I'm done torturing him, and I get on my toes to put a quick kiss on his lips.

Liam finally looks down at me, with a pout.

"That's it?"

I bite my lower lip, a bit excited now that I've had a taste. Plus, we are both naked, alone, and under the shower already...

"...Come and get it," I mutter, feeling a bit sexy.

His eyes light up all of a sudden, and his surprised expression turns into a cheeky smile. He wraps his arms a bit tighter around me, and I feel his naked body against mine... Oh, it's definitely not so cold in here anymore. I smile and with a movement, turn the water temperature up above us, right before he suddenly starts kissing me.

Moon Goddess, his kiss... I could cry of happiness just from feeling Liam's familiar, gentle kisses against my lips. It's so wet, and cold yet hot somehow. We take it unbearably slow, as if we were kissing for the first time all over again. It's soft, the water rolling down our faces and washing the remnants of that long, long night away. I kiss Liam, again and again, getting lost in his arms, holding on to him as if I was about to lose him again. I just want him. To touch his skin, feel his heat, the lines of his body, the way he moves and reacts to me. And he does react to me... I chuckle in between our kisses as I feel him poking me, but just as I do, Liam's tongue gets a bit wilder against mine, forcing me to focus again. I'm feeling really hot, and not just because of the water this time... I tighten my grasp around him, our kiss getting more passionate. Our breathing is getting louder too, the two of us getting more excited. I want him. I know I really want Liam, right now, and he definitely wants me too. I give more of myself in our kiss, hungry for more, more of his lips and his caresses on me. Liam's in the same state, he's getting more... handsy. His hands go down on me, following my curves, making me shiver. I forget all about the pain of my injuries, my body is giving me much more agreeable sensations right now.

When his fingers get between my legs, I gasp, my body reacting right away. Oh, yes... I gladly let him touch me, caress me, but I'm so hot already, this feels like torture. I feel him smile against my lips, and he moves on to kiss my cheek, my jawline, and starts nibbling my neck. I grimace because he does bite me a bit, but the sensations he's giving my lower half make up for it. I hear myself moaning a bit, feeling shamelessly wet and eager right now.

"Liam..." I groan.

"Yeah, I know."

He lets out a long sigh and moves his body against mine, his hands on my butt. I lift my leg around his hip, and let him in... I feel him fill me, and I wince involuntarily. I can't even tell if it's pleasure, pain, or a devilishly good mix of both. Oh, it's just so good to feel Liam inside me right now... He kisses my cheek gently, his other hand moving up to caress the nape of my neck.

"You okay...?" he asks in a whisper.

"Yeah... Move, please."

"Okay..."

He starts moving right away, but slowly. I like that. This is what I need right now... Liam's gentle pushes, slow but deep, filling me up and sending delicious shivers throughout my body.

"I like that..." I mutter without thinking against his shoulder, holding on a bit tighter.

"Yeah, me too."

I smile, and he keeps going at a balanced rhythm. I try to breathe, but Moon Goddess, it's good. I gasp and hear my erratic breathing echo his own groans. This feels so good, just having simple, gentle sex after everything. Feeling... just me and him, so desperately alive. We're alive, and together, and this is happening.

Liam keeps going, although he can't help but accelerate a bit, and I don't hate it. I move my hips with his, our breathing in sync, as we still try to kiss and caress each other non-stop in the heat of the moment. It's so steamy in here, and my whole body is going crazy from all these sensations. I'm tired, but so into this. I caress Liam, his skin, his face, so glad to feel him against me, inside me. I move to kiss below his ear, and feel him shiver when I bite his lobe a bit... I smile.

"...I love you," I whisper against his ear.

Suddenly, I hear him groan, and we both freeze. I open my mouth, completely stunned.

"Did you just–"

"Don't say it."

"–come...?" I chuckle, biting my lower lip.

He sighs, and leans against my shoulder. I can't believe it!

"This is so uncool..." he grumbles.

"Oh, this is so cute..."

He suddenly bites my shoulder, making me grimace.

"Hey!"

"You started it... you cheat."

"Well, it's not my fault you're so cute..."

"You'll see if I'm cute," he retorts with a pout, suddenly lifting me up.

"What are you doing?!" I protest.

"Your turn now, and I'm not stopping until you come too."

"Oh, Moon Goddess, Liam!"

But it's too late to cry wolf. He starts moving again before I can do anything, and by some Dark Magic, my body sensations pick up right where they left off, taking me with him in a new, dangerous, but so exciting dance...

Half an hour later, I'm pruny, exhausted, and definitely clean. I quickly put on a T-shirt and some shorts from my wardrobe, while Liam is moving around the kitchen in some jeans he borrowed from Ben's stuff he had left here. I'm probably never going to allow him to wear a T-shirt ever again at this rate.

"Cheeseburger and Mara for breakfast," he chuckles. "My new favorite."

"I was already sore," I sigh, sitting down on the floor. "Now I can barely walk without looking like a duck..."

"You're a cute duck."

"Thanks..."

He smiles like the devil and comes to sit behind me, the two of us facing the bay window. We're eating on the floor just so we can enjoy the full might of the sunrise, and also because I can't stand right now. We silently dive into those cheeseburgers, a strange mix with the cold coffees, but not too bad for our empty stomachs...

For a few minutes, there's nothing but some chewing and licking mayonnaise off each other's lips playfully. We're too tired for words, and I'm happy to lean my back against his torso, in my favorite seat. I'm on my second cheeseburger when Liam kisses my shoulder gently.

"Mara..."

"Hm?"

"What happened to me?"

I slowly finish chewing, feeling a weight go down my stomach. I knew I wouldn't be able to avoid it, but it's... hard.

"...Did your brothers say anything?"

"They said I should ask you."

I swallow, and let out a long sigh before turning around to face him. He gently smiles at me, caressing my cheek.

"Babe, don't worry. Whatever it is, I'm strong enough to take it. I have a bit of an idea too."

"...You died," I finally let out. "You died, and I..."

I can't put it into words. It's... hard. Not just to tell Liam the truth, but to relive what happened. After a second, I decide to do things differently. I take another deep breath, and lean my forehead against his, taking his hand. I look for the right way to do this, not using magic, but our deep bond, our mind-link.

I show him everything. I quickly pass on his actual death, but I show him all that happened with Luna, what I learned and the choices I had to make. I feel his fingers tighten around mine, but I keep focusing on that intense moment between us. I give him everything, all of my feelings, all of my suffering too, and the relief when he came back. After a few seconds, it's over already. I slowly pull back, a bit torn inside. Liam reopens his eyes.

"That's... a lot," he mutters.

"Yeah. I'm sorry I... made that choice for you."

His Blazing Witch

He stares at me for a long minute, without saying anything. I see the sunrise in his clear eyes, but he's looking at me, and only me. After a few seconds, he lets out a little smile, and leans in to give me a quick kiss.

"...So stubborn," he whispers.

"...Anything else?"

"Yeah. My brother was right. I hate that you gave up half your life for me, but... I would have done the same for you."

I smile. I suppose that's okay, then.

"I'm still sorry," I mutter. "We won't get to... grow old together."

"We'll live together for the time we've got," he retorts. "That's fine by me. Also... just because we have a few years doesn't mean there isn't a ton of stuff we can't do."

"Really? What do you have in mind?" I ask, getting a bit closer to him with excitement.

"Well, we should really think about spending more time together, so we should live together."

"Agreed. You can move here, then."

"Why don't you come to my place?"

"Your place is too big, and I love my current roommates. Let's just share with Ben and Kelsi."

"...Okay, I like that. What else?"

"I want to get my own bike, and a proper license," I announce. "Let's go on a road trip, just you and me. I want to go and visit Amy, and meet that useless father of mine. I need to look for young witches too, and teach them what Luna wants me to teach them. It's probably going to be one long trip."

"Deal. ...Is it okay to leave Silver City, though?"

"Silver City will be just fine," I chuckle. "There's your brothers, Nora, Selena... Moreover, I think Ayesha wants to stay. She can watch over while I'm gone. And we can come back whenever we want... I think I found a very nice way to get home very, very quickly if we need to. A new little spell in my book. So, let's just go as far away as we want."

"Oh, I like that. Just you and I on a honeymoon..."

"Honeymoon?" I repeat, raising my eyebrows. "Liam Black, aren't you getting ahead of yourself there?"

"Why not?" he chuckles. "My understanding was that we have to live fast. I want to call you Mara Black soon."

"I never took you for the ceremonial type. Wait... Then, I get to see you in a suit?"

"I get to see you in a pretty dress."

I try to imagine it for a second.

"Alright, but it will be a black one, then."

"Now we're talking, Mrs. Black... Also, I want to have a Liam Jr. or a Mara Jr."

"You want kids?" I repeat, blushing all the way up to my ears.

"You don't?" he asks, visibly worried.

I take a second to think. Well, it's not like I'd be against the idea at all... I can definitely imagine us with a baby or two... A mini Liam and me. I smile.

"No, I think I'd like it... having our own baby."

"Right? My nieces and nephews are too cute, I want you to have my baby too..."

"Okay, but first I want to finish university."

"You're still going to study?" He raises an eyebrow.

"I want to get a proper job by myself! I can't keep living off my sister..."

Liam chuckles.

"Damn, does that mean I'll have to get a job too?"

"Find a job where you can stay half-naked, then," I chuckle, caressing his abs.

He shivers.

"I don't think I can do that..."

"Come on, you've never thought of getting an actual job?" I chuckle. "You can't keep being the rogue wolf of the town!"

"I promise I'll think about it... Perhaps something to do with security, then?"

"Oh, I could see you in a uniform..."

"...Mara, you're becoming a real pervert now."

"You make me a pervert," I laugh.

We laugh and joke for a while about our plans for the future, our list of things we want to do together, half joking and half serious about it. After a few minutes of laughing about Liam's top ten restaurants we ought to try, I let out a long sigh, and he gently caresses my neck.

"...How do you feel?" he asks.

It's not the first time I've been asked that this morning, but the way Liam says it feels... different somehow. How do I really feel right now...? I'm tired, and my body is giving me hell, but Moon Goddess, I feel... good. I feel alive and relieved. I am so thankful he's here with me. I caress his cheek as well, and smile a bit weakly.

"I'm just... fine," I mutter. "Still a bit... you know, tired, and feeling the losses we went through, the hardships, the injuries, and all that mess, but... I'm glad we made it together. You, and our family, our friends... our pack. I feel... home. It's a bit strange, though. For a long while, I was... desperate to find my identity, where Mara Jones was from, get all the answers, and now... I just feel like I need more questions, even if the answers don't matter as much. Now that I have a home, I want to leave and explore the world with you. Now that I have found a family, I want to... make another one with you, and spend time with my friends. Do a ton of stuff together, and give myself new things to think about. I'm ready to... I don't know, just live the next chapter of my life. My new life."

Liam simply smiles back at me, and I feel a bit embarrassed. I just said a lot, and he's just staring right back at me with his cheeky smile, and those tender eyes... I blush.

"...What?"

"I love you."

I blush even more now, taken by surprise. He can't be that brutally honest without a warning...

"I love you," he repeats. "I really love all of you. How you're... my girlfriend, my mate, and my best friend. How you care about everyone, everything, but you're still... you, just you."

"Liam..."

"I'll follow you," he continues. "I'll follow every freaking where you want to go. To meet witches, your family, to the end of the world if you want. Anywhere, Mara."

I take a deep breath, as if he was filling my heart with love, all by himself. I'm so happy I have Liam... I smile and lean in to give him a long, deep kiss. A bit warm, with a taste of sunshine... and cheeseburgers. We don't want to separate, and I think we're not going to for a long while... Liam smiles against my lips.

"That's my hot stuff..."

"You mean your witch."

"...My Blazing Witch."

The End.

Epilogues

6 Months Later

I take a step in, as quietly as possible. The apartment is so quiet, as expected. Well, it's early in the morning, so those two must be sleeping. I walk up to the fridge, opening it as silently as possible.

"Babe, can you grab some breakfast too? There's nothing in here..."

"Gotcha."

I smile, and close the fridge before heading to my bathroom. We've only been gone for a weekend, but it sure feels good to be home! I take a quick shower and get ready for the day, grabbing black tights, a short but long-sleeved dress I know Liam will love, and a jacket to put on top. I'm still putting on my earrings when I hear someone knock.

"Mara, is that you?"

"Ben!"

I smile and walk over to hug him, his chuckle welcoming me. He probably just got up, judging by how he's only wearing his pants, and his red hair is a complete mess too.

"Who else were you expecting?" I ask with a frown.

"Sorry, I forgot you said you'd be back this morning... How did it go? Liam isn't with you?"

"He went to get breakfast first, he'll be up in a minute. And everything went fine, as usual. ...How are you?"

To my surprise, Ben grimaces.

"She made me sleep on the floor again..."

"What did you do?" I ask as we walk back to the kitchen.

"Why do you assume I did something?!"

"Ben," I laugh, "I know Kelsi. She doesn't get mad for no reason! Come on. Is it because of a scary movie again?"

"No! I've been careful not to pick those kinds of movies anymore... No, it's just... I've been busy with work as a Beta lately, and last night, we finally had a date night, but I acted like an idiot..."

"What did you do?"

"I got... a bit too jealous..."

Well, that's a surprise. I'm about to add something when I see my Spark jump on the kitchen counter, coming to me with much purring and rubbing his nose against my arm. I hug my cat, but still turn to Ben.

"Jealous? Since when are you even the jealous type?!"

"I've never been! It's... just..."

He lets out a long sigh, ruffling up his already messy hair, and crosses his arms. I've noticed he's whispering and keeps sending glances toward their bedroom door. He's probably worried about either of us waking Kelsi up, but if I'm not wrong, her alarm should go off soon anyway...

"Kelsi... She's been even prettier lately."

"...Prettier?" I scoff, unable to hold it. "Ben, Kelsi's always been pretty."

"I know! Of course, I know that, but... you know, she's switched back to contacts, she changes her clothing when we go out, her hair, she's even putting on makeup... I mean, I love Kelsi regardless of what she does, whether she dresses up or not. You know I find her the cutest nerd ever. But... You know, all that stuff makes her stand out, and I've noticed at the university, she's getting more attention, and when we go out too. It makes my werewolf instincts get all upset about other guys checking my girlfriend out!"

Oh, Moon Goddess, I swear those two are so cute together... I sigh, and start setting the table for breakfast.

"Ben, relax, Kelsi doesn't care about those guys. Plus, who do you think she's making herself pretty for?"

Ben doesn't answer, but he seems to be brooding over this... He can think about it as much as he wants, I'm really not worried. Those two are still a bit awkward even after six months of dating, but they love each other like crazy. Kelsi getting back to sexier clothes and allowing herself to look "pretty" again just means she is finally comfortable enough to do so, and it's all thanks to Ben who loves her regardless of her nerdy looks.

Liam finally walks in, carrying our coffee and breakfast. He walks up to me right away and, while I take it all off his hands, he leans in to kiss me.

"I missed you."

"It's only been twenty minutes!" I chuckle. "Go shower, you hungry wolf!"

He gives me a wink and walks around the kitchen, greeting Ben quickly before he disappears into the bathroom. Thank Moon Goddess, coffee and donuts! With Ben's help, I get breakfast ready for all four of us, adding a few slices of toast and omelets for the werewolf stomachs.

As Liam and I decided a while ago, we're now sharing the apartment with Ben and Kelsi. Liam gave his former apartment back to his brother, since it didn't feel like his in the first place, and I asked Amy to pay her rent for real, so all four of us can share equally and live together like normal roommates. This arrangement has been working surprisingly well so far, most likely because the four of us aren't actually glued together or anything. Lately, Liam and I are rarely in town on the weekends, and since all four of us have occupations during the daytime, plus the time we spend with our respective families or friends, we just get to have breakfast or dinner together like this from time to time.

"How is Bonnie?" I ask Ben while taking a sip of my coffee.

"Oh, she's doing great. I think she's dating a guy, but she didn't want to talk about it yet, so..."

His Blazing Witch

I smile and nod. Bonnie is still rather private, but I do see her almost each time I'm in town, and she comes here when she can. She's always more curious about how we can apply some of the witches' healing methods to wolves and humans... Just as I am about to ask something else, their bedroom door opens, and Kelsi steps out. Her long hair is a mess and her eyes are half-closed, but she still automatically runs over to hug me, wearing that gigantic bubblegum pink T-shirt I bought for her birthday.

"Boo! I missed you so much..."

"I missed you too. How are you?"

"I'm good... Do you have any tips for curbing a wolf's territorial issues?" she asks, sending a frown toward Ben.

"A leash? A collar?" I suggest with a chuckle. "Sorry, no tips from me. Oh, come on, don't fight when we just got home... We got you breakfast too."

"Oh, yes, donuts!" she exclaims, taking a pink one enthusiastically. "So, how did it go? You met the witches as planned?"

"Yep," I nod. "Two young Fire Witches, teens. They were pretty nice and open. A bit surprised to have me come for real and help out, but it was high time. One set her own school on fire, and neither of them had received any guidance from older witches before... In any case, they should be fine now, and they can call or write to me anytime."

"You must be a real superstar among witches now," chuckles Kelsi. "You've met more than a hundred across the world now, right? I mean, the new dean did say they were receiving more applications than ever for the paranormal course. Silver City is turning into the place to be for all the werewolves and witches around. Did I tell you? I got an email from the professor last week, she actually wants me to become an assistant..."

"Really? That's great!" I exclaim. "You love that course, and that professor we have now only came to temporarily fill Vutha's spot, right? Wouldn't you be interested in becoming a professor eventually?"

"I don't know," she sighs. "I love occult arts and being able to help you out, but if I accept, I'll have less time for my blog and I'll have to fulfill a ton of obligations... plus, you know I'm not very comfortable with public speaking."

"You'd do great!" says Ben. "You're super passionate and you already know more than that teacher anyway!"

"That's true," I nod, grabbing a donut too before the boys eat them all.

"I don't know..." mutters Kelsi, blushing a bit. "I'm still not too sure about taking Professor Vutha's... you know."

Just as she finishes her sentence, Liam comes back, half-naked with a towel over his head, and sits next to me, grabbing a donut. He puts his other arm around my chair, and we exchange a smile, but first, I take Kelsi's hand.

"Kelsi, Vutha was arrested three months ago now. Everyone knows she isn't coming back to teach at the university, and they need a professor. You should just accept the assistant's job for now and see if you like it! You did great at taking over to organize her things with Ayesha!"

"Yeah... I'll think about it."

We move on to chat more about the university, but since we are both taking free classes now, we have a much more flexible schedule. Even Liam and Ben have fuller schedules than we do as they work for the packs, although both are seriously thinking about their careers. Ben wants to become a paramedic to help out his sister while keeping his position as Selena's Beta, and Liam is seriously thinking about taking the exam to become a cop next year... Kelsi goes to her bathroom to get ready while Ben updates us on the pack matters, although everything is going as well as usual in Silver City.

Since there are no more borders of any kind, all werewolves just live together in harmony with the humans, and the Alphas and Lunas now only intervene to resolve issues between the wolves or when foreign packs appear outside of town. It sounds a bit utopic, but since the curse is gone, Nora and Selena both agreed there has been a lot less conflict. For a while, wolves and humans were just focused on building back what was destroyed in Silver City, and it helped create new friendships. Of course, there was also a period of mourning for those we had lost... The first few days were hard, but we all had enough to keep ourselves busy and not think about it too much, and slowly heal. Then, life went back to its usual course. Everyone wanted to cherish their loved ones and spend some time in peace, while Liam and I left at the first occasion to spend time together outside of Silver City while looking for new witches. I didn't abandon Silver City, and I was there when they needed me, but I was glad Selena and Nora could handle a lot without me, and Ayesha stayed around to help too. We actually came back so often, I don't believe they noticed much of our absences until we began leaving for longer periods, or whole weekends like we do now.

"Nora invited us for dinner tonight," I suddenly remember as we all get ready to go to work or university. "Are you guys coming?"

"Sure!" Ben smiles. "We're having fondue bourguignon! The whole family will be there so prepare yourselves, it's going to be packed and cramped for sure!"

"We will," I chuckle.

Liam gives me a little wink and takes my hand as we leave the apartment. I'm sure he and I can find the right time to escape the craziness...

The four of us walk to the car; as usual, Ben will drop us girls at the university while he and Liam go to the other side of the city. My mate and I get in the backseat, but I notice Liam doesn't want to let go of my hand at all, even as we drive away. Ben turns on Kelsi's favorite pop music to try and have her stop pouting toward him, both of them unaware of the two of us flirting behind them.

"*...What are you doing?*" I ask Liam as his hand caresses my knee.

"*I don't want to part with you... We've been together the whole weekend and now I don't want to spend my day away from my witch.*"

He leans his head on my shoulder and I chuckle. I feel that too... He and I are almost inseparable lately. He sticks to me like a bodyguard at all times, and since we get to spend every day, night, and weekend together when I don't have classes, it feels odd whenever we can't be close to each other...

"Come on, we have to live like normal people. Remember, this is what we wanted. A normal young adult life. Having fun with our friends, working or studying, having a place that we actually pay for instead of living off our siblings?"

"...Do you think your sister will like me more once I get a real job?"

I grimace.

To my surprise, Amy didn't care much about me having two male roommates, but one being my boyfriend did make her raise an eyebrow... I think she takes Liam for some hooligan or something, and she literally grilled him with all her questions when we went to see her. Although, she did say she'd respect my choices. I think she was more worried about me "meeting" my father at that time, but that was really nothing special. He just turned out to be the arrogant prick I had figured he'd be... at least he agreed to answer my questions. He confirmed he was a werewolf, although an Omega who didn't give the gene to his children, and decided to live like a human and forget his previous pack. Strangely, the more I listened, the more I felt he was someone who had a difficult past with no desire to go back to it, so I didn't ask. He did give me information about Clarissa's birth mother, so we managed to find and visit her grave two months ago...

The relationship with that estranged biological father will probably remain a bit odd, but I don't care anymore. Amy, however, calls me once a week, and we see each other when there's an opportunity. I think she's the only person I consider my family who doesn't live in Silver City...

"Can you have a... man-to-man chat with Ben?" I ask Liam.

"With Ben? Why?"

"He and Kelsi keep fighting lately, so... I think he could use a little pep talk from an expert."

"Oh, so I'm an expert now?" he asks, kissing my temple.

"Kelsi isn't a werewolf... and I'm not just a werewolf, either. I think they just need some assurance that it can work..."

"Well, there are other ways than a bond between mates..."

I smile, and my eyes go down on the ring on my finger.

It's not a fancy one, just a simple silver ring with a little black diamond on it, but it matches the one on Liam's finger. We didn't even have a fancy ceremony or anything like that. We just bought these on a whim last month, but in our hearts, we were actually engaged long before that. This was just... another token of our promise to stay together.

"Alright, ladies, we have arrived, please don't forget to tip your driver!" announces Ben with a chuckle.

"You silly..."

Still, Kelsi puts a shy kiss on his lips, making him all happy again. Liam gets out of the car to take the passenger seat, hugging me before I go.

"Stay out of trouble, hot stuff," he whispers.

"You too, babe. See you tonight..."

We kiss each other a couple more times, unwilling to part, until Ben honks to remind us where we are. I chuckle and let him get in the car while Kelsi pulls on my bag.

"Come on, he's had you all weekend, it's my turn!"

I laugh and walk to university arm in arm with my best friend as she doesn't even wait before telling me all about their messy date night. I won't tell him, but I also enjoy spending time without Liam; Kelsi being human allows me to forget all about the witch and werewolf matters for a moment, and just be a young woman like any other living her life. Plus, it makes it twice as exciting when we reunite...

I think this new, strange, and busy life balance is exactly what I needed. University is just the right dose of boring I needed in my life, and as I sit down to take notes for my first class, I leave all the crazy outside, just chatting with Kelsi like any other duo of girls complaining about our clingy boyfriends... She even insists on redoing my black nails as that class is even more boring than anticipated, and I don't say no.

I know she has noticed I grew a few visible gray hairs in just six months, but Kelsi didn't ask about it. Either she already knows, doesn't want to know, or knows I don't want her to, I can't tell. Perhaps both of us know we don't want to talk about it, so we don't; I don't care about it, either, I'm just glad the way things are. She knows her witch of a best friend has her secrets, like I always have, and we are both okay with it. It's even cute how she is an expert on witches and witchcraft so she can help me, but we also have random conversations about video games, our latest dates, and any gossip we can get from the university. I still get weird glances or people whispering behind my back from time to time, and I'll never really blend in with the other people our age, but I don't care.

I've got the greatest friends I could possibly need by my side already.

After our last class of the afternoon, Kelsi and I decide to walk downtown to grab a coffee, outside of the university campus; this might only be our first year studying there, but neither of us want to stay longer than needed. Without much of a surprise, Spark appears at the corner of a street to greet us with a loud meow, and I happily grab my cat to carry him in my arms, the usual purring following.

"I just wish he'd be more... human, at times," sighs Kelsi, "and at the same time, I hate that I'm almost forcing him to be less of a werewolf! I feel like I'll never compare to the chicks in his pack..."

"Wait, Ben has girl... friends?"

Kelsi pouts, brushing her long black hair back. She does gather some attention now that she's not hiding in her oversized clothes nor behind those ugly glasses... She went from the typical invisible nerd to one of the prettiest girls on the campus, and our duo doesn't go unnoticed anywhere.

"More or less," she sighs. "Well, he has two sisters so it can't be helped, I suppose. Plus, he is a Beta and super outgoing too. I just feel like if I have him out of my sight for more than ten minutes, some other werewolf girl is just going to jump in and mark him..."

I chuckle. It probably won't happen anytime soon. Is Kelsi thinking about how quickly Liam and I marked each other? It's very different, though, we are both werewolves, and fated mates too... I put my arm around her shoulders, glad I put my high-heeled boots to match her height.

"Kelsi, relax. From what I can see, Ben is the one worrying about you dumping him. He was super worried about you being upset this morning, and plus, each time he makes a mistake, he tries so hard to make up for it. Don't worry, you guys are rock solid, and his furry butt is crazy for you. I promise."

She gives me a shy smile, and Spark meows as if to agree, getting another smile from her too. We finally reach one of our favorite coffee shops, a chain cafe but with nice servers and an amazing selection. We quickly put our orders in and take a table right by the bay window so we can see the Silver City river and people passing by. Needless to say, a few guys stare back, but once they catch sight of my black nails, the black cat on my lap, and golden eyes, they go on their way.

"How about you and Liam...?" she asks, a wry smile on now that this is about me instead of her.

"What about us?" I blush a bit.

The server comes to give us our drinks, sending an extra long unnecessary glance toward Kelsi, and goes back.

"Come on," she smiles. "You guys are turning the heat on whenever you're in the same room together, and it's not from your magic! How was your weekend together?"

"It was... really nice," I confess, even redder. "You know, since we get to travel together, it's one surprise after the other, and we don't have time to get bored, either. I just feel a bit sorry for him when I'm with another witch and he has to wait, but he always says he's fine as long as he can stay around."

"Well, it's almost your job now," she nods. "You've inherited a ton of responsibilities, it can't be helped... but it's getting better now, right? No more headaches?"

Oh, that's one thing I'm glad is over...

After I received so much knowledge, and worse, the ability to mind-link all the witches I wanted, it just became too much for me to handle. I was so overwhelmed that I couldn't focus on the present at all. It was as if I had just... too much going on. Someone was talking to me from the other side of the country, and all of a sudden, I was living the same scene over and over again, unable to tell the difference between my foreseeing and the present, trying to remember if something had really happened or not. Each time I tried to control my foreseeing abilities, I ended up having a hard time remembering what had already happened, or if I had only foreseen it and it was about to.

His Blazing Witch

It did become too much, after a while, to be the greatest witch or something like that; I just couldn't take anymore of all those voices calling me, controlling my magic, the werewolves, and all the knowledge in my head. At that time, Liam was once again the one who saved me. He took me to that little chapel where we had our first conversation, surprisingly still there, and we stayed there together in the silence, until I could overcome it. I know it's just an old abandoned building full of dust and spiders, but I love that place. Liam even asked his brothers to see if we could somehow save it, and now, his older brothers promised they'd try to keep it safe from destruction, at least.

"No, I'm a lot better at handling it now," I smile, spinning the ring on my finger. "Plus, most young witches who needed help already had the talk with me once, so it's not like they'll reach out this way unless there's a major emergency again..."

And there have been a few! I never realized how problematic it would be for a young witch to be completely unsupervised, but it did happen a few times, most young orphans with no idea about why they could suddenly provoke a flood in their village or provoke an earthquake on a whim...

"So, um... Can I expect to be a bridesmaid soon?" she chuckles, her eyes on my ring.

"I don't know..." I admit. "I know Liam would marry me anytime if he could, but you know I'm not fond of ceremonies or crowds. I think we might do something simple this summer, just with close friends and family. I'm pretty sure Nora is just waiting for me to say the word to get on it."

"That's for sure," chuckled Kelsi. "Her hints last time weren't very subtle..."

I chuckle. Nora suggested we borrow their garden, and did mention a few ways we could hold a quiet but still very nice wedding, at least before I get pregnant or something. I think they are all expecting that me and Liam will have a child soon, but we agreed to wait at least until I finish university and he passes the exams to become a cop, so...

"I'm fine with how things are for now," I say, sipping on my coffee.

"Me too... I love having you guys as roommates!"

"We are the best roommates ever," I laugh. "We're away almost every weekend and we bring you guys breakfast on Mondays!"

"Don't say it like that," she pouts. "You know I'd rather stick with you all the time... To be honest, sometimes I miss when it was just you and me; between Ben's snoring and having two young and energetic couples under the same roof, I don't know what is worse..."

I can't agree more. Our bedrooms are right next to each other, and as we have all noticed, not fully soundproof...

"Oh, Kelsi, would you come with me to the cemetery later?" I ask. "I want to take care of the graves..."

"Sure. We can even go now if you want. It'll be a little walk, and I'll bring some flowers for Ben's brother too..."

I agree, and we take our coffees to go, Spark leading the way as always. I'm rarely cold anymore, but from Kelsi half-opening her jacket, it's probably a bit warmer in the sun. It's almost mid-November already... Now that I think about it, I have been in Silver City for a while now, although I always come and go. Liam and I have gone to almost all the neighborhoods and tried tons of restaurants and places. It's like coming home to this city gives us an excuse each time for a new date elsewhere... I smile helplessly as we walk by another sandwich shop where I know my mate's favorite pick. We certainly have been glued together for about six months now...

"I thought about introducing Ben to my brother," Kelsi drops suddenly as we keep walking.

"Seriously?"

I'm surprised. She almost ran away from her family so she barely has any contact with her parents anymore, but I know her brother and her have gotten closer as of late. For Kelsi, this would be a potential first step to making things a bit more official with Ben... She nods, looking a bit nervous.

"Just... you know. I've mentioned a couple of times I was seeing a guy, so my brother said he'd come around next month, and since I'll most likely spend Christmas with Ben's family..."

I can't stop smiling, happy for her. They don't look like it, but those two are definitely taking their own baby steps together... Kelsi doesn't add anything after that, her cheeks a bit pink, and I don't get more inquisitive, either. I know they need to take things at their own pace, and after what my poor Liam endured with my sister, I really can't blame them. I was lucky that Nathaniel and Damian were rather blunt in their attitude toward me since the beginning. Of course, it's a lot better now, and we are regularly invited to the family brunches. Nathaniel loves to complain that instead of taming Liam, I made him twice as wild... and I accept the compliment each time, of course.

We reach the cemetery, buying some flowers outside before going in. It's a bit strange how I feel fine going into that kind of space, but I think death is... somehow a part of me. I may have lost my Earth and Water Magic, but I can still feel the soil beneath us, the quiet and calm atmosphere floating between the tombstones. We quietly part, Kelsi naturally going toward Levi Lewis' grave. Meanwhile, I walk to the pair of white tombstones a bit farther. As expected of a former Alpha and Beta pair, they are well taken care of. I smile at Lysandra and her lover, and put down the purple flowers I chose. The truth is, their bodies were cremated with everyone else's after the battle. After what we had witnessed, it felt like a much better solution, and something that would appease both werewolves and humans, too... Still, we raised many tombstones here, so we could have a place to pray. I didn't cry at the funeral, and I never cry when I come here either. I can't really explain why... perhaps I had already grieved enough at the hospital. I apologized to Boyan, over and over, but he was the one who comforted me instead... That big guy hugged me despite his own state, telling me that at least his sister was gone with her mate, defending the pack like a Beta. His words in my mind make me choke up more than the sight of their names on the white stones... Lysandra was a part of my family too, and I'm grateful for what I learned from her. I mutter a silent prayer, and once I feel a bit better, I move on to the next place.

Little Mara's. It's been cleaned, and now, I take care of it whenever I can. I had Clarissa's name added to it, so they can be together in death once more... and that's my own way to not forget them either. I leave them a big crown of flowers, and spend a few minutes in silence, going to what I call my mindspace to share my latest memories with them. I still feel as if a little part of them is with me. I don't want to ever forget how I came to be, my strange history, and our unique bond. They will always be in my heart... I chose not to tell the whole truth to Clarissa's older sister, and I'm sure this is what she would have wanted. Perhaps Amy already knows that her little sister has changed into... someone different, but she won't ask. It's perhaps better left that way.

"...*Babe?*"

I smile, and walk back to the cemetary's entrance, letting Liam feel my position. I hear his bike a couple of streets away from the cemetery, and wait until he parks it right in front of me. He takes off his helmet, his hair sexily untamed, and I lean in to kiss him.

"Hi, there," I chuckle against his lips.

"The cemetery, of course. Where else could my witch girlfriend be...?"

"Don't mock me," I chuckle. "I know you're not fond of it, but I still need to come from time to time."

"Yeah, yeah... I know."

We playfully exchange a couple more kisses, and I'm grateful I walked a block away from the cemetery because this is really not the place to act like we are... Liam already plays with the bottom of my skirt, making me shiver despite the clothing covering my skin like a barrier under his fingers. I love the smell of leather on him... it gives me naughty ideas. I think again about Kelsi's observations. I don't think we are over the honeymoon period yet. Moon Goddess, what will it be like when we actually have a wedding and a honeymoon? I can't imagine!

"You two really can't part for more than five minutes!" sighs Kelsi's voice behind us.

Liam and I exchange a complicit glance, and he wraps his arms around me, his head on my shoulder as we both turn to her.

"Sorry, not sorry," I chuckle. "What now? Any news from Ben?"

"He's still working, but I'll go and meet him," says Kelsi with a smile. "I love a nice walk in the hispanic neighborhood with him! Plus, I can't stay around you two, I don't want to be the third wheel... We'll see you tonight at Nora's, okay?"

"Okay. Bring an extra jacket, though, I think it might snow..." I say, glancing up at the sky.

"Snow?" Kelsi repeats, surprised. "The sky is clear blue!"

I shrug, but she knows I'm rarely wrong. After a while, she sighs.

"Alright! But we have to go party after, right? We have classes late tomorrow, and I miss going dancing with you guys!"

I exchange a glance with Liam, and he nods excitedly. It's true we haven't gone partying in a while, and if we go to one of Nathaniel's clubs, we get free drinks too.

"Deal," I smile. "Don't be late, though!"

"We won't! Don't get naughty!"

She walks away with a smile, taking out her phone, probably to call Ben or Bonnie and meet up with them. I chuckle as we watch her walk away, but Liam is restless. His lips are all over my shoulder already... After a while, I can't take it anymore, so I turn around and kiss him.

"So naughty," he smiles.

"You started it."

"Shall we go back to our place? We would be alone..."

I hesitate, but eventually bite the tip of his nose playfully, making him grimace.

"We just came back. Let's spend time with the family instead. I want to see Rose! I'm sure Nora will be happy to have us over sooner so we can play with the kids too."

"You mean play the nanny," he laughs, "but alright. I love those brats too. Oh, shall we bring them snacks? How about some warm churros or donuts?"

"...Babe, are you hungry again?"

He smiles playfully, and puts a quick kiss on my lips.

"Hungry for food, most of the time. For you? Always..."

I blush. Oh, this wolf... I slap his butt, a bit excited.

"Come on, let's get going before we both get arrested for indecency..."

"I'll get as indecent as you want with you anytime."

"Save it for the club tonight!"

"...You'll let me rip your tights?"

"No!" I laugh.

Well, he always ends up ripping them, anyway...

I'm so used to being behind Liam on the bike that I can just close my eyes and lean back, feeling the wind on my face. I hope I can get my own soon, but I know I will miss riding with him. We have taken countless rides together, whenever we can go somewhere without using a spell. Even if we had to spend hours on the bike, neither of us cared. Moreover, being able to mind-link is just great to let the other know when we need a break or to communicate anything.

"*...Babe? Do you mind if we make a detour?*" he suddenly asks while we're already on the highway.

"*Sure, but... where?*"

"*...Just some place.*"

I feel like there's something more going on, but I don't ask anymore. I let Liam drive and decide, yet I can't help but get more curious as we drift away from our usual path. Liam takes the next exit on the highway and rides through

653

the streets, taking one turn after another in a neighborhood I don't recognize. Perhaps we came here before, but it doesn't look like the kind of place we would hang out in. It's nothing but old residences and quiet streets. There's only one little convenience store, an abandoned square, and a fast food restaurant. Liam slows down as we take a narrower street between the buildings... Where are we? After a couple more streets, he finally stops in front of a large residence.

There's a "Sold" sign in front, and the entrance is barred, yet this is definitely the place. Liam doesn't say anything for a while, simply staring at it. After a few seconds, I get off first, and he follows.

"...Do you know this... place?" I ask softly.

He lets out a long sigh and slowly takes my hand. His fingers are cold... He finally nods with a complex expression, his eyes still on that old residence.

"It was... our family's."

Does he mean his... childhood home? I turn my eyes to the property again, a bit stunned. I didn't even think of that before, but the Black Brothers all once lived together, under their horrible father's reign... I never thought about where they had actually lived. This looks like any other residence one would find in Silver City. A bit old, with red bricks, a tall black fence, three floors, and six windows facing the street.

I hold his hand a bit tighter, and Liam finally moves to go in, ignoring the sign. I follow him, neither of us talking while we push the doors in easily. Nothing is locked, but there is some tape on the doors, and signs to keep out. It looks large enough to have three or four families living there... Liam goes straight for the stairs, and I follow him. He goes to the top floor, and stares at the entry door on the right. He stands there for a few seconds, his hand holding mine.

"...Are you okay?" I ask.

"Yeah, it's just... I'm not sure what I'm going to find inside, or what I'm... expecting."

"I'll stay with you," I simply mutter, holding his hand with both of mine.

He slowly nods, and finally pushes the door.

It's... surprisingly empty inside. There are only a couple of pieces of furniture, a large cardboard box in the corner, the kitchen sink, and... that's it. It is so empty, our steps echo in the room, and even I feel a bit colder. Liam slowly looks around, a bit surprised. I wonder what he sees...

After a short while, he slowly moves to one of the rooms, his hand tightly holding on to mine. That place was... clearly meant to be a bedroom, but it's completely empty now. Liam doesn't step in. He only stands in the door frame, looking at that small space with a confused expression.

"It's so..."

"Empty?"

"Small," he scoffs. "I guess I haven't seen this room since I was a kid, but..."

"Was this your bedroom?" I ask.

"...Our bedroom. Nate slept there, and Damian on the other side. They were always sleeping facing the door to know first when my father would come... I had a bunk bed above Nathaniel's. But I... rarely slept in it. Most of the time, I slept with Damian, or under Nate's bed to hide from my father. He actually destroyed my bed at some point, not long before he..."

Before he died.

I remember the story I was told, many times over, it seems. Damian Black killed their father, Judah. Although it was a crime, it was to protect his younger brothers, as well as the whole pack and Silver City... Liam was so young back then. I feel bad, looking at that room. It should have been filled with fun childhood memories, but it's just... dark and empty. The window is so small, and there's barely any space for three boys to share.

"It's funny," chuckles Liam. "I haven't seen this room in years, but it doesn't feel like... it was once my bedroom. I recognize that ugly wall, though, and it still stinks of old wood."

"Liam... Why did you want to come here?"

He sighs.

"My brother... just sold this place. They are going to tear it down, and build something new instead. To be honest, I didn't even realize we had inherited it until a while ago. I think Damian didn't want to think or talk about it at all. He let an agency manage it until all the people that lived in it left. He told me for the first time when he learned the last of the people living here had left, to ask Nate and I what we wanted to do... To be honest, all three of us wanted nothing to do with it anymore. I don't even have memories of my mom in this house... so we agreed to sell it, and give our shares from the sale to a charity. So, I guess this is just me... checking I didn't leave anything here."

I know he doesn't mean that literally. I can feel what he's feeling inside, it's like... a bittersweet mix of nostalgia, grief, and resentment. Liam probably has more bad memories than good ones in this place, but that doesn't take away what it means to him. He still... slept in this room every night with his brothers. A part of his childhood is rooted in this place, even if it's a painful one. Since he was younger, he probably needs this closure more than Nathaniel or Damian. Liam told me how they constantly protected him from seeing the worst of their situation, but it doesn't mean he has no feelings left behind. I sigh faintly and put my chin on his shoulder, not adding anything else. I understand his need for closure.

Perhaps seeing this room, smaller than he imagined, is also the best way to say goodbye to that part of his life. Once this place is destroyed, it will be chapter closed.

After a few minutes, I hear him take a deep breath, and he nods.

"Alright... I'm okay. Let's go now."

I don't discuss it, and follow him out, letting him close all the doors again behind us. I wish I could heal the scars and bad memories he kept from that part of his childhood, but that is not my part to play. I'm glad he's honest with me about it, though, and able to find closure by himself.

655

We walk out of the residence and stop for a second in front of it, Liam staring at the third floor with a slight frown.

"You know, as a kid, I told myself I'd never have children. I was afraid I'd be as bad and terrifying as my father one day…"

"What made you change your mind?" I ask, curious.

"My brothers," he chuckles. "After my dad died… Damian buried himself with work, and Nate had so many women. Then, all of a sudden, Nora and Elena appeared, and they both turned into amazing husbands and dads. When I see Damian with his kids, or Nate with his daughters, I'm crazy jealous these days."

"Are you jealous of them or the kids?" I tease him.

He rolls his eyes and turns to me, wrapping me in his arms.

"I'm over my brother complex, okay? Plus, now I have this sexy witch girlfriend I want to have babies with…"

I blush uncontrollably hearing Liam talk about me having his babies… To be honest, if it wasn't for him, I wouldn't be so sure about having children. I still don't feel like becoming a mother yet, although I feel like it will happen in the future. I'm glad Liam is willing to wait, although he's dying to become a dad himself. I put a quick kiss on his lips.

"You're still cute when you talk like that about your big brothers," I whisper playfully.

"You witch…" he sighs. "Come on, let's go grab some food and then see the rest of the family."

I nod happily, and we get back on the bike. I notice Liam doesn't even look back once before driving away, but I say nothing, just holding on to him, and glancing toward the residence myself. I hope whatever is built here instead only hosts good memories from now on…

This time, Liam heads straight toward Nora and Damian's neighborhood, much more lively and crowded. It's Monday, after all, and at this time, kids are finishing school and some people are leaving work. He parks the bike in front of Nora's children's favorite donut shop, and we get in the queue behind a group of teenagers. They are a bit loud, but Liam has decided to be naughtier… He wraps an arm around me, and keeps kissing my temple, my cheek, and my hair so much that it embarasses me a little. But of course, the more I push him away, the naughtier he gets. His flirty hand travels lower, to my butt, and his kisses keep going. I'm glad we are a few steps away from the young ones because this is not appropriate at all in broad daylight!

"*Stop it…*"

"*I'm hungry.*"

"*You're being pervy right now! Even the teens in front of us are better behaved.*"

"*I don't care. I'm a young adult and I want to be pervy with my girlfriend…*"

"*I'm going to burn your hand again.*"

This time, he pulls away, giving me a pouty expression, but I don't give in. He has no choice but to pull his hands higher up, although he still wraps them tightly around my waist, and puts his chin on my head. I turn around, leaning against him while staring at the delicious looking donuts ahead. I hear him sigh faintly.

"...I wish we had met sooner. We could have gone to school together... Damn, if I had a girlfriend like you in high school, I wouldn't have missed a single class!"

"Are you sure? Nathaniel told me you were quite the runaway."

"Damn it, Nate told you that? Since when did you guys get so close?!"

I chuckle. Liam has no idea... He often falls asleep first when we stay late at Nora's or Selena's place, so I can chat all I want with Nathaniel or Damian, and both of them have tons of stories about their little brother... They obviously love him, and are glad to share his cuteness with me. Let's just hope he never finds out that I have some of his baby pictures.

"We would probably have missed classes together," I chuckle. "If I had you in my class, I would never be able to focus..."

He holds me a bit tighter, agreeing with me in a chuckle, and we stay like this for a little while, waiting for all the teenagers to be done ordering. Some keep sending glances toward us, either because we're shamelessly snuggling in public or because I am visibly a witch... I've gotten used to it, though. It's not nearly as bad as it was a few months ago, either. I went from the most hated person on the campus to overnight celebrity, which was somewhat more annoying. Some girls even harassed me about becoming a witch, as if all it took was getting a pointy hat and a couple of lessons...

Finally, the young ones leave and it's our turn to order. I have to remind Liam a couple of times that we're not ordering for ourselves, but we still leave with a large box and a donut in each of our hands. My werewolf stomach got the better of me... We take our time going to Nora's house as we'll be there early anyway.

As soon as we get to the familiar, less crowded streets leading to their house, I can't help but smile. This feels like visiting the family, our big, warm family. It's strange yet sweet how close I've gotten with each member of that big family. Regardless of whether we are blood-related or not, I just feel at ease as soon as I see the big, white house and its fence and, as usual, some wolves scattered in the garden.

Liam parks his bike, and sure enough, as soon as we get off, a bunch of young wolves and children run to us. I can't believe how fast they grow up! James is already all about Liam's bike while we make our way to the garden, ready to greet all of the Black children. Lily, Will, Estelle, Aurora, and Rose are all there, playing in the garden on a large cloth. Boyan is there in his wolf form with his daughter, Mary, right next to him, entertaining the younger kids. Rose is the first to get up and run to me, and I open up my arms to hug her.

"Hi, Mara..." she says with her cute voice, hugging me back.

"Hi, sweetie. How are you?"

I put a strand of her long, dark hair behind her ear. She's growing up so fast… She stares at me with those big blue eyes of hers, definitely getting cuter each time.

"I'm okay…"

"How is Mommy?"

"Mommy is okay," she nods.

"That's good."

She nods again, and suddenly jumps on me to hug me again, almost making me fall back. Moon Goddess, she's the cutest little girl ever! Ever since I discovered my connection with her dad and Rose herself, I've been visiting Rose a lot and chatting with her mom, Tiffany. Although she is too young to understand, Rose can feel that connection between us, and her wolf probably lets her feel that I'm part of her family… that I'm related to her dad. I will explain it properly when she's older, but for now, I'm just glad to be part of her life like this.

"How are you, Boyan?" I ask the big brown wolf.

He simply nods, and his daughter leans against him. Surrounded by kids like this, he probably can't get much rest, but Boyan is definitely happier when he's babysitting this rocky bunch. I chuckle and sit among them, and sure enough, the rest of the group comes back, James making a bit of a fuss behind Liam.

"Mara!"

Nora comes out of the house, looking a bit exhausted but with a large smile on.

"Need help?" I chuckle.

"Everyone inside!" she shouts at the children first. "It's getting late and cold now, you should play inside…"

The children obediently get up and most follow Boyan inside, except for Rose, still holding my hand, and James. After a few seconds, Liam sighs and grabs his nephew to carry him inside for the second half of his tantrum. Nora sighs, following them with her eyes.

"This boy… He can be an angel at times, but Moon Goddess, he is so wilful!"

"Alpha blood," I chuckle. "You'd better be ready…"

"Oh, you should see Lily, she's the little princess of the house already, Damian can't ever say no to her… I don't know how Nathaniel does it with two girls."

Rose giggles, and I brush her hair with a little wink. She definitely knows how to get her way with her uncles too…

"Mara, I have a little thing for you…"

"For me?" I repeat, surprised.

"To be honest, Elena and I weren't sure when to give it to you… We wanted to wait until your birthday or Christmas, but we don't really know when you'll celebrate the first, and the latter will definitely be crowded with the kids and all, so…"

Now I'm curious to know what she is talking about... She takes out a little box, and I have no choice but to put Rose down for a second. I take it, wondering what she and Selena came up with...

Moon Goddess... A necklace? I'm in awe, staring at the rose gold necklace. It's a short chain with what looks like a five-pointed star for a pendant with red little rubies.

"Nora..." I mutter, shocked.

"It's just something small," she smiles. "I have this moon necklace, and Elena has a sun one... Since you're... part of the family now, and such a big one at that, we thought it would be a great way to... welcome you in."

I'm in shock, I don't even know what to say. I did notice their necklaces, and I thought they were beautiful, but... I never thought they would go as far as to gift me one! Damn it, I can't start crying now, but I am still touched...

"Thank you..."

"Let's put it on you," she chuckles.

She takes it and helps me put it around my neck. I don't really care to see how it fits me, I know it will be perfect... Nora smiles and nods, visibly satisfied.

"Perfect," she says. "...Now you're an official part of our little trio... The third Luna of the Black Family."

"...Thank you, Nora," I manage to say, a bit choked up.

"No," she shakes her head. "Thank you for coming to us."

I nod, and we hug each other. Oh, Moon Goddess, I love it... I really feel like I am part of this family now. This is where I belong, with all of them. We hug for a long while, hearing the children shouting and playing in the house. I finally hear Nora sigh, and we part, holding each other's hands with big, silly smiles on.

"Alright, let's go inside before those kids tear the house apart..."

I chuckle and follow her inside to reunite with Liam, the kids, and the rest of the family coming here.

I'm home.

#

His Blazing Witch

10 Years Later

"You're doing great," I encourage her. "Now try to hold it there. Take deep breaths and focus on the sensations inside."

The massive body of water between us trembles. The shape is changing in irregular shapes, little drops falling on the floor, but nothing alarming. She's doing amazing, considering the size, and slowly moving it across the area. I see her frowning a lot, her fists clenched, almost glaring at that huge bubble she's holding together. It keeps moving, floating in the air until it is almost above the half-empty pool.

"Alright, now slowly release the pressure, slowly. Just let go as if you were opening your hand..."

I hear her breathe out, and I try to feel her magic. Her pressure is strong, but she's too scared to let go. She gently releases the pressure, but she's still holding on, and the water falls too faintly, a few drops at a time.

"It's okay," I encourage her. "Trust yourself, you're doing great. Just a bit more..."

She listens, and soon, the water starts falling back into the pool, several liters dropped one after the other, making splatters but still going where we want them. I see her smile on the other side, witnessing her success. I say nothing and just let her go on. She suddenly gets a bit too confident, and as soon as she looks up to glance at me, all the water suddenly falls, splashing both of us in the process. She gasps, and runs over.

"I'm so sorry!" she exclaims. "I lost focus, I didn't think it would fall like that..."

"It's okay," I chuckle, wiping my face. "You still did pretty great! Don't worry, it's just water, and it will dry in no time. But you did amazing! See? You just need to focus on your power, and trust yourself with it. Really, you're doing great for your age."

"Thank you, Mara... I wouldn't have done it without all your help and advice... I feel so much better than before now, I'm really so glad... C-can I hug you?"

"Oh, sure."

She hugs me right at the end of my answer, tightly. I smile and hug her back. She's a sweet kid, just a bit lost... and a great future witch, I can tell. After a while, we part and I wipe the tears off her cheeks.

"Thank you so much..." she cries.

"It's alright, stop crying!" I chuckle. "That's enough water for the day. But promise me, the next time you get angry, just dive into the pool, alright? No need to try and drown everyone around with a water bomb."

"I promise," she replies, half laughing and half crying.

"And you keep training, okay? With time, this will be nothing. You'll be able to help a lot of people around you with your power. So don't waste your time with teenagers like that being mean to you. Just move on, and grow stronger from it. Even witches can't change people's opinions, but we can act whatever we want to regardless. Be a strong witch and be yourself. Don't be scared to be different, okay? One of my best friends said weirdos are cool."

"You're the coolest," she smiles.

"Thanks," I chuckle.

She takes a deep breath in, wiping her tears.

"Do you have to leave?" she asks with a sorry expression.

"Yes, my family is waiting for me... but don't hesitate to call me if you need, okay? Humans don't have magic, but technology is still useful and you can chat with other witches like I told you too. You'll see; everyone has issues, but we're stronger together."

"Thanks, Mara. Thank you for everything. I promise I'll get better at all that."

"Train," I nod, "but keep studying! Make memories at school, and become someone great. We need more cool witches."

I take a few steps back, and wave at her, my magic circle appearing beneath me. She keeps waving from afar, crying again a bit, but soon, she's gone.

I let out a long sigh and close my eyes, letting my circle bring me home. What time is it in Silver City? It's probably pretty early... I can't help but smile, a bit excited to go home. It's always the same, no matter how long I leave, a few hours or a few days. As soon as I'm gone, I'm looking forward to when I'll be back.

I arrive in our living room, as usual. The furniture is actually set so I have space to arrive, just in case I land a bit farther than planned or something even though I've used this spell so many times I can do it without thinking now. I take a deep breath and stretch. The sun is up already, but the house is so quiet. It's a Saturday, after all... With everyone sleeping, I feel a bit lucky to be awake already. I make a quick stop by the bathroom to dry my hair and put away my wet clothes before I soak the whole house... I glance up at my figure in the mirror. No dark circles this time, but my hair is going to be a nightmare later... Oh, well. I push a few white strands out of my face. I'm really getting used to it now. It looks like a real witch thing...

I grab a pair of sweatpants and a shirt from my dressing room right next to it. I'm tempted to cross it and go into our bedroom, but I want to go somewhere else first.

I smile and go back into the hallway to sneak into the first bedroom on the left.

The little crib is hidden in the dark, just a few phosphorescent stars shining above it, and the thin light filtering through the curtains. I quietly walk up to the little bed, and lean over. Moon Goddess, he is so cute... Sleeping with his body spread like a star, his little mouth open, Milo is deep asleep. His little hand is still holding Spark's tail, just like when I left him. I chuckle quietly, exchanging a glance with my cat, curled up in the corner with his golden eyes glowing.

"Thanks for watching him," I mutter with my lips.

His Blazing Witch

Spark lets out a cute little meow, and puts his head down on my baby's belly. I smile and go back to watching Milo sleep. I love his frizzy black hair and his golden skin... and those cheeks! I could squeeze them all day long if he didn't hate it. Plus, he inherited his dad's eyes behind those closed eyelids. All his aunties and I are certain: he will be unbearably handsome when he grows up. However, for now, he's still an adorable toddler with a very heavy sleep and a dangerous appetite of a little wolf when he's up... He's got his little pajamas with the words "Watch out: Baby Wolf" written on them that Selena gifted him last Christmas. I pull his blanket to cover him, and put a little kiss on his cheek, provoking a little pout on his face. It's cute, and not enough to wake my little Milo up. I exchange a wink with Spark, and quietly walk out of the bedroom, closing the door without making a sound.

I get back into the hallway, but don't dare enter the other bedroom. Unlike her little brother, she'd wake up right away for sure... so I quietly sneak into our master bedroom, opening it once again as quietly as possible.

Oh, Moon Goddess, what a sight...

He forgot to close the blinds again last night, which he always does when I'm not here. I guess he hasn't gotten used to it yet, it's only been two months since we moved here... I won't complain, though. In fact, I have the chance to witness my adorable husband, half-naked, sleeping across the disheveled bed like his son, with the lines of his abs hit by the sunlight... I bite my lower lip, a bit too excited. Oh, I could devour him right now. Instead, I chuckle and slowly climb on the end of the bed, trying not to wake him up.

He's snoring faintly and it adds to his charm. He's wearing patterned pajama bottoms... Still no top, of course. I have a matching set, which I only wear on weekends when we have to watch out for those little ones barging in the bedroom. The rest of the week, it's sexy black lingerie only. For now, though, I'm not wearing either of these, but it doesn't stop me from climbing over my husband. Although he doesn't open his eyes, I can tell exactly when he wakes up as I feel his inner wolf excited by my presence. I put a kiss on his lips, and he immediately pouts to ask for another. I chuckle, and happily indulge.

"Good morning, my wolf."

"Good morning, my witchy wife... How did it go?"

"The usual. Troubled witch teenager almost drowning her classmates... How about you?"

"The usual.... Our daughter tried to charm her godfather, our son tried to bite everything... including his dad and his mom's cat."

"Oh, poor Sparky... So you spent the evening with Ben?"

"He brought the twins too. Kelsi kicked him out, she's still working on her essay thing... I don't know which one between him or me missed their wife the most. Although the pizza party was fun."

"You had a pizza party with my babies without me again?" I chuckle. "They must love when Mommy isn't here..."

"They still miss you, though. Milo cried for a bit... and Cynthia asked when you'd be back, like, three times."

"I'm sorry, babe. I thought it would go faster."

"It's okay."

He wraps his arms around me, and I chuckle, hugging him back. Oh, I missed him... He smells just like my Liam.

"I missed you too," I sigh.

"Me too. ...Aren't you tired?"

"A bit. But it's alright, I'll nap later. Are we still going to Nora's this afternoon?"

"Yep. Still, you should rest. You're always running left and right these days..."

He pulls the blanket over me, and I happily snuggle against him. It's true I am tired, but with the sun already up, I don't feel like sleeping right now... and I want to enjoy my time with them.

"I'm worried," he sighs. "You're always running around on top of your work here. You're going to overexert yourself again."

"Don't worry. I promise I'll stop and let some of the other older witches help if I'm really tired. The older ones are starting to get real good now, a handful can even use the teleportation spell... I just went this time because I've been following that girl for a while, she's really got no one to help. Next time, I'm sitting out and staying with my babies, I promise."

"Hm. Good, then. ...But what about your husband? I have been feeling super lonely too. Very, very lonely, you know. I'm super pitiful."

I laugh, and give him a bunch of kisses on his cheeks to apologize. Oh, my Liam... I hope he never stops being playful and childish like this. It really helps me stay focused on what matters and relax. He's like my inner strength. I just need to go home to him, and everything else can be blown away.

"...I'm sorry," I sigh after a while.

"What? Why?"

"I feel like I'm a bit... you know, always leaving you with the kids. You have your job at the police station, the werewolf stuff, the house and stuff, while I'm... super focused on witch stuff. I just feel a bit bad..."

After a while, he suddenly starts laughing. Why is he laughing? It's not funny! I'm really trying to be sincere here... I slap his shoulder, a bit annoyed.

"Stop laughing!"

"Sorry... Damn, I love you, witch!"

Before I can even react, he suddenly overpowers me and makes us roll on the bed, him getting on top of me.

"You're not funny..." I grumble a bit, annoyed that he's not taking my apology seriously.

"You're the funny one," he chuckles. "My wife is sorry about being a super badass and busy witch while I get to stay home and play with our babies? Excuse me?"

I sigh, but he shakes his head, and puts a quick kiss on my lips.

"Mara, I'm super proud of you. You're doing a ton of stuff at the same time, and unlike what you're thinking, you're here for our family, okay? That's why our kids notice if their mom is gone even for one night. Sure, it was a bit hard at times, but we always decided and did things together. And we have a big family exactly for that, so we can rely on our pack when you and I are both busy. Don't apologize for being a kick-ass mom who's helping tons of little witches without a mom out there. Cynthia understands, and she is super proud of her mom too. And Milo... Well, he'll just keep biting his dad and pulling Spark's tail for now, I guess."

This time, I chuckle, and surrender, putting my arms around his neck. It sure was hard sometimes... although I did take real breaks when our babies were born, or when the family needed us. Silver City is still my home, after all; wherever I go, I'll come back to this place. Moreover, it's not like we didn't get to enjoy ourselves... Liam and I traveled a lot together before we finally decided to move out and have a family of our own. Even Kelsi got a taste of motherhood before I did with her twins... although her pregnancy wasn't really planned, as it happened when she was still studying. It wasn't so easy for me either. Liam and I had a full two years of focusing on our careers and other things before I finally got pregnant. Now we have our two babies, our new apartment, the cat, and even our daughter's magic turtle...

Suddenly, we both turn our heads as we hear running from the hallway. Here she comes...

"Dad! Dad, I lost Gem again!"

Cynthia barges in, still in her pajamas, her hair in an utter mess and looking panicked. She frowns when she sees the two of us hugging, with Liam on top of me on one edge of the bed.

"Miss Cynthia, what did we say about running into a room without knocking?" growls her dad.

"Mama!"

I smile and push him away to open my arms as my daughter dives into the bed and into my embrace.

"Hi, my baby girl!"

We laugh and hug for a while, Liam completely left on the side. I hug my daughter and sit up, facing her. I try to brush her hair a bit while she excitedly starts talking.

"Mama, when did you come back? We had pizza last night! Uncle Benny came and the twins too! And we had fun playing tag with Spark! Oh, and Milo bit dad again, and then he cried a lot too... Oh, and I put nail polish on Gemma!"

I frown.

"Baby, I'm not sure about putting nail polish on your turtle... Also, where did my seven-year-old daughter get nail polish?" I ask, turning to Liam who shrugs.

"Have you tried keeping three girls out of their mom's nail polish drawer? Because Ben and I tried everything, I swear..."

664

I sigh and turn to Cynthia, only now noticing that pink nail polish on her fingers. Oh, I would never wear that one, anyway... I chuckle and show her my dark blue nails.

"Alright, how about you and Mommy go and buy some appropriate nail polish for your age, and we try to keep it off poor Gem, okay? I know your turtle is very fashionable, but this and trying to take baths with Spark is probably not a good idea, Cynthia. Alright?"

"Okay... but then can we also get makeup?"

"I'm sure there's going to be makeup for little girls," I nod. "Actually, how about you ask your cousins this afternoon? I'm sure Aurora and Lily have some they can lend you."

"Oh, yes!"

We keep chatting for a while, Cynthia being a real wordmill... Meanwhile, Liam comes to hug me from behind, leaning his head on my shoulder without a word, probably snoozing before the real trouble starts...

"Oh," Cynthia suddenly says.

Indeed, we can hear her little brother's tantrum from the other side of the apartment. She jumps out of the bed and runs to Milo's bedroom even before us. Liam sighs, and puts a quick kiss on my shoulder.

"I'm glad we waited before we had Milo," he sighs. "A five year gap should be the minimum, for any parent's mental health..."

I laugh.

"Says the husband who wouldn't stop asking for another baby as soon as we had Cynthia?"

"Cynthia slept her full nights when she was two weeks old! I didn't think her brother would make me wake up at 4:00 a.m. every day for nine months... I was the only guy at the police station who would gladly take on the early morning shifts. They still remember."

I chuckle, and give him a quick kiss on the cheek.

"Well, baby alarm clock still likes to wake up early... Let's go see before Cynthia decides to put something on his nails too."

He nods, and we get up, hand in hand, to go and free poor Spark.

It's a morning like any other in Silver City... and I hope it goes on for a long time.

His Blazing Witch

About the Author

Jenny Fox is a French author, born in Paris in 1994.
She reads alone for the first time at 6 years old, Harry Potter and the Philosopher Stone, and writes her very first story at 9 years old. Her teacher reads it in front of the whole class, and from then on, she will never stop writing, from short stories to fanfiction.

His Blue Moon Princess is her first story to be entirely written in English, inspired by her experience overseas and her love for Fantasy Novels.
She lives in London, UK, improving her English while working on her next story.

Follow her at **@AuthorJennyFox** on her Facebook Page.

Novels by Jenny Fox

THE SILVER CITY SERIES
His Bluemoon Princess
His Sunshine Baby
His Blazing Witch
*

THE DRAGON EMPIRE SAGA
The War God's Favorite
The White King's Favorite
The Wild Prince's Favorite (Coming soon)
*

STAND-ALONE STORIES
Lady Dhampir
The Songbird's Love
A Love Cookie
Hera, Love & Revenge
The HellFlower
Dhampir Knight
A Love Cookie 2 (Coming Soon)
*

THE FLOWER ROMANCE SERIES
Season 1
Season 2